Delilah

MARCUS GOODRICH

Delilah

WITH A NEW INTRODUCTION
BY CAPTAIN EDWARD L. BEACH

TIME Reading Program
Special Edition
TIME INCORPORATED · NEW YORK

TIME
LIFE
BOOKS

EDITOR *Norman P. Ross*
TEXT DIRECTOR *William Jay Gold*
ART DIRECTOR *Edward A. Hamilton*
CHIEF OF RESEARCH *Beatrice T. Dobie*
ASSISTANT TEXT DIRECTOR *Jerry Korn*

EDITOR, TIME READING PROGRAM *Max Gissen*
RESEARCHER *Ann S. Lang*
DESIGNER *Lore Levenberg*

PUBLISHER *Rhett Austell*
GENERAL MANAGER *Joseph C. Hazen Jr.*

TIME MAGAZINE
EDITOR *Roy Alexander*
MANAGING EDITOR *Otto Fuerbringer*
PUBLISHER *Bernhard M. Auer*

COVER DESIGN *Jerome Martin*

This volume contains the first of two separate novels concerning its subject. Nevertheless, the two books are assured an added general continuity by the author's having planted some seeds in the pages of the first novel that will be seen to burgeon in those of the second now in preparation.

Delilah *is a work of fiction, in the writing of which no character was designed to bear resemblance to any actual person, living or dead.*

MARCUS GOODRICH

Editors' Preface

When Marcus Goodrich sent his novel *Delilah* to press in 1941, he was 44 years old. He had run away to sea when he was 18, had had a ship sunk under him in the Mediterranean in the First World War and had spent much of the next 20-odd years writing *Delilah*. Its acclaim was swift, and so was the pressure on him to fulfill his promise to release the second half of the book, which was even then written but in need of some final reworking. This last rewriting was interrupted by World War II, which sent him back into the Navy as a Lieutenant Junior Grade. When it was over he was a Lieutenant Commander with a record of amphibious operations in North Africa, Sicily, China and Okinawa. That experience had such a profound effect upon him that he has never been able to return to *Delilah*.

He has published nothing since, and this has led some to think of him as a writer who wrote himself out in one book. He disappeared so completely that others thought of him vaguely as having died. But, precisely for the same reason that he was not able to complete the second part of *Delilah*, he has spent the years since World War II writing more intently and under greater pressure than ever before. Hidden away, dropped from view, and with the golden tongue that once enlivened New York literary circles now so silent that there are weeks on end when he seldom hears his own voice, he has been writing steadily. In fact, he has in these years since World War II written three more novels—"All finished, but not quite," is the way he puts it.

With Marcus Goodrich, "not quite" has a different meaning than with most authors. And one must understand those words in his terms to learn why the second part of *Delilah* has not been published, indeed never will be published (which may also be true of his other novels) in his lifetime.

"The Second World War was a traumatic experience for me," he explains. "I was first astonished and then troubled by a fundamental change in the men I found there compared with the kind of men I knew in *Delilah*. The change was so deep and so remarkable that it has made the men of *Delilah* obsolete. I found I could not write about them any more. For as time went on I came to know that it was not a passing change. I saw it again in the Korean War. And my urge, literally my obsession, is to find out why this change has come about."

Goodrich will not be pinned down as to exactly what this change is that he has observed in contemporary man, nor will he conjecture as to the forces in history that have produced it. His readers may find a mystery here. Many a veteran of World War II, reading *Delilah* today, will agree with Captain Edward L. Beach's conclusion, in his new introduction to this special edition, that the U.S. sailors of the *Delilah* and those of modern times have much in common. Goodrich himself indicates that he is not sure where the difference lies. "Writing about men doing what they do is my only way of finding out why they do it," he says. And until he has completed the "not quite finished" novels he is working on, he will not have the answer to his own satisfaction.

"Discovering what makes men do what they do is my sole reason for writing about them and I must keep on working until I know. The first volume of *Delilah* is complete; there is nothing I would change after all these years. When I reread it I know that I have solved all its problems. And it is because of this, when I reread what I have *since* written, that I know these are not yet ready for publication. I find in them problems still to be solved and authenticity still to be proved, and until I am satisfied that I have met these tests I must keep on working and working."

The story of *Delilah* must be read and one must hear Goodrich talk about it, all these years later, to know how he meets his tests and what an extraordinary man he is. The destroyer *Delilah* is an aging craft, a four-stack coal burner, driven by spent machinery and put down in the public books as antiquated. Suddenly she is flung into a search for arms and war materials which the Moro tribesmen of the Philippines had reportedly stockpiled among the hundreds of islands of the Sulu Sea, to help them in their revolt against control from Manila. The time is the half year or so before April 1917, when the United States declared war against Germany.

Unseen orders govern the life of *Delilah* and force her into speeds which all but wreck the vessel and exhaust her men, and there is smoldering resentment among the officers against the officialdom which sent them and in particular against the "fat Tagalog politicians" in Manila who they feel have made of them a cat's paw. But this anger does not keep them from driving *Delilah* through vast areas of semicharted seas, her deck plates so hot from her own fires that they char the wooden sandals the men have fashioned to walk upon them; nor does it reduce the spirit of the landing parties going ashore in whaleboats through roaring surf on some of the most exciting and mysterious searches of uninhabited islands in the annals of literature.

The book opens with *Delilah* under forced draft and Ordinary Seaman Warrington, a slight, sensitive youth, pitting his meager strength against both the demands of the roaring furnaces and the challenge of a massive veteran of the fiery ordeal. Then, as *Delilah* moves feverishly around the South Pacific, we come to know the test-tube world aboard her and the lives and motivations of the 71 men who live in her forecastle and wardroom.

There are extraordinary images which rise in Goodrich's fertile mind—such as the similarity between the turreted ship and a turreted walled town standing against the unfriendly world—which sweep him far from the Pacific and into a full-length description of the battle of the Alamo, in whose shadows Goodrich lived as a boy and within whose walls his kinsman stood and died.

There are scenes of great profundity, such as the portrayal of the men at mail call when each, in receiving and reading letters from his wife or mother, is subtly transformed. A curious change sweeps the crew as the "she" from home momentarily supplants the "she" of *Delilah*. And the ingrained power of authority over those trained to obedience is startlingly noted in the scene in which Lieutenant Fitzpatrick subdues the crazed seaman O'Connel in the midst of a barroom rampage. All others having fled, Fitzpatrick, shielded only by his shining white uniform, confronts O'Connel, who stands before him bloody, drunk, and fired to attack, and quells the revolt by simply saying to him, "Come along," and then turning his back.

The book ends abruptly, with the dramatic reading of the Secretary of the Navy's message to the crew at ship's quarters: "The President signed an act which declares that a state of war exists between the United States and Germany." The fact that this sudden ending does not dissatisfy the reader may be a comment on the freedom of the modern novel from the traditional formalities of plot. Goodrich says that he brought the first volume to a close here "simply because the manuscript had become so bulky that it was convenient to cut it in half, and the declaration of war seemed as good a point as any to split the book."

Of course he has paid a price. Warrington, for example, one of the two most important characters in the novel, inexplicably fades away. Equally inexplicably, an entirely new character, Seaman Rowe, is introduced. These deficiencies are readily admitted by Goodrich, who, all these years later, says of them: "Warrington was not lost. He was simply waiting for his cue. And it does not come until the second volume, where he plays a very important part. As for Seaman Rowe, he has one of the most dramatic roles in the book. He was introduced as a reluctant, hesitant man because it is this characteristic in the next volume which brings *Delilah* to disaster. It is Rowe, at the wheel, who reacts so hesitantly in a crisis that *Delilah* is finally sunk."

Delilah is usually considered to be a story about a ship and the sea—and, indeed, it is in that sense that Captain Beach writes of it. But it was never intended that way, says its author. "I placed it aboard a destroyer because a man must write about the things he knows best and I know the Navy. But it is about men that I write. Nothing else really interests me. I could have placed that novel anywhere else and come out the same." For *Delilah* is not simply a work of realism; it is a factual and informative account of life aboard a destroyer only in the sense that *Moby Dick*—which in a way it resembles—is a factual and informative account of life on a whaling ship.

"The novel," says Goodrich earnestly, "is the most honest form of art in existence. Its base is truth and authenticity. Authenticity of a writer arises from authenticity of background and surroundings." In the search for truth, "each writer has his own tests, but there can be no compromise. My own search, and my method, involves time. When I am in doubt I put my books away in the icebox and wait. Each rereading, sometimes months apart, shows up new problems of honesty or authenticity. Sometimes I solve them. When I cannot, I put them away again and wait for another reading. There are times on rereading when a solution is suddenly clear. Others remain murky. For these I wait still longer."

Rudyard Kipling advised, when he described what he called "the higher editing": "Read your final draft and consider faithfully every paragraph, sentence and word. . . . Let it lie by to drain. . . . Re-read. . . . Finally, read it aloud and alone at leisure. . . . [Then] let it go, and 'when thou hast done, repent not'." Marcus Goodrich describes such a process in dealing with an incident in *Delilah*. "When Lieutenant Fitzpatrick picked Mendel out of the bay, crushed and dying, I faced a major problem. There was a submarine out of control, its crew aboard dying and the craft circling wildly in an unguided course. Fitzpatrick was under pressure to get aboard it, and the problem of what to do with Mendel stopped him. And it stopped me, for weeks. Finally Fitzpatrick drops Mendel back into the water and makes for the submarine. For years that troubled me, but I tested it over and over by reading and rereading and it proved itself to me and that is the way I left it.

"But the original version of the explosion aboard the submarine was another matter. There was something wrong about it, and it took me years to understand what it was. That episode was written in the nineteen twenties. Anti-Semitism was strong in the Navy then, and I was a product of my time. The story of that heroic action was drawn closely from an actual event I had witnessed. It was the story of an extraordinarily courageous officer. The officer was a Jew. But when I came to write it, I automatically changed him to a non-Jew. Deep in my senses was the conditioned, unthinking belief that Jews were without courage. Then the truth —something very deep—came to me. Courage, or the lack of it, is the property of all men. Neither knows any boundaries of race or creed. Five years after I wrote the first version I rewrote it and Ensign Schiff, the Jew, took his place at the wheel of the submarine in that terrible ordeal, bringing his craft ashore. In that experience I saw my own anti-Semitism clearly, and in that experience, I lost it forever."

Just as his writing has deepened his understanding of himself, Goodrich's life and experience—like any author's—is the well from which he draws the water for his characters. He delves into both more deeply than most writers and his relationship with his characters is therefore very solid and personal. "I like Captain Borden," he exclaims. "The reader doesn't like him, or Fitzpatrick. They're naval officers. And people don't like naval officers. But I do." His eyes have turned to the distance and he is back in time. "They're men. I never liked Warrington, though. But I can't leave him alone. He fascinates me. I'm not through with him yet. He's still got a lot of uncharted courses and rough storms ahead of him."

Much of the course behind Marcus Goodrich has been uncharted, too, and often stormy. He has, for example, been married five times, the last time in 1946 to Hollywood actress Olivia de Havilland, whom he courted and married in three weeks' time. The marriage lasted six years.

Goodrich received his pre-college education in the public schools of San Antonio, Texas. He served briefly with the Texas National Guard on the Mexican border before running away to sea. It was during this Navy hitch, while he was aboard ship on the Asiatic Station, that he first tried to write. After the First World War he attended Columbia University. He wrote for the *New York Globe* while at college, and during the same period served as stage manager for several Broadway productions. Later, after college, he was a reporter at various times for the *New York Tribune,* the *World* and the *Evening Post,* and contributed also to *The New York Times Book Review.*

In the years preceding and immediately following World War II Goodrich traveled extensively in Europe, wrote for an advertising agency, and worked periodically as a script writer in Hollywood. Hollywood, he says, was the Mecca of superficiality, and he would not sell his own *Delilah* to any studio there. "I have always made it clear that if Hollywood was going to do anything with it that I must have complete and unquestioned control over the script, and there's never been anyone in Hollywood crazy enough to give me that authority."

Today Marcus Goodrich lives in Richmond, Virginia, which is the approximate scene of his present novel. "I had thought at first," he says, "to place it in New England. But after a long visit there I realized that New Englanders are religiously and emotionally unstable and that the South would provide me with a people more nearly normal." This novel, presently entitled *Malagueña Salerosa,* is concerned, like the two which preceded it, with the theme of the changed American.

"Ever since I dropped *Delilah,*" Goodrich says, "I have been at work explaining the contrasts between the mainstream of American life in the 1900s and of present day America. People have changed not because of the machine or because of the pressures of modern society, but because something very much more profound has happened. I am held to the subject with such fascination that I cannot get away from it in any moment of consciousness and it is this that I am testing again and again in these novels. When they have stood the test and I know that I have it right, I shall then say what this change is and how it came about."

In Richmond, Goodrich lives in a third-floor walkup in a now shabby but once elegant apartment house in the heart of the downtown district. It is, in fact, a retreat. Surrounded by books, which overflow shelves and lie in heaps alongside yellowing stacks of documents and clippings, he has cut himself off from the world.

Goodrich's working schedule was fixed years ago. He writes six days a week. On the seventh he attends services at the Episcopal church and then goes for a walk in an area requiring further research for the book. His writing day begins at 7:30 in the morning and if he is at a point of action or exposition he writes straight through until 1 o'clock. If, however, it is character development, or action which reveals character, he cannot write more than two hours. "I am so exhausted by then that I have to leave it," he says. "That is the most demanding and enervating activity I have ever known."

Goodrich says: "My life is now in what I have written and what I am writing. Sometimes I find moments in it that thrill me. But there are dark periods, when I face what I've done and what is left to be done, when I am depressed. Sometimes when I reread *Malagueña Salerosa* I feel that I shall have it finished in eighteen months. Then I read it again and I know that it will take more time. I live under pressure. The second part of *Delilah* is behind me. I shall probably burn it. But I must get on with the rest and I've only got six or seven years left. There is no time for anything else. I no longer write to anyone and no one writes to me. I've become a hermit.

"When I die, I know I may be unknown, or I may be a criticized man. But I've lived to fulfill my function. I'm never sure why a man writes or paints or carves in granite. But writing is why I'm here—why I was born. And I'll continue writing till my time runs out."

—THE EDITORS OF TIME

Introduction

Captain Edward L. Beach, author of this introduction, has been a U.S. naval officer since 1939. His novel, "Run Silent, Run Deep," was a 1955 bestseller. From 1953 until 1957 he was President Eisenhower's naval aide. In 1960 he was commander of the submarine "Triton" when it completed the first underwater circumnavigation of the world.

A novel set on the sea cannot be a great novel unless its thrust is on the development of its characters. The background against which the characters are set, though vital to the story for other reasons, can be only incidental. That is why *Delilah* has joined the slowly growing group of enduring novels.

Delilah is the slightly unbelievable name of the U.S. destroyer which forms the setting for the book. Marcus Goodrich actually served in *Delilah*—whose real identity was U.S.S. *Chauncey*, Destroyer Number 3. The annals of our Navy state that *Chauncey* was sunk in a collision with the British steamer *Rose* off Gibraltar on the 19th of November, 1917, and that 21 of her crew died with her.

Although there is really no central character in *Delilah* other than the destroyer herself, if one had to be selected it would probably be the young sailor Warrington, for it is he with whom the author spends the most time. The thought even intrudes that, just possibly, Warrington might have been a synthesis of Goodrich himself—in which case his fate is even more intriguing. Still, despite the emphasis on Warrington, the book ignores that fussy rule of writing which holds that a single point of view must be maintained, that one central character must be described from within, as it were, while all the others should be treated with rigorous objectivity. Instead, Goodrich goes into considerable subjective detail with at least 15 members of *Delilah's* crew. Some of them are so deeply dissected that they probably would be least of all recognizable to themselves. The author's intent, in short, was to write about people—not so much to tell their stories as to tell *about* them.

Within the closed society of a ship, the essence of a man's personality becomes sharply delineated. At sea, one learns to know one's fellow man intimately—his strengths and, inevitably, his weaknesses—simply because one is with him constantly. The cliques on board, the concealed struggles for supremacy, the misunderstandings over trifles, the deeper misunderstandings of personalities, the witnessed as well as unseen heroisms, the secret degradations, the growing and grudging admiration for the character who can survive the destructive influences—all these serve to throw into unusually vivid relief the personalities of the men who serve on ships at sea.

When I first read *Delilah* in 1941, I was living through all this as ensign in a younger sister of the ship which gave her name to the book. My destroyer, Number 118, was named *Lea* and had been launched some 20 years after *Delilah*. Shortly after reporting aboard I found a brass plate attached to the varnished lower portion of *Lea's* wooden foremast which recorded for posterity the fact that she had been launched down the ways of Cramp shipyard on the same day that I was launched in a New York hospital.

To me this fact was significant and private. *Lea,* when I came to her in 1939, had for several years been gently moldering in mothballs. The war in Europe called her back into service and my footsteps on her rusting steel decks, among the first she had felt for many slow, nodding months, presaged the beginning of a new life for both of us. The coincidence of dates symbolized a relationship which, I felt, would be a growing, fruitful and busy one. It proved to be so. During much of my time aboard, exactly two years as it turned out, there were only four officers in *Lea's* complement—as in *Delilah's*—and I was the most junior, the busiest, and in my own estimation at least, the happiest.

Like *Delilah, Lea* had four tall, slender smokestacks. Her hull, about 60 feet longer than *Delilah's,* had the identical tall, knife-edged bow, flaring delicately outward as it rose from the water; even at anchor or moored to a pier, she trembled with the same taut energy. *Lea* displaced just over 1,000 tons, twice as much as *Delilah,* and burned oil instead of coal, an advance no one regretted. A less obvious difference would have pleased Ensign Woodbridge: the wardroom and officers' cabins in the *Lea* were directly under the bridge and it was barely a couple of dozen steps up two ladders from where I slept to where I stood eight hours of watch every day. The space aft, where so much of *Delilah's* life took place, where her wardroom and the red-shellacked quarterdeck under the awning were located, was devoted in *Lea* to a crew's berthing compartment and elongated depth-charge racks.

Much of *Delilah* was identical to *Lea.* Many of her crew closely resembled men I knew and worked with. In retrospect I can as well imagine myself in Subic as in Guantánamo Bay, or off Olongapo instead of Charlotte Amalie with a returning liberty party coming alongside. The liberty parties that came after midnight were usually a little boisterous; once in Santiago, I was hurriedly relieved as officer-of-the-deck in order to dive into the filthy water of the bay to help two of our just-returned liberty party who unaccountably had been unable to remain upright on deck. (I later found this laconic entry in the gangway watch's log: "Three over the side and back aboard.") But far more important were the target practices we fired, the meticulous care the torpedomen lavished on our torpedo tubes, the perfect order in which the Chief Boatswain's Mate insisted our foc'sle always remain, the pride in our boasts that *Lea* had never failed a commitment.

So it was with *Delilah,* and this common heritage remains unchanged in the new greyhounds of our Navy. But, though the heritage is there to see, there have been many changes too. For years, destroyers carried powerful, long-range torpedoes of great accuracy. Now these are gone. Today their main armament is composed of electronic equipment and self-powered missiles able to sense the presence of an enemy aircraft or ship and to destroy it.

For power to run its machinery the latest of the new destroyers

—like its natural enemy, the submarine—relies on nuclear power. Gone are the days of shoveling coal into the white heat of a gaping furnace, of spewing smoke high into the clean sky, of working in the grime and filth and sweat of the boiler room. Today, a new generation of engineers works in sealed and air-conditioned cubicles, facing panels covered with instruments monitoring the working of their science, squinting at ubiquitous slide rules, guided by heavy loose-leaf tomes containing intricate instructions and calculations.

New weapons and new power have changed these ships, and the men who serve in them today are likewise outwardly different from those who served in the ships of the past. Most of *Delilah's* crew would not have known what to do with a family if they had had one, whereas in today's Navy most of them would be doing their best to maintain a normal family relationship while at the same time fulfilling their obligation to the service. Such a man as Warrington would not have been a misfit in the new Navy. His taste for literature, poetry and music would have struck kindred sparks in every crew. He would have been understood by most, and tolerated by all. His yearning to maintain his personal integrity would have been echoed a hundred times over. Borden, the introspective captain, dedicated to the old Navy, would also have found a place in this new Navy. So would the brilliant Woodbridge and the thoughtful Fitzpatrick. Rowe, the failure in *Delilah,* might not have failed in the new Navy.

Better educated, possessed of higher personal standards, today's destroyer crew has nevertheless one great point of sameness with those rough and ready crews of yesteryear: integrity. Their working lives are dedicated to the service of their nervous racehorse of a ship, but they like to play together, too. There may be fewer occasions, in these more recent times, but the cry, *"Semmes!"*, *"Truxton!"* and *"Bainbridge!"* in a crowded quarter of a foreign city is likely to evoke the same magic today as the ancient one of *"Chauncey!"*

We all feel a sense of nostalgia for the ships which have passed, and respect for the men who served in them. This we shall never give up, for from this was distilled the grim determination of the destroyermen at Okinawa who reaped the harvest of the Japanese suicide air attacks; from it came the esprit which drove the *Johnston*, *Hoel* and *Samuel B. Roberts* into the teeth of the big gun broadsides of Japanese battleships that fierce 25th of October off Samar to save five of the six escort carriers trapped there.

Chauncey, which Goodrich called *Delilah* (doubtless he felt that so feminine a creature should have a feminine name), never fought an enemy except vicariously. But her bloodlines have been in our Navy ever since she slid down the ways, and the loyalties she bred in the men who served in her have been bequeathed to her descendants and intensified through the years. To me, *Delilah* and *Lea* were one and the same, and every old destroyerman can make a similar identification.

One of my treasured keepsakes is a little gold watch with an inscription on the back, an admonition I shall always carry with me. It says "Remember the *Lea*."

Like *Delilah*, who could ever forget her?

—CAPTAIN EDWARD L. BEACH, U.S.N.

These, in the day when heaven was falling,
The hour when earth's foundations fled,
Followed their mercenary calling
And took their wages and are dead.

Their shoulders held the sky suspended;
They stood, and earth's foundations stay;
What God abandoned, these defended,
And saved the sum of things for pay.

—A. E. HOUSMAN

The poem appearing on this page is "Epitaph on an Army of Mercenaries" from *The Collected Poems of A. E. Housman,* and is reprinted by permission of Holt, Rinehart and Winston, Inc. Copyright 1939, 1940, © 1965 by Holt, Rinehart and Winston, Inc.

Chapter
One

1

She was very slim and light. She was always tense, often atremble, and never failed to give the impression of being a mass of almost terrible power wrapped in a thin and fragile blue-grey skin. The materials that went into the making of her complete being were more curious and varied than those that went to compose her creator, Man,—for Man, himself, formed part of her bowels, heart and nerve centres. She ate great quantities of hunked black food, and vented streams of grey debris. Through her coiled veins pumped vaporous, superheated blood at terrific pressure. She inhaled noisily and violently through four huge nostrils, sent her hot breath pouring out through four handsome mouths and sweated delicate, evanescent, white mist. Her function in existence was to carry blasting destruction at high speed to floating islands of men; and her intended destiny, at the opposite pole from that of the male bee, was to die in this act of impregnating her enemy with death. It was, perhaps, for this reason that she carried her distinctly feminine bow, which was high and very sharp, with graceful arrogance and some slight vindictiveness, after the manner of a perfectly controlled martyr selected for spectacular and aristocratic sacrifice. Her name was Delilah.

2 ≈≈≈

The suave, glistening Sulu Sea parted before Delilah's sharp bow and slid under her flat stern with great but smooth rapidity. It was only in her wake, where was left a white commotion, that there was betrayed the adequate evidence of the effort of her

3

progress. A few feet above the cause of this foaming propulsion—two whirling typhoons of metal—an old Irish monk sat on the edge of a camp cot and gazed intently forward along the destroyer's narrow steel deck at what was taking place amidships. He seemed unmindful of the sweat that exuded from his tonsure and leaked down the white fringes of his hair and over his big hands, in which he was resting his head. He seemed unmindful of the very sun, itself, which so fiercely inflamed the universe with white glare that it was difficult to look at the opal circle of the sea and impossible to look for long into the sky. Yet he was sitting in the full blaze of it, because even the quarter-deck awnings had been furled as possible hindrances to the attainment of maximum speed.

The ship, too, seen from one of the small islands she occasionally passed, must have appeared insensible to the limitless conflagration, a compact creature skimming easily along the water, naked to the sun and docile bearer of the few visible people ensconced along her thin length.

Deep inside of her, however, the Engineer Officer, who was also the Executive Officer, was thinking that she was a skidding shelf of hell. Stripped to the waist, he was standing Machinist Mate's watch in the Starboard Engine-room. He was used to this sort of thing only in theory and in the pleasantly inauthentic reputation he enjoyed amongst the lounges and bungalows ashore. "Fitzpatrick," said the Service people who gave parties in Manila and Zamboanga, "is one Engineer Officer who really gets acquainted with his engines. If he had to, he could stand a watch shoulder to shoulder with his Machinist's Mates . . . Most promising youngster the Academy has turned out in a long time" . . . . . . But now, in the midst of just such an emergency, Lieutenant Fitzpatrick (Junior Grade) was not shoulder to shoulder with anybody. He was alone with what he was wont to refer to importantly as "my starboard engine," a thing that suddenly had turned out to be chaos of scorching oil jets, hissing steam tentacles, pounding verticals of steel, and wet heat that brought him almost to the fainting point. The oil-splashed floor plates and gratings made even standing precarious, and a slight movement of the ship often sent him careening threateningly towards the

4

maze of flashing, metallic pandemonium beneath the three cylinders. As he performed the dangerous ritual of feeling bearings for excess heat, he said to himself: "This business is more dangerous than sticking *banderillas* in a Muros bull . . . poor old Hemple, who does this all the time . . . he ought to be rated Chief . . ." Lieutenant Fitzpatrick groped gingerly with his right hand for a bearing the size of his neck. It was necessary first to synchronize his hand with the up and down movement of the bearing, which was moving so fast that he barely could distinguish its location. Finally he caught up with it and reassured himself that it was not running too hot. ". . . This certainly is risky business . . . next month I'll manage to give Hemple his Chief's rating . . . the 'Old Man' will kick . . . there are already more Chiefs than the complement calls for . . . do something for that new man, the Oiler, too . . . soon as I can." He looked up longingly at the brilliant blue oblong of the open hatchway. Privately, he did not think that they would get there in time.

The Machinist's Mate and the Oiler for whom Lieutenant Fitzpatrick was substituting were in the fire-rooms exigently shovelling coal into the flaming areas beneath Delilah's sensitive boilers: and so was everyone else except Ensign Snell, who, like Lieutenant Fitzpatrick, was standing the watch of two men in the other engine-room; Ensign Woodbridge, who was acting as helmsman; the Captain, who had succeeded himself on the bridge as Navigator and Watch Officer ever since eight o'clock in the morning; and the elderly monk, who was sitting meditatively on the camp cot—where the Executive Officer had urged him to nap—turning over in his mind how best he could help speed on this craft that was rushing him along to what might prove his destruction.

3 〰〰〰

On the galleons of old, the highest part of the hull was astern in the form of a gallant, elevated deck called the poop. Delilah had one of these rearing decks, but it formed part of her high, sharp bow. This forecastle deck extended sternward for about one-fifth of the length of the ship, then fell sharply away like a steel cliff down to the destroyer's main deck, which was a convex strip of thin steel twenty-one feet wide stretching back for two hundred and fifty feet to the low, flat, rounded stern. Almost on the edge of the cliff formed by the break of the forecastle deck, was a thick steel conning-tower. It contained on its inside an auxiliary steering wheel. On its roof were mounted the regular steering wheel and a three-inch gun; and this conning-tower roof was Delilah's only equivalent of a navigating bridge. Also, the squat tower shouldered, in appearance, a bold but graceful mast much after the manner that a soldier shoulders a rifle with fixed bayonet. The Captain invariably referred to this mast, as well as to the one which was similarly shouldered by the After Conning-tower, as a "signal stick." Squeezed into the space between the foremast and the conning-tower was the "Radio Shack" into which fitted comfortably one man and his apparatus.

Down the narrow convexity of the main deck—it really was like the back of a thin whale—stretched in single file the external structures indispensable to Delilah's purposes and functions. First came the short, formidable, stream-lined Smokestack Number One, leaning backward toward the stern as if unable to meet upright the strain of Delilah's fierce, forward leaps. Back of the stack, side by side, came the two capacious nostrils of the big blowers that sucked a heavy pressure of air down into the Forward Fire-room. Between these was the air-tight little hatch that provided the only access to this fire-room. Next came Smokestack Number Two, precisely similar to the first and succeeding stacks, and after that the rectangular hatch of the Starboard Engine-room, echeloned to port of which was the hatch of the Port Engine-room. It was not mere coincidence that Lieutenant Fitzpatrick was sending his longing glances staggering up towards the fresh, blue mirage framed in the Starboard Engine-room Hatchway, while Ensign Snell was glancing up as desirously at that framed in the Port; for as Fitzpatrick was senior to, and took precedence over Snell, so the starboard engine took precedence over, and set the pace for the port engine.

Mounted between, and swinging over the two engine-room

hatches, Torpedo-tube Number One—which was about as long as the ship was wide—marked the middle of the destroyer, and, like a lengthy, grey womb, ever harboured one of the polished steel seeds consecrated to her deadly fertility.

Following the torpedo-tube and the engine-room hatches, after a longer interval than any of those between the other stacks, was Smokestack Number Three, followed by the After Fire-room blowers and fire-room hatch. Behind these came Smokestack Number Four, then the square, iron box of the galley or kitchen. Abaft of this galley was a sizeable space centred by a Hotchkiss Rapid-fire Six-pounder, which overshadowed the hatch of the Chief Petty Officers' sleeping compartment. Forming the after limit of the space was the After Conning-tower; and this marked the border line where manual labour and implicit obedience ended and intellectual effort and supreme authority began: For the After Conning-tower, besides mounting on its top another three-inch gun, enclosed within its exclusive, steel walls the sacred hatchway down to the officers' Wardroom, and, with its whole, conical bulk, shielded from the forward, vulgar seven-eighths of the ship the gentle after eighth. This miniature quarter-deck between the After Conning-tower and the stern was shaded, ordinarily, by a smart, well-cut awning; and its steel deck area was handsomely covered with red shellac. In its centre was a spruce, little skylight, fitted with lace curtains that delicately filtered down into the Wardroom the *mélange* of light that diffused through the white awning and reflected up from the red deck. It was the only part of the destroyer's exterior, with the exception of the bridge, that could be kept anywhere near clean; and it was there that, on ancient fighting ships, stood the altar of the gods.

Four more six-pounders, like grey claws, projected from either edge of the ship's long body: a pair on the main deck at the break of the forecastle, which partially protected them in battle, and the other pair on the main deck just forward of Stack Number Three.

And all this, Delilah's top side, was fenced in from bow to stern by a railing formed of four bronze cables arranged one above the other at twelve-inch intervals. The narrow, bulging deck of the craft provided such insecure footing that without the railing there was proven danger of people tumbling over the side. Even with the railing, men sometimes went over,—through the interstices.

4 〰〰

The monk on the starboard side of the quarter-deck had been for thirty-five years in the multitudinous islands that stretch from the Malay Peninsula to the Kamchatka Peninsula, and he had been used, exploited or persecuted in so many of the crises that had splattered these brilliant archipelagoes with blood that his body and soul seemed to have assimilated certain aspects of them. People who encountered him even superficially were prone to imagine that "if he had lived in the Middle Ages he would have been a saint." Yet, as Lieutenant Fitzpatrick had observed to the Captain that morning after the monk had boarded Delilah alongside the Zamboanga dock, "The old boy seems to have too much of a sense of humour to make a good saint."

"I don't know," the Captain had answered, "he evidently hasn't enough of it to make him unimportant."

The monk's arrival had been preceded by urgent, emergency orders to get Delilah under way immediately he boarded her and proceed at the utmost speed possible to Isla-Sulu, one of a cluster of coral islands that lay at the southern limit of the Sulu Sea. On this small island the Moros had risen. Some of the dozen or so white and Chinese traders on it were dead or wounded. Survivors were besieged. The order surprisingly further instructed the Captain to land the old holy man on the island, and under no circumstances to send ashore a Landing Party unless the monk called upon him to do so or failed to communicate with Delilah within an hour after landing. The Captain had been ruffled by this order.

"Well, if they want to kill off a priest or two, I suppose it's none of my business."

Even Lieutenant Fitzpatrick, who had an emotional leaning towards confidence in the monk, had not been able to help feeling uncertain about one or two aspects of the affair. As he had hurried about preparing to get Delilah under way, he had told himself that "it was a very curious idea . . . paradoxical . . . this trying to pacify a bunch of Mohammedan fanatics by dumping a Catholic monk on them . . . as if he were a damn barrel of oil on a rough sea . . . And what the devil would happen to the people who were besieged during the hour the Landing Party held back . . . if the Father failed to straighten things out?"

Shortly after Delilah had steamed westward through the Straits of Basilan, it had become clear to Lieutenant Fitzpatrick that his short-handed fire-room gangs could neither meet the demands made upon them nor even survive in the fierce heat developed in the ship by the sun and the four boilers. The Captain, still worrying in a minor key over having to do with the monk, had dismissed what Lieutenant Fitzpatrick had considered a formidable difficulty with swift efficiency, not appearing to dispel wholly from his mind its preoccupation.

"Put all hands below, Mr. Fitzpatrick, in short shifts. You and Mr. Snell stand the engine-room watches; that is, if you think Snell can handle it. Mr. Woodbridge and I will take the bridge." His pleasant, ugly face had set amiably as it often did when he was dealing with younger men whom he liked. "We have to get there, you know."

The crew's astonishment at the radical rearrangement of its duties, as well as its uneasiness at having the monk on board, had given way as soon as it was miserably immersed in the black and fiery struggle to drive Delilah along at a steady twenty knots, a cruising speed that no longer was the easy matter it had been for her some sixteen years before when she and the century were born: But the Captain had peered back over the bridge railing once or twice, and had been relieved to find that apparently the monk was sleeping soundly back there, his lanky frame stretched out passively on the cot Lieutenant Fitzpatrick had had rigged for him.

About three o'clock in the afternoon the monk had sat up in a manner that seemed to indicate that he had not been asleep at all. Now, two hours later, some complication in what he was gazing at forward made him get to his feet. As he balanced himself against the starboard railing, with his worn, black galoshes showing up drably against the shining red deck, and with the edges of his dark robe flapping slightly about the hairy angularity of his spread, bare legs, he appeared a rather terrible and thrilling figure; and his blue eyes, intense with a sort of aggressive sweetness, contained as much violence as the scene upon which they were fixed.

A thin man, named Poe, under normal routine the Chief Electrician, was being hauled up through the After Fire-room Hatchway, black with coal dust and stricken with heat. He was sobbing raspingly in rhythm with the pulsing engines.

5

It is probable that the early torpedo-boat destroyer, which is practically all raw engine and boilers, was not designed with a view to Sulu Sea operations in the hot season. Even in cold weather, with fire under all four of Delilah's boilers and the engines running under maximum steam pressure, it was necessary to wear thick wooden sandals in order to tread the burning expanses of deck over the fire- and engine-rooms. This also was more economical, because it took longer to char away the wooden sandals than it did leather shoes, and the sandals could be sawed out of any thick board as fast as they were needed. Now, even though shod with the thick wood, the men waiting to relieve those below in the fire-rooms climbed off the scorching deck onto every shelf and corner that would hold them. A number even perched on the bronze cables of the railing, a thing normally not permitted because it stretched the cables.

An Ordinary Seaman, a young Texan named Warrington, with nothing on his body but a thin, sleeveless undershirt, dungaree trousers and a pair of wooden sandals, was crouching on the torpedo-tube base, two feet above the deck, waiting for his turn below. He, too, was staring at Poe's agonized face. Three men dragged the Chief Electrician off the After Fire-room Hatch rim, where he had collapsed, and hung him on the railing. Another, who was playing a vigorous stream of salt water on the deck in an attempt to keep the heat down, turned the nozzle on the fainting electrician to revive him. He screamed as the column of cold sea water broke against him. From Poe, the Texan's glance slid down the iron perspective of the deck and encountered the formidable figure of the monk. The association called up in his memory a story of Inquisitional torment . . . the men hung on the bronze wires like black, rotting victims of some ancient torture rack . . . soon he'd have to tackle it again . . . the hour wasn't nearly up, but the other gang seemed to be passing out for good . . . fifteen minutes up . . . fifteen minutes down . . . for an hour . . . then try to rest . . . for an hour . . . like this . . . on an incandescent deck . . . fifteen minutes up . . . fifteen minutes down . . .

As a matter of fact, in this heat very few were able to stick out the full fifteen minutes below, and only the most rugged of the "black gang," the regular coal heavers, were expected to. When a man was on the verge of collapse, he crawled up the ladder and those above hauled him through the hatch onto the deck. Then the man whose turn it was next climbed down in his place. There was no question of anyone being a quitter: the crew knew instinctively and at once when a man was all in, and every one realized that they knew, so there was no shame about giving up and no thought of giving up while there was still strength enough to shovel. Some stuck it out eight minutes, some nine, some ten, some twelve and some thirteen minutes; even Rene, the bulky Chief Machinist's Mate in charge of the resting gang to which Warrington belonged, had stayed the full fifteen minutes only twice.

"Stand by, you guys!" yelled Rene.

His gang had been seriously reduced by the necessary transfer of two members to the other gang as replacements for four men who had suffered permanent collapse; and in the resulting rearrangement of pairs to work below, which now took place, Warrington, the Ordinary Seaman, found himself linked with the one thing in his hated surroundings that he hated most, a thing that infected his consciousness with an unrelaxing dread of terrific power coupled with devastating irresponsibility. This thing was O'Connel. Warrington and O'Connel, the Water-Tender, were the antitheses of each other in everything; even in the quality of their indubitable honesties: the boy's honesty was like that of an old steel blade, and the man's like that of the sea. One was seventeen, the other thirty-four. The Texan, who was born in a high, blue room pervaded by the scent of magnolia blossoms, fortified himself with poetry and hunted out his strength from the tunnels of his soul; while the Irishman, who was born in a canal barge, fortified himself with whiskey and sucked up his strength from the magnificent stretches of his great body. The one steered his aggressiveness against the universe and its enemy; the other shattered the faces of every one in the Squadron who was as big as he was. For the youth, this environment was a valley of repellent futility down which he had fled blindly from an intolerable situation in his home; for the man, it was a high place vivid with significant life. The Texan was ever on the verge of annihilating the Irishman on the level of significance; and it always seemed as if O'Connel were about to rend Warrington bone from bone. Both looked life squarely in the face, but they saw there different things.

6

O'Connel was heavyweight champion of the Squadron, and he was too tough to serve on anything but the black boats. He had been in the Navy twelve years, and his service was a record of turbulence. For much of it, he had been deprived of advancement and pay and slammed in the brig; but for some of it he had gotten the Congressional Medal of Honor and a reputation for being a "hard egg" in the face of things that were likely to smash him as well as in situations where he was the one able to do the smashing. It was for this reason that people looked upon him as a wild man rather than as a bully. It is probable that the function of introspection was but primitively a part of his mental operations, and his test for human authenticity seemed to be a formula involving physical force, elemental simplicity and "guts."

In 1907, when he first went to destroyers, the thing had occurred that gained him the Congressional Medal. A cylinder head blew off at sea while O'Connel and three others were in an engine-room making emergency repairs on the engine. The splattering steel and steam killed one man outright and wounded the other two. The right side of O'Connel's head was crushed in. Nevertheless, he seized the Engineer Officer, who was one of those knocked out, and dragged him up out of the lethal cubicle onto the deck. Then realizing that the scalding steam was intimidating the Rescue Party that had gathered to extricate the men remaining below, he flung himself angrily into the midst of the fat, white death billowing out of the hatchway, and tumbled back down into the engine-room. Those on deck could hear his wild and private curses spouting up with the steam. A moment later, in rapid succession, the limp bodies of the other two men shot up through the steaming hatchway as if they had been hunks of lava flung skyward by the violence of an erupting crater.

When O'Connel had made his raging leap down the hatchway, his intention had been to make his way to the steam manifold and shut off all the steam making its way from the boilers to the engine. But in landing on the steel floor plates he had broken his left leg. It would have taken him so long a time, he had felt, to crawl first to the manifold, hoist himself up and turn off the steam, cracked up as he was, that the lungs of the men he was trying to save would surely have been burnt out by the steam. So he had heaved the men up first; and then afterwards, though the boiled flesh had been peeling from his hairy legs and arms, and his cracked head had assumed something like one of those grotesque shapes usually seen but in the distorting mirrors of a penny arcade, he had rolled and clawed his way to the manifold and shut off the steam. When the rescuers reached him, his slowly relaxing, blood-spattered body was doubled over his broken leg; but his big hands were fiercely gripping a polished engine stanchion after the manner of a wrestler holding to the limb of an opponent, and he was enunciating, more as if in realization than as if in supplication, "Peace, you son of a bitch, peace . . . peace . . . peace . . ."

With his bronze medal on his breast and a silver plate in his skull, he had lain for a long time in hospital bunks and champed restlessly in places good for his lungs. But he finally went back to destroyers seemingy cured of everything but a curious, elemental rage at something too far beyond the horizon of his consciousness to assume definite objectivity. When he raised hell, the men said: "You see, he's got a silver plate in his head."

7 ≈≈≈

The Irishman hit the floor plates first and stood with his fists on his hips watching the Texan descend the ladder. Through his back the boy felt the wild, blue gaze plunging hostilely at him, and his heavy prescience that this was to be a significant encounter seemed to suffer instant confirmation. He helped the two worn-out men they were relieving up the ladder, slowly lit the taper of his bunker lamp, glanced a little helplessly from the great, iron visage of the boiler that formed the forward wall of the cave in which he found himself to that which formed the after wall, and then, almost shutting his eyes, crawled through the low door into the port coal bunker.

For some seconds O'Connel stared at the bunker hole, where the dim gleams from the Texan's paraffin torch flickered. Finally he stamped over and looked through into the bunker, which, like that on the starboard side of the ship, was a crevice only a little more than two feet wide, but extending the height and depth of the ship. It served the double purpose of carrying fuel and pro-viding a protective belt of coal for the engines and boilers,—the only armour of any sort that stood between these and an enemy's shells. In the depths of this narrow, towering frame, O'Connel saw the Texan leaning for a preparatory instant on the handle of his shovel as if it were a crutch. His eyes, across which there was a sweeping smear of coal dust, were gazing at the deep darkness just above the level of his head, and the squirming light glowed uncertainly amongst the curls of his dull blond hair.

The Irishman lunged back to one of the firebox doors under the after boiler, flung it open and shot in a shovelful of coal from the heap on the floor plates. As he was withdrawing the shovel from before the flaming door, some arresting pattern formed on the stream of consciousness rushing through his great, battered head. He grinned, and the red gush of brilliance from the firebox flashed and shone on the long row of his upper teeth, which were all gold. The sweat pouring down his face was curiously diverted into two deep channels that formed in the flesh on either side of his thick, flat nose as he grinned, and his hair, stiff with coal, seemed to bristle uncannily. His grin burst into a delighted, braying laugh. He banged the shovel on the floor plates with fierce zest as a man might bang out his delight with a spoon on some cabaret table.

The mad banging and laughing penetrated into the bunker and startled the boy. Hanging the bunker lamp to a hook on the bulkhead, he crawled back to the low hole that served for door and peered out into the fire-room. For about as long as O'Connel had stared in at him, he was held by the lurid apparition before the flaming furnace; then he went back in where the coal began and commenced getting it down. After a few shovelfuls, he paused to readjust his grip . . . He was holding the shovel too tight . . . but then if he held it looser the sweat made it slip . . . the heat seemed to be getting him already . . . he'd have to get the coal out fast . . . felt like the air pressure was bursting in his ears . . . blowers turning up too much . . . O'Connel used a lot of coal . . . too much coal they said . . . but the officers weren't watching the smoke on this run . . . deadly hot . . . He moved down to the door and shovelled through it onto the fire-room floor plates the coal he had knocked down. The infranatural laughter bit at him again. His breath stopped for an instant.

8

The interior of the coal bunker was so narrow that he could maintain himself at any depth in it by the centrifugal pressure of his legs: But now he had shovelled his way to the bottom again, and somewhat farther away from the entrance into the fire-room. He'd fed O'Connel a lot of coal . . . this was about the end . . . as far as he was concerned . . . coal was as hard as rock . . . wasn't the coal, after all, but the steel side of the ship . . . this would never do . . .

couldn't make the shovel go where he wanted it to. In a spurt of irritation he drove the shovel into the lumpy implacability before him. The force of the movement threw him forward into the coal, a section of which, jarred loose, caved in upon him. For a time he lay there in the hot, primordial smother, relaxed, at rest, losing consciousness, much as a snow-beaten man surrenders to the lethal peace of a deep drift. The uninterrupted noises that in the first moment of his recumbency had seemed to have a soothing, lullaby effect upon him, slowly began to wear through their disguises: the malevolent, high-pitched purr of the sea as it slid viciously along the thin skin of the ship, and the pounding struggle of the propellers as they tore and twisted at its waters . . . He began to think or dream or remember: "The sea . . . the sea . . . the unutterably horrible sea . . . an infinite, biological solution in which coiled and gasped monsters and living slime beside which the images of man's diseased obsessions and insane fears become delicate symmetries . . . a festering, amorphous mass pouring over the areas of the earth, licking and pounding in insentient fury at the few rocks up which man has fled . . . a distraught gesture of Creation" . . . Slowly he pulled himself up out of the coal and tried to stand erect. But he could not maintain himself in that position. On all fours he crawled over the hot bunker plates and coal towards the ruddy flicker of the fire-room entrance. His under lip curled out instinctively to catch the dark sweat that poured from about his head. He reached the door. Like a dying animal, covered with black mud, he glared through the hole at O'Connel.

With the heat and the air pressure assaulting the borders of his last province of strength, the Irishman, sweat-drenched and inflamed, was probing the conflagration before him with an enormous, iron slice bar. In proportion to the extent that his body succumbed to tiredness and weakness, he furiously revenged himself upon it by demanding of it heavier and grosser performances. He was left-handed and his right arm had been a little wasted by a series of injuries; but when he found that exhaustion was creeping into his good left arm, he flung it from him as if it had sentient personality; and, in no sense to get relief, but rather to defy his own strength and to humiliate his left arm, he swung angrily about to grip and handle the slice bar with his right hand alone. It was then that he saw Warrington staring at him from the hole.

This confrontation unloosed a considerable emotional and mental convulsion in each of them. The effort to reinstate the image and idea of the boy in his consciousness, which had been intensely monopolized by a quite different problem, and the sudden realization that "the little, white-necked louse was still at it" unpoised the Irishman. He emitted a raucous bleat, such as might come from a gargantuan calf.

"A-a-a-A-a-a! What the hell! Quittin'?" He sneered with both corners of his big mouth.

The instant the boy saw the great creature fighting with the fire, he had succumbed to the torturing obligation of maintaining the authenticity of his difference from him. He *couldn't* quit. The flaming power of his abhorrence of the Irishman and of the idea of admitting any sort of inferiority to him, openly or secretly, concentrated what little physical energy was left in him and strengthened the waning current of his blood. It began to pound unbearably within the sick regions about the back of his head. If his miserable body would only keep up with him . . . see him through . . . Were O'Connel a person like himself there would be no question of keeping on . . . he could say, "I am so tired, help me up the ladder" . . . even sink into the arms of an enemy . . . like himself . . . but this . . . this *thing!* When the Irishman shouted his question at him, the boy, still on all fours, turned about and faced back into the bunker; then he paused there as if endeavouring to marshal before him in the black path, in one convenient obstacle, all the ramifications of the dread necessity for going back.

This manoeuvre confounded O'Connel; so he went over to the hole and gripping Warrington by one of his slim arms dragged him out onto the floor plates of the fire-room. The boy jerked himself free and crawled back into the bunker. Until the thought of his fires called him back to the boilers, O'Connel stood in bewilderment staring at the hole and listening to the spasmodic coughing that began to come through it.

In his first excitement over being down with O'Connel and his fear of not getting out enough coal to meet shovel for shovel the Irishman's effort, Warrington had gotten down, and heaved out into the fire-room considerably more coal than the fires needed; so

17

that the frantic, almost futile efforts that his exhausted body now engaged in, with his eyelids tightly pressed together as if to shut out the feverish dimness that enveloped him, held things back not at all for the moment. To load his shovel from the pile that he knocked down onto the floor of the bunker, hoist it to the level of his knees and then project its load through the hole to O'Connel was demanding more intense mental concentration, attention to bodily balance and physical sacrifice than he ever had been called upon to suffer before. To get a load in the shovel, he felt with its blade for a clear space on the steel near the coal as a blind man searches the way before him with a stick. When he had found such a space, he laid the back of the shovel upon it and then lunged forward on the handle. Such coal as the edge of the shovel encountered slid into the shovel. At this point the terrible phase of his repetitious struggle was upon him. He balanced himself unnaturally on his heels, which he kept wide apart and opposite each other, and rested his back against the bulkhead. Then jamming the end of the shovel handle into his stomach just above the loins, he slid his hands half-way down the handle and slowly began to pull. The force of the lift was taken by his stomach, as a fulcrum, and each shovelful seemed on the verge of sending his straining intestines bursting through the pit of his abdomen. When the shovel hung poised at about the level of his knees, he opened his eyes with an effort, located the red bunker hole, closed his eyes again, and fell toward it. The shovel of coal proceeded through the hole until his body brought up sharply against the steel wall above it. This jerked the coal forward from the shovel. Often he missed the hole, and the coal and shovel clattered tauntingly against the bulkhead.

The Irishman could not get out of his head the idea of this "punk" actually trying to battle it out with him. Every time a shot of coal spat into the fire-room, he turned his head towards the hole. Eventually, the strange manner in which the coal jumped off when the shovel stuck through into the fire-room caught his attention. After watching for the rather long time required by three of these reappearances of the shovel, O'Connel could not resist the temptation to look into the hole. He leapt over, as the shovel was being withdrawn, and peered in. Slowly, as he watched the agony-drenched ritual develop in the reddish haze of the bunker, a crude, eerie revulsion proceeded within him. Some strong attitude, which particular one he had not the faculty to determine on the instant, began to disintegrate. Some handhold to his immediate situation seemed to be giving way. He slumped back uneasily into the centre of the fire-room, where he slung his head from side to side lionesquely, as if seeking to sight something which he could rush upon and smash to reaffirm that all was right with his world. His eyes found the air-pressure gauge. It indicated an excessive pressure of air in the fire-room. His rage, blasting him along the channel provided by this, swept him up the ladder. With his sweating, tightly clenched fist, he crashed open the little, air-tight hatch-cover and, like a gleaming wet demon rending up through the earth, projected his coal-blackened upper bulk into the midst of the group clustered on the deck.

"You crummy bastards!" he howled at the ship in general, "watch them blowers!"

The senior Chief Machinist's Mate, Stengle, a small, coffee-coloured man, was jerking about between the two huge nostrils that sucked air down into the fire-room, trying to regulate their speed. The mechanism that controlled them from below had broken down early on the run.

"Keep your shirt on! Keep your shirt on!" he said, shaking a big Stillson wrench at the Irishman as if it had been a forefinger. "I'll have to let 'em run high, or shut 'em down . . . Can't do that."

9 〜〜〜

When O'Connel had dropped back down the hatch, leaving the abrupt banging of its cover as the period to his final, vituperative roar, the men awoke to the fact that the pair below already had survived for thirteen minutes. This was the record so far, for although several individuals had lasted the full quarter of an hour, one or the other of every pair that had gone down up to now had been relieved before the thirteen-minute mark. O'Connel always lasted it out; but no one expected or demanded of Warrington to stay down more than five minutes. As the fourteen-minute mark was approached, the situation took on the aspect of a prize fight in which some "dark horse" was putting up a totally unexpected and wonder arousing show. The men, including the resting gang from the Forward Fire-room, crowded a trifle excitedly around the hatch expecting every second to see it exude the sweat-soaked body of the boy; and the man whose duty it was to relieve him hovered preparatorily about as if made restless by a feeling that he should have been down long ago, but that it was no fault of his that he was not. A red-headed Oiler, named Feenan, who was in the habit of making clumsily sarcastic remarks about the boy's careful and rather over-elegant manner of speaking, stepped to the railing, his unpleasantly freckled face set with primitive primness, spat accurately into the sea, and said:

"He'll never stay down the fifteen minutes."

As if by sudden, unanimous consent, the sporting attitude of the crew gave way to a general feeling of uneasiness.

"Maybe the kid's passed out in the bunker and that wild guy has forgotten all about him."

"What time is it now?" Stengle was asked for the third time.

"Maybe the big harp got sore and smacked him."

Everybody laughed restlessly.

Stengle moved over to the hatch, pulled it open and stuck his dirty, little, grey head down into it. O'Connel feeling the pressure of the air jump suddenly from off his chest and ear drums, and perceiving the white fire he was feeding begin to turn red, raised his face questioningly to the hatch. It seemed to Stengle that the Irishman was more all in than he ever had seen him before.

"Time up?" shouted O'Connel.

"Minute to go," Stengle screamed back. His voice barely pierced the barricade of mechanical uproar between them. "How's the kid making out?"

At this question, the alien, about-facing disturbance within O'Connel burst into clear recognition. He flung his two great fists into the air as if they were gonfalons he was bearing into battle, and shouted triumphantly, half-incidentally up to Stengle,

"Going strong!"

Stengle popped his head back out of the hatch and permitted the cover to spring shut.

"Going strong," he repeated to the men around him.

A wave of surprised admiration swept up the deck, and even swirled for a moment about the bridge when "Unc" Blood, the Chief Quartermaster, was summoned there to relieve Ensign Woodbridge at the wheel for a moment.

Blood stationed himself upright behind the wheel, as motionless and set as a carbonized, baroque statue, and fixed his lecherous, little eyes steadily on the Captain in a suggestive fashion, a fashion that often caused the Captain to preface his Wardroom stories about the Chief Quartermaster by saying, "Blood came up bursting with news . . ."

These two had "been together" going on six years, and the Captain never failed to assume what he felt was a discouraging attitude towards the man's propensity to gossip. He assumed this attitude now. For several minutes he would not look in Blood's direction: But when he finally—as he always did—shot a quick glance at the aging mariner to see if he still was "bursting," Blood's sanguinary glance nailed him. Before the Captain could escape, the point of Blood's blackened beard, which curved to one side in a satyrlike manner, dropped an inch and a half, the bright red cavity of his mouth twitched about his decayed teeth, and the two spikes of his mustachios, which at one moment resembled those of a Western sheriff and at another those of a Chinese gentleman, see-sawed slightly from one side to the other. When the Captain could bear this grin no longer, he said shortly:

"What's the matter?"

Then he stepped quickly over to the binnacle and glanced at the compass in the hope of catching Blood off the course; but, as always in these encounters, the Chief was dead on. In a twanging voice, as if he were saying something slightly vindictive, but really believing himself bathed in a fine, jesting manner, Blood said:

"You know, Cap'n, that new lemon from the Galveston they dumped on us last month at Cavite? . . . He's been down fourteen minutes and is still going strong! . . . Running neck and neck with O'Connel."

"You mean that new youngster?" said the Captain a trifle

incredulously; then turning in good-natured and pleased surprise to Ensign Woodbridge (who, arriving back on the bridge in time to overhear Blood's news, already had exclaimed, "Well, I'll be damned") he said: "Woodbridge, that little Ordinary Seaman they gave us is down with O'Connel and sticking it out."

"Well, I'll be damned," said Ensign Woodbridge again, not so much with the feeling of surprise that had first engendered the remark, but with a sense of getting his exclamation in its proper rank and order.

10 〰

O'Connel no longer was exiled in the depths of fire, coal and steel with a despicable alien. As his stark delight ascended flight after flight of sweet and fierce recognition, he pounded his shovel and shouted, "Guts! Guts! Guts!" He thought: "He's probably Irish after all! . . . Shovel for shovel with me, O'Connel!" He rushed over to the bunker hole to roar in some greeting as if to a well esteemed newcomer.

But the glimpse he got of the Texan down this new perspective brought him up sharply. A veritable incarnation of distress, the boy was struggling with the shovel as if it were some awkward, slippery burden. O'Connel gave a start that seemed to indicate that he was about to leap into the bunker to rescue his wounded comrade.

As he hesitated, Warrington jammed the handle of the shovel into his stomach for another try, and O'Connel realized the other's agony so intimately that his being began to function somewhat as if it were he, himself, fighting there in pain. He dove in to put an end to it.

The boy, sensing the great creature crowding the obscurity before him, glared toward it desperately and emitted a hawking, defiant sound, a sound electric with the sharp anomalous authority that often concentrates in even the meanest man in the throes of physical anguish. It arrested O'Connel and slowly pushed him back into the fire-room again, where he found himself, lost in a wilderness of uncertainty and pity, clumping along a network of unfamiliar mental and emotional trails. "I'm gonna stop this," he told himself truculently, "time must be up . . . them tight bums on the top side holding out till the last second . . . the bastards!" It entered his mind that the thing to do was to "tell the kid the time was up."

"Time up!" he shouted with the relief of having hit upon an actable line of conduct.

The next instant he was at the bunker hole yelling again:

"Time up! Time up! Time up!"

When the boy finally heard him, he sat slowly down cross-legged about his shovel, drifting into the incomparable luxury of oblivion, slowly pulsing away from an acute crisis of high-pitched, kinetic agony.

For a second O'Connel's eyes lingered on the wet haft of the shovel, along which the light from the bunker lamp flickered. It projected upright from the dark mound of the small body like a limb stuck into the cairn marking some isolated and valorous death.

Seeing that his end was gained there, O'Connel swung back into the fire-room, kicked open the door of the coal bunker opposite to that in which Warrington was, and with furious surreptitiousness heaved out nine or ten shovelfuls of coal from that as yet untouched supply. After soundly reclosing this bunker hole door, he fed a shovelful to each of the fires, and then, steadying himself angrily on his slightly swaying legs, he rapidly transferred the remainder of the coal he had gotten out to the diminished pile in front of the Texan's bunker hole. It was a custom that the relieving watch should find a small supply of coal out to start with. As he heaved the last shovelful, he felt the air pressure rise from off of him. He dropped the shovel guiltily. A relieved, victorious feeling surged through him.

"What th' hell!" he yelled up at the open hatch.

The murky bodies of the relief followed one another quickly down the ladder.

The Irishman's figure, assuming a slight exaggeration of its usual arrogant, hard-boiled stance, shuffled over to the bunker hole. He stuck in his head and shouted,

"Hey! Lay off! Time's up!" Then, as he crawled through the hole, he added in loud, incompetent dissimulation, "Hold up, I'll give y' a hand."

Morrow, the relief coal heaver, knelt by the hole and pulled the boy's body through as O'Connel shoved its shoulders within his reach. Morrow and his watch-mate, Whorley, started to carry him towards the ladder; but O'Connel, arising from the bunker hole, snatched the small body from them and climbed up the ladder unassisted, maintaining the boy on his left shoulder and chest with the pressure of his right arm. As the two heads arose from the hatchway, the crowd of men surrounding it, comprising nearly the entire ship's company, let out a triumphal yell. The big bruiser, shaking off all the black hands that shot out to relieve him of his burden, climbed to the deck and stood for a moment glaring in a squinting manner at the slick sea, which the sun, burning the first suggestion of colour for its setting, had raddled a greyish pink.

As he stood there swaying above the crowd of heads with the boy in his arms, he seemed to the monk on the quarter-deck like one of the bulky Pietas, absurd of colour and strangely awkward of workmanship, that the Italian mountaineers bear down the trails to their devotions on feast days.

11 〰〰〰

Throughout the day the monk had confined himself rigidly to the exact area assigned to him by Lieutenant Fitzpatrick when that officer had led him to the camp cot and said with authoritative cordiality: "Here, Father, you stay right here." For the past twenty minutes, as the afternoon ended, he had stood in precisely the same spot by the railing contemplating the nearer of those two implacable square holes down which the young men slid with jaunty energy, and from which they were dragged a few minutes later like sooty cadavers. The glimpse he had gotten of Poe's tortured face had dismayed him in an unprecedented manner. The whole

24

spirit and system of violence that was doing for these men appeared to him more detached and mystical than any he had ever encountered before. The smooth slide and play of the ambient discipline, the rush of the steel boat over the water, the throb and beat of the machinery, the pert sway from side to side of Delilah's rounded, little stern—like the hip movement of a young Moro girl when she walks with a basket of mangoes balanced on her head—and the crouching shadow of nausea that lurked in the pit of his stomach as if about to spring upon him in full force, combined to intimidate him. His usual certitude and clear vision in the face of violence and misery became dimmed. He did not know quite what to do. His invincible surmise that his purpose in life was to place himself without reserve between all the Tortured and their Torturers remained, all the while, clear-cut and coruscant; but here there seemed to be no torturers to set himself up against, no tangible, apprehensible sword to which to bare his breast: only the tortured and their agony were there before him. Now, here was another one! The old man clenched his fists feverishly as the crew propped Warrington against the railing and turned the hose on him.

"Give him another shot," cried one of the men supporting the boy's shoulders.

The monk jammed his two clenched fists up under his chin against his neck and waited for the impact of the water. When it crashed against the sick, slender body, the monk nearly went down under the spiritually multiplied smash and bite of it. The second dose of salt water had washed away some of the coal dust and much of the thin undershirt that formed Warrington's only upper covering. For a fraction of time, after the stream of water had shifted from it, the boy's thin chest shone smooth and grey in the soft glare of the sun like a wet river stone; then on it, here and there, the blood broke out in bright channels from the wounds he had received in flinging himself against the iron wall to empty his shovel into the fire-room. The monk glared until the vermilion threads had dripped as far as the boy's heaving stomach, at which instant, as if it were a signal, he pulled up the dark flaps and edges of his gown and girded them about his hips, securing them with the sash that encircled his waist as he tramped forward towards the group amidships. The profound and magnificent indignation, the ever tense mainspring of his being, finally had projected him clear and undubious up through all the intangibilities and uncertainties that had been cluttering his ordinarily clear pathway: Yet he looked quite ridiculous as his bare, bony legs swung along beneath his upper bulk now enlarged with the packed tucks and folds of his voluminous skirts. He looked somewhat like a combative rooster prancing forward to encounter an enemy.

The exhausted and startled group of men fell back before him. Cavendish, the blond Second-Class Quartermaster, began to laugh with nervous embarrassment.

"I see that you are getting short of men," the monk said firmly, addressing a man whom he had picked out at random from the crowd, "give me a shovel."

No one made a sound. The only movement was a unanimous, definite turning of eyes upon Olgan, the Cook, the luckless man at whom the monk was sending his demand and his gaze. Olgan stood there miserable and pusillanimous, his patchy haired, lobeless-eared head hanging, and his milky eyes shifting unseeingly from one of the ecclesiastic's rectangular knees to the other. With silent, instantaneous assent the small community affirmed the leader that opportunity had indicated to represent it in this flabbergasting crisis, and dumped the full load and unprecedented responsibility of it upon his contemptible shoulders. For the first time in his shapeless life, Olgan was obtruded as a social spearhead, and although it shattered him, he pierced the situation before him rather well.

"There ain't any up here, sir . . . They're all down there below," he said plaintively.

When he finished saying this, he backed, slightly doubled up, through the crowd until he brought up against the four bronze cables of the railing. But this effort at putting his fellows between himself and what seemed to him a kind of assault was automatically frustrated by the crowd, which parted, leaving a clear lane from him to the monk.

Stengle, before any possible operation of the inevitable seniority and authority machinery could "pass the buck" to him, hustled over to the Starboard Engine-room Hatch and dropped half-way down the ladder.

"Hey! Mr. Fitzpatrick," he shouted ominously but respectfully, "the priest is askin' for a shovel and is headin' for the After Fire-room."

Lieutenant Fitzpatrick lifted his white, grease-streaked face to Stengle with an expression that said clearly: "Damn it, what next?" Yet there was not much surprise there, for Lieutenant Fitzpatrick, almost with his emotions alone, had apprehended immediately what the situation was.

"Take the engine-room," he ordered.

Stengle climbed the rest of the way down the ladder, and the officer mounted the ten feet or so to the deck. As he emerged into the air he had to grab hold of the upright hatch cover, for he began to sway dizzily as if he suddenly had arisen from a too hot bath.

"Father, Father!" he called to the old man, who was then stooping over the fire-room hatch, feeling for a hold.

The monk straightened up and fixed upon the Second-in-Command a gaze that seemed to be travelling over a long stretch of foreground.

"Look here . . . come aft for a minute . . ." the young officer's voice was thin and uncertain with exhaustion and emotion.

He walked nervously over to the monk and, oblivious of the oil with which he was spattered, tried in a friendly, coercing manner to put his arm around the monk's shoulders. He missed this hold and his arm drifted about the old man's neck. The monk, to steady the officer, put an arm around his waist. Thus they made their way along the starboard side towards the quarter-deck: But before they had gotten as far as the galley, Lieutenant Fitzpatrick halted as he felt the swiftly moving ship sway into a turn. He darted a glance over his shoulder. Then he abruptly swung the monk towards the railing. With his free hand he pointed emphatically.

"Look! . . . see . . . it's not necessary . . . it wouldn't help . . . we're there!"

Within clear view off the bow, far across the immobile stretch of unctuous, murrey sea, there lay what seemed to be, under the prismatic splendour of the setting sun, two great chrome-splashed rings, from the sharp perimeters of which there sprouted vague green clusters of monstrous ostrich plumes.

12 〰〰

The monk, who knew Isla-Sulu well, wanted the Captain to proceed at once through the narrow break in the coral wall that served for entrance into the larger of the lagoons; but the Captain, smiling amicably, and breaking into the Pidgen English which served him as a sort of slang, and which he seemed to fall into whenever his natural disinclination for forcing his will upon people was unmasked by his friendliness or good humour, said that he wanted "to have a look see first." So Delilah whipped around the atolls on a perfectly circular course, close inshore, while the Captain steadily examined through his binoculars the segmentary beaches, the palm clusters, the matted undergrowth, the stretches of coral and the flashes of the distant interior lagoons that broke through where the vegetation of the rings was thin. His probing encountered only the rounded, colourful implacability that the two conjoined atolls presented all along their circumferences: But the tranquillity seemed definitely malignant,—like that which pervades a brilliant stalk of bananas in which lurks an aroused tarantula.

When Delilah had arrived opposite the narrow, jungle-framed entrance to the large lagoon for the second time, the Captain ordered a decrease in propeller revolutions that slowly brought Delilah down to about eight knots speed. He stooped, as the knife edge of the bow headed for the exact centre of the entrance, and pushed the button of the General Quarters bell.

Delilah and her men had begun to relax and cool off under the greatly decreased speed and the blue twilight. The men had lined the railing and were staring at the shore in much the same subdued manner, compounded of affirmation, curiosity and relief, with which they would gaze at the empty coal barges alongside after a grilling day spent in loading Delilah with coal. But at the

28

sudden, exigent goading of the bell, the men came alive again and lunged towards their battle stations. The fire-room hatch covers were slapped shut once more, the blowers whirred back to life, the ammunition gangs dragged and banged the shell cases to the guns, and Lieutenant Fitzpatrick and Ensign Snell turned over the engine-rooms to the battle crews and hurried to their posts, the first to the bridge and the second to the top of the After Conning-tower.

Delilah, ready to leap and strike, drifted with menacing quietness to the middle of the round lagoon that formed the island's centre. The unobtrusive purring of her machinery imbued the immanent silence of the place with the feline, intimidating quality of a pard-infested cavern. The Captain took to his binoculars again. In them the lustrous evening world became a shadow elusive of detail . . . the compact cluster of nipa houses, dark and deserted, that waded on high stilts out into the water . . . the group of brown, out-rigged *bancos* on the pale beach nearby . . . the feathery growth beyond them . . . some cindered ruins near the profusion of tall palms that drooped over the entrance to the lagoon . . . the rickety, planked pier that reached out some thirty yards towards Delilah . . . and the high wall of orchid-clotted jungle that received the broad trail leading from the wharf . . . all these betrayed nothing but their apparent utter lifelessness. It might have been an artificial scene. Only the weighty fragrance from the flowers of the *ylang ylang* tree—white, feverish, little blossoms like very young girls burnt out by excessive, unrecognized desire—affirmed the living quality of the environment. It lay on the lagoon as if it were an invisible fog.

"Mr. Fitzpatrick, I'm going alongside the dock," said the Captain finally, letting go of the binoculars, which hung from a strap around his neck. "But I don't want to put out any lines. Keep the six-pounders manned. Have the starboard guns ready to open fire on the jungle around the mouth of the trail, and the port ones trained on those *bancos* over there. Get fifty men ready to go in the Landing Party. You had better take Mr. Woodbridge with you . . . if you have to land."

As Delilah swung warily in towards the dock, men scurried after their regular shoes and the two Gunner's Mates and their striker issued out rifles, bayonets and ammunition belts. Those told off to go in the Landing Party jerked and snatched at the equipment, working themselves up out of their fatigue and the nervousness that inevitably preceded the rough and tumble business they believed to be ahead of them. The measure of what experience had taught them to expect was taken by the care with which they tested and examined their bayonets. They looked to their bolts and ammunition only when they were ordered to. Their curses became more restless and venereal, and they charged them with an unwonted, rubefacient viciousness.

Delilah's side touched the face of the dock and slid lightly along it. The timbers of the structure creaked and crackled. The Captain ordered the engines "Full speed astern" . . . then "Stop!" Delilah halted in her tracks on the still water alongside the dock. The armed men rushed to coagulate against that part of the railing opposite the pierhead. Some were bare to the waist, others wore tattered, sooty undershirts that clung transparently to sweating muscles; and their coal-stiffened hair bristled as with ferocity.

Among them, with a rifle in his hand, Warrington, the young Ordinary Seaman who had "stuck it out" below with O'Connel, leant dizzily against the bronze railing wires, which bulged and gave with the turbulent knot of men. It occurred to him that these straining wires alone formed the barrier withholding a furious gust of steel and violence from bursting into the quiet, green blot of land that loomed before him.

"Take it easy!" shouted Ensign Woodbridge in his pleasant, uproarious voice, and grinned into the face of the Carpenter's Mate, who was gesturing with the axe which he carried in place of rifle and bayonet.

The men clanged gun butts on the iron deck, unconsciously pointed truculent bayonets through the railing in the direction of the trail as if their victims were in sight, and twisted their open breathing mouths into baroque grimaces. They reincarnated one of those raging Gothic squads, depicted in old woodcuts, about to roar through the shattered gate of a city.

Little Lieutenant Fitzpatrick stood in the centre of the men carefully examining through his binoculars the terrain over which he probably would have to take the Landing Party. He was just as he had come up out of the engine-room, bare-headed, clad in the khaki athletic clothes that had survived his graduation from the Naval Academy, and smeared with oil and grease. But he was, nevertheless, as neat as a pin. When Ensign Woodbridge shouted, "Take it easy!" at the men, Lieutenant Fitzpatrick pulled his head away from the binoculars, which he continued to hold straight up in front of him, as if just then becoming aware of the commotion about him. The crisp glance of his small, brown eyes darted from one to another of the men, and left each, as it were, sucking in on his inflated restlessness. As his eyes came back towards the binoculars, they lit upon Ensign Woodbridge, who was leaning, a little detached from the group, against a stanchion of the railing.

In most men Ensign Woodbridge's posture certainly would have seemed affected, a nonchalant stance copied from some actor surveying the fictitious battle into which he was about to dash: but Ensign Woodbridge was unquestionably genuine, actually the almost mythical thing the actor, himself, imagines he looks like as he poses before the audience fired by the footlights and his own exhibitionistic certitude. He had managed, as always before what he called "a row," to change into an immaculate uniform whose whiteness had been tinted a delicate coffee brown to decrease its visibility: But its brass buttons were highly polished and the gold in its shoulder straps glistened. His shoes were shined and his cap sat on his carefully combed hair at a precise and interesting angle. He was, as Lieutenant Fitzpatrick had once put it, "the perfect target."

Lieutenant Fitzpatrick's lips caught up into a wry, complicated smile as he clamped his eyes back onto the glasses. He murmured distinctly to the man at his elbow:

"Would you mind going down into my room and bringing up the cap in the second drawer under my bunk, the one with the white cover on?"

Hardwood, the Seaman, a white youth who talked like a Negro, said, "Yes, Suh!" and swung away in a hurry, as if he feared something would happen before he got back. When it arrived, Lieutenant Fitzpatrick hastily jammed the new cap on his head. Its broad gold strap shone luminously even in the twilight. Standing there with it on amidst the crowd of the Landing Party, he looked something like a short, begrimed, gold-headed poker stuck into a coal pile.

The Captain came up with the monk and the men straightened to attention, from which they gradually relaxed as the conversation between the skipper and the tonsured old man proceeded.

"... I'll give you a Very pistol, and if you need the Landing Party you fire a red ball; if you don't, then fire a green ball ... so we'll know how things are."

"If you don't mind, Captain, I'd rather not have anything that's like an arm," the monk said with a touch of apology in his tone, "you see, I ..."

"All right, all right, whatever you want to do, Father, but we've got to hit upon something. What do you say to this? When you get in there," he pointed to the beach, "if you find you need us, try to get back far enough down the trail for us to see you. Keep your arms stretched straight out sideways from your shoulders and work 'em up and down ... like wings. If I don't see you within exactly one hour," he took his watch out of his fob pocket and looked at it, "after you hit the dock, the ... uh ... Mr. Fitzpatrick will come out and look for you."

The old man smiled in humorous understanding of the Captain's slight hesitation. He kept nodding his head slowly and easily up and down. The Captain continued:

"If you straighten things out, will you come down within view and stand for a moment with your arms stretched straight up over your head without moving them? Then we won't worry about you any further."

The Captain made a friendly, homely grimace, and curiously enough the same sort of apologetic colour that had tinted the monk's refusal of the signal pistol now leaked into the Captain's smile. It never once occurred to him to suggest to the monk to cry out if he were in imminent danger on the chance that the ship might hear him: the idea was so out of proportion in the perspective the monk engendered, and so off the course of ideas that his attitude set up.

Hardwood and Cruck, the Chief Boatswain's Mate, cast off a section of the railing with a solemn expertness that seemed to take on the significance of a ceremony uniting the dangerous land with the fierce, little ship. Ensign Snell, who had been standing amongst

32

the men, indistinguishable in his dirty dungarees except for his amicable quietness and assurance, lowered himself over the side to the dock and held his hands up to help the monk down. The blue eyes in Ensign Snell's broad, likeable face looked up at the old man much as they would have beamed down at a child their owner was about to hoist up piggy-back. As the black-gowned figure went over, the men became tense and immovable; they might have been watching him walk the plank. He stood on the dock for a moment with his hand lightly poised against Delilah's side, as if he were surreptitiously blessing her. He raised his face, the long chin of which reached just to the deck line, and looked at the Captain, who leaned over somewhat to look back at him. The two antipodal men smiled at each other. Then the ecclesiast turned and swung unhurriedly along the dock, up the trail and into the jungle. Delilah remained rigid, still, expectant, listening for the slightest inimical sound. Finally the Captain walked up the deck towards the bridge. His footsteps drummed out a hollow solo in the stillness. Lieutenant Fitzpatrick kept his glasses fixed on the spot where the monk had disappeared.

At the end of a quarter of an hour several men had drifted aimlessly away, one after another, from the Landing Party by the rail. When Lieutenant Fitzpatrick finally noticed this, he sang out:

"Everybody in the Landing Party stand by."

The sound of his order rang startlingly along the deck and out over the breathless, darkening water. The stragglers rushed back to the Landing Party, and the crews at the six-pounders, attaching over-importance to the order, sprang alert and glared at their respective target areas. Even the Captain reached hastily for his binoculars: when he tried to use them he noticed that it was getting dark and replaced them with others that could be used at night. He took up a second pair of the night glasses and walked from the bridge back down to the clenched, fistlike group by the hole in the railing, where he handed the second pair of night binoculars to Lieutenant Fitzpatrick and told him that he didn't "want any lights in the ship for a while yet."

Ensign Woodbridge's mind was painting, and his will promptly dissolving, distraught illustration after illustration of the fate that possibly was overtaking the monk. In a moment of nearly physical effort to clear his mind of a horror, he made a just perceptible, un-localized gesture; but every movement and attitude he made were so thoroughly impregnated with the tradition that had produced and supported these men, their situation and their medium, that they received the impression of it instantly, as a photographic plate receives an obscure and minute shadow. They seemed to take it as a signal that they were no longer obligated to bear the strain in silence.

"What the hell kind of business is this anyhow?" broke out O'Connel, leading the burst of indignant demands they made of one another.

This imprecation in the riotous voice of his enemy awoke the Texan, who had been heavily asleep on his feet. His suddenly opened eyes, muddled by dreams and conflicting reality, struggled in alarm with the dark, encircling shore.

"Unc" Blood rotated the point of his beard nervously and in-dulged in the curious sound he habitually made by first drawing in suddenly through his nostrils, then grunting bluntly from the re-gion of his tonsils.

The Carpenter's Mate, a middle-aged man with an angular, in-timidating face, waved his axe slowly above his head and spat out:

"By God, in the *old* Navy there was none of this stuff of puttin' a priest ashore! We'd 'a been in there long ago kickin' the guts out of 'em!"

Above the high, stiff, white collar of his blouse, Ensign Wood-bridge's slim face again smiled jeeringly, nepotically at him. The Carpenter's Mate had served with his father when the Navy went against the Boxers.

But the tenseness was not relieved. At no given moment the upper stretches of dull blue air exploded silently into a silver in-finity of pulsing, glowing fragments. Under this equivocal star-light, despite the apparent illumination, the lagoon water remained black. An occasional leaping fish gored in it a cloudy spiral of phosphorescence.

"There he is!" abruptly shrieked a gunner from forward.

Into the murky circle of Lieutenant Fitzpatrick's hungry binocu-lars there moved, amidst several lesser lumps of shadow, the tall, unmistakable, black erectness topped with silver. The monk came down with a sort of dignified swiftness to a spot just clear of the jungle. The long lines of his drape slowly extended themselves straight up towards the sky, and the faint brilliance of his up-turned face, framed between the ebony columns of his lifted arms, seemed to be in some unfailing, daedal communication with the radiant direction of his reaching.

Chapter
Two

1 〰️

The forced run that Delilah had made to Isla-Sulu had deranged her insides. One of her condensers was impaired. A main bearing had burnt out, permitting the starboard shaft to disturb its alignment, and there was a nervous knock in one of her cylinders. She barely had been able, after a remarkable session of make-shift, emergency repairing, to falter back to the dock at Zamboanga.

The combined storm of these interior penalties had been dreaded secretly all along, as an eventuality, by the Captain; whose conviction, for many months previous to this run, had been hardening about the idea that if he was going to lead her the kind of life upon which they seemed to be insisting, he would have to get her into some kind of shape. Every time of late that he had given the engine-rooms or the Helmsman an order that called upon her for some rigorous performance, there had loomed faintly and distantly, but very sombrely on the edge of his small stock of permanent apprehensions, a disturbance that, forced into the inadequate channels of a ready, mental phrase, seemed to warn that all that was left of him was somehow inextricably committed to all that was left of her. In his mind the apperception of this impression had been like the recognition of a covenant; and quite unconsciously, on the occasions when he suffered this impression, he had regretted her neglected condition, a condition—enforced by governmental economy—that her extreme age made increasingly dangerous. Years ago the Department had put her down on its public books as an antiquated, slow creature fit only for coast defence: after which it promptly had flung her into a savage, semi-charted region, where she was called upon to engage in active service, at high speeds, far from bases.

Now the Captain (in rank he was a Lieutenant-Commander)

forwarded to the Department, through his proper superiors in Cavite, an urgent, radioed request to put her out of commission long enough for a major repair operation to be performed upon her. He had it in his mind that once in the Navy Yard, under the operation, he would "take the bull by the horns" and, legally or illegally, regardless of the risk to himself personally, see to it that her boilers and cylinders were replaced, her steering cables renovated and new steel plate laid into her deck and, where necessary, into her hull. Her serious condition now, which even the most economical could understand, would be a pretty good fulcrum upon which to lay his lever.

At lunch in the Wardroom he told the Executive Officer what his intentions were, and asked him to get up a list of everything that could be done to her from bow to stern.

"Even if we get everything," he ended, "it won't bring her up to what we're making her do."

These last words blew into the celebration that was flaming within Lieutenant Fitzpatrick over the ship's recent faithful, victorious performance as a gust of rain might sweep a triumphal beacon. He read into them an implication that faintly lowered the whole tone of their existence in her, and twinged his uncompromising partiality.

"Twenty knots wasn't so bad, Captain; the new boats cruise at only five more."

The Captain smiled and rather ceremoniously took off his big, horn-rimmed spectacles, which sat amidst the weather-tan on his small precociously wrinkled, thirty-three-year-old face with a kind of flagrant incompatibility. His blue eyes blinked for a moment as if testing themselves in the new freedom. His wearing these spectacles was, more than anything else, some notion of his wife's. She had said that he was to wear them whenever he used his eyes; but, really, she had an idea that they smoothed him down a bit. He inevitably took them off and put them in their broad, thick brown case whenever he felt a poignant, impracticable urge to dispense with the routine pretence behind which even the simplest of human dealings must manoeuvre, whenever he felt an urge to let down, for the particular person opposite him, the mask that disguised the full, detailed inexpressibility of what actually was behind the stand that he was being forced to take. And nearly always, when he took off the spectacles, he would make a compensatory sweep at the cowlick that disordered the uneven, sandy hair parted on the side just above his low forehead. He made this gesture now.

"And look at her," he replied. "As a result of it she'll have to limp all the way up to Cavite at six or seven knots."

There were many things that Lieutenant Fitzpatrick would have replied to Snell or Woodbridge; who, on their parts, sat staring into their coffee cups and thinking of the clear points that could be made with "the Old Man," that *should* be made by anybody who "drew as much water as an Executive Officer." It was clear by the expressions on their faces that their pleasant feeling of being subjects for approbation was being slowly deflated, deflated by the apparent discovery that the Captain felt so ordinarily about the feat they and the ship had performed.

Lieutenant Fitzpatrick flicked the ash off his cigarette and glanced away through the port-hole. The water, which quivered a few inches below the port like a slab of blue jelly, flashed and stabbed recklessly with the beams it caught from the sun . . . "the Captain didn't seem to understand fully what she'd done," he thought . . . "didn't seem to be inside the situation . . ." For three years, now, Delilah had been the Lieutenant's first ship. For only a slightly longer time she had been the Captain's first command.

As if he already had received the favourable answer to his request, the Captain next morning headed Delilah out of Zamboanga, and put her on the first leg of the course that would take her up through the islands to Manila Bay. She pounded awkwardly through the smooth purple water in a wounded and creeping way that emphasized the intended swift precision of her life. There had not been much, in the way of amplifying the emergency repairs achieved by the crew in Isla-Sulu, that Zamboanga had been able to provide.

The unnaturalness of her situation affected the men with a kind of exposed-nerve over-alertness. They closed hatches, turned cocks, shifted the rudder, much as if they were fighters pulling their punches. There was about the whole ship, as a matter of fact, the neurotic quality that pervades a training camp compelled to send a boxer into the ring with a hand broken and imperfectly healed.

The men frankly were relieved when, just out of Basilan Strait, with Bototindoc Point abeam, the ship was put about and headed back towards Zamboanga. At once the rumour whirled through the ship that Delilah was not to leave Zamboanga after all. The rumour had little to go on, perhaps, besides the almost palpable wish of the men, a burst of strident, mechanical hum in the Radio Shack, and the rapid trip aft of Portness, the jockeylike Radio Electrician; and it proved to be false. The demonstration of its falseness, however, was of such a quality as to set vibrating through the general atmosphere of ill-being a high-keyed expectancy, a sharp apprehension that, as Arnold, Quartermaster, Second-Class, put it, "something must be up."

Once alongside the dock again, the order was given to stand by; and the Captain, leaving Delilah with steam up and everything in readiness to get under way at a pull of the engine-room telegraph, went ashore to confer with the Governor-General's representative. At noon Delilah still was standing by. The folding tables were let down into the layer of intense heat under the re-spread awnings, and the sweating men ate hastily, almost surreptitiously, with an eye up at the head of the dock. A glimpse there of a small, gold-spotted, white figure would have sent them, working at huge mouthfuls, hurrying to their stations for getting under way: But it was the middle of the afternoon before the Captain was seen coming down the dock. He walked slowly into the white-hot motionlessness of the universe as if he were a bit of its circumference that had begun to melt and drip towards the centre. His appearance of labouring over the broad planks of the long dock probably owed less to his perturbation or the heat than it did to the confusing, oppressive intensity of the light. He kept his eyes lowered as if even a glance towards the sky would have injured them. The masts of the ship, the palm trees, the distant radio tower shimmered blackly in the infinity of still, bright confusion as if they were fragments of filament at the core of some frightful luminosity.

His three officers and the Quartermaster on watch, saluting stiffly, met him at the narrow timber that served as gang-plank. He stepped aboard with an obvious gesture of relief that he, himself, thought was the result of getting in under the awning out of the sun; but his perspiring face was more than usually ruffled with the mild distemper that nearly always coursed through the wrinkles in his face after an official session with the civilians ashore. After a quick appraisal of the Captain's face, Lieutenant Fitzpatrick withheld the question that would have satisfied their curiosity.

"All right, get under way at once, Mr. Fitzpatrick," the Captain said. After a moment of hesitation in which he was both thinking and taking a step in the direction of the quarter-deck, he added:

"Lay your course for Taytay Bay."

"Taytay Bay. Aye, aye, Sir." Despite himself, Lieutenant Fitzpatrick had been unable to keep his enunciation of "Taytay Bay" from becoming an exclamation of astonishment: Nor could the group of men lounging or occupied at tasks nearby, very ostensibly not listening, keep itself from mirroring, in its moist expanses of work-soiled skin and dungarees, its superior's surprise.

Later, with the jungle-framed, red roofs of Zamboanga hidden astern behind the rise of Caldera Point, the Captain joined Lieutenant Fitzpatrick on the bridge. He had taken a shower and changed his clothes. Lieutenant Fitzpatrick was at the pelorus; Bidot, the Quartermaster, First-Class, was closely watching the chronometer in his hand; Ferguson, a stout, truculent Seaman a trifle over five feet tall, was leaning forward across the wheel to stare intently at the compass. Ferguson's grimy, stubby hands were delicately poised on the spokes of the wheel, and each time he was precisely on the course, he would sing out, "Mark! . . . Mark! . . . Mark! . . ." So slowly was Delilah limping ahead, that the light, stern breeze streamed the smoke from her stacks out before her on the bright air, and its billows swept a shifting roll of shadow over the translucent surface of the bridge awning. Somewhere aft, a man was singing, in a voice shrill, quavering, beautiful against the hum of the blowers, a slight, nostalgic melody whose words begin: "O, we won't go back to Zambo' any more . . ." The business of taking a bearing on Teinga Island engrossed the whole attention of the three on the bridge; but, like some sensitive cell-unit, they were aware of his presence the moment the Captain came up the ladder. An expectant audience before whom, they felt sure, the Captain now would raise the curtain on this new and provocative act of the ordeal through which they must push their crippled ship, they yet fumbled no single minute of time or space in overlaying the glistening strip of water between Delilah and the green lump of frothy island with a great triangle, invisible but informing.

Anxious as he was to hear what the Captain had to say, Lieutenant Fitzpatrick, under stimulation of the Captain's patient, interested presence, could not resist the temptation to make a slight display of the virtuosity he so indubitably and effectively enjoyed in the elegant precisions of his navigation. When the final leg of the bearing was taken, he stepped jauntily to the chart-board and applied his data with just a trace of the decorative pomposity that might distinguish a member of a French eating club noting, for purposes of judgment, an item of deliciousness for some dish entered in a contest. When he had quite finished with his final gesture, the Captain frankly smiled at him.

"We've got a big job of navigating to do," he said, "we'd better talk it over. My request to take her back to Cavite for repairs is granted all right; but on the way we've got to take her all around Palawan and then around through the islands between Palawan and Mindoro" . . . Here his indignation broke through his information . . . " '*on the way*,' for God's sake! Get that! On the way!"

Lieutenant Fitzpatrick was knocked clean off his balance by the unexpectedness of the information, aggrandized as it was by the unwonted force with which the Captain empowered it.

"Why, Deacon," he ejaculated, using the off-duty nickname by which his intimates had addressed the Captain ever since his Annapolis days, "what on earth for?"

"We've got to look for caches of guns and ammunition . . . and for fellows running them in."

2 〰〰

For the Captain, it was days before Delilah's mission was regarded as anything but the absurd and somehow indecent affair that it had been for him at first impact. In the first place, he could not help but see this mission in the light of his sympathies. He was not so sure that his sympathies were not actually with the Moros for whom the smuggled arms were intended. Decidedly, his sympathies were not with the tricky, little, half-breed, Manila politicians and their helpless American masters who had bungled him into this position. The real basis, however, for his strong emotion was the unfeeling ignorance, the downright unpractical ignorance of the civilians ashore who insisted on sending a disabled vessel chasing around in the bad weather season through hundreds of miles of uncharted waters looking for trouble . . . "risking thousands of dollars' worth of government property and seventy-one good, white lives just to coddle the guilty fears of a crooked gang of Tagalog *politicos*." He shied away from Lieutenant Fitzpatrick's way of putting it . . . "like sending a delicate, injured woman into some arduous activity" . . , but he wanted to get his ship up to Cavite. He wanted to get her in shape.

The first night out, he had welcomed with relief the sudden torrent of rain that had driven at the gently rolling ship as he had settled himself under the sheet of his bunk. On his back, with his hands clasped under his head and his knees drawn up, he had lain comfortably listening to the drumming of the rain, the giant throb of the propellers just beneath him, and to the quiet, regular creak in the cabin following each roll of the ship. His mind, unused to dealing consciously in symbols, struggled nebulously with the feeling that this cloudburst would wash his ship clean of its contact with the people in Zamboanga. As he thought of the hot hours he had spent pawing over charts and maps in that office ashore, and scrabbling about amongst the pretentiously disguised fears of the politicians, he became oppressed by the confinement of his white, over-sized pyjamas, which through habit he wore even in hot weather. He sat up, pulled the jumper over his head and dropped it on the deck beside his bunk. The atmosphere in the small, boxlike cabin, very little larger than a couple of piano crates joined back to back, was so realistically humid that he had not noticed until he was about to lie down again that the rain was deflecting in semi-mist from the wind-catcher of the port-hole onto the foot of his bunk. He couldn't close the port . . . too hot . . . he had to have one port open anyway . . . he turned the wind-catcher so that the rain would deflect up towards the ceiling. As he lay down again, his gaze flattened by the steel ceiling less than four feet above him, he had a restless instant pressured by the illusion that he was smothering under water that had filled the cabin. The bulkheads seemed to distend and become concave under the tremendous pressure of the illusory water. A slight gesture had served to dispel this impression. He had raised his forearm and, with its hairy, outer surface, rubbed instinctively at a tingle just above the right nostril of his sizeable, triangular nose.

Through the dim, subaqueous glow that pervaded the cabin as the rain stopped and the stars came out, he could distinguish, hung on the bulkhead at the foot of his bunk, the precise blur of the frame that held his wife's picture, and across the cabin, more dimly still, the generous puff of almost imperceptible shadow that marked a vaseful of intensely white flowers. The flowers very faintly tainted his breathing with dank, fragrant difficulty. As the port-hole would swing slowly through the beam of a cluster of stars, an occasional glint, a minute, preternatural absence of shadow, would flicker over the invisible surface of the mahogany desk, over the back of the chair, across the glass in the frame, along the sides of the silver vase . . . The flowers should have been put in the wardroom . . . it was nice of her to send them down to the dock . . . he liked her best of all his wife's friends out here . . . if he came south again for any length of time he'd get Laura to come down from Manila and stay with her for a visit . . . they'd both enjoy it . . . only that would mean he'd have to spend a lot of time ashore in Zamboanga . . . some of those people were probably all right if you didn't have to have official dealings with them . . . just the same as in Manila . . . or as in Washington, for that matter . . . What a shifty crowd they all were! . . . That Governor-General's man! . . . Even with all their shiftiness the politicians they sent out to Manila couldn't handle the Tagalogs . . . he couldn't ever get people like that out into the open, couldn't ever get at what they really were after, except by suspecting it, no matter whether it was good or bad.

Suddenly there spread throughout his memory, like an instantaneously grown weed, the rank pain and shame of his first important experience, years back, with the politicians. He had landed with a hundred-and-ninety men, under orders to take a Latin-American town and drive its garrison of seven hundred some ten miles back from the coast line. The local Consul's order to the cruiser had been confirmed by Washington despite the Commanding Officer's warning that on account of the garrison's size there would be a stiff fight. "Take the town" . . . well, he'd taken it. As long as he lived he'd never forget Henderson, the Coxswain, stretched out in a row with the others in the twilight, stiff, blue, the front of his throat a bloody gap. Next to Henderson had lain the Mail Orderly, his long white face lined with a weird agony. A finely sharpened bailing hook had clawed out his testicles and lower intestines. "I saved as many of the boys as was possible, though." His innermost private conscience assured him of that. The simplicity of the tactical problem involved should have made his actions clear to almost anybody . . . a National Guard lieutenant with only a smattering of tactics would have understood what to do in that problem.

The enemy had concentrated on the water-front of the town, waiting for him behind cobble-stone breast works. The cruiser had shelled them out of there; but they'd taken to the windows and roofs of the water-front houses. The Commanding Officer had been afraid to throw many shells into the houses . . . destroying those would have been almost impossible to explain to civilians at home. "I'm afraid you'll have to chance it," the Commanding Officer had said, "but we'll keep them off the beach until you get there." As the boats had approached the town, its whole face had blazed with rifle fire. He had seen with his binoculars that even women were firing from some of the windows. Watching carefully the volume and area of splash in the water, he had become certain that his party would not have been able to survive on the beach in face of that fire. When his boats had almost reached the jetty, he had swung off to the right, as if he were going back, and, to the complete surprise of the enemy, had landed at a little village a mile below the walls of the town. From there he had marched two miles inland to another village, almost in the rear of the town. The undisciplined garrison, in a panic lest their avenue of retreat be cut off, had then fled back into the farm land for almost the ten miles. Everybody had congratulated him . . . he had taken the town . . . he had kept the casualty list way down . . . the civilians in the place had been exposed as little as possible.

But some kind of political turmoil had arisen in the States over the move, and the politicians who were responsible had scrambled around saving their faces. They had recalled his Commanding Officer and him to Washington and hauled him up before a gang of Senators . . . "Watch out for yourself, Deacon," the Chief of the Bureau of Navigation almost had whispered to him, "the President's man in there, Senator Stalk, has orders to prove, right or wrong, that you exceeded your authority, that all you were supposed to do was a little harmless police duty. But remember, you are representing the Navy in there. It's going to be hard."

Senator Stalk, a well-dressed, little weasel of a man, had bored at him relentlessly with the same technique that criminal lawyers use on a witness. He was a lawyer, when he wasn't a Senator, a coal company lawyer from up in Pittsburgh . . . "Where's your mathematics, Lieutenant? Can't you figure percentages? You say you lost eleven men in taking the *three* towns; yet you ask us to believe that you lost less men than if you had taken only *one* town."

"Well, Sir," he had attempted to reply, "the tactics of the situation . . ."

"Never mind about the tactics of the situation, Lieutenant, let's stick to common sense."

Senator La Bandia had been almost as much of an ordeal as Senator Stalk. He had understood vaguely that La Bandia had been taking out some kind of personal, irrelevant vengeance on him, that the man's questions and jibes had smacked of something like a petty, suppressed envy. Old Admiral Fellows had told him afterwards that La Bandia had practically been reared on his place out in San Francisco, that his father had been the gardener there. In the end, they had summoned, as an expert witness, Commander Kerns. It was a mystery how Kerns ever had gotten as far as he had. He was dull, unprofessional, without energy, and up until the time he had testified at the hearing, he had been passed over for promotion by the Selection Board. "Yes, the town could have been taken without taking the other two villages," he had testified. "Yes," in his opinion, "the garrison would have retreated if the Landing Party had gone straight in. Yes, probably without a fight . . . Yes . . ."

The Navy, from Manila to New London, had been profoundly

disturbed by the phenomenon of Kerns' appearance before the Senatorial Committee.

On the day after Stalk and La Bandia had put him through that third-degree, backed by Kerns' testimony, he had smiled in honest entertainment in the first moment that his eye had caught the headline in the newspaper: SENATORS UNMASK BUNGLING MILITARIST . . . then the bitterness of what all this meant had bitten into him . . . "Why! Why! I have studied all my life for my country; so that I could do things like this properly for it when the order came . . . And I did do this properly. Any tactician in any country anywhere would say so." For years his country had educated him, schooled him, drilled him, tested him, and then because he had served it properly in the way his books and drill prescribed, it had thrown him to the first gang of temporary office-holders that had howled for a victim. He remembered how the whole event, a year later, had returned to his memory just as it was doing now, and how a kind of fear had taken hold of him when the rumour spread of how the politicians were trying to re-ward Commander Kerns and the few other officers whom they had persuaded or forced to play their dirty game: And there was no recourse to the people of the country themselves, for early in the Navy's history an iron-clad rule had been established that no officer could make a public speech or write for publication with-out permission of the Secretary of the Navy, and without first having submitted his utterance to that politician for censoring and approval. This rule was aimed exclusively at protecting the Navy's technical secrets; but it had not taken the politicians long to pervert the rule in behalf of the most dangerous kind of pork-barrel chicanery or dubious, demagogic manipulations. Now it was merely a gag that forever blocked all frank communication between the nation and its Navy.

Stalk . . . La Bandia . . . now this Governor-General's man . . . They hung lividly before his mind's eye like exhibits in a gallery of wax criminals . . . What a pity there wasn't something like the British Admiralty to stand in between the Navy and the risky ex-pediency of people like that . . . that Governor-General's man was a bad one . . . he'd been a lawyer, too, a second-rate criminal lawyer back in Kansas . . . "But won't your boat run, Captain?"

this Governor-General's man finally had asked. The memory of the man's question evoked all too clearly the stocky image of the man himself: smelling slightly of sour perspiration, a mussy, greying head, tobacco stains seeping from the corners of his badly shaven mouth.

"Well, she'll make six or seven knots; but it's dangerous."

"Captain, isn't it your business to risk danger in an emergency?"

Before he had had a chance to reply to this, the small Chinese-Tagalog quarter-breed, comically gotten up in a new, ill-fitting Constabulary Officer's uniform, had hastily put in, throwing a frightened glance through the large, horizontal window as if he had expected to see a horde of Moros pouring from the green restlessness of the nearby jungle:

"And this certainly, *certainly* is an emergency! Why! Supposing all the Moros got guns?"

It had been on the tip of his tongue to say that he wished to hell the Moros all would get guns; that he didn't see why the natives of Luzon should have them and the natives of Mindanao shouldn't; that . . .

"We have sent for some more warships that are in good order to look into the situation thoroughly," the Governor-General's man had continued, spitting inaccurately into the ring of discoloured mucous around the cuspidor, "but meanwhile, right now that is, we have got to know what is going on in Malampaya Sound, for instance; and Major Mendoza here has gotten word about some activities in Saint Paul Bay, in some kind of an underground river there. We've got to know. They can't get those other boats down from China before next week. The Governor-General has put pressure . . . the Governor-General has arranged," he corrected himself, "for you to attend to this; so I am afraid you'll have to tinker up that boat of yours and co-operate." He had said the phrase "good order" and the word "co-operate" as if he were indicating to the Captain some failure or fault. Major Mendoza had seemed to shudder slightly at the mention of the "underground river."

As he had walked onto the head of the dock, he had felt, despite the cabled instructions in his pocket confirming the orders to proceed at once on the mission, a surge of relief. There at the far end, leaning with an air of pert assurance against the face of the dock, had waited for him his world of open and apprehendable life. He couldn't quicken his pace . . . The heat wouldn't permit that . . . But it had helped that the instant his foot had touched the first plank of the dock, he had felt a kind of relieving reconnection. Marching heavily down the dock between high-piled bags of copra, he had struggled, at the outermost borders of his consciousness, with the tentatively puttering, unrecognized feelers of a mood of depression. He had thought it was his unusually keen repugnance, that day, of the stench swirled up by the heat from the tide mud and the dried, almost rotting, coco-nut flesh. "I must have developed in the night," he had guessed, "a little irritation of the nose and throat." Never in his life had he consciously suffered a mood of acute depression. Probably, if he had, he would have been so spiritually confounded, so intimately outraged, that, in sheer protest, he would have destroyed himself. The magic, rarely failing fuse, which permits into the circuit of each individual consciousness only bearable loads, unfalteringly protected him from what he would not bear—this faithful fuse equipped with illusion, with symbolization, with forgetfulness, equipped even with the exaggerations of these for the penultimate boon that Society repudiates as "Insanity."

He became physically sick, in some almost visual way uncomfortable, when his mind filled up with the hints and premonitions begotten by conferences such as he just then had been through. On this occasion, as in all such moments, he had been approached obscurely by intimations of how completely his world, this world awaiting him but a few paces away at the foot of the dock, was built upon and surrounded by the tricky mud and filth from which he was walking away. It had been his fear of these intimations, perhaps, that always had blocked his avowed purpose to study the politicians and their methods so that he could deal with them "without making a fool of himself": for it was powerful, if not clear, in his consciousness that such a study might too definitely reveal for him all the solid, reassuring world that was the Navy— the hard, clean, polished world of steel within unequivocal lines, where men like the lines lived by *Articles For The Government Of The Navy* like the steel—as *not* being a bright planet revolving on its own axis in clear space, sufficient in itself. It might instead, such a study, reveal the Navy as something like a submarine sunk deep in the mud of unscrupulous politicians drooling tobacco juice, ignorance and lethal opportunism . . . where someday, through a rusty rivet, through a sprung seam, the mud would sneak and claw its way in . . . as it had into the Russian Navy that the Japanese engaged so confidently because they knew it was filled with the mud . . . as it had into the Spanish Navy that succumbed to the Americans only because it first had succumbed to the mud. These implacable intimations, fluttering at the entrance to the brightly lighted areas of his mind, poised him, inevitably, on the brink of conscious depression.

3 ~~~

For Lieutenant Fitzpatrick as Executive Officer and Engineer Officer, the outrage in Delilah's assignment at first had loomed jaggedly; but it slowly had been dissolved in the beauty and danger of the rare problem before him as Navigator. Bit by bit, under this solvent, he had come to persuade himself that, despite the constant fear at the back of his head to the contrary, she could "go on forever at six or seven knots." As he and the Captain had worked it out tentatively, her itinerary began at Taytay Bay, worked back down towards the equator through the bays and shelters of Palawan's east coast to Balabac Island; north again along the mysterious, almost uncharted west coast of Palawan; and then into the labyrinth of small islands that sprays out from its northern tip, amongst which the mission was to be permitted to dissipate itself. It was, however, the Island of Palawan, itself, stretching in thin, glamorous outlandishness for two hundred and seventy miles over the rarely navigated water between the South China and Sulu Seas, that seductively had engaged his anticipation. The mere, non-committal shadow of it on the chart there had eddied through his senses like mist from a hypervolatile drug. Nearly uninhabited, its jungle unexplored, its writhing, unknown coast line shunned by all save wary, groping ships forced through storms or irregular needs to approach it, the dark sliver of island, ostracized in an un-mentioned area of sun-drenched sea, promised for him the great navigation adventure of his life. "The shores are faced by numerous islands and coral reefs," read the *United States Coast Pilot*, reluc-tantly blurring the cold exactness of its virtually scientific prose, "and, owing to the unfinished surveys, navigation is conducted with difficulty." On the chart, itself, across the nearly blank stretch representing the complicated surface of sea to the west of Palawan, through which his skill, his intuition and his glistening instruments must guide the ship to the mouth of a strange, under-ground river, was brusquely printed the warning: "Dangerous And Unsurveyed Ground."

By the time Delilah had reached and subsequently left Taytay Bay, he literally had memorized every item of the meagre informa-tion relating to the itinerary that was contained on the charts and in the reference works carried in the ship. Whenever he closed his eyes, in the first few seconds the lean, weird blot of Palawan Island glowed on his retina, solid, bright, purpureal, like the silhouette of a vase in a sunny window that lingers behind closed eyelids. He got little rest, for in addition to the four-hour watch he stood ev-ery eight hours under way, he visited the bridge at least twice in each of his off watches. He even slept there on a cot during dark hours when Delilah would be creeping slowly across a patch of particularly dangerous liquid mystery.

He took advantage of the ship's two-day stay at Puerto Prin-cesa, which was, in any realistic sense, the only known town on Palawan's great, wild length and varying ten miles of breadth, to include in his making-ready operations things that could not be gotten at handily under way. He and "Unc" Blood, the Chief Quartermaster, who was almost a jeweller and an optician at such matters, furbished and adjusted his sextant until it fairly glowed with polish and precision. The instrument, which had been pre-sented to the Lieutenant by the Captain's wife on the occasion of his second birthday on Delilah, lay ready in its red satin case like some angular, be-mirrored device of esoteric sun worship. His en-thusiasm of preparation communicated to the rest of the Quarter-masters, Bidot, Cavendish, Arnold and their striker, Warrington, spurred them to the overhaul of every other piece of equipment on the bridge that pertained to navigation. They turned the awninged, circular top of the Forward Conning-tower, monopolized though it was by the grey, three-inch gun, into a kind of temple where the sharpened pencils, parallel rulers, dividers and course protractor lay enthroned on the creamy spread of the chart-board in all the punctilious array of holy implements set and ready to supplement the ritual of the splendid sextant.

After Delilah had left the port, this sense of especial alertness and preparation tinctured even routine procedures, and so far did it extend into the realm of extraordinary precaution that at all hours of the night, men aroused for a moment by the heat, which had driven them from the forecastle bunks to sleep on cots stretched along the deck, would raise their heads to listen, as in a dream, to the melancholy quaver of Bidot or Cavendish chanting up to the bridge the marks and deeps of the lead line.

Ordinarily, the voyage south-west down the east coast of Palawan, close inshore, would have been considered by all concerned a major piece of business in itself; but to Lieutenant Fitzpatrick it had become mere practice and schooling for the precarious opportunity ahead: the unexampled voyage, without benefit of beacons, lighthouses or adequate data, up the west coast of the island, through nameless coral clusters, in and out of bays like tropical fjords, past threats labelled falteringly with such phrases as "Shoal patches reported by H.M.S. Merlin in 1885."

So little did he spare himself in this preparation that the Captain, aroused by his officer's bloodshot eyes and the dark symptoms beneath them, began waiting patiently for the chance to check, within Lieutenant Fitzpatrick, himself, the ravages of the intensity that the whole ship had come to sense as a kind of magic fever in whose heat and visions their chance of security rested . . . "That guy," Arnold assured a ring of washed and combed men, resting in clean undershirts through the moments before evening meal, "could take her in and out of a keyhole."

The Captain's chance came while the officers, too, were waiting for their dinner. It was Ensign Woodbridge's watch on the bridge; but the Captain and Ensign Snell were relaxed in deep wicker chairs on the starboard side of the throbbing quarter-deck. Between them sat Lieutenant Fitzpatrick, who was perched on the edge of his chair, bent tensely over a pencil that worked at a note pad on his knee. A tall, frosted, glass pitcher of lemonade, framed off from the heavy heat by a sort of corona of coolness, stood on a small table before them. Each time the victrola, lashed to the carriage of the torpedo-tube, would come to the end of its record, Ensign Snell would get up slowly, pause as if he were about to stretch himself, then step over and stop the machine. Going deliberately through the box of records, he would make a selection, usually a record he, himself, had bought and carried back to the ship. It innocently never occurred to him to inquire if the others would like the selection: he simply started it playing and sat down again. In succession, he had chosen and set going: *When It's Moonlight On The Alamo; Just A Little Love, A Little Kiss; Down The Old Green River On The Good Ship Rock and Rye; Dreamy Eyes; Don't You Remember California In September?; If We Can't Be The Same Old Sweethearts Let's Try And Be The Same Old Friends.* From away forward, below the break of the forecastle, came the shouts of a group of belated bathers, shouts that were recognizable, even with the event hidden, as coming from naked bodies suddenly being drenched with buckets of water to clear themselves of soap; but these shouts from forward there, from the glistening wet bodies flexing like shafts of meaningful whiteness in the layers of brilliance and shadow beneath the awning, would seem to burst forth as if in ecstatic response to some chord in the music, a seemingly elicited shout, like the yell, wild and glamorous, that rips from the lips of men in a Mexican crowd who suddenly feel themselves at one with a phrase of melody to which they are listening.

Ensign Snell, his gaze lost in the uncertain yellow and vermilion softness of the evening horizon that pulsed delicately on the far edge of sea like the throat of a moth, was thinking: "What a damn shame it was when they took away our liquor!" He almost smacked his lips when he thought of how good the stuff his glass contained would have tasted with just a shot of gin in it. "Aiming to abolish it in the whole country eventually . . . that's what mother said . . . don't see, though, how they'll ever get away with it . . ." He smiled wryly as he thought of his mother talking about "drinking," smiled at the glass in his hand resting on the arm of the chair as if that pleasant, cool object were somehow her representative here.

The Captain, seeing him smile at the glass, thought, as he looked from him to Lieutenant Fitzpatrick, who still was figuring on his pad: "Fine thing it was only lemonade the boys could get hold of on this trip . . . there would be plenty to worry about if Fitzpatrick, with all this navigation and these engines on his hands, were able to start kidding his nerves with pick-me-ups." He had protested as vehemently as the next one when they first had prohibited "wine" (that was the euphemism he and the rest had used) in the ships . . . "taking their damn, experimental spite out on the Navy which had no way to protect itself" . . . but he slowly had come to see the point in it; he was seeing it very thankfully at this moment. His mind, however, drifted back to the days when the point had not yet even been thought of, sauntered nostalgically along through old memories that rose before it as it went along, friendly, valorous memories washed clean by time of all the headaches and vomit and lapses of efficiency . . . "but," he said to himself, precipitated back to thought by the first glimpse of Chief Machinist's Mate Stengle walking toward the quarter-deck, "ships were slower in those days . . . the whole thing was slower . . . you had more time to retrieve yourself . . . mistakes . . . not so much ticklish machinery . . ."

Stengle came straight aft and stood informally at attention. He, as a matter of fact, could stand at attention in no other manner. His entire being, washed and clean garbed though it now was, was somehow irremediably informal and dirty; not soiled, but dirty in a kind of pure, smeary, earthy way. He was about five feet, six inches tall and he could not have weighed the proper amount even for that scanty height; but they waived that, each time he was up for re-enlistment, just as they waived his stomach trouble. He had fifteen years of impeccable service behind him, and in the opinions of the Captain and Lieutenant Fitzpatrick he knew more, from the practical aspect, about reciprocal steam engines than anybody else in the Navy. Lieutenant Fitzpatrick once had told him so, and on that occasion, Stengle's habitually contemptuous face had betrayed no pleasure, no emotion of any kind, as it certainly would have done if this compliment had been paid him by any enlisted man associated with him in the black gang. Officers had come to mean, for him, something quite impersonal, something theoretical, not human, mere gold-bedecked symbols of the irresistible power that gave pattern and compulsion to the world about him. Now, he fixed his small, restless, black eyes on Lieutenant Fitzpatrick's bowed head until the officer looked up and stared at him without recognition for a moment, struggling to slow down and divert to the man before him the stream of consciousness that had been pouring along over the figures on the pad. With what bordered on a grimace he finally synthesized the shapeless, oil-soaked oxfords ... the clean, worn dungaree trousers ... the small paunch above the tight, black belt . . . the thin, brown arms hanging loosely out of the white, cotton undershirt on the texture of which spots of sweat had begun to widen . . . the little, brown face . . . "All right, Stengle, what do you want?"

There almost was hostility in his tone; but it was not because he disliked Stengle. He did like him. He would have said definitely, if he had thought about it, that he even was fond of him. Here, now, however, the man's presence had struck him importunately, as if he were in some way an unpleasant reminder.

"Sir, I would like to get a couple more days lay-up in one of these bays we go into. We'd oughta get at those bearings again ... have to if my say counts for anything."

"Why!" said Lieutenant Fitzpatrick in surprise, his sensitive, arched eyebrows going up, "are they going that bad?"

The Captain quickly put in: "How will tomorrow morning do, Stengle?" He spoke from the depths of the chair where he had slumped, almost stretched out as if asleep, his arms akimbo across his face.

"It'll do fine, Captain." Stengle saluted as he spoke. He always saluted the Captain when he had any contact with him whatsoever, even of the most casual, passing kind. If he had passed him twelve times in one hour, cap on or not, he would have raised his hand in his inept gesture precisely that many times, and without appearing ridiculous.

"That will do then. You may go."

Lieutenant Fitzpatrick and Ensign Snell were startled. Even with danger hanging overhead like a sword on unravelling thread, the Captain never interfered with his three officers, never failed to give them a chance to go through with it, unless, as Ensign Snell phrased it, they were "about to drop the ball."

Ensign Snell looked away from the confusion that began to spread over Lieutenant Fitzpatrick's face, and fixed his eyes on the glass of lemonade in his hand as if this action would remove him from consciousness of what was happening. If he had been able to think up some utterable excuse he would have left the quarter-deck. He got very red in the face.

A flicker of sadness held the region about the Captain's mouth as he sat up and looked at Lieutenant Fitzpatrick. A person looking at the Captain an instant later would have thought that the expression on his face, if there was any definite expression on it, was one, or recently had been one, of extreme reluctance. He put on his glasses, tossing the case on the little table, where it jangled warningly against the base of the lemonade pitcher. Here was the repugnant opportunity for which he had been waiting so carefully.

"Mr. Fitzpatrick, how did you come to miss the trouble about those bearings? We oughtn't to have to wait for Stengle, you know." The anguish on the tired face, on which surprise still lingered, almost stopped him. "Stengle is a good man; but you are the Engineer Officer, remember. I think lately you're leaving too much of the job to him."

The pound of the ship's propellers, the mellow roar of an infinity of small bubbles bursting under her frothing stern, the hiss of the water along her sides, all combined to draw about the three men on the quarter-deck an effect of congealing silence. Ensign Snell was unsettled by a fear that Lieutenant Fitzpatrick, weakened and upset as he was, conscious of how much he *had* done, might try to excuse his neglect of the engines, might not "take his beating standing up." He got hold of a package of Fatima cigarettes on the table and lit one, lit it fumblingly behind cupped hands, which he kept up in front of his face even after the cigarette was lighted. With what was for him a nervous gesture, he stepped to the rail and looked at the sky. Turning around, his heavy face ingenuously lit up with a quite artificial smile, he said in a tone of voice appropriate to one just arriving through a doorway of a room full of friends, said briskly with no slightest intention of irony but only in a desperate, confused attempt to help his friend in this intolerable moment:

"It's a nice day . . . cooler."

4 〰〰

With the contingency upon them of no prostitutes, no barrooms, no restaurants, nothing but the narrowness of the ailing ship struggling near breakdown in an ornate vacuum of bright fish, sea and light, and the toiling forays upon the unreal land, the men soon became even more restless than before under the general tension and concern, which now was aggravated by much loose talk of the uncertainty ahead. The very leisureliness of the business pointed and underscored the tension. Delilah made only a hundred and sixty or so miles even when she steamed for a steady twenty-four hours; but this she rarely did, for, like an easily fatigued invalid, she paused almost every afternoon, to linger for the night, in the shelter of some convenient, purple bay or in the lee of a jungled shoulder. Disabled as she was, the Captain was reluctant to risk any but the most necessary chance of her being caught by rough weather or of breaking down entirely, especially at night, while at sea: But these pauses, even when there were no Landing Parties, instead of providing a recess for the men, seemed only to call attention in another way, a delaying, retarding way, to the peculiar quality in their condition of ill-being.

Delilah's temperament, always a thing calling for skilful handling, now exhibited its most cross-grained aspects. In apparently deliberate recklessness of the careful persistency of their nursing and attention, she seemed to be doing everything in her power to make the lives of her men miserable. Not being able to range above seven knots, her most uneconomical speed, she kept the watches below feeding her an inordinate amount of coal. Her infirm condensers extracted so paltry a supply of fresh water that, when no safe supply was found ashore for her small storage tanks, the men were forced to wash less and drink water reminiscent of the sea from which it came. Almost continuously in her frequent stops, and often while she was under way, Stengle, his Machinist's Mates, the Boilermaker, the imperturbable, bald-headed Blacksmith and Lieutenant Fitzpatrick (who now with grim, exacting impartiality devoted half his time to the engines and half to the navigation) had to work at her ailing organs; and whenever she was not at anchor during the warm, heady nights, disturbing enough in themselves, she kept many of the men anxiously awake with the knocking and thumping of her bad shaft and cylinder.

All this anxiousness and ever-increasing stress concentrated upon and penetrated the Captain as if he were the vital element in a barometer at the centre of a gathering storm. Sleep, for him, at anchor or under way, day or night, became a matter of occasional naps dozed into semi-consciously while he stood on the bridge, a steadying hand on the grey-painted, canvas wind-breaker, or as he was stretched out on his bunk, fully dressed except for his shoes and cap, or as he sat in a chair on the quarter-deck, the backs of his joined hands over his eyes. At any hour of the night or early morning, if Delilah happened to be anchored, the Quartermaster on watch, pacing the starboard strip of deck, automatic pistol on his hip and long glass under his arm or night binoculars slung on a strap from his neck, would hear the Captain's impersonal, almost mechanical:

"Quartermaster."

When the Quartermaster sprang towards him with, "Here, Sir," he would ask:

"How's she holding?"

With the Quartermaster's answer, a look over the side at the water, a long gaze into the star-configured sky and then a glance at the nearest bulge of land, he would go back down below. His presence in the ship was so relentlessly supervisory, so powerfully at the back of its life, that his contact was almost exclusively an indirect one, devoid of the savour and satisfaction of doing or finding out things for himself. He even did not dare to stand and watch the men working on the engines. They would get nervous, drop their tools or something of the sort.

A woman had asked him once, while he and Ensign Woodbridge had been dining ashore with some civilians:

"Just what do you do on the ship, Captain?"

For a second he had tried to think of something he actually did
do. Finally, he had had to answer truthfully:

"Not much of anything, I guess."

Ensign Woodbridge, seeing he was going to let it rest at that,
had said sardonically:

"Oh, he just takes the responsibility. If I run the ship on the
rocks, or the man in the engine-room fails to stop her and she piles
up on the dock, they court-martial *him*."

"But suppose he's not to blame; suppose he's in bed or something like that when it happens?"

"No matter; he's to blame just the same; even if it happens
while he's ashore."

This had startled the civilians. They had found it almost incomprehensible. The impact in it for their sensibilities had been unintelligible but threatening, something like the flash of steel for
the bull beneath the folds of the matador's bright cape.

One of the deeds that did fall within the nameless categories of
his province was an attempt to lessen still further the concentration, almost the fever of concentration, that had tightened itself
about Lieutenant Fitzpatrick's being. Into the half of his time that
he now permitted himself to devote to navigation, he strove to
crowd as much effort as he had given it before. "It had helped
some," the Captain told himself, "raking him over the coals about
the engines. But it wouldn't do to ride him too hard; he's so damn
touchy . . . the devil only knew what course he'd take if I did
. . . but I have to keep him in shape somehow . . . he's a marvel at
this kind of business . . . almost guessed himself from one patch
of deep water to another . . . it was astonishing . . . but he's making
himself sick . . . and that damn stretch of west coast still ahead."

He suggested to Lieutenant Fitzpatrick that he take ashore one
of the Landing Parties that they sent over at each anchorage to
search about for caches of arms or anything that looked like traces
of gun-runners.

". . . It'll do you good. You need the exercise."

Lieutenant Fitzpatrick almost lost sight, then, of the fact that the man before him was his close friend, as well as the Captain of his ship. The idea flamed up in his temper that the man was nagging him . . . "What, in Christ's name, did he want anyway?" . . . His smallish, dark, Irish face, almost Spanish in impress, frankly betrayed his indignation . . . "First he lands on me about leaving the engines too much to Stengle; now, when they really need attention, he wants me to go scratching around in the jungle ashore . . . God damn him anyhow!"

"Is that an order, Captain?" Lieutenant Fitzpatrick said thickly, standing at attention, his perspiring, grease-smeared chin pulled a little too high, a little absurdly high. From the Port Engine-room Hatchway, alongside which they were standing, arose the sickening smell of burnt oil and dead steam, and the raw steel deck areas that a momentary drench of fierce rain had been able to reach beneath the awnings exhaled in the heat an acrid breath of oxidization.

"Of course not, Fitz. It's just a suggestion about which . . . when you get yourself together . . . you're to use your own judgment." He walked away.

Lieutenant Fitzpatrick climbed back down the engine-room ladder, gripping with a kind of ferocity at the greasy steel rungs, which felt hot and elusive on his sweating palms. Resentment and anger, the first anger his friend ever had aroused in him, pumped muttered exclamations to his lips and the blood in such a whirl to his head that he had difficulty in keeping his balance on the ladder.

In the end, dressed for the shore duty, he had walked aft with the natty swing of arms and legs that naturally pervaded his walk even with his face showing clearly the collapse of all tone and crispness in his being. He apologized formally to the Captain.

"Good!" said the Captain, the word plainly not being a response to the apology, but an accompaniment of his obvious taking in of the Landing Force uniform, "Enjoy yourself, Mr. Fitzpatrick, it looks fine country over there through the glass."

Then impulsively, his whole frame relaxing, Lieutenant Fitzpatrick had put out his hand as he had been in the act of turning to go. At once the Captain had taken it in his firm, dry grip.

"You're making a mountain out of a mole-hill, Fitz . . . out of a mole-hill. As a friend, if you'd treated me as badly as you're making out, I'd take you ashore and give you a trimming; as the Commanding Officer, I would have had you confined to your room long ago . . . They're waiting in the boats there for you, Mr. Fitzpatrick."

5

These Landing Parties on Palawan aimed at exploring the land borders and approaches of the bays that might serve as bases for gun-runners. Usually the boats beached on great crescents of fine sand, glowingly pale, that stretched back past the high water mark, where an occasional, rebellious trunk leant wildly toward the sea from the vast palm groves, as silent and passive as abandoned cathedrals, in which the beaches lost themselves. These groves the Landing Parties would explore thoroughly, meeting tenaciously the demands of this mission in which they had no slightest confidence or belief. When, after floundering through the shaggy, dry slipperiness of palm debris layered for centuries beneath the great trees, they came to the barricades of jungle that inevitably walled in the groves, they looked for paths and openings. Failing to find them, they then attempted to break through the entanglement of often swampy vegetation, buttressed by heavy creepers with huge hairy leaves, ferns as tall as trees and massive vines armed with shiny spikes, that festered in the gloom beneath towering limbs from which orchids drooped. If they could not break through, they concluded that no gun-runners had broken through either. They never found what they were looking for, nor even a sign, save now and then a cluster of lost-seeming natives clinging to the margin of the sea, that any men of any kind ever had been there before them; nor did they come upon a single one of those formidable relics of the Spaniards, a rampart, an esoteric flight of steps, a whole fort even, ruins all but obliterated in jungle, such as they had encountered everywhere else on their comings and goings throughout the archipelago.

The emptiness of the luxuriance through which they so faithfully and stubbornly made their search did not, however, permit them to subside into unalertness. Once a Landing Party, tenaciously pressing along in a compact group through the obscurity of a less resistant avenue of greenery, jerked itself to a swaying halt on the very brink of a cliff so extensive, so faced with immense depth that it seemed the precipitous edge of the world. What had helped to save them, to bring them up so abruptly just in time, was the unexpected blaze of the sunshine into which they had plunged from the gloom of the forest. It was as if the universe had silently exploded in their faces. Under this vast illumination they gazed down into, out over, the profundity at their feet. Far below there, the delicate, close-packed tops of the tallest jungle trees stretched away as far as the eye could see in every direction like the surface of a green ocean rippled by a light breeze. Here and there on this limitless surface, hazy with distance and leafy depth, there glistened like spreading patches of vermilion and cream-coloured foam the clusters of those blossoms, blossoms of the creepers, of the parasites, of the trees themselves, that, reaching for the sun, had risen out of the dark smother beneath to waste their flagrant beauty in the brilliance of this high desolation.

Sometimes they landed against shores from three to ten feet high, like ancient sea walls over which vegetation runners and thick roots had matted. They secured the boats to tide-exposed roots clustered with large oysters, dark roots which they could see, in only faint distortion through the weirdly clear water, extending down into bright nothingness where fish like bursts of pigment swam flickeringly about the tangle of submerged tendons as if these harboured some hidden desire. The men climbed the roots to the land, the boat-keeper passing up to them their haversacks, rifles and ammunition belts. At the end of each day's march, often bleeding from scratches in which the vegetation had left some stinging ichor, their bodies slowed down dangerously under the heat and humidity, their necks and wrists tense with the cling of black, puffed leeches in which the gorge of blood showed darkly, they would rush to the sea, fling off their sweat-drenched clothes and swim frantically for a few minutes. The boat-keeper, roused from his nap beneath a tarpaulin stretched across two thwarts, would climb a tree and keep a lookout over the clear water for the deep sight of a shark, a projectile in liquid crystal, hurling itself toward the swimmers.

Bidot, the Quartermaster, First-Class, climbing up to put on his clothes, would pause on the way up to pick a dozen or more of the great oysters bared by low tide. Holding on with one hand, his slim, white body entwined with the black roots, he would select each shell carefully, as if he were an epicure in a familiar restaurant, and fling it up to solid ground. Up himself, he opened the oysters with his bayonet and sucked out the cool flesh with a loud and enthusiastic ripple. No one else would touch them; but, half persuaded, they gathered about Bidot as he ate, the expressions on their faces ranging from sheepish envy to smiling repugnance. Perhaps the great, juicy hunks of life were too dark, too generous, too apposite to the hard monstrosities, encrusted and misshapen, from which Bidot extracted them. Once Cruck, the Chief Boatswain's Mate, his rugged, aggressive nakedness leaning over the sitting Hardwood to pick off some clinging leeches, had held one of the small, bloated things out to Bidot with the remark, "Here, you, you might as well eat this too." The men had howled in delighted revulsion; but Bidot had gone on undeterred sucking at the oyster. Mixing the sucking motion of his lips with a soft, artless grin, he irrelevantly had nodded his head, from which the long, straight, wet hair hung down evenly as from the head of a Japanese.

On the occasion that Lieutenant Fitzpatrick went ashore with the Landing Force, they found a village composed of a dozen or more nipa shacks built out over the water on thin, cane piles, as if the dwellers there wanted to maintain themselves as far out as possible from the mysterious land. The inhabitants appeared to be Moros. Lieutenant Fitzpatrick searched the village thoroughly. The children peeked in solemn hostility from behind their bewildered, smiling mothers and fathers while Lieutenant Fitzpatrick, Cruck and Ferguson went through each tawny, fish-scented house to discover, as always when they encountered the occasional village, nothing much besides a scattering of rice, mangoes and coco-nuts. It came out that one of the natives here could speak broken Spanish. Lieutenant Fitzpatrick, who could speak Spanish well, seized upon him eagerly as representing the first opportunity to make inquiries that had offered itself since the ship left Puerto Princesa, in this fantastic world where the rare voices spoke a dialect as strange as the world itself.

Standing face to face, their mouths aimed almost obtrusively at each other, the officer and the native shouted in the way men shout in seeking to communicate through a language that is but imperfectly mutual. They stood on a platform in the centre of the village, a platform made of thick, bamboo stalks laid and lashed with fibre side by side. Behind the spruce officer, his cap with its broad, gleaming ribbon of gold sitting at a slight angle on his neatly combed, black hair, the natives had gathered in loose order, forced there, in a sense, by the squad of sailors leaning on rifles that had lined up behind the Malay who spoke Spanish. This man was naked except for a width of bright green cloth draped around his tobacco-coloured hips and a sparse twist of similar cloth about the womanish coiffure of his stringy hair. His small body, smaller than Lieutenant Fitzpatrick's, was wasted by some organic disease. His knee and elbow joints glistened bulbously in the intensely bright sunshine. His puffy lips, towards which his whole head and face appeared to stretch and strain, seemed unable to close, and about the lips and his blackened teeth seeped the bright vermilion of betel nut juice.

To Lieutenant Fitzpatrick's question as to whether there were any more men or villages near here, the sick man pointed up the coast, north-east, saying, "Far, far away." To this phrase in Spanish, he added a clicking, resonant word that was merely a pregnant sound for the officer, who then pointed inland and asked if there were any men in there. The native answered simply: "Never."

Lieutenant Fitzpatrick asked him, at this, if he knew anything about a great cave somewhere across the island. The man did not understand, nor did he understand any elaborations or simplifications of the idea, until the officer got it into a Spanish equivalent of "underground river." Then the man's eyes widened as if he were a child just past infancy before whose gaze something wondrous has arrived. He fell back a step, shifted his eyes to the natives over Lieutenant Fitzpatrick's shoulder and flung them a restrained, staccato phrase. The smiling faces instantly reposed into shapely, expressionless ovals. Almost as one being they had flinched back without moving their feet. A very small baby, like a chocolate blossom lying confidently on the thin, hard symmetry of its father's breast, closed its great, liquid eyes at its parent's sudden movement, clutched more tightly in its minute hand a beflowered sprig of jasmine and began to cry.

Lieutenant Fitzpatrick looked at his men. He thought one of them must suddenly have waved a pistol. The Malay did not answer him, made no further sound. He gave off an unmistakable impression of having been a victim of trespass. The thin crying of the child, the lapping of water under the platform, the slight knocking of a tied boat against a pile, the suck-suck of water struggling in some small cavity below took possession of the silence about them. From the shore, out of the great mass of sunward pouring green, against the background of which the clustered blossoms of a fire tree shone brilliantly like small, bloody wounds, an elongated bird sailed out over the sea, its colour lost and indistinguishable beneath the incandescence of the sky, its pursuit relentless and calm, its victim mad with light and the failing flutter of the great, dark membranes that served it for wings.

6

The officers always ate below, even in the warmest weather. There was no room on the small quarter-deck for the comfortable spread of a table, and under way, a veritable rain of cinders from the stacks swept and dribbled in under the awning. If Ensign Woodbridge could be said to have had a stock set of conversational subjects, one of them certainly was his complaint that "always sticking the officers' quarters aft was an inconvenient bit of conventionalism." He had all kinds of arguments to support the contention that in designing each individual ship the Wardroom should be allocated to that portion of the vessel, wherever it might turn out to be, that would prove most comfortable and most adaptable to the officers' needs and functions. He was developing his idea again at dinner, putting into his conversation fresh material in the form of items derived from his actually having redesigned the ship in the hours of the previous night, when he had been unable to sleep.

"Take us now," he was saying, gesturing with his soup spoon, the handle of which he held droopingly by its tip between right thumb and forefinger, "here we sit skidding around in this little box with the propellers trying to knock us out into the water. Cinders, noise, motion, we can't eat, sleep or think. We're packed in here, the most uncomfortable spot in the ship, like one of those four-masters Chips carves inside a bottle."

He was waiting for the Captain to say to him, as he usually did, "Well, what would you propose? What scheme have you to take the place of this one?"

This time he was ready for him. He had a design roughly but carefully laid out on paper. It would take only the slightest rise to the bait on the Captain's part to send him striding into his room after the three sheets of paper on which he had a redesigned Delilah, clear and shipshape, to meet the Captain's invariable demand, in discussion, that if you tore something down, something had to be supplied in its place. But this time the Captain did not rise to the bait. He did not rise even when Ensign Woodbridge, struggling hard for his long-deferred chance of victory on the field of this subject, said:

"You'll never convince me this ship was designed by Naval Constructors . . ." he paused, looking hopefully, then ironically at the Captain . . . "it was designed by politicians."

Even this absurd remark did not get hold of the Captain's attention. The whirr of the small electric fan for some seconds had no other rivalry than the clash of silver on china and the occasional blurred intake at Ensign Snell's lips when he forgot and sucked at his spoonful of soup instead of drinking from it. He had done this ever since he was a little boy . . . each time it happened now he remembered how invariably and patiently his mother had rebuked him for it at home. This slight action, never failing to remind him of his mother, carried with it a faint, pervading haze of pleasure. The old rebuke, which was what he thought he remembered, became the rebuke of the action now whenever it occurred. Abashed, he always stole a glance around to see if anyone had noticed. It was as if his mother were at the table, whispering a little too loudly: "William, don't suck at your spoon!"

Nobody at the table, really, had taken in anything Ensign Woodbridge had said. To one side of the stream of thought running through the head of each had been the realization that their friend was talking about the Wardroom; but they knew what he had to say on that subject; they had heard it before. As the Tagalog Mess Attendant carried out the silver soup tureen and returned for the soup plates, Lieutenant Fitzpatrick, as if impelled to utilize the temporarily clear space of table before him, pulled out his pad of note-paper and pencil. The pencil poised above the surface of the pad, arrested by the very thought it hung there ready to deal with. The direction of his stare seemed to indicate that his thought was concerned with the faintly visible spray of white leaves woven into the still whiter background of the table-cloth.

The Captain was turning over in his mind the incident ashore, which Lieutenant Fitzpatrick had reported to him in detail. Stripped of its drama and colour, the reaction of these natives to the question about the subterranean river was, in his thought, an item in the business to which he was turning his hand just as if it had been a gasket or a screw-bolt used in the repair of his engines. He was thinking about it still when the boy brought in the fruit.

"You know," he said aloud, "the way those people acted over there," he pointed to the port-hole full of sunset in which the cluster of bestilted, little houses was deeply framed, "is, at bottom, the way people acted in Puerto Princesa when I asked about that subterranean river." He laughed uncertainly. "The whites treated my question as a joke; said they didn't believe there was such a thing, that most likely it was just another native superstition. The natives, that fellow in charge of our coal barges, for instance, skeetered away from the question as if it had poison in it."

"It's marked definitely on the chart as being there, Captain," Lieutenant Fitzpatrick said, halting a golden slice of mango just below his lips.

"Oh, I guess it's there all right; but I wouldn't put too much faith in where the chart places it. The charts are very nearly bluffing when they deal definitely with that west coast."

"The island is probably honeycombed with caves of one kind or another," said Lieutenant Fitzpatrick, "I saw an enormous bat over the village this afternoon."

"Probably a *tree* bat," said disgruntled Ensign Woodbridge.

"The native Constabulary Officer there at Puerto Princesa took it as a personal affront when I kept after him about it. Finally, he said to me in a sullen sort of way, as if I had been forcing him to eat dirt about something: 'Captain, the reason I haven't been over there yet is because you can't get there overland. It's directly across the island from here, but the jungle is impassable.'"

"Oh, but he's wrong about its position," said Lieutenant Fitzpatrick, "that is, if the chart's right. It's about opposite Tinitian, that little village off which we lay overnight, a couple of days before we got to Puerto Princesa."

"Likely as not they're both wrong," said Ensign Woodbridge.

The Captain pulled the band from a very thin cigar, slit the tip with a fruit knife, and lit it. Ensign Snell was smoking his cigarette between seemingly solid swallows of coffee.

"Partridge, that fellow with the general store," said the Captain, "told me that the former Constabulary Officer stationed there, an American, had a good deal of information about the region where it's supposed to be, Saint Paul Bay, they call it. He said the American often had hiked across a trail that leads from somewhere in Honda Bay through a pass to Ulugan Bay, which is right next door, theoretically, to our underground river, and he said that this fellow once set out to climb some mountains there, mountains around five thousand feet high; but the natives quit him cold when they got the idea these were the mountains under which this river was supposed to flow."

He smiled. Some amusing pattern had dropped, for a moment, over the puzzle in his mind. He continued to smile. Finally he leaned forward in his chair. Ensign Woodbridge knew at once that the Captain was going to tell a story. The others did not realize it until he said, after taking two short puffs at his cigar:

"These fellows all remind me of the man in Paris who got a note from a girl he'd picked up in a cafe." The Captain stopped and looked, slightly abashed, at Ensign Woodbridge. "I guess you've heard this all right." Ensign Woodbridge had; so had each of the others. Lieutenant Fitzpatrick, to be exact, had heard the old story fifteen years ago if it was the story he was sure it was: But they all said quickly, almost together:

"I don't believe I have."

"Let's see."

"No, I haven't."

In this deceit lay no flattery, no hypocrisy: it was an act like recounting a fairy-tale to a child. Telling a story, around a table like this, was the only non-professional accomplishment after which the Captain strove. For him, somehow, the telling of a story was more than a device, a simple pleasure of gregariousness. It would have seemed ridiculous to him, for example, to have heard it placed in the same category as playing poker, a game at which he long and profitably had surpassed, and from which, as a result of the solemn, changeless expression his wrinkled face infallibly assumed throughout a game of it, he had gained his midshipman nickname, "Deacon." For him a story or a joke well told in an atmosphere of coffee and good tobacco was a splendid thing, the execution of which was to be classed with playing the violin, painting a picture or singing a song. He *knew* that it really was not, and he would not so have classified it outspokenly for others; but in the privacy of his own secret standards, standards maintained by feeling rather than by thought, the classification held. To Ensign Woodbridge, who could not tell a short joke but who was a master at telling a pointed story, he paid a manifest deference that extended over into their professional relationship. It was quite realistically an attitude akin to that which musicians assumed towards Paderewski or Rachmaninoff. He always took Ensign Woodbridge with him to dinners ashore if he could manage it; and when the young officer had skilfully and colourfully brought the whole table with him right up to a telling climax, the Captain would beam around at the guests with the assurance that he had brought along to the dinner something quite as fine as the duck and sherry of the hostess. He consciously attempted to profit by the technique he observed in Ensign Woodbridge's narrations, and he sensed nothing to the slightest degree absurd in this. The Captain told his stories well. The trouble was that his memory for them was so bad that he could not remember a story unless he had heard it three or four times. By the time he had heard one often enough to remember it, it was wilted, dead, superfluous. His Wardroom, however, stuck by him. Lieutenant Fitzpatrick, certainly, would have accepted a bullet wound in preference to depriving the Captain of this luxury, this one release into, what was for him, fine art.

"This man, this American," the Captain continued, "had smiled at the girl, who was sitting at the table next to his. Of course," he put in hastily, "she probably had smiled at him first." Ensign Woodbridge was thinking: "He put that in because he sees himself as the man in the story." The Captain went on: "The girl stood up, looked speculatively at him for a moment, started to walk off with another smile over her shoulder, when she changed her mind and sat down at the table again. She pulled out a pencil and paper from her pocket-book and quickly wrote something on the paper. She leaned over and laid the paper on the man's table." Here the Captain, savouring to the full his position in the midst of the narration, stopped to look around at the faces of his audience. On the face of Ensign Woodbridge he could detect plainly the play of sincere delighted engrossment; for Ensign Woodbridge was entertained with the vision of the Captain playing the part in this comedy into which he unconsciously had projected himself. This satisfactory look on Ensign Woodbridge's face kept the Captain from seeing too deeply into the faces of the others, on which was clamped the smiling, faintly over-enthusiastic expression that takes hold of faces whose owners do not want the true state of their reactions to a story disclosed.

The Captain blew a cloud of smoke at the low ceiling. It impacted, spread, recoiled down the surfaces of the four walls and clung in the dark green folds of the gathered drapes at the portholes and the door to his room. The walls and ceiling were painted a very light, creamy green; the floor, on which there was a green rug, was shellacked a deep red. These colours took on a misty, delicate quality through the ambient smoke. The fragrance of the tobacco struggled pleasantly with the faint aroma of salt water and disinfectant that pervaded the Wardroom. "She then walked quickly away before he had time to make up his mind to do anything about her. He walked towards his hotel thinking about the note in his pocket. At a street lamp, one of these polyhedron affairs, you know, that lean lopsidedly from the top of a post, he stopped and tried to read the note. But it was beyond him; he only knew a few words of French. There was a policeman on the corner; so he asked him, on the chance that he could speak English, if he would translate the note for him. The policeman could speak a little English. He would be 'delighted, enchanted' he said with that pompous, tricky way those fellows have. He took the note, his eyebrows went up, he got insulted, mad, then strode off saying he ought to arrest the man. He threw the note back at him.

"The poor fellow reached his hotel, his curiosity at fever pitch, but afraid to ask anyone what the paper said. He saw the bellboy then; you know, one of those birds that are always after you to let them get you a girl. Here was somebody that wouldn't be bothered by the damn thing. He called the boy up to his room, and asked him what the note said. The boy took it, read it, stared incredulously at the man and fell back a step. 'Monsieur!' he exclaimed in shocked horror and disgust, and fled from the room. And this was a boy, mind you," here the Captain pointed seriously with his cigar, "that would do anything, absolutely anything.

"He was now determined to get to the bottom of this thing before he went to bed; so he went out again and walked into the hooker district, where he searched around until he found the lowest dive in the place, a place where the vilest kind of degeneracy was the order of the day. Well, here he called the madam to one side and asked her if she spoke English. She said no, she didn't; but she had a fellow there who did. She summoned him, a horrible, slimy pimp, who took the note and read it. At once he screamed something at the madam, and both their faces took on a look of great disgust. They grabbed the poor man, others piled on, and they all threw him into the street, yelling horrified names after him.

"Now he was afraid to do anything more about the note; but his curiosity wasn't dead. Quite the opposite. He'd wait until he'd found a close friend, he decided, who wouldn't misunderstand the thing, to translate it for him. He stowed it away in his wallet.

Finally, he went home on the steamer, and one of the first people he saw on board was an old and close friend, who he knew spoke perfect French. As the boat sailed out of the harbour, he called his friend to one side and told him the whole story. His friend said laughingly, 'Here, let me have it, I'll translate it for you in a jiffy.' He pulled the wallet out of his pocket. Inside it was the note. Eagerly he took it out. Unfolding it, he held it out to his grinning friend. The friend reached out his hand for it . . ." the Captain paused and looked from one of the officers to the other with a kind of warning clearly contained in his expression . . . "when the wind snatched the note and blew it overboard!"

The Captain relaxed back in his chair, delighted, relieved. Ensign Snell roared exclamations. Lieutenant Fitzpatrick laughed adroitly. Ensign Woodbridge alone of the three was laughing sincerely: he was laughing at the spectacle, even the fictitious spectacle, of the little Captain in a situation like that of the man in the story.

They were quiet for a time, their faces ruffled pleasantly by the smiles that lingered there, as the memory of a storm lingers on the sea's surface in the quiet atmosphere after the gale suddenly has vanished. Striving to prolong the pleasure of this dinner . . . the first easy-going minute they seemed to have had since leaving Taytay Bay . . . the Captain said:

"If there is any contraband in these parts, that subterranean river is probably where it is, because the Japs or whoever are running in the guns would think it the last place in the world where anyone would go prowling about . . . You know, it would have been a real help having that American Constabulary Officer along. Might have saved us a lot of trouble."

"What's the idea of replacing him with that little Tagalog?" asked Ensign Woodbridge. "Why, if a Moro stuck his head around a palm tree and shouted, 'Boo!' that bird would jump right in the bay with his eyes shut."

"That's the new policy," was the Captain's reply.

"I know, Captain, but why a native from way up north strutting it around down south here? . . . And that other one in Zamboanga, especially! This isn't Tagalog country. Mindanao certainly isn't. Why not put Moros in these two jobs, for instance, if they must have natives? It *is* Moro country; and at least they'd be able to speak the language they use around here . . . I don't think that clown in Puerto Princesa could speak a dozen words of this dialect."

"That's the new policy too. They're putting the whole shebang, every branch of the government, into the hands of the natives of Luzon and the other northern islands. That's what's behind all this trouble we're having now. The Moros think we've sold them out to the northern Philippinos, and they've started to fight. That's why the Manila crowd are so scared some firearms will be run in down here."

"But that's the rottenest thing I ever heard of!" exploded Ensign Woodbridge. "These people south, here, these Moros, are the only sound groups in the Philippines. Why! The Tagalogs, Bicols and such riff-raff used to be their slaves. . . weak, barbarous trash that didn't even know how to grow rice until a few Chinks came down and conquered them. Hell, everybody's conquered them, done what they liked with them, Chinks, English, Spaniards, Americans. Everybody knows they used to run to the hills like rats whenever a few Moros would sail along their coasts."

The Captain shrugged his shoulders. He believed this too, believed it all the more as Ensign Woodbridge touched it with the quality of eloquence. "It's rottener even than that," the Captain said. "Not long back, our politicians got most of the Moros to disarm and quit fighting. They even surrendered their arms as a sign of good faith, and they had plenty of them then. Came in and piled them up in the market places before the American Constabulary Officers. The deal was that the encroachment on their territory by Tagalogs and such like, protected by American arms, would stop . . . that if independence ever was granted, they wouldn't be left holding the bag with Northerners placed in authority over them." A faintly puzzled expression, perhaps a touch of shame took possession of the Captain's face. "As soon as the Moros had surrendered their arms, the politicians turned the poor devils right over to the Tagalog bosses. They're even putting northern native Constabulary Officers over them, as you see. That's why the southern half of the islands is so dead set against what the northern half calls, 'Independence.'"

"Well, the Northerners are Christians," defended Lieutenant

Fitzpatrick. He immediately was embarrassed by having uttered this phrase. It had not sounded like what he meant at all. What really was in his feelings was that these people that the Captain and Woodbridge complained of were Catholics, like himself; but his intellect would not permit his emotions, for some reason or other, to make precisely clear what he would have said.

"Christians!" exclaimed Ensign Woodbridge. "Bare-assed Christians! They'd be anything . . . Christians, Buddhists or anything else their conquerors were."

"But look at the Moros," continued Ensign Woodbridge, "the real Moros in the hills back of Zamboanga and Jolo . . . and incidentally, if you want to go by size, Mindanao is damn near as big as Luzon . . . has anybody ever conquered them? Not so that you can notice it! We're still battling them, and we've got way farther than anybody else. But . . . Why! We can't even send a liberty party ashore *inside* the walls of Jolo without issuing out automatics."

Lieutenant Fitzpatrick started to say that it was far from his intention to defend what was going on; and Ensign Snell launched a question; but Ensign Woodbridge, as if he had not noticed this, resumed:

"And what are the Moros fighting to defend? A real culture . . . the only culture that ever has flourished in these islands, a culture that takes in beautiful brass-work, and weaving, and real sculpture and poetry. That's why it's so sickening when the dispatches to the papers in the States call them bandits. The Moros are literate, and they were literate, too, before we or the Spaniards or anybody else got here. With my own eyes I've seen, in every part of these southern islands, gangs of little children gathered around a schoolmaster with a Koran, learning to read . . . and that same thing's been going on for centuries."

All at once he stuck his face across the table at Lieutenant Fitzpatrick, bent on ignoring the evident probability that that officer really might be agreeing with his position almost in detail. His curly hair, his blue-green eyes, the pastel-like texture of his skin, his long clean-cut face over the high, starched collar of his white blouse seemed literally to glow with youngness, aroused and alluring, as if over him had been poured some magical, golden liquid that seduced and compelled. He was becoming excited, which had a tendency to dispel the adroit, Mephistophelean atmosphere that habitually surrounded his speech and attitudes; and under the stress of this excitement his southern accent became more pronounced.

"Did you ever see any of those gooks up north with a book that the Americans, English or Spaniards didn't bring? Did you ever see a book anywhere up there outside the Manila region, for that matter? Everybody knows that illiteracy in the northern islands, in any and all languages, is just about one-hundred per cent. Christians, for Christ's sake! What's that got to do with it?"

"Some Caloocan skirt must have left you waiting in a *carromato*," said Lieutenant Fitzpatrick sarcastically, helplessly.

"Sure she has," replied Ensign Woodbridge, "but not very long! . . . And that's a point too, if you want to bring it up. That's just what the crowd on Luzon, Samar and Leyte are, a gang of whores . . . and pimps . . . and bootblacks."

"Come, come, now, Woodbridge," interjected the Captain.

"Let me ask them just one more thing, Captain," pleaded Ensign Woodbridge, including in his attack poor Ensign Snell, who had been congratulating himself, with a touch of deprecatory smile on his face, on being well out of this. Ensign Woodbridge lowered his voice as if restrained by the fact that he was addressing the Captain, "Just one more thing and then I'm done. Tell me this: Have any of you ever encountered on Luzon a whore, a pimp or a bootblack?"

"Not as many as you have, probably," jeered Lieutenant Fitzpatrick.

"You bet you have, and not just around Manila either, but in every *barrio* from one end of the northern islands to the other. On the other hand, did you ever encounter a Mindanao or Jolo whore, pimp or bootblack?"

"Sure!" testified Ensign Snell firmly.

"Where?"

"In Jolo."

"O that!" grudged Ensign Woodbridge scornfully. "All right then, Tulai Mary, a couple of her friends . . . a couple of whores in the whole of Mindanao and Jolo; but how about pimps and bootblacks?"

"Cheap sophistry," said Lieutenant Fitzpatrick.

"Cheap sophistry, hell!" answered Ensign Woodbridge, "It brings out just the point you, yourself, dragged into the discussion. The Tagalogs and such mongrels are tribes that take easily to whoring, pimping and bootblacking . . . while the Moros, even these water Moros that hang on around the coasts . . . Why, man, the proof of the whole thing lies in the fact that wherever the Army stations a garrison down south here they have to import a couple of housefuls of Jap girls to keep the boys from going crazy. But they don't have to import any for the posts up in the northern islands!"

At this moment, some general vision of the remote and alien tragedy in which he was being forced to take part sailed full-rigged out onto his consciousness. His excitement recalescing, his accent deepening, his voice seemed to take on a shadow of the orchestral quality that soars with the pain and beauty of some great, tragic phrase in minor.

"The Moros are a fine, literate people who look you straight in the eye. Take them now, out all over their islands ready to face all comers . . . machine guns, battleships and all. They've got nothing to fight with but a few knives. But they get out there and die . . . you've seen them, I've seen them . . . in the open sunshine, dressed in gay silks and gold filigree buttons, dying in defence of their weaving and their sculpture, their brass-work and their decent traditions, their poetry and their pure women."

The other three were powerfully disturbed by this final outburst. While Ensign Woodbridge, silently filling his pipe with hands that almost trembled, sought to regather about him the folds of his usual urbane manner, they looked down steadily as if their eyes were held by what they saw reflected in some morose pool deep within their beings. It had been a clear implication, a too clear implication, of the tension at the bottom of the whole business of their life out here, a business that inevitably was a perversion, somehow, of the life they had taken solemn oath to lead . . . "It isn't really the intention of the politicians to sell out like this . . . bad as they are . . . I don't believe that," the Captain told himself, as he unconsciously drew and redrew a triangle with his thumbnail on the elusive pattern of the table-cloth . . . "They weren't doing it deliberately. They just couldn't help following the path of least resistance . . . a kind of moral laziness . . . The native Manila *politicos* wheedled around the weak American office-holders out here as kept women wheedle and nag things out of the men that keep them . . . the Moros scorned that kind of stuff . . . and here I am out here ready to kill off all the decent people in the islands for the sake of the scum . . . to put the finishing touches to the destruction of a fine, free people . . . And for what? . . . Simply to turn them over to a wretched crew of half-breed intriguers whose only previous relationship to them has been the occasional one of slave . . . The whole American position here was wrong . . . it was like those unhealthy combinations you see in a boarding school where the nasty little boy, protected by the bully for dubious favours, goes around hitting the decent children . . . and the Moros were the decent people out here, there was no doubt about that . . . nor much doubt that the Americans were the bully and the northern islanders the nasty little boy . . . By God! It was worse even than that! . . . It was exactly like the Reconstruction when we sent an army into the Southern States to put niggers and carpet-baggers in all the offices over the whites . . . and all because these poor devils of Moros had the courage to maintain their integrity while the Tagalogs and such like were smirking and lying on their backs for anybody who happened to beach a ship in their vicinity . . . What was eating these northern tribes anyhow? . . . They weren't content with running their own show in their own islands and letting the Moros settle down and run theirs . . . They seemed to have some kind of feverish, fixed idea about acting the part of conquerors over the Moros . . . with the help of the American good right arm, of course . . . And what the Moros wouldn't do to them if the Americans weren't there to back them up and take the Moros' guns away! . . . In those old days, before the occupations, the Moros really had been something . . . they were organized . . . even to the point of sailing large vessels, war vessels, in fleets and manoeuvring them . . . That monk said they used to signal from ship to ship with red flags . . . a wig-wag system . . . Even in his time, the monk said, he had seen a column of these *praus* swing, on signal, right-front-into-line in a stiff breeze off Sarangani Island . . ."

Portness, the Radio Electrician, climbed down the conning-tower ladder and stood in the doorway looking at Ensign Woodbridge. He stirred about, rustled the radio message in his hand to attract attention. Ensign Woodbridge, who was the Signal Officer, looked up.

"All right, Portness, what have you got?"

"Code signal from Cavite, Sir." He stepped over, handed the message to the officer and swung back up through the conning-tower. As Ensign Woodbridge looked at the ominously long message, he realized that it was in code used only for signals of extreme secrecy and importance. His eyebrows arching and his lips assuming the stance of a whistle, although no sound issued, he pushed the message past the silver vase of flowers in the centre of the table towards the Captain. As the piece of paper, this last straw of complication, travelled along the surface of the table-cloth with all their eyes following it, their moment of relaxation slowly died. Once more they became tense men on a crippled ship, whose hard-pressed, short-handed crew was growing dangerously restless, creeping through intense heat and ever-threatening waters into punishing mystery, creeping relentlessly to ensure the destruction of weird and gallant men who aroused in them only pity and admiration.

The Captain and the Signal Officer rose from the table and walked aft into the Captain's cabin where the Confidential Code Book was kept. It was heavily bound in lead so that it would sink quickly with the ship or when thrown into the sea.

The Captain, as he went through his door, the curtain of which was being held aside for him by Ensign Woodbridge, waved the piece of paper apologetically at Lieutenant Fitzpatrick and Ensign Snell. Lieutenant Fitzpatrick, in a voice that did not seem quite to succeed in tone and purpose, said smilingly:

"Captain, don't let the wind snatch it and blow it overboard."

7 〰〰〰

The legal limits and caste barriers, more formidable than iron and steel, that are placed between commissioned officers as a group and enlisted men as a group are no mere markers of class distinction, although they fit with seeming final appositeness into the aspects of this. They extend, too, with their rigidities slightly disguised under amenity, even into the more comprehending precincts beneath the quarter-deck, where each subordinate is separated by them from the officers above him in rank. This separation takes the concrete form of dividing into distinct wardrooms, where the size of the ship permits it, the three general classes of officer rank: junior officers, senior officers, Captain. The case of the Captain, that remote symbol of impeccable and irresistible power who even must dine alone when the facilities of his ship provide adequate isolation, is, in extreme degree, an explaining example of these limits and barriers which are as indispensable a part of war on the sea as are the guns and the compass.

The Captain never can be just a man from Illinois who sleeps in rumpled pyjamas, makes mistakes about history and uses his finger, when he thinks no one is looking, to push food onto his fork. Familiarity, when it is permitted to prevail, if it does not breed the proverbial contempt, certainly breeds between the giver and receiver of an order, an order that may lead to death or frightful mutilation, at least two things impairing the confidence, the aggressiveness and the speed with which a battle crisis must be met.

First, in the giver of the order, it breeds a realization that if he takes this step, which in his judgment is exigently indicated, it may convert into a gory horror that tall, ruddy-faced man who has the next chair at dinner, who likes radishes, which he eats with a loud rending noise, and who smiles with pleasure when his home town of Baltimore is mentioned. The order may be given; but the doubts, emotional stresses and temptations to rationalization, set up then, distract from the almost inhuman concentration on the development of the battle that must prevail, if those already dead in the struggle are not to have died in vain and the battle is to be won.

Second, in the receiver of the order, familiarity breeds the constant reminder that the giver is merely a human being like himself, that the tactics on which he bases the summons to death may be as faulty as his familiar table manners, that he may be as mistaken here, in this fatal matter, as he was the other night at dinner in regards to the basic causes of the War Between the States. In the end, the order may be obeyed; but the slight taint of hesitation, dissatisfaction and lack of confidence in the obedience may be quite sufficient to infect a hundred surrounding men, lead to a half-hearted spurt where fury, accuracy and decisiveness are imperative. It was no crowd of cronies that responded with lethal alacrity to the command, "Damn the torpedoes! Go ahead!"

These limits and barriers are a device, operating constantly, in battle and out, afloat and ashore, in work and in friendly conversation, to remind all concerned, keeping it protected and vividly functioning, that it is not this nondescript, little individual in glasses, this mere human being, who gives the order, who must be saluted, in whose presence all must stand; but that it is something essentially non-confusable with his personality that gives the order, and to which the deference must be paid, something that is but reposed in him as a jewel is placed in a rough and makeshift casket with which its ultimate quality is not to be confused.

The order to engage the enemy may come from lips belonging to a man familiarly describable in terms of human failings, possibly of vulgarities; but these defects are hidden and made nontainting behind the limits and barriers within which the man has been isolated and consecrated. If happily this man, in his person, is valiant, kindly, glamorous, then the order enjoys all the added benefit of this personal setting, much as the jewel is more advantageously displayed in a beautiful case: Yet it merely is *through* the man, through his years of training and testing, his consecration, that the order to steam into death roars out to his crews, roars straight up out of the living depths beneath a hundred million people fighting for a richer and more significant life, depths where a band of lonely Pilgrims still make the first covenant to "submit to such government and governors as they should by common consent agree to make and choose" . . . where gentlemen still rear the spacious and graceful mansions on the fragrant margins of tidewater . . . where a frozen Army, dying and forlorn on icebound Pennsylvania hills, still bleeds out a gleaming pattern within the loom of its dreaming, iron leader's will . . . where women, like rare, embattled flowers, fighting back to back with their men in a fantastic ordeal of isolation and raddled death, earn for themselves an unparalleled freedom . . . where the dream of schools free and open to all of whatever creed and aim is passionately realized even through famine and corruption . . . where Poe and Bierce sing of desire and hope lost in the ferocity of a lovely and monumental wilderness . . . where Willard Gibbs still launches the theorems that gave to the modern world the chemistry of its very life . . . where prairie schooners still breast the mystery of vaster landscapes than men with women and children ever had dared before . . . where two brothers still conquer first the yearning desert of the sky . . . where a lesser, seven hour a day slavery to the machine is substituted for the bestializing, dawn to dusk slavery to the land . . . where Melville, with his pale monster, still chants in mephitic, beguiling frightfulness his rebuttal to Dante's *Comedy* . . . the cogent summons from these depths it is, in times of clear right or inescapable wrong, crystallized, reposed within the essentially irrelevant person of the Captain, together there with the covenant pledging the decision of their efforts to Death or Victory, this it is before which the men of Delilah's world stand, salute and obey.

These rigid limits and barriers, set between superior and subordinate Commissioned Officers in the attempt to differentiate and preserve from being lost in the individual the power reposed in him, are graphically understood by those concerned: But between the Commissioned Officers and the crew, the limits and barriers, like foundations that grow broader and vaster as they sink deeper into the earth, become less matters for understanding than for apprehending, and intangible though they are, their formidable cleavage makes of the group in the Wardroom a different order of beings from the group in the Forecastle.

To the enlisted men, amongst whose various grades of Chief Petty Officer, Petty Officer, Seaman and Fireman the rigid limits and barriers are not set up, the Commissioned Officers loom as a kind of golden, incomprehensible cloud ever on their horizons, a removed, privileged existence almost beyond aspiration, beyond envy, a cloud to be understood, as an entity, only through portents, signs, visitations and, in a measure, through long experience, an aureate nimbus from which the inescapable lightning plays, supervising every detail of their existences, advancing them, demoting them, giving them money, taking it away, feeding them, imprisoning them, leading them to die. However, Chief Machinist's Mate Stengle, for example, a man impossible to think of as sentimentally patriotic, could be brought to say, as the result of a more definite realization than this general attitude of the enlisted man implies, that it was not Borden, himself, that he saluted when he stood before the Captain, but that it was "the two-and-a-half gold stripes on his shoulders."

To the officers, the group in the forecastle is a murky clot of being quite as mysterious in their eyes as they are to it. They apprehend this group much as if it actually were a part of the ship, its thrilling and brutal blood, a thing, like O'Connel to Warrington's mind, of wild and formidable power coupled with devastating irresponsibility, which at all costs must be confined within the vital veins and organs of the ship. The officers peer respectfully into this phenomenon at the foundation of their existences with something akin to the strange sensation that is aroused by a primordial odour . . . by a sight of the tentacles of a great, uprooted tree, dark, moist, bowel-like . . . by blood pulsing in regular spurts from a hole in a bulge of white skin above an artery . . . by the labyrinth of an opened ant heap . . . or by the mystic confusion of entrails from an animal. Despite this sensing of the wild, primordial power beneath them, and their respect for it, the officers yet go jovially about the business of keeping this power harnessed within its courses, go about it as assuredly as a *mahout* keeping a giant elephant at piling teak. This joviality the men recognize as a proper omen. They accept, too, its absence in the mere, grim hardness of a truly bleak nature; but the smirk on the face of an officer who in confronting them confronts something that he fears, or the defensive hardness on the face of an officer who is intimidated by them, they instantly scent out as a danger to their very lives.

It was across these legal limits and caste barriers separating them, chasms and walls that have resisted mutiny, boredom, political pressure, death and ridicule, that Lieutenant Fitzpatrick, the officer, and Warrington, the enlisted man, in a night watch as Delilah loped slowly along over the glassy plains of lonely water under the Malay moon, were swept towards each other by an incalculable current, a mere, off-routine eddy of humorous warmth, which was to hurl them, much before they realized it, deep into the proscribed territory of each other's personal orientations.

It is probable that no other powerful combination of the frail elements composing the event would have served to breach the great wall between them, that no other synthesis of time, place, droll crisis, laughter and careless remarks would have served to plunge the officer so suddenly and quietly through into the disturbing universe of the boy's mind, leaving him no time to administer a mutual curb, nor even to derive a warning that one might be necessary. He had mounted the bridge ladder to go on watch, as he had done countless times before, followed by a seaman in dungarees, by a man enlisted to serve his time in the world's toughest corps of mercenaries. Then suddenly this trained barbarian from the depths of the forecastle, who was to obey his slightest order and give him manual assistance in driving the ship across four hours of sea, had been veered around by a tangential gust of humanity. The officer had found himself played upon, with unbalancing unexpectedness, by the very kind of human power to which he was most susceptible, found himself face to face with a strange, gentle being, fierce with idealism, equipped with the traditions of formal scholarship, and alluring with all those responses that most clearly are delineated by suggesting that, being present in the personality of a man, they complement the sound subtleties and spiritual disciplines of a finely bred woman.

In the previous watches that he had stood with Warrington since the forced run to Isla-Sulu, he, as Executive Officer responsible for the training of the crew, had taken advantage of leisure moments to coach the boy for an examination for promotion to the Petty Officer rating of Quartermaster, Third-Class. Although the new hand had been assigned on the bridge to strike for this rating when he had first arrived in the ship, his achievement of it had been then but a distant possibility, for he was only an Ordinary Seaman; but after his display of indomitable, emergency quality in the fire-room, the Captain, in effect, had ordered Warrington advanced to Seaman. The Executive Officer, pleased to find his original prejudice in assigning the boy to so important a station as the bridge thus speedily confirmed, immediately had set about help-

85

ing to prepare him for the further promotion; for which he now was eligible. He had arranged, in order to enlarge the opportunity for this instruction, that Warrington, acting as his Quartermaster, stood nearly all his sea watches with him.

It was neither Lieutenant Fitzpatrick nor Warrington who first realized that this program of instruction had been deviated from, that their conversation had ceased to deal with quarter-decks and signal flags, soundings and bearings: It was Saunders, the Seaman at the wheel. From his post in the darkness at the rear of the bridge, he listened with surprise, then with increasing uneasiness, to the officer and enlisted man warmly, personally giving and taking long sentences and big words over some subject that significantly had nothing whatsoever to do with the watch, the ship or even, any longer, with the laughable incident in which they had found their predecessors of the watch involved. At the end of the first two hours, when his relief, Cruck, came up to take over the wheel, Saunders shot a few surreptitious words into the Chief Boatswain's Mate's ear regarding what was going on, and Cruck, setting himself at the wheel as some rugged neighbour woman might position herself at a window to get the full benefit of a next-door event, prepared to satisfy himself as to just what had so astonished Saunders.

By noon the next day, the whole crew was astir with the report of the conversation as rendered by Saunders, who in speech, spiritual equipment and person was a slightly fatter and smoother version of Cruck. The latter, relegated to the status of corroborator by a sort of crude dignity he insisted on maintaining in the varying degree that, at any given moment, he realized his prestige as Chief Boatswain's Mate, was turned to by Saunders at almost every punctuational point in his report with such interjections as, "Ain't that right?" . . . "Didn't he?" . . . "He says that to him, I'm a son of a bitch if he didn't, didn't he, Cruck?" The portentousness with which Cruck's brutal face and head gestured assent and backing to the narrative lent a kind of sanction to the curiosity of the men, framed as it was in the nerve-pressing bareness of their present situation. It almost was as if—forced by the absence of usual interests and stimuli, women's bodies, alcohol, restaurant food, shore brawls, new people—they had tuned down their receptivities to the substitution of such stimulation as this unique event. On each succeeding day for nearly two weeks, men off watch gathered in the forecastle to hear whatever pair of helmsmen that just had stood a watch with Lieutenant Fitzpatrick and Warrington repeat, in necessarily approximated and caricatured terms, the progress of the continued conversation.

Beginning when they laughingly had exchanged remarks about the ridiculous event introducing the watch, they had drifted without thinking about it into a sequential discussion of the human trait, as old, no doubt, as consciousness itself, that causes men to project into entities that by definition are lifeless, such as the sun, a mountain, an abstraction or a ship, the sentience of a human being or an animal. They had gone on from this to the difference between an "emotion" and an "instinct," and when Lieutenant Fitzpatrick had to speak to the engine-room near the end of the watch, they were dealing with the possibility that what in one race bordered on being an "instinct," might in another race border on being an "emotion." They resumed the conversation every time they were on the bridge alone, alone, that is, save for the routine, mechanical presence of the helmsman. Oblivious of him, and all unconscious that through him, whoever he might be, the entire enlisted personnel was their eager audience, they soon were hunting down the apparently safe valleys of mutual readings, stalking along the not quite so safe ridges of parallel thinking, strolling arm in arm through the recalled visions of pleasant places they both had visited, and darting, their sympathies and recognitions seeming almost miraculous to them, amongst the perilous intimacies of their innermost philosophies and moralities.

The commonplace fragment of humorous incident that started them off, the mere breath of assault upon the barrier between them, proving efficacious only through some millionth chance by which the angle of incidence and very gentleness of the assault coincided with some pattern of weakness in the barrier, was in itself an outgrowth of Delilah's stricken health, her precarious situation and her persistent venting of her distress upon her men. On account of her high, thin, sail-like bow, Delilah was very sensitive to a wind, and had to be handled, especially at the low speeds to which she now was restricted, much as if she were a ship under sail. In her present mood, she continually had managed, on the night in

87

question, to take the shifting, uncertain breeze on first one bow and then the other in spasmodic succession, driving the helmsman, struggling to keep her accurately on the course, further and further towards a crisis of impatience.

Ignorant of what the Captain's long code message had contained, and of the fact that it was this message that had led the Captain to reverse the schedule on which Delilah travelled by day and sought the shelter of the bays and inlets by night, Hardwood, the helmsman, had cursed the Captain to himself and ruminated on the evidence that the officers really did not know what they wanted, what was the best thing to do . . . "It was just plain murder to push this ship along through these crazy waters on a flickery night like this . . . and then hide all day in some damn bay like a galanipper in a hole . . . The way they'd mostly been doing before had some horse-sense to it . . . travellin' by daylight . . . restin' up at night . . . that was the way to do it . . ." Standing there at the rear of the bridge, a bulky blot beneath the low, scallop-shaped, conning-tower awning, a shadow marionette flicking a shadow wheel, he suddenly had been forced to transfer all of his irritation and attention to Delilah; for the ship, as if she deliberately had been out to make a final attempt at breaking the uncommon patience with which he had borne her perverseness for nearly two hours, quickly had flung her head way off to starboard. When he rapidly had wound the wheel to the left to offset the puff of wind he had felt she must have been taking on her port cheek, she instantly had shaken clear of the fitful breeze and answered his rudder by jumping smartly past the course to the left. Ejecting soft, warm Alabama curses from the depths of his indignation into the golden glow of the binnacle bowl, Hardwood had stopped her swing, had disgustedly given her what he knew should have brought her properly round, and then had lifted his head to glare at her arrogant nose trembling on the silvery horizon.

"You damn bitch, get back on thea!" he had flung at her.

Ensign Snell, on watch with him, had been slightly bent over the wind-breaker, staring down contemplatively for a moment at the fulsome, glistening, white furrows Delilah was turning up out of the black-green sea: but at this shout hurtling out of the night he had turned about and stared. So had Bidot, his Quartermaster of the watch. Lieutenant Fitzpatrick and Warrington, coming up to relieve, startled by the astonishing exclamation up on the dark bridge, had paused on the ladder, one behind the other, with their heads and shoulders just above the level of the top step. When it finally had seeped through Ensign Snell's leisurely comprehension exactly what the sputtering Hardwood's situation was, he had begun to laugh, a laugh from which his not inconsiderable reputation in the Squadron probably took its personal tones, a solid, lifting fugue that mounted easily from his muscular stomach, shook his body somewhat, twisted his pleasant, Americanized Dutch face into honest puckers and charged his eyes with amiable blue light.

"What's the matter? She teasing you?" he had said.

"I declah, Suh, evah since we pushed her outa Zambo' with that monk aboard she jes' won' seem to do *nothin'*."

8

The daylight watches on the bridge were not those that found Lieutenant Fitzpatrick and Warrington, in any real sense, resuming their conversation. Throughout the day under way, the bridge, in addition to being the station from which the vessel was controlled and navigated, was the headquarters for numerous reports, instructions and orders regarding ship's work. Too, Lieutenant Fitzpatrick being the Executive Officer, the bridge absorbed, when he was on watch there, all the traffic that surrounded that general-managing function; and the Captain was forever mounting the bridge ladder in a casually determined manner, binoculars in hand, to inspect, with an air slightly redolent of the hesitations of courtesy rather than of apology, the compass, the Rough Log, the reaches of the ever-looming land and the expanse of glittering sea towards whose horizon he was trusting (there was never any doubt of that) the three on the bridge safely to pilot his ship. Consequently, it was in the night watches, especially in the bitter vigil from Midnight-to-Four in the morning, watches free from interrupting visits to the bridge by any save the Captain, solitary watches in which there was little to do through four long hours of darkness but keep a look-out over the sea and hold the ship on her course, that their opportunity virtually was forced upon the Officer and the Seaman who had so much to say to each other.

Always, at the beginning of each of these watches they stood together, Warrington, who usually preceded Lieutenant Fitzpatrick by some minutes in taking over the watch, would hasten through the preliminary routine involved and stand stiffly on the starboard side of the bridge, against the curve of the wind-breaker, gazing intently ahead over Delilah's bow at the horizon as if he hoped to see arise there an assurance that the officer would reopen their communion. Each time, his hope that this would come about, as well as his fear that it would not, or that the Captain's also coming on the bridge would prevent it, was definitely desperate. Fatally exiled as he saw himself to be in this lost and brutal world of the forecastle, that first memorable watch, when he and the officer had been swept away from their moorings, had burst into the murk of his general, dangerous despair like the white flare on the life-preservers that are flung at night; and at the end of it, as at the end of the succeeding watches in which they talked, he had swum feverishly through the ship's routine towards the next possible descent of the saving illumination as if that possibility were the only purpose of his presence in the ship.

The hours that Delilah spent in the brilliant, obscure little anchorages, jungled retreats naïvely pigmented with strange fruits, rare flowers, with now and then a tiny cream-coloured woman and soft-eyed children who never before had seen an occidental, streamed between him and his next sea watch with Lieutenant Fitzpatrick like bright barricades of delay. Forced to leave in the Landing Party, a necessity he formerly had viewed with relief, he now was inundated by a feeling of deprivation, as if he were being driven perversely from a scene where something might happen of which he longed to become a part; and he would welcome the sailing out again of the ship beset by the same intensity of eagerness with which the rest of the crew had greeted its steaming in. This served still further to ungear him, within himself, from the alien turbulence of men in which he was immersed.

Before, the common anxiety, which he shared, to flee the oppressive ship had drawn him, in a kind of minor, mechanical sense, to an occasional participation in their community. To this degree he had been a real part of them, part of the Landing Party that would pour over the side as a man might seize, without permitting his desire to come up definitely to the surface of recognition, a chance to get away from a sick wife, whom, even before she was sick, he had thought of vaguely in terms of desire for change.

In the first hour after the men would land, while they were tramping or resting in the jungle, the sudden remembrance of the ship and the necessity for going back to her would depress them; yet, after the expedition ashore had extended through hours of bizarre fragrances and vegetation, under the increasing pressure of strangeness pointed and compacted by the flash of an incredible bird, the sting of an iridescent insect, the threatening droop of an eerie and monstrous tree, they would dash back out upon the beach almost cheering for sight of the grey little craft, usual, known, understood, floating trimly and safely there, a quick antidote for their dim feeling that they had been trembling on the verge of being lost in a brilliant and intolerable wilderness. Then on their way back, once more, with each stroke of the oars that brought them over the clear water closer to Delilah, the burden of their ordeal aboard her, a perceptible tightening of their nerves and spirits that was unconcealable beneath their loud ejaculations and laughter, would again settle down about them.

Warrington, however, now approached the ship with satisfaction. In this situation too, now, his attitude was polarized oppositely from these men. The former flash of unity with their vibrations, which he as well as they unconsciously had enjoyed, rising when in the brief moment of celebration on reaching the shore they had smiled together in the same way, at the same thing, at being free of the ship, now was no more. For him now the ship, with all its vacuous suffering, was a setting for, an indiscerptible part of, the rich contact with that mind and spirit which might, which must occur again. He approached the ship, the inimical emptiness of the world there, as if he had been an Epicurus approaching fanatical abstinence in an iron garden to deny himself all food so that, when eventually he did place on his tongue so much as a crumb, the poignant taste of it would spread like a revelation through his whole being.

The descent of night at sea, with its long lonely watches, now plunged him into a warm shadow of febrile anticipation. This was true, perhaps especially true, even of those nights on which he was scheduled to stand the dreaded Twelve-to-Four, that watch through the four most dark and lifeless hours of the ship's night. In the time before he and Lieutenant Fitzpatrick had broken into their first conversation, Warrington often had paid Arnold, Cavendish or Bidot two dollars, out of his salary of twenty-two dollars a month, to trade the Eight-to-Twelve or Four-to-Eight for this mid-watch when it came around to him. He, like most people in the ship, had found this watch to be one of the minor but miserable ordeals of his routine existence. The ordeal, which lasted sluggishly, like a hangover of dissipation, quite through the working day following the night of the watch, arose out of the mechanics of the relationship between his being and sleep. After the hour of taps when he was free to do so, he would get to sleep between nine-thirty and ten o'clock. Better than this was seldom possible in the crowded forecastle of the noisy little vessel. After he had fallen asleep, it seemed to take the two hours or so of unconsciousness for his tired muscles, his tight nerves, his pressured brain to unwind their tensions and relax. Then just at the death-like moment when sleep had begun to possess him completely, to pour through his being in soothing triumph the warm luxury of its healing peace, at the very moment when he was drugged most heavily but had not yet had time to gain any restoration from the drug, there would come a nightmare tug at his shoulder . . . "Twelve o'clock . . . You've got the Twelve-to-Four haven't you? . . . Come on, sailor . . . On your feet." He would sit up heavily, mechanically in the darkness, like a dead body responding reflexively to stimulation. Painfully his eyes would open wide under the dimly sensed necessity not of seeing but of convincing the oppressive shadow hovering impatiently above him that he actually was awake. Infuriatingly, the shadow would never disappear until he was on his feet. Then with all that made him think, feel and live, writhing, helplessly abject and betrayed, within the heavy recesses of his mechanically aroused body, he would totter about on vague legs adjusting his clothes. The hurried mug of hot coffee from the big copper pot near the Forward Fire-room Hatch enabled him to breathe deeply, and he would smile at the one or two others, recently awakened like himself, who were gathered around the pot; but he smiled in precisely this same fashion, a tight, sharp grin in a face whose skin felt drawn and slick, even when no other men happened to be there at whom to smile. The brief lift of the hot stimulant carried him steadily enough up the bridge ladder and through the effort of officially taking over the watch from the man who had awakened him; after which he just stood there on the swaying top of the conning-tower until four o'clock in the morning, moving only to perform some occasional task or to keep himself awake until the time when he could return below for three more hours of sterile sleep, just stood there in the dark fighting for alertness, while his nerves slowly rewound their tightness, his brain its pressures and his muscles their tense resistance to fatigue.

What, for Warrington, had raised the routine abomination of this mid-watch to the power of a formidable dread was that it had been in this watch, in the darkness through which the ship slowly struggled across an infinity of surface as insubstantial yet as implacable as the darkness, that the clear terror and despair of his fate, ambushing his relaxed spirit and thoughts suddenly severed from their drug of sleep, always had closed down in full force about him. As the black minutes passed, the despair and terror would press closer, closer, closer, to the muted pulse and beat of the machinery in which he was isolated, press in ferociously about him from all sides like the walls of Poe's torture chamber, until his successor, arriving with chronometerlike promptitude, had served as the touch on the lever throwing back, at the final crushing moment, the limits of contracting pain.

A determination to destroy himself had found in the despair of this particular four hours the empowering mechanism for its accomplishment. He had rigorously practised timing his resistance to the disaster of these four hours so that the resistance would reach its last limit of possibility at precisely four o'clock in the morning. If ever at this moment his relief were seven minutes late, he determined, he would take this as his signal. At the seventh minute of lateness, after having permitted for these minutes the unresisted, searing constriction of the walls as they burst together upon him, he would plunge, already dead, over the ship's side. In the water he would maintain himself close to the side of the ship so that the two propellers, when the stern caught up with him, would suck him into their blades: But now in this all too brief Twelve-to-Four, in the glorious privacy of this dark hole in the night, the jagged crystal of his fatal necessity was dissolved by the monopolizing intoxicant of his hope . . . He would cling, waiting, to the horizon . . . would hear the officer climbing the ladder behind him . . . would hear him step to the chart-board back of the helmsman and snap on its shaded light . . . would strive to gain a favourable premonition from the crisp, pleasant accents that went so surely about the responsible business of taking over the watch from Ensign Snell. "Will he relax from that official manner? . . . Will the conversation start once more?" Now the officer was coming towards him. He could sense him circling the faint redolence of the well-greased gun that partitioned the centre of the bridge. He dared not glance around as Lieutenant Fitzpatrick ranged alongside him at the railing, his clean, starched uniform a tidy mass of blurred white angles and surfaces smudged with gold in the obscurity. Warrington had not the immediate courage to precipitate by a glance or a word the probable disaster of finding that, after all, the only fellow being whom he had reached in the dreadful desert of his situation had become again the inaccessible officer.

But Lieutenant Fitzpatrick, on his part, had gotten his curiosity, his emotional and mental integrity, as well as his vanity, too deeply into this new, arresting personality, this challenging, unsuspected intellect, to withdraw from it summarily. Sometimes he did wait for the rigid figure in dungarees to open the conversation. Once he waited for half an hour; but in the end, as always, he had to do it himself. Neither of them realized that once the boy had tried to carry the conversation to him, had tried by as much as a glance to point the obligation of their relationship, it might have served to check the officer's own advances, might have served in that mysterious way that makes one hesitate when the person towards whom one is struggling suddenly makes a gesture of encouragement. Such a hesitation, such a slight mechanical movement of withdrawal on the officer's part might have sufficed to remind him that certainly this was no relationship for him, might have made him, in the instant of pause, look about him in bewilderment at the territory he already had entered. But it actually was not until the opportunity for this withdrawal was quite passed, until he and Warrington after days of conversation, beginning to understand what manner of individual each had before him, had commenced instinctively the marshalling and aligning of forces for the inevitable struggle whose issue, when it can be decided, is moral supremacy, that Lieutenant Fitzpatrick realized fully the unusual, heretical plunge he had taken.

Once at the end of twelve hours of fiery sunlight through which they had lain at anchor behind Arrecife Island, lurking there in the tranquil inferno of coral reefs, sunken rocks and shallows of Island Bay like a ship in hiding from a powerful enemy, the other officers almost had gotten hold of a hint of this relationship growing up so swiftly between Lieutenant Fitzpatrick and Warrington, a hint of so extraordinary a thing as a breach in the everlasting social and official barriers between officer and enlisted man. On this occasion, the tang of something out of the ordinary had aroused the Captain for a critical second or two from the preoccupation that had of late settled upon him. He had sat up in his chair and looked speculatively at the Executive Officer as if he had been about to look into something; but the fierce current of thought and feeling, like a heavy, exclusive illness, that had welled up out of the code message and swept him along, drowning everything but his preoccupation with it, had sucked him back before the intention had crystallized. The look, the question, the suggestion that would have resulted under ordinary circumstances, which, like a flash of light on a dark horizon, would have pulled Lieutenant Fitzpatrick up with the astonishing realization that he was dangerously off his course, never developed. The Captain had sunk back in his chair, the stimulus of something slightly wrong on the quarter-deck about him submerged, the brief moment of interruption unable to compete with the flood of danger, uneasiness and despair pouring from the code message through his consciousness.

All the officers were sitting together on the quarter-deck: the Captain, Lieutenant Fitzpatrick, Ensign Woodbridge and Ensign Snell. Delilah being at anchor, the Quartermaster of the watch, Warrington, was pacing soberly back and forth on the starboard side, the curt brim of his small, round, white hat turned down all around in non-regulation fashion to protect his grey eyes from the glare. One limit of his pacing was the small log desk fastened to the side of the After Conning-tower; the other limit was a point abreast of Smokestack Number Four. He would pause now and then to study through his long-glass, which he braced for steadiness against an awning stanchion, the upward lick of the thin empty, black, horizon line to seaward, the rising, evanescent twist of white above a reef, the shimmering unreality of one or another of the numerous small islands above which an occasional palm tree hung like the dark framework of a burnt-out star. The day was cooling off. It soon would be possible to look steadily at the slick surface of the sea; but there was nothing for him to see there. There was nothing of importance for him to see on the land side either. It trembled there, the land, behind its screen of diminutive, feathered islands, like a flat, green and blue illusion stretched between the sky and sea. The high mountains, the nearer ones a glowing, mystical blue, those more distant betraying their greater height and distance only in appearing soft, grey and doubtful, hung above the misty, new green heaviness of the jungle as if too light to sink down to it. The bright, disconnecting drifts of white vapour extended like ragged space between the jungle and what seemed the suspended base of the graceful mountains. There even was no sign of life, despite the cooling of the day, at the mouth of the little river shortly up which was hidden a tiny village. The one movement he had detected on the shore turned out to be, when he trained the glass on it, a flight of white rice birds circling up from a marshy stretch beyond the orange-grey beach.

Warrington turned his gaze away from the quiet wildness of the land and let it rest upon the ordered scene beneath the quarter-deck awning. The officers were sitting tiredly—with a tiredness that wore somewhat the guise of hopelessness—in their comfortable wicker chairs clustered about the little hatch and the breech of the torpedo-tube that ranged fore and aft the length of the quarter-deck. The Captain, the smoke of a cigar periodically beclouding his youthful, deeply wrinkled face, was leaning back in his chair with his eyes closed; Lieutenant Fitzpatrick was reading *The Beloved Vagabond,* which a girl had given him in Zamboanga; Ensign Woodbridge, with pencil, paper and a general chart of the Japanese Islands spread on his knees, was marking away as though he were trying to solve some engaging mathematical puzzle; and Ensign Snell, bulky and immaculate in his white duck and gold, was waiting patiently for dinner time, smoking one Fatima after another as he gazed steadily, unseeingly, his eyes twin areas of slightly amazed speculation, at the conning-tower.

Now, as always when Warrington stood watch on the quarter-deck with Delilah at anchor, his glimpse of the life aft flooded him with a non-invidious, exquisite sense of envy. As he resumed his pacing back and forth he could feel, at the precise moment that he stepped each time across the line where the red shellac of the quarter-deck ended and the raw steel of amidships began, something barely perceptible but definite and complete, like a flick, happen to this feeling of envy. It was hazily as a man might feel whose duty forced him, on a windy winter day, to march back and forth across a line sharply dividing a patch of wind-swept gloom and a strip of sunny, sheltered ground.

Some shadow of this sensation, this feeling of Warrington's, seemed to drift out and interfere with Lieutenant Fitzpatrick's determined reading of the light novel. It was as if he had been subconsciously aware of that boy's presence all the time beneath his quite real attention to the book; as if, sensitively attuned to what was going on in the Seaman's feelings as he paced his station, some intuitive part of him had been unconsciously disturbed, suffered a twinge of pity on receiving the impression from the peculiar quality of envious feeling rising in the boy's emotions. All at once the officer permitted the book to drop to his knees, and he laughed out in a quiet but dramatically pleased way. This sound overtook Warrington as he was on the round of his pacing that carried him away from the quarter-deck. A little shock as pleasant as the laugh vibrated up through him, brought him slowly to a halt. He knew, knew as definitely as if they had been alone together reading the book aloud, that the laugh was for him. He stood still there, with his back to the officers, and looked steadily forward towards the forecastle. After a few seconds, Lieutenant Fitzpatrick raised the book to his eyes again. As if in response to this, Warrington resumed his pacing. Abreast of Number Four Smokestack, he turned around fearing to find, as at the same time he hoped to find, that Lieutenant Fitzpatrick was still smiling and looking in his direction. He started aft again, a trace of self-conscious deliberation in his step, with his gaze focused on only the non-sentient objects on the quarter-deck: the curtained hatch, the red deck, the life-preserver hanging on the bronze cables of the railing, the colours drooping from the flag staff, the long grey cylinder of the torpedo-tube . . . When he was almost on top of the officers, and about to pause at the log desk, Lieutenant Fitzpatrick again put the book down on his knees and laughed once more. Despite himself the youth caught the laughter and smiled. When their glances met, the officer spoke to him:

"I'm laughing at onion soup." He laughed again and nodded at the book. "It's very amusing. When I finish, I'll let you take it."

"Thank you very much, Sir," Warrington replied.

For many seconds the Seaman gazed unseeingly at the broad pages of the Rough Log before him. He made no attempt to organize his feelings. They seemed to be doing a confusion of unrelated things on different levels of his consciousness. His mind had not yet taken hold of the open, public, warm thing that just had happened. It was thinking clearly and slowly: "They ought to get rid of that torpedo-tube . . . put it somewhere forward like the other one . . . it clutters up this fine little space . . ."

Lieutenant Fitzpatrick was irresistibly moved by this incident. For him it was a somehow significant unit from the instant that a delicate wrench at his attention had made him drop the book the first time and look up at Warrington, until this final moment in which his friend turned to stare down with such heavy intensity at the pages of the log. The officer got up restlessly from his chair and laid the novel on the base of the torpedo-tube. It occurred to him that he had better make out his work list for tomorrow . . . He'd just about have time before dinner . . . As he climbed down the conning-tower ladder to go to the desk in his room, his intention changed to another. He knew they were having onion soup for dinner. He had himself the night before told the Steward to have it. He had been looking here and there in casual appraisal through the same novel he just now had been reading up on the quarter-deck. A paragraph devoted to appetizing mention of the soup had held his attention; and he had given the order. Remembering this, instead of going to his desk, he walked to the miniature pantry off the wardroom, where the Tagalog Mess Attendant and Ah Lee, the Captain's Steward, were sweating under the final preparations for dinner, and told the Tagalog that, as soon as the officers were served, he was to take a bowl of the soup up to the Quartermaster on watch.

"Here . . . Put it in this," he ordered, pulling out from its green woollen bag a small, elegant silver dish belonging to a set that the wardroom used only on formal occasions.

Going out to his room, a niche whose closed curtain formed the starboard wall of the short passage leading from the wardroom to the conning-tower ladder, he wrote on a piece of personal stationery:

> "Drink this and you will enjoy the book more when you read it."

As he went to give the note to the Mess Attendant with instructions to take it up with the soup, he was thinking: " . . . the poor devil . . . fish out of water with a vengeance . . ."

9 〰️

The Captain was the only one who was not busy eating when, in the middle of dinner, the Tagalog took the silver dish of soup up the ladder. He was looking straight at the pantry door; but he did not see the dish. He saw only the decision he finally had come to, saw it clear and bright and strong. "All right, I'll go in for the coal . . . but I won't intern! . . . Let 'em catch me, damn 'em, when they could . . . if they find me along this coast in the daytime they'll have to pick me out of one of these Palawan bays like meat out of a crazy nutshell . . . and I'd like to see the whole damn Japanese Navy try to catch me at night! . . . They'll get me in the end, there's no doubt of that . . . like they got the Emden finally . . . smash me to pieces in the bight of one of these God-forsaken headlands . . . No they won't! . . . not here, by God! . . . I'll work her into Japanese waters . . . and they'd never expect that . . . when they finally do get me, it'll be right on their own door-step and I'll have my mark on their shipping and a couple of their coastal towns . . ." They might have put in the message, he felt, what the war was going to be about. He guessed it had something to do with the absurd religious dream of empire within which that tricky, semi-savage people worked and strove. The message had said that the government feared war to be inevitable. This brought a bitter, an almost ferocious expression to his face. He knew how heartily successive administrations had laughed at the possibility of war out here, and with what tolerant smiles they had repelled the admirals who had insisted that if they were to keep any part of the Navy out here at all, it should be adequately based and able to defend itself in just such an emergency as it now was called upon to face.

The Japanese Fleet, the message further informed him, already had put to sea. It already controlled by position the approaches to Manila Bay and the northern islands. It was waiting only for the first shot, the first word of war to put the control into effect. There was a Japanese cruiser squadron heading south, probably for Bala-bac Strait. "To avoid being destroyed by this squadron, if a state of war ensues," the message said, "it is suggested you intern your vessel in nearest Dutch port of Borneo, coaling immediately at Sandakan against possibility of voyage involved" . . . "Well, I won't!" was the decision he finally had come to in regard to the "interning" part of the code message; and from this seed of de-cision all the rest of his plan had risen before his mind's eye, risen like a hard, metallic, spiny plant, glittering, deadly but satis-fying. The message had gone on to instruct him that until the actual outbreak of hostilities, he must continue to carry out as much of his mission as possible, inasmuch as arms reaching the rebellious Moros at this juncture would seriously aggravate the danger of the new situation: but *that* fitted in with his plan, fitted in perfectly. He would get out of Sandakan, once he had coaled and provisioned, slip through Balabac Strait if it was dark, through North Balabac Strait if it was light . . . He could not help smiling grimly at the vision of that Japanese squadron trying to hook him

100

from out of the labyrinth behind Bugsuk Island. Once through the Strait he would lose himself in the mysterious two hundred and seventy miles of that Palawan west coast. Each day that he spent looking for the gun-runners in there would be a day of hiding from those cruisers. He would be travelling, too, towards Japan every night . . . "let them wait for me off Luzon . . . let them hunt for me down here . . . let them!"

The combined pressures, great and small, sliding quietly one after another atop this little man and his ship had aroused him, tranquil, gentle, uncombative as he was, to a pitch of fury. Indignant and resolved, he had become like a tortured steel framework from which a wind, increasing gradually to a devastating storm, finally had blasted away everything save those girders that determined its fundamental form and strength. He was caught out here with his ship in dangerous, unknown waters, engaged on a dirty, political business, caught in his ship that was antiquated, broken down, ready to be transformed before the first gust of wind into a steel coffin for seventy-one men; but it would have been lost, in the face of this culminating threat of war, even if it had been in good condition. Her limited food, ammunition and, above all, fuel capacity (due to her low tonnage), made of her a ship designed to operate from naval bases; and there were no naval bases, save the single distant one in Manila Bay. It occurred to him in scornful bitterness that just a short distance away was Malampaya Sound, which only a few of the dollars that go into each administration sustaining political chicanery could turn into a naval base commodious enough to shelter and supply the whole United States Fleet . . . and there were still other adequate sites away south in Mindanao. The Navy often had thought of Malampaya Sound: deep, extensive, sheltered from all weathers, strategically located and capable of impregnable defence on all sides, it was perhaps the greatest natural naval base in existence. He could not help thinking, much as a person desperately pressed by poverty thinks how it would feel suddenly to find fifty dollars on the sidewalk, of the haven Malampaya Sound would have offered to him if he and his ship had been in the English or Japanese Navies and these islands had been developed by one or the other of those nations. The Americans did not even have a coal pile there. In a few hours more he would need coal, too, and then he would have to risk going into an English port to get it: There was no possible way for him to get more ammunition and torpedoes. It was strange, he thought, how Englishmen, Japanese and Frenchmen understood things like international trade, navies, trade routes, areas of trade influence and naval bases, while the Americans, despite the classic masterpiece by Mahan, did not. "Americans, when they tried to deal in these matters," he reluctantly admitted to himself, "were like young boys suddenly projected from a country family of women into the tough neighbourhood of a big city."

Every way his mind had turned through these last nights and days it had collided with the walls of the corner he was in. Every development, every turn of events, pressed him closer into the angle of his disastrous predicament. When he forcibly cleared his mind of this torture, it only was to make room for the spectacle of his men growing more desperate every day in their endless, fruitless searching ashore, under the oppression of the sterile brilliance in which they were immersed with their little ship full of fire and failing machinery. The men had begun to dart searching, stolidly fearful glances into their officers' faces as if the new expression they had at once sensed there was an omen that in some hidden way the very core of their universe was beginning to crack. This end of it, the men, he kept trying to reassure himself, he could do something about. When the time came, he would line them all up and give it to them straight. He felt, he *knew*, that they would back into his corner with him and, shoulder to shoulder, face what he had in his mind to do, face it as uproariously, joyously as he once had caught them, backed against the front of a saloon in a Shanghai alley, facing with unrecreant fists the combined crews of a whole British squadron.

It was, however, when he turned from his crew to another element in his situation, what seemed to him the fundamental element of his situation, that he became most frantically aware of just how cornered he really was. He could face anything . . . maybe he could not, but he would try . . . if only his country really was behind him, if only it would not get him into these inexcusable, abominable corners: But his country was not behind him. Only those successive administrations of politicians were behind him. There they were,

102

always in between him and the country itself, marauding little cliques of businessmen, untrained, with rare exception, in history and statecraft, calling themselves Republicans, Democrats or whatever else might be necessary, and encouraging, strengthening, through ignorance, blundering and idiot-optimism, those with whom sooner or later they would call upon him to fight. As he gazed down into the circle of creamy soup before him, he remembered what Woodbridge once had said at the end of a discussion regarding the way the country permitted its leaders to blunder into one economic panic after another. Woodbridge had said: "A country always maintains as good a government as it deserves." Suddenly, as this phrase writhed in his mind, the circle of soup seemed to widen and spread throughout the whole field of his vision. He saw only white, wild, creamy, ugly white, clotted with all the successive, compounded suggestions of his fate, a perverse fate in which the whole universe, even his country, was against him . . . "All right. All right." He silently roared his defiant acquiescence. "If it all sums up into the end of the ship, I'll end her! . . . But I'll end her right, by God! . . . End her right in the middle of Japan where everybody responsible for her situation can't miss getting an eyeful of their handiwork . . . that's the way I'll end her! . . . smashing the hell out of everything in sight . . . smashing . . . smashing as long as Cruck and I or somebody is left to press a trigger!"

10 〰〰

There was a flawless quality of assurance behind the Captain's passionate acceptance of his ship's fate and his determination that the acceptance should be given significant form. It arose out of his invincible surmise that the human links of the chain, his crew, with which he must dominate that stark acceptance, were not only adequate to the form he envisioned, but also worthy of it. If, in the very moment of his determination, he had consciously recalled the adage that a chain is no stronger than its weakest link, it would have but increased the exultation in his assurance.

In most organizations of civilization the axiom, "A chain is no stronger than its weakest link," is a commonplace but utterly abstract and diluted principle. Usually the links are so duplicated and complex that even if a dozen or so break, the failure is absorbed and the load manages to get lifted just the same. Of course, there often is considerable trouble if a bank fails, the firemen are delayed in getting to a fire, a politician votes for the wrong measure or the policeman is tardy in summoning up his courage. Usually the worst that results is the temporary impoverishment of a few homes, a new job for the builders, a politician out of office or a gangster saved the cost of another acquittal. The great ointment of "flexibility" whose lubrications prove such a boon in the civilian areas of the earth soon heals the wounds. "We must be tolerant" ... "They did their best" ... "We must not question motives" ... and that pleasant section of the world rolls on, on through its formidable plenitudes of gold, oil, cotton, wheat and labour, where fortunes can be lost and regained a half-dozen times, where Presidents can lead through cesspools of graft and corruption, where scientists can be brilliantly mistaken, where authors can reach the hall of fame with works jaundiced by myopic eclecticism, where University heads can bend pedagogy to dubious political devices, where religions can suppress even the technical truth and propagate even the technical error, where business leaders can wallow in criminal opportunism, and editors can beget bilious journals clogged with sloppy thinking and inverted sentimentalism, and yet where all can emerge mysteriously in the end amidst monuments, prizes, longevity, glory and fine raiment.

But in the stark sphere where Delilah speeds out her life, the magical ointment of the civilian, that luxury for which only the slangsters have a name, must be hunted out and obliterated as if it were the deadliest contagion. Here one must be right or he perishes. In this chain there is no room for duplication, no time for retrievement: on each link depends the fate of the whole. Let the Navigator's pencil misplace but eight or nine degrees on a dark night, and Delilah thrashes out her delicate life on a lurking reef; let a coal heaver feed but one shovelful too many and a smudge of smoke betrays her to scouted enemy monsters who crush her to the bottom with torrents of steel; let a commander decide for a wrong measure, as at Trafalgar, and an Empire dies.

104

It is for something like this reason that, aboard a fighting ship, what appears to landsmen to be undue and exaggerated recognition is given to minute and seemingly trivial morsels of efficiency and competency. Based deep in the consciousness of every soul in the craft is always alive and restless the awareness of how much depends on each single man and lever. It is that the very life, purpose and significance of this specialized community rely so desperately on what in ordinary existence is taken as a matter of course, to be demanded, expected, but to be safely if not freely pardoned in remissness, and things that normally would loom large in the foreground, here are etched in dim relegation. Thus for Delilah and her Samsons, bound inflexibly together with a tape that makes civilians see red, emphases are shifted and life given an inverted perspective.

"Drink yourselves into periodic oblivion of your sparse fates, if you must," says Delilah to her men, "worship God or the Devil as you will, and brawl away your lives in the gutters of the world; but hold me ever on the course, keep my engines turning over, and the cross-bars on the target."

It is remarkable what high courage and pure endeavour is required to remain faithful to this adjuration. Not the least simple requirement is that which demands that each man stare boldly at his fellows' weaknesses, efforts and motives and then arrive at appraisals in loud, hard voices. To be swayed by hate or love towards distorted criticism, to indulge in easeful self-deception, tolerance, prejudice or kindly pretence is to mechanize for veritable failure and annihilation.

Here, incidentally, is a hint that it is no mere "romantic lure" that accounts for the Navy's "old timers," the large and steady company of the re-enlisted. It may be that a man once committed to the life system of Delilah and her kind is perhaps forever lost to the civilian world. No matter how many filth-ribbed oaths he may swear never to ship over, no matter how passionately he may detest the sea or love the land, he will surely find himself inadaptable to the life ashore, find resentful backs and cold shoulders there turned against him, find that his life formula will not serve, and that he has forgotten how to make the world safe and comfortable for those who want to be called good but are not good, who must be big but are small, who demand their share of glory without being glorious, and who insist that they see their world yet never face it. In short, he is repellently naked, he has lost his magic anointment of "flexibility" somewhere on the arc of the sea . . . and the only arms held welcomingly open to him are those from which he is trying to flee.

The uncompromising pattern through which Delilah must trace her life is not so much a freak of modern warfare, or an offshoot of current specialization, as it is an intact anachronism. The wave of relieved, delighted surprise that swept across Delilah when the boy, Warrington, was discovered to be, after all, a sound and tough link in the desperate little chain, had been forming for thousands of years. It began when the first group of people gathered together to live, love and die securely within the organized confines of a protecting wall, and delegated to a selected few the duty of manning the wall's vital spots.

It does not seem to have taken long thereafter for these embattled spots to have become towers, nor long for these towers in turn to have developed a special kind of crew inured to their cramped interiors and committed to their fatal exactions. It took longer to push these towers, floating, out upon the sea: But even thousands of years later, Delilah's men referred to all the world and life beyond her decks as "the outside"; and they were organized in duty watches almost precisely after the fashion that prevailed on the towered wall around Agamemnon's hollow ships, when the Achaians fought, behind the glamour of a woman's name, for the trade routes of their world.

On almost every spot where men found life good, in the fertile valley of the Nile, on ancient slopes in the Western Hemisphere, on the shores and grass-skirted crags of Europe, are to be found the relics of Delilah's ancestors and kinsmen. Some of these towers still stand, dauntless monuments to just how thoroughly their men planned to function within their fates. There is a notable one on a flat plain between Marseilles and the Spanish Border. True, it was constructed long after the fighting tower first took to the sea; but it is the thirteenth-century perfection of the long-lived tradition that produced it, and can well be taken as the representative and summation of all the fighting towers that had gone before.

Rising from the walled town of Aigues-Mortes, it presents on its moated exterior an aspect as smooth and implacable as a grey egg-shell; but its rounded walls are stone armour six metres thick. Within the tower are three circular turrets, one above the other. These provide, not for one hysterical "burning of all bridges behind," but for three planned and deliberate abdications of retreat, each complete in itself, yet each more hopeless than the last.

Should the hostile forces from without succeed in bursting into the ground turret, a massive system of compartmentation shuts it off from the upper second and third turrets in which the survivors of the crew concentrated to carry on the fight. When the second turret was penetrated, an enemy-tight door made of the final, high turret a unit in itself.

From the second turret it was possible to pump down into the ground turret, when the enemy got into it, a veritable expelling pressure of huge, round, stone balls, arrows, bolts and scalding oil; and this lethal pressure could be directed from the topmost into the second turret also, if the invasion reached that.

The tower, thirty-three metres high, dominated the town, and was able to send a storm of missiles, the great, cannonball-like stones and clouds of arrows and bolts, into any part of it. Any possession of the town would be only nominal that did not include the tower or bring about its destruction. Conceivably, its destruction might have been obtained through some vast undermining of its foundations. In such event the great structure, cracking and sliding amidst the reek of blood, the smell of burning oil and the mystical effluvia, pungent, dangerous, electrical, that pervades confined scenes of terrific activity, would have gone down: But with its men, *if they had been what the tower intended,* clinging in undaunted possession to its topmost, tottering fragment, hurling a final salvo at the enemy and a last roar of defiance at the sky. It is, perhaps, sufficient to record that no enemy ever defeated or captured The Tower of Constance except through treachery or failure of its personnel . . . except when there were weak links in the chain of its defending crew . . . except when there were links that had not delegated to Death or Victory the difficult decision of when the battle was to end.

Of all the old land towers, it is in this one especially that the man-of-warsman is flooded with a strange, dreamlike feeling of having been there before. Even details seem familiar . . . *the way the structure is compartmented against the entrance of external forces . . . the provisions for bringing expelling pressure to bear in these compartments if external force should flood its way in . . . the ladderlike stairway thrusting up through circular, armoured space . . . the massive armour at vulnerable points . . . the fanatically economical contours and close quarters . . . the names of its parts, like "tower," "castle," "barbette," "port," "turret" . . . the enforced intimacy and interdependence of officers and men that the close quarters would give rise to, and the iron, mortised discipline that this, in turn, made necessary amongst these picked and specialized tower fighters . . . the omnipresent apertures through which to spout death and destruction, within whose circle these men ate, slept and were merry . . .* all these details must fragment the mists before the man-of-warsman's mind and feelings and permit him to realize that actually he is in no alien place, that this tower is, in sinew and spirit, a man-of-war, that those who manned it were what he is; for he and his shipmates are indoctrinated, also, with the same attitude towards life that made possible the confined battles to the death in this ancient tower; they too, like the bygone crew here, must establish themselves amidst a hostile element in a structure with no secret passage to saving flight, must "burn their bridges behind them," fight concentrated at the centre of an even more ruthless loneliness and die unconquered, if called upon, in a yet more horrible sinking into unspeakable depths infested with monsters and slow suffocation.

When the sea became, comparatively late in man's existence, his most vital battle ground, and taking his towers and castles off the hills and crags, he launched them on the sea, he was effectively arranging for the preservation of the tradition that flourished in those towers, arranging for it just as effectively as if he had painted it on a deep cave wall in Altamira: For the sea, with all its formidable insulating power, is a cave where customs, habits and ideas are preserved from the weather of life that whirls and flows upon the land, a weather that changes the patterns within which men think and believe and behave no less than the very contours of the hills upon which they live. It is no mere aquaphobia that oppresses the spirit of a man isolated in a boat at the centre of an unblemished circle of sea; nor were the ancients mistaken when they feared to sail too long for fear of falling over the edge of the world.

Thus "Fight her till she sinks and don't give up the ship!" is much more than a melodramatic cry rising from the lips of a dying commander, more than a plea to shed more blood where too much has been shed already. It is a prehistoric fragment of stag bone magically carven with fish and reindeer . . . a charging bison painted on the quaternary rock . . . a bit of pattern engraved on the day when the survivors of the first successfully defended tower paused to think and feel about their victory.

To these first tower fighters it must have been clear that no matter how thick their walls might be, victory depended on the maintenance of a constant, defending, human pressure within them. Defeat set in at the moment this pressure was relaxed. This pressure, then, must be maintained as long as there was hope of victory. But how were they to recognize this point beyond which it was hopeless to maintain the defending pressure? A vote taken in a tower at the most bloody and frightful climax of an action as to the prospects of the fight, would disclose almost as many opinions as there were varying personalities there. A man permitted to decide when the fight was over would have been found to have compounded his judgment of many counsels extraneous to the actual fight, and he would have been unable to include in the compound things hidden by fate or time or even by the very walls of his tower. The perspectives of history are strewn with the regretful debris of many defeats bearing witness to fights that were given up too soon. In the tower, hope and strength must be bare of any complicating reservations. The decision, then, could be left to no man; it must be delegated to Death or Victory.

As The Tower of Constance, even though its date comes long after that on which the first tower moved out to sea, is permitted to represent the tradition that produced it, so a crew of tower men coming later still may exemplify, in the classic perfection of their functioning, the kind of defending group that the towers, from the beginning right down to Delilah, sought to develop. In the case of The Tower of Constance, the standing stone and metal intact speak truthfully for the tower's own virtues; but the ancient truth of what men did in such towers is tainted with myth and the enhancement of successive generations seeking to bask in an increasing reflection of glory. The facts regarding events even so recent, say, as the death of Roland at Roncesvalles have drifted and dusted away to leave behind only the bright aura of a fabulous boast. Therefore tower men must be selected for example whose feats are fresh enough to be examined in authentic record and detail.

Even in myth, no tower seems to have witnessed a more flawless adherence to the fatal pattern than that which grows, like a golden-brown, rectangular fungus, from a field in Texas. The field is so gently sloping that a nearby stream loops sinuously back and forth as if in torpid indecision which way, under the bright sun, to stretch its length. On its banks blue-bonnets grew, and the clustered cottonwood trees, in which mockingbirds sang, blurred their symmetries with long streamers of firm, grey moss. The two-hundred-year-old tower, itself, is no such formidable structure as The Tower of Constance, for it was designed primarily as a shelter for prayer to an all-powerful God; but its walls are thick, its entrances armoured and its vulnerable approaches covered by apertures from which to fire.

What men did in this tower, which was then the military key to the region in which it stands, is told in the records of the army that stormed it, in the testimony of women who survived their men of the tower's crew, and in the reports of those who witnessed the fight from a distance. No boast or excuse from the tower men, themselves, remains. "Thermopylae had its messenger of defeat. The Alamo had none."

For many hours before the enemy arrived around the tower's walls, those within knew of his approach . . . a long, well-equipped, well-officered column thousands strong. From the walls of the large, fortified corral, of which the tower formed one limit and the citadel, it was possible to see the dust of this column some miles away.

With a kind of deliberate, assured ferocity, the column closed in one evening on the tower. Taking up the positions from which the attack was to be launched, it paused to let the tower's crew foretaste to the full the power of the impending assault. In one

110

direction from the tower, a way pointedly was left free for flight.

Denied even the final boon of knowing that there was no way out, the tower's crew set about testing the links of their thin chain under the pressure of this initial blow from their enemy, a blow as shrewd as it was bloodless. With his sword, the commander of the tower marked a line on the ground from wall to wall. On one side of the line he mustered the one hundred and forty men of his crew. Then he gave each man, as he called his name, the choice between escaping out the way left free or signifying by stepping over across the line that he would remain, relegating all his fate to Death or Victory. When the calling of the roll was finished, only two men remained on that side of the line where all had stood before. One was a sick man on a cot. He ordered his friends to carry him over the line.

In the warm night, blurred delicately with the scent of magnolia blossoms and the strange fragrance that streams breathe off towards the west, the tower crew lifted the other man, a man with the name of a lovely flower, over the wall to safety.

Thirty-two friends and kinsmen of the besieged marched from a nearby town to take in, from the top of a hill crowned with tall cypress trees, the plight of the tower. They observed the way left free by the besiegers. At three o'clock in the morning they crept through it, climbed into the tower and accepted its stark covenant.

For days, while the drums and brasses of a band on the river bank vaunted his coming triumph, the enemy marshalled his forces, infantry, artillery, cavalry, in plain view on three sides of the tower. Reinforcements increased the besiegers to five thousand. Once, twice, they launched intimidating attacks, were bloodily repulsed. They destroyed the aqueduct supplying the defenders with water. Artillery kept up a steady bombardment of the tower, whose men still scorned the way left free.

At last the besiegers grimly closed the circle around the one hundred and seventy-two Texans, and gave them the choice between immediate surrender or battle without quarter. The tower answered with cannon-shot.

Then, with the first light of day on Sunday, March the Sixth, 1836, the enemy leapt forward to the climactic assault. Cannon-balls smashed at the doors, ricochetted within the roofless corral.

Thousands of rifles sprayed unremitting streams of death at wall tops, ports and windows, at every spot from which a defender could fire. Covered by this deadly storm, the enemy flung scaling ladders against the walls on every side. Men roaring the intimidating shouts of certain victory that need no language streamed up the ladders. Time and again these streams were met by little dams of defenders, bunching recklessly on the wall top wherever a ladder touched and clung. At breached walls and doors the torrent of attack smashed to a stop, bleeding and dead, as if against some magic barrier.

It would have taken five hundred men, in calculation, to defend this poor corral thirty minutes; but with such ferocity did the few defenders keep their covenant that the morning, too, had begun to die before the five thousand besiegers found themselves in possession of its earthen, sun-browned walls. If the struggle had gone no further, if there had been, at this point, no single defender left to die, the historical purpose of their sacrifice would have been assured: Never again would this enemy attack these men, in the persons of their kith and kin, save through the morale-destroying memory of their terrific effectiveness here . . . And in the distant nerves and cells of those whose destinies hung upon the battle, there blossomed rich and strong the courage of a new Republic.

But there were a few tower men left. With ammunition exhausted, and probably with no man left unwounded, they abandoned the shattered corral to the flood of the enemy and concentrated in the cool, cavernlike compartments of their tower. Within each sculptured door and port they formed a rebuff of steel, waiting for the swarms that hacked at roof and door and wall roaring demands for surrender that fell like pebbles of non-meaning into the chasm between dark Death and gleaming Victory . . . A door crashed in . . . a section of wall gave way . . . at an inner entrance, the sick man on the cot, armed with a cutlass, carved round himself a mausoleum of hated dead before darkness covered his eyes . . . Now round his ship the Achaians and Trojans warred on each other hand to hand, nor far apart did they endure the flights of arrows, nor of darts, but standing hard by other, with one heart, with sharp axes and hatchets they fought, and with great swords, and double-pointed spears. And many fair brands, dark scabbarded and hilted, fell to the ground, some from the hands, some from off the shoulders of warring men, and the black earth ran with blood.

11 〰️

All this, the harvest of the fatal principle upon which are founded every custom, every ceremony, every hope of those who war, is barbarous and ghastly; more horrible, perhaps, than the peaceful struggles men are constrained to make in wards drenched with the pus and pain of wet leprosy . . . than battalions of little children distorted in the reflections of guiltless syphilis . . . than custom-driven souls writhing frantically within the labyrinths of carefully labelled madness . . . than streets and highways littered with the corpses, the mangled bodies of men, women and children struck down by peaceful machinery while seeking no greater thing than to go from one place to another . . . than female legions reduced to the existence of but one organ of their bodies . . . than tall honeycombs packed with helpless men forced to spend every sunlit hour adding meaningless digits or making fragments for objects even in whose assembled wholes they would take no joy . . . But it is these horrible towers, these barricades with their uncompromising sacrifice of bright blood, that ever have sustained man's upward flight from the mud toward his dream of Freedom. As independent of the successive patterns through which man has envisioned his dream as morality is of the many religions that have exploited it, the tradition of these towers armed the victory when Freedom meant the triumph of feudal lords over kings, that gained the victory when it meant triumph of market-place over feudal lord, that will gain the looming victory for a Freedom that now means the triumph of him who makes and him who grows over him who runs the market-place.

Since the far beginning, too, it has been these towers, consecrated to Victory or Death, that have been man's antidote for his own inevitable passion to ravage and destroy the very things he has so hardly wrested from chaos. It was just such towers that held back the barbarians from destroying the incipient clusters of civilization long enough for the barbarians themselves to become infected by the germ; and it was behind such towers and the unrecreant corpses of their defenders that Aristotle founded Science, Giotto painted, Dante sang, Christ was permitted his sacrifice within significant organization, and Pericles' Athens marked the period to man's emotional and mental attitude towards life.

12 〰〰

It also was up from the depths and perspectives within which The Tower of Constance and the Alamo are monuments that the Captain and Ensign Woodbridge impulsively had heaved their exclamations of relief and pleasure when "Unc" Blood had told them about Warrington, the new, untried link, sticking it out below with O'Connel: And it must have been the same kind of influence that, together with the unmitigated support of O'Connel, his pointed advancement to the rate of Seaman, and the fact that he soon was held to have "a bigger education than Mr. Fitzpatrick," now coerced the crew to accept this unassimilable individual and his outrageous range of accoutrements.

This acceptance shielded the Texan, in large measure, for the first time in the fourteen months since he had signed the enlistment papers in San Francisco, from the unrelenting efforts of his environment to protect its sensibilities against him. In the moment of his first arrival on board Delilah, when Cruck and Arnold, reaching down, had helped him to heave his bag and hammock from the Galveston's whaleboat up onto the deck, the bristling, emotional wall behind which it clearly was his intention to reserve himself, had antagonized everyone from the Captain down to the Cook. He had stood for a moment in the bright morning

114

sunlight, with legs spread to balance himself in the tossing boat, his head rising and falling just above the level of Delilah's deck line, to glare with tense aggressiveness up and down the narrow, iron length of this new embodiment of his prison. The Captain and Ensign Snell, on the bridge, and the crew, along the rail, leaned over attentively from beneath the shade of the awnings to watch him climb aboard. This he did in a manner that quite increased the antagonism already charging the atmosphere; but at the same time his manner did faintly enrich this atmosphere with the kind of dauntless integrity, like a stark fragrance, that envelops a courageous enemy stepping, by an act of deliberate will, to a fate from which there is no return and beyond which there is no hope.

In that moment Arnold, a Quartermaster, Second-Class, who once had been a prizefighter but who had been disqualified for that activity by some accident to his feet, had studied the bruises on the boy's face with an eye whose findings later were translated into the phrase: "He certainly has been taking it plenty on the chin." One eye was underclouded faintly with the yellow and purple stain from an old blow; the flesh around the other was darkly discoloured from a recent one. The skin upon his forehead and his left cheek had been broken in several places, which were in varying stages of healing. The single flare of prejudice in his favour had been in the consciousness of Arnold; and this prejudice, arising from some synthesis in the ex-prizefighter's perceptions of the boy's light weight, the unchastened quality of his indubitable pride and the several layers of bruises, had been increased and sustained when he had discovered, in helping to lift the sea-bag aboard, the thing that almost immediately was to usher in the conflicts with authority and the social persecution into which Warrington, with grim foreknowledge, had climbed from the whaleboat: The sea-bag, which should have been packed with clothes, was filled with books.

The books had served as a reasonable, material pretext upon which to base an almost unanimous, verbal condemnation. Knowledge of them became a general scandal when Cruck, the Chief Boatswain's Mate, had escorted the new deck-hand to the small, wedgelike hole under the forecastle deck that served as crew's quarters, but which could be occupied only in the fairest weather, to assign him his bunk and locker.

"Put your duds in there," Cruck said, pointing to an empty locker. For some reason, perhaps because Warrington's manner was too eloquent of waiting for him to be gone, he had not gone; but had stood with his big, grimy, misshapen hands resting on his hips near the skirt of his dungaree jumper, and his Chief Petty Officer's cap, the visor of which was crinkled like a field of dried mud, pushed far back on his unsmooth, bucket-shaped head.

"Go ahead," he said belligerently, "stow your duds. I got something for you to do on the topside."

"Give the guy a chance," said Arnold, who had followed them in, "what's it to you when he stows his stuff?"

Four men lying in the tiered bunks in their drawers and undershirts tried to sit up to give their attention. There not being sufficient space between bunks for a sitting posture, they got out upon their feet and stood watching.

"And what's it to you?" shot back from Cruck.

Cruck was a short mass of muscle, bone and hard fat. He never laid anything down. Whether an object was light or heavy, he *threw* it down. One knew where he was at work by the sound of a hammer, a coil of line or a bucket crashing and banging onto the deck. When he passed his plate at table, he threw it with a kind of sailing motion. He seldom wore any socks, and when he undressed he took his shoes off last. Four or five seconds after his shoes were heard to impact on the deck he would be in a dead sleep. At sea, or with an emergency in prospect, he slept with his shoes on; otherwise when he slept he was quite naked. For him, life seemed to be a kind of soft, encircling activity, which penetrated not even in degree the outermost layer of his permanently grimed and blackheaded skin. In a fist fight he employed only one type of blow, a kind of quick slug; and being worsted, he attempted to hold on with his left arm and hand while he reached with his right for some heavy object to use as a weapon. He never used anything for language but a few nouns and verbs. In place of adjectives he used four or five variants of words uncommonly designating the most extreme kinds of filth. These he sprayed about continually, in a penetrating, staccato bellow, as if they were the foul froth whirled off by the pressures of his tremendous energy.

Arnold had not given back an inch before Cruck's advance. He knew that Cruck was not sure that he could best him, and he knew as well that Cruck never willingly engaged in a fight of whose outcome he was not fairly certain. Then Cruck suddenly remembered, as he saw that the formidable, splay-footed figure before him did not give back, that Arnold was a friend of O'Connel's. This would mean trouble with O'Connel. He was not prepared for that. Quickly he had swung back to the source that had generated his irritation. He reached over, knocked the new man's bag free from the rolled hammock coiled around it, and, gripping the bag by the bottom with one hand, held it up, heavy as it was, halfway out from his shoulder. With the other hand he undid the bag's lashings. The books cascaded out upon the deck, piling up in a multi-coloured profusion that seemed impossible ever to have been contained even in the deep bag. Glowing in the bright path of light from a port-hole, the angled mass of bindings seemed like an esoteric heap of finished splendour stored away and astoundingly discovered in this murky catacomb of shabby steel.

Warrington, steering slowly and desperately around the emotional upheaval that had risen to the level of his throat, and nauseated by the heavy, sweet vapour of dead steam and burnt oil that seeped in from the steering engine and smothered the forecastle, had stooped on one knee at the feet of the silent, sweating group gathered around the books. One by one, he had picked up and fitted into the locker, where the Chief Boatswain's Mate had ordered him to put his clothes . . . *Moby Dick* . . . *The American Commonwealth* . . . *Rasselas* . . . *The Hound of Heaven* . . . *Les Misérables* . . . *Barrack-Room Ballads* . . . *Marius The Epicurean* . . . *The Iliad* . . . *Compensation* . . . *The Meditations of Marcus Aurelius* . . . *Crime and Punishment* . . . *The Bible* . . . *Unto This Last* . . . *Don Quixote* . . . *Essays in Pessimism* . . . *The Way of All Flesh* . . . *The Cloister and The Hearth* . . . *A Modern Symposium* . . . *Lamia, Isabella, The Eve of St. Agnes and Other Poems*

. . . Maxwell's Grammar . . . The Plays of Aeschylus . . . Tales of Mystery and Imagination . . . Typhoon . . . The Works of Shakespeare in One Volume . . . The Broad Highway . . . The Decline and Fall of the Roman Empire.

13 〜〜〜

"Come on," Cruck had said, "this is a job for the Exec," and he had led the way out onto the deck. As Warrington joined him for the trip aft, they met the Executive Officer, who was heading for the bridge.

"Mr. Fitzpatrick," requested Cruck grimly.

"Well."

"This new Ordinary Seaman has no clothes."

"No bag?"

"Yes, Sir, he has a bag."

"Well then?"

"The bag has nothin' but *books* in it, Sir."

"Books!"

Lieutenant Fitzpatrick had shifted his gaze in amazement to the new deck-hand. The boy was standing so stiffly and tensely at attention that he appeared to be a trifle sway-backed, a little like a wooden soldier, a marionette into whose back the artist has put just a trace of caricature. His grey eyes were almost glassy with the intensity of their seeming concentration upon something scorned but dangerous behind Lieutenant Fitzpatrick's head, through which they appeared to be staring. The officer almost turned around. In an instant he realized that the boy had frozen his whole being in a frantic attempt to halt some kind of disintegration of self-control. Repelled by the ugly tenseness of the spectacle the boy presented, and hoping to give him a chance, in some measure, "to thaw out," Lieutenant Fitzpatrick had turned towards the forecastle entrance, saying:

"Let's have a look."

It had been Warrington's perception of the very insight and sensitiveness gaining him this respite, perceived in the first moment he stood before the officer, that had brought about so suddenly the disintegration of his self-control, so painfully impaired his power of resistance. The element of surprise also had contributed to the emotional emergency in which he had found himself; for, in the previous months of his ordeal, he had resisted blows, ridicule, every device of irritated brutality, with an arrogant competency that had satisfied even himself; satisfied him even when, in the isolating privacy of darkness, lying breathlessly still amongst sleeping men so that not even an alien consciousness of his awakeness could intrude on this privacy, he had reviewed, at its end, each day's struggle . . . reviewed it critically at the rigidly exacted cost of an hour or so of the blessed oblivion brought by sleep.

Under the eyes of this officer, the lively, brown liquidity of which as they appeared in that moment he never was to forget, he had been projected into a struggle for self-control that was superficially embodied in a violent, physical effort not to burst into tears. In the midst of this struggle, almost beyond the pale of his consciousness, as his eyes met the officer's, there had fountained gracefully, but in detached, dim irrelevance, the memory of an incident several years back, an incident that seemed like the memory of a dream of what was happening to him now . . . He had addressed some infuriating phillipic to the assembled student body of his high school regarding their apathy when called upon to cheer at football games. He had used the phrase, "Southern laziness," which had exploded the assembly hall into a bedlam of hoots and jeers. Unable to go on, he had stood on the platform smiling coldly like an adolescent tiger into one face after another . . . until, in a small, oval face like a white cameo set in the surrounding fury, he had met a gaze that had seemed to envelop him in a kind of bemusing sensitivity. It was as if he had been taken in gentle arms and some unbearable nectar poured into the hidden crevices of the deep wound he was receiving. His eyes had filled with tears, tears which she ever after had helped him fiercely to deny . . . All his life he had been haunted by a poignant dread of crying in the face of a punishment or an enemy who might be trying to wring from him the thing of which he felt tears were the symbol . . . and here suddenly, before these two men, he was betrayed to the verge of tears in the midst of battle, betrayed by

119

influences that were not in the battle: but to the battle, neverthe-less, his tears if they came would be ceded as tribute. They would be ceded to the battle not only by his enemies, but, paradoxically, by part of his own consciousness as well. At the beginning of this incident, as he had followed the Chief Boatswain's Mate out of the forecastle in search of the Executive Officer, he had marched high-headed, unconquerable, as to a small sacrifice at the hands of creatures that he despised, inferiors amongst whom he recklessly had plunged to be irremediably snared. Then suddenly, before he had had time to realize that it was not the mechanics of being dragged before authority that was undoing him, he had not been able to dispel the trembling weakness toward which he felt himself drawn; and he had tried to reassure himself with furious reminders that this was a mere routine matter, a trifle of punishment for an offence that a year from now would seem humorous. It had been at this instant (the instant in which, blighted by the sudden weak-ness and mistaking its cause, he had erected, almost as a vision against the hazy, purple-green cone of distant Mariveles Moun-tain, his frantic reassurances and was staring fixedly ahead at them as if seeking to extract through his gaze regeneration, courage, significance) that Lieutenant Fitzpatrick had shifted his look from him and moved towards the entrance to the forecastle.

"Come on," Cruck said to the boy.

Inside the forecastle, with Arnold and the four half-dressed spec-tators gazing on intently from a respectful distance, Cruck had flung back the cover of the new man's locker, pulled out the folded, empty sea-bag and displayed the books that Warrington, when faced with the choice between carrying either his clothes or his books in the only luggage permitted to him, had been unable to leave behind on the Galveston. Lieutenant Fitzpatrick had looked down at the neat rows of backs for a length of time more than adequate for reading all the titles. Then he had permitted the fingers of his left hand to drop to the back of *The Cloister and The Hearth* and sweep slowly, as if in guidance to his eye, or in casual caress, across *A Modern Symposium* and Keats' poems. The faint fragrance of a cologne, combined with that of his well starched and laundered "whites," had surrounded the officer like a delicate aura protecting him from the heavy miasmas of the forecastle. Warrington had felt the gesture on the books as if it had been a caress on his forearm.

"There is no harm in the books," Lieutenant Fitzpatrick had said to Cruck, "but he's got to have clothes. Take him ashore to the Store-Keeper and get him a complete outfit. Everything on the list. By the time he gets another payday after that, he'll think twice before leaving his gear behind."

Cruck had grinned with pleasure. This was an official vindication of his stand regarding the boy, and of his clash with Arnold in defence of it as well. This order had been, in effect, a heavy fine, a deprivation of funds that, if it had been inflicted upon Cruck, himself, would have been a major disaster depriving him for many weeks of the bar-rooms, the brothels and the restaurants for which he lived, and in which he suffered the only shadows of the religious experience permitted to his existence.

But all that had splashed onto the boy's whirling consciousness and clung there was the phrase: "There is no harm in the books . . ." His eyes had followed the officer's smooth, thin hands as they had lifted Keats' poems and turned the pages.

Feeling, without looking up, Cruck standing there in gloating indecision, the officer had said to him:

"Jump up on the bridge and tell the Captain I'll be with him in a moment . . . that I've been held up for a second or so."

As the final syllable of Cruck's "Aye, Aye, Sir!" had sung back through the forecastle entrance, Lieutenant Fitzpatrick had turned to the index. He had located the title he was looking for, and then, in the middle of the book, the poem. The brightness of the moted path of light from the open port-hole had caught his eye. He had moved into it and turned the book slightly to intercept its light. After a moment of reading, he had moved up closer to the port-hole, without looking up from the book, and leant with his shoulder against a bunk stanchion. Very faintly through the sunny port-hole had come fragments of a high-pitched, sing-song shout from a *banco* passing in the distance.

Warrington had stood, silent and motionless, as if afraid that the slightest sound or movement might make him less aware of the delicate but exquisite breath of satisfaction that was playing about him. It was as if, pausing for an instant on a sultry day, he

had felt himself in a barely perceptible current of perfumed coolness. Every time the officer had moved, each time he had changed
position, this breeze of sensation playing upon Warrington had
eddied and swirled as if the slight movement had changed its direction, as if the movement had been a special, personal gesture for
him in a dazing current of intimate, glamorous service. Up the
back of his head there had showered delicately a fine mist of parti-
cles, tiny fragments of poignant sensation . . . The delicately playing, surging shower had drifted to his shoulder . . . to his back . . .
over his chest . . .

14 ≈≈≈

In the weeks that his money had been withheld to pay for his new
outfit, Warrington's puritanism had stood him in good stead.
Even with his pockets full of money, he never drank or smoked;
and he made it a conscious point of self-discipline never to eat any
but the most simple and humble foods. He never would eat, for instance, ice-cream that had been coloured . . . only white . . . and
pastry such as cream puffs or éclairs was on the index of his
distaste.

His work about the ship, he made an instrument of the self-
discipline that always had been part of his life, but he had intensified and extended the rigours and scope of this self-discipline once
he had felt deeply the necessity for resisting, at every point of contact, the suctions of his environment. If he were set to chipping at
an area of rusted metal or polishing a stretch of brass-work, tasks
particularly odious for him, he cleaned the stretch of metal with a
self-punishing supererogation from which he derived a definite
sense of pleasure, a kind of aesthetic surge arising out of self-
discipline precisely and generously wrought. If in the routine of
his daily conduct he forgetfully passed over some detail, forgot
some trifling item, some private or quite unimportant remissness
that if disclosed no one ever would take the trouble to call to his
attention, he would stop whatever he was doing at the moment he
remembered or discovered the slighted detail and, as if savouring

the intricacies of a kind of ritual, go back and fully attend to it.

From his new clothes, also, there was an inexhaustible store of pleasure to be mined. He would wait until half or more of his clothes had been soiled, then taking a bar of salt-water soap and a bucket of water a trifle too hot for the comfort of his hands, he would find a sunny spot in the deck area assigned to washing and bathing, just forward of Smokestack Number One, and scrub the clothes between his knuckles with purposeful vigour and craftsmanship. The movement of scrubbing the clothes also permitted him to think or imagine or contemplate, for he could engage in any of these three things, while not lying on his back with an arm pressed over his eyes and conscious that it was night, only to the rhythm of some regular movement such as walking or this scrubbing. The clothes, themselves, moreover, after they were clean and dry, rolled and stowed neatly in his sea-bag, which he kept on top of his locker, reflected into his consciousness a minor but indubitable ecstasy . . . a sensation compounded of the satisfaction that came from contemplating the results of the chare well done and an aesthetic delight in the sheer cleanliness.

His books, however, were the rich and incomparable anodyne of his existence. It was an easy matter for his will, groomed and nurtured constantly as it was, to resist the besetting temptation to slip away during some lull in the ship's work and, finding a hideout, finish the chapter in which he happened to be suspended: But even after working-hours, when he morally and legally was in possession of leisure in which to read, the pleasure he took in reading, the intoxication, the utter luxury of it, impelled him to a kind of routine of restraint, a gesture in self-denial. This took the form of settling himself comfortably with his book, usually in the narrow seclusion of the two-foot space between the Forward Conning-tower and the Radio Shack, and then, no matter how eagerly he had anticipated taking up once more the thread of the book, forcing himself to study, in painstaking review, one lesson in the dry precisions of Maxwell's Grammar before relapsing to his reading. This may have been part of his struggle to restrain his thoughts, his contemplation and his imagination from succumbing entirely to the books, a struggle to prevent the books from becoming the final objective of his existence, the struggle to keep his being aimed, drawing the books, too, within this aim, at the high and coruscant, but unidentified, target to which he ruthlessly was consecrated.

At that time, and perhaps under stimulation of the fanatical wardenship his consciousness had assumed about all the borders of his integrity, prayer became an increasingly important scalpel in his case of mental and spiritual instruments. He used prayer almost exclusively in a negative attack upon his fears and the obstacles to his hope. Before each act, intention and thought, he marshalled the possible, even improbable, bad results of the act, the hindrances to the intention or the evil trailers of the thought, and intoned in his mind, much as some Roman Catholics cross themselves in the interest of not drowning before diving into the water, a short, blunt prayer against each contingency. Around a single intention, for instance, there often would arise a dozen or more ideas of hindrance. Carefully remembering all these ideas, he would abstract the first one in order of occurrence and issue his prayer against it. In the act of praying against it, there would arise in his mind a number of further possibilities contingent only on this particular secondary idea of hindrance. He would then take up and pray against each one of these new ideas, twice removed from the original intention, before going back to pray against the idea of hindrance, and its progeny, occurring second in the series of twelve or more that had arisen around the original intention. Thus, for example, in a moment of foreboding, he threw against the screen of its prophecy the determination never to "knuckle under to Cruck." Around this intention there at once sprang up a number of ideas embodying possible hindrances to his ability to carry out this intention. "Supposing that I should be alone, lying on my back in my bunk, humming a melody, and that Cruck should come into the forecastle and, in a gesture of sheer, personal bullying, standing with his fist raised like a club above my face, demand that I stop humming. Would I be able to carry out my intention not to knuckle under? Or supposing that I should be talking to someone and should make a simple statement of fact that happened to irritate Cruck and he should say, 'Admit right now that that statement is a lie or I will beat you to a pulp.' Could I stick to my intention? Supposing that . . ." When all these ideas embodying hindrances to the intention had been lined up, he would take the first one and pray: "O God, Almighty God, be sure that I keep humming the melody even under the rain of blows, that I do not give in and stop." Then around the idea of this contingency against which he prayed, the further series of ideas would arise: "What if I compromised by keeping on humming, but by just lying there passively at the same time until I was beaten unconscious? What if . . ." Then for the moment carefully storing in his memory the series of ideas beginning, "Supposing that . . ." he would leave it temporarily to pray through the new series of ideas: "O All-Powerful God, see to it that I do not lie there passively, that I do not fail to give fight to the utmost of my ability. O God Almighty, make me . . ."

He would pray thus concurrently with any other act he might be performing; as he was washing his clothes, as he gazed out over the sea from the bridge while on watch under way, as he polished the bright-work or as he hauled a strip of fluttering, tugging signals to the yard-arm . . . praying whenever an act, an intention or a thought sprouted its necessities. On this praying, he had a profound reliance and a cloying dependence that was in direct contrast to the repulsion that swept out to him from all religious services and churches, a repulsion that, starting in early boyhood as a faint nausea over the hymns, had deepened and widened until it had engulfed even the lovely silver plate in which the offering was collected: But his prayers, like heat-darkened slabs of prismatic crystal, grew and multiplied around him at fabulous speed, crowding, extending to, the breathless limits of infinity, as if he were a piece of string, hanging in one of those magical bottles of liqueur, on which crystals grow, coagulate and mass.

Most of Warrington's prayers were concerned directly or indirectly, because that was the trend of most of his thinking and feeling, with keeping him different from, and protected against, the stream of life in which he found himself being swept along . . . He was an enlisted man in time of peace! . . . a gentleman in that ignominious quicksand of being enlisted with no end in view but the hire itself . . . he had plunged in amidst the scum of the earth, and he was writhing there with pain, ignobility and sterile violence . . . and there was no way out of it for years. Nothing could have assuaged his racking despair over this, except that he had been suffering the situation for his country in time of war: But his country was not at war.

The thought of desertion, even in the first days, never had entered his head. The image of himself in the act of deserting from the United States Navy was a figure his imagination would have found dissolved, as surely as if it had been an image of incest, the instant when it swam against the outermost bulwarks of his consciousness; and he could act, if the act was a significant one requiring strength, only if the act first had been sown in his mind as a seed of imagination.

For two years more . . . two long years . . . he must breast this stream into which he had fallen . . . breast it honourably and stoutly, taking the utmost care that it did not sully and distort him . . . that it did not batter him into any relaxations that might unfit him for the distant, future good, the effulgence of which, just over his most distant horizon, was as significant for him as it was undistinguishable. The natural mechanics of his spirit were well adapted to this struggle; for his apparatuses of contact were such that he could not well apprehend the things that were near, immediately around him. Only those things at a distance—both behind and ahead of him—were cogent for his vision. The near good almost was unavailable to him. He could but to a painfully small degree enjoy what was about him at the moment; and never could he disregard what the enjoyment might lead to. He sacrificed the present ruthlessly to the formless but perfect future good; and he meant by this futurity nothing contained in the sanctified promises of the churches: all his horizons, fine, sweet rings beyond which inevitably flourished perfection, encircled, to his vision and intuition, areas of actual mortality.

The moment, occurring about two months after he had enlisted, in which he suddenly had realized, under the stimulation of no particular event, that he must bend every effort to preserve himself from his environment, literally had saved him. It had given him, this realization, lost as he was on the vast sea of his despair, a point of departure for struggle. His whole instinctive, emotional and mental being had rushed to the confirmation of this realization, and then unreservedly to its support. The certitude had brought him erect. "I will not be downed and sucked in!" All the pain and blows and items of illth would be badges of honour in resistance to this. From that moment on, his glance had flashed with a different interest over the planes and perspectives of his environment, to which he related himself as a wild animal relates itself to the interior of a cage. He had now a struggle of significance to engage in, a struggle to preserve his fitness as a part of the pictures he sensed so dazzlingly in the distance ahead and his appositeness with the pictures he saw so clearly far behind. He told himself that, "I will resist to the death"; and by death he meant the common, realistic implication of the word. "They can starve me, imprison me and batter me, but I will preserve myself against them." He now had regained a point around which to centre his pain, an honourable reason for suffering, a conception of defeat, if it came to that, in terms of his tradition. The number that should symbolize his life in the end would be no mere opportunistic algebraic sum; but a glorious, round figure arrived at by adding to each other only beautifully positive, even numbers.

With an added intensity, he refrained from cursing, from using slang, even from humming any common tune the general category of which might be familiar to the life of those wallowing lustily in the mud about him. When he lived, thought or worked to the accompaniment of melody, he hummed, with only occasional, equivalent substitution, the aria from *Samson and Delilah* or the thin phrase of noble pity that writhes from the violin throughout the latter half of *Ein Heldenleben.* There was but one descent from the levels on which he selected his melodies. This was when, thinking of the young girl at home, he would hum, almost breaking into quiet song, the melody of *Mighty Like A Rose,* because this was intertwined inextricably with his memory of her.

For illumination of his strength, he read and reread passages in *The Meditations of Marcus Aurelius,* a small, crimson volume containing the words, deeply buried in the text, "Such as are thy habitual thoughts, such also will be the character of thy mind; for the soul is dyed by the thoughts." So vividly had this sentence suggested to him a manner of saving procedure, that his mind had found some way to ignore the implications of the sentences that follow this in the paragraph. In this way he read the whole book, marking in the margin with a pencil all the passages that gave him light and guidance. When he reread the book, he went from one of these marked passages to the other as if they alone had formed the text matter. Read in this fashion, the book seemed to him like a mysteriously pertinent message, devised for his personal assistance in this ordeal. From his standpoint, he had been led to it miraculously, picking it up casually in a book store in San Francisco and opening it at once to the words that so vividly had caught his eye. He had an emergency supplement to this, a verse by Emerson, which in moments of general terror and despair, when there was no current point of resistance around which to centre his struggle, or when he was tossing in the wake of some brutalizing disaster, he would recite invokingly, resonantly to himself, with his eyes tightly closed in order to see better:

> "And all that Nature made thine own,
> Floating in air or pent in stone,
> Will rive the hills and swim the sea
> And like thy shadow follow thee."

15 〰〰

That Warrington abstained also from the use of such women as drifted or were flung within the currents against which he was striving, could not be attributed to the rigour of his fight for self-preservation; although this did lend contemporary colour and heat to the workings of this abstention. His body seethed, around the perpetual fulminations of his imagination, with desire for a woman's body; but he could not face even the possibility of using the body of a prostitute. The spectacle presented by a prostitute, either in reality or in the more vivid realm of his imagination, flooded him with an infrigidating pity and a kind of tragic repugnance, with much the same kind of iron melancholy that had shot through him when he once had gazed, in a side-show, at a white, human body headed by a hairy, animal snout. Despite the rumours that had seeped into his ears throughout the previous years of his youth, and despite the torrent of experience that had poured about him in recent months, he believed definitely that a woman could give herself only within the beauties of some pure and immaculate formula. He believed this just as he believed, and with the same mechanism, that two times two equals four. If it were possible, under any conceivable set of circumstances, for a woman to let herself be used in the darkness beyond the limits of this prescription, it was because she was a monster, inhuman in some vital physical and spiritual particulars, a creature born with some key part missing or aborted.

Often in his imagination, he would evolve one of these enabling formulae and, within its glistening precincts, enjoy with passionate, violent tenderness the slim, featureless perfection of a woman he had created. He never imagined thus in his arms the body of a girl whom he knew in the real world; for, with one exception, each had some insuperable defect the consciousness of which punctured any amorous attitude that he might strive to set up. It never occurred to him that it was ridiculous for his appetite to reject one because a segment of her petticoat habitually hung below her dress. Another was forever lost to his imaginary embrace because she coughed slightly to clear her throat before she began to speak; and another because he never forgot her as having been under the care of a physician when she was about ten years old. Sometimes a girl that flashed by him in the street would have left an impression with him perfect enough to serve his passion. Her he would take after an elaborate and painstaking seduction of such beauty and sensitive preparation, and within a formula so tested by virtue, that, he assured himself, could she have become aware by some magic of what had happened to her in his imagination, her integrity would not be outraged. Always, however, this unknown, when she reached his arms, was featureless . . . he never could remember the details of her face.

The exception to the fatally blemished women of his amorous universe, the girl whose sympathy, encountered then for the first time, had swept upon the school platform and melted him to weakness before his enemies, was forever placed, by some bright swordlike mechanism of his will, religiously beyond the uses of his body's desire. He would be unfaithful to her in the dissipations of his imagination; and he could conceive of being unfaithful to her in reality if he should chance upon a woman without some desire-killing quality, providing that he, then, did not find this woman also at once projected into sanctified unavailability by the very force within himself that permitted him to see her as perfect . . . but the throbbing, glowing perfection of his little love in the fine past, dancing like a slim shaft of delicate splendour just beneath his lips . . . his precious love, framed in febrile rings of iridescence, swaying towards him in her chair . . . like a crimson leaf vibrant in sunshine . . . his whole desire of grace and glamour and fragrance dissolved in night beneath magnolias, an ineffable tension, an unbearable, mystical sweetness somewhere before his throat . . . her he would never touch in reality, in idea, in imagination . . . until the far day, within the purity and brilliance of the ultimate formula, a formula whose borders he never had permitted even his contemplation or his imagination to approach, when he would fuse himself with her so splendidly, so beautifully, so powerfully in consonance with the mighty essence of God that his being, at last, would burn through into the celestial relaxation towards which he ever was struggling.

16 〰〰

The fullness of Lieutenant Fitzpatrick's sympathy with Warrington, and the ease with which his pity for him arose at the slightest provocation, was, it may be, an indication of how fundamentally similar their beings were, how much of himself the officer unconsciously was witnessing under torture in the person of the boy; for such deep concern about others seems to be the convenient mechanism for pitying oneself, that proscribed indulgence, in projection.

The differences between them, and these were multitudinous and complex, were those that naturally would occur in radically different patterns cut from the same material. The very sameness that drew them together, made them one, the very force that constrained them to this, also was the agency that emphasized and opposed their differences on the common foundation; as if its definite purpose in doing so was to obtrude for obliteration the differences, to smooth out the variations in the sameness. Thus their association was one that could not hope, except in the desire for its persistence, to run a smooth course. There could be no room in the midst of it for any peace.

Clear gauges not only of their unity, but of the quality, sharp and delicate, of their differences within it as well, were their respective attitudes towards the distant women whom they loved. The officer, once thinking about this girl whom he loved, had felt that somehow she was like a sinuous burst of bougainvillaea against a white wall. He had at once written a letter and told her so. The young seaman, too, had come upon a symbol that on the instant strangely had wrenched his heart with memory, longing and glamour. He had written the girl that evening; but he had not told her that she was like the beauty that had stirred him. Instead, with a precision quite lost in the impact of the impersonal passion and colour he had put into his descriptions, he had told her about the strange people, about their stilted houses, how the gold of the beaches blended into the purple and green of the jungle, how the palm trees looked against the brilliance of a black and white sunset. Nevertheless, the symbol that actually had inspired the letter remained in his imagination, remained there with its aptness as untarnished as in the moment when first his eye had caught, on the limb of a shrub projecting out over the jungle trail, the slender gracefulness of a single leaf, and he had thought of her, an exquisite, crimson leaf vibrant with sunshine against the patch of overhead blue sky.

The first battle for supremacy between Lieutenant Fitzpatrick and the Seaman, when it came, on a night just one week after the start of their conversations, formed itself around, and disguised itself in, a discussion of poetry. In attempting to clarify a generalized preference for English over French literature, Warrington had classified lyric poetry, in terms of the ultimate, spiritual impact of art, as being clearly secondary to epic poetry.

"Why, I'm amazed that you could go that far wrong!" leapt from Lieutenant Fitzpatrick's lips. His tone contained a personal aggressiveness that up until now had not touched their exchange.

The classification that he just had brought forward seemed so reasonable to Warrington that he became slightly indignant with the other's failure to agree with it. He had a faint feeling that some ulterior, unfair manoeuvre was involved with the disagreement. Without it even occurring to him that the soundness of this feeling needed examination, without really taking the time necessary for his intellect definitely to realize the feeling and assay it, he instinctively permitted this feeling to load his reply with a combative quality; as if within him a resting army, suddenly hearing its king challenged, had risen to its feet as one man and fiercely flung its banners to the sun. It was in this spirit that he shot back:

"It is no more amazing than that the philosophical novel is of more significance than the novel of manners. Lyric poetry, marvellous as it can be, is merely a surface business, a decoration, a comparatively unimportant tassel hanging on a throne. While epic poetry is a philosophical medium, a road clear down into the spirit of things . . . into existence . . . all the way down . . . as far as human expression can go!"

"Oh, that's just rhetoric, Warrington! Philosophy has quite as much opportunity in a lyric poem where the poet has to use his skill in symbolizing what he wants to get over . . . subtly . . . delicately . . . as it has in a long-winded, stark affair like . . . like . . . like *The Iliad*."

"Or like the supreme poem, *The Divine Comedy!*" shouted the Seaman.

The officer lay flat for a moment. He was a Catholic. He could not deny the incomparable glory of *that* poem: Yet it did not occur to him that Warrington really had scored a point. It was as if his opponent suddenly had reached over, gripped his wrist and struck him in the face with his own fist. Warrington sensed the temporary victory; but mistakenly judged the cause of it as being the cogency of his argument. He had not even an inkling that, if some curious accident had not made him, at the last split second, substitute *The Divine Comedy* for *Paradise Lost,* which last poem came, as an example, much more naturally to him, Lieutenant Fitzpatrick would have sailed down upon him, undaunted, with a broadside as full of energy and assurance as before. Neither of them realized, furthermore, that here no argument, no use of logical explanation, regardless of its perfection, could influence either of their positions to the slightest degree. Each was battling egoistically in defence of his own fundamental kind of integrity, in defence of the symbol, the particular, significant sentiment in the projected, spiritual environment, that most interpreted and apotheosized the quality of their respective souls.

Lieutenant Fitzpatrick was up again: *"The Divine Comedy* is *filled* with lyric poems."

"Yes, and they are merely its decorations, its surface colour, its tassels. Take them all out and the great poem would still be there like a great, granite throne."

"Any one you took out could beautifully represent the whole poem. You wouldn't need the damn granite throne."

"You mean to say that you could get everything from one of the lyric stretches of the poem that you get from the whole thing?"

"Yes!" They glared at each other through the obscurity. "Especially if the lyric poem had been written with that end in view."

The officer had forgotten his rank; but he resentfully laboured under a strange sting of irritation, an acute feeling that partially had to do with the difference in their ages coupled with the goading power the boy put behind his missiles. Not at all conscious of this goading power, Warrington exclaimed his answer with devastating incredulity:

"Do you really believe that you could make a tassel, no matter how much you had the end in view, do everything that the throne does upon which it hangs? Could the king and queen sit on it? Could . . ."

"Don't go crazy!" almost screamed Lieutenant Fitzpatrick, "Don't call everything I bring up a tassel! I won't stand for it!"

"Well, you're driving camels through the eye of a needle."

"The trouble with you," said the officer more quietly but with even more ferocity, "is that all your analyses are quantitative."

"And the trouble with you," replied Warrington, losing in the intense spiritual heat his steadying awareness of the preciousness that he attached to his relationship with Lieutenant Fitzpatrick, "is that you won't admit that literary subjects can vary in degree of significance. You won't admit that some tunes can be played on a piccolo, while others need a symphony orchestra. You . . ."

"A piccolo! . . . Why you pompous little bastard!"

Lieutenant Fitzpatrick's interruption came like a fusillade of verbal bullets propelled by deep, personal fury. It shattered the remaining form and outlines of these two beings' protective coverings, unloosed twin torrents of silent, final, denuding communication. Their chins strained toward each other. Their eyes glowed with pain. They shouted confusedly, reckless of everything and everybody, isolated, as far as they, themselves, were concerned, on a swaying disk of steel at the centre of an equatorial waste of sea.

"Light, ho!" burst from the dark depths of the bridge where the listening Cruck stood panic-stricken at the wheel. His hoarse voice, usually cocksure with a kind of brutal presumption, was tainted with uncertainty, bewilderment, and with primitive relief at the pretext for interruption. It was perilously near a warning scream.

Silenced instantly, Lieutenant Fitzpatrick and Warrington swung about and faced, on the lonely, livid horizon, the evidence of how thoroughly they had been swept from the course of their proper function. Taganak Light, which their eyes should have caught the moment it became an uncertain, golden stain beneath the drift of paling stars, was already high. A stiff breeze had sprung up. It swept a flight of spray across their peering faces. They licked the salty dampness from their lips. The watch was over. They had travelled far up the blind alley of intimate enmity and friendship ineluctable.

17 ≈≈≈

Despite the fact that the ship might find itself blocked up in the port by the Japanese cruisers, the officers anxiously looked forward to anchoring in Sandakan. All of them had become uncomfortably alive to the crew's increasing restlessness. It hung upon the men like an ear or an arm that, through a tenacious heaviness or the shadow of a pain, becomes unnaturally an entity in a person's awareness. The restlessness was fevered also by a vague storm of superstitious uneasiness arising out of "Unc" Blood's dramatization of the talk between Lieutenant Fitzpatrick and the Water Moro about the cave toward which the voyage was carrying them. "A bottomless pit," according to "Unc" Blood, "protected by something so mysterious and horrible that men shunned even the strip of coast where it lay."

Throughout the past week this oppressive restlessness of the men had broken out in a series of sudden, bloody flare-ups. Men, being halted in their work by some routine disagreement over the exact tool to be used or the method to be followed, would begin splattering each other with stinging, verbal filth in bursts of fury which they later found it hard to account for. They sprang upon each other, slugging viciously, at the slightest provocation. Cavendish had beaten Mendel, a Fireman, so severely that he was not able to leave his bunk. Wembly, the First-Class Gunner's Mate, a small, thin, nervous man with a large Adam's apple, had received a sudden blow on the nose, which had so crushed and flattened it that he would be disfigured for life. The blow had come with such unexpectedness that it had not been preceded within himself by an instinctive impulse to dodge, landing while he was staring in bewilderment, his face hanging unguardedly forward, at the red anger spirting and twisting up over the features of Saunders, to whom he had made some seemingly innocent comment. These encounters were nasty, instantaneous, almost clandestine affairs about which everyone kept morbidly, tenaciously silent. The officers saw only the blood and the ugly wounds left in their wakes; whereas, normally, if two men insisted on settling a difference by fighting, it became a public matter fought out according to prize-ring rules, in a clear space ringed by the crew and refereed by the Officer of the Deck. The Executive Officer was counting heavily on an over-night liberty in Sandakan to decrease the tension. It was a torpid little place less than six degrees above the Equator, where the resident Englishmen talked in uninteresting fashion of almost nothing else but the war their relatives and friends were fighting on the other side of the world; but there were restaurants, brothels, a moving picture theatre and a dance hall.

The accuracy of the Executive Officer's hope was borne out amply by the wild anticipation of the liberty ashore that boasted and speculated in the talk and preparations of the men. The way in which they counted their money, calculated the promised payday and got their clothes ready was eloquent. Even a civilian stranger to the ship, perhaps, would have known that Cavendish, the Quartermaster, Second-Class, and the dandy of the crew, was preparing for an important liberty ashore. He got out his fine suit of white duck, cut to a quite non-regulation smartness by a Chinese tailor in Shanghai, its hip fit skin-tight, the bell-bottoms of its trouser legs beautifully exaggerated, and laundered it with the care that a photographer devotes to the development of a cherished plate. His white hat, which had been built up carefully from a regulation start into the bit of pastry that it was, he scrubbed delicately with a nail brush that he kept specially for the purpose, after which he hung it up in the sun covered with salt to dry and bleach whiter, if that were possible. The crown of this hat was soft and regulation like a skull-cap; but the short upturned brim was as stiff and hard as a cylinder of creamy wood. It had achieved this quality at the hands of the same Chinese tailor, who had sewn round and round, over and over, this brim in close stitches on his machine with white thread. The hat sat on the back of Cavendish's very blond head like a white, upward-flaring halo appropriately terminating the superb symmetry of his slim, strong body.

Cavendish knew that he was taking all this trouble for mere whores, native ones at that; for enlisted men in the Orient were allotted strictly to the company of such women: But he had in his mind his somewhat inauthentic reputation for sleeping with whores without paying, which, in the Orient especially, is a difficult reputation to maintain. When he was in the States, his preparations usually had a different end in view; for there, with a kind of sexual arrogance, he stayed strictly away from prostitutes, associating with them only through accident, deception or spectacular conquest. When he was with the Atlantic Fleet, in New York, Philadelphia or Boston, he always was able to play upon the curiosity and stirring attraction the picture he created aroused in some incautious waitress or shopgirl. He would manage to persuade her into an isolated place, skilfully encouraging her mental reservation that there always were ways to handle a man, always a method, in the final moment, to escape with nothing lost but a kiss, an embrace, a tearful struggle. Once secure with her in the isolation of some lonely room, a cluster of trees, a stretch of deserted beach, and convinced that there willingly was no surrender beyond this, Cavendish would reach up, quietly, suddenly, unexpectedly, and strike a short, gentle blow on the point of the chin. The girl would be stunned or knocked completely out. As he had wrapped his hand with his black silk neckerchief before delivering the blow, this wrapping process being carried out under the guise of a nervous gesture in the midst of distracted pleading, there would be no serious mark left, especially as he carefully had studied the force and delivery of this blow, practising it on a punching bag. It never had gotten him into trouble: the outraged girl with retribution in her mind, when she was willing to face the disgrace, had little or no social or legal case: she had gone into a deserted place with him, there had been no outcry, her clothes were not torn, there was no evidence of struggle.

In Cruck's case, on the other hand, the preparations were as simple and straightforward as their object. When they called away the liberty party the Chief Boatswain's Mate just would put on some clean clothes and go ashore. He would have dropped whatever he was working at and gone ashore dressed quite as he was if he had been permitted to; but he could not get over the gang-plank unless his shoes, clothes and hat were clean and in good order. Meanwhile, across the plexus of his anticipations poured the visionary impact of beef-steak, fried potatoes, rice pudding, straight whiskey and women's bruised and exhausted bodies. It never occurred to him to seek out any women but whores; and he probably would have resented an implication that he associated with any other kind. By some obscure thing common to the tastes of both of them, he and Arnold, the Quartermaster, often were led to the same brothels; and this was a particular irritation to both Cruck and Arnold, for both invariably described their evenings in detail next day, and from their respective descriptions it sounded as if they had been to quite different houses.

Arnold's conception of what the land held for him was projected with clear definition into a conversation that he and Warrington, the Seaman, engaged in as they stood at the windbreak of the bridge immediately after Delilah had anchored off the town. Arnold was trying to persuade Warrington to go ashore with him. His gentle, brown eyes, which always seemed to harbour a pained expression, were fastened avidly on the little Asiatic town, and his small, pugged nose, of which the nostrils were large, exposed and almost on a plane with the surface of his face, sniffed at the warm off-shore breeze that swept out to taint faintly the atmosphere about the ship with a disturbing, living redolence. Arnold's head was a bit too large for his body. Above his face this was not so noticeable, for his hair was a soft dust colour and downy in texture; but his face was big and rectangular, and his small mouth, nose and eyes were set into it in such a manner that the somewhat brown face, seen at a distance sufficient to lose the expression of the eyes, would strike the observer at once as being that of what in the language of the prize ring is called a killer.

Arnold never had been ashore here before, and his hope and his hunger led him to exaggerate Sandakan's possibilities in terms of what he knew about Manila. Sandakan was little more than a large village; yet as he talked persuasively to Warrington, what he really and plainly had in mind was the large city. Warrington already knew that for Arnold "going ashore" in Manila meant simply and almost exclusively a prolonged visit to one or another of the houses in the restricted district of Caloocan. Warrington knew this because after each night ashore, Arnold would discuss, in quiet, unsparing rumination, the visit that had monopolized his hours of liberty. The manner in which he would discuss it, within whatever group he happened to find himself in a moment of relaxation, was precisely the same manner in which he would have related, if he had been a stock-broker living in the suburbs at home, the eventualities of a last-night's dinner party. It was the retained impression of this authentic social quality, this unquestionable respectability, only incidentally and as a matter of course spotted with lust, that, habitually dominating Arnold's attitude towards the houses of his visits, almost had persuaded Warrington in the end.

"These women is different," Arnold assured him, thinking of the brothels up north around Manila, "they're small and quiet. They're like butterflies in their funny dresses. And they won't pester you like them bitches on the Barbary Coast. You got to buy drinks, but you don't have to drink 'em, see. And you don't have to take no whirl at the quiffs. Jes' take it in as a show, see. Christ, you probably been to plenty of shows where the actresses was just as much of bitches as these girls. Come on with me and have a look. They've got fine records for the victrola and they always have a big bouquet of flowers on the table in one house I know."

If this persuasion had come before Lieutenant Fitzpatrick and Warrington had opened their conversations, the chances are that Warrington would have gone with Arnold. As it was, he nearly succumbed; for even the prospect of being cut off from the officer's friendship for the two days the ship was to be in port had begun to spread before his eyes again the threatening panorama from which the new relationship had beguiled him. However, this relationship had reopened and extended all the multifold petals of his sensitivity, as if his apperception had been one of those flowers that closes up tightly in gloom but uncoils under the first ray of warmth and brightness. Because of this, all his repugnance of prostitutes, all his sensitivity to the repellent vision of them that persisted in his mind and feelings, was more poignant than it had been in a long time at the very moment Arnold's singular display of them was on the point of seducing him. Uneasy with a kind of jealousy aroused by Lieutenant Fitzpatrick's being forced to remove himself totally beyond his pale for two days or more, and sensing his former loneliness crawling in upon him again from all sides, he stood on the raw steel deck and stared with hungry eyes at the fragrant land where quiet butterflies played a victrola in a room decked with flowers.

The water licked and slapped gently at the sleek grey side of the ship just beneath them. Arnold talked on. Suddenly Warrington, more to reassure himself, more to convince himself by the clear objectivity of feeling organized in definite sound, than to inform Arnold, interrupted with a blunt explanation of his feelings about prostitutes. The Quartermaster was astonished, almost as upset as if suddenly he had been confronted with a threat of maniacal violence. His expostulations took the bewildered, time-marking form of demands for clearer, more detailed explanation. To these Warrington, with a shy, fanatical look in his eyes that lent to his words an insuperable authenticity, explained that he could as soon embrace a female pig or monkey as a whore.

Arnold literally did not know what to say. Nothing but a half-whispered exclamation came to his lips, an exclamation called out more by the turmoil and power flaring in the boy's face than by his words. "Jesus Christ, man, you're bug-house! . . . You got a crazy slant on this," muttered Arnold.

A wild necessity to clear up the shameful consternation swirling about this dumbfounded friend drove Warrington deeper and deeper into self-exposure. For this crude man, in whose walking, talking and thinking there was the flavour of a trained wild animal, he opened up his insides in a desperate manner that had not been approached even in his conversations with Lieutenant Fitzpatrick. From behind the very altar of his being he abstracted the ineffable purity and beauty of his beloved. Confused, distraught, his finely chiselled face bent forward solicitously, his large grey eyes flaming with exaltation and a plea for understanding, his thick, shapely eyebrows arched high in a sort of uncertain innocence, he described the girl in detail, quite unaware that it was beside the point. He used her as an example, offering her as a clear foundation upon which to erect his proposition that a normal woman could not be seduced, that she could be taken, and then only despite her sacrificed spiritual and physical reluctance, within marriage or its equivalent. He added to this the statement that the man who so took her was the only one to whom it was possible, through some definite, material hindrance, for her ever to give herself. When it was out there before him in uttered words, it mysteriously did not sound right. This only increased the boy's effort, drove him floundering, here and there, frantically. He told Arnold, as one might rush to fling bits of debris into a hole in a dam, told it in a clear passionate voice, that this girl could not swear, could not speak obscenities, that something in her mental and spiritual being, something physical in her vocal chords even, surely made it impossible.

Arnold, his eyes fastened on the boy's face, his own features and body obviously tortured by a spasm of embarrassment and revulsion, backed away by unconscious degrees until he bumped against the base of the gun a few feet away. His feet hit the spread of the conical base first, so that he fell awkwardly back against the gun. He leant there for a moment. His averted, flickering gaze landed on the bridge ladder. He turned and threw himself towards it.

"I gotta get ready," he faltered.

140

As Arnold landed on the deck below and swung in through the forecastle door, his mind and feelings struggling stickily in the confession he just had received, he went unseeingly past Feenan, the red-headed Oiler, whose initial dislike of Warrington had only been aggravated by his spectacular endurance in the fire-room on the trip to Isla-Sulu. In the midst of that occasion Feenan had gone on record, publicly and contemptuously, with the prediction that the boy never would stick it out below.

The Oiler, having just come off watch in the Starboard Engine-room, and having paused on his way into the forecastle to look at the town, had heard all of the disclosure Warrington had made to Arnold. He had been almost under their feet, hardly three yards away. His large pale, freckled face was alight with a leering grin as he looked after Arnold, the kind of grin people direct at the back of a man who has been made the victim of a piece of ridiculous, obscene madness.

18 〰〰

Nearly all that were going ashore had gone, with the exception of a few in the black gang who were late in washing up as a result of having stood the watch that brought her in. One of these exceptions was Feenan. He stood with large legs aspread over his bucket, the soap and water dripping about on his naked, bulky, thirty-four-year-old body and over the rotundity of his developing waistline. Large and husky as he was, his body skin was of an almost unhealthy paleness. Only at the back of his short, thick neck was there any colour. There, below the line of red hair, the skin was roughened by a series of cracklike wrinkles and was coloured with a freckled grey-ruddiness. He scrubbed himself with complacence, as he did everything else in this society in which his position was excellent, of which he was, as a matter of fact, a self-respecting and respected pillar. His mature age and the fact that he had definitely committed himself to the Navy, in which he already had spent nine years, caused him to view his surroundings with much more resignation than prevailed in the spirits of those who lived, or thought they did, only for the day when they would be handed discharge papers. This, combined with his naturally domestic nature, led him to endow his life and equipment with all the flavours of permanence that were possible to him. His locker in the forecastle had been waterproofed and neatly lined with felt. He bought numbers of handy implements, such as a sheathed mirror, adapted especially for the kind of life that had to be lived aboard ship; and he often brought back from ashore a glass of preserves, a box of shredded wheat or a carton of Life Buoy Soap with which to garnish the routine of his life. The handle of his bucket was attractively braided round with white cord, which he kept scrubbed decently clean. He read the *Saturday Evening Post* and the sports pages of the old newspapers that reached him regularly about once a month, read them slowly and carefully while he puffed importantly at a five-cent cigar, a box of which he kept in his locker. He had very little to say, and for this was credited with having sound common sense by those who appreciated his leaving the saying field quite to themselves and by those who, unable to say anything either, valued the comfort of his unchallenging presence. When he did speak, the tough pomposity of his voice, the solemnity with which he spat as a mark of punctuation or puffed his lips before he began, begot for his shortest inanity the praise that, "When Feenan speaks he's got something to say."

Now he smirked at the other three men who were washing with him, a smile that seemed to say, "Watch this if you want to see some fun," as Warrington, who had finally decided to go ashore, walk around and eat dinner, came out of the forecastle door with a change of clothes in his hand. Feenan waited while Warrington heated his bucket of fresh water under the noisy steam jet, then he shot at the boy, in a falsely jovial, vulgarly pedantic voice, a question that summed up what Warrington had told Arnold; but summed it up so brutally, so obscenely, that the question seemed to bear almost no relation to it. However, the question disclosed to Warrington how thoroughly his explanation had been overheard. Stunned with mortification, he hung above the bucket he just had laid on the deck. He could think of nothing to say. The only things he was trying to think of to say were things that would pacify or choke this man into silence. He turned his body so that his face would be shielded from the four men and pulled off his undershirt. He kept silent.

"Listen," the Oiler went on, "the sooner you learn this the better. Any woman, I don't give a damn who she is, married or single, will lay on her back when the right man comes along."

The boy kept silent.

"Not only that, she'll do it a dozen times a month if a dozen different right men come along . . . And give her a couple of shots of hootch and she'll think every man she meets is the right one. They're all the same. The whores is just the unlucky ones, the ones that got caught too often."

Warrington was praying, praying mechanically, tensely, for the continuance of the bloody deafness that his surging, pounding mortification had whirled about his ears.

His little eyes fastened on the boy's back, Feenan paused in his dressing and waited for a response. His one hundred and seventy-five pounds of body were balanced on one leg and a shoulder resting against the screen of the starboard blower. He was in the act of pulling on his trousers. One thick leg already was encased; the other was jack-knifed above the trousers, ready to be lowered. He began to feel humiliated. The fun somehow was not developing. The three spectators waited, solemn, puzzled. Under the boy's silence and unresponsiveness, the visible accoutrements of the man's prestige began to crumble and tarnish. Feenan's face became redder and a trifle puffed. The situation hung like this amongst them as if it were a vivid, immaterial image projected by a powerful magic lantern against the dark side of a building above a crowded street. Feenan finished dressing, and stooped to gather his gear. The flesh of his hips and legs strained and bulged at the clean, white surfaces of his trousers. As he stooped, his face grew still more crimson until it vied unpleasantly with his damp, crinkly hair, which was brushed as straight back as it would stay. He stowed his soap, towel, comb and brush in his empty bucket. All at once he straightened up and stepped towards Warrington. He grabbed him by the shoulder and shoved him back against the forecastle bulkhead.

"You swell-headed little punk! Say something when a man talks to you . . . You God damn white mouse anyway!"

A "white mouse" was a man who informed on the crew to the officers. The three onlookers knew Warrington was not that. So did Feenan; for Warrington's conversations with Lieutenant Fitzpatrick had been reported to all hands in such detail that there was no real doubt in anybody's mind as to their subject. It was in the very fact of their talk not having been about the ship or even about the Navy that the scandal had lain.

"Aw, lay off the kid," said one of the men.

Warrington shook off Feenan's gesture, which had been halfway between a shove and a blow.

"Well, what do you want me to say?" Warrington asked.

Feenan screamed his answer in a shrill, thin, nasal torrent of sound into which the whole lusty bulk of his being seemed to be goaded.

"You understand what I'm telling you! Any woman will lay on her back the first good chance she gets! I don't give a damn who she is! Do you get that? They're just as hot after it as men are. Do you get that?"

"No," said Warrington, with a kind of incandescent deliberation, "that is not true."

"You crummy little son of a bitch, are you calling me a liar? Are you?" The man's big fists obviously were trembling on the verge of a series of blows.

To Warrington, the beating looming close before him was a terrible thing. A heavy, spirit-attacking fear always would sicken him at the mere hypothetical prospect of a broken nose, a battered eye or a bleeding mouth. For him a fist fight over some trivial cause, more for the joy of battle than anything else, such as school grounds witness every day, was a thing of sterile brutality. In the extreme case, he stood ready, he believed, to die for certain significances of his being; but he prayed if such an occasion should come, its exaction would be death and not wounds. Here once again before him, however, were blood and wounds, petty, horrible, meaningless wounds. Already he could feel once more the flashing smash upon his eyes . . . taste the destroying warmth of his own blood . . . He could escape . . . he had but to say, "No, I'm not calling you a liar. You're probably right." The whole business was without real meaning anyhow.

He stepped (and with the two short steps all the thing within him that was not mere bone, liquid and flesh dropped one notch nearer to the extinction that had progressed with each of these catastrophes) to a clear space of deck. He said, the thin, glowing air of his breath making the speech difficult, as if he were drawing it on the indescribable heights where the figure of a young girl glistened as a symbol of glamorous purity:

"All right then . . . you're a liar."

19 〰

Two of the men picked Warrington up and carried him into the deserted forecastle to his bunk. Even after the Seaman had been knocked to the deck unconscious, Feenan had attempted to hold him up with one hand while he pounded at him with the other; but the men had shoved Feenan aside.

"He's not hurt," said one of the men, probing with his fingers at the boy's jaws, neck and limbs, "just out like a light."

"Too bad Doc's already gone ashore," said another of the three, referring to the Pharmacist's Mate, Heller.

"I'll watch him," said a voice from the gloom at a level with their heads. It was Mendel, the Jew. His bunk, where he lay, silent and inscrutable, recuperating from the beating he had received at the hands of Cavendish, was in the centre tier, directly opposite Warrington. He had been able to hear most of the words and blows that had comprised the fight.

Mendel made no further sign in recognition of the boy's plight until the two men had retreated through the forecastle door to the deck outside, where Feenan was talking loudly and heatedly in justification of what he had done. The Oiler seemed bent on eliciting some approving word, some word consonant with the attitude the crew always had held toward him.

When they were quite alone in the forecastle, Mendel, one of whose ribs was broken, hoisted himself painfully out onto his feet, and looked into the boy's bunk, observed the items of damage, gazed at the crushed excellence in which he had taken so much private and distant pleasure. The way the boy, without fear though without physical strength, had become a free member of the formidable O'Connel clique, his locker full of intellectual furniture, the precision and skill of his talk, the almost fanatical nobility of his gaze, and his obvious rejection of the life about him, had made the boy seem a fine thing to Mendel. On the night when he heard the report of how Warrington, the lowest man in the ship, had in some miraculous manner dared to stand eye to eye with the Executive Officer and establish his intellectual equality if not superiority, a rush of exultation had swept through Mendel. In sheer theory, the world had seemed for him, at that moment, a more tolerable place. He would have liked nothing better than to have struck up some kind of relationship with Warrington, found some way to participate even slightly in his life; but he had not dared. To talk to Warrington, even to listen to him, except at a distance, Mendel would have had to risk getting within range of O'Connel, the Water-Tender, and it was this that he had not dared; for much of the Jew's waking life was spent keeping beyond the notice of O'Connel, whose custom it was to set upon him verbally and physically on the slightest pretext or none at all.

The unreasonable antipathy that Mendel inspired in the Irishman seemed to take objective form on every occasion that O'Connel was reminded of him. If someone no more than mentioned the Fireman, O'Connel was likely to interrupt with the exclamation, "That dirty Kike!" and look around in an aggressive manner to see if Mendel was in sight. Once O'Connel and Mendel had met in a narrow passageway. The Jew had flattened himself nervously against the bulkhead to let his enemy by. O'Connel had looked at him with disgust for a few seconds, then reached over and given him a a short hook to the stomach with his fist.

For this reason, for this scourge of his life, Mendel had been forced to participate indirectly, at a secure distance, in the kind of splendour with which he had endowed Warrington. He would sit out of sight around the angle of the bunk tiers or in the obliteration of a deep shadow and listen to Warrington and Arnold argue. Periodically, as he listened, he would nod his head approvingly, savouringly, a faint flick of oriental smile at the corner of his large mouth. But now here it was, all his splendour and fineness, lying wrecked and blood-smeared on this blanket. He got a clean under-shirt from his locker, moistened it from a bottle of antiseptic he had been using on his own wounds, and dabbed the boy's face and neck clean of the blood. After this he crawled back into his place again and lay on his back with his eyes closed, his sharp, beaked face quite expressionless. Warrington was crying stertorously, as if he were alone, unmanned by his perception of Mendel's sympathy and assistance.

Outside on the deck, Feenan still was arguing with one of the men. The other two had gone. The Oiler seemed to have been driven frantic by the heat, the white glare and some incomprehensible frustration inherent in his crisis.

"What do you want to do?" expostulated the Seaman, "kill the poor kid?"

"He ain't said he's had enough," droned Feenan shrilly, "he's not going to get away with calling me a liar." He exploded in a fusillade of obscenity. Stamping about the deck in front of the forecastle door, he kept swinging his right fist in a tentative, hungry manner, as if its unwonted taste of blood and feel of tearing flesh only had aroused in it a desire for more.

When, in the end, Feenan shoved past him and stepped into the forecastle door, the Seaman looked helplessly down the vista of the deserted ship. His concern had risen to such a pitch that he was on the point of running aft for the Officer of the Deck, a dangerous, uncanonical expedient, one which was likely to bring down on him the contempt of the crew. He succumbed to this temptation only under the pressure of the Oiler's persistent and bewildering savagery; but he was halted, even as he turned to run aft, by a frightful, hysterical yell from the depths of the forecastle. It had halted Feenan too, stopped him in the doorway, where he hung bent for the low opening, swaying uncertainly.

The wild threat came from Mendel, who now was standing beside the boy's bunk, his thin, half-naked, somewhat absurd figure leaning stiffly forward in a fierce gesture. The dark liquid of his eyes had turned to glaring metal. They were insanely threatening in his unshaven face, like the eyes of a large rat cornered in the murk of the forecastle. Dirty, bruised, he was a grotesque monument to the projected pain under his left hand that pressed at his own broken rib, and to the outrage and world-agony, fused by this contingency with his personal suffering, that seems to burn and sing through the typical Jew whenever he is forced to witness physical oppression. In his right hand he grasped a short, jagged length of broken crow-bar, which since his beating he had kept hidden under the mattress of his bunk.

Feenan was staring at the hand that held the unexpected weapon. In the twilight of the forecastle, clenching the bar so ferociously that the blood and skin seemed to have disappeared from the bones, the skeletonlike hand, pale, indistinct, hideous, was like a certain portent of death. The Jew had yelled at the figure in the doorway:

"If you come in here, you son of a bitch, I'll kill you!"

20 ≈≈≈

The crew returned to Delilah next morning in a kind of relaxation that dimmed momentarily the contracting rings of torturing necessity and bad luck which they would begin to feel again as soon as the anchor was hoisted. Those who habitually smiled, smiled easily. Those who were sullen, were merely sullen once more. The news of the trouble between Warrington and Feenan appeared to them, therefore, not as being one of the outbursts that had punctuated the days before the ship reached Sandakan; but rather much as it would have struck them under normal conditions, as a somewhat unpleasant and quite unnecessary public occurrence. O'Connel backed Feenan against the guard rail in his engine-room and, glaring down into his face, rasped threateningly:

"Listen, fumble-foot, lay off the kid! Get me?"

To emphasize this, he delivered one of his characteristic short jabs to the red-headed man's stomach. The Oiler, his face puffing with indignation and pain, sank to the floor plates, hugging his stomach with both arms.

But Arnold was not satisfied so easily. As he listened to the Seaman who had witnessed the whole thing, his large face lost more and more the saving gentleness of his soft eyes. The lids by imper-

148

ceptible degrees almost met to obscure them in a minatory squint. All day he went around in this manner, obviously brooding over something in the situation that his being found indigestible. It was not that the Texan had been given a beating; even his partisanship of the boy did not exempt him from Arnold's unformulated dogma that a strong man had a right to beat a weak one if the weak one got in his way: But there was something, in this particular situation, that the formula did not cover, something that kept flaming up to demand defence, redress. Towards supper time his brooding developed into his saying to himself: "He's always hated the kid . . . hated him because he could talk out of books . . . said once they ought to take the books and throw 'em overboard . . . the red louse! . . . And that time the kid talked it out with the Exec he'd almost went crazy." It probably was this feeling, this wrench at one of the most powerful and absurd superstitions of his make-up, a sensing that Feenan somehow had done violence to the mysterious world of book learning, that kept crying to Arnold for some kind of action.

He leant over and rolled up the bottoms of his dungarees and tied his shoe-laces tight and secure. Straightening up he shifted his weight from one leg to the other, testing his feet. Then he went aft to the galley and got a cup which he filled with water at the scuttlebut. Carrying this in a careful way, as if he had some business with it forward in the forecastle, he padded slowly past the group in which Feenan was listening to someone recounting adventures ashore. Abreast of Feenan, he put out his elbow so that it bumped against the Oiler spilling some of the water.

"Gangway, you punk!" Arnold shouted angrily.

Everybody turned inquiringly to face the two men, arranging themselves automatically in a semicircle of spectators. Arnold was the smaller and weaker of the two, but the men could see that it was he who was bent on aggression.

"What are *you* getting tough about?" said the Oiler, quick anger deepening the colour of his face.

"Well, if you want to find out come on up on the forecastle and I'll show you."

"All right, you God damn trouble maker," answered Feenan,

throwing his cigar over the side with a vicious jerk of his big hand, "you're asking for it and you're going to get it."

"Fight!" someone shouted.

The cry echoed up and down the ship as the two men walked deliberately towards the forecastle ladder with the growing crowd behind them. Ensign Snell, the Officer of the Deck, heard the cry and got up from his chair on the quarter-deck. He stared forward a moment at the throng moving up the forecastle ladder, then he, too, walked forward. The pair already were thickly ringed and striking blows by the time he had pushed through the crowd that formed the ring on the narrow, tapering forecastle deck. When they clinched, he separated them.

Arnold was relieved when he saw the white, starched arms prying them apart. He couldn't handle this heavy in the clinches, but given regulation, open fighting he was sure he could do the job he had in mind.

Respected as Feenan was, the crowd was with Arnold. They roared encouragement to the smaller man carrying the fight so silently and aggressively to the Oiler, whose big arms were swinging and slugging dangerously. Finding and utilizing his chances with machinelike precision, Arnold was using all his memory, skill and ring experience to cut the Oiler's face to ribbons. He accepted no opportunity for a blow, except for tactical reasons, that was not to the face. He deliberately passed up two sure chances to deliver knockout hooks to the jaw, because Feenan's face was not yet cut up enough to suit him. Fighting this way, he was afraid he would be knocked out himself or that on account of the blood Ensign Snell would stop the fight before he had done what he wanted to do. So far, Arnold had boxed himself clear of every really serious blow; but he knew that if he kept on tempting Providence that eventually one of those powerful haymakers was going to catch him. He lashed both of Feenan's eyes closed. He opened up a gash just forward of the left ear with a twisting hook that almost broke his wrist. He mangled Feenan's mouth into a puffy crater that sprayed red as the big man panted and swore.

Ensign Snell was worried. He could not quite understand this fight. He was surprised that apparently Arnold had not punch enough to knock the man out. Feenan was not even winded. He did not feel like stopping this thing, with Feenan still so fresh, until the big fellow had done a little damage himself. If he only could land one of those swings . . . he didn't like the bird, but it wasn't justice not to give him his chance after the mangling he'd taken . . . yet this was getting altogether too bloody.

The men were yelling:

"Put him out, Freddie, put him out!"

"What's the matter, Feenan, land on him, land on him!"

Suddenly Feenan could not see at all. He could not manage to wipe enough blood out of his closing eyes. Every time he used his hands for anything but fighting, his enemy seemed to twist another burning knife in his face. He slipped in his blood and fell in a sitting posture to the deck. The blows on his face ceased. He remained sitting there with his back to the railing, from which the crowd had cleared as the fighters manoeuvred against it. The sun had set and the sky was drenched in deep, smooth red, against the background of which the man's hair and uplifted, blood-covered face formed one of those ugly contrasts that arise out of conjoined tones of red.

"Get up, you *ignorant* bastard," said Arnold in a voice as vicious and machinelike as his blows had been. The way he said the word, "ignorant," seemed clearly to indicate that in that word lay the clue as to the real cause of the fight.

21 〰〰

It was very dark and raining when Delilah steamed out of Sandakan. Long, slim, compact, with port-holes agleam, she speared into the torrential slant of rain like an anomalous animal of the rain and night, reckless of her fate, swaggering out over the black sea into obscurity.

The rain continued all night, and its interminable, leaden lines filled the desolate newness of the daybreak, grey, vast and lonely. Lieutenant Fitzpatrick and Warrington, standing well in from the bridge rail in an effort to escape some of the rain that slid in between the awning and the top of the wind-breaker, silently and dejectedly watched the blackness of the night turn to emptiness. For no particular reason at all it had turned out that since an hour before, at four o'clock, when they had come on watch, they had spoken no word save sparse syllables connected with the blind navigation of the ship. Finally in what might have been an effort to save himself from succumbing to the pale desolation, Lieutenant Fitzpatrick said:

"There's nothing so depressing as rain in the early morning before sunrise."

The drum and purr of the rain on the awning had blurred his voice.

"I'm sorry, Sir, but I didn't catch what you said," the Seaman answered, turning toward him.

Lieutenant Fitzpatrick swung about a trifle irritably to face the boy and repeat his comment. "I said . . ." His words smothered to a stop on his lips. The shade of irritation on his face gave way to shocked pity and distress as he gazed in the dead light at the boy's battered features. Unconsciously, in a quick unobtrusive movement, his hand went out as if reaching to make a gentle, impulsive gesture of pity and support. As unconsciously, Warrington's hand rose in response. Suddenly feeling drops of rain on the backs of their hands, they stared at them there, suspended gropingly, nearly meeting, half-way between their bodies. Startled, they drew them hastily back.

22 ∼∼∼

The series of incidents growing out of the beating he had given Warrington quite ruined poor Feenan's position. Abandoning the secure and easy shelters of silence and untestable assumption, he had entered the sphere of action, where, in quick succession, he had gained a pitifully easy and thoroughly unpopular victory, been forced to back down before the Jew, taken an ignominious admonishment from O'Connel and in a fair fight with the much smaller Arnold been given a spectacular cutting up in the midst of which he had quit, in the feelings of the crew, like a craven.

Men who usually protected themselves from brawls by an unfailing show of good humour in the little incidents that so readily lead to them, now took no pains with Feenan. They gave the appearance of simply brushing him aside with the mental comment that it really did not matter whether he liked it or not. He seemed to be, for these men, no longer a person to be reckoned with. Hardwood, whose hooting, loud-mouthed, negroid ragging spouted and spread through every moment of work and leisure that found no officer present, respecting no target from O'Connel down, soon came to pass over Feenan entirely. As far as Hardwood's ragging was concerned, the Oiler just might not have been a member of the crew. This was the most salient outward sign of the change in Feenan's social position; and it was the most important one, for an informed person, studying the relative positions of the members of the crew on the basis of Hardwood's jibes alone, could form a very accurate opinion as to the social standing of each man. On Feenan's face settled a permanent, irritating look of bewilderment and self-pity. It was as if he went around the ship with a sign on his breast like a beggar reading, "I am now an underdog."

On the other hand, Mendel's fate suffered quite as great a change in the opposite direction. The whole crew believed he certainly would have tried to kill the Oiler; Warrington became his close friend; he was seen on afternoons after five o'clock reading one of the boy's books; and now Warrington persistently stood in between him and O'Connel. Finally, on one climactic occasion, when Rene and O'Connel were trying to organize a pinocle game around the Blacksmith's lowered cot on the port side in the shelter of the Amidships Torpedo-tube, and having difficulty in finding a fourth, O'Connel had invited Mendel to play. Mendel, Feenan and Saunders had been scrubbing clothes in the wash space. When the Irishman's prowling for a player had brought him there, he had surveyed the three for a moment, his big face chopped by a meaningless grin. Saunders did not know how to play. It was a choice between Feenan and Mendel. Then he had roared belligerently, annoyance and surrender plainly dominating his voice:

"Come on, Kike, sit in."

Mendel had gotten up at once, dried his hands and sat down at his place in the game, an inscrutable look on his narrow, beaked face. From that occasion on, he suffered a continual hooting bombardment from Hardwood that must have been very difficult to bear. In some manner the Seaman had discovered that Mendel had allotted a large share of his salary to a bank in Brooklyn. It was easy for the crew to understand an allottment to a woman, a wife or some member of a family; but to allot one's wherewithal to get food, drink and women to a bank was in most of their eyes a kind of mean absurdity. Merely to mention the fact was, for them, a joke: and Hardwood managed to bring it out in some connection or none at all at all hours of the day or night. Once Mendel, crawling up out of the fire-room hatch at two o'clock in the morning, had dropped a clinker out of his clothes onto the deck as he straightened up. Hardwood, passing forward to go on wheel watch, had heard the slight ring as the piece of slate hit the deck. He had half hissed in the chortling voice of a Negro on a secret spree:

"Hey! . . . Kike . . . There goes your dough! . . . What's happened to that bank in Brooklyn?"

Mendel watched for these sallies (that for others when aimed at them were like linked drops of water eternally pounding away at the head of a torture victim) as if they had been nuggets of gold and he the miser that Hardwood ever strove to make him out. They were his symbols that he had been pulled within the pale, that the most heavy pressure of his present existence had been lifted. They prepared a table before him in the presence of his enemies, they anointed his head with oil, they filled his cup to running over.

23 ≈≈≈

For the crew as a whole, however, there was no lasting peace or exultation. The moment they were under way again, the pounding threat of breakdown expanded once more at the backs of their minds; and the ever strengthening suspicion that there was some deadly secret thing hidden behind their officers' faces received further support from the manner in which the ship lay at anchor in Coral Bay all the next day after leaving Borneo. It was clear to everybody that this was an act of hiding; an act of hiding ominously pointed up by the standing order given to those on watch: "Call the Captain immediately at the first sight of smoke on the horizon." The little more that was needed to definitely and heavily mark the end of the brief relaxation in Sandakan, to throw it far back into the poignant nothingness of pleasant memory, was the putting ashore of one of those chastising Landing Parties to search the wild reaches from Bancal Bay to Madrepora Point.

Once Delilah had rounded Cape Buliluyan and progressed but a few hours up the west coast, the whole life and being in the ship sank beneath an oppressive, specious space. The surface of the crew's consciousness became used to the threatening pound of the shaft much as people come to accept the roar of a great city as an unnoticed part of their environment; while the fear, confinement and drudging ordeals of the forays ashore assumed the proportions of a terrible normality. The ship seemed to drift through a monotony of strange air, utterly clear, palpable. The dangerous and unknown sea was so motionless and reflective under the brilliant sun that it was difficult to tell exactly where it was beneath the ship or where it extended to in the direction of the merging horizon or where it met the hard unreality of the towering land. Existence became so dreamlike that their vigilance relaxed. Their acute sense of time and space was benumbed. There were here no ships, no blurs of smoke against the intense nothingness beyond the horizon, no villages on the shore, no floating debris except when a sudden torrent of rain and wind swept out a branch of leaves or a cluster of blossoms, no lights at night to challenge the still nightmare of the white-fire flecked infinity above. All life, all existence save items in illusion seemed to have ceased. The peace grew over their festering tension and their ill-being like a marvelously smooth scab.

One morning, as if the arrival bore no relation to their conscious efforts, they found themselves off Saint Paul Bay, a broad, unsheltered bite out of the stark coast-line backed by towering cliffs, by formidable, dome-shaped hills through which swift water courses ran riot, and by a great blue mountain over five thousand feet high whose summit was blurred with bright, white clouds.

"Hmm . . ."

The Captain, through his binoculars, was studying the line of sandy beach that stretched on both sides of the place where the cave was marked on the chart. Foaming white and rich with a splendid swirling wash far up the yellow beach, the surf looked enticing and lightly beautiful; but the Captain judged that the combers were pounding in there at terrific speed from ten to twenty feet high. It appeared as if the great sea, calm and polished as the early morning disk of sun, suddenly aroused by sensing the still and reticent limbs of the exotic land so near it, was predaciously flinging itself forward in all its tremendous force.

"I'm afraid you're going to have to land your boats through the surf there, Mr. Fitzpatrick," said the Captain.

"It's going to be a nice little job, too," replied Lieutenant Fitzpatrick. Standing beside the Captain, he also was examining the land through binoculars.

Still studying the strip of beach, the Captain said:

"I can't find hide or hair of that river . . . ought to be issuing somewhere along there." Then he added quite irrelevantly, removing his eyes from the binoculars for a moment to take a general look around at the supernaturally peaceful and artificial-seeming world. "If it comes on a blow while you're in there, I'll have to take her around into Ulugan Bay. There's no shelter here. If the blow should keep up, we'll try to push some stores overland to you across Piedras Point. It looks pretty tough, though, through there. If we couldn't get through, you'd just have to make out."

"O, don't worry about the Landing Party, Captain, we'll make out all right," said Lieutenant Fitzpatrick. He glanced off over the dead incandescence of the China Sea. "This calm will probably last for a hundred years; and anyway, I'll bet there are plenty of bananas and coco-nuts and orchids and God knows what else in there . . . not to mention those obscene oysters of Bidot's."

"Well, you can't eat orchids," said the Captain.

"O, hell, Deacon!" protested Lieutenant Fitzpatrick with a wry twist of a smile.

The two boats selected for running the surf were beautiful objects of art whose sculptured forms perfectly and glamorously followed their intended function. They were whaleboats evolved by those unparalleled seamen who hunted the whale out of New Bedford, boats which are the same today as when the Navy first inherited them, except that the freeboard is higher, the thwarts are higher and more roomy, and opportunity for coxswain and oarsmen to exert their strength is improved. Very light, smooth-bottomed, a tendency toward broad beam, single-banked, six-oared, both ends a sharp cutting bow, the whaleboat inspires confidence and even enthusiasm in the men who have to handle it in a race, in a heavy sea or in a landing through surf where their very lives are at stake.

To give the two whaleboats their best chance in the effort at hand, they should have been stripped of all load except the coxswain, the six oarsmen and their oars; but this could not be. The boats each had to carry a cargo of Landing Party with weapons and ammunition in addition to their crews.

With the men working in brusque, over-emphasized movements as if trying to shake themselves free of the dream-lethargy that still seemed to bemuse them, the boats were dropped in the water alongside, after Delilah had anchored a mile and a half offshore. Rifles, ammunition belts, bunker lamps well filled with paraffin, food and a few pounds of other equipment were lashed in the bottom of each boat amidships. Bidot, the Quartermaster, First-Class, and Cruck, the Chief Boatswain's Mate, each of whom had coxswained boats through surf before, personally distributed and lashed these loads in the respective boats in which they were to handle the steering oars. For this dangerous operation, the modern rudders of the whaleboats had been unshipped and replaced by long, heavy steering oars, oars which the old whalemen invariably used and which give the coxswain a more powerful and delicate control over his boat, but which are inconvenient and unnecessary in the routine business of paddling about a roadstead.

Barefooted, the six oarsmen took their places on the thwarts of each boat; the coxswain standing in the stern. Their shoes, into which their socks had been tucked, were hung around their necks by joined laces. At the command, "Toss Oars!" they swung their oars up vertically and held them there, while seven members of the Landing Party crawled into the bottom of each boat between the thwarts. Pushed away from Delilah's side by the coxswains in the sterns with boat-hooks and by the bow oarsmen with their oars, the two whaleboats became separate units, independent of the ship and of each other, ready for the strenuous venture.

Cruck roared his orders; Bidot sang his. "Let Fall!" The oars came down to just above the surface of the water. "Give Way Together!" The boats slid swiftly in towards the beginning of the surf, Cruck's boat leading because it contained Lieutenant Fitzpatrick. Just outside the well-defined line where the great, smooth calm of water mysteriously aroused itself and began to charge violently toward the land, the two boats paused. The men rested on their oars while Cruck and Bidot studied the problem before them.

Suddenly the standing Cruck braced himself and felt for a good grip, with his hands, right elbow and hip, on the great steering oar trailing out astern. The six oarsmen facing him, as they saw this, felt for holds with their bare feet, curling their toes down as if to grip, while their hands flexed preparatorily on oar handles. At the stroke oar of this boat was old Blood, who had had every venereal disease known to medical science; behind him was Hardwood, silent for once, his heavy shoulders poised and ready over his oar; behind him his friend, Horner, a pug-nosed man of hard, well-packed flesh, who had fled into the Navy from his driver's seat on a Cincinnati brick wagon after impregnating an idiot girl; then came the straw-haired, pimply-faced Wright, the Seaman who had started running for the Officer of the Deck when Feenan was bent on renewing the fight with Warrington; back of him Ragatzo, medium-sized, smooth, ugly, coffee-coloured, who was a fugitive from some kind of trouble with the Hudson Dusters gang in New York; and at the bow oar, Forsythe, out of a small cattle town near Fort Worth, whose long, lean, tough being had felt, one afternoon, the intolerability of the great prairie spaces surrounding him, and had tried to escape through a bright Navy lithograph pasted up in the post-office. The passengers crouching in the bottom of the boat had complete confidence in these men. They were the best boat's crew in the ship. Lieutenant Fitzpatrick, pleasantly scented, elegant in gold and white, sitting on his heels at Cruck's bare, clutching feet, restrained his impulse to make suggestions and looked steadily and smilingly at the land as if there were no crisis at hand.

"Give Way Together!" yelled Cruck, digging his steering oar deep into the sea.

Their bodies stretching, their heads bowed, the searching illumination of the slanting sunlight turning the hair of their bare heads and Blood's beard into tangles of dark, distinct lines, they pulled smartly forward to battle the great walls of blue water rushing landward.

They stroked swiftly and steadily in with the surging water until Cruck, in a periodic turn of the head, saw roaring down upon them the first and greatest of the pursuing waves. Looking terrible in its great height and velocity it blotted out the seascape . . . and overtook them.

"Oars!" shrieked Cruck.

The oars came out of the sea, paused for a few seconds just above it, dripping blades parallel to the water and in line, waiting for the swiftly following command.

"Stern All!"

The blades of the oars turned, dipped. The straining bodies now pushed against the oars. The boat stood still for an instant before it reversed its direction.

Cruck, his feelings exaggerating this perilous stationary moment as his eyes glared back into the charging, monstrous mass of water, screamed wildly, raising his eyes instinctively to the sky:

"Stern All! . . . Stern All! . . . Christ! I'm out here with a gang of pansies!"

The boat, however, had gained momentum. It was backing water straight out to sea, straight at its great enemy, which the oarsmen now could see plainly. Towering in cold, dispassionate ferocity the wave scooped down upon them at terrific speed.

By the time the stern of the whaleboat had met the base of the wave, the boat was travelling fast enough to neutralize somewhat the speed of the sea. The boat stood comparatively still while the comber passed under it; but this is not what seemed to happen. As if it were going to loop the loop, the whaleboat appeared to dart up the massive, concave front of the wave towards the scintillating ridge of foam that had begun to sprout all along its length.

This was the moment on which hung the fate of all in the boat.

They waited consciously, waited so consciously that the period of waiting seemed to them grotesque, for their craft to climb upon the crest of the wave. This it would do if the boat's crew had plied their oars with the proper strength and evenness, if the cursing Cruck had handled his long steering oar with skill and accuracy: in short, if the whaleboat had been backed at a precise right angle into the wave at a speed sufficient to maintain that angle before the force of the wave, and thus prevent her from being carried along in front of it. Otherwise, the boat would end for end, spilling, like peas from a pod, the helpless men into the sea in a chaos of oars, boat and tons of insane water that meant pounding, smothering destruction; or the boat would jerk broadside on to the sea, be roared along before the wave out of control, like a piece of flotsam, to fill with water and capsize.

With Cruck fighting his oar in a raging, brutal aggressiveness that seemed to lend personality to the liquid monster that gripped it, the whaleboat leapt onto the top of the wave. Those in the other boat waiting beyond the broken water glimpsed it for an instant there, hull and blades bereft of water, hanging atop the burst of immaculate and dazzling white foam like a dark water-beetle, its legs, fine straight black lines against the morning blue, waggling slightly as the men in swift desperation renewed their grips on the oars.

As the whaleboat slid down the long, slanting back of the wave, the crew at Cruck's order now pulled vigorously with it. For the time that they could cling there on the wave with their oars, the boat travelled shoreward in a gale of speed. Soon, however, the wave left them behind amidst an uncertain series of small peaks and troughs through the spume of which they continued to pull strongly in the wake of the vanishing enemy. Cruck roared the time for their stroke:

"Yo! . . . yo! . . . heave! . . . heave! . . . yo! . . . yo! . . . yo! . . . heave! . . ."

The battle was not over by any means. Behind them curled and thundered another monster almost as large as the first. Again the boat reversed its direction, met the enemy, was flung high in the air to come down precisely on the wave's back and speed shoreward. Time and again they thus met the immensities of water, escaped their ferocity and tricked them into becoming beasts of burden. The last one, much smaller and much easier to deal with than the others, carried the boat out of deep water onto the slope of the beach.

When Cruck felt bottom with his steering oar, he yelled, "Trail Oars," threw his oar at the water and leapt overboard. The boat's crew almost at the same moment dropped their oars into the water and jumped after him. The oars, on short trailing lines, dragged sternward, clinging close to the sides with the onward motion of the boat. The crew, nearly waist deep in water, seized the gunwales and with the help of the sea's rush dragged the boat up on the beach before the back-wash could develop. For a moment the men became a clot of wild gesticulation, an exultant shout. Over the raging field of water came an answering cheer from the other boat waiting the signal to come in.

Lieutenant Fitzpatrick had told Bidot to hold off, unless disaster overtook the first boat, until he got a signal. The officer wanted to locate the mouth of the river so that the second boat could, if possible, head right into it. Not only would this be easier than landing on the beach, but it also would save all the work that now faced the first boat in getting to the river once it was located.

As Lieutenant Fitzpatrick looked about him, he could see nothing of either a cave or a river: a graceful curve of fine sand . . . a background of impenetrable-looking mountains . . . a high, barren cliff down which writhed a thin, lacy waterfall . . . a small cove to the right seemingly choked with bamboo and fantastic vegetation.

"It's probably in there," thought Lieutenant Fitzpatrick. He had not been able to detect the mouth of this cove from the ship because its small entrance channel ran almost parallel with the line of the beach. As soon as the boat's crew had put on their shoes and everybody was in possession of a belt, rifle and bayonet, he made for the little cove. The moment he was at its mouth he saw the "river," a creek some fourteen feet wide, sneaking unctuously in a quick turn towards an indentation in the beach that almost reached the cove's mouth. Slow and obscure as the stream looked, a sounding, taken with a rod of cane cut from a cluster that sprouted from the precipitous side of the cove's entrance, proved it to be quite deep enough to float a boat. Clambering along the border of the stream, they got inside the cove, a groinlike niche of a pool at the base of a bare, belly-shaped mountain. The place literally was clogged with lush creepers, stiff aggressive clusters of delicately leaved cane and great orchidlike plants that drooped from every fungus-spotted vantage point of damp shade. A heavy fragrance, equivocally agreeable, like a strangely perfumed perspiration, seemed to stir and drift, now faint, now strong, in the confined air. The men turned their faces up towards the rough triangle of intense, vague blue that covered rather than served as sky. The mouth of the cave, in a globular bulge of smooth rock, formed the triangular pool's farther limit, its apex. It was a round, repellent hole some fourteen feet in diameter, imbued with a quality of being alive and surrounded with a tangle of hairy vegetation. It was plain, as had been rumoured, that the only way to get into it was by boat. At the entrance to the cave there was no place for a man to get a foothold on either edge of the stream, which, for all its remarkable pellucidity, somehow gave the impression, as it issued from the hole, that it was a spurt of excrement.

With the topography of the situation clear in his mind, Lieutenant Fitzpatrick wrote out a short message to Bidot that described in detail the course of the stream from the beach into the pool. On the beach where the hidden stream slipped into the sea between breakers, the men erected, as markers, two oars with undershirts hanging from the blades, one on either side of the channel's mouth. Lieutenant Fitzpatrick gave his message to Warrington, a member of the Landing Party in his boat, who, with the piece of paper between his teeth, climbed up the seaward face of the shoulder that formed one side of the cove. When the Seaman found himself in front of a dark clump of vegetation against the background of which the movements of his arms would be plainly visible from the sea, he turned about and braced himself. He could see the other whaleboat out there tossing patiently. Fastening the paper to a projecting twig so that he could read it merely by turning his head as he squarely faced the boat, he extended his arms and semaphored, "Attention." Almost at once one of Bidot's arms went up in a motion that signified he was ready to receive. The end of the semaphored message precipitated the boat into immediate action. It headed quickly into the troubled water.

While Bidot had been waiting for the signal ordering him to come in, he had spent his time studying the characteristics of the enemy with which he was to grapple. He observed that the big combers charged one after another in groups of three and that between these groups there were stretches of comparative calm broken only by smaller waves that to him seemed not so dangerous. Giving his commands in a strong voice that had the quality of a high, broad, mellifluous whistle, he nursed his boat right up to the heaving edge of the rough water and held her there, backing water if he got too close, working slowly forward again if he drifted away.

When he got the order to come in, he counted off three of the big waves that seemingly first took form and being but a few yards to landward of his bow, and at the moment when the third one just had gotten under way to his eye, he sang out:

"Give Way Together!"

In the wake of this third big wave, he timed as fast a stroke as his crew was capable of maintaining . . . "stroke! . . . stroke! . . . stroke!" . . . With his tall, slim body somewhat bent in the direction of his steering oar handle, about which he appeared to sway slightly as if he were not quite able to resist entirely the fight in the oar, he headed straight for the beach, regardless of the intermediate waves that dashed water in the boat and struck frantically at the stern trying to shove it to one side or up in the air. Every trick these smaller waves tried, Bidot met and bested with his steering oar, and he was nearly half-way in before one of the big waves of a new group loomed up behind the whaleboat.

The Captain, watching from Delilah's bridge with Ensign Snell and Ensign Woodbridge, was so entertained by the manner in which this boat had evaded most of the big combers that his wrinkles rearranged themselves in a smile that took in his whole face. He shook his head in a manner that seemed to partake of pleasant, hopeless envy, and turning his head from his binoculars to Ensign Snell, he said:

"Slick as paint, that fellow."

Bidot's boat quickly backwatered into its first major antagonist, mastered it and rode so far in on its back that the following giant, after the boat successfully had mounted its crest, carried her all the way to the beach. In the broken water, flung along at great speed by the rush of foaming sea, he used the long, heavy steering sweep with such effective grace, a grace compounded of beauty, power, intelligence and intrepidity, that the sight of him there, his straight-hanging hair almost framed by the morning sun, his willowy body swaying surely on his long legs in the pointed stern of the whaleboat, from which it seemed to grow, this sight of him elicited shouts and whistles of admiration from the intently watching men on the beach.

Dead on at the beach shot the whaleboat, as if it had been a well-aimed torpedo, clean between the two upright oars erected as markers. As the boat passed into the mouth of the stream, Bidot sang:

"Toss Oars!"

The momentum carried the boat smartly forward, and Bidot managed the turn with his steering oar partly levering against the right bank. The boat passed the entrance to the pool, cut across the still water within and drifted to a stop just before the entrance of the cave, its six oars pointing stiffly up like a cluster of skyward-aimed spears. The rowers were gasping with their effort. The perspiration poured down their bare arms, drenched their eyes. When they had unshipped and stowed their oars, they kept clenching and unclenching their hands.

It took considerable work to get the first whaleboat into the river. They cut thick tubes of bamboo and using them for rollers under the boat trundled it up the smooth beach near the edge of the sea until they got it to the channel's bank. Every now and then one of the bamboo rollers would sink into a soft patch of sand and then Lieutenant Fitzpatrick would make them lift the heavy weight ahead. He was afraid that if the boat were dragged over the sand it would injure the bottom.

To those on the distant ship, relaxing, into a reawareness of their normal oppression and fundamental fatigue, from the exhilaration of watching their friends run the surf, the men working with that boat off there all at once became a cluster of barefoot alien pygmies struggling frantically on the margin of golden membrane that bordered this remote and demoniac shore, a shore almost lost at the base of the mountains that towered above it. Like a blue-hazed phantasmagoria, the mountains rose in a brilliant confusion of sharp, cream-coloured cliffs without perspective, of great, flat, cloudy peaks in uncertain ridged outline, and of vast explosive-looking domes, insubstantial, green-spotted, pregnant, unnatural.

Well before noon the two boats were lined up on the surface of the pool, Cruck's boat, containing Lieutenant Fitzpatrick, in the lead, ready to penetrate the river. The rudders had been shipped in place of the steering sweeps. A man was stationed in each bow armed with a boat-hook, and fastened to the hull in front of him was a lighted bunker lamp. Several more of these small paraffin torches were distributed down the lengths of both craft. It was impossible to use oars because the cave was too narrow, and so men with long lengths of bamboo posted in the stern of each boat made ready to pole them upstream.

There on the sunny, still surface of the pool, the thud and roar of the surf outside seemed abstract, incredible, faintly threatening. The men, tensing a little forward on the thwarts, rifles with fixed bayonets beside them, stared resolutely at the ugly, secretive hole to which the bows of the whaleboats pointed.

24 〰

For many yards the cave went straight in, its low rounded roof and sides gleaming wet and unhealthy in the eerie white daylight that followed the boats in and mixed uncertainly with the yellow sway and flicker from the paraffin torches. Every now and then a man would throw a quick glance over his shoulder at the diminishing circle of white glow that marked the entrance. Even after the narrow gut, barely a few inches wider than the whaleboats, had made a ninety degree turn into deep gloom, intense concentration on the shifting walls of the passage was rewarded by a sense of faint, white stain that had managed to make the turn and pierce in from the bright world being left behind.

The young Seaman, Warrington, sitting between thwarts in the bottom of the first whaleboat, was suffering the impression that he was penetrating the body of some huge living animal, an impression suggestively abetted by the heavy smell of bats and the illusion that the walls of the intestinelike passage were tentatively contracting and expanding, in the twisting play of the torch light, as if preparing to eliminate this foreign matter clawing along within it.

In the bow of the boat Lieutenant Fitzpatrick was straining his eyes ahead into the implacable darkness, seeking for the moment when this thin tube would widen out or merely change. He was struggling with a faint obsession that the tube was narrowing and that the boat would jam suddenly and be caught there. He restrained an order to the man with the pole to go slower. As if he were one of a group of conspirators huddled in a moment of precarious silence, he was startled and irritated on the instant by Hardwood's voice crashing confusedly in the passage with jibes at Cruck because the Chief Boatswain's Mate kept a firm grip on the tiller.

"Whea do y' think the boat's a goin' to if y' take y' hand off?" hooted Hardwood.

The men in the boats tried to laugh at this, but the ugly, funnelled, ear-torturing roar their combined laughter became, discouraged them. No one, however, could bear the silence of the unending push through this stream of liquid winding down against them. Men shouted to each other from boat to boat meaningless phrases that set up wild, hollow whirlpools of sound in the musky obscurity. The shouts only accentuated the confinement and unnaturalness they were intended to relieve. At the stern of the second boat, the pleasantly taciturn Petrie, who in the sunlight was a very red-faced man with glistening black eyes, could resist neither this unnaturalness nor the impression that what he was thrusting into with his pole was not water. More than once in relapses of silence that seemed to have conquered and benumbed the others, he had shouted:

"This stuff never gets very deep."

The minute-after-minute sameness in appearance of the passage walls in the murky flare and waver of the torches, and the monotonous progress of the boats under the slow, even thrusts of the

166

polers gave rise to bickering discussion as to whether the boats had made any progress at all. It finally seemed to them that they had been in that labyrinthine pall all morning, that the current of the stream and the efforts of the polers served merely to neutralize each other. A man insisted on replacing Petrie at the pole, and this change was emulated loudly in the first boat. Someone tried to start a song, but when two or three others took it up it became mere uproar that quickly subsided, leaving in its wake curses, protests and the inexorable scourge of Hardwood's sallies. In the midst of this, some cavities, like giant black flowers blossoming above them to right and left, appeared in the wall of the passage. The darkness of their areas was so profound that, like surfaces, they appeared to repel the yellow stabs of torch light; and as the boats passed the spots over which the cavities leaned, they seemed to absorb and change the quality of the noise that arose from the boats. This intimidated the men. Some of them lowered their heads while the boats floated past as if they expected something to rain down. Only a grisly, mothlike creature, evidently disturbed by the noise, drifted flutteringly down from one of the cavities and then up again into another.

Some distance past these cavities, a dim, liquid rumble began to grow in their ears, a smother of sound like the sustained repercussion of a drum. Never violent, the sound increased in volume as the boats progressed.

Warrington was realizing uneasily that Heller, the Pharmacist's Mate, who sat close to him, was getting nervous. When Heller, struggling a trifle with his breath and looking straight up at the close, dank top of the passages, said "Christ! . . . This is just like being buried alive," Warrington felt clearly the urge to make some kind of joke. The urge did not arise from any desire to relieve Heller's nervousness, nor from any desire to protect himself from it. There appeared to be merely the coincidence that the same moment that had produced Heller's remark also had clarified his own feeling of need. No joke, however, to shout or dramatize in action would grow in his mind. He waited for minutes trying to think of one as a man listens for an expected sound. Then in a query shouted up and down the boats in what for the Chief Boatswain's Mate was a pleading tone,

Warrington sensed an opportunity for his unfamiliar exigency.

"Who's got some chewin' tobacco?" Cruck's repeated shout began to drum through the general stress like a pointed chant. It searched out the reluctant Petrie and forced him to reach into the pocket of his white jumper and pull out a tooth-marked plug a few seconds before the grimly resisting Ferguson was ready to admit that he had some. The man beside Petrie, catching a glimpse of the tobacco in a flash of the torch light, yelled:

"Here's some . . . Petrie's got some."

"Pass it forward . . . Pass it forward." Cruck was by no means an addict nervously dependent on chewing tobacco; he took it in the general run with food and drink; but his voice now, if it had been overheard for the first time, would have given the definite impression that he was.

Petrie prepared to pass the plug of tobacco forward, half standing in the moving boat and steadying himself against the jerky impulses of the poling with one hand on the gunwale. A man a couple of places ahead of him reached aft to receive the plug so that he could pass it on. At this moment, Warrington shouted in a shrill, antagonistic voice, completely devoid of the humour with which he had intended to fill it:

"Never mind passing it now . . . He's found some."

With his nervous appetite complicated by astonishment and irritation over this incomprehensible check, Cruck's mental machinery made no effort to solve its purpose. He stuck persistently to the material objective before him:

"God damn it!" he roared, "Pass that tobacco!"

Petrie again got the tobacco ready to pass, thinking there had been some misunderstanding.

Embarrassed and bewildered over the added situation into which he had projected himself, Warrington uncertainly but stubbornly held to his role.

"There goes some," he shouted, shrilly trying to disguise his voice, "He's got some now, Petrie."

Having recognized the way Warrington pronounced his name, and having been led away by this from perceiving that Warrington was trying to disguise his voice, Petrie took the shout seriously and put the plug of tobacco back in his pocket.

Cruck had stood up in the stern of the boat, an aroused bulk distorted by shadow and the flicker of torches, to watch the progress of the tobacco being passed up to him. When it had not come, and he saw no passing movement amidst the shadowy clots that represented knees, hands and elbows down the length of the other boat, he screamed raspingly:

"Where's that lousy tobacco?"

He began to stamp ferociously and swing his fist. The din and the wildness of his movements agitated the men in both craft.

"Sit down! . . . You're rockin' the boat," somebody yelled at him from the boat behind.

A furious sense of injustice was racking Cruck, and this shout from one who was not even in his boat seemed the last straw. Not trying to shout anything intelligible, simply emitting a crescending, frantic hurricane of sound, Cruck roared. He jerked out the tiller and brandished it.

Petrie, as if he were somehow guilty, again dove into his pocket with quick furtiveness for the plug of tobacco. He held it straight up in the air and kept it there. Before he spoke he swiped at the perspiration on his troubled red face with the sleeve of his stiffly raised arm.

"Here it is . . . Warrington said you had some."

His mouth twisting and almost drooling with rage, Cruck lunged forward toward Warrington in the bow, trying to strike, even at this futile distance, with the clubbed tiller.

"I'll brain *that* bastard!" he yelled.

He lurched into a stumbling fall over the men before him. A bulky tangle of bodies struggled in defensive turmoil, breathed ugly sounds of fear as the boat rocked precariously. Even in the other boat men instinctively put out steadying hands against the wall of the narrow passage as if to keep their craft from capsizing, and their poler permitted it to drift with the current back away from the tumult ahead.

There simmered a brief moment of heaving silence, amidst which the sound of water rippling past the boats became the most definite sound. Then Lieutenant Fitzpatrick's voice could be heard cutting through this turbulent stillness like an authoritative lash:

"Pipe down there! . . . Pipe down ! . . . Keep your places!"

The swad of men slowly disentangled itself in the stern of the wildly rocking boat. Cruck sat up sullenly, a little confused but still clutching the tiller as if he were going to use it as a club. Warrington sat stiffly in the bottom of the boat, hot with self-stultification.

"Let's have that damn tobacco," ordered Lieutenant Fitzpatrick.

Petrie still was holding it up in the air. Someone snatched it and passed it forward to the man in the bow, who, with a shout of "Stand from under!" tossed it accurately across the widening stretch of spectral water into the first boat. It hit Wright in the chest and fell at his feet. He stooped to pick it up, calling out with a trace of triumph and relief:

"I got it, Sir."

"Pass it to Cruck," said the officer shortly.

With a gesture reeking of petulant, half-ashamed satisfaction, Cruck received the plug and fiercely bit off a large wad of it.

"You with the pole there," commanded Lieutenant Fitzpatrick. His voice, as it left his lips, bloated into a monstrous resonance that pounded and surged back upon the words that followed. "Keep her moving."

The poler, who had been holding the boat stationary by using his pole to jam it against the side of the passage ever since he feared it might capsize, gave it a responsive shove forward. The boat scraped around a turn into a deeper gloom caused by leaving the other boat and its lights behind around the turn.

There was only one torch left burning in the front boat. The others had been smothered or knocked overboard in the struggle. All at once the poler ceased his effort and held the bamboo high poised while he stared intently ahead. The man with the remaining torch attempted to hold it aloft so that the scene ahead would be better illuminated. It fell from his fingers and sputtered out in the water. The darkness contracted heavily. The poler could be heard levering the boat against the wall. The men tried to stare before them, struggling with superstitious dread that was becoming panic. The darkness, dank and horrible, was almost alive, palpable, vegetable, like an enveloping fungoid growth.

"Strike a light," ordered Lieutenant Fitzpatrick. His voice came through the obscurity over-controlled, tense, unnatural; but this quality was disguised by the way his voice vibrated shudderingly, in this part of the cave, like the deep tones of an organ. It seemed to strike and enter through the body rather than the ear.

The rear boat swung around the turn, casting before it a spasmodic glow from its torches.

"I want my tobacco back," said Petrie plaintively, almost apologetically, as he caught shadowy sight of the forward boat.

No one listened to him. Every faculty, every fixed gaze was thrusting ahead, beyond the dying rings of the feverish, aborted joke that had racked them like a delirium, to where, in the near distance up there, it could be indeterminately sensed that the narrow, oppressive tube in which they were floating, this place of slimy entombment, had come to an end.

By the added light of the two torches that finally were lit in the first boat, Lieutenant Fitzpatrick saw, certainly enough, that they had gone as far as they could go in the boats. The river came to an end against a towering cliff whose pale, livid surface, fading into the gloomy heights above, was of the waxy colour inside a mouth. From the face of the cliff, some twenty feet above the level of the river, there projected a sort of giant nipple, elongated and obscene, out of which water oozed thickly and cascaded down with a blurred, drumming sound to the stream on which the boats floated. On the left, in the wall of the passage just before it reached the cliff, a long thin cavity hung a few feet above the stream's surface, shadowy and grim like the parted lips of an unhealing wound.

Reluctantly, Lieutenant Fitzpatrick saw that this forbidding slit was an opening through which he could take the Landing Party if it led anywhere. He ordered the boats to approach the cavity. The disinclination of the men behind him fairly beat upon his back. Nevertheless, the first whaleboat cut through the water and came to a stop beneath the opening. It rested against the wall there almost noiselessly as against a buffered and well-oiled dock face. The other boat crept up.

In the combined glare of all the torches available it could be seen clearly that the floor of the cavity mouth was indeed a sort of natural dock, coming down to a little less than two feet above the gunwale of the boat.

"Up you go, men," said Lieutenant Fitzpatrick brusquely, and swung himself up on the ledge.

Cruck followed heavily like a bull charging at some unnatural obstacle slumbering in darkness. The rest of the men followed one by one. The floor of the ledge, where they put their hands on it to pull themselves up, was repulsive to the touch, lubricious and slightly yielding. Although they were dripping with moisture, the odious atmosphere of the place seemed to pulse out at them in dry, bubblelike gusts from the interior of the cavity. It seemed to them as if they were beginning to smother. Deep in this gloomy maze, lost and helpless within the vague, feculent recesses of this monstrous mountain, the men silently revolted against the hole full of sable nothingness before them. Their eyes sought the officer uncertainly. In him, too, the nervous tension of the past days was finding its opportunity to claw and twist up to all the surfaces of his being; and on the outside of him, on every area beneath which flinched a nerve, there throbbed the blurred drum of that water-fall.

"Line up!" He flung the order at them with the sharp arrogance and inhuman assurance that so arouses resentment in the civilian who witnesses a professional officer about his duties. The flick of this order, devoid of any sympathy that might have abetted the weakening of their strength, restored these men in measurable degree to the exacting world of steel and regulation in which they belonged, and in which, under the assurance of this superior being's tone, all still was well. They lined up, rifle butts planted firmly in the fleshlike muck under their feet.

"Atten . . . tion! . . . Count Off!"

"One, two, three, four . . . One, two, three, four . . ."

"Front! . . . Right by Squads . . . For . . . ward . . . March!"

Far in the murky, horror-tainted entrails of the world, their serried bayonets flashing in the torchlight, the detachment marched forward, its slim officer poised aggressively at the obscurity and mystery ahead.

25 〰〰

As they left the river well behind, the narrow tunnel began to expand so rapidly that they soon found themselves in what appeared to be illimitable space. The visceral dampness gave way to an intense dryness that seemed to have turned the very air into dust. The smooth powder underfoot swirled up about them to form a great, rotund cloud in which the torch flames, now small distinct spirts devoid of illumination, leant steadily backward as in a still mist. Their numerous feet striking in heavy unison seemed to beget only a blurred "puff, puff, puff." The dust mixed with the perspiration on their faces, necks and hands to cover them with a finely textured mud.

It appeared to them that they were marching across a vast plain in hazy night. Actually, it was darker than it had been in the passage, for now the light from the torches had no walls to confine and reflect it; but it felt less dark, as if there were a pervading, nocturnal glimmer through which they could not see. There was an illusion of the sky being somewhere above them, and now and then a marching man would bend back his head as if straining to find a star or the glimmering delineation of a far horizon.

26 〰〰

They had been marching a long way it seemed, doggedly, knees a little bent as the plain tilted upward, heads bowed with growing fatigue. The dead world through which they marched seemed greedy to suck away their strength, to turn them into the drooping, albino things one finds growing in darkness. It made them silent.

Too, the sound of a voice, when it came, was so empty and lost that it intimidated them. The hill they were climbing grew steeper; then suddenly they were going down the other side. Without an order they stopped.

"Rest," said Lieutenant Fitzpatrick.

Huddled together there in the darkness, beneath the unseen dome of a blind sky, on top of this high, pale, powdery hill at the tenebrous core of a buried universe, they unconsciously ringed themselves in with pointed bayonets. They held futile torches out into the gloom, sought to pierce it with long, fixed stares.

"I wish to hell we was gettin' back to the ship," said Wright softly, running his hand over his pimply face and through his straw-coloured hair. His hand felt strange in the slime of dust and sweat that mired his head. He absently pulled his hand down near a torch and looked at it.

"Him wants to get back to mama," essayed Hardwood loudly, trying to mimic a child. His negroid voice seemed to spurt down from somewhere, thin, muffled and weird, its attempt at caricature redistorted. For an instant, men at some distance from Hardwood, not recognizing the sound, opened their eyes wide and gripped their rifles tighter. There was not even a shadow of laughter.

"Cruck." Lieutenant Fitzpatrick spoke sharply.

"Here, Sir."

"Take a look at this compass."

Using the top of his stiff, white cap, laid on the dust, as a miniature table, the officer displayed a small, pocket instrument at which he had been glancing as he marched along. Beside it he laid a pad of paper.

"You see, I've tried to sketch our course here since we left the mouth of the cave."

As Cruck peered down through the flicker of a torch, drops of muddy perspiration spotted the top of the hat and the sheet of paper. With a preoccupied gesture the Chief Boatswain's Mate briefly raised his big head and tried to shake it free of the moisture.

"Yes, Sir."

"The lubber-line lies with the flow of the river as we left it."

"Yes, Sir."

174

Lieutenant Fitzpatrick stuck the point of the pencil on the piece of paper.

"And here we are now."

The men crowded forward about the pencil point, stared down intently at the mark it made. Some of them straightened up to look hopefully from that mark around into the inert, surrounding gloom.

"I want you," continued Lieutenant Fitzpatrick, "to take five men and march at right angles to our present course," he pointed the direction with his arm, "until you come to the wall of this place in that direction. Look along the wall both ways and then come back and report. Understand?"

His big blunt finger-nails fumbling slowly at the top of his scalp, Cruck said once more, but with a kind of aggressive uncertainty:

"Yes, Sir."

"If you get out of sight, the glow of our torches above us will mark our position. Don't lose that."

Cruck stood for a moment looking down at the compass and piece of paper as if these were the last, vanishing fragments of a familiar and regretted shore-line. There was no sound, no movement. Then:

"Ferguson!" Cruck's voice was challenging.

As if this summons were a tricky and personal affront, Ferguson made a deliberate jerk with both hands at the top of his trousers, spat truculently at the vague dust and stepped clear of the others.

"Here!"

"Forsythe!"

"Here."

"Saunders!"

"Here." He reluctantly stepped out to join the other two.

"Horner! . . . and Ragatzo!"

"Here," came the uneven chorus of the two voices.

"Let's go."

The six men suddenly tramped straight out into the unnatural night without a look behind. The others stood staring after them with eyes that were troubled with concern.

"Sit down and take it easy," said Lieutenant Fitzpatrick.

A few sat or lay down in the dust; but all eyes continued to watch the slowly fading glare in the distance. Just before the little group had dropped from sight beneath the cloudy reflection of its torches, it had glowed for a moment, sharp, clearly delineated, miniature, atop a far-off knoll like a squad of tin soldiers caught by a livid gust of light.

There was no taking it easy. Lying there in the fine, soft dust, their feeling of being in a mysterious and unnatural place piled up about them like a smothering mound of the strange dust in which they lay. As if the thought had been spoken and all emphatically had agreed on it, the idea fastened itself in each man's mind that the only possible thing to do now was to go back. Their restlessness increased. They became unhealthily conscious of their skins, their ears, their armpits. Apparently, the only thing holding them from starting back at once was the absent reconnoitring party, and they concentrated their whole attention on its possible manoeuvring and imminent return. Orlop, the tall, dapper Chief Gunner's Mate, got to his feet and stared in the direction of the place where he last had observed the glow of Cruck's party. Little wisps of dust, like smoke, slowly drifted down from about his body. He shaded his staring eyes with his hand. Other men on the ground, observing his action, arose and gazed also.

"I don't see them any more," Orlop said.

A quick, portentous murmur swept the men.

"I see them," said Lieutenant Fitzpatrick definitely.

He did see them; but the glow was now but a thin, flat blur, very faint in the distance.

"Make a bunker lamp fast to the tip of a bayonet and set the rifle up on that rifle stack," ordered Lieutenant Fitzpatrick, "It'll give them a better bead on us."

27 〰〰〰

The far darkness, across which one of Cruck's men nostalgically swept his eyes, suddenly was pricked by a rising point of light.

"Look," he said, "they must be comin'."

Like a great, ill-humoured rat looking for a hole, Cruck had fumbled along the smooth, precipitous wall for two or three hundred yards in each direction. Now he swung about and stared at the point of light belligerently.

"Naw. It don't move. It must be a recall," he said.

"They've got a Very pistol," said Ferguson.

"Yea, but this means *something*," insisted Cruck in a tone carrying with it the implication that he would brook no interference whatsoever in this.

He was fed up with stumbling along this wall. Anyhow, he had carried out his orders. There were no openings or anything else. "That light," he told himself, "was gonna be recall whether it meant that or not."

28 〰️

Lieutenant Fitzpatrick observed with satisfaction the rising glow in the distance that indicated the return of Cruck's party. He shared silently the exclamations of relief that popped around amongst the men as they also observed this sign. He sensed that this feeling of relief involved not only the safe return of Cruck's party, and the relaxation of the curious emotion twisting at the members of a group that has been forced apart, but also the feeling that now the whole detachment would start back out of the cave. Probably he sensed this because he was experiencing the tug of the feeling himself. As Cruck's party rejoined, there was a clamour of profane celebration, blurred eerily by the cavernous environment. The officer's participation in this was a smile and an instinctive turning to his friend Warrington. Their eyes met through the sombre, shifting glow in a brief, gay glance.

Sharply, the officer ceased smiling and looked away as if he had caught himself off-guard. He struggled constantly now to keep the open play of their relationship confined to the watches on the bridge. Although he invariably took Warrington with him when he led the Landing Party ashore, he tried meticulously to preserve the same attitude toward him that he maintained toward each of the other enlisted men. Somehow he could not bring himself to leave Warrington behind. He told himself that "that would be leaning over backwards"; but what deeply impelled him was, in part, the foreknowledge of the distress that such a measure certainly would inflict upon Warrington. Moreover, he found repugnant the expedient of explaining the necessity for such a course to him, found something tainting in that prospect, something clandestine and esoteric that the spoken words of such an explanation would evoke and admit. He preferred the impossible compromise of confining the active life of their proscribed friendship to the hours on the bridge and attempting to preserve as hiatuses the periods that stretched between, safe, static stretches in which their relationship would neither die nor live. That Warrington understood his effort did not seem to save the boy from being wounded by it. Each time the officer, in a moment of forgetfulness, looked at his friend as a friend, he would find in his eyes a clear, cerebral resignation to the necessity; but deep beyond this was an eagerness, a welcome, and a resentment as well, the perception of which poignantly complicated the general stresses that each day seemed more fiercely to be rending the very sanity from the officer's being.

He stood there now, ankle deep in that repulsive dust, dejected, nearly at the end of his physical endurance, fighting down the hysterical threat of his rebellious nerves. With his strength going, he was almost at the mercy of this rebellion. It was not in his nature to dissipate it by probing analysis. For him it was a surface entity in itself, like joy or hate. He apprehended only, as he felt Warrington there, that this was his friend, more disturbingly than anybody ever had been his friend before . . . yet it must not be his friend . . . it must be merely one of these men . . . these men for whose lives he was responsible . . . buried here in this ghastly place . . . They wanted to get back to the living world . . . so did he . . . but he must push them on . . . deeper . . . deeper . . . to the end . . . What did it matter anyway? . . . The ship was broken down . . . every turn of the screw might be the last . . . the first bit of weather would finish her . . . or those Jap cruisers, hunting, hunting, hunting . . . even if she held up and no typhoon came . . . even if the Japs didn't get her . . . he wouldn't be able to keep her off the hiding dangers of that malignant shore . . . the whole west coast of Palawan shimmered before his eyes in liquid realistic relief . . . beneath the surface of the purple water dodged and stabbed a multitude of sneering, jagged spearheads . . . he was only kidding himself and the ship . . . he could never get her through . . . one of those lurking spearheads would find her . . . she was doomed . . . God! . . . they were all doomed . . . It was hard to breathe here . . . it wasn't air . . . it was some kind of horrible dust . . . and he was breathing the stench and smoke from the burnt paraffin . . . that's what he was breathing . . . pressure . . . pressure . . . pressure! . . . day and night . . . day and night . . . pressure . . . it was filling up this lost gut of the world like crushing gas . . . it was compressing his skull . . . his chest . . . he was being burst in! . . . he was going to burst in a great, screaming explosion . . . he could feel it starting from his stomach . . . it was at his chest! . . . he gripped at his chest hard with both hands trying to hold it . . . it was at his throat! . . .

"There's nothing there, Mr. Fitzpatrick, except blank wall . . . We went along it for about two hundred yards each way from the point we struck it . . . It runs about parallel with the course we been travelling."

"Fall In," said the officer.

"We're going back, ain't we, Mr. Fitzpatrick?" ventured Petrie.

"Let's go," said the officer, ignoring the question.

He swung mechanically around and headed for the wall from which the reconnoitrers just had returned. He held one of the torches at about the level of his knee and his head was bowed. His eyes were following the disturbance in the dust left by Cruck's party. Less man now than years of drill and indoctrination, the officer was marching heavily, mechanically to the beat that rose in his mind . . . "hateful mission . . . hideous tomb . . ."

The men drew together and watched him tramp off into the darkness in a direction that crushed their conviction that they now were going back. They were aghast, almost enraged.

"Gee, Mr. Fitzpatrick," called out Ferguson, "I'll be a son of a bitch if there's ever been anybody in here."

Through the ensuing moments of silence they stared in terrible reluctance at the fateful flicker and blur of their officer's form slowly assuming distance.

"Come on . . . You bastards!" ground out Cruck.

Heavily averse, the mob of men moved slowly forward. Their shoulders were hunched, their knees bent, as if they were bucking an elastic, yielding obstacle.

"What time is it?" asked Wright. His voice had a stertorous, plaintive quality.

"What the hell do you care? You ain't goin' no place," said Hardwood.

"Keep yer God damn traps shut!" raged Cruck.

They began to progress a little faster. Orlop, the Chief Gunner's Mate, and "Unc" Blood, the Chief Quartermaster, moved ahead through the gloom and overtook Lieutenant Fitzpatrick. To the men who had formed Cruck's reconnoitring party the climbing and descending march along the ridge now seemed much longer than when they had made it before.

At the wall, Lieutenant Fitzpatrick stopped. He gazed at the smooth, scabrous surface before him. Holding high his torch, he let his eyes follow the wall up to where it dissolved in the equivocal night. Then his gaze came down to where the wall stretched relentlessly on ahead.

"Where to now, Mr. Fitzpatrick?" asked the Chief Gunner's Mate. The tall man always spoke suavely and with good humour.

"I want to follow the wall as far as it goes, then follow it back on the other side to where the boats are."

Orlop stepped forward and began to march along the base of the wall. "Unc" Blood, his beard thick with the mud of sweat and dust, trudged after him. Cruck and the crowd of men, slogging through the dust as if it were deep snow, were almost upon the officer before he too began to move again. Every now and then Cruck would turn around, walking backward for a few steps, and glare at the massed sway of faces struggling close in his wake beneath the flat ruddy cloud of smoky torch light. They glared back at him as if fiercely reflecting the aspersion in his stare.

Marching steadily on and on, pressed unremittingly against this smooth, pale, unending wall to the left as if by the unliving violence of the sick, lunar void to the right, the massed marching slowly became the only manifestation of their beings. Heads down, often with their eyes closed, their thoughts, their voices, their very personalities became dissolved in the entity of the marching. They became a clot of heavy, hypnotic liquid, alive only with idiot movement, seeping through the arid murk.

They would have marched forever, now, in this manner, through this vast, nihilistic smother, until they dropped unnoticed one by one, slowly to be absorbed and covered there by this bottomless sediment of patterned nothingness through which they struggled.

All at once those in the lead sensed that the wall on their left was no longer there. Another wall loomed before them. Automatically they stopped. Like dim echoes of far sounds, Lieutenant Fitzpatrick's thoughts were shouting spasmodically: . . . "This is the other wall . . . the place narrows here."

The spot that marked the furthermost limit of the void in which they had been marching, the rotund angle to which it narrowed, was pitted by a stark, vertical slit about as tall as a man and as broad as three. Its edges seemed to reach and quiver in the shadowy, red glare cast by the torches. In calm delirium Lieutenant Fitzpatrick surveyed the hole; then he walked into it. With a cumbrous lurch the clot of men resumed its marching. To penetrate the narrow passage the mass had to attenuate. This slowly began to restore its submerged units to individuality. Men here and there raised their heads, used their eyes and sniffed alertly like startled animals. The wispy air in the passage seemed to feel for them, fumble about their ankles, their hands, their faces, their necks, then steal past them. It was moist, odourless, bestial.

They became conscious of a persisting sound, an indistinct but immense, gurgling rush. Resonant and oppressive, it turned the thin passage into a living tube suffering monstrous strangulation. The men themselves seemed unable to breathe. They had difficulty in commanding their feet. Some pawed roughly at their throats, clutched at the close walls to keep from tumbling. They were drenched with sweat. Their eye-balls appeared to stretch and protrude painfully in the torch light now revivified by sudden confinement. The passage narrowed. The ceiling gradually closed in upon them. Their miserable desperation expanded, pounded at the contracting walls, grew vague, tenuous, but not less poignant.

181

They strove forward as against a barely resistible, repelling force.

Suddenly the three in the lead jerked to a stop. They held themselves rigid, then bent over something at their feet, their bodies leaning in tense curves. More men slowly crowded up from behind. There in the firm, hardly impressible substance underfoot was the imprint of a boot.

Thin, stabbing, electrical currents, eerie and breath destroying, rained against their loins, their wrists, their lungs. The pits of their stomachs dissolved, became painful space.

The print was like nothing they ever had seen before. With its sharp, pointed toe, flaring sole and small, deep heel, it was both brutal and womanish. There was only one.

Lieutenant Fitzpatrick raised his eyes and glared in the funnelling darkness ahead. His throat began to beat in giant throbs that jarred rhythmically the sick pain at the top of his head. Groping with his pistol before him, he crept forward, cringing over the stony surface close to the wall, away from the ugly, firm clay in which that print glistened, insolent and otherworldly.

Men fell to all fours, dragging their weapons after them, like prognathous animals clawing and battling forward to undefeated death. Their breathing came in ugly gasps. They were covered with sweat and pale dust-mud that turned them to the colour of the walls. The noise, jittering like the drums of a monstrous rumba, the ever-increasing tenseness, the slick, sucking surface up which they crawled, the fluttering current of air, all seemed to merge in the leprous darkness before them and push them back. Two yards forward . . . three more . . . Lieutenant Fitzpatrick in the lead had ceased moving . . . He was stretched, stiff and ominous, on his stomach with his chin thrust forward as if he were staring fiercely. As they held there, they realized that the noise had changed. It seemed to pour straight up now, clearer, heavier, more insistent. Without moving his head, Lieutenant Fitzpatrick slowly reached back and fumbled for the arm of the man behind him who held a torch. The man gave it up as if against his will. The officer stuck the torch out before him. Like a fatal, ritualistic gesture, this called into shadowy being, there a few yards in front of them, an uneven gash of a chasm brimming with thick, black swirls of tortured liquid. On the bank of the chasm was a boat.

Lieutenant Fitzpatrick dropped the torch, retrieved the pistol from his left hand and rearing back on his knees raised the weapon before him. In slipping, blundering ferocity, the men massed up at his back. Their eyes stabbed at the blank wall that ended the passage . . . at the torrent at its foot . . . at the surface to the left from which the liquid sprang . . . over the surface to the right into which it disappeared. Nothing . . . nothing . . . only the boat, lonely and formidable in the gloom.

Lieutenant Fitzpatrick fastened his gaze on the boat. The intensity of his concentration brought his tormented consciousness up to a fever of attention as a blast of air drives nearly expended embers to incandescence. It took all his being, all of him that was stricken with the horror of isolation in these slimy buried depths, all of him that smouldered with despair over the disasters that threatened his ship and his personal world, and drove it into the grim outlines of that mysterious, small boat.

Glowing there, a precise phantom, the boat struggled with his attention like something on the horizon that barely escapes identification. High of bow and even higher of square stern, the quality of the short craft drifted over him, took hold of his driven and lacerated sensibilities, called poignantly to his sense of recognition.

He crept closer. Strange as the boat was, it was not Asiatic; every line of its form protested that. It came to him dimly that in some inexplicable way this boat was what he was, that it, too, was an alien in these hideous depths, clutched horribly in black, intangible destruction.

Closer still . . . there was a name on the stern . . . it was a ship's boat! Cruck was staring over his shoulder. Their bodies moving in weird unison, they leaned precipitously in the direction of their gazing, as if their very flesh was striving to pour itself into the effort at seeing. The faint, barely clinging words were words formed of the alphabet they knew. That was certain. The question of that never even arose in them as an explanation of the illegibility. A name, a name that they could almost read, that tantalized them with the impression that it would be familiar if it could be made out. They moved closer. Still the words blurred there, illegible, as if glimpsed down a vista of obscurity. The officer seized a torch and held it a bare yard from the words. Hanging there like shadows of letters, they formed a half-forgotten name in the mind, maddeningly on the tip of the tongue.

Through the dusk and horror of this last, innermost recess, through the malevolent, breathless tension and the aura of stricken bodies, Cruck, grinding his teeth, flung his heavy body up in a gesture of final, catastrophic impatience and lunged forward. The crowd of men flinched down, as if such a movement would provoke some occult horror. Cruck loomed for a moment over the boat, his head bent truculently towards its stern. The distinct yet indistinct words still evaded him. To jerk the stern of the boat around into the light, his arms shot out and roughly seized it by both gunwales. The boat, down the whole of its unspeakably ancient length, crumpled like a morsel of delicate ash into dust.

Chapter
Three

1 ∼∼∼

At about the moment that Cruck laid hold of the small boat in the cave, the Captain, on board Delilah, received a radio message that lanced instantaneously the deadly gather of tensions oppressing the ship. Without explanation, the message informed the Captain that danger from the Japanese cruisers no longer was to be expected. Also, Delilah was detached from the duty of searching for the gun-runners and was to proceed, at the discretion of her Commanding Officer, to Cavite for the repairs requested. It was relief, poignant delighting relief, rather than surprise, that rose through the Captain as he read this message. It was as if there never had been in his mind any question but that the relief would come, as if his distress had been merely a matter of its persistent and perverse delay. Now he could head his ship straight away from this hateful coast-line, in the secure light of day, taking shelter as he pleased if he scented threatening weather, or if that shaft began to cut up too badly. Not even what some might consider the flaw in the relieving message impaired his delight. It would mean only a few hours more. That was nothing after what they had gone through. The message instructed him to stop in at Romblon on his way and take aboard the body of an Army Officer who had died there.

Ensign Woodbridge had helped him decode the message, had exclaimed, with a long exhalation of breath, "Thank God for small favours!" and had then lain down on his bunk and fallen swiftly and quietly asleep. With the message in his hand, the Captain climbed up to the quarter-deck; but Ensign Snell was asleep too, dozing patiently, with that extreme patience that characterized him as much as did his laugh. His heavy, white-encased legs were stretched straight out from his chair across the red deck, the weight of his big white shoes resting on the edge of the heels, and his head was thrown back, with his arms bent across his face. Every now and then the wicker chair emitted a crackling murmur under the breathing of his heavy body. The Captain stood looking down at him for a few seconds as if considering waking him up; then he walked around the torpedo-tube and sat down himself. The only outward sign of the Captain's impatience to take advantage of the message was evidenced in his quiet, occasional scrutinies of the beach where the boats had landed. For each of these scrutinies he would walk all the way forward to the bridge before as much as glancing in the direction of the shore; and once there he would focus his binoculars with unusual care as if some unnatural difficulty were to be expected in piercing the thin brightness of the space intervening.

These visits by the Captain to the bridge aroused Arnold, the Quartermaster on watch, to a point of restless competition. "What the hell! . . . The Old Man knows I'll get it to him the minute those birds show as much as a hair over there." He would, he swore to himself, spot them before the Captain did. But, in the end, it was the Captain who sighted them first.

The boats suddenly appeared in the little channel leading from the cave pool to the sea. Men leapt from them, shouting and exuberant, to run wildly up and down the beach. Some of them literally danced, flinging their arms up in wild gestures of freedom towards the sky. Others just walked away from the boats onto the land with an air of finality, in the manner of men walking away from the climax of some punishing and exhausting physical effort.

Cruck, his little eyes blinking and his short brutal nostrils flexing tentatively, stood with his legs spread and pounded his deeply breathing chest with his two fists as if he were exercising. Between Lieutenant Fitzpatrick and Warrington, standing almost face to face, there flamed a smiling glance of intimate celebration.

On the ship, the Captain's mouth, too, was smiling broadly beneath his binoculars levelled on the outburst ashore. In the first moments, against the background of his own knowledge of release, the turbulent rejoicing in the distance seemed to need no explanation. He turned his back, not at all on the scene on the beach but on the fabulous beauty of the repellent land that held it, and, with utter relief, said to Arnold:

"Hoist the recall."

2 ≈≈≈

The Captain's news of release, spreading rapidly through the ship in one form or another, affecting especially the sensibilities of those who had been projected into the ecstasy of relaxation on returning out of the cave, seemed to absorb the ship and the men in a soft, clear solvent of slack weariness. Delilah appeared to drift effortlessly along an undefined groove in the sea, her illness dormant, the threat somehow gone from her pounding shaft, her perverse and sensitive will bemused. The sounds of her swaying progress through the smooth water were lost in soothing regularity and rhythm; and in the daytime the heat of her personal fires, even her dominant body odour of heated metal, seemed to lose identity amidst the fiery brightness of the calm world in which she relaxed. It appeared as if the crew simply permitted her to go her own way; and it was as if by accident that she encountered Romblon Island, drifted past the long reefs shimmering in beautiful patterns just beneath the surface of the transparent sea, through the narrow entrance, and came to rest almost in the centre of the tiny harbour's round, deep tranquillity.

This harbour was embedded in a circle of high, wild hills smothered under jungle that was intimidatingly luxuriant; and the village, a precise blur of stilted nipa houses, seemed barely able to preserve itself from the excesses of the sporelike vegetation towering about it. A stone cathedral, yellow-grey, startlingly over-sized, leaned out of the village toward the harbour like one of the distorted churches in Russian paintings.

It was from somewhere in this cathedral that they carried down the body of the Army Officer, twelve barefoot little men distributed around a hastily carpentered coffin, trotting calmly along through vistas of shade, the marvel of cool shade in the tropics, toward the beach. They placed the coffin on a large outrigger canoe and, with some of the bearers squatting along the limbs of the outrigger to steady it, paddled across the water to Delilah.

The crew stood around unceremoniously, but with their hats off, while Cruck, Petrie, Ferguson and Wright took careful grips on the coffin and hoisted it aboard. They experienced a flurry of difficulty at the last moment and Cord, the Boilermaker, although he was not expected to interfere in the duties of the deck force, stepped forward and bent to their assistance his tall, very thin frame, which, with its solemn, narrow, Saxon face and profusion of straight, blond hair, presented a somehow humorous aspect.

Some of the men watching his assistance there realized for the first time, although he had been with the ship for years, what a remarkable man he really was. He knew much about boilers that decidedly lay beyond the pale of practical mechanics and in the realm of educated, theoretical engineering; but in some unobstructive way he managed to escape the prestige of this, to transform the substance of his theory into the matter of the everyday practical mechanics. He was like a country doctor who seemed to prescribe nothing but castor oil, but who impregnated his treatments, as one found by looking into it, with the abstrusities of Johns Hopkins and the Rockefeller Institute. The possibility of excitement to the slightest degree seemed incredible in the Boilermaker. He was never known, even once, to have had an altercation, and he presented an appearance of unpointed detachment, not only from the life of the ship but from the very life of the world, that was complete. There always was a faint taint of droll self-depreciation about the expression of his face; and his weapon for meeting most crises was a slight, childlike smile, not the defensive smile of the Jew, but a passing movement of droll good humour. On his upper lip he wore a pale miniature of a Norseman's drooping mustache.

When the coffin had been carried aft to the quarter-deck and placed there on a cot alongside the torpedo-tube, on the starboard side, just where once the monk had tried to rest, Cord returned with the four deckhands to the outrigger and helped unload the *papayas* and mangoes with which the spaces of the canoe beneath the coffin had been packed, a gift from local authority to the ship;

and then he had stepped back into the crowd of spectators as if he had had no part in this event.

With the coffin securely aboard, Delilah waited only on the return of Lieutenant Fitzpatrick, who was making an official visit ashore, to steam back out through the channel and resume her northward passage. The arrival of the dead man in the ship had ended the extreme relaxation, had precipitated them all into a quiet, normal functioning and awareness; but an awareness in which there still was no fear of the time ahead, no restlessness about the weather, nor about the possibility of total breakdown. When they looked into their officers' faces the men saw there little more disturbing than fatigue. Now they merely were men taking their ship back to Cavite to be repaired.

When Lieutenant Fitzpatrick was sighted coming down the narrow dock, the order was given to weigh anchor; and very shortly after the officer arrived alongside in the whaleboat, bearing a long, brown envelope and an armful of small, weird, white flowers for the Wardroom table, Delilah was steaming slowly for the entrance. Then the men let down the folding tables from under the awnings and, as if labouring under the delusion that they had not had a regular meal in days, ate great quantities of fried chicken, fried potatoes, stewed canned corn and the *papayas* that had come in the outrigger with the dead man. Only the men eating at the tables on the starboard side gave any sign that they felt his presence aboard. Once or twice a man slowly stopped eating and stared aft towards the quarter-deck. After such a glance, Hardwood swung himself slightly to the right on the bench so that his back was turned definitely to the direction in which he had glanced.

Lights, warm and golden bright, but as yet without illumination, sparked into steady glow throughout the ship. Night imperceptibly was draining the vividness from the long evening. One by one, as they finished eating, men got up and left the supper tables. They moved slowly, almost carefully, as if they consciously were balancing the packed globes of food in their torsos, as if they knew that all the energies and juices of their bodies had been conscripted to deal with their loaded stomachs. Orlop, the tall Chief Gunner's Mate, had paused at the railing. He was gazing down in pleasant torpidity at the water-line, watching the guard rail sway steadily beneath the water and then above it . . . down . . . up . . . down . . . up . . . then in barely willed casualness he permitted his eyes to lift from this rearward slipping edge of water that flipped at the ship's side. His gaze drifted his consciousness on and on out through the vast, vague evening tint that filled the universe and absorbed the sea, until, far, far away there, his gaze and his inert being were blurred, dissolved, lost . . . A faint cloud of tobacco smoke wafted across his face. He turned his head. A few paces forward along the rail Hemple, the Machinist's Mate, was smoking his pipe. He too was staring into the soft, desolate, amethystine depths that still seemed day. His large, solid-looking head was thrust slightly forward in the direction of his gaze, and despite his mature, commonplace figure with its paunch, the healthy vulgarity of his firm, rounded face and the down-to-earth quality that pervaded his plenitude of coarse, dark hair, he somehow seemed pitiful and alone standing there in this fashion gazing into infinity. Orlop let go of the railing's top cable and absently glanced at the palms of his hands. The cable had felt greasy with salt. Hemple, as if this movement near him had reached out and brought him back to the ship, turned his head and looked at Orlop. These two thoroughly ordinary men stared at each other for a second, glanced back out into the immensity, looked at each other again, and smiled. Remembering the perspiration that had clung about his face as he ate at the table, Orlop lifted the back of his hand to his forehead. His forehead felt dry and pleasant. The two men moved nearer to each other along the rail.

"Damn fine," said Orlop.

"I didn't notice it before," said Hemple, taking in deeper breaths as if to savour the breeze to which he referred.

"It's going to be a fine night for sleeping," said Orlop.

"I wish it was time to put the cots down," said Hemple.

This wish seemed to have pervaded the ship. It was as if it were a part of the slight, steady breeze that just barely was fragrant of the distant islands across which it was passing. Men appeared only to be killing time until they could turn in for the night.

Cruck stomped in a very leisurely manner about the deck fumbling with little details here and there, tidying up, much as if a persistent storm had denied to him, up until these tranquil moments, the opportunity for this business. Others sat about in the forecastle, with the breeze blowing in through the open port-holes, sewing, reading or playing cards.

Ensign Snell stepped through the After Conning-tower entrance onto the quarter-deck. He stood there for a long moment in the gathering darkness looking peacefully, heavily about. He looked at the victrola, then at the coffin sleeping in sombre self-possession on the cot. A flicker of something indefinite but alert travelled through him. Then he relapsed, as by an act of will, into his peaceful, unseeing gazing about . . . at the wake . . . at the torpedo-tube . . . forward, past the conning-tower, along the deck. His gaze was held by the distant bulk of the forecastle, alive with patches of electric light. He strolled forward. On going as far in that direction as the engine-room hatches he encountered a robust murmur of talk and laughter that drifted down in careless bursts from somewhere up on the forecastle. He climbed the ladder to that deck and came upon Arnold overhauling signal flags, the rack for which was at the brink of the forecastle. It was almost dark now and Arnold was working in the rectangle of light cast from the open door of the radio shack, before which several men were squatting, talking with him and Portness, the Radio Electrician. The latter was on duty at his instrument, sitting there with his headphones askew so that one ear was free to listen to the conversation of his friends. They all stood up as Ensign Snell paused.

"Sit down, for Christ's sake," muttered the officer with what an alien in the ship might have taken for an abashed manner. He took out a Fatima and lit it behind his cupped hands. The men kept their faces turned to him, grinning respectfully in complete, sympathetic friendliness.

"Why don't you go aft and get the victrola?" asked the officer at the end of a considerable silence.

Ragatzo and one of the Carey brothers jumped to their feet in precipitate acceptance of the offer. They were already going down the ladder before the exclamatory murmur of surprise and pleasure had run its course amidst the group of men. Half-way down the deck, Ragatzo said to Carey:

"He's a swell guy."

"He's the whitest son of a bitch that ever wore a gold stripe."

Abreast of the After Conning-tower, they came to a dead stop, shoulder to shoulder, as if they had collided with a soft but repulsing barrier in the darkness that had finally settled upon the sea and the throbbing ship. Their eyes were fixed on the coffin. Then slowly, on tip toe, they moved up to the victrola and unlashed it. Ragatzo carried it forward. Carey pulled two handfuls of records from the chest and hurried after him. As Ragatzo went up the forecastle ladder with the victrola, Hardwood, scrubbing clothes beneath the electric light bulb in the washing space, hooted after him:

"You all look like you seen a ghost."

"Crazy bastard!" Ragatzo muttered fiercely under his breath.

He placed the victrola on top of the signal flag rack and indiscriminately selected the top record of the pile that Carey laid on the deck. There was no awning over this section of the ship, and the breeze, suddenly shifting for an instant in a strong puff from aft, swirled down about the group there, still uncomfortable with the reminder in Hardwood's shouted gibe at Ragatzo, a cloud of acrid fumes and cinders from the nearby funnel. Even after the breeze had shifted to its former direction they kept hawking and spitting as if they could not get the stench out of their throats and nostrils. Ragatzo blew the cinders off the disc and set it playing. Ensign Snell leant against the side of the Radio Shack, Portness resumed his seat before the instrument and those who had been squatting on the deck relaxed there again.

Up on the bridge, where he was standing the Eight-to-Midnight Quartermaster Watch, Warrington was leaning, motionless and waiting, against the wind-breaker. He felt himself to be a victim of some peculiar quality in the deepening night, attributing to it his poignant restlessness. The breeze, warm, caressing, delicately scented, did not calm him. It seemed, rather, to combine with the living, reciprocative swaying of the ship in preparing his being for the disturbance that possessed it. He felt as if he were at the bottom of the transparent, blue-black night and resisting the necessity to plunge up through it for relief, wildly up through it past the stars that cascaded in arrested torrents toward the soft, metallic line of the horizon. Like dense, black velvet the sea smoothed away in every direction from the phosphorescent swath Delilah was cutting through it, parting in two even billows of flickering green flame before the knife of her bow, flashing along her sides, trailing back into the infinity of her wake, a contrast, cold, alluring and unearthly, to the red glow above the smokestacks. It gave Warrington satisfaction to glance back now and then at this glow above the smokestacks, this glow of a fire that could consume and burn through even the smothering beauty of the night; but it did not steady the unevenness of his breathing nor quiet the torment of his waiting . . . waiting . . . *that* was what this desperate feeling was . . . a kind of waiting, not with the expectancy of the something splendid in the far future, but disturbingly for something now . . . imminent . . . something just as unidentifiable, yet something that also was climactic, fulfilling.

The melody from the victrola below, as if the restless night itself had summoned it, rose to colour and define his torment. He said to himself: "They must have borrowed the victrola from aft . . . that's that *Song Without Words* . . . What's the matter with me anyhow . . . with him?" He knew that Lieutenant Fitzpatrick, across the bridge there, was as restless as he in this moment; yet here they were together, his cherished friend and he . . . with everything as it always had been in their best watches together . . . talking until there had seemed nothing more to say . . . He made a frantic gesture of impatience that was almost completely internal . . . but he continued to stand there waiting . . . waiting . . . And nothing sustained occurred to divert them, to help them, no slightest business of sighting a ship or a light, nothing, until the commotion around the coffee and cornedbeef sandwiches, set down near the Forward Fire-room Hatch to fortify the oncoming watch, aroused them to prepare for their reliefs. They simply had stood there silently on the bridge of this thin, dark ship swaying through the perfumed night with a corpse on the quarter-deck, stood there, desperate with imminence, staring ahead into the deep sky at strange, low stars, bright, implacable and pure.

3 〰〰〰

When Delilah steamed past Corregidor Island into Manila Bay, tied up alongside the dock at the Cavite Naval Base and discharged the coffin, a few naval people remarked casually, "I see Delilah came in today." Once or twice somebody troubled to make negligent answer to the effect that, "Yes, she's been down south after the body of an Army Officer." Delilah, however, in her own view had steamed triumphantly into harbour, surrounded by the aura of a dauntless victory over wounds and ordeal. Her men, when they went ashore on their first liberty, assumed that peculiar, modest manner of men who have behaved very well in a dangerous and exacting crisis. They had unconsciously settled into an emotional arrangement on sighting Corregidor that somehow, as far as it concerned the outside world, was based on the assumption that that outside world knew and felt as much about their long expedition south as they did. They actually would not have been surprised if they had been called upon to parade through streets lined with people cheering approval and admiration: But most of the people they met did not even know that their ship had been south. This vacuum in the attitude of these people where Delilah's men, without saying so or thinking about it, had expected a positive plenty, made them vaguely indignant: And the people whom they encountered were irritated, on their part, by this inexplicable quality that tinctured the destroyer's crew. The crew was like a college football player who, falling into the idea that he was in a vital game, had run seventy miraculous yards with a broken rib, only to find, when he staggered up to be helped heroically off the field, that the stands contained not a single person.

A few, such as Cruck, Ferguson and Saunders, found it particularly difficult to adjust their expectancy to what it met, and finally, although they would have been outraged if this had been explained to them, attempted to satisfy this expectancy with public attention earned by new and irrelevant feats. Ashore together on the afternoon of the first liberty party, Cruck, Ferguson and Saunders seemed to sense something disregarding and inhospitable in Cavite's principal street as they strolled along with its trickle of natives, Chinamen, Navy people and dowdy American civilians; and almost as if seeking shelter from this strange bleakness of the angular, sun-baked thoroughfare, the usual mercantile street of little sea ports bequeathed by the Spaniards to tropical countries, they turned into the dusk of a drinking place. They stood for a moment, almost posing, just within the doorway. No one in the crowd there noticed them except an acquaintance of Cruck's, a Machinist's Mate off a submarine, who waved cordially and turned back to the glass of beer on his table. Cruck, speaking loudly to the whole room, but ostensibly addressing Saunders and Ferguson, said something that involved the word, "Delilah," raising and strengthening his enunciation as he pronounced the word. This begot no attention from the crowd in the drinking place. Saunders then replied to him, also using the name, "Delilah," talking in a mumbling manner until he reached the word, which he shouted clearly and distinctly. Not a head turned. For a moment the three stared hard into the long, low-ceilinged room filled with the thin murk of unventilated tobacco smoke, then they swaggered to a table against the middle of the left wall and sat down, talking loudly. They ordered beer. The empty moments before the arrival of the drinks became intolerable in this place that for them was proving as perverse and unsatisfactory as the street. Saunders' gaze, scouting belligerently here and there, caught and held that of a man at the next table. He found himself grinning and asking:

"What ship, sailor?"

"Brooklyn," was the reply. "What ship you off of?"

"Delilah!"

"That's the new transport, ain't it?"

"What the hell navy do you come from?" jeered Cruck angrily.

The tone in which he said this nettled a big Coxswain with the other party. He replied carelessly for his friend:

"What the hell of it?"

Cruck's glare appraised the six or seven men sitting with the big man; then slowly he seemed to dismiss them, and looked down at the glass of beer being set before him. A little beer had slopped over the edge of the glass and formed a puddle about as large as a dollar on the table. Impatiently he flicked at the little puddle with his forefinger. His whole hand got involved with liquid in this gesture. Without thinking he put his wet hand down and gave it a drying stroke across the leg of his white trousers. Such dust and smear as his hand previously had collected, now being dissolved in the beer, wiped off in a long, dark streak on his trouser leg. Looking down and observing this, Cruck put his clenched, uncomfortable hand back upon the table. His coarse nostrils sniffed at the air about him. It was malodorous with that stench peculiar to superficially cleaned bar-rooms in the Orient, of warm matting and stale urine, of Manila tobacco smoke and spilled drink slopped over with crude soap. For Cruck, this always had been a kind of homely fragrance; but now a mysterious feeling of being ridiculous surged through him and brought him to his feet, saying with some fury:

"This place stinks!"

"Aw, sit down," yelled someone from the other side of the room, "you're rockin' the boat!"

A blinding, scorching short-circuit seemed to explode somewhere in the middle of Cruck's body. At one and the same time he was here in this hostile bar-room and back in that boat in the cave being tricked about the tobacco. He kicked the chair over from behind him. At the end of an animal-like, lunging trot, he was behind the big man at the next table who had said, "What the hell of it?" He took a firm grip on the man's black neckerchief with his left hand and swung him around. As the man's face came about, Cruck drove his right fist straight into the centre of it. The man fell to the floor on his back, his knees bent upward like a stricken insect's. The Coxswain's friends stood up and stared down at his face masked by the blood which also was drenching the front of his white jumper. His legs slowly unflexed and straightened out along the damp gritty boards. Then they tried to get at Cruck. He upset their table in front of them. One tripped on a leg of the overturned table and sprawled over it. Saunders, who was now on his feet, kicked him in the throat. People at tables near-by got hastily to their feet and crowded away towards the ends and centre of the room, while those at a distance stood on chairs to see. Ferguson promptly had lunged from his chair to Cruck's side, but he no sooner had arrived there than he had been dropped to his knees by a blow from a man who hurdled the overturned table. In groggy instinctiveness, Ferguson clutched at the flaring ends of the white trouser legs about the ankles planted before him. He jerked them fiercely upward and towards him as he rose again to his feet. The man crashed to the floor in a sitting posture. Ferguson stepped quickly across him, kneeing him accurately on the jaw in the stride of his step. A thin noise was coming through Cruck's teeth as he clung and twisted with his left hand and slugged with his right. This noise was like a wild, steady scream pitched so high that it almost escaped the ear only to slash hor-ribly at nerves buried deep in the body. A kick, then another, drove Cruck to the floor clutching a patch of ripped cloth. He landed nearly on his back in a semi-sitting posture, his fists braced widely on either side of his body, his eyes staring frantical-ly. A beer glass shattered explosively near his right shoulder. A man swung a chair and knocked him flat. Before the chair could land a second time, Saunders had its wielder in a strangle-hold. Cruck rolled his body away with a swift, violent movement, and kept rolling in this convulsive fashion between the tables until he brought up, as if he were a log crashing down a hillside, against the legs of the spectators crowded against the tables on the far side of the centre aisle. There he got to his feet and backed along the aisle to the door, where he stood, his uniform covered with dirt and blood, his knees giving spasmodically, staring semi-conscious-ly in the direction of the fight.

Ferguson, jabbing and hooking effectively as he backed away, was himself half-way to the door when he saw Saunders, pressed against the wall near where they had been sitting, slide helplessly to the floor. A man reached down, clutched Saunders by the un-dershirt where it projected above the V-neck of his white jumper and, as he pulled him up, pounded him in the face. The undershirt gave away. As the man reached down for another hold, Ferguson stopped backing towards the door and charged in again, head down, through the two slugging enemies in front of him. His hurtling, stocky body cleared a tumbled path and felled the man leaning over the disabled Saunders. Two men, one armed with a broken bottle, were making for Cruck, who still stood there unsteadily in the doorway; but now they flung about and leaped for the charging Ferguson. Ferguson kicked at the face of the man he had knocked over, gripped Saunders by the beltline of his trousers and dragged him away along the wall toward the front of the place, upsetting tables behind him as he progressed. His eyes fixed desperately on the doorway as he dragged Saunders along, Ferguson began to shout at regular intervals, wild, sustained cries of defiant need:

"Delilah!" . . . "Delilah!" . . . "Delilah!"

This cry ascended from a dirty, remote drinking place, a summons from the cheap murk of a petty brawl; but a brawl, nevertheless, in which Ferguson and his unconscious friend were facing much of what the individual has faced in many a decisive battle of the world. The shout, rising from his bloody lips with all the terrible lilt of cries heard above the frenzy of a Hastings or a Gettysburg, swept up and down the street outside, arrested the two Carey brothers, who just had left the ship, and pulled Orlop, the Chief Gunner's Mate, out of a nearby restaurant onto the sidewalk. As if it took more than one pulse of the cry to launch them, each paused where he stood there in the street until the cry had rung again and again in their ears; then the two Carey brothers, tall, slim, boisterous men from Tennessee who were viciously effective in a fight, began to run. Orlop, walking deliberately, followed them.

The Carey brothers plunged through the door of the drinking place as if they were crashing it in. Their furious ingress knocked Cruck to the floor and brought them, unseeing in the sudden change of light, deep into the interior and up against the crowd trying to keep clear of the fight. The Careys struck out blindly against the bodies in contact with them . . . "Delilah! . . . Delilah!" . . . It was behind them there on the other side of the room! They swung around and leapt towards it, one after the other, like a man and his vivid shadow in a turmoil of obscurity and danger. Now they could make out the struggle against the wall, a crowded tangle of quick, vicious movement.

Cruck's head had cracked hard on the base of the cashier's cage when the Careys had knocked him down. Almost reflexively now, he pulled himself up once more by clawing at the door jamb. He leant there helplessly, just barely able to raise his arms in front of him as one of the nearby spectators, one of those whom the Carey brothers had struck in the first blind moment of their entrance, jumped at him with swinging fists. As the man's first blow landed, Orlop appeared in the doorway. With movements that seemed somehow leisurely and authoritative in all that frantic cruelty and panic, Orlop pulled the man off Cruck, backed him against the opposite door jamb, measured him there for an instant and then hit him accurately on the point of the jaw. This blow, struck so efficiently, so deliberately, and illuminated as if by a spotlight in the rectangular beam of afternoon sunshine that cut the murk just inside the doorway, seemed to concentrate, for the beholders, the deadly, blood-spattering reality of the violence around them. There ran through the crowd trying to keep clear of the fight a murmur of gathering shock that broke here and there into revolted exclamation, into sadistic cheering; then a girl began to scream, the thin, high, chattering scream of a Malay woman in bewilderment and terror.

A waiter, almost on all fours, darted through the door, paused outside for an instant to look wildly up and down the street for the Marine Patrol, and then started running as if goaded by a savage gust of the mad sounds behind him. Other battle cries arose now, cries as enraged and pleading as the "Delilahs!" that had summoned Orlop and the Carey brothers.

"Brooklyn!" ... "Brooklyn!" ... "Submarines!" ... "Monadnock!" ... "Monadnock!"

A rapidly increasing crowd had gathered in the street. Struggling vainly to see inside, some pressed close up to the doorway. Others, forced to rely only on their ears, massed before the huge screen of matting that served virtually as the front wall of the semi-open place. They had winced back when the woman's scream issued from behind this matting, back still further before the catastrophic sound of an unseen crash that involved glass. From the dark chaos in there hidden by the screen, a man's voice, exigent and horrible with agony, staggered out into the sunny air of the street:

201

"O-o-o!... O-o-o!... My God!... n-n-n!... n-n-n!...
n-n-n!..."

A barefooted, stocky Tagalog, his sun-blackened face twisted
into a truculent mask, leaped forward from the crowd on the sidewalk, reached in and fumbled for a grip on the matting. He gave
a fierce jerk. The screen gave a little. He gripped the edge of it with
both hands and threw his body back with all his might. The great
area of thick matting came completely away with the suddenness
of a storm-ripped sail.

The white glare of the sunlight exploded into the smoky dusk
of the embattled room as if someone had set off in there a monstrous flashlight cartridge. All motion was arrested instantly, paralysed by the mighty impact of the light. The back of the room
seemed to have flashed forward, and the shallow place, cluttered
with dirt and blood and rigid, distorted figures, erect or fallen, was
for a moment like a gigantic peep-show suddenly exposed to the
sun, tawdry, livid, unreal.

"The Patrol!... Patrol!" somebody shouted.

Delilah's men hurled themselves out into the street. Before them
the crowd out there surged away as from a burst of maniacal danger. The six of them, clawing at each other in frenzied cohesion,
clustered briefly on the sidewalk, glaring wildly up and down the
sunny ambush between the two rows of shabby, exotic buildings.
A Marine Patrol was double-timing up the street from the water-
front; another was just rounding a corner in the opposite direction.

"In there," panted Ferguson.

Dragging the almost helpless Saunders with them, they charged
from the street into a narrow dry-goods shop. The Chinaman behind the counter closed his eyes at sight of them and dropped to
the floor. They brought up, staggering with the inertia of their
charge, against the back wall of the store, where their collective
breathing sounded like some unnatural boiling in the cool, cloth-
scented gloom. The two Carey brothers swung around and faced
the front door belligerently. Cruck and Saunders, drunk with
blows, swayed against the counter, holding on to one another's
arms. Saunders kept sniffing at the blood that blocked his nose.
Orlop, his feet slightly spread, stood with bent head and mopped
at his handsome, perspiring face with his handkerchief like a man

who had been outraged but who also was disgusted because he had lost control of himself. Ferguson, the lips in his round, hard, full face tightly pressed together, was pawing and jabbing at the shadow of the back wall. He gave a tug and then a shove. A shaft of diffused daylight bluely tainted the right half of his body.

"Let's go!" he shouted, and they crowded after him out the rear door.

4 〰️

Back aboard ship the next morning with their wounds, they recounted to the rest of the crew what had happened, recounted it in a manner that very definitely crystallized in many a feeling that there really was something wrong in the attitude ashore towards the ship. With all the sincere passion of victims of injustice they told a tale of having been generally slighted, of having been put upon verbally and of finally having been mobbed. That Chief Gunner's Mate Orlop had been with them in the trouble lent to their view of it a respectable colour and a strong support. They could think of no other explanation for this persecution save that the other ships and the Base were jealously resentful.

"Them sons of bitches," said Cruck, "are sore because we showed 'em up. While we was out doin' somethin' they was layin' around on them God damn fake submarines and tin cruisers . . . But we showed 'em!"

Through the Base and in the other ships, news of the fight had spread quickly because it had been a more fierce and bloody affair than usual. The news was ribbed with indignation because none of Delilah's men, who had started the thing, had been apprehended by the Patrol; whereas others who merely had defended themselves had been caught and returned to their ships under arrest. The consensus was that Delilah's men now, for some reason, thought they were "salty" and were looking for trouble. They were, seemed to be the general determination, going to get plenty of it.

Within two days there were two more such fights; one of mob

proportions in the big dance hall at Caloocan, into which even Wembly, the First Class Gunner's Mate, sober, placative, sensitive of his broken nose, had been drawn. The opinion, agitatingly sponsored by Cruck, Saunders and Ferguson, grew rapidly now amongst Delilah's men that what many had believed from the first was true, that they were deliberately being resented and bullied; and when, a night later, there was a wild mêlée at the very gate of the Base in which Poe was hit with a bottle, Warrington received a cut over the eye and Hemple had his jumper ripped off, the most stable men aboard admitted "that there must be something to it." From this riot the Patrol had dragged the two Carey brothers and taken them to the hospital. Their injuries were such that they were kept there.

Delilah's crew, almost to a man, now had lost its perspective. Men who habitually suffered a taint of cynicism in estimating the quality of such life as touched them saw in this petty, incidental violence an affront to some fundamental significance. A kind of red irritation swept many of them when they thought of the Carey brothers lying in the hospital. They suffered this even in the face of knowing that also in the hospital were seven men from the ranks of those whom they had come to look upon as their enemies: three Marines, one Tagalog civilian, two men from the submarines and a man from the Brooklyn. Most of them now, including Cord, the Boilermaker, stood ready to answer with their embattled presences whenever there should arise, from the depths of even the tawdriest brawl, the summons to defence.

Actually feeling themselves to be a small tribe of unsubmitting men isolated amidst persecution and injustice, they prepared for the next liberty party ashore. They organized into little fighting parties of from six to eight men and pledged themselves to remain within these groups while on liberty. By a process of natural selection the units that would run the chance of meeting the most active violence contained the most pugnacious and experienced fighters; thus, from the ranks of those who wanted to spend their time in saloons and brothels were formed units that contained such men as Cruck, Saunders, Ragatzo, Ferguson, Whorley and Rene; while those who wanted to go to the restaurants, the shops and the picture-show drew men like Orlop, Feenan, Petrie,

Cord, Portness, Warrington, Poe and Barnes, the Blacksmith.

Warrington really did not want to go at all. The kind of meaningless brutality he was being called upon to face ashore revolted and intimidated him, made him feel cheaply helpless; but in the sensation, bordering on nervous nausea, that gripped him as the time drew near he detected fear, so he forced himself to go, forced himself as a defiance and a punishment of the fear. For a moment, in the zeal of this self-discipline, he even contemplated going to the saloons and the brothels with those who were sure to be set upon.

There was one group of men who did not know where they wanted to go, who insisted that they "just wanted to bum around." Of these were O'Connel, Morrow, Forsythe, Arnold, Hardwood, a wild, formidable fighter, and Horner.

"Unc" Blood scornfully refused to remain even in the vicinity of any group and prepared, as usual, to disappear from sight and knowledge until the time for his reporting back to the ship.

When two bells struck, the whole number of those who were going on liberty lined up in two rows along the port railing to be checked out in a body by the Quartermaster on watch. On larger ships this invariably was the custom, those having liberty being permitted to leave the ship only at scheduled times, and only after having been inspected by the Officer of the Deck; but on Delilah, alongside the dock or anchored where bumboats were plentiful, a man left whenever he had a mind to after the first liberty party was called away, and the Quartermaster on watch did the inspecting. For this reason the sight of the two long lines of spotless white uniforms astonished Ensign Snell, the Officer of the Deck, as he took the first paces of a casual stroll from the quarter-deck to the bridge. The surprised look on his face slowly gave way to one of naïve curiosity. His lips breaking into his heavy smile and his throat rumbling faintly with the beginnings of his laugh, he took the few steps necessary to bring him beside the Quartermaster, who was about to begin the inspection. At his appearance, the Quartermaster stood at attention. The two long lines of sunburned men, clean and smelling of soap, also stiffened to attention. Ensign Snell glanced up and down the ranks, then at the Quartermaster. The pleasant flood of his smile and the words of his short question seemed to come out of a little storm, carefully hidden somewhere deep inside himself, the minor pleasure, wonderment and excitement:

"What's the idea?"

"It's the liberty party, Sir," answered Cavendish, the Quartermaster on watch.

Ensign Snell looked away up the length of the deck and back as if he might have been trying to convince himself that he really was here beside Delilah's midships torpedo-tube, that these really were her small engine-room hatches projecting from the bare steel of her deck, that he was not amidst the bright, clean order of some large and formal cruiser. Cavendish, as if assisting him at this effort, volunteered, when the officer's eyes came back to his:

"They just all happened to come aft at the same time, Sir."

Ensign Snell, under the influence of the impression engendered by this unusual sight of the men lined up there in regulation fashion to go ashore, fell into the prescribed routine with which an Officer of the Deck on a large man-of-war dispatches a liberty party. As he moved along the double line of men in the glowing shade beneath the tightly stretched awning, scrutinizing carefully the dress and appearance of each, he noticed a long bulge below the left side of Heller's fashionably snug jumper.

"What's that?" he asked the Pharmacist's Mate.

"That's a shoe, Sir. I'm taking it ashore to be fixed."

"Take it out and carry it," said the officer. "That's no way to go ashore."

Heller stood there without moving.

"Take it out."

Heller, with calm helplessness, lifted his jumper to display a length of iron pipe sticking above the waistline of his trousers. A hole had been drilled near one end of the pipe. A shoe-lace was looped through the hole. Heller pulled out this deadly weapon and tossed it on the deck. The officer stared down at the thing for many seconds as if he were giving his slow, good-natured thoughts time to run their course. When he finally looked up he was hard, clanging, dangerous, like the weapon on the deck.

"Any more of you got these things?"

No movement or word flickered from the two long lines of faces, which remained monotonous in their simple range from stubbornness to grimness.

"Quartermaster, search these men."

Cavendish's eyes darted nervously from end to end of the front line of men, his face expressing clearly his loathness to obey the order. At the climax of this brief hesitation, he moved to the end of the line and planted himself in front of Wembly. The two stared at each other for a moment; then Wembly, puncturing the tension of ignominy, reached beneath his jumper, produced a homemade brass-knuckles and, with a gesture of aroused independence rather than recklessness, heaved it on the deck close to Heller's primitive blackjack. All down the deck men now emulated this gesture, until Ensign Snell found himself staring down at a sizeable heap of metal and wood that seemed fairly to shimmer with a threatening and sinister emanation.

Still staring at the heap of weapons, the officer said to Cavendish:

"Ask the Captain if he can step up here."

In exactly this position, the officer looking with a kind of impersonal harshness down at the heap, the men staring straight ahead with an expression that closely resembled the quality of Wembly's gesture in producing the brass-knuckles, they waited for the appearance of the Captain.

Followed by Cavendish, the Captain came around the galley and paused at sight of the extraordinary tableau. He looked from the liberty party to the pile of weapons as if struggling for a preliminary estimation of what the scene meant; then he walked to Ensign Snell, who had faced about and come to attention upon first hearing the two sets of footsteps approaching along the steel drum of the deck.

"Yes, Mr. Snell?"

Ensign Snell's posture relaxed slightly and he barely made a movement with his hand of indicating the lines of men.

"This is the liberty party, Captain." He said this as if it still were an astonishing thing. "They all had these gadgets stowed under their jumpers." He pointed at the heap.

"They all had them, hey?"

"All but a few of the Chief Petty Officers and O'Connel there," replied Ensign Snell.

Instantly, without thinking, O'Connel almost imperceptibly offered his two great, clenched fists in a displaying manner as if scorning the technicality that permitted him to escape the full charge of having joined his fellows in their arming.

The Captain stooped and lifted several of the weapons one after another, delaying over each one, in this stooping posture, as if in careful inspection. When he straightened up, he turned to Cavendish:

"Quartermaster, throw this stuff over the side."

As Cavendish gathered up an armful of the weapons and moved past the torpedo-tube towards the starboard rail, the Captain got hold of the leather case that held his spectacles, deliberately took them out and put them on. Looking impersonally, dispassionately at the men, although afterward each one of them retained the impression that he had looked straight at him part of the time, the Captain said, naming Ensign Snell as the person he was addressing:

"Suspend all liberty from the ship indefinitely."

As the men moved forward, on Ensign Snell's order of dismissal, the Captain stood staring after them for a fraction of a second, a moment that seemed much longer because of the quality he concentrated in it. He had been swept, as he stared after the men, with the same feeling of warning, with that impression like the recognition of a covenant, that had come to him every time he had called upon the poorly conditioned ship for some rigorous performance. To these men, too, these tested men who knew every eccentricity of her life, every weakness, every individualized strength, he somehow was inextricably committed. They seemed to him, as he stared after them, these particular men in relation to each other, an indispensable part of her that he must keep intact and operative if he was to get her in the condition upon which he had set his mind and spirit, set them so powerfully that, in a man of his even balance, it could be called nothing less than an obsession.

This strength of his feeling as it applied to his crew had impressed Admiral Douglas in their conference that morning. The Admiral had summoned Delilah's Commander ashore to his office and told him that everything he had requested for Delilah's rehabilitation was granted, that the work was to begin immediately. Lieutenant-Commander Borden nearly had recoiled before this statement. He had been prepared to fight so strenuously for only half of what was on his list that this complete surrender, amounting in the light of the normal past almost to eagerness, had left him with a feeling of uneasiness. It was as if in getting what he wanted, he had gotten much more, something mysterious and dangerous yet unapparent; but his frank pleasure had broken out all over him. His eyes sparkling and his wrinkled face smiling unrestrainedly, he had stood in the doorway of the shabby, frame room, shaded to an illusion of coolness behind lowered Venetian blinds, and shaken Admiral Douglas' hand. As their hands had parted, the Admiral had said:

"And by the way, Borden, before we're through with you, your crew as well as your ship will be brand new. We're going to turn you out of here really shipshape."

At this, Lieutenant-Commander Borden had closed the door behind him and stepped back into the office. The man past whom he stepped held within the operation of his will and prejudices, to a vital degree, the future of his career and his fate; but he had stepped past him with all the defiance, all the preparation for struggle that he so long had been mustering to gain his ends regarding the repairs to his ship. Startled as he had been by the implication in Admiral Douglas' casual statement and despite its heavy tug at his spirits, he had reassured himself that he was prepared. He had not expected the difficulty to take this form; but it was, essentially, the same struggle and he had felt his commitment to it no less powerfully.

He had turned around near the centre of the office and stood in relaxed alertness. He seemed more like a person who had heard something rather than one expecting to hear something; and the impression he had given had been so fatefully that of a man over whom a victory would prove of a cost out of all proportion to its worth, that Admiral Douglas had been surprised and a little flurried. His speech slowly regaining authority and fluency in the face of his subordinate's deathlike barrier of nonacceptance, he positively had argued his point before Lieutenant-Commander Borden had said as much as a word.

"Delilah's crew," he had contended, "has gone sour. As everybody knows, this sometimes happens . . . And the only thing to do in such cases is to break the crew up. These fights all over the place have upset the whole establishment . . . and even the civilians are complaining. This is the thing to do and it's been arranged. Why! A number of people already are laid-up in the hospital. It will do the men good to get new offices and new associates."

To all this, Lieutenant-Commander Borden had answered simply that he did not agree with the idea. A flick of irritation had cut through Admiral Douglas' sensibilities. Up to this moment he always had liked Borden. He never had seen him like this before in all the years the man had been in and out of his life officially and unofficially. He would put an end to it. He would tell him that this was what he had decided and that this was the way it was going to be. The Admiral was tall and thin and his curly hair and mustaches were white. He had leaned aggressively over Borden to tell him just this; but he had found himself arguing in the same fashion once more when the words came out. He even had found himself tolerantly trying to talk down to Borden as one would to an unreasonable being. This had plunged their conference still deeper into failure, for Borden was not an unreasonable man. Anybody in the Navy would have been surprised by an opinion that he was unreasonable, and would have felt, no matter whose it was, that in some way there was something wrong with the opinion. Always he gave the impression of being calm, subordinate, co-operative, and he had given that impression even then, as he had stood there, a mature man with eyelids slightly lowered behind the lenses of his horn-rimmed spectacles, repeating over and over, in different form each time an answer was required of him, that his crew was fitted and trained for its duties to an efficiency that would be hard for him to duplicate . . . that it had not gone "sour" . . . that he understood and could handle the situation satisfactorily . . . that he requested permission to do this . . . that he "personally" requested the responsibility.

Admiral Douglas, irritated though he had been, had shied away from this "personal" element in the situation; yet he had felt that somehow this was a very personal matter to Borden, a vitally personal one, and there had grown in him a reluctance to apply the remedy (a remedy that he had grown less certain of as the conversation had progressed) by overriding so much personal issue in a man of such unquestionable, such impressive integrity.

In the end, it had been decided that the crew should be held together; but that while the ship was going through its extensive repair period two of the officers and a number of the men should be detached temporarily for duty elsewhere in the seriously undermanned Asiatic Squadron. Delilah's Commanding Officer had had to be satisfied with this. For him, it had held off the dissolution of his crew as an accomplished fact, and it had given his determination, his unmitigated and active determination, something to go on. He knew, however, how this arrangement would work. When the time came, simply to save themselves trouble, the Personnel Office would try to give him new men who happened to be near at hand: But he would handle that somehow, he told himself. He brought to this promise the same kind of adamantine resolution that had carried him through the struggle with Admiral Douglas; but his very existence seemed to be disorganizing and scattering to the four winds as he thought of his officers leaving for other commands . . . of little groups of his men, their packed bags and hammocks on their shoulders, turning their backs on the dismantled ship and tramping away . . . "temporarily," he said loudly in his mind as if the word had some exorcising quality . . . But he would get them all back . . . even the two in the hospital . . . just as he would get the ship back together after they finished tearing her apart. He would reject any new men they tried to foist on him. He did not know just how he would find the way to do this; but he would . . . And he would get all his men back . . . every last one of them!

5

On that first evening when Delilah had steamed up from the south and sought out the dock in Cavite alongside which she was to remain for repairs, the men simply had tied her up in this more or less familiar place, eaten their supper and turned in for a night of sleep free of uncertainty and vigilance. The next morning, however, they had gotten up to look about them with a feeling of being landlocked in the midst of the surrounding scene yet definitely insulated from it. Their voyage south seemed to have unfocused their sense of time so that they instinctively had looked for signs of the changes that must have taken place since last they were here; and, as if striving to detect with their nostrils the signs that escaped their eyes, they sniffed at the air about them, repeatedly unconvinced by the accustomed aroma, bold and becalmed, that pervades places where many ships seek shelter and repair. Here was the dock, which they knew well, a long repair quay quite out of the traffic of the Yard. They often had tied up to it before; yet as far as they could see its every detail remained unchanged. There across the narrow stretch of dead water was the Submarine Dock. Close in sight was the antique, moored hull of the Receiving Ship, a relic that had spread its sails in the War Between the States; and on every hand, confining Delilah as if she were a slightly hysterical invalid, were the sprawling sheds, temporary, with corrugated iron roofs, and the old Spanish buildings, one story and of stone, that housed the Base's machine shops, foundries, laboratories, storehouses, magazines, offices and barracks: all unaccountably unchanged, as if this place, drugged with heavy sunshine, had dreamed away in suspended animation the formidable lapse of time through which they themselves had returned. It was days before this feeling of their environment being strangely the same had readjusted itself or become dissolved in their turbulence over the change they had managed to find in the people ashore. Struggling in this unworded mood with the scene that imprisoned their ship, the men had had then no slightest suspicion that many of them were to be dispersed into and even beyond this stagnant-seeming outside world, nor that its inhabitants were about to begin on Delilah a labour so extraordinary in degree as to amount to prophecy.

Still in this mood on the third morning, many of the crew had gathered after breakfast along the starboard rail to smoke through a traditional moment of idleness before beginning the day's work. They were staring in calm curiosity across the muddy channel at the submarines. Three of the submarines, moored flank to flank, projected from the dock, while a fourth was hauled up on a small ways such as might be used in caulking and painting a comfortably sized sail-boat. Delilah's men all had seen submarines before and a few had served in them, and often they had seen the conning-towers of these very boats bobbing loggily about Manila Bay or drifting uncertainly close in along the coast between Corregidor and Olongapo; but none of the men had ever seen one of these A-Boats out of the water before. It was hard for them to believe that the primitive craft on the ways there actually was a vessel in the United States Navy; and they stared at the thick, blunt, grey egg, ridiculous and incredibly small, much as men might stare who, although they had seen street-cars every day of their lives, were confronted for the first time with a horse-car that had clung on to use in some backward corner of the world. If O'Connel had had any idea that in a few days he would be serving in that awkward lump on the ways over there, he never would have exclaimed loudly:

"That damn thing is so old it's about to fall apart!"

Instead he would belligerently have said, despite the fact that these first submarines of the modern Navy were many years old: "Aw, they're all right. Still kickin' right along." At what he did say, Mendel, standing within three feet of him, flinched spasmodically as if O'Connel had made one of the old gestures of aggression towards him; and the Jew continued to stare at the small, aged death-trap as if he had some prescience that soon he, himself, was to be serving in one of the things.

From where he stood, abreast of the galley, O'Connel's loud exclamation had carried clearly the short distance back to the quarter-deck, where Lieutenant Fitzpatrick also was looking across at the submarine on the ways. The Irishman's voice, brash and obtrusive, shot out of the general murmur along the rail like something that, taken by itself, was offensive and to be suppressed; but Lieutenant Fitzpatrick required only a few seconds to rid himself of this impression, only as long as it took him to connect the voice with his established vision of the Irishman. Against the background of this vision the voice became quite another thing: it became a roaring emanation of risible wildness, of rough and ready glamour, of terrible but sympathetic valour. As if the better to establish this connection, Lieutenant Fitzpatrick leant out over the railing and looked forward to where the voice had risen . . . there he was . . . the crazy Irishman . . . what a lot of gold there was in that big loud mouth . . . the Jew on one side of him and Warrington on the other . . . The smile on Lieutenant Fitzpatrick's face slowly relaxed as he noted this. That, he told himself, was a queer combination . . . unhealthy . . . and now that he came to think of it, he had seen it often these last few days. His eyes shifted from Mendel's dark repellent features to those of O'Connel. He knew what those Irish features meant, knew with his blood and the deepest nerves in his body. Then his eyes went to Warrington, and as he took in the blend of the boy's curly blond hair, the firm, pure sculpture of his face and the utterly youthful tension in the curve of his body, he could not restrain his irritation . . . "Out of the whole damn crew these are the two Warrington picks! . . . What the devil is the use in trying to help him anyway? . . . Anybody would think he was tied to O'Connel's apron strings . . . That was what he probably liked really . . . that greasy Kike and that Irish roughneck." There writhed through his feelings a thin conviction that Admiral Douglas was right . . . "the crew needed breaking up . . . a change all around would be a good thing" . . .

At this instant Warrington turned his head aft and, observing the officer leaning far out over the rail staring in their direction with an emphatically disapproving expression on his face, concluded that it was a sort of order to O'Connel to pipe down. He quickly communicated this impression to O'Connel, speaking warningly almost out of the side of his mouth. O'Connel flashed a look in the officer's direction. Then Lieutenant Fitzpatrick saw him smile recklessly down at Warrington, a smile of reassurance, appreciative affection and defiance.

A sudden, astonished shout from the port side of the ship interrupted O'Connel's smile and swung all eyes from the submarine to the general direction of the dock. Down it was pouring a mass of native humanity, heading for the ship like some plague of small, exotic animals that had sighted a carcass to be picked. There ensued, at this sight, a moment during which no explanation of it occurred to anybody, and in which the attitude of the crew in-stinctively became that of men tensing to repel boarders; but the tools on the shoulders and in the hands of the little Malays trans-ferred, rather than dispelled, the astonishment, transferred it to the realm of the proper explanation. This horde was coming to work on Delilah! It seemed to O'Connel that never before had he seen so many Navy Yard workmen at one time, not even at five o'clock leaving the gate. It seemed incredible that so many men and tools were coming to belabour one small ship.

"Jesus!" he shouted, "they must be going to do plenty to her . . . and in a hurry."

The crowd of workmen swarmed all over her, jostling and iso-lating her men as a herd of stampeding cattle engulfs a group of riders. In the first moments of this ferment, O'Connel was ex-asperated to the act of striking a native workman in the face with a shoving blow of his open hand, and he had to be hurried up into the Forward Conning-tower by Rene and Warrington, where, to escape identification by the natives, he smouldered in hiding for almost an hour. To the consternation of the crew, who instantly had formed a conspiracy to shield him, he kept sticking his great head out of the door to emit general imprecations and exclama-tions to the effect that "all this means something." However, by virtue of the fact that the Radio Shack screened the door to the Forward Conning-tower, O'Connel managed to remain undiscov-ered by the affronted man and his friends, to whom the Executive Officer had promised justice if they could point out the culprit. Ensign Snell had observed O'Connel being rushed into hiding and had concluded that he was the guilty party; but all through the excited complaints that the blow gave rise to, he said nothing. It seemed to him useless to disclose the man, just about as useless as the blow had been, like an incident of opposition that loses its very meaning before some irresistible march of events.

The protest over this incident exhausted, and O'Connel more or less secure from assignment to a Summary Court Martial, the workmen, armed with oxy-acetylene torches, cold chisels, saws and sledge-hammers, set upon Delilah and ripped off the plates of her deck. They tore her boilers out of her and flung them, a twisted mass of discarded intestines, on the dock. They hauled out the three cylinders and dumped them beside the boilers. They dismembered her so relentlessly, in fact, that even by lunch time she seemed to be a ship that was ceasing to live save with the repellent abstraction of life that a swathed figure manifests on a surgeon's table.

To O'Connel, everything they did to her appeared in the light of mysterious and frantic preparation. He was sure that "all this means something," and he loudly voiced this conviction every time the full power of it swept through him just as he had voiced it in the first moments of the workmen's descent. For the speculative function of the rest of the crew, sensitively over-alert to any possible variation in Delilah's fate, the quality in O'Connel's exclamations was like a spark in a charged cylinder. It drove the feelings of the men to near turmoil of curiosity and foreboding. Anyone who tried to maintain that this impressive rush of workmen meant merely a normal repair procedure was passed by derisively. Arnold wondered if it meant that the United States was going to join the war against Germany; but that explanation was unsatisfactory, as far as Delilah was concerned, because there were no Germans out here to fight. The last of them had gone years before with the valorous Emden and the raiders. Finally, they tried to be content with a guess at a new Japanese threat; but this neither satisfied nor settled them.

Much of what O'Connel's exclamations had aroused in the men, had already been aroused in the officers by the attitude that Ensign Woodbridge instantly had assumed when the Captain had returned from his conference with Admiral Douglas and told them that Delilah was to get every single one of the repairs requested and more besides. Ensign Woodbridge's attitude, insinuating, vivid, slightly irritating, had resulted in no light on the event, not even as much as a reflection from the Captain; but it had agitated Lieutenant Fitzpatrick and Ensign Snell to the point where their minds and feelings continually reverted to restless conjecture. The Captain could not be drawn into this conjecturing; and when they had enveloped him with the pressure of it, he had simply put on his glasses and told them, as if they had not been pressing him for something quite different, about Admiral Douglas' intention to break up the ship's company. Lieutenant Fitzpatrick had offered, as a probable explanation, that inasmuch as England was finding it necessary to call home to the war nearly all of her naval forces, America was preparing to take over entirely the International Patrol of the Chinese Coast. This suggestion had satisfied no one, especially not Lieutenant Fitzpatrick, himself, who, as Second in Command, thought that the Captain should rightfully share with him even the most guarded secret that concerned the ship. Not one of them doubted for an instant that the Captain did have a secret, and they felt that by refusing absolutely even to recognize their conjecturing he was withholding the just hint, the generous gleam from the satisfying light he must be hoarding within his dry, neat person, that would have enabled them to make proper deduction. It had not minimized the slight strain arising between the Captain and his officers over this situation when Ensign Woodbridge had smiled in an amused and dismissing manner at Lieutenant Fitzpatrick's suggestion about the International Patrol. He had behaved as if he were sure just what the remarkable repair concession meant, as if he had some definite information, as if the Captain, perhaps, had taken him into his confidence. This slightly had nettled the Captain, himself; for he had no secret. He merely had a conjecture like the rest, a conjecture with which he felt he had no business to disturb them. What really had nettled him more than anything else was the suspicion that Ensign Woodbridge, as so often happened, had guessed what was in his mind; but the assurance with which his young officer accepted as valid what he had guessed, lent, even as it annoyed him, a confirming weight to the Captain's guarded conjecture that the Captain, himself, had not given it in the first place.

Ensign Woodbridge could not be manoeuvred into sharing the item of his assurance. When Ensign Snell asked him point-blank what his opinion was, he had simply looked at the Captain and smiled. Then he had gotten up from the luncheon table as if he had been about to make some momentous preparations, asked the Captain for the key to the Signal Book locker and had gone aft with a portentous air into the Captain's room. For a few seconds after he had disappeared, the Captain had sat looking from Lieutenant Fitzpatrick to Ensign Snell, seeking to find on their faces whether or not they were accusing him of countenancing in any way this absurd game. As if he had not liked what he had found in their faces, he too had arisen from the table. He climbed to the topside, where very shortly the two left in the Wardroom had heard him pacing slowly back and forth, the deliberate pulsations of his steps resounding on the thin plate above their heads like some function of the ship. Conflicting for their attention with the regular sounds of this pacing, yet supplementing it, had been the sounds Ensign Woodbridge made back there in the Captain's room. He was in there spasmodically rattling papers, Signal Books, charts and other such paraphernalia. Once he emitted a long, deliberative sigh. At this, Ensign Snell, looking as if he were about to rush in there and knock things about, had said aloud to himself in a vain effort to dismiss the whole matter from his mind:

"Aw, hell, he doesn't know any more about it than we do."

Of all the people in the ship who had caught the fever loosed by O'Connel's exclamation forward and Ensign Woodbridge's attitude aft, only two were sure: Ensign Woodbridge and Olgan, the Cook; and the latter took the trouble to inform not even himself as to what was hidden beneath the general effect of his certitude. He simply stood silently, sullenly over his cookstove, succumbing to a growing terror and heaviness of heart that rose like symptoms from the nameless certainty deep within his ratlike being.

6 〜〜〜

Under stimulation of the trouble ashore, the disorganization attendant upon the presence of the workmen and the restless pressure of foreboding and conjecture, the tension that had relaxed when Delilah turned her back on Palawan would have begun to gather again if the repair operation itself, which now was so largely responsible, had not involved its own antidote in the form of the partial dispersion of the crew and the dismantling of the ship. For some of the last of those transferred, it was a relief to escape the obligatory brawls ashore as well as the feeling of being left behind that ensued when the first batch of eight men were shipped away and Ensign Woodbridge was detached for some far-away duty up the Yangtse Kiang. Those of the men left behind soon found themselves forced to move from the ship to the dock, the ravages of the repair operation now having made uninhabitable every section of the vessel except the Captain's room.

Camped there alongside the ship with their cots and a cookstove, they spent a good deal of their time watching the efforts of the workmen. To some of the crew it seemed that the natives were unnecessarily violent in their work. A few even felt that they were taking it out on the ship for the blow O'Connel had struck; and although no one put this impression into words, two or three of them actually watched carefully for the impact of a hammer or a spirt of the torches that would serve as a basis for protest. Strangely enough, the man most swayed by this idea was the taciturn and utterly practical Stengle, although he did not think of it, perhaps, in connection with the blow the workman had received. He was the first to observe something on which a protest could be based. He was standing on the dock looking down into the shallow, ragged cavity that had been the engine-rooms, where a group of the natives were attempting to remove a long section of pipe. When one of the workmen lifted a sledge and struck the pipe several times in an effort to loosen the threads, Stengle emitted a loud exclamation of disgust, jumped aboard and hurried aft to where the Captain and Lieutenant Fitzpatrick were engaged in a discussion.

Standing at his version of attention, Stengle told them that the workmen were ruining the whole pipe line system of the ship, that if something was not done at once the lines all would be crystallized from the sledge blows, that the rests and fittings where the lines passed through bulkheads would be worked out of fit and that he thought they were going about the whole dismantling procedure in the wrong manner.

The Captain and Lieutenant Fitzpatrick stared at him in surprise. Coming from him this almost was an hysterical outburst. Lieutenant Fitzpatrick knew that Stengle's statement was largely a dramatization of a shred of truth, the first such over-emphasis he ever had observed in the manifestations of this matter-of-fact man with whom he had been so closely associated. He, himself, had been watching every detail of the dismantling, and he knew that as little harm was being done as was possible under the circumstances, that really things were going satisfactorily: Yet he too had gazed down in dissatisfaction at the work of the small, brown labourers.

In the effort to restrain his own dissatisfaction, Lieutenant Fitzpatrick had asked himself why, in the face of the acceptable work, he should have felt it, and there had passed through his mind, vaguely, rapidly, that what disturbed him was the different philosophy of technique, or the lack of it, guiding these Malay workmen. These men from the jungles and thatch-roofed villages *knew* imitatively about the machinery amidst which they worked, but they did not *feel* and *believe* it; whereas he and most of his men, like their forefathers, were part of a nation that from the very beginning had sought the realization of its dreams through machines. In its homes, on its farms, in its cross-roads stores were machines. It had filled the air and the roads with them, the surface of the sea and its depths. Tales of machines passed in the stories from father to son, and its folk sang *My Merry Oldsmobile, Steamboat Bill, Casey Jones* and *Hello Hawaii, How Are You?* Its poets had found beauty in the precise flight of telegraph wires across the sky, and the senses of its people first awake to the singing, the odours and the symmetries of machines, just as the senses of these jungle men first awake to the sounds of birds, the perfumes of flowers and the patterns that grow from the earth.

Confronted now by the authentic concern of the Chief Machinist's Mate, this man in whose very cells was an evolved receptivity to the manner in which a pipe should be threaded or a throttle pulled, Lieutenant Fitzpatrick took it for granted that it was this cultural discrepancy that was stirring at the bottom of Stengle's discomfort. He smiled at Stengle, and it was the strange quality in this smile that instantly informed Stengle of the unusual error into which he had fallen, informed him that in some way he was being what he called "soft." His small, dark, mottled face seemed to heat to a dull red. The colour looked artificial beneath a smear of grease across his forehead. However, Lieutenant Fitzpatrick said to him without a shade of difference from the tone he habitually used to him:

"All right, Stengle, I'll have another look right away."

Stengle swung about in a sagging fashion and got away as rapidly as possible from what he felt had become, somehow, an exhibition of himself. With an air of being in moral support of Stengle, the Captain stood there for a few seconds before he too turned and went below. He knew that Lieutenant Fitzpatrick was right, calm and right in a superior attitude, and he was thankful for it; but he was on the side of Stengle in this matter, and if he had known how the men were standing on the dock suspecting the worst, he secretly would have wished, despite himself, to be standing with them there watching grimly for an overt act. As he had tarried in Stengle's wake he had been stubbornly grim. His wide lips pressed together in a firm line had given his face the expression of a grandparent who, hearing an obviously exaggerated tale of inefficiency at the hospital in which his grandchild is undergoing a treatment of which he disapproves, discounts the detail and silently but solemnly endorses the principle. An outsider observing the two in that moment might have gotten the impression that Lieutenant Fitzpatrick was the Captain and the other his officer.

When the Chief Machinist's Mate had interrupted them, the Captain and Lieutenant Fitzpatrick had been discussing the question of the Captain going ashore to live while the heavy repairs were in progress. Lieutenant Fitzpatrick had suggested this once before, pointing out that the ship just would not be liveable; and he had been urging it upon him again.

"You can come on board every day, Sir, and look things over . . . If anything comes up I'll report to you at once . . . (Lieutenant Fitzpatrick and Ensign Snell were sleeping on the dock with the men) . . . Staying aboard here you're just taking a beating for nothing."

The Captain, however, would not hear of it. He even, the better to resist his friend's urging, maintained on the surface an air of listening to some sort of official report. He was, as a matter of fact, a little annoyed, because he suspected that behind and added to Lieutenant Fitzpatrick's concern in the matter was the instigation of his wife, who had insisted that he was wearing himself out uselessly sitting around all day in the noise and dirt. His sleeping aboard the dismantled thing, she thought, was utter nonsense, especially in view of the fact that previously he habitually had spent his nights ashore in their bungalow whenever Delilah was in the neighbourhood of Manila. The Captain did not mind her going for him herself, personally, about this; but he objected very definitely to her influencing or entering into relations with the business of the ship in any degree. His annoyance, whenever he did detect some such item of influence, always was quick; for just beneath the surface of awareness was the suspicion that in some not clear way her influence on the life of the ship was considerable, and he was against this on principle. Every evening now at four-thirty, he would go ashore and join his wife, a tall, well-proportioned, blonde girl with a faintly freckled, shapely face that held an expression of calm frankness: But at midnight he would return to the demolished ship, and he would sleep there in her, the only person aboard this forlorn metal shell cluttered with tools, debris and oily dirt, as if any other course would have constituted a kind of abandonment.

7 ≋

Laura, the Captain's wife, was the only woman any of the crew ever had seen aboard Delilah, and even her visits were rare. Nevertheless, the ship was populated by women, women who never had seen each other, women who slept and ate in houses often thousands of miles apart . . . a prosperous woman who knelt in a clean New England church . . . a whore in Brooklyn . . . a spare, barefooted woman slowly dying on a dank field in Alabama . . . a white-haired matron who chaperoned dances in Baltimore . . . a woman who each day filled a dinner-pail in Akron . . . a woman in the Green Mountains . . . a cloud of women, nostalgic, powerful, ever-present, that rested upon the ship as a cloud embraces a mountain top. They exchanged opinions, these women, whenever two men fell into a conversation about one of those subjects that men habitually delegate to the province of women: They criticized Olgan's cooking; they discussed marriage and how a home should be run; a woman on the San Francisco water-front agreed, in essentials, with a woman in Cincinnati about Sarah Bernhardt. Another hummed, in the depths of the bunkers, a melody that she loved and which she often sang over her housework. One of them stood behind Ensign Snell at table and told him how to eat his soup. One placed a muffler around Petrie's neck when he went on watch on a damp night; and to another, a bedraggled woman on an Illinois farm, a man had made his last appeal when Delilah crushed him in an engine-room: "Mom," he had whispered, "Mom . . . Mom."

It was no sensing of his wife's being one of this pervading crowd of women that the Captain objected to. His objection was to an influence more material, more directly political: But his wife *was* amongst these women, powerfully amongst them. The men seemed to feel her there in his cabin, and it was not only out of respect of him and his power that they felt like intruders, uncertain and subdued, when they entered it. She had arranged the place for him, put pictures and things around. Her photograph was there and, Warrington thought, a breath of the scent she wore. Men entered this minute cabin almost aware of the feeling a man experiences whose business forces him into the bedroom of a woman whom he deeply respects but does not know.

Although the men knew little about her, save her appearance and that she was a Senator's daughter, they did deeply respect her. Perhaps if Wright, the Seaman, for example, had been asked quickly in private by the right person why he respected her, and he had answered just as quickly before stopping to think that he did not know, he might have answered:

"Because she loves him."

Once when she had started off on a trip to be gone for a few months, she had sent him a radiogram back from her steamer at sea. Delilah's apparatus being temporarily out of commission, the message, "I love you," had been received by the station ashore and then semaphored out to Delilah, anchored off Cavite. Bidot, the Quartermaster on watch, had been profoundly embarrassed on receiving the message, and as he had delivered it, carefully folded, to the Captain, he had stood more rigidly than usual at attention, his face almost lifeless with formality. The rest of the crew had been just as acutely disturbed by this message, for its transmission had been observed by a number of men about the deck who understood semaphore, and who had instantly made public this unprecedented communication. It was not because his wife was in love with him that they were upset. They would have been definitely indignant if she had not loved him, this man whom they accepted so thoroughly, who aroused in many of them a warm enthusiasm; but it was because the message, as a message to him, seemed somehow outrageously inappropriate. Never again, however, would they envision him, small, wrinkled, his hair ineptly combed, save through the added cogency, the glow of this woman's love.

In this same way but more dimly and in much smaller measure, nearly every other person in the ship was illuminated for the others by the quality of some woman's power over him. This quality betrayed itself most perceptibly at mail time, when Chief Gunner's Mate Orlop, who served as Mail Orderly, having returned aboard with the monthly sack of mail and first distributed their letters to the officers, would stand up on the base of the midships torpedo-tube with an armful of mail. Starting with the topmost letter, he would call out the name on it. There would be a quick answering, "Here!" and he would hold the letter down at arm's length in the direction of the voice. He did this without looking away from the next letter, as if he were studying the inscription on it, or as if he deliberately were restraining his eyes from a trespass within the off-guard expression on the face of the man to whom he was holding out the letter.

The instant Orlop was sighted approaching the ship with the sack, the cry, "Mail Ho!" would ring up and down the deck, be taken up by voice after voice until the ship's company would be crowded about the base of the torpedo-tube waiting for the appearance of the stack of letters under Orlop's arm. When it did appear, a current of emotion would leap through the ship, a current blocked and confined within the armful of letters; and its pressure would hold there until the last letter was handed out, for the stack of envelopes was not arranged in alphabetical order. The pressure of this emotion took many hours to subside, and it tainted even the most laborious day (this invasion of the fabulous world in which they slept and ate and worked by bits of paper from the world lost to them save in dreams and memory but in which alone they believed) with a kind of heady unreality.

Crowded there waiting for the letters, some of the men behaved as if they actually were keeping an appointment. One would smooth his hair. Another would roll down and button the sleeves of his jumper. Over Ragatzo's face would come an expression of sensual eagerness in the midst of which his lips would knot into a small smirk of confidence. Saunders would become a little sullen like a man waiting to exact a customary accounting from a woman whom he bullied. The elder Carey brother just stood there a trifle sheepishly, shifting his weight from one foot to the other, smiling as if in anticipation of some minor, intimate miracle that had happened before and was about to happen again. Stengle, too, was expectant, but there was nothing excited about his expectancy. There, in that moment, waiting for the letter he received each month, he became, this remarkable little man dangerously exiled on fantastic alien shores, simply a tired, middle-aged mechanic, crossing a drab threshold after a hard day's work for a family that would have resented the idea that he could be anything more.

Olgan, the Cook, never received any mail. When the cry, "Mail Ho!" would go up, Olgan now invariably walked into the forecastle and lay down on his bunk. If men came in there to read their letters, he put his arm over his eyes as if he were sleeping. A year or so before, he used to stand around watching the men receive their mail. He even used to watch them read it, his little, shiny eyes steady and alert. Once Heller, the Pharmacist's Mate, whose persistent, routine gambling smacked of professionalism, had looked up from the reading of a long letter to find Olgan's eyes fixed upon it. The letter was from Heller's sister, a girl three years younger than he, who regarded his constant teasing as the thrilling and complimentary condescension of a hero. For an instant, as he was trapped, Olgan's eyes had wavered up to meet Heller's. In irony and disgust Heller had asked him, holding out the pages:

"Here . . . How would you like to read it?"

An expression of eagerness had come into Olgan's face, and he had quickly extended his hand for the letter. Heller had jerked it back.

"Why, you bastard! . . . I believe you would," Heller had said.

The Pharmacist's Mate, who had a slim, hard body that was just above medium height and a handsome, reckless face, the clear definition of which was a trifle blurred by a corrupt aura, had been impressed by this incident. He had recounted it to Rene, and the two of them, although Heller never before had been known to play a practical joke on anybody in the ship, had planned a trick on Olgan. They unearthed a big pink envelope somewhere and had it mailed to him, timing it so that, in all probability, it would be distributed with the monthly mail from the States. As Heller would have put it, the trick "got by" smoothly, "got by" as he, himself, and most of his manoeuvres usually did. He was the sole member of the crew, for example, who managed to wear his hair really long in civilian fashion; and he kept this head of hair, brushed straight back from his forehead in a precise, oiled sweep of brown luxuriance, even through inspections. There were others in the ship, notably a Fireman, Second-Class, named Easterly, who wanted to wear their hair in this manner, who were quite improved in appearance by wearing it thus; but just as surely as one of them would permit his hair to grow an officer would dart a glance at him and say: "Better get your hair cut." Easterly was the only one who was regularly persistent in the effort to emulate Heller, and each time he was ordered to cut his hair, he would grind out, almost audibly, in the wake of the order, as if Heller, himself, were giving it with some usurped authority, "That God damn pill-pusher gets away with murder." To Heller's face, however, Easterly always was good-humoured about this; for the Pharmacist's Mate once had arisen in the midst of a crap game and struck the gigantic Rene in the mouth and "gotten by" with it without further fighting or backing water. To have come in conflict with this peculiar quality in the fate of Heller would have been like defying some thoroughly believed in superstition.

Orlop, standing up on the base of the torpedo-tube distributing the stack of mail, had taken a genuine second look at the name on the pink envelope before, in a surprised tone, he had called it out. This was the first time in the two years he had been Mail Orderly that he had seen it on a letter.

"Olgan!"

The Cook had had to be nudged by some one in the crowd before he had realized that it was his name that was being called, that there at the end of the outstretched arm was a large, intimate, pink envelope with his name written expansively across it in pencil. He had stood there staring at the envelope, his breath quickening. "Watch this . . . Watch this," Heller and Rene had passed around the word. Impatiently Orlop had commanded, slightly waving the envelope:

"Take it away."

Olgan almost had snatched the envelope, then looked around for a rift in the crowd about him through which to escape with it; but as no one had stepped aside for him he had remained where he was, ineffectively picking at the flap. Another name was called, and as the man had pushed forward, Olgan, under the cover of the man's action, as it were, had made haste to tear open the envelope and pull out the folded strip of toilet paper within, holding it in such a manner that the long strip had slowly unfolded clear down to the deck. The crowd had roared with laughter, and those nearest him had kept poking him with their fists in a jesting way. His eyes darting unseeingly here and there at the wall of hilarity that encircled him, and the curve of his stooped shoulders increasing as if he were trying to take shelter beneath it, he had stood there like a helpless animal that waits for surrounding danger either to destroy him or sweep on.

It would be difficult to believe that what Olgan had been observing, in the days before Heller and Rene played the joke on him, was the transformation that took place in a man as he read his letter from home. These transformations, often dramatic, sometimes ridiculous, did take place, however. They took place in obedience to a law that burgher philosophers love to repudiate with such absurd dicta as, "Be natural," "Be yourself." There is no "naturalness," no "self" in the sense suggested by these personal slogans. Even in introspection a man "acts" a different personality according to which of the various backgrounds of his life, past or present, his thoughts and feelings may be dealing with. He cannot see himself in essence; he can see himself only as an actor before some other person either actual or ideal . . . "I often," Warrington once told Lieutenant Fitzpatrick, "separate into two personalities at the same time, one of which stands off and watches or judges what I am or what I am doing." Warrington, moreover, actually was more nearly "natural" and true to "himself" than anybody else in the ship; that is, in the degree to which he approached being one character, because the parts he consented to act, the people he chose as audiences, regardless of what other individuals might face him, virtually were restricted to three. One was the part he acted before the idealization of himself as judge, the second was the part he acted before the vision of the girl at home, the third was the part he acted before Lieutenant Fitzpatrick. It was for that reason that so many of the men regarded him as what in a civilian group would have been called a snob, the reason that made Cavendish, for example, say of him, "I don't get that bird." On the other hand, a man who acts the different part required by each of the different people whom he meets, setting each up as a particular audience and skilfully acting the character required, is a "good fellow" and is understood by all even though the part he acts before one is Hamlet and before another Falstaff. It is a common occurrence for a man to come from a stimulating meeting with a friend and, continuing to act the person he was before that friend, find himself adjudged "strange today" by someone whom he subsequently joins before remembering to abandon the old part and step into the new: And the man who is remarked upon as being nothing in a crowd of people who know him well, who is neutralized when faced with the necessity of acting so many various parts at the same time, but who shines as an interesting personality when alone with any individual in that crowd, is as common as the remark: "What can she see in that man?"

This law, in its operations on Delilah's men, tended to make them seem abnormally alike, strangely simple, in the way that leads civilians to remark on observing a ship's crew at work, "Why, they're just children playing." Each man in the crew who submitted to his environment became more or less the compound of all the characters he would have acted when face to face with each man in the ship individually. He faced, so to speak, the entire crew as if it were a single individual, an individual whose components included many who were immature, even insignificant, but an individual with whom he was inescapably confined, under incomparable intimacy, to eat, sleep and work. Thus the complex character he acted, clear and simple to the point of childishness in appearance, was no more elementary than a beam of pure, white light whose bright simplicity imprisons the conflict of seven individual colours as well as a myriad of vibrations, high and low, that escape the eye.

At mail time, however, waiting for a letter from a woman vital in his life, taking hold of an envelope with her handwriting upon it, reading her actual thoughts and words, a man behaved as if he were in her very presence, as if suddenly the emotions that arose had isolated him with her and obligated him to play only the character he acted before her. This character, which the man otherwise never acted in the ship, the crew forgave him, as they expected him to forgive each of them; and gaining from his behaviour some idea of the mother, wife, sister or whore behind him, transferred the whole responsibility of the business, this ambush of his control and his integrity, to her.

There was but one other person in the ship besides Olgan who had no woman behind him, and that was Ensign Woodbridge; yet Ensign Woodbridge received more letters from women than anybody else. Behind Olgan there was a vacuum besetting him with all its melancholy stresses; but behind Ensign Woodbridge there simply was a crowded meaninglessness, women who had been his mistresses and others who would be his mistresses, no doubt, if he troubled to manage it. Having no mother, no sister, no female relatives who had a hold on him, women formed for him little more than a part of the mud and beauty and danger of a world created for him to conquer and use. It was inconceivable that any woman ever would crack that thin, hard shell of glistening armour in which he strode through and over them. If he had received a public message saying, "I love you," the men merely would have grinned and shaken their heads in a manner that would have said for him, in sincere admiration, "Another one . . . That bastard!" and for her, in sincere pity, "The poor little bitch."

Although Ensign Woodbridge thought in a very cogent manner about other things (in the field of astronomy, for example, he was on the road to becoming learned) he did not think much about women: he mostly just took them for granted. When he did think about them at all, it was in bright spurts of thought that had to do with the idea that woman was a semi-human creature built around and for that organ of the body whose equivalent in the male was tacked on the outside of him as a sort of afterthought. He would have been astounded if he had been told that he did not respect women, and so would any of the women who knew him. He literally would have given his life in defence of any woman who had committed herself to him, and his considerate handling of them as well as his undeviating courtesy towards them were remarked upon from Shanghai to Zamboanga. Much as one evolves a code with which to deal with horses or children, partly to protect the children or the horses, partly to protect oneself, Ensign Woodbridge had evolved a code that rigidly governed his relationship with women. He would not, for example, be lover to a woman whose husband had introduced him to her; nor would he take advantage of a situational or economic need in a woman's life. Those men who used liquor to condition a woman for their advances he looked upon with much the same light contempt that he bestowed upon men who cheated at solitaire; and he scrupulously forbore, even when it would have helped him in his campaign for a woman, to imply by so much as a dropping of the eyes that a given woman had been his mistress. He scorned the idea that because a girl was a virgin she must not be touched; and he went for any woman that he desired, aged between sixteen and thirty and who was not beyond the pale of his personal proscriptions, as a bullet goes for a target. This code was not an affectation with him. He summoned to its enforcement all the formidable moral power within him, summoned it to such an extent that he actually would have looked upon becoming the lover of a close friend's wife as the most obscene of treacheries, as a thing almost as reprehensible as incest. His fastidiousness ably complemented the moral force that he brought to the maintenance of this code, because it prevented him from simply taking a woman because she was a woman, from taking her for the mere primitive release inherent in the culmination of the act with her. He never once, as Ensign Snell often did, left the ship with the intention, private or avowed, "Well . . . guess I'll go ashore and get bred." This same fastidiousness restricted the province of his desire to the choicest women, so that months sometimes went by through which he lived a continent life. Those who sought for flaws in him either did not credit these periods of restraint or, on the other hand, affected to believe that male prowess was unturbulent within him. However, even women who had not been in love with him but who had accepted him only once out of sheer desire, remembered what he had been to them.

What made it difficult for the women who could not resist him or who did not want to resist him was his conception of them as objects of his desire and the swiftness with which he sought to attain them. It seemed to him that in the instant he saw and desired a woman, he should have her; because what came through to him from her in that instant was she, herself, in essence. The form of her body, the spirit with which it was carried, the individual life that glowed in her eyes, the primal thing she did to the vibrations around her, these were really she, the she he wanted to hold in his arms and possess: And he felt that the moment she began to speak, to be what the world had made her, to act the character, too, that she must be for him eventually, she obliterated the essence he had desired in the first place and became, to the degree he was forced "to know" her before he possessed her, a being quite different from her he had wanted in the beginning. When a woman had been able to hold him off for a considerable period of "getting-to-know-each-other-first," he would then find in his arms, not the thing he had desired, not the woman, herself; but something compounded of all the schoolteachers who had had a pronounced effect upon her, her father and mother, the books she had read, the characters in plays she had seen and the other men she had known.

A number of women had said to themselves, "That is the man I am going to marry"; but when they did not succeed in this they harboured no bitterness. Some of them, for years after they saw him for the last time, persisted in gleaning news and gossip about him, as if he were some great and inaccessible personage who, in passing, had touched their lives with fire. They were not women, but only men of a certain type, who contended that he "let women down," that he was not the man for a decent woman to associate with. Usually, however, these were not the men who had women as a responsibility: the latter knew exactly where they were with Ensign Woodbridge: they knew that their wives were safe and that they had to be on guard over their daughters or sisters. Parents did what they could about their daughters, warned them, discreetly forbade them to be alone with him, or helplessly "trusted" them; but if a man had had to commit his wife to a brother officer for safe-keeping in an emergency, he would have chosen his friend, Woodbridge, and felt secure.

Ensign Woodbridge was a falconlike being, a person born to victory, an officer who got excited but who inspired in the men, when they found it was he who had been selected to lead them in a skirmish ashore, a surge of relief and confidence. When one asked Ensign Woodbridge how he was, he invariably said, "Very well, thanks"; but one got an impression from his smile and the energy radiating from his body that he had said, "Splendid!" and there was, in fact, a kind of splendour ever about him. This splendour was not merely the illumination of the wealth that always had been in his family, nor his consciousness that for hundreds of years his blood had flowed through men who had led in law, religion and war: It derived from a kind of untarnished virtue, a shining virtue still perfect with lack of irresistible ordeal and clouding test, a virtue of which the years had not yet had time to prove the tragic truth that "The hardest knife ill used doth lose his edge." Nevertheless, Ensign Woodbridge was the kind of man whom prosperous grocery or hat store magnates, or those who should have been, passionately resented.

On the news spreading around Manila Bay that he was detached for duty in China, even his enemies, in a sense, regretted it. His departure seemed, in some unaccountable way, to decrease the significance of the community from which they, themselves, derived significance. The women, including those who were quite beyond the range of his amorous attentions, had been stirred by the report of his arrival when Delilah steamed up from the south, and now the news that he was to leave gave them a moment of poignant dissatisfaction, like the passing of some bright danger.

8

Delilah's crew had been thinned out considerably. It had been reduced, as a matter of fact, to a skeleton crew; although this status, which would have implied for them a kind of unsettling rele-

232

gation to the stagnant backwaters of life, was not fully realized by the men. They had been led to understand the absence of their shipmates more or less in the sense of their having gone off on unusually extended missions from which, however, a return was a matter of course. Thus, as far as it occurred to them to be concerned, there being little work to do, the ship merely was temporarily depopulated in much the same way she always was when large working parties or expeditions were sent ashore, as she had been many times, in the immediate past, down south. What seemed the only unusual thing about it, the greater duration of the condition, could be viewed with complacence (no more than just tainted by over-emphasis) since she was held up for repairs. They felt directly very little of what tormented the Captain, who, gaze as he might at the grimy Commission Pennant still fluttering from the mainmast, never for a moment faced away from the fact that his ship was in pieces and his crew really dispersed. The men began to grow casual and relaxed in their movements in the way men do who live on land and take on flesh. Their muscles and inner-ears seemed to be losing the memory of years spent on decks alive with the breathing of the sea; and they expected, and were granted, longer hours of liberty in Cavite and nearby Manila.

The most arduous duty that fell to them in those days was the rigging of the dock for a dance given by Lieutenant Fitzpatrick. They entered into this with enthusiasm. The Executive Officer had required of them only that they stretch a large tarpaulin for a dancing surface and set up a few strips of nipa fronds to screen the more unsightly portions of the dock. He had asked this favour of the deck force only; but the whole ship's company turned to. In the boats, towed by the motor-dory, they invaded a swamp down the shore and literally denuded it of nipa. With this they transformed the roofed dock into a pavilion that from a distance looked like the palace of an island king. From the jungle trees they hacked away whole limbs on which orchids grew and set them into the walls of the pavilion so that the blossoms now actually grew there. They hauled up boat load after boat load of all the creepers, flowers and shrubs that seemed to them decorative and laced them into place to form panels around the top edges of the walls and around the broad, low portal that occurred in each side

233

of the pavilion. Within the precise luxuriance of these panels they concealed strings of coloured electric lights.

When this paradisiacal bower was but half-finished, Lieutenant Fitzpatrick was so impressed by it that he instantly changed his mind about the kind of dance it was going to be. In the beginning he had asked just a few intimate friends to "dinner," people who would understand his asking them to a party on a dirty stretch of dock; but when he looked at that utterly neat expanse of waxed canvas dance floor being so gorgeously and originally enclosed, he invited everybody, even those before whom he never chose to appear save in all the protective social armour at his disposal.

The dance turned out to be the most notable informal event of several years, and this was influenced, in important degree, by the fall of those circumstances that made it an effective spectacle for the crew as well as an object of their uncalculated solicitude. At the start of the dance, nearly all that was left of the crew had gathered on Delilah's darkened deck, opposite one of the portals of the pavilion, to have a brief look; and then, even including many who were free to go ashore, they simply had stayed there all through the party, sitting on the Port Engine-room Hatch, the base of the torpedo-tube and two rows of mess benches, listening to the music and watching the dancing.

Highly critical of the dancers and their deportment, estimating the women's figures, smiling in admiring approval if the Captain, Lieutenant Fitzpatrick or Ensign Snell achieved some little spectacular success or grinning sheepishly if they met with failure, the men were unexpectedly delighted with the whole thing, as if this officers' affair were a spectacle staged especially for their entertainment. Warrington, thankful that he was in darkness, sat between Mendel and O'Connel on the base of the torpedo-tube. Each time the orchestra launched the first bar of some personal melody, a wave of feeling, yearning and nostalgic, would surge upon the beach of his memory and leave him brooding over the music, the gowns of the women, the good manners, the delicate drifts of perfume, the rhythmic friction sound of dancing feet on canvas as if these were, not so much the ghosts of excitements lost in the graceful world he had abandoned, but premonitions of some happy time wandering into his mind from that distant future that one day would be the glorious past. Horner, the Seaman, however, thought that the music was not lively enough . . . "that was no way to play *When You Wore a Tulip.*" Ragatzo said it was too bad Mr. Woodbridge was not there . . . "he'd make that Jg. from the Navy Yard look like just a punk." Cruck contemptuously said that the women were "only egg-shells, only egg-shells"; but he ferociously admonished any man who, in the most hypothetical degree, was guilty of a noise, an exclamation or an action that might have disturbed the party.

This crowd of enlisted men who sat out there in the darkness and watched the dance with an almost entranced attention were, for the officers and their women, something not less powerful than an audience but something much less formalistic. They were something that made the officers play quite consciously to the gallery, as it were, that made them bring to the fore such masculine dominance and gallantry as each was capable of, and they behaved somewhat as men do who want to give the impression to other men that they are the masters of the women around them. This compounded the excitement in the atmosphere and lent to the party an unusual gaiety and voltage. Women, who long had grown accustomed to the submission of their husbands, to their uxoriousness or to their indifference, responded with a surprised spark of alertness, resistance or a delightful inquietude. Some thought the especial virtue of the party lay in the unusualness of its site and the decorations. Some of the women thought it was because they were rediscovering in their men a little of what had been alluring in the first place; while others attributed the success to Lieutenant Fitzpatrick's punch, and they pressed him for the recipe. On the whole, however, they drank less than usual, restraining themselves from the very nectar they thought was making them gay, restraining themselves, automatically, because they were under the eyes of the unseen men they sensed out there in the dark, the influence that was giving them, in large measure, what they attributed to the alcohol.

This restraining influence, extemporaneously imposed upon the party by the watching men, more accurately indicated the nature of the crew's intrusion than did the "life" their unseen spectatorship induced. The crew formed there, in effect, that formidable ring of dowagers who sit about the perimeters of ballrooms, smiling, nodding, raising eyebrows, silently maintaining by the sheer pressure of their chaperonage a bias in favour of graciousness and a pervading avoidance of an appearance of evil. The Captain's wife, who was having a quite successful evening, felt this pressure now very definitely. She felt, each time she danced with a man other than her husband, a little as if she were circling the floor in the presence of a self-deputized batch of her husband's relatives, and she even was a bit defiant when she walked out on the margin of the dock, to cool off between dances, with the handsome Jg. from the Navy Yard who clearly had established himself as the lion of the party. She would not be surprised, and she smiled impatiently as the absurd little idea scuttled through her mind, if she were to hear, in case she stayed out there too long, the warning clump of heavy footfalls in the nearby shadow and "Unc" Blood's voice saying something like, "O . . . Excuse me . . . I'm looking for my hammer."

The dance climaxed, although it was sometime later before the band played *Goodnight, Everybody,* with an impromptu gesture consistent with the tone that had characterized the affair from the first: Admiral Douglas' wife, on taking her leave, glanced at one of the orchids on the wall and commandingly hinted that she would like to have it to take home. Lieutenant Fitzpatrick tried to get it for her, but it was too high to pluck, and the limb on which it grew was too firmly fastened for him easily to pull it down. As if appealing for assistance, he instinctively glanced out the portal in the direction of the ship. Immediately, in response to this glance, Hardwood jumped from the ship, across the intervening three feet of water, to the dock. He made straight for the orchids, holding an open jackknife out before him as if to advertise his purpose and apologize for his intrusion. A tipsy officer shouted, "Gangway for a sailor!" The crowd of white and gold uniforms and scented organdy dresses parted smoothly before the hurrying Hardwood as if engaging in some kind of ceremony, and the Seaman, locating the heavy brace on the outside of the nipa, climbed it to the branch of orchids. He cut it free and leaped to the floor, where he plucked a blossom and handed it to Mrs. Douglas with a deep, graceful bow which he unexpectedly summoned from the cumbrous mass of his muscular body. Out of the darkness of the ship there burst a roar of spontaneous cheering. As if inspired by this, Hardwood turned to another woman and, saying, "One for you, ma'am," plucked and presented to her another of the orchids. Then, as he proceeded right along the dock renewing his supply of blossoms from the wall and presenting them to the ladies, the officer who had shouted, "Gangway for a sailor!" began singing, and the others joined in:

"Stand Navy down the field,
Sails set to the sky . . . . . ."

When Hardwood had jumped out so intrusively to help with the orchids, the materialization of the crew's pressure upon her, which the Captain's wife had half-jokingly expected, had caught her unprepared. Coming suddenly at her from an angle somewhat different from the one over which she had smiled impatiently, it had brought to the expression on her face a twinge of anxiousness, of hope that the boy would be understood and handled sympathetically, the kind of look that takes possession of a woman's face when her precocious child suddenly dashes into the midst of some grown-up activity in a burst of innocent, exuberant helpfulness: And her blue eyes had smiled with relief (a smile reflected in Ensign Snell's eyes, too, in that moment) and then with more than relief when she saw that Hardwood not only was all right, but that he was triumphant.

9

The day after the dance there were still further transfers of people from the ship. Ensign Snell, with a small party of men, was assigned to a Landing Force that was to march across Luzon; and

O'Connel, Mendel and Warrington went to the submarines. There was no little surprise at Warrington's transfer. He was the last man they expected to see on a transfer list so long as Lieutenant Fitzpatrick was Executive Officer; but late in the afternoon this surprise was swept away and forgotten before the resurge, now magnified and affirmed, of the astonished speculation that had hit the ship when she had been flung so urgently into the midst of more repairs than she had bargained for. What happened was the Delilah's four sister ships, each of which was identical with her in every detail save the number on the bow and the identification form at the masthead, steamed into the bay and tied up alongside various docks at the Base. Within two hours after tying up, even before some of the people around the Base knew the destroyers were down from China, the ships were set upon by crowds of workmen who began the same extensive repair operations being suffered by Delilah. This, certainly, "meant something." It may have been that, now, no explanation, even the most surprising true explanation, would have proved adequate to absorb the psychic geyser that swirled up from the crew and spread to make itself felt wherever, from Jolo to Hankow, there was a handful of Navy people to receive news of the portent. Even the few days' headstart, apparently, that the work on Delilah had gained could not be spared: Delilah's men, staring through the dusk, realized that the work on the other destroyers was to progress through the night.

This disturbing event, combined with the fact of his finally having to sleep in his bungalow ashore because the repair work now had extended to the propeller shafts beneath the floor of his cabin, achieved with the Captain something no other power had seemed able to effect. It divided his loyalty, tore him away from Delilah and set him up in an office ashore; for he was not only Captain of his own ship but Division Commander as well. This command of the five ships as a unit always had remained for him, except briefly at torpedo and target practice, almost entirely a theoretical concept, a sort of official technicality. Although he used the pronoun "my" in connection with those under his command, he rarely had been heard to say, "my Division."

Even days after the other destroyers had arrived, when he was imperceptibly losing his identity as Captain of Delilah and gaining another as Division Commander, and after being immersed for hours in conferences with the other four Captains over drawings and plans that did not concern Delilah, he still said, "the Division" and "my ship." If, on one of the daily visits the Captain scrupulously made to Delilah, no matter how exacting his duties grew in the administration of this unprecedented Division activity, he had been heard to say, "my Division," his relationship with Delilah's men would have suffered a subtle dislocation that would have left them overtly disquieted. As it was, the intimacy between him and them, tacit and highly formalized, an intimacy far greater in essence than that between them and any other officer in the ship, underwent a dilution; and this negative barrier tended to isolate him from the men much as his refusal to give the three officers a clue to the meaning of these extraordinary repairs had detached him a little from them. He was distinctly aware, when he came aboard now, of a feeling that he was being received there, not simply as the Captain of the ship, but also with a strain of that larger attitude the lack of which he would have resented on boarding any other ship in the Division. Sensing it there, in his own ship, it somehow gave him an uncomfortable feeling, as if he had been made the victim of an excluding gesture. It was this, perhaps, that made him go poking about the ship on his visits in an aggressively proprietary manner no one ever had observed in him before. He would descend to his room and rearrange a few objects there in seeming accordance with some precise intention; or he would lean over an engine-room hatch and fasten his gaze on one thing after another below in a way that gave an impression that it was his hands he was using rather than his eyes. Once he climbed up to the signal rack behind the Radio Shack and began pulling out the signals and looking at them in a purposeful way. When he felt eyes gazing down on him from the bridge, he apparently felt a kind of justificatory pleasure, for he began jerking the flags around with brusque, rightful gestures. Bidot, Cavendish and Arnold, watching him from the bridge above, smiled broadly, sympathetically, a flush of understanding touching their feelings . . . the Captain, down there, was declaring himself "in," behaving intimately with the private mechanics of the ship, a privilege denied, by regulation and tradition, even to the Admiral, much more to the Division Commander.

A rumour began to circulate that he was to be relieved of his command of Delilah so that he could devote all his time to the duty of Division Commander. On the night that he first got wind of this possibility, he walked straight out of the house where he was dining, after the most perfunctory of excuses, and headed for his ship . . . That would be a fine thing . . . to step clean out of the rank of ship commanders up into the high company of those who commanded only units . . . the ladder was presenting itself free and clear for him to climb . . . all he would have to do was climb . . . climb . . . climb up out of the necessity of getting his ship back together again . . . of getting his men back in her . . . the two Carey brothers . . . and Woodbridge . . . and yes . . . himself, too, by God! . . . If he played his cards right now, he would be Borden, Division Commander . . . then Borden, Flotilla Commander . . . then Borden . . . He stood on Delilah's quarter-deck and stared across the dark film of water glinting unhealthily under the covered moon. The thickness of the night seemed to lie in the miasma, esoteric and musky, that rose from the ring of oriental tidewater in which were mired his ship, the hovels of the Base, the four other destroyers in the distance, the few blurred stars close overhead and the whispered rise of his fate. In his feelings and in the soul of his mind he could not seem to get his apperception of reality significantly past this ship upon which he was standing and his personal relationship to it. He fixed his gaze determinedly on the other destroyers one after another. Flaring over there in the unclear darkness with the orange and blue fires of forges and welding torches, they seemed like long cauldrons boiling frantically in the night under the sinister impatience of witches who knew dreadfully and surely what they wanted. He congratulated himself again as he stood staring at the apparition of his new opportunity, congratulated himself like a small, neat Macbeth there in the fetid darkness, while the many

240

wrinkles of his face grew elongated and stiff, and his hands clutched tensely the topmost of those bronze cables that kept Delilah's men from falling overboard.

10 〰️

It had seemed as improbable to Lieutenant Fitzpatrick as it had to the men that he ever would put Warrington's name on one of the successive draft lists he was being called upon to make out. That he finally did so could not be attributed to the reasons that had crept up on him after the event. He had put Warrington's name down, he *now* told himself, because he had to be more strictly impartial in his case than in regard to any other; and Warrington had been the youngest and least valuable man on the bridge. However, when the demand first had arrived for two men out of the Engineer's Force and one signalman to be sent to the submarines, there had been no such thoughts in his head.

He had had little difficulty in selecting O'Connel and Mendel as the two men out of the Engineer's Force to be sent to the dangerous little craft; and he had actually been conscious of a hope, as he had written down their names, that circumstances might keep them there, that somehow in the mix up of this transfer business he might get back a couple of other men in their stead. He had been a trifle surprised at finding that this was his attitude towards O'Connel. He had thought that he believed that the Irishman was part of the cherished tone and colour of the ship, that he believed what he once had said in describing O'Connel to a cocktail party ashore: "Destroyers should be manned exclusively by men like that wild Irishman" . . . That, however, was just the trouble . . . he was wild and crazy and unpredictable . . . he was TNT on the loose. Lieutenant Fitzpatrick had put his name down with the feeling that he ought not to get him back, that he ought to transfer him to the submarines, that the submarines ought to transfer him to some other station, that that station in turn ought to transfer him and so on to the day of his pensioning. The Navy was no place for crazy men . . . nor for Jews . . . one could imagine a Jew dying as Christ on a cross, but not as Horatius at a bridgehead. He would transfer them both.

The demand for the signalman had puzzled him. He never had heard of a signalman being sent to a submarine. He thought they must have made a mistake. He had queried the Personnel Office at the Base and had found that there had been no mistake. The submarines were going to engage in a new kind of surface manoeuvre and they wanted a good signalman on each boat. As a matter of fact, he had told himself, he could spare people from the bridge at this time more easily than any others. He would send Arnold. Then, on the instant, with pencil poised to write Arnold's name, a strange cloud of revulsion had swept through him, a revulsion that had had nothing to do with Arnold, but that yet had kept him from putting down the man's name. It had been a kind of nameless, hidden fear flaming into the open as if to illuminate the imminent, fatal loss of a saving opportunity, a flame that, as it had persisted, had chemically changed some dominating attitude of his emotions, burning away the supports of his feelings so that he had seemed to be dropping down suddenly through great clear depths with a painful vacuum at the pit of his stomach. He had written Warrington's name on the transfer list. Then in utter, empty, unhoped-for relief, he quickly had handed the list to Bates, the Yeoman, saying: "Copy and post it."

Lieutenant Fitzpatrick had not been present when O'Connel, Mendel and Warrington had left the ship. Immediately after ordering the list posted, he had gone ashore feeling released into a kind of new, fresh being. He would not have been able to explain really how he felt, nor, if he had been able to, why he felt that way. As he strolled along briskly in the sunshine, he was exultant over a new sense of freedom. He had mysteriously got himself back again. He had plunged out of an unhealthy storm back to solid ground. Even if Warrington had been an officer or an equal ashore, such an involving friendship would not have been too sound a thing. Never again would he get so deep into anybody's being; and he must never let anybody get so deep into him . . . "But it's over . . . settled very simply for good and all . . . I'll see to that," he told himself. He was almost drunk, physically drunk, with the feeling of belonging to himself alone once more. He gave a light pull at the visor of his cap, setting it slightly to one side. He glanced, alertly gallant, into a passing *carromato,* and smiled exuberantly at the pale, little *mestiza* sitting alone in the shadowed corner of the semi-open carriage like an impassive, delicate insect poised on the wings of her full mango cloth sleeves. As her carriage passed him swiftly, she let her handkerchief flick out and trail almost imperceptibly for an instant in the light air beside her. With a free and easy promptness, but just faintly shadowed by a strange self-consciousness of its freedom, he swung toward a carriage waiting for hire at the nearby curb. Again, some kind of strength seemed to be dissolving warmly, exquisitely away from the pit of his stomach. It interfered with his breath, as he tried to call sharply to the dozing driver and horses:

"Let's go! . . . There . . . just turning the corner."

For Warrington the break had come with none of this heady bursting into discovery of unexpected release: But he, too, was free, calmly, tragically free, free of the nameless, restless pressure within him that he had come to regard, come to regard aggressively, as the price of that friendship the lack of which, even in this heavy moment, he found difficulty in facing. As he had stared at the posted list, he had told himself that this blow was not unexpected, and his mind had seemed to use the word, "blow," as one customarily uses the word, "solution." Not for a moment did he regard his transfer as the temporary expedient that included the others who had gone; he knew that it was to be permanent, that it was a dissolution. He had walked stiffly forward along the deck to say good-bye to the bridge crew. Then he had gone below to pack his bag. The same fierce glaze had come to his eyes that had been there in his first moments aboard the ship. The air that he had breathed had unsettled his throat and his lungs. It had seemed to him that he had been walking through an abandoned house in which he once had lived.

In the forecastle, through whose cagelike tiers of grey metal bunks the port-holes were sending beams of yellow light, he had been observed by Mendel the moment he had come through the doorway. After staring at him for many seconds through the centre tier of bunks, Mendel finally had circled around to Warrington's locker and silently helped him pack his books. Those for which there was no room the Jew had packed in his own bag. Mendel had kept darting looks at Warrington's face as if covertly seeking there the very words of comfort and exhortation he had wanted to speak to the face, that he had been tortured to speak into the welter of pain, discomfiture and anger that had smouldered behind it. In oblique desperation the Jew had been struggling for something to say that would have borne not at all on the cause of his friend's suffering but that yet would have served accurately as anodyne for it. At last he had said, gesturing with one of the books, while his wide lips had almost sneered with the frustration of his compassion:

"This will fix us up with the real thing . . . just reading about danger and stuff isn't enough . . . those submarines are the works . . . they're lousy with danger . . . they got plenty of excitement."

Warrington's brain, apparently, just had not identified the words. He had said, "Yes," and had begun lashing his hammock. While Mendel had been speaking, Warrington had been struggling with his astonishment, with his heavy resentment over the fact that so much that was deeply personal could have been dismissed with such an impersonal gesture as that posted order. Mendel, conscious of how far his distorted effort would have missed the mark, had been relieved that Warrington had not heard him.

11 〜〜〜

Lieutenant Fitzpatrick, at a quarter to nine the next morning, stood at the end of the dock, near Delilah's stern, and watched the little submarines lumber out through the breakwater toward Corregidor. There were four of them, one behind the other at about hundred yard intervals, struggling and foaming along in the quiet brown water of the bay like over-fat grey pigs with awninged howdahs on their slightly awash backs. To Lieutenant Fitzpatrick, they appeared somehow clean and definite out there under the sun-blue morning sky. He glanced around at the greasy, splintered dock on which he stood, now completely denuded of the greenery that had transformed it, and then at the dishevelled ship alongside him. It looked rusty and deserted despite the animal-like little workmen crawling about it. He moved his shoulders restlessly. He would, he thought, like to serve in a submarine . . . "not in one of those Noah's Arks out there . . . they could barely creep along . . . but in a capable, modern one . . . like one of those fast K-Boats at Pearl Harbour . . . That would be real Navy . . . on one's own with a handful of picked men in the depths of the sea." He glanced reluctantly at his own ship. ". . . just a God damn coal barge when you came right down to it . . . ferrying back and forth." With a sense of futility that spread in calm malignancy into every reach of his being, he glanced out again over the muddy glitter of the bay. The last submarine in line had fallen a considerable distance behind. He watched mechanically as it gradually lost headway and relaxed into a stupid rolling and drifting with the almost invisible motion of the placid water. "Break-down," he guessed, ". . . The whole, stinking, antiquated Fleet is breaking down." He wondered if any of the men he had transferred were on her. "Must be hot as hell drifting out there in that blistering calm . . . A lot of help Warrington would be to them in this fix if that was the one he was on." The water splashed restively around the piling beneath his feet. Through the wide cracks in the planking a stench of some floating dead thing thrust vaguely up at him. "Every man on those boats had to fit in and do more than his share . . . no room for excess baggage there . . . only twelve or so men . . . and all of them crowded into one little compartment along with everything else, torpedoes, engines, tools, ballast, periscope, storage batteries, men . . ."

The submarine, which now had been left far behind by the others in the assurance that if she could not continue on she could signal the Base for a tow, drifted into such position that Lieutenant Fitzpatrick could make out the number on her. "Schiff's boat . . . *Ensign* Schiff, phooey! . . . it *would* be his boat that broke down . . . a Jew had no business being a naval officer . . . much less in command of a vessel . . . Schiff was clever as hell, you had to hand him that . . . but their guts and blood were sour . . . no iron in them . . . they . . ." Lieutenant Fitzpatrick's hand had come quickly up to shade his eyes, which had levelled in a stare of amazement. Out there three men had been spat abruptly up into the air from the conning-tower in the most ridiculous fashion. Like acrobatic clowns in a vaudeville act, they sprawled laughably for a moment in the air between the submarine and the blazing sun. Then they splashed successively into the water. He watched for them to swim back to the submarine; but there seemed to be no movement where they had fallen. There was no movement on the submarine either, not a sign of a man between the four stanchions that had held the small awning. The awning had disappeared too: Only a ragged wisp hung at the tip of each stanchion where its corners had been fastened. The submarine was moving, moving uncertainly and very slowly in a meaningless direction, moving, he thought, through the still heat like an abandoned derelict in a light breeze. Suddenly Lieutenant Fitzpatrick began to shout, nearly screaming as if under the assault of some desperate awakening.

"Man overboard! . . . Man overboard! . . . Get away the life-boat!"

"No, by God, that wasn't it," he told himself. "Explosion! . . . that's what it was . . . that thing had exploded without a sound, without a puff of smoke!" Lieutenant Fitzpatrick swung around and faced the men that were springing toward him along the dock.

"Get away the Rescue Party! . . . Explosion on submarine six hundred yards due north!"

A number of men automatically followed him as he leapt from the dock onto Delilah and made for the starboard whaleboat, which still hung forlornly at its davits. Most of the men on the dock, however, had been thrown into helpless confusion by the officer's shouts. Nobody knew what to do marooned there out of the ship on the cluttered dock. The regularly organized Rescue Party had been broken up by the transfers . . . "Who goes? . . . Where's the boat? . . . What gear? . . . What tools?" Cruck, the Chief Boatswain's Mate, had sung out, in response to the officer's order, "A-w-a-y-y-y the Rescue Party!" in a chant that had been heard clearly far beyond the limits of the dock and which had alarmed that whole section of the Base into concerned alertness;

but around him men did nothing but shout back uncertainly and mill towards a view of the bay. Cruck grabbed Wright by the throat and flung him ferociously towards Delilah. The Seaman's pimpled face crashed stunningly against a railing stanchion as he grabbed frantically to keep himself from falling into the narrow crevice between the ship and the dock. His dirty hands groped childishly at his straw-coloured hair as his stunned senses struggled with the meaning in the bellowing behind him:

"Lay aft the Rescue Party! . . . Lay aft all hands! . . . The starboard whaleboat, you dirty bastards! . . . *move*!"

The men had stood there, a sweating, wildly disturbed mob, frustrated in the face of Cruck's uninforming violence, until he uttered the words, "all hands" and "starboard whaleboat." Then they charged at the ship as if, like Wright, they had been flung there.

Lieutenant Fitzpatrick and those who had followed him had gotten the boat down in the water. Forsythe, the Seaman, stood in the bow fending her off with a boat-hook. Easterly, the Fireman, Second-Class, was at the stern, awkwardly holding her in by clutching at one of Delilah's open port-holes. The officer, a thick streak of grease disfiguring his white cap-cover, balanced himself on spread legs in the middle of the whaleboat and with grim impatience fixed his eyes in the direction from which, on the other side of the ship, came the fury of Cruck's shouting. All at once the whole ship's company flooded across the ship and massed at the railing above him, a great, arrested wave of staring eyes. His gaze met, for an instant, that of a man in the crowd. He lashed an order at these eyes, an order that was fatalistic rather than calm:

"Get an axe" . . . Then to another pair of eyes: "Get a fire extinguisher" . . . Another: "Get a bucket" . . . "sledge" . . . "bar" . . . "line" . . . But he was thinking: "Warrington's on that boat . . . it couldn't be any other way . . . that's the way life works . . . Christ!"

After Chief Machinist's Mate Stengle had climbed down, armed with a Stillson wrench and a hacksaw, the boat started to pull away; but when Lieutenant Fitzpatrick saw Heller, the Pharmacist's Mate, fighting his way through the crowd at the rail, he ordered the boat to back water. "Got to have this man, God damn him." The Pharmacist's Mate, who evidently had been taking a bath, was wet and naked save for a pair of drawers and his emergency kit slung by a strap over his shoulder. Even at that, for two or three minutes Delilah's boat, badly manned and overloaded, was the only one on the way to the submarine, which still was circling slowly in the smooth water like a small whale tortured into imbecile helplessness by the relentless sun.

When they were some three hundred yards from the stricken craft, the atmosphere of being abandoned that pervaded it was abruptly dissipated by the figure of a man emerging from the small, black hole of the conning-tower hatch. Out waist high, he bent at the middle in an eerie manner and writhed face down across the bulge of the submarine's top-side into the water. Those pulling at the oars in the whaleboat could not, of course, see this; but the cry that arose from the others in the boat, a cry of consternation and discovery, empowered their pulling with furious desperation. That helpless figure sliding awkwardly, blindly into the sea there had slugged through the abstraction of disaster with the personal reality of tortured men trying to claw their way up out of frightful confinement. Another blind figure arose from the submarine's hatch, tottered around for an instant as if trying to locate the water, then leapt insanely as if trusting to chance. The unseen splash of his body, counterpointed by the involuntary sounds this tore from the mouths of men who could see it, shattered the self-control of some of those at the oars. Easterly, the Fireman, Second-Class, missed the water altogether with his blade. Confusion swept the stroke of the six oarsmen behind whose backs something horrible was happening. Easterly fought viciously with the oar defying his sweaty, blistering hands and screamed silently against the injustice of his own incompetence and the fate that had driven him into this intolerable corner: He never had touched an oar more than a dozen times in his life.

Lieutenant Fitzpatrick had begun to shout the stroke:

"Pull! . . . Pull! . . . Pull! . . ." The officer's eyes were clutching at the figures in the water. ". . . Stroke! . . . Stroke! . . . (He probably was pinned inside the thing) . . . Stroke! . . ."

It occurred to Easterly to heave the oar that was defeating him over the side. As he did so, he flung his head around in a reckless, relieving gesture that permitted him to see behind him . . . "The hell with the God damn oar! . . . Doing more harm than good with it anyway." However, the instant he had adjusted himself to the scene behind him, he semi-consciously leapt at the idea of some compensatory act, something that would assuage his own agony under the pressure of the horror only a few yards away there that he just had betrayed by flinging away his oar. As a result of his defection the boat had swung off its course, almost broadside to the direction in which the submarine slowly was moving. In the intervening strip of water, near the whaleboat, his searching eyes found a head and an arm. Further disrupting the efforts of the oarsmen to get reorganized, he stood up in the boat pointing wildly and trying to shout above the roar of recrimination that rose around him. He prepared to jump overboard after the man barely afloat in the water. Somebody knocked him back on the thwart. He arose again, was knocked back once more; and as the whaleboat was oared toward the figure in the water he crouched there, half out of the boat, every feature alive with frustration because he could not jump overboard after that man.

It was Lieutenant Fitzpatrick, leaning authoritatively far out from the stern, both hands extended eagerly, who got hold of the man. Mendel's head was denuded completely of hair, and the flesh of his skull and face had turned a strange, parboiled white. His hawklike nose was bulged out of shape, and the closed lids of his eyes had become very thick and purple. The officer grasped him violently under the armpits and shook him.

"Mendel! . . . Mendel!"

The line of the Jew's wide, sensuous mouth slowly changed its shape, like a small, torpid serpent that had been disturbed. His breath was coming and going with the sound of a jet of air fluttering a loose strip of membrane. Lieutenant Fitzpatrick half lifted him out of the water and, putting his mouth close to the Jew's ear, said:

"Where's Warrington? . . . Is he inside? Did he get out?"

The Jew's wet face was a mask of unrestrained resignation and submission, like the face of an invalid who has had enough of pain and of life. He partially opened his eyes for a moment to look at the face close to his as he said:

"He's on another boat."

In the spasm of exquisite relief and comfort that struck through Lieutenant Fitzpatrick, his hands and arms unconsciously relaxed, permitting Mendel to slip back into the muddy water. He simply sank beneath it without another movement, as if he somehow had expended the last fateful vestige of a pretext for remaining above it. The momentum of the whaleboat carried it several yards past where the Jew sank before those in the stern of the boat, including Lieutenant Fitzpatrick, himself, fully realized that nobody any longer had hold of him. The moment this generally was perceived, the oarsmen began to swing the boat toward the spot. With a kind of ferocity Easterly once more prepared to dive into the water. Lieutenant Fitzpatrick now, however, insuperably was possessed with his obligation to the disaster as a whole; and from the depths of this obligation his voice, irresistible and calm, rose to hold the men back from their excited effort to return to Mendel. Into the face of their confused, unexpressed averseness he shouted, as he pointed astern at other small boats that were coming up swiftly:

"They'll get him."

When the whaleboat, dominated by the first real semblance of order that had prevailed since it had left Delilah's side, was almost upon the submarine, Lieutenant Fitzpatrick was astonished to see the stricken craft suddenly increase its speed. As if this had been a symptom of further disaster, he stared belligerently at the ominous little conning-tower expecting to see its dark mouth vomit more victims. The cry went up:

"It's going under!"

What it was doing was careening erratically around a turn of its unguided course before the thrust of its greater speed. "If it would only turn this way," thought Lieutenant Fitzpatrick, "a man could jump onto her deck and take the wheel . . . steer her into the dock." He tried to direct the whaleboat across the submarine's new course, but in the very moment he thought he finally was intercepting her, she changed direction once more. If those other boats would only get up they could corner it! He glanced helplessly in their direction. The nearest boats had stopped to pick up the men in the water. One was hauling in a man whose glinting leg bone had been stripped of flesh by the plunge from the searing heat of the explosion into the water.

"Lay on those oars, damn you!" yelled Lieutenant Fitzpatrick.

The oarsmen did not hear him. They were semi-conscious under the desperation of their sustained effort. Their faces were red and dripping perspiration. Their teeth were clenched. They heaved at each stroke as if it were the last act of their lives. Lieutenant Fitzpatrick fixed his gaze in an agony of intensity on the small surface-steering-wheel, swinging helplessly first one way and then the other, on the deserted deck of that grey death-trap fleeing through the muddy water . . . If he watched its swing he might get an idea which way the thing was going to turn . . . it was getting farther and farther away . . . If only he could get a man at that wheel!

As if the fury of the wish he shot along his gaze at that forlorn little steering-wheel had a power too strong for reality and fate to resist, an apparition, a long, distorted object of blood and rags, and flesh that looked unreal in the sunlight, rose from the hatch of the submarine and crawled fumblingly on all fours to the steering post. Grasping the spokes of the wheel, it pulled itself upright, a horrible caricature sharply outlined against the luminous background of the sky. It even straightened its shoulders in a grim and ridiculous gesture as if bracing itself for an ordeal; then it swung the wheel and the submarine headed for the breakwater. A veritable scream of relief rose from the boats struggling to come up with him. Those nearest him shouted his name in frantic encouragement:

"Straight ahead, Mr. Schiff!" . . . "Stay with it, Schiff, old boy!" . . . "Schiff. . ."

Ensign Schiff did "stay with it." He stayed there at that wheel, a tall, gaunt figure, stiff and appalling, and steered his vessel through the breakwater entrance and straight at the Submarine Dock, steered her on and on in some miraculous fashion, the soiled, glistening skull his youthful head had become, in which only the aquiline nose still seemed to live, bent far back so that the eye sockets were aimed rigidly, sightlessly up into the topmost depths of the glaring and pitiless sunshine.

The crowd of watchers lining the shore-lines of the Base, and those in the welter of boats in its wake, grunted spasmodically when the submarine finally crashed bow on into the Submarine

Dock, grunted as if they had been a single individual struck violently in the stomach. Those on the dock grappled the submarine and made her fast. Then, for an instant, the rush aboard her of a Rescue Party was checked by the stench, acrid, fleshy, nauseating, that poured from the hole in that steel maw. In that instant, Ensign Schiff turned, holding onto the wheel behind him with one hand, and said to the people on the dock, speaking as a man speaks who has fought to hold his breath for a long time:

"Batteries . . . hydrogen . . . Get the men out please."

Then he swung slowly about and faced in the direction of the bungalow, not far away, where he lived with his wife. It seemed for a moment as if he were about to walk off in that direction right across the intervening strip of water; but instead he sank reluctantly to his knees, then onto his side, and pillowed his head on the odious thing that had been his arm.

12 〜〜〜

For the Captain, Mendel's death was an item of unequivocal defeat. There was one man Delilah never could get back. They would beat him there; be able to, have to give him a new man to replace him. It was not a fair defeat though. It was as if he had been standing fist to fist with an opponent and the referee had slipped in a blow from behind. It made him restless, so restless that he spent the day after the accident goading along the work on his ship in an effort to reduce the period in which such things could happen. He must manage to get to the point, as soon as possible, where the ship all came back together again. There was trying to arise in his mind a vague, irritating conviction that forces beyond his control, even beyond his contact, were eating around the edges of his plans and his purpose. He was struggling unself-consciously against this conviction when he sat down in his cabin to the miserable task of writing a letter to Mendel's mother in New York regarding the manner of his death. He wrote the letter very rapidly, almost mechanically, to the tempo, as it were, of the current of thoughts running below those concerned with the letter . . . He had two

more men in those submarines . . . he was going to get them back
. . . get them back right now! . . . He had not figured on this
kind of sniping . . . He made a restless error with his fountain
pen, spoiling the letter, when another idea clotted this current of
thought, a kind of idea particularly repugnant to the essence of
his personality, the kind of thing he objectively would have regarded as hysterical nonsense: It was queer under the circumstances that it had to be one of *his* men that was killed, was the
substance of what had risen in his thinking. "But, hell . . . hadn't
eight other men been killed too!" he had instantly reprimanded
himself as he laid down the pen and picked up the unfinished
letter. When he had read what he so far had written, he knew
that he would have to write an entirely different letter. What he
had written was true enough; but what that woman would want
was something definite and comforting about the way he died.
He could make it definite enough, he assured himself, "but there
was nothing comforting about it . . . being blown to smithereens
into the water and dying hard there for ten minutes . . . this was
a tough one." What vaguely but cogently complicated the difficulty of writing the letter was his remembered impression of Mendel about the ship, as if from this impression there was reflected
to him some disturbing hint of qualities where his letter would
be received that peculiarly incapacitated him as the writer of the
letter. He would have found himself at a loss in writing such a
letter to the mother of any of his men; but to Mendel's mother
the effort became mysteriously more difficult.

He strove to envision the mother reading this letter, or a good
one if he could manage to write it; and there rose in his perceptions the figure of the only mother of any kind he really ever had
known as such, his own. He could guess uncomfortably at what
to say to this woman, this firm-fleshed angular woman of English-
Scotch ancestry whose controlled, reticent spirit had patterned his
boyhood; and he took up the pen again to say it . . . to say it to a
short, swarthy, obese woman, into whose great, moist, black eyes,
complaining and ever on the alert for misery, there flooded, at the
slightest release, all the frank power of her emotions . . . to say on
a piece of paper words about the death of her son, the son, an
appendage of her body, like one of her breasts, whom a ruthless

God had given her to immerse in a dank and exhaustive maternity
. . . words on a piece of paper telling the wrath of the God she so
long had propitiated . . . propitiated standing beside her mother
in the gallery of the synagogue on Delancey Street, staring down,
tortured with emotion, at the shawled male heads below that
swayed rhythmically before the passionate, masochistic lash of
the rabbi, who intoned with inspired detail the insults, the injuries
that preserved their nationalism of ignominious pain, intoned it
until her mother, who had seen pogroms in the Balkans, sobbed
so terribly that she disturbed the service and had to be helped out
by the *Shamus* into the street . . . a piece of paper that began:

> "Dear Mrs. Mendel:
> This is a hard letter to have to write to you. By now the
> Navy Department will have informed you of your son's
> death out here in the line of duty. As his Commanding Of-
> ficer, I thought you would like to know something more per-
> sonal about it, and that we did the best we could for him."

As he poised the fountain pen for the next paragraph, he shifted
his body with dissatisfaction, shoved the butt of the pen through
the unruly area of his sandy hair. He was no good at this kind of
thing . . . what he was writing was as dry as dust . . . that boy was
probably the apple of her eye . . .

> "He was a fine, clean boy and served his country bravely
> to the end like a true American. And I can only say to you
> that we liked him and hated to lose him and I feel the deep-
> est sympathy for you in your terrible loss.
> "We have carefully gotten his things together and will
> send them to the Navy Department, which will forward them
> to you. He would have been promoted soon because he was
> intelligent and never neglected his duty."

Now for the hard part . . . this is what she really wants to know
. . . where were those eye-glasses . . . He located them and put
them on . . . What a thing to have to tell a boy's mother! . . . He
wrote:

"Your son was assigned temporarily for a few days' duty on the submarine. On its way out for manoeuvres an explosion occurred. Your son was at his post. He was blown out into the water, where he died before a boat picked him up.

"It is small comfort to you, who have lost a son, to say that the manner of his passing on has aroused the greatest admiration in all who know him. I wish there was something I could say to comfort you. All I can say is that you and your family have the deepest sympathy of the officers and men of this ship amongst whom he lived and served his country."

The Captain read the letter over. It occurred to him to show it to Lieutenant Fitzpatrick; but almost immediately he rejected this impulse. He read it over again; then his small blue eyes stared hard at the paragraph about the manner of Mendel's death, stared at it as if for some reason he was not seeing it. He started to call in the Yeoman to have the letter copied on the typewriter. No . . . he had decided in the first place that it had to be written personally and he would write it that way . . . He still was staring at that paragraph. Then with a kind of finality he laid the letter down on the desk again and picked up the pen to correct it . . . He *would* correct it . . . and copy it over himself. With an abrupt gesture he took off his spectacles. He changed the words "was blown" to "got" and put the word "instantly" after "died." As he recopied the letter, however, he wrote: "almost instantly."

It certainly was true that O'Connel, for one, had been filled with admiration and a kind of exultant sadness by Mendel's death. This was apparent when he and Warrington had returned back aboard Delilah, returned as a result of the Captain's insistence at the Personnel Office that he now needed them and the submarines did not, those craft having been laid up for alterations in an effort to preclude another disaster. Warrington, on the other hand, had not yet developed any poignant memory of Mendel. The man's death remained almost an abstraction for him, an abstraction illumined by a general pity that at one moment was intense and at another almost theoretical. His feelings were claimed preponderantly by a kind of heavy relief at being back aboard the ship; and the appreciation, the admiration that arose in him whenever his consciousness was completely caught by the events

255

of the explosion, was for the magnificence of Ensign Shiff's effort, an effort by a man he did not know, and which, therefore, he was able to appreciate in essence, an effort that reflected glory on the death of his friend, Mendel (whom he knew only too well), to just about the extent that this death participated in that of Ensign Schiff. He almost smiled at the way O'Connel (for whom Ensign Schiff's end was little more than the background, heroic but abstract, for the death of the man that he, O'Connel, knew personally) carried on about Mendel, at the boisterous persuasiveness with which the Irishman became touched on the occasions when his name came up: But it was the hardy dye of the big man's emotion that soon coloured the attitude of all the rest of the ship's company. Even the blond, stable objectiveness of Cavendish, the Quartermaster, was affected by it. In the first hours after the accident, O'Connel's mind and emotions had fused three elements that, together as a crystallized whole, became for him Mendel and his elegy: the extraordinary manner in which Ensign Schiff had permitted himself to die only after he had brought in his stricken men, together with the conviction that he, O'Connel, had been Mendel's recognized friend, had become one with the fact of Mendel's death in a spectacular disaster. With that remarkable ability available to some people, the Irishman swept out of his consciousness the memory of all the disgust and hatred, all the violence, he up until recently had visited upon Mendel; and he would have been astonished and indignant if anyone had seen anything inconsistent in his attitude. Standing with an arm thrown around Warrington's shoulders, he would mourn Mendel for minutes on end, almost clinging to the Texan as if they two were the survivors of a triumvirate that only such a death could separate. Feenan slowly detected the one unconscious flaw in O'Connel's attitude, when periodically O'Connel would interject, "He must have had some Irish in him," and the Oiler, whenever he thought it was safe, would respond, turning away to spit over the side, "Yeh . . . he was different from regular Jews."

Easterly, the Fireman, while he remained susceptible to O'Connel's influence in this matter because it pointed up Mendel's death, was not concerned with it greatly in its guise of tragic heroism. His main concern with the event seemed to be that it was the source of the unpleasant feeling that kept pawing at his insides, a restless feeling of being humiliatingly unsatisfied. He thought of this feeling simply as anger over his having been treated unjustly; but he could not get rid of it . . . "the sons of bitches . . . Why, I tried to save a man's life!" he kept insisting to himself, "Tried to dive over after him! . . . And they cursed me and socked me . . . and held me in the boat . . . and Fitzpatrick bawled me out . . . made a fool of me!" He tried to convince himself that if they had not interfered with him he could have saved Mendel's life; but his normal critical sense mitigated that conviction with the unquenchable probability that the man was dying when they came up with him in the water . . . But that was not the point, he told himself over and over, it was the idea of the thing. He had tried to dive over to save a man and they had made a fool of him!

Lieutenant Fitzpatrick had reprimanded him, spoken to him sharply and impatiently before most of the ship's company, while the fires of Easterly's frustration still were burning brightly. It had been in the moment of release after the whaleboat had pulled back to Delilah's side. The sweaty oarsmen, their breath and strength spent, were hunched over on the thwarts, with their arms extended rigidly out at their sides for support. They probably had not paid much attention to the reprimand; but the men crowding Delilah's rail had. In order to listen to it they had halted the questions they were firing down at the boat. The others in the whaleboat, those not at the oars, who were waiting for the officer to be first out, also had listened attentively while Lieutenant Fitzpatrick told Easterly that when he wanted anybody to jump overboard he would give orders to that effect . . . that Easterly had held up the Rescue Party in the first place by losing his oar, and then had thrown everything into confusion by trying to jump overboard like a damn fool . . . He ought to put him on the Report . . . Next time he was in a boat he was to see to it that he sat tight and obeyed orders.

As Lieutenant Fitzpatrick had turned his back and climbed up onto Delilah's deck, Easterly had stared after him in a daze of mortification and resentment. He had hated that back more than he ever had hated anybody in the world; but he had continued to stare at it because there was no face in it, and keeping his eyes there saved him from looking into those other faces lining the rail. "The dirty little punk!" he had raged to himself, "I'd like to show him . . . I'd like to smack him in the mouth." It seemed to him that he had sat there before that crowd stripped naked, by brutality and injustice, of everything that made him human. It did not occur to him for a second that in their eyes he looked like nothing more nor less than a shipmate who had been rebuked by an officer, appeared as he always appeared, a healthy but hollow-cheeked coal heaver with dark, stringy hair and prominent, square, slightly separated teeth in a wide mouth. It was true that his full lips, which usually had colour, had paled, and that the slightly fuzzy area across his eyes, an area with a womanish quality, had become drawn and tense. His easy smile had gone for the moment; but he had the same touch of wild handsomeness about him, had been, for them, the same quite ordinary youth. When Lieutenant Fitzpatrick's back had disappeared over the rail, Easterly had shifted his eyes into the perspective of smooth, dirty water that led up into the Base . . . Why the hell didn't they get away from the rail and let him come up in peace? . . . He had wanted to dive over after that man . . . the sons of bitches. He appeared to be gazing at the spectacle, in the distance there, of the native workmen on the other destroyers already at their labours again, as if not even death and disaster could halt for long their furious efforts in behalf of some fatal and hidden exigency.

13 ≈≈≈

The relief of both Lieutenant Fitzpatrick and Warrington, over the latter's return to the ship, was so extensive that, not being able to perceive its limits, they almost ceased to recognize it. They soon breathed the atmosphere of their reunion as a swimmer might breathe the air an hour or so after rising to the surface from a deep, lung-torturing dive, unconscious that it was a boon, that it was a thing whose deficiency had been experienced, a precarious thing to be reckoned with. Shortly the officer found himself spared even the poignancy that at first remained in the memory of the long, violent moment through which he had suffered the false premonition that Warrington was on the wrecked submarine; and for some reason he found himself thinking: "I had nothing to do with getting him back aboard . . . I tried to transfer him." It had become implicitly clear to him, while Warrington and O'Connel were in the very act of officially reporting back aboard as members of Delilah's crew, formally lined up before him on the dock with their bags and hammocks, that there now persisted between himself and his friend a barrier that seemed insuperable, an unidentifiable barrier that yet was like the aftermath of some final quarrel. The officer's mind, however, never reached the point of envisioning what had brought about this state of affairs: There had been no quarrel: Their relationship simply had encountered a great, passionate, nameless obstacle, on one side of which was himself and on the other Warrington.

Warrington, on his part, although his mind seethed continually with a hunt for the cause, never for a moment seemed to attribute his own participation in the result of the implicit quarrel to his feelings over having been transferred. That cruel and curt act, it appeared to him, was not a cause but a consequence; and he now seemed to perceive that the clearly remembered feeling of finality that had swept him on seeing his name on the transfer list, the feeling that the transfer was to be permanent, really had been a confused realization of the end of their friendship. Neither of them spoke to each other now save in the line of duty. "Hand me the Rough Log Book," Lieutenant Fitzpatrick would say sharply, glancing at Warrington impersonally in the routine way one glances at the man to whom an order is given. Warrington's "Aye, Aye, Sir," would come out in a voice that was detached, almost aggressively prompt, illusively condescending; or, Warrington being on watch and observing the Captain entering the head of the dock, he would report to Lieutenant Fitzpatrick in much the same manner and tone of voice that the officer had used to him in giving an order: "Captain coming aboard, Sir"; and then the officer, borrowing the repellent quality, but not the forced respect, of the tone in which Warrington had said, "Aye, Aye, Sir," would pronounce, "Very well," and, turning his back

259

with pointed casualness, would walk to the gangway to meet the Captain as if Warrington had been merely a slightly annoying bell whose summons had interrupted him. Often the officer struggled with the impulse to recognize the enlisted man's attitude as contemptuous and insubordinate, and put him on the Report for it. He tried to condone the presence of this temptation, succumbing to which would have procured for Warrington a General Court Martial, by telling himself that "the man was begging for it." On the other hand, he literally would not have dared to make a gesture of reconciliation toward his friend, nor speak the word that would have launched them, in some empty moment of one of the many long, careless days that were smothering them there alongside the dock, on one of the old conversations. Neither could Warrington have made the gesture or spoken the word. He could not have done it if it would have saved him from being hung at the yard-arm. Fortunately for him the disaster to their relationship did not return him completely to the desert of meaningless ordeal that the Navy had been for him up to the moment of their first conversation on the bridge. The very stress between them, largely monopolizing his emotions and reflections, was, in its polarization, a misery rich with significance, as rich, in that sense, as their harmony had been. Like the officer, if he could not restore the harmony, he clung to the conflict that still bound them. However, the striking thing was not that they clung to the only bond that still seemed possible to them; but that they both actually seemed to be striving to protect and preserve, striving carefully and with a kind of cold desperation, the framework of their tacit quarrel as such. It was as if beneath their consciousness some deep prescience was battling, indirectly in the dark of their spirits, to save them from the illumination and strange grace into which an overreaching reconciliation, now, might plunge them.

The breach between Lieutenant Fitzpatrick and Warrington had been noticed neither generally nor importantly by the crew. This probably would not have been the case if Delilah, when the breach occurred, had been in a seagoing way of life, with the crew, as normally, a crowded, close-textured community confined within her and patterned by her routines. As it was, many of the men were gone, and most of the remainder, breeding private projects

260

ashore or recovering from alcoholic depressions, lolled in the deceptive shade on the covered dock amidst the clutter of cots, cookstove, fragments from the gutted ship and glistening torpedoes, or went ashore on more frequent and extended liberty than they usually enjoyed. Of course, there was work for some at odd jobs here and there on the dock and in the ship, which they went at in a disconnected manner under the pressure of but the one officer left to them. They even sent their laundry out to some Chinaman in Cavite. Their life, apparently, no longer was of a quality that made them susceptible to the minute hints and indices that, when they were at sea together, would have aroused them.

It is true that there had been the moment of group surprise when Warrington's name appeared on the transfer list; but that had been swept away by the storm of astonishment, both collective and individual, that had arisen around the incredible way the repair operations had been extended to the other four destroyers. Their susceptibilities, their community susceptibilities, all seemed keyed now to the heavy potentialities in these repair operations; and as a crew they remained almost unresponsive to anything of lower tone. The rapidly decreasing, sporadic fights ashore had quite begun to lose meaning for them as a definite collection of people; and even the accident to the submarine, with Mendel's death, had but briefly jogged them from the current of disorganization that, on the one hand, was tending to make of them mere individuals, and from the cross-current of mystifying interest that, on the other, still swept them along in a tenuous community of larger curiosity above what formerly had been their concentrated daily life.

Once Saunders did notice the manner in which an order was given and received between Lieutenant Fitzpatrick and Warrington. His heavy eyebrows had gone up in surprise and he had nudged Cruck, saying:

"What the hell's up between Whoses and Whatses?"

"Aw, I guess they got sore in one of them arguments or something," Cruck had replied negligently.

Even if Cruck's interest had been what it normally was in this category of event, it is doubtful if Saunders now would have been impelled to do much about it; and even if he had been impelled, managing to present the anecdote in its most catching form, he no doubt would have found that his item no longer possessed the impact and spread of live gossip.

Ensign Woodbridge and Ensign Snell, if they had been present through the development of this situation, might have sensed something a trifle disturbing in it, although the friendship between the Executive Officer and the Seaman never had gotten through, as a clear realization, to either of them. Ensign Woodbridge's only clue to the existence of some special relationship lay in his having twice interrupted the two, deep in talk about books, in order to relieve Lieutenant Fitzpatrick on the bridge. He had made nothing of it except that Lieutenant Fitzpatrick was being eccentric and that Warrington was some kind of freak; and he had made nothing else of it simply because such a friendship would be quite beyond possibility for himself. He would have been astounded, rather than scandalized, if his brother officer had confessed to him how far the association had gone. Neither the Captain nor Ensign Snell could have made him believe it. He would have had to hear it from the lips of Lieutenant Fitzpatrick, himself; and his feeling at such a confession would have been, in point of astonishment alone, a little like what it would be if he were to hear a friend back in Virginia confess, not to a quite usual deep regard and esteem for a Negro, but to an equal friendship with one. When he had overheard the literary discussion between the officer and the enlisted man, his mind casually had dismissed it as a piece of bizarre nonsense on the officer's part, a piece of nonsense that did not concern him, Woodbridge. It never would have occurred to him to discuss literature with an enlisted man anymore than it would have occurred to him to discuss astronomy with a woman. It just was not in the nature of things that it should occur to him. If it *had* occurred to him, on some inescapable occasion, he might have done it; but he would have felt that the occasion was uninteresting and inauthentic. However, if he had met Warrington ashore as a civilian, or in the person of a brother officer, the range of knowledge that the Texan possessed, as well as the tradition of his attitude toward it, would have attracted him and held his interest. As it was, Warrington, an enlisted man here in the ship, was not an individual who was available to "attract" or arouse "interest" in that sense; nor was he to be suspected of being such for anyone else abaft the mainmast.

Ensign Snell, on the contrary, was quite capable, with slow intuition, of building a good-natured structure of suspicion on any clue in this regard that might be blown his way. He was, as a matter of fact, quite on the verge of sensing out the relationship between his friend and the enlisted man; but it would have taken a kind of thing other than hearing them discuss books to give him a clue. It never would have occurred to him, either, to discuss novels and poetry with Warrington; nor with anyone else, for that matter. He did not know anything about novels and poetry.

People had a tendency to say of him, "Snell always wants to talk shop"; but such talk of the Navy and his work in it, or of the sports that interested him, was the only conversation for which he had a mature and adequate set of thought patterns. When he tried to express his feelings, deep and well developed though they were, they encountered the pattern barriers deposited by the only literature that ever had been permitted a real opportunity to influence his instincts and emotions: for he had graduated from the childish romanticism of Henty and the preparatory school fables of Barbour to rise no higher than a share of Kipling and the shoddy formulas of typical adventure prose. For this reason he talked less than Lieutenant Fitzpatrick or Ensign Woodbridge, restrained by a deep-seated sense of proportion from discussing things of which he knew little or from trying to express his feelings about them in a pattern and power of words that were less than they deserved. This sense of proportion handicapped him most in the face of a passion for a woman, because he had almost no language of love save his slow smile and the charming energy in his eyes. The finishing verbal stroke of a seduction, for him, could be little more than a bashful murmur, faintly touched with truculence: "How about it, Hon?"

The things he discussed with people, things like baseball, boxing or his work, he would have felt no hesitation whatsoever in discussing with the enlisted men about him if it were a question of passing a stretch of waiting minutes or a dull hour on the bridge. In such opportunities he once had talked of baseball with Barnes, the Blacksmith, and of boxing with Arnold, the Quartermaster.

On another occasion he had outlined to Warrington his ambition to resign from the Navy someday and become master of a merchant vessel. He had talked for twenty minutes or so about his feeling that life in the Navy, as much as he liked it, was not strictly speaking a constructive life, not really in the swim of things . . . while working a merchant ship was helping the wheels of the world go round . . . carrying necessities from people who produced them . . . to people who needed them . . . and a man could make money that way, make his proper share of that measure by which the world judged whether a thing was constructive or not . . . not that he wanted to make money . . . he didn't "give a damn about that really." Ensign Snell never would have made such a confession to the Quartermaster on watch if it had not been very dark on the bridge, so dark that what, unexpectedly, had existed chiefly for him, in the personality hidden opposite in the night, had been the pull of the youth's especial quality of being receptive to confidences that required particular understanding. This short conversation had not been a success, however. He had not, as he would have put it, been able to get his point over.

Warrington, who liked but did not admire Ensign Snell, had replied uneasily to the effect that he, personally, would rather be an Ensign in the Navy than president of a bank . . . that a great manner of life must be judged by standards that had nothing to do with making money . . . that it was only the lower levels of effort that could be judged by the measure of money . . . that money was merely the fertilizer of the world's effort, and that one mustn't confuse the merits of the animals that produced manure with the merits of a Burbank whose creations the manure fertilized . . . that, really, the merchant ships and all business, everything that was "constructive," even law and order and the very idea that held the nation together, existed solely by grace of the Army and Navy Officers behind these things, by grace of their arms, their knowledge, their position above the market-place and what they were prepared to sacrifice. Warrington had not stopped there, but had gone on to make clear, in a tone that, while it was utterly respectful, implied that the case had to be stated in simpler terms, that merchant ship officers were, in his view, mere aquatic truck drivers or floating hotel men; whereas a Naval Officer not only was a navigator, but a warrior, a diplomatist in the highest foreign circles, a scientific man and a disciplined repository of the national faith.

Tolerant Ensign Snell had not been irritated by this oration, in which he had detected, he was sure, much that was reflected from Lieutenant Fitzpatrick's opinions. He simply had stopped talking; and never, with this man, had tried it again. In this conversation with Warrington, despite its confidential character, Ensign Snell had maintained the same attitude that had dominated his chats with Barnes and Arnold, an attitude something like that of the college senior on the football team conversing with a member of the freshman squad. This was his invariable formula for dealing with enlisted men whenever he relapsed into a personal moment with them, an attitude, nevertheless, in which they sensed no unpleasant condescension. So thoroughly did they not sense such condescension, that many of them suspected, on occasions when a swimming party was roughing it up in the water or some hilarious horseplay was going on forward, that he would have liked to take off his gold stripes and get in there with them; but this never permitted any of them to forget even unconsciously that Ensign Snell, drunk, embarrassed by a moment of slow thinking or informally smiling, was an officer. It was this idea of forgetting that he was an officer, of nullifying some fundamental force making the machine work, that would profoundly have disturbed Ensign Snell if he had come into a full perception of Lieutenant Fitzpatrick's friendship for the Seaman, Warrington. His near approach to such a perception might have led him now, if he had been present and witnessed the exchange that had been noticed by Cruck and Saunders, to say to his friend, his big face lighted up with jeering amicability: "What's the matter with teacher's pet?"

As for the Captain, his opportunity to detect the unregulation friendship, once so nearly grasped, had not been presented again. Certainly at this juncture there was no field for such an opportunity. He visited the ship for but a few minutes each day; and he was preoccupied with getting his crew back together, and with maintaining his original relationship to it, maintaining it despite those other destroyers, his command over which could be neither evaded nor reconciled to his fateful necessity. Not that he neglected those other four ships; he positively leant over backward in his attentions to them. He was preoccupied, too, with getting through with the work that was to be done on his own ship alongside this dock. That would mean, he told himself, that two-thirds of what was to be done was definitely done. He could breathe then a little less like a man in an undecided battle. Things, the most sizeable jagged segment of things, clearly could be considered at that point to be on the mend. He thought distinctly of her in this way, as of a person nearly finished with operation and treatment in a hospital, who soon would be out and on the mend under his care. It was scheduled, as a matter of fact, that he was to take her out of this place as soon as the work here was finished, take her out, her insides all strong and new, down the bay, through the entrance into the open sea and then up the mountainous coast to the floating dry dock at Olongapo. It did not bother him much that he was taking her only a few miles from one bay to another, nor that they were going to hoist her clear out of the water in the dry dock. She was on the mend. They were going to lay some new plates into her skin and make a few, final, finishing touches that could not be accomplished here in the water. That would not take long. He almost could begin now to prod them about getting his men back. Perhaps he could wait until she was in dry dock. At any rate, it would be a pleasure to get rid of all these alien workmen mauling about in her, and put back in place all her things exiled on the dock. It did slightly cloy his sense of moving to a conclusion that she would have to be towed out by a tug and up to Olongapo. He could not get steam up in her until after they had finished with her there: But she soon would be a ship again now . . . Or at least he could say so as soon as she had begun to move away from this dock.

14 〰〰

About this time the old monk arrived in Manila. He had not seen fit to stay long in Isla-Sulu, not long, at any rate, after the investigators of the Government Judiciary had found their way there blatantly convoyed by a too large force of Philippine Constabulary. He had not been of much help to these agents, nor, when they saw that he was there, had they expected him to be. Most of the time, in their eyes, he just had walked slowly up and down in the shade of a mango tree reading some kind of religious book, and every now and then, for their irritation they were sure, rattling the large, unneat beads of his rosary. They had found him a source for very little information more than that the Navy had not found it necessary to land, and that the "outlaws" evidently now had gone away. Neither the surviving copra traders, whose lives he had saved in some miraculous manner, nor the officials, who knew him well, had cared to press him too hard. They had not, for one thing, wanted to force him to go into that "song and dance of his," that is the way the principal American official in the region once had put it, about "these poor children rising in childish rebellion against the trickery of Godless traders." They much preferred to offer no hindrance to his boarding the small transport that had brought the officials there and steaming away in it to Zamboanga. This he had done; leaving a couple of them standing on the dock staring after him and wondering what in the world it was he had wanted out there all these years, wondering why he was not "with" them. Heavens knew, the game they were playing out there amounted, when you came right down to it, to the Catholic game.

In Zamboanga he had learned that the transport was to voyage on up through the islands to the north, and he had arranged to sail with it, the time being ripe for his periodic visit, in which he took small pleasure, to the Capital on Church business. In Manila he had found something, quite irrelevant to the business in hand, that interested him. It was a long letter from a friend, a Jesuit missionary in Hankow, expressing appreciation, among other things, for the aid that his brother in Christ had even unknowingly put in his way. In the midst of a very difficult situation it had saved the day.

The letter told of how two barges loaded with medical stores and vaccines, provided and sent to China by right-minded people in the States, had come up the Yangtse Kiang to be distributed to the multitudes of sick and dying that bordered both sides of the river from Nanking to Hankow. On one side of the river, a ravaging complication amidst the starvation and small-pox, was the army of one revolutionary faction. On the other stricken side of the river was another desperate army opposing it. The barges had sailed right up the river between the two armies and had anchored, along with the American gunboat protecting them, off the mud flats some distance below Hankow. The boy in command of the gunboat had supposed that everything would be all right, because they had come on an errand of mercy, to give away medicine to the sick. In order to protect all concerned this officer (the Jesuit didn't think he could have been a day over twenty-three) had wanted the distribution of the stores to begin immediately. However, the missionaries who had come up on the barges, they having been selected as the proper persons to take charge of the distribution, wanted first to organize their situation so that it would bear fruit. They wanted to restrict the distribution of the stores only to those amongst the sick there on the banks of the river who would accept or had accepted Christ.

The writer of the letter confessed frankly that he had agreed to this arrangement solely because the assortment of Methodists, Baptists and Presbyterians with him in the venture had been determined upon it. There had not appeared to be any other way for him. It was, apparently, God's Will. The young Naval Officer, however, was disgusted with this plan and had retired to his tiny gunboat, saying he would have nothing to do with it. Then each of the armies on either bank had flatly demanded all of the stores for themselves. When their demands were refused, they started to come and get them. Upon this the boy and the fourteen sailors with him had manned their one little cannon and set up four machine guns on the rail of their toy warship. He told the emissaries of those two armies that he would begin shelling both banks of the river if any armed men came within a half mile of him. It had seemed ridiculous for such a David to threaten those two wild Goliaths on either side of the river: But he must have known what he was doing; for the forceful youth with his little grey cannon, out on that river across which eddied the stench of death and disease from the surrounding land, was successful with the threat. The writer of the letter said that, like the soldiers, he personally had not thought that it was an empty threat, that he had been certain the boy would go through with it. However, clouds of the Chinese soldiers still had hung about in the distance back from both banks of the river as if only waiting for a chance to sweep down.

"We spent the next day," the letter went on, "trying to come to some arrangement whereby the stores could be distributed according to purpose, and how a just apportionment of the converts could be made amongst the Church and the various sects." Late in the afternoon, the young officer suddenly had come over from his gunboat to interrupt the detestable haggling with an ultimatum. He was not going to stand for this outrageous delay any further, he said. If the stores were not in actual process of distribution by eight o'clock in the morning, he would distribute them himself. "Tiglath Posner, you know him, that Baptist, replied for us that rather than see God's Work thwarted, we would throw the medicine into the river. The boy replied that if so much as a bundle dropped overboard, he would open fire on *us*. Posner yelled back that we would defend the stores with our lives. The boy's answer to that was that that was just what it would cost us. Those poor, astounded, furious men just stood there and stared at him. It was clear that, pushed to the last point of desperation by the soldiers on the land and us on the river, he really meant to do something violent. Those around me on the barge did not know what to do. You know the type. Men who started life as carpenters, teamsters or farmhands. I dared not offer counsel, not even as much as the others. You know how they regard anything a Jesuit offers.

"Then everybody began to shout at him at once. They threatened him, they vilified him, they whined at him. Disgusted by all this, the boy went back to his gunboat, where he stood watching us across the thirty feet or so of intervening water. All the rest crowded to the end of the barge to continue their yelling at him, but I sat down and tried to study the boy out at a distance. Imagine him, all white and glittering, standing out there on the graceful stern of that little ship, scorning those people like a young Centurion beset on some Palestinian beach by a horde of screaming, verminous Israelites.

"I couldn't make out much about him except that he appeared

to be a person of parts, a person with something behind him. I envied then your experience in dealing with these military men.

"When my associates on the barge began crowding around the medical stores and shouting that they were going to throw them into the river, the boy got one of the machine guns and trained it on us across the stern of the boat. Then he got a chair and sat behind the gun and smoked his pipe, watching us, all through the setting of the sun. Every once in a while that Tiglath Posner would stand up in the most barbarous fashion and yell the name of Our Lord and other things up at the sky. The others responded with 'Amens' and the ugliest shouts. The coolies that manned the barges were frightened sick. My heart was wrung with pity for that boy caught out there in that sick desolation between those two armies waiting to spring upon him, and tormented by the wild threats of God's Vengeance screamed spasmodically from our barges.

"I finally got up and walked straight at him. He did not move the muzzle of that gun out of the way an inch. When I reached the edge of the barge, I smiled across the intervening strip of water. He said: 'Well?' So I questioned back: 'Well?' His reply to this was: 'We came out here to distribute those stores and I'm going to do it in the morning.' I said: 'Good. Let me come over and talk to you about it.' He looked me over from head to foot before replying, then he said: 'I'll send a boat for you.' When the others on the barge saw me going across in the boat, there was a positively unmentionable outcry; but he paid no heed to it whatsoever."

The Jesuit had confessed to the officer, on boarding the gunboat, that he had not come, necessarily, to talk about the trouble. He said he was lonely and bored out there with those men, that the officer and himself were educated men, that there was no reason why they should not enjoy each other's company through this evening that seemed to promise sleep for no one. This had caught the officer fairly and squarely on a vulnerable spot, had added to his burdens the further, mandatory one of hospitality. He was that kind of person. The writer had figured that out when he had been studying him from a distance on the barge. He had ended up by inviting the Jesuit to dinner, relegating the watch by the machine

270

gun on the stern to a man who was instructed positively to call him at the slightest sign of activity amongst those on the barges.

"The dinner was the most punctilious affair imaginable, starting off with his informing me that he was an Episcopalian. He relaxed a little in telling me about his regular ship, of which he spoke as of a living creature. She was down in the Philippines, he told me, where he had left her to come and take up this temporary duty; and it was plain that he eagerly looked forward to getting clear of this situation and rejoining her. The subject of those Islands thus brought up, I soon was inspired, by the Grace of Our Lord Jesus Christ, to mention your name as one who knew the Islands well. The effect of your name on the youngster was magical. In the most charming manner, he pushed the identification of you in a series of quick questions that brought him certainty. He told me of some adventure that you and he and his friends had engaged in on their ship. You were, in his words, 'a great old boy.' His name was Woodbridge. Do you remember him? At the end of a story I told him about you, he fell silent for many seconds. As he remained in deep thought, I thanked Almighty God. I knew then that I had found a base to build on, that I should be inspired with a vision of the way out of our difficulties. Finally he asked me if you were a friend of mine. I told him you and I had been friends for many years. 'Close *personal* friends?' he persisted. I trust, in the name of Holy Mother Church, that you will forgive me for giving him an affirmative to this. He then burst out with: 'Father, what in hell's the matter with those crazy men over there?'"

The upshot of this question eventually had been that the Jesuit had said to the officer: "My son, you know that you are not going to be able to handle the distribution of those stores. You don't know these people, the language or the medicines." The frank answer to this had been a simple: "That's true." In the end, they had decided to distribute the stores together, the Jesuit agreeing on his word of honour not to act in a religious capacity, not even, in the process, to mention anything in any way connected with religion. The two solemnly had shaken hands on this agreement; but the officer, the letter related, had smiled at him in a quite ironical way, and the Jesuit had received an impression from this as of his being conscious of making a repellent concession, a concession that stopped at bare practicability, to a necessity that was inexorable.

"This arrangement, My Brother In the Lord, you will see was a righteous thing all around. First, and above all, the poor, frantic sufferers around us quickly secured the medicines that God willed they should have. Secondly, there was no betrayal of my associates, those missionaries of the sects, because, although I participated in the distribution that the officer's previous ultimatum made clear was inevitable with or without us, I abstained strictly from uttering any word to the heathen that could have been construed as an enlightening one. Thirdly, although I uttered no such word, I could not prevent the poor sufferers of the region, amongst whom I freely went (protected by the guns of the boy's boat, the bayonets of his men and the Infinite Mercy of Jesus Christ Our Lord) from recognizing in me the same shepherd of the True Church who had worked throughout their countryside these many years. This last, happy, accidental concomitant of the result of our agreement, which displayed a representative of the True Church alone distributing the stores, enraged the uncompromising missionaries of the sects to a point of madness. But young Woodbridge would not even permit them off the barges; and finally, after the barges were empty, they went off down the river in one of them, the coolies sweating distractedly at keeping it in the current, amidst a nightmare of blasphemous prayers and yells."

The writer expressed his fear that the boy had ruined himself. "Alas, you know what that Tiglath Posner is. He and his friends will devote themselves to stirring up the millions of misguided souls who follow their sects in the States. Can't you just see all those wild, little Methodist and Baptist villages working themselves up? We shall hear even over here the roar of protest that will go up over the story of how an arrogant whipper-snapper of a Naval Officer, living off the taxpayers' money, had used his power and government property to persecute men of God, had even turned guns on them to keep them from the religious duties they had been sent out by the Churches of America to perform! Yes. I am afraid that that splendid young man is to be sacrificed. Tiglath Posner will be satisfied only when the Navy Department and Congress, itself, serve up this boy to him, when he can shout triumphantly to the multitude:

'O Lord . . . Thou hast smitten all mine enemies upon the
   cheek-bone;
Thou hast broken the teeth of the ungodly.'

Yes, it is a sad thing. They no doubt will ruin his career. The ways of Almighty God are inscrutable."

The letter went on to deal with other things; but the old Irish holy man did not go on with it. He laid it down on the stone floor in front of him and, sitting forward in his chair troubled and intent, gazed into the distance beyond the bare walls that framed him. He had been in many ships, known many groups of men in his time, still could remember many of them vividly; and certainly that little Wardroom family was to remain among the vivid. They were such a sound, spirited little family. Perhaps what quite held them in the undissipated realm of his sentiment was that they were so mutually kind, so mutually, unresentfully dependent . . . Or perhaps what held them there was that the four of them in their ship had appeared to him to form an almost perfect thing of its kind in this world where everything was perfect save what was human. The precise blue fire beneath his heavy, ancient brows began to glow so fiercely that it seemed to deepen the shadow in the hollows of his long cheeks. He did not want anything to happen to this family; he did not want any smiting upon cheek-bones or breaking of teeth; he did not want the ways of God to be inscrutable with that boy. A fine, proud lad he was, that boy, all shining with youth and those golden badges of authority . . . He arose, pushed the chair out of the way with his long, heavy foot, and began to pace up and down over the flagstones . . . He told himself that he was feeling strongly, very strongly about this matter, and where feelings could be so strong it must be because a course of fulfillment was open to them . . . But he couldn't feel his way through a situation that involved that strange chaos across the ocean where life was governed not by a pattern of authority but by a fear of it and a worship of a lack of it . . . Through any authoritative régime he might have been able to feel his way; but through that one he would have to think it . . . Congress . . . the Navy Department . . . little rampant Methodist villages . . . for him flat symbols of mere thought . . . things he had studied and memorized about for years so that he would not be lost in the situations like this one . . . but he couldn't feel about it . . . he would have to think about it . . . Certainly he could think as well as Tiglath Posner . . . God bring light and calmness to that man! . . . But Tiglath Posner was of over there . . . he knew all about it . . . the whole chaos was created to be the instrument of such a man . . . He, himself, had never been there . . . he had been only here, since his youth, since long before the Spaniards left, in these many islands of God's lovely wilderness. With the same terse, well-co-ordinated movement that had characterized his body when he had launched himself at the fire-room hatch to demand a shovel, a movement that reflected itself in the response of his rosary and the folds of his worn gown, he suddenly swung towards the door.

Out in the hot glare of the old Spanish street, he stalked along purposefully, mopping with a bandanna at his weathered face and the sunburned tonsure framed by his white stringy hair. He would find out where that Delilah was. Maybe he could reach it. At least he could get in touch with it. Those boys (he included even Captain Borden in this conception) surely could help him think, let him know if it was necessary. Perhaps he was feeling too strongly about this. Perhaps they would laugh away his feelings as simply as they would actually be able to sweep aside the trouble he might be exaggerating for that young man . . . After all, they were powerful people in a powerful world . . . What need had such as they of a humble ignoramus from the uttermost backwaters of the universe? . . . He was bound, however, to find out where his feelings were . . . and on that ship, it was a certitude, it would be safe to try . . . As he strode along past the portal of a church, a breath of incense drifted out to him . . . That was one of the things that made them vivid for his sentiment . . . in any honest terms, good or bad, you could know where you were with them . . . He took hold of the first bead . . . Those boys would provide him with a sign, the clearest kind of sign.

15 〰

The moment Captain Borden called down to the civilian Master of the tug, "All clear!" in a significant tone, the tug summarily hauled Delilah's lifeless little stern a few yards out from the disordered dock, and then began to back into the channel with her. There was an air of impatience about the tug's proceeding, as if the people on it had suspected beforehand that there was going to be a lot of nonsense in the attitude of those aboard the destroyer, as if it were a ridiculous thing to be so solicitous about such a small old hulk. Repeatedly, while the tug had come alongside and made fast, and while Delilah's men had cast off from the dock with an air of elated relief, the Captain and the stout Tug Master, who wore a cork helmet, had shouted at each other through megaphones, and everybody else had stood silent and watchful. Even through the preparatory moment of uncertain motionlessness, with the two conjoined vessels hanging there between the blazing vastness of the sky and the still brown flatness of the water, totally free of the land and at the mercy of the deceptively absent current, these shoutings had continued to punctuate the event. The word-structure of these communications had contained nothing that was not absolutely canonical, nothing that had not been bandied formally back and forth a hundred thousand times in similar circumstances; but a non-seagoing watcher on the dock would have felt certainly that he was overhearing an exchange that was critical if not defiant.

The Captain, however, standing stiffly on the bridge with Lieutenant Fitzpatrick, both in fresh, spotless whites, enjoyed an impression of there being a little less of unpleasantness in the situation than he had bargained for. In the first moment of looking forward to this departure for Olongapo, his mind had fallen into the use of the word "towed," and his anticipation had neglected to rid itself of the unpleasant connotation, which could have been achieved by an instant's reflection on the technic of what was in store for his ship, until the tug was alongside. The true case was, of course, that he was not to be "towed" at all. He was to be brought out by that tug secured alongside bow and stern. This arrangement would leave his ship completely out of his control, Bidot at the wheel, himself and Lieutenant Fitzpatrick on the bridge mere helpless formalities. They would simply be dragged along like a bulge on the side of the tug; but he preferred this, definitely, to being towed, much greater though his participation in the control of Delilah's movements would have been, at the bitter end of that tug's hawser. "That man," he alertly warned himself, "must get her stern out more before he backed . . . Even a landlubber would know she was all screw back there." He picked up his megaphone:

"On the tug there! . . . Haul her stern out a little more!"

As he turned away from the Tug Master's scornfully patient acknowledgment of his admonition, a slow movement of the extended arm and hand that that double-chinned man could have defended as responsive and placatory, a surprised, jubilant shout went up from the passive silence amidships. Then a scattering cheer rang the whole length of the ship, followed by yells of:

"Run for it, Father!"

"You'll make it!"

"Jump, Father, we'll grab you!"

Uproarious and goading as these cries were, there was no disrespect in them. They were simply roaring encouragement, in all sincerity, to a bizarre personage who had aroused, did arouse, their enthusiasm, and whose effort, in this moment, they were interpreting in terms of the quality he had made most memorable for them. Moreover, the old Irishman appeared, as he sped down the dock in long, hurried strides, as if he were about to run for it, as if he had already run for it through the dust and the heat. The Navy Yard orderly beside him was experiencing difficulty in not breaking into a trot to keep up. Although the old man did not run, he managed to arrive at a point directly opposite Delilah's bridge before the widening strip of water between the bow of the ship and the dock had exceeded four or five feet. Impulsively, Lieutenant Fitzpatrick started for the other side of the bridge to shout instructions at the tug to put them back against the dock; but he checked himself in time, and instead, before his critical faculty began to function adequately, stared impatiently at the Captain, from whom he expected to receive instant authorization for his impulse. The Captain, however, made no such extravagant use of his authority. Nodding emphatically two or three times, he smiled his welcome down into the venerable face, perspiring and slightly baffled, that looked up from the edge of the dock.

"You wanted to join us, Father?" he called to him.

"I did," the monk called back.

Raising his voice in opposition to the ever-broadening strip of water between them, and with his face assuming a friendly, homely grimace that was a trifle apologetic, the Captain shouted:

"We're only going to Olongapo . . . Come out in the morning . . . on the boat from Manila."

The monk cupped his big hands around his mouth and shouted back:

"What about young Woodbridge?"

"What?" shouted the Captain. He grabbed up the megaphone and placed it at his ear as if the better to catch, in all its tone and content, the corroborative repetition of this extraordinary question.

"Young Woodbridge . . . Is he going to get out of that trouble all right?" The monk bellowed his question this time.

At this, under the intent scrutiny of the aged cleric on the dock, there took place in the Captain's face a change of expression that, in suddenness and violence, was patently uncharacteristic. It was as if some darkly poisonous cloud had sailed between his unhandsome, wrinkled features and the amiable light of his spirit. He glared hatefully, savagely at that tall, dark-robed harbinger looming there like an apparition drawn by the blinding fire of the sun from the muck of water beneath him. "Woodbridge! . . . And now Woodbridge!" He was swept, totally possessed this time, by that repugnant idea, now powerfully, personally emotioned, of unnatural forces beyond his control eating away malefically at the edges of his fate. He leant out over the wind-breaker to stare back across the by this time considerable distance from ship to dock, as if the unrelenting gaze from there were trying still to hold him, as if it had not yet finished extracting the required truth from the radiation of his eyes and the furor in his face. It seemed to him that he was forever standing on a ship staring down at that old man on a dock with some dubious question between them.

Lieutenant Fitzpatrick, fearing that the almost past opportunity would be spent before all was learned that could be, took it upon himself, instinctively leaning as far out as he could, to shout:

"What trouble? What's the trouble?"

It could not be ascertained at the distance that now intervened, all that really could be made out was the long black robe and the white hair glistening in the sun, whether he shifted his gaze from the Captain to Lieutenant Fitzpatrick to reply; but many on the deck of the intently listening ship heard most of the blurred answer, a reply, bellowed and strained as it was in the effort to pitch it across the water, that nevertheless carried a quality of tenderness and some kind of exhortation:

" . . . missionaries . . . serious quarrel with missionaries . . ."

These words struck powerfully at Lieutenant Fitzpatrick's assurance that whatever trouble it was that their friend was in, he, of all people, surely would find the way out of it . . . "but this was damn serious trouble . . . if the mixup had been serious enough . . . there would be no fit way out of that sort of thing . . . those Psalm singers! . . . That reckless ass!" The tug was swinging the ship through the entrance of the breakwater. Lieutenant Fitzpatrick hastily stepped forward around the motionless Captain to scrutinize the manoeuvre; but as he stood there on the alert, while Delilah, like a large, dead, empty model of herself, was dragged out into the reach of the bay, he managed for several seconds a sustained waving signal with his upright arm, a signal of friendly recognition, of gratitude, of farewell; and it seemed to him that he received a last impression of the bold mediaeval figure in the distance, of his standing there alternately mopping at his face and neck with the bandanna and fluttering it at the ship in a gesture that evoked an illusion of some kind of shyness, even of appeal.

16 〰️

It took the tug all that afternoon and a good part of the night to haul Delilah the fifty miles or so along the coast to Subic Bay and then half-way up the bay's eastern shore to the land-locked port of Olongapo. Most of the next morning was spent off the Naval Station there jockeying the helpless destroyer in between the walls of the submerged dry dock, and it was evening before that great cradlelike structure had pumped itself up out of the water to leave Delilah braced high and dry between its towering walls; so the ship was just barely ready and free to receive the monk about the time the puffing little freight and passenger boat arrived from Manila: But the monk had not taken the boat; nor did he subsequently take it. There now was no need. On the dock he had received, across the widening strip of water, the clear sign for which he had sought.

It was fifteen days before the Captain knew definitely, through official channels, how that part of Delilah stood that was represented by Ensign Woodbridge. The Captain's mind was not the mechanism to extract and face the fact that the ship, without the prospect of Ensign Woodbridge in it, would not be the ship at all, that it certainly would not be what he was having so much difficulty in relinquishing for the early career of higher command. All the turmoil that this unfaced fact whirled up in his awareness, he attributed simply to the occurrence, itself, of his officer having got into ruinous trouble, and to this new loss assuming a climactic place in that fatal series of personnel losses that he detested to view as supernaturally assaulting the texture of his life. It would have been hard for him to make out that the loss of Ensign Woodbridge did not take on much of its importance through the power of feeling at the disposal of friendship. There was, in fact, a closer bond of friendship between the Captain and Lieutenant Fitzpatrick; and the loss of the latter officer would have been more of a personal loss, a loss with quite more intimate pain in it. Such a misfortune, however, would have been of a kind that his view of life obligated and prepared a man to bear. The loss of Ensign Woodbridge, on the other hand, loomed in the category of disasters less personal but more devastating (although Lieutenant Fitzpatrick was a more responsible and operative member of the ship's company), a disaster, as it were, comparable to the loss of Spring from a world whose poetry and traditions were based on its eternal resurrection, a disaster that struck obliteratingly, for the Captain, at the very essence and colour of the thin swift universe to which invincible premonition had committed his fate. For almost anybody else on the Asiatic Station but the Captain the aspect would have been very nearly reversed; thus, for example, if the ship had gone down, carrying with it the Captain, Lieutenant Fitzpatrick and Ensign Snell, there would have existed, amidst the general shock and grief, no sense of a lack of fitness in the disappearance of these three into the memory of the ship; and there would have been sensed, even amongst those who did not like him, no lack of fitness if Ensign Woodbridge had survived, for he seemed to be identified less with the personality of the ship, any ship, than with the breadth of the peculiar spirit that held them all within the word, the careless, worn word, "Navy."

No one quite could bring himself to believe, because of this sense of Ensign Woodbridge's "fitness," that he would really be stopped even by this trouble, which for almost any other would have appeared to be the end. Nevertheless, it was clear to the Captain, and to everybody else under the official necessity for seeing it, that the officer had been, or would be when the missionaries and their politicians got through with him, stopped dead in the steps of his career. Admiral Douglas had communicated an idea of the lengths to which the missionaries were prepared to go, already had gone, for that matter. The Admiral had received, along with others of Federal authority in China and the Philippines, protesting letters or visits, as well as news of protests on the way across the Pacific to elements in and close to the Government who would be forced to make the most of them. The Captain had received from his superiors the plainest sort of intimations that he was not to count any further on Ensign Woodbridge, that on the Ensign's return to Delilah he was to be regarded in a kind of detached light, as if he merely were awaiting in the ship the arrival of mail from the States ordering the Board of Inquiry that would reluctantly sacrifice him to the voracity of the churchmen.

Reviewing these intimations, as he paced the brief quarter-deck in a routine manner, the Captain told himself once again that it was useless worrying in this way, that he must put this concern from his mind and attend to practical business. He told himself that now again; despite the fact that it had done no good for him to tell himself the same thing over and over before. He would put it from his mind as a pattern of thought that perfected only a vicious circle; but it would always, almost immediately, come back, until his consciousness was filled with a series of these troubled, vicious circles in the way that a room is filled with smoke rings for the amusement of a child. There was nothing, absolutely nothing, he could do about it . . . Woodbridge was lost . . . just as surely as Mendel was . . . and it was getting to be a disorderly thing for him to carry on in this fashion . . . It was proper and necessary to fight uncompromisingly for what was right . . . but one must be sure that a fight for the right really remained such and did not degenerate into mere rebellion . . . There was no such thing as a man's purpose being right and the world wrong . . . One must continually check his bearings by the scheme of things . . . there could be no messy tampering with the rules . . . If one was tempted to do that knowingly or unknowingly, he fell into the hole of fooling himself with such stuff as "bad luck" and that kind of thing . . . A man must be sure that his trouble was not caused by running afoul of the scheme of things.

He paused at the stern near the limp colours, rested one hand on the breech of the torpedo-tube as if bracing himself against the afternoon's pressure of scorching heat, and looked broadly about him as if the scheme of things was in the scene before him, as if he would find something in it upon which his state of mind could get its bearings. The mood of the impression that he took in, however, was not one to help him derive any point of view such as he had been urging upon himself. Nearby, the scene met his eyes in unreal, distorted perspective. In the distances it was glowingly blurred by the ruthless sunshine and the equivocal vapour that helped make uncertain the long line where lush vegetation ended and the glare of smooth sea began. Even in the shadow cast by the jungled rise of land on the left things, that appeared vivid at first glance, melted into uncertainty of limit and outline under scrutiny. He could not make out, over there on the left, the mouth of Boton River. He knew it was there, though, near the thick screen of vertical glinting lines where the grove of bamboo came down beside the coal dock. The eye could be sure of only extensive masses like the blue brilliant surface of Subic Bay stretching out of sight to the right, or its broad entrance in the distance almost in front of him beyond Grande Island. So powerful was the illusory property in the extravagant frankness of the sunshine that, for an instant, as he glanced at the nearer shimmering green of little Mayanga Island off there to the right, in the middle of the bay, he seemed to see it as part of the far shoreline on the other side.

Everything that he gazed down on, near at hand, was in varying degrees of appearing abnormally below him owing to the ship being braced high up between the two tall walls of the dry dock, the tarry steel floor of which extended beneath most of the hull. The stern of the ship, however, including the quarter-deck, projected out beyond the floor, over the water. All the rest of the vessel, except the upper heights of the masts, was lost in the vast roofless tunnel of the dry dock. Being accustomed to look from the deck of the ship, which normally was very close to the water, at a sea and things floating in it that virtually were on a level with him, it gave him a moment of startled adjustment now to look unexpectedly over the side or beyond the quarter-deck and find nothing but space. His vision, forced to go on down past where the water should have been to where it was, could not seem to find ordinary reality there. Things below there, at this range and angle, took on somewhat the quality of things seen in a dream. It contributed to the dreamlike quality of the aspect that from here he often could see on down through the incredibly clear water to the pale, sandy bottom of the bay. It seemed that on some occasions when he looked down he could see the objects on the bottom in more clear definition than objects above the surface. It was like looking down through the glass bottoms of those boats at Catalina Island, only on a grand scale; and at life that was more prodigal and fantastic: immense, branching plants full of purple and orange and bright green that swayed strangely with the solid movement of the invisible water, giant slugs that appeared to live only in the vermilion of their colour, spiny bursts of magenta like microbes magnified to the size of a fevered summer moon and as brilliant, a wilderness of huge blue streamers flecked with gold and unknowable hues, fish like weird feathers maddened by an exquisite debauch of tints, a writhing, darting, festering display of living unreality in the clear depths of the still water. Instinctively he would turn away from this vision and look up the narrow grey and black perspective between the taut, weathered awning and the steel deck, as if for some kind of reassurance; or he would look up at the dazzling sky for a sign of rain, perhaps because this was a diversion for his faculties or because when it rained sight could not penetrate the surface of the sea. Once it had given him a slight feeling of relief to reflect that if a man actually were down there beneath the water, all that mad, repellent colour would be suppressed for his eyes almost to a mere variety of flat tone.

At this moment, he could not see plainly beneath the water because the Swimming Party, which included nearly the whole ship's company, was breaking the surface with the turbulence of their sport. The water seemed to be transmuted by the churning, plunging, sunburned bodies, all ashine with the molten gold of the sunlight, into something less than liquid, something that was pale blue, milk white, crystalline. Even the shouts of the swimmers rising up to him impressed him as a little strange, a little unlike what they would have been if the ship were floating down there alongside them, impressed him as being more like the shrill, blurred drifts of alien sound from the native band practising in the town that, travelling disconnectedly the heat-smothered distance, sculptured in the air about him awkward, nostalgic curves of melody, blurred fragments of *If We Can't Be The Same Old Sweethearts* . . . *Tipperary* . . . *Dardanella* . . . "Those fellows just couldn't handle those tunes," he thought, "just couldn't get at them . . . they did something funny to them . . . as if they were singing them with a

Malay accent." Into the midst of his feeling about the music, there intruded the memory of his impression of the gaudy nightmare beneath the water in which his men were swimming. He did not struggle for an instant to make anything out of this. He simply shook himself free of the whole level of consciousness on which the memory occurred and tried to listen to the hollow, muffled hammering of the dozen or so native workmen at the bottom of the dry dock, where they were repairing the hull of the ship. How he would like to hear normal sounds about the ship once more! . . . the clatter of the ash buckets in port . . . the roaring hiss of the ash ejector under way . . . the living throb of pumps beneath the deck . . . the rhythmic churning of the screws over which Woodbridge insisted it was a crime to place the Wardroom. Automatically his mind reverted to the constructing of another of those vicious circles, the repellency of which had driven him to pause at the stern to gaze about him. His mind took hold once more of the Board of Inquiry and General Court Martial awaiting his officer . . . Woodbridge, of all people, to fall into the jaws of the missionaries . . . and the politicians . . . It was unthinkable that that was the scheme of things . . . but his own helplessness, everybody's helplessness, in the situation seemed to indicate that it was . . . The heat and smells of this coast made a man sleepy all the time . . . drugged him . . . There seemed to be a film of perspiration between his skin and his clothes . . . But he didn't see how anybody could manage to sleep below in this heat as Fitzpatrick was doing now . . . even at night he, himself, found it impossible below . . . He gave a twist to relieve his legs and chest where the sweat made the cloth cling . . . It probably was in the rules, too, that he shouldn't be struggling with everybody and his brother to do what he alone thought was good for this ship . . . no doubt it was the scheme of things that he should let the ship go and be Division Commander the rest of the way . . . It was he that was in the wrong trying to buck the way things were going . . . that was what was the matter with him . . . why he got strange ideas about bad luck cutting at him from the dark . . . It was the scheme of things that was breaking up his crew . . . promoting him out of the ship . . . that killed Mendel . . . that was losing Woodbridge . . . that same scheme that built things up and made

284

them good . . . You had to have the right bearing on it, that was all . . . and he didn't have it . . . he was sighting only on this one little ship, which, after all, was just a collection of steel plates and some boilers . . . All ships were the same . . . Divisions of ships . . . Flotillas of ships . . . Squadrons of ships . . . Fleets of ships . . . He took out his spectacles, polished them carefully with his handkerchief and adjusted them on his prominent nose. One of the tortoise-shell hooks failed to settle properly behind his ear. He fidgeted with it for a few seconds and then decided his skin was too wet with perspiration to wear the spectacles. He took them off, followed them with his cap, which he laid, spectacles inside it, on the torpedo-tube, and mopped at his sandy hair and wrinkled face with the handkerchief. He couldn't do anything about Woodbridge . . . that was clear . . . it must be in the scheme of things that Woodbridge was to be cut to pieces and dragged under by those people . . .

17 〰〰

The Swimming Party, nakedly enjoying an illusion of relief from the heat in a liquid whose temperature provided little contrast to the heavy, incandescent air, an illusion that permitted wild expenditures of energy impossible on the shore, surged continuously back and forth in exuberant fractions between the end of the dry dock's floor and the water. If the Captain on the stern of the ship high in the air above the mass of swimmers had been a different man, it might have occurred to him that the dark end of the dry dock was bursting and bubbling into life under de-equilibrizing pressures like those that found the first strip of primordial mud, swollen above the bare surface of steaming swamp, being stricken by the sun to everlasting restlessness.

The swimmers, themselves, would have preferred to be fewer in number or not under the necessity of confining their sport to a congested area immediately fronting the dry dock; but Lieutenant Fitzpatrick had insisted on these conditions as a precaution against the numerous sharks that could clearly be seen infesting the bright, wild depths in which the dry dock floated. All but the habitually perverse had accepted these limitations with good grace, because it was common knowledge and common sense that sharks would not attack in water that was confused by a large mass of men. Orlop, the tall Chief Gunner's Mate, who was in charge of the Swimming Party, stood on a pile of spare timbers, like those that had been used in bracing Delilah in the dock, and watched out with smooth, good-humoured alertness for anyone who might detach himself from the crowd. Every now and then his clear shout, pitched at variance with the prevailing tone of noise for distinctness, would crack out over the turmoil with, "Hey! Ragatzo! . . . Get back in there!" or "Petrie!" and when Petrie, a trifle startled, not so much by the admonition as at finding himself out of bounds, would raise his red face and glistening black eyes from the water to look around, Orlop would beckon curtly with his whole arm as if in irritated disgust. Not that he was either irritated or disgusted; he remained as usual a dapper Chief Petty Officer, dressed in clean, sleeveless undershirt, dungaree trousers and smart visored cap, doing his duty; and that was the way it was done. Even before this gesture had completed itself, Petrie would be diving forward under the water directly toward the core of the swimming crowd. Ragatzo, on the other hand, would skirt the edges of the crowd in a semblance of evading the command to return, swimming with deliberate grace as if he were on exhibition; but his course would lead him back within the fold. Saunders, on being the object of Orlop's reminder, would flop onto his back, as if he had not heard, and float slowly in amongst the other men, using an almost imperceptible flutter of his palms to maintain direction and motion. He would do this even on the occasions when Cruck was in charge of the Swimming Party. Once, in the first days, when everybody still harboured unadmittedly a certain amount of doubt as to the truth of there being no danger from sharks in a vigorously moving crowd, Ragatzo and Forsythe, swimming side by side, had found themselves, unnoticed by the man in charge, some distance from the others and on the verge of drifting around the wall of the dry dock. Under sudden, mutual impulse they had struck off along this wall in a beautiful, surreptitious dash that had carried them all the way round the dry dock. Gasping for

286

breath and exhausted by the long sprint, they had brought up triumphantly amidst the cheering and enthusiasm of their friends only to be ordered out of the water for their daring and denied the right to answer Swimming Call for two days. Their feat, however, which no one attempted to emulate, served to draw much of the threat out of the surrounding water. They now doubted that it was as dangerous as they had been led to believe. At any rate, they begot a complete faith in the mass method they had been using to prevent shark attacks, somewhat the same kind of faith a man has who learns to cut semi-mechanically across a stream of traffic that includes careless, drunken and myopic drivers, cut across it with the experience-taught assurance that, dangerous as it may or may not be, he will get safely through.

In the last few days it was realized that a number of sharks, lithe grey fellows from four to five feet long, who almost from the beginning had been sensed shadowing the edges of the broad commotion set up by the crowd of swimmers, had taken to mixing with the men in the water. It was as if they, too, had become convinced (despite the dark, thin, little fish that darted about them, clung to them, whispered to them) that there was no danger. They joined the revel in that warm water, whose surface it agitated to a kind of milky translucence, as if it now belonged there, belonged like the shivering, unedged rays of sun that pierced down to illumine the gardens growing from the sand, where lived things too bright, too slow, inedible. The sharks took the sport casually, almost disinterestedly, as if they had been obligated to play, swinging and looping in a professional manner even up amongst the confusion of legs and torsos of the men, never once touching, nor changing pace, nor making a spasmodic movement to get out of the way. Men who could dive well now dove deep, as close to the fantastic bottom as they could reach, in order to get a glimpse up through the equivocal perspective, while rising as slowly as possible, of the beautiful acrobatics these graceful monsters performed amidst the glowing, blurred chaos of the swimmers' bodies near the misty surface.

Those who wanted to dive for this view of the sharks, took turns plunging off the pile of spare timbers on which Orlop stood, it being the highest point available. There was a standing order against diving from the top of the dry dock, a high dive that only three or four of the men would have been willing to make even if there had been no such order; but the drop of twelve feet from the top of the timber pile to the water really was sufficient both for those who wanted simply to dive and for those who found their pleasure increased by having something to dive for, the deep view of the sharks. At this moment there were six men in line for the diving position up on the stack. Warrington, Wright and Easterly were on the top beside Orlop, while three more men clung to the sides of the stack waiting until there was room above for them. It was the Texan's turn, and, as on several previous dives, he stood so long on the brink of the stack before diving that the three men clinging part way up began shouting:

"God damn it . . . go ahead!" . . . "Quit posing" . . . "Aw, cut it out and let the men dive."

As a matter of fact, Warrington was neither posing nor reluctant. He was in process of adding the further complication that inevitably seemed necessary to him. He was not amongst those who could enjoy diving simply for diving's sake, but amongst those whose satisfaction was empowered by giving the act a definite objective; and within this pattern, on almost each succeeding day of swimming, he had privately managed to add something beyond the accepted objective, the view of the sharks, that remained sufficient for the others in his category. What irritated everybody, especially the waiting, naked men forced to hang on to the splintery, clifflike side of the timber pile, was a dim sensing that it really was not timorousness or exhibitionism that delayed him up there for the extra seconds, which failings they would have regarded more tolerantly; but rather another of those perversities, annoying yet unnamable, that that irreducible youth persistently flaunted in the most unconscious manner. It did not do them complete good to hurl curses and protests at him, even though it sometimes hurried him off, because they could not get missiles quite suitable to the target, which was not convincingly the appearance he presented up there. What he was doing seemed very simple to him, however. He was exposing himself as long as possible there to the full brunt of the sun, and taking in a glaring full view of the terrestrial panorama spreading before his eyes. At the moment when the heat and the view became intolerable under his free reception of them, he would leap forward, straighten out, cleave the water and then, when he felt the momentum of the dive expiring, open his eyes and his feelings to the miraculous contrast, the cool different universe beneath the sea, while they still were flinching with the half-memory, half-reality of that above. For the dive he was about to make he now took his full time, disregarding the jibing shouts behind him, because on his last dive he had been urged off before conditioning himself for receiving all that was to be gotten out of plunging almost instantaneously between the extravagantly contrasting worlds. He stood there until it seemed to him that his dry skin was about to crackle into flame in that blaze of sun, and Grande Island, like an object in a bright window stared at too long, was burned on his retina forever. Down he went. The water roared in his ears, sped up along all the surface of his skin with an impression of calm, terrific speed. He felt himself slowing down. He opened his eyes and gazed over the luminous, blurred landscape that he divined rather than saw as spreading away illimitably in all directions just beneath him, opened his eyes to gaze as if he were a bird gliding through air that suddenly had caught fire and changed into something dense and pellucid, pale green and cool, above an earth become a dead wilderness of vague forms and tones, beautiful, lonely and fabulous.

He bent his body and with the last remainder of impetus swung upright. Working his extended, upturned palms in upward thrusts, he strove to maintain his position at the bottom of the dive as long as possible. Struggling against the positive buoyancy of his body and the protest of his lungs, he swept his gaze around for a last look about before rising to the surface, when his eyes would be directed straight up at the play of the sharks through which he would ascend.

At the far end of a tangled, quivering vista that cut through the opaline wilderness toward the floor of the open sea, he sensed an oncoming immensity of speed!

In a devastating instant he lost all sense of his dimensional relationship to the external world. He found himself wildly entangled in what must have been an effort to scramble through gravity and the dense pale greenness toward the glow of sand on the bottom. He became frantic with the confusion of whether that immense hideous swiftness was hurtling from above, from below or from the side, whether the plane of illumination under him or the one above him was the surface of the water. The universe began to drum monstrously with the rhythm of the heart beating beneath his tight throat. His arms were twisting from his shoulders. His legs had become something vague and useless. He felt he no longer could see . . . but there blazed frigidly in his consciousness the vision of that horrible, majestic speed filling, obliterating the rift in that delirious jungle beneath the sea . . . like an enormous drop of mottled grey liquid streamlined to a point under pressure of a furious fall through space. Clawing insanely through his consciousness, he could find no recourse. His intelligence succumbed. He flung himself on the mercy of his body's animal will, struggled in blind, uncritical desperation to do what it wanted to do . . . It exploded in an infinite flare of intense, colourless nothingness . . . his throat pumped out horrible, ragged sounds into this expanding blaze of existence.

With his mouth strictured into a wide, terrifying rectangle that destroyed the form of the sounds issuing from it, he continued to yell as he threshed and tumbled through the foam, through the welter of shoulders and heads toward one of the great chains that moored the dry dock. He reached it, clutched a link the size of his head and hauled himself in one movement out of the water and up on the chain. He was nearly knocked off, before he could climb to the dry dock floor, by the following rush of those to whom he had communicated his panic. Without even a questioning hesitation, everybody in the water had flung himself, swimming wildly hand over hand, at the dry dock the moment Warrington had shot waist-high above the water in their midst, with his piercing voice half screaming, half bellowing some irresistible thing that sounded like, "Horror! . . . Horror!"

An instant before Warrington had shot to the surface, Wright, the slight, straw-haired Seaman who never could rid his face of pimples, had launched himself on his dive from the timber pile. When he came up, treading water and giving a jerk to his head to get his straight hair out of his eyes, he found himself all alone in the smoothing stretch of bluish-white water. A vast yell enveloped him from the men massed on the end of the dry dock. He tried to shake his ears free of water to get what it meant. He stared at them expectantly, a trifle bewilderedly, bobbing up and down gently with the barely perceptible ground swell; then he disappeared abruptly beneath the surface as if he had been a float on a fishing line that had caught a fish. A flood of repellent silence swept the world clear of sound and movement, save where the dispassionate blazing of the tropic sun caught and flashed at the widening ring that centred the spot where Wright had gone down. As the mass of eyes focused on the spot, Wright's head and shoulders rose precisely there, a startled look on his face that would have been incomprehensible had it not contained so much of outrage and despair. In a long, hoarse, wailing cry, he shouted the word, "Shark!" a cry that was more a warning than an appeal. He was jerked part way under again. As he started another shout, he sank out of sight as completely, as suddenly as before, the sound he was making ending in a brief bubble of hollow noise. From one in the mass of dripping men packed into the end space of the dry dock beneath Delilah's stern, a single, hysterical exclamation sailed out to lose itself in the flaming stillness of sea and jungle:

"Jesus Christ Almighty!"

There was nothing anybody could do. It was a catastrophe beyond the impromptu expedition of human courage and power. The water there had begun to moil with the presence of many long, swiftly circling, darting bodies. A dim cloud of crimson drifted up and hung within the widening circles on the surface of the whitish water. Up on the timber stack, Chief Gunner's Mate Orlop was facing the fact, facing it with a heavy regret from which he never completely was to recover, that he could not bring himself, thus on the instant, without adequate preparation by his imagination, to make the unexampled attempt that he felt his duty there demanded of him. Unseeingly, uncomprehendingly, he shifted his eyes to Easterly, the Fireman, who suddenly had stiffened himself on the edge of the timber pile, arms raised above his head. There was a determined, triumphant, almost fanatical look on the Fireman's white face. His stringy hair was hanging down over his forehead. His wide mouth had become a thin grey line. He was going to jump over after that man. As he flexed his knees, a tense, barely audible mass sound burst from the men below; then Easterly jumped straight at the pale, bloody water as if, for minutes, he had been aiming at that very spot.

The front of Easterly's body hit the surface of the water flat, with the sound of a gigantic slap. A radial of dark lines fled out away through the water beneath him as from an explosion. As he began to sink in the water, Wright's head rose beside him, the arms that framed it making an awkward effort to swim. Easterly clutched at the straw-coloured hair above the desperately closed eyes and kicked furiously toward the mooring chain, his free arm splashing and reaching out before him as if he were deluded by a wish that the chain was close enough to seize.

Cruck flung himself down along the chain to the water's edge, lost his balance and fell in, then boldly stroked to Wright's side and grabbed him under the armpit. Men crowded down the chain with arms tensely outstretched to take hold of them as they came within reach. They dragged Wright onto the chain.

"Haul him up, you bastards, haul him up," Cruck spluttered.

To this end Cruck reached beneath the water to get a grip on Wright's leg; but he suddenly let go of him completely, flinching away into the water as if he had encountered something frightful and obscene. He had gotten hold of the beveled stump of the Seaman's leg, bitten off just below the knee-cap. In an instant, however, he was back beneath Wright, giving him a mighty shove up the chain.

They laid him on his back on the floor of the dry dock, where he smiled queerly up at the crowd that ringed him as if he did not know that anything serious had happened to him.

"Give me that undershirt," Heller, the Pharmacist's Mate, said to Orlop.

Orlop whipped it off and said to the crowd:

"Get back . . . get back . . . give him a chance."

Feenan, pompous and distressed, stood silently near Wright's head, his freckled arms outstretched protectingly against the crowding.

Heller tied the undershirt around the mutilated leg above the knee, looked about searchingly and shouted:

"Give me a stick . . . a big nail . . . anything!"

The crowd of naked men looked around wildly, at the floor and walls of the dry dock, at the bottom of the ship, at the knot of tensely impassive native workmen, at the propellers, at the sea. Some of those on the outer fringe of the crowd then saw that Easterly, strangely dazed and helpless, was still clinging to the mooring chain down near the water's edge. He appeared about to topple off. They crawled down and dragged him up to the dock, where he lay retching, on his face, his nerves in complete revolt. They swung him over onto his back, but as soon as they let go of him he turned on his face once more.

Warrington, when Heller's voice rose in a shout of, "Come on! Come on!" grabbed a small, round chisel from the hands of a native workman and shoved his way through to the centre of the crowd, where he held the chisel down near Heller's face with a frantic, tentative movement. The Pharmacist's Mate seized the chisel and stuck it between the encircling undershirt and the wounded leg of the youth, who continued to lie quietly on his back as if he were dreaming there in a pool of blood under the violent sunshine.

Holding firmly to the chisel, which he had twisted round and round with a vicious exigency until the cloth looked like a white ring about which the flesh of the leg partly had grown, Heller got to his feet and said, naming the hospital ship moored in a basin some two miles away:

"Get him to the Relief."

Orlop and three other men picked him up and, falling into step behind Cruck, who strode along a few paces in the lead, marched up the length of the steaming, shadowy dry-dock floor, across the gangway, onto the land. Before they had gone more than a few yards along the dusty road, Cruck stopped and half held out his arms crooked belligerently.

"Hold it," he shouted, and pointed to a small, open waggon loaded with bundles of laundry that was about to drive into the main road from the trail to the coal dock.

While they waited for the waggon to approach, Heller and the men carrying Wright stepped with him beneath the broadleafed shade of a plantain tree. The close-packed, following crowd, its rear ranks not yet fully emerged from the dry dock, roared with discovery and relief when it sighted the horse and waggon. At this mighty shout, the Tagalog driving the waggon, mystified and aghast, jerked his horse to a stop before it reached the turn into the road. He had been half asleep, the brim of a stiff straw hat shielding the eyes of his low-drooping face, the reins almost un-retained in his unconscious hands. He stood up, leaning back on the now tightly clutched reins in astonishment and growing terror, and stared at the yelling, naked mob on his left that seemed to fill the view, then at the blood-smeared men on his right grouped beneath the green curve of the plantain tree who clutched a man-gled body that dripped blood onto the dust, then at the dismaying figure ahead of him, where Cruck stood in the middle of the road beckoning fiercely with his arm and mouthing impatient curses. A spasm of blind fear and repudiation beset the driver. He gave frenzied pulls at the reins, trying to turn around and flee. Cruck was yelling:

"Bring me that rig! . . . God damn . . . son of a bitchin' . . ."

Part of the crowd, in a torrent of impatience and indignation, already were charging down upon the waggon. Corum, an Elec-trician, Second-Class, a slight man whose black hair usually was parted precisely in the middle, reached it first. Forsythe was right at his heels. Corum seized the Tagalog and attempted to pull him off the waggon. When the man hung on blindly, Forsythe struck him in the face. Corum flung him to the ground. Then Forsythe, climbing to the seat, drove the frightened horse in a fury of haste off the trail, across a drainage ditch, through a tall patch of cogon grass, in a short cut straight to the plantain tree beneath which Heller still was twisting tightly at the chisel in the red-drenched undershirt.

Long after the waggon had careened off up the main road, and the naked horde had crowded back out of sight onto the dry dock, the native continued to lie stunned at the side of the trail in the centre of that drowsing landscape. His thin, brown body, from which the shirt nearly had been ripped away, heaved in the man-ner of an ambushed animal. His thin, bare feet were cowered together and his face was burrowed into his tightly folded arms as if he felt sheltered there between the warm, familiar smother of the heavy sunshine and the soft earthiness of the dust, re-assured, sheltered from the ineffable storm of blood and vio-lence that had come mysteriously up from the sea to invade the land.

18 〜〜〜

The Captain, high up on Delilah's stern, had observed carefully every development of the event below him that had added Wright, the Seaman, to the list of those whom he never could get back, of those swept away in the flood of that implacable current that seemed determined to engulf them all. He had felt that throb of fatality again even before the boy had been struck, in the mo-ment that he had bobbed alone there in the water as if waiting for the shark to take him. He had not expected anybody to go in after him, and he had been startled, thrown a little off his balance, when the Fireman had leapt into that act so extravagantly far be-yond the borders of intelligible courage, beyond, in fact, what he understood to be useful and normal heroism. He had spotted the big shark beneath the surface of the farther clear water just before it had sped out of sight under the confused, foaming area left by the swimmers, and he had begun the shout of his warning; but that fellow, Warrington, had been ahead of him. The manner of that other warning, too, had produced swifter and more effective results than any shout from him would have. When he had ob-served how the other sharks had been maddened by the example and the blood, he had noted thankfully that the extra seconds gained in clearing the water had been a very good thing. The Fire-man had dived right into the midst of that inferno. "Good heav-ens, what a thing to do!" His reaction had been partly as if to some fantastic act of wastefulness. The man could not help getting the Congressional Medal for this . . . certainly . . . He had better enter this whole business in the Rough Log himself. He had or-dered the Quartermaster on watch to get Mr. Fitzpatrick up on deck immediately when he saw that they had succeeded in hauling Wright out of the water to the floor of the dry dock. Through his binoculars he could see that the man was unhurt save for the amputated leg . . . no, there was a wound above the knee also, where the shark evidently had taken a first, hasty grip. That Easterly . . . What a thing to do! The impact of his body had scared the sharks away all right. He did not see how anybody could have figured that out beforehand though. However, he had approved, step by step, of everything they had done down there in meeting the emergency. They had met it promptly and efficiently . . . no fumbling, no panic . . . Fitzpatrick seemed to think that that Pharmacist's Mate was a wild man . . . he did look dissolute . . . but there he was, not missing a trick. Only once had he been tempted to call down; but they had gotten around to that too . . . Easterly . . . gotten him up off the chain. He had looked over Easterly's body through the binoculars . . . no wound . . . just the wind and nerve knocked out of him. When the whole crowd had followed Wright up the dry dock he had realized that it was unfortunate that they had no clothes on. He could not have them flocking across the countryside in that fashion all the way to the Relief.

He turned expectantly to the door of the conning-tower. He had but a second to wait before Lieutenant Fitzpatrick came through it, heavily drugged with sleep, a startled expression on his perspiring face.

"Mr. Fitzpatrick, Wright has been struck by a shark. The Swimming Party is starting with him to the Relief. Get down there with these men." He nodded at half a dozen or so who had not been in the Swimming Party and who, having invaded the quarter-deck to watch the event below, were bunched at the rail nearby. "Take over the wounded man and carry him to the Relief."

Lieutenant Fitzpatrick said, "Aye, Aye, Sir," and began the long climb down the ladder to the dry dock floor as if he were in the throes of a nightmare coiling through the sleep from which he just had been awakened. The Captain leaned over the rail to say to him:

"Mr. Fitzpatrick . . . and send all those naked people back aboard here immediately. Do everything you can," he added, "for the boy."

Relapsing deeply into some mental absorption, the Captain began pacing slowly back and forth in the pervasive quietness, upon which the sun had begun to go down. He paced now with his head lowered, as if he patiently but rather reluctantly was calculating the regular fall and direction of his hollow steps upon the deck. Now and again as he reached the stern and swung about, he would glance back out over the world in a calm gesture of detecting, of suspecting, what more might be brewing out there, out there on the face of that world shielding itself from the decadent sun beneath a thin mask of burnished sea and illusory land upon which the angular rays glinted and flashed. He was deciding to do something of a kind that all his mature life in the Navy he had dreaded and hated, something he objected to almost superstitiously. He slowed to a halt abreast of the conning-tower door. He paused for a second before walking to it, his face turned attentively toward the sea in an attitude that might have been mistaken for one of listening, of listening for the faint, spasmodic strain of cheap music drifting out from the heart of the land. What he was doing was noting the distant, somehow ominous approach, towed through the polished water by the persistent, ugly tug, of two other destroyers of that Division over which he might have retained command, approaching under pressure of the fateful race against time that suddenly had seemed to enmesh everything. He continued on through the conning-tower door, down the hatch, to write a plea to his wife's father, powerful in the Senate, urging him to intrude himself and his politics into the clean life of the Navy in behalf of Woodbridge, who was being dragged under by those missionaries out there.

19

A few hours after Wright lost his leg, there returned to the ship, led by the reckless exuberance of the two Carey brothers just released from the hospital, twenty of those "lost" men who had been transferred from her back there in Cavite. They had arrived on the two other destroyers the Captain had observed being brought in by the tug. Their rejoining the ship seemed a kind of signal that the period of dismantled, pressured detachment was at an end and that the ship was to plunge back into her normal life. The Captain, despite the presence amongst them of one new man, accepted their arrival as the first sign and increment of his victory; and it heralded the positive blazing of the spirit of reunion that arose two evenings later when Ensign Snell and his small force, ragged, weary and full of wild tales of their days in the jungle, marched down the dry dock floor and climbed the ladder to Delilah.

There began, the next day, a great flurry of preparation to re-launch the ship. Men began to tighten up on the way they conducted themselves, as if they felt that already she were once more afloat and faced with the natural exactions of her duty. Some of them, especially the "old-timers," men on their second or third enlistments, were carried so far by this feeling that in their leisure hours aboard they fell energetically upon those personal or semi-personal details the condition of which is the true symptom of just how shipshape a man-of-war is or is not: Cruck, for instance, started two new Turk's heads to cap the fenders of the Captain's gig; and from the same kind of thick, white cord others wove fresh coverings on the handles of their wash buckets. Two or three men began work on patterned belts of this cord for their dungarees, trim stiffly woven belts that could be bleached regularly in soap, salt and sun to a spectacular whiteness; and Bidot sand-papered his Indian Clubs and revarnished them. Even Warrington, that fanatical non-communicant, betrayed a response to the stirring of the ship's spirit. He reawoke to the rigid self-discipline that, for example, had forced him, when he sat down to read in his leisure hours at sea, to review a lesson in Maxwell's Grammar before succumbing to the luxury of the thing he wanted to read. In these lax, latter days he had gotten so absorbed, so indignantly absorbed, in magazine and newspaper accounts of the havoc being wrought by the Germans in Europe that he had been swept out of his reading routine into a feverish wallowing in the atrocity columns of all the publications that he could buy ashore or that came in the mail to the men of the ship. He seemed to have forgotten his books and his Grammar in order to torture himself with nothing but the reading of every reported rape, every destroyed cathedral, every executed civilian as if each were a personal affront to his own human dignity. Most people in that ship, exiled amidst the bright wilderness of the antipodes, paid virtually no attention to news of the war; for them such news was a vague, massive rumour, to which they had grown accustomed, of something wrong in a legendary part of the far world that did not concern them; but Warrington, who ever appeared so anti-social in the eyes of the crew, was, like the old monk, a righter of wrongs, a defender of the weak, a partisan of justice; and he projected his sympathy (as some men project theirs into a dog, a horse or a son), all the sympathy of his passionate youngness, into whole groups of people, into nations, into mankind. He could not savour his food because men were starving in Belgium, nor enjoy the setting sun because helpless villages were being sacked and burnt beneath it, nor sleep at night because its darkness hid the rape of young girls. He brooded, as if he were culpable, over his inability to act, even fruitlessly, against this injustice; and he prayed at night, as he used to pray in his own unprojected behalf, that the United States would enter the war so that he could strike against the doers of this evil. Nevertheless, under the stimulation of the ship's imminent return to the sea, he that day got himself back within what had been his normal discipline, forced himself to review a lesson in the Grammar before taking up the latest news of the war.

There was a sharp revival, also, of those industries that inevitably declined when the crew had a long stretch of continual access to the well-furnished life of a port, declined in the face of the land's varied, expert competition both for the business of the customers and for the attention of those who served them: thus the Ship's Tailor, who was Corum, the Electrician, overhauled his hand sewing-machine in readiness for the mending and alteration activity he sensed was about to beset him; Horner, the pug-nosed Seaman from Cincinnati, and Morrow, the Fireman, announced surreptitiously that they would resume their illicit laundry business for those who wanted to evade the regulation duty of washing their own clothes; and Wembly, the Gunner's Mate, unofficially but definitely recognized as Ship's Barber, publicly honed his razors, scissors and clippers. Perhaps the clearest possible symptom that Delilah considered herself free of the land, once more a bird of passage skimming along its shores, was given by Cavendish, the blond Quartermaster, who, in his next liberty ashore, made the first gestures of conditioning himself and his Ilocano girl, whom he had found up Boton River, for the inevitable farewell.

It was into the fever of this renascence, like a fitting climax, that Ensign Woodbridge returned. Men trooped up to him and shook hands, with words of pleasure over his being back. Their grins of approbation, the buzz of their comment to one another and their noisy, respectful greetings to him amounted virtually to a cheer. Feenan and Chief Machinist's Mate Stengle, of the minority who disliked him, exchanged a glance in these first moments that might have been a comment on the corner of fine linen handkerchief protruding delicately from beneath the sleeve at his wrist. Lieutenant Fitzpatrick genuinely was delighted at his friend's return; but he suffered a flare of irritation over the man's unconscionable disregard of the trouble he had gotten himself into; and it was clear that Ensign Woodbridge really seemed to regard the matter lightly. It was doubtful if even the Captain was going to be successful in impressing him with its weight. He was, in the most nettling way, charmingly unconcerned, splendidly unconcerned against a background of general, personal manner that made inconceivable the fact that he had been in any kind of tarnishing conflict, or even that anyone ever would have had the effrontery to oppose him after the fashion of the event that by now had become notorious. He quite sincerely referred to the missionaries, in a brief exchange with the Captain and Lieutenant Fitzpatrick, as "those unfortunate fanatics." Although he did not show it, this attitude irked the Captain profoundly because it abetted an attitude of his own that he had to keep rejecting with annoyance, a kind of game he had found himself on the verge of playing with his feelings, a kind of make-believe that had tried to arise within him some days before when he had been officially notified that his officer was returning, a make-believe that the return was settled and all right, that it was not a mere prelude to a detachment for a Board of Inquiry and then a Court Martial.

Despite this, dinner on this night of Ensign Woodbridge's return was a luxury for the Captain: here was his ship renewed and ready for the sea, his officers, all of them, fitted around the table in the miniature wardroom at ease and in aroused sympathy with one another over coffee and tobacco, and Ensign Woodbridge, launched on a story, gesturing extravagantly with his pipe. The Captain enjoyed a realization, only faintly tainted with hope, that it was just like old times. His weathered face, wrinkled and youthful, assumed a rapt, almost childish expression as he listened to the story Ensign Woodbridge was telling, a story so detailed and so controlled by the verbal precision with which Ensign Woodbridge could be inspired, and yet so emancipated by his imagination, that it gradually became transformed there, in its impression, from the quality of a tale of events told casually into that of one of those written pieces of fiction in which the creator is capable of disclosing not merely the acts of his characters but their thoughts and feelings as well.

The Captain, as he listened, was flooded by a quiet but poignant sadness that he accepted, without thinking about it, as a pigment of the story's content. There was no opportunity for his mind to perceive that this especial emotion derived not from anything within the story, but from the story's climactic position, as an achievement, in that field where, for the Captain, Ensign Woodbridge's achievements already stood notably high. It entered the Captain's mind, during a moment when the young officer paused to puff at his pipe, that the man never could surpass this . . . this was a blaze of glory. It even might have occurred to the Captain, given his opportunity, that Ensign Woodbridge was trying to go out in it, trying to give all there was to give in one final, farewell burst; and under the peculiar pressure that now lay upon the Captain's being, that had lain upon it ever since the day in Zamboanga when he had submitted to the premonition that he and the ship fatefully were committed to each other, he now would have faced this climactic quality of the story as an omen of his officer's fate, faced it as, in the same moment of awareness, he would have been repudiating the idea of any such thing as an omen. It then would not have reassured him much to have reflected that, after all, Ensign Woodbridge's life had been built one climax upon another; nor could he have sacrificed himself to the doubt with the

301

abstract speculation in relativity that a farewell may be celebrated by him who stays as well as by him who departs.

This story had been evoked when Ensign Snell, who had had no hint of the trouble until he returned out of the jungle to the ship, bluntly had inquired:

"What the hell did you get yourself into anyway . . . up that river?"

The Captain and Lieutenant Fitzpatrick had been pleased with this forthright question. It expressed their sentiments exactly. Although their bodies had made no movement, there had arisen about them an atmosphere as of leaning forward expectantly. Ensign Woodbridge had smiled a bit scornfully, a trifle glitteringly in the face of what this question and this expectancy had called up within him. He had replied, with a restless raising of his shoulders:

"Oh, those birds wanted to blackmail the sick Chinamen into coming to Jesus, and I wouldn't be a party to it." He had shrugged his shoulders again. "I knew that Jesuit was putting it over on me . . . in a way . . ." He gestured with the pipe. ". . . But not really, because I did what I went out there to do . . . distribute those stores without any nonsense." The handsome mouth and chin in his profoundly young face had hardened for a silent moment and his green-blue eyes had fixed in an unseeing, slightly arrogant stare upon the silver bowl in the centre of the table, from which the fragrance of ripe mangoes rose like incense to blend with the blue drifts of tobacco smoke; then his features precipitately had brightened as if some irrelevant sun had dawned within him. "Say!" he had exclaimed, not as if he had been changing the subject but as if succumbing to a surge of eagerness, "That Jesuit told me a good one about our old monk . . . about when the monk was a young fellow and first came to the Islands . . . Away back in the old days out here."

The Captain had relinquished his expectancy, without even a murmur or a shadow of protest at Ensign Woodbridge's sudden flight, and he had relaxed, alert but already bemused, to receive the pleasure he had found instead. Lieutenant Fitzpatrick had followed him almost as readily; although on this particular occasion he might not have done so if the story had not promised to deal with the old monk, the memory of whom had gotten, with some kind of glowing permanence, into his feelings and his brain. Ensign Snell could not follow any such lightninglike and bewildering shift as this; and he had not wanted to. There had been, however, nothing he could have done about it, nothing but wait the story out, shielding himself silently in the cloud of his monumental patience.

It seems, Ensign Woodbridge had gone on, that in those days Manila was just a sort of village surrounded by the high stone walls. The Spaniards were losing their grip even then, and the place was a cruelly administered refuge for dubious Spanish careerists, exiles, and a scatter of rather desperate island traders of all races, an edge of the world morass of torpid whoring, gambling, drinking and the debauching of helpless natives. The only decent class of people in the place seemed to be the Chinese shopkeepers.

Trading and government did not extend very effectively beyond the easy reach of Manila's walls. Some of the more distant islands, Jolo and Mindanao for instance, practically ignored the authority of the town and its Spaniards. Anybody who would and could trade amongst those fierce Mohammedans of the southern jungles and estuaries was welcome to what he could get. The Spaniards rarely interfered seriously with foreigners who made the attempt to trade out there, but they never protected them. Probably, such foreign traders were not much of a threat even when, for any considerable stretch of time, some of them occasionally appeared to be making headway. If they began to intrude on those nearer areas where trade, though less quickly profitable in a lucky strike, was comparatively safe and easy, the authorities flatly told them to move on. Eight or nine trips in some small, old sailing vessel or native craft was about all most of them lasted. Eventually they seemed just to disappear. Perhaps they retired, for a new start, to more practicable coasts with the small stakes they had gained; or perhaps they made "one last voyage" too many, drifting leisurely out of life over the purple water into the sunshine, the mystery, the deadly wilderness of the archipelagoes, lovely and ominous, far to the hazy south.

The most successful of these foreign traders was neither a

303

ruined man desperately risking all on the chance of a new start, nor a hopelessly defeated one crushed outward helplessly into danger. He was a sourceless American named Parker, a person who preferred, evidently, to snatch, slash and trick his subsistence from whatever place was the end of the world and amidst degeneracy, mystery and danger. This man often had sailed his disreputable little schooner right into the Gulf of Davao, a place to this day barricaded behind a legend of sanguinary terror, going ashore to trade in every little death-dealing village he could find along its coasts. When anybody asked him how he managed it, he laughed contemptuously, in a strident, maniacal, profoundly irritating manner, not at the Gulf of Davao or the question, but at the questioner.

Whenever he laughed in this way, no matter what it was he laughed at, it made people want to strike at him; but people seldom tried this, because it inevitably entailed fighting of a sustained and lethal character. Parker never would permit such an incident to remain within the proportions of a mere bar-room brawl; but released into a repellent storm of underdog violence, he always tried to make the encounter deadly. His favourite manoeuvre was to seize a bottle by the neck clubwise, crash off the bottom of it on something as he charged in, and attack his opponent with the remaining jagged circle. If he had been knocked out on the occasion of the first encounter, the next day or the next or the next the man who had struck the blow suddenly would find himself confronted by Parker, charging in wild precision, brandishing his horrible weapon with deadly intent, driven by an incommensurate ferocity. When his opponent had a revolver and threatened to use it, Parker simply went and got a similar weapon. He did this not as a gesture but as a necessary part of a sincere effort to kill or mutilate his enemy. He gave it as his reason for not habitually carrying a gun that he did not want to shoot anybody foolishly in a moment of excitement.

The monk and Parker came together as a result of the holy man's unquenchable conviction that the new field of his labours included also those Moro-inhabited islands to the south. Nothing could dissuade him. The authorities made a strong try, because his would be a death that, in the end, they would have to explain.

They promised him that whenever a strong military detachment ventured into one of those Moro regions he could go with it. They gave him the example of the priests who, finding themselves in Jolo, kept sanely within the high stone walls surrounding the town on that island. This, the monk tried to make clear to them, was not the sort of thing that would serve his purpose; so they appealed to the diocesan head of the islands. The Bishop replied that he did not feel his authority was indicated sufficiently in this irregular and very perplexing matter; but he did speak to the monk, rousing himself momentarily for the occasion from a kind of continual, hollow-eyed siesta. He, too, came off second-best with his meek but indomitable, and thoroughly unwelcome, recruit, who possessed an exhortative letter, instructional papers signed by double authority, of Rome and of Madrid, which made it very unclear whether or no this foreign monk was to be restrained from stirring up about all their heads those hornets' nests of Moros. As a matter of fact, the Bishop felt that the monk was to be pardoned for reading into these writings an outline of a reconnaissance mission amongst those people . . . "but that kind of thing just wasn't practicable . . . the Moros were a unique problem . . . Authority was Authority; but was he rash in feeling that it did not really intend to operate thus through the blindness of five thousand miles?" All the Bishop could do was to argue against the wisdom of the monk's interpretation of the letter . . . "the vineyard was not ready . . . a tomorrow would come when the time was ripe . . . tomorrow . . ." but the young monk held firmly to his own interpretation. He kept his papers always about him, and whenever he was summoned to a mansion or an office of Authority, of Church or of State, he would carry them in his hand ready to point out certain passages. However, he received no help from anybody. They all smiled painfully. They shrugged their shoulders helplessly. It was in the face of this situation that he finally was thrown upon the information and mercy of those dubious ones who alone knew much about the southern islands and who alone ever dared their shores in any general manner.

The monk was assured that of these foreigners the only one who really might help him with what he wanted, the only one who had been making it out there and back regularly for any considerable length of time was "that devil Parker." It took him two days to find the trader, two days of winding around through the thick of whore houses, gambling rooms, saloons and stilted nipa hovels beyond the walls where the man had left the spoor of his appetites and his lust. He had looked for him in these places because an American sea Captain at the trading wharf had told him that there he was to be found, "throwing away every last dime of what his last trip brought him in . . . But don't you have no truck with *him*, Father," the sea Captain respectfully but indignantly had insisted, "he's a raping, roaring, hell-bending son of a bitch."

The monk found Parker late at night in a dance hall outside the walls. It was little more than a vast nipa roof above a torch-lighted space crowded with moist bodies suffering or simulating excitement. The warm, nearly living air was smothering there in a musky blend of female perspiration, rank perfume and the pungency of native tobacco smoke that clung and eddied around the torches. A scatter of beings flickered constantly back and forth in the jaundiced moonlight between the shelter of the roof and a row of palm-screened nipa huts a hundred yards distant, these a shadowy, angular source of woman sounds: degraded giggling, sharp cries and staccato pleading. The orchestra strummed provocatively its Malay-Spanish rhythm, as on the very nerves of the dancers, strummed almost silently, like the beat of blood, save when the scream of a cornet rose to stab and goad. Along the unpolished wooden stretch of the long, dark bar, festooned with paper streamers of red and yellow, the sweating Spanish soldiers, Chinamen and crews of ships in the bay slopped beer with unsteady hands, snapped at liquor with prehensile lips and, to prelude or stave off the trip to the shadowy huts, bought volleys of drinks for clouds of little aphrodisiac creatures with glistening black hair, winglike blouses of stiff, billowing mango cloth and glossy skirts formed of a single piece wrapped tightly about miniature hips and limbs.

With grim timidity the monk, a dark tide of action and reaction tumbling in the mysterious breath-caverns of his young body, had tramped straight into this from out of the warm, surrounding shadow, through the corona of stench, of urine and ordure, that edged the place; and he stood there near the bar, naturally ignored as if he had been a plantain tree, a shaft of moonlight or the iron-laced door of the nearby convent, looking about for somebody who might be able to point out his man. This office finally was performed for him by the alert *patron,* himself, Señor Bocanegra, a fat, merciless ex-sergeant of the army, who came up not because he was disturbed by the almost theoretical presence, as he definitely would have been if it had been that of a mere, practical priest, but, virtually out of habit, because here was a man maintaining a pointed, questing attitude in his establishment.

The monk was surprised, after all he had heard, to find in the one pointed out to him as Parker a person so slight. For minutes, in his astonishment and an effort to readjust his conceptions, he watched the trader dancing and walking impudently around in his shirt-sleeves out there like some thin, loose-jointed animal about five feet, nine inches high. His stringy hair was the colour of dirty straw and he wore it low at the temples in front of his large ears and in a kind of disordered lock over his medium-high forehead. The colourless skin of his small, long, thirty-year-old face was slick, like an oriental's, and the whiskers came out on it in only smudgy patches. His mouth was continually grinning and in this aspect it was a wet, pink rectangle bordered with blunt, separated, grey teeth. There was something unspeakably shameless and bold, but at the same time genial, about this grin between the rather sharp nose and the firm, pointed chin. His brown eyes were very large, full of white and were sparsely fringed with long lashes the colour of his hair. They always were restlessly on the move in an unhurried, liquid fashion. What he was like when he was asleep it was impossible to conjecture, but awake he appeared to be in the grip of an unending spasm of optimism and impudence. When he danced he slid his feet gracefully around in extravagant patterns over the floor, holding the girl tightly in his thin arm against the right hollow of his loins. His left arm he permitted to droop almost free in a reckless gesture as if it ever were about to engage in some groping manipulation. His shirt-tail seemed on the point of working out at any instant, and, as he danced, he kept his buttocks projected as if in deliberate derision not so much of his partner as of the onlookers. When he walked, he swayed impertinently from side to side, bending slightly at the waist in an apparent effort to favour the hang of his notoriously oversized genitals.

Parker never came to the dance hall for the purpose of using one of the women. He came there to listen to the music. When he wanted a woman, he went after something more choice; his usual procedure being to tempt, with a handful of money, a poverty-maddened father or husband into permitting him the use of a young girl he would spot in some wretched vista of nipa hovels. Although he came to the dance hall for the music, standing for twenty minutes or so listening to it with that good-natured grin on his face, his head on one side and his disreputable body swaying in time, he sooner or later would find himself dancing, and then finally making his way through the moonlight with a girl to one of the huts in the shadow. Drink had little to do with this because, although Parker drank continually, gulping slowly and obviously, one drink sometimes lasting him as long as an hour, he rarely was under any detectable influence of alcohol. Señor Bocanegra hated these occasions of Parker's visits. They usually tested to the limit the power of his authority and the order of his administration. The trouble was not with Parker: he simply stood there all through it in the best of humour, radiating the inexhaustible abundance of his violent energy and erupting the roars of his maniacal laughter. The trouble was with the women. The type he inevitably picked did not want to go out there to a hut with him.

Whenever Parker appeared at the dance hall, women whom he had taken before were swept by a panic of physical fear. They tried to hide, their friends explaining to the alert Bocanegra that they had become ill and had gone to the wash-room; or they made up frantically to the men they were with in an effort to get taken immediately away out to one of the huts. There was a tacit conspiracy that whenever Parker appeared all the biggest girls were to envelop him and keep in his way in an effort to divert him from the other smaller ones, some of whom were strikingly tiny and doll-like. The big girls would sway out to the attack, glowing with a kind of feminine, oriental boldness and smiling, for all to see, their contempt of this formidable man and the scandal of his violence, for which, nevertheless, there was in their attitude a flaw of something that, incredibly, suggested enthusiasm, admiration. No doubt the preponderance of their confidence lay in the fact that Parker never failed to ignore them. He would light upon one of the smallest creatures in the place and, aroused and grinning, indicate that she was to go out with him. The girl, literally stricken, would plead that she was sick, that she had gonorrhoea, that she was with child, any frantic, useless excuse that flashed into her mind. It did no good. Parker would take hold of her and grin his insistence. Her friends would circle at a distance and hurl ridicule and reproach at him that would have crumpled a less shameless man. Other men witnessing the scene would get away quickly, laughing evasively, spreading on the gathering storm of their outrage and uneasiness such rationalistic oil as: "It's just a joke." "Aw, that's what she's here for." "It's none of my business." "Christ! . . . He can't help it if he's built like a mule." This was the first stage of these affairs that enraged Bocanegra. He would fling himself into the scene shouting apoplectically that it was a lie, that he never had women in there who were "sick or no good." For an hour after he had driven the fearfully reluctant girl out into the moonlight with Parker, he would prowl around expanding and repeating this denial to all who got in his way, swinging viciously at the air with the thin club that habitually hung from his wrist by a leather thong, and yelling by no means empty threats at the women, now launched on a subtle and disastrous sabotage that reduced the number of drinks bought and the number of men entertained, that he would put them in jail . . . that they all owed him money . . . that they were "a herd of ungrateful cows." A number of men always left the place after one of these scenes; and Bocanegra, sullen and helpless, would watch them go, muttering vindictively to himself that they were "just a bunch of fairies" . . . and there was no way to get at that Parker . . . there was no pretext for excluding a man who was so sober and orderly . . . who paid good money for everything he got . . . "and who, the filthy goat, violated no rule of man or God."

Music, any kind of music, provided it was produced by more than one voice or instrument, fascinated and drugged Parker. It got hold of both his solar plexus and his brain. He would even stand on the porch of a church, spitting thinly now and then from between his teeth, and listen to a choir and organ. Once he had sailed his dirty, little, black schooner all the way to Singapore to hear the performances of a travelling opera company he had found out was going to appear there. On that occasion he had encountered for the first time a stretch of song, the Quartette from *Rigoletto,* that literally had possessed him, taken hold of him for good as the memory of a woman does. It had wrought in him something akin to the religious experience; and he had set it up, then and there, as a vague but poignant standard, as an object of his existence. He had paid out the last of his stock of money to the four singers, just before they sat down to lunch the next day, to have them repeat the song for him on the noon-tortured verandah of the hotel where they stopped. The music had made him so strangely drunk that it had not occurred to him to make an effort at getting hold of the thin, sad woman who sang the soprano part, a woman who happened to be one of the few white types that attracted him. From then on, no matter where he encountered a musical group, a piano and violin in a restaurant, a band in a dance hall, a group of singers around a bar, he attempted to elicit that composition. It was a perverse arrangement of his fate that he rarely was successful. He had bribed the leader of the military band in Manila to include it in the program of his public Sunday concerts; but that mustachioed notable had never gotten around to completing the deal. Whenever Parker reminded him of it, he emitted a shower of abrupt excuses, smiling but impatient, and hurried off on the round of pressing duties that seemed to have caught up with him at that very moment . . . "The arrangement had not yet been finished . . . it would have to be rehearsed too . . . however, very soon . . ." Parker, who knew nothing about music, was only half deceived by this evasion, and he would not have accepted it with the grinning docility he did if the bandmaster had not been an acknowledged priest of the one powerful magic in his universe. In reality, the bandmaster was desperately determined never to play that composition. Virtually in the moment that Parker had taken up with him the matter of the Quartette from *Rigoletto,* he had realized that he hated the piece; and this hatred had gone so far, on the occult wings of a memory of how Parker had carried his Mimosa, dead drunk, out onto the schooner and kept the little bar-girl prisoner there for three days, that it came to include all of Verdi, whose music he excommunicated from the band with a determination that was not understood by the musicians but respected. At best, a rendition of the piece by the band would have been but a compromise for Parker; nothing would have satisfied him, really, but to hear the four allotted voices sing it after the manner of that first encounter. The nearest he ever had come to this was one night while his schooner was anchored in the bay. The song, powerfully played by an accordion on a distant ship, had poured through the heavy, land-musked night down the glittering water-track of the moon and enchanted him, swept him out of himself. The next morning he had shoved off in a heavily manned boat to find that ship and get the accordion player for himself, at no matter what cost of money, effort or conniving; but the ship already had sailed away.

The monk had waited patiently near the bar for a chance to get at Parker, who all the while had been dancing or talking to one of those girls. The monk had not wanted to interrupt, but when he decided that the couple were preparing either to leave the place or to launch themselves into what appeared to be the beginnings of a quarrel, he dared not permit his opportunity, so arduously searched out, to escape him. He walked out across the dance floor when the music stopped, embarrassingly conscious of his growing isolation as the dancers dispersed towards the edges of the hall, and came to a stand about ten feet from the couple, whom Señor Bocanegra had now joined. The *patron,* like a menacing cloud, was leaning tensely over the little girl, whispering down at her, his piglike face thrusting in a remorseless, explosive manner, while his thin club pounded in unconscious painfulness against the calf of his leg.

There was something decidedly wrong here, the monk told himself. It was, no doubt, some bicker about money. That was the usual issue in a place like this. It could wait, he told himself. He must seize his opportunity. He called out in a resonant voice, full of richness and deprecation:

"Mr. Parker . . . Could I have a few words with you?"

The determined English sentence, its intent and tone so positively different from that which prevailed there, dropped into the place as if it had been a large stone impacting the surface of a lake. A widening circle of silence eddied swiftly to the farthest corners. The whole population of the hall finally was staring, surprised and

311

expectant, at the two men and the girl facing, in no little astonishment, the tall dark figure at the back of whose long head, on the surface of the precise tonsure, the wavering torchlight seemed to gather and glow in the suggestion of an aureate disk. Everybody understanding perfectly the situation that gripped Parker, the girl and Bocanegra, attributed the same understanding to the holy man and concluded unhesitatingly that it was the cause of his interference. Parker had swung slowly about, casual and good-humoured, into the direction of the question. His face was ablaze with that easy, dissolute grin, which seemed to signify, in all its effrontery, that the questioner and the others about him were just a trifle crazy or daring but that he, Parker, sympathized with this and in some measure condoned it. As he stood there, his absurd body sagging almost imperceptibly at the knees, a cigarette drooping loosely from his thin, protruding lower lip as if it were glued precariously there to the beginning of pink inside exposed by the grin, Parker maintained a ruthless grip on the girl's arm above the elbow. There was something abominable, something beyond simple cruelty or an intent to imprison, in the way that powerful hand sank into the little column of pain-whitened brown flesh. The monk jerked his gaze free of this, as if to leave it struggling there with what was inexplicable and obscene would but increase his bewilderment, his uneasiness. If, as it would have later in life, his gaze had gone next to the girl's face and interpreted that in terms of what was so repellently besetting the childish but exquisitely mature body, that watching mob of revellers would have gotten what they expected. Instead, the monk's gaze swung directly, with the directness of youth or of determination caught in uncertainty, right past the misery and oppression near at hand to the man who, he had decided in the calm, controlled time of planning before this confusing happenstance, would lead him to the need and pain crying in the romantic darkness of the far distance. He repeated his question, staring rigidly at Parker in a way that seemed to make non-existent that girl beside him. She was leaning hopelessly toward her tortured arm, her small breast heaving with excitement, with fear, with loathing that seemed about to burst from her slightly parted lips; but her face, which reached about to Parker's heart, was a heavy mask of un-dead lifelessness, that typical scab behind which rages, in moments of ambush, all the festering terror and helplessness of those who are at the exploited bottom of humanity.

"Sure," said Parker. "Go ahead."

"I am obliged to get to the islands in the south . . . to make a trip around through them. Yours seems to be the only boat . . . that . . . I would like to go south in your boat the next trip you make." He ended the speech firmly, but it appeared as if he had intended to say more, as if he had intended to explain why it was very important, and that he could pay a little for the trip.

For an appreciable, silent moment, Parker simply bathed the monk in the effluence of that grin from his repugnant mouth and big, quizzical eyes; then, tightening his grip on the girl and jerking her to him, he lashed at the space about and above them with the roar and screech of his laughter. He swung his gaze delightedly along the surface of the crowd as if taking in the massed approval of admiring cronies to whom he had presented, and was handling superbly, a very funny entertainment. The men in the crowd shifted about uneasily, the women gritted their teeth or clenched their fists.

"Sure!" Parker finally said, his nasal voice genially insolent, penetrating. "Tomorrow. Be down at the trading dock at seven o'clock in the morning."

Upon this the situation abruptly disintegrated, the monk swinging around and striding directly away, swiftly, as if fleeing from an odious cavern of decay and viciousness out into the clean and normal world of the night. That was in the days of his youth before he realized that there was no place to flee. As quickly, but more casually, Parker and Bocanegra turned around, hustling the girl between them, and made out in the opposite direction, toward those huts. The soles of her slippers sometimes hissing their resistance against the floor, the girl was clinging to Parker in the strange way that a person clings to the rock that is crushing him or the wild beast that is ripping at his vitals. Through the sweating, torchlit crowd under the great nipa roof there swept a murmur of disappointment and betrayal, of resentment against the monk; but it subsided, almost at once, into the hot night, the smoky perfume, the stench and the gathering movement of bodies, before

313

the sudden rip and thrust and rise of guitars and mandolins, the visceral th . ud . . beat . . . throb . . . th . ud . . beat . . . throb of drums, the gasp and scream of the cornet.

The monk found it impossible to get to sleep. He kept quite still on his back waiting for it, restraining himself with difficulty from tossing about. Periodically he would drift vaguely to the semi-conscious borders of it, then throb quickly back to awakeness, as if some sound, some sharp thought had struck him back. In these returns, when it seemed to him that he was acutely awake, he told himself that what had hold of him was the anticipation of his voyage in the morning with that man, "that foul, brutal scoundrel." A twinge of restlessness and antipathy shook his body. He suffered, heavily impatient, an attack of remorse for this recurring view he took of the man. He reproached himself fiercely for it. "This man, like all men under the sun, was a child of God, the Almighty . . . lost, misguided, tortured with iniquity, he nevertheless was under the glorious, all-seeing eye of God . . . inescapably . . . like all the children of the flock . . . He had but strayed away amidst the thorns and the stones . . . our sweet Lady, our blessed Lord, lead him safely back to the fold . . . The arms of Jesus Christ, our Lord, so sweet, so compassionate, had opened wide upon the terrible Cross for him as well . . . for him too . . . that child of God, made brave and wild that he might seek out the fierce lost tribes beyond the daring of other men . . . and yes . . . that he might lead God's poor, sorry servant amongst them in the name of our Lord and his holy work . . . the Father . . . the Son . . . the Holy Ghost . . ." Aroused, as by a shadowy movement of his hand, he shifted un-easily as if to free himself from the heavy air that seemed to be precipitating moisture over his body. He called upon God to for-give him if he restrained himself from praying, because it stirred him further and further up out of sleep . . . and he must be ready for the Lord's voyage in the early morning. When he opened his eyes he realized he was not as acutely awake as he had supposed, that his being, with the heavy, stone walls that sheltered him, was lost and dim beneath the moon-blurred smother of the night, of night that was layer upon layer of darkness like warm fur, dead, nameless fragrances from the living garden outside the barred win-dow, lingering incense from the chapel down the corridor and cogent dimensionless memories of unknown things . . . sweetest sanctity wafted from a lone lily, a thin column incarnadine, blossoming on a mountain of dung . . . take this, the precious body and blood of Jesus Christ, our Lord . . . th . ud . . beat . . . throb . . . Parker . . . Parker . . . poor little child wandering desperate, lost in the strange wilderness of the deadly leprechauns . . . Parker . . . would lead him into the wilderness that God's work might be done . . . thus, thus ever, ever from the dung heap grew the lily . . . beautiful like living threads of fire in the black fever of the night . . . holy martyrs' blood glowing on the grey sand of the vortex . . . th . ud . . beat . . . throb . . . the body of the dead Saint breathing off intoxicating sweetness where man's nostril expected the breath of corruption . . . th . ud . . beat . . . throb . . . th . ud . . beat . . . throb . . . Mary, Holy Mother of God . . . one Mary . . . two Marys . . . three Marys . . . Mary, the Amber Saint, faithful and lost on the alien marge of sand and sea . . . down . . . down . . . down into the black fire of the tropic night . . . O, burn bright the blood of the Lamb . . . the Golden Heart . . . Parker . . . the glorious, inscrutable ways of God . . . down . . . down . . . the Dark Mary writhing in the grip of Parker's hand . . . th . ud . . beat . . . throb . . . th . ud . ." On the instant desperately wide awake with a rush of violence that had swept him up from the pallet to his feet, he stood in the leprous darkness and faced the intolerable realization that, in all the gathered pressure of its tardiness, had slugged and hurtled through him: the full, true realization of what that scene between Parker and that helpless child signified.

He stood there for many seconds, stressed against the torrent of his feelings like a steel mast in a heavy wind. Then slowly he began to relax, to make the first resigned move back to his pallet; but as he did so the wavering storm of violence resurged upon him, surprised him with such force that he struck his body insanely with his fists. He grew sick at the stomach. He ground his teeth. Wildly, horribly, he used the name of the Lord as a club and a curse, as if he were a sailor in the dark of a swaying forecastle battling the shadows of drunkenness. Jagged obscenities, ready and hideous in the deep, ineradicable cesspools filled with the debris of early youth, rose and hacked about him like unclean knives, only to be flung back by the walls to quiver in his own breast.

In a pause of the storm, he became aware of the feel of the stone against the flat of his bare feet. Its hardness, its illusion of coolness, its persistent reality struggled impassively, negligent of repulse, up the reaches of his limbs, towards his heart, against the consternation and the fury that possessed him. The hard reality of the world crept back in upon him from all sides; his body and his emotions faltered before the strengthening of his mind and spirit. Here at the first real encounter with an example of what God meant by one of His children being lost from the flock, he, weak and corrupt, had crumpled like a man of little faith. He had taken the name of the Lord in vain. He had wallowed in blasphemy and hatred of his brother. He fell on his knees in the darkness, up through which shimmered heat waves that would have been semi-visible in the light, and hid his face in his hands. Dared he beg of God to try him once more? . . . Yes, to forgive him for mistaking the distorted, evil surface wrought upon Parker by the world for the immortal soul beneath? He sought no escape from punishment for his own apostasy. Let it be as fierce as the Lord saw fit . . . but, Almighty God, try him on the difficult way once more! The Blessed Virgin and the Holy Saints intercede for him. Let God's forgiveness of Parker, His child, lost and blind, come many times sooner than his own. His words now came out upon his lips, clearly and frankly, the last of them bursting forth passionately like something thrusting its way up through solid rock, "Show me, in the light of Thy infinite mercy, O God, how to love my . . . my brother!"

Long past dawn he rose from his knees, took up the bundle he had prepared before going to bed the night before and, hoping that he was not too late, strode down to the wharf. The little black schooner was still there, sulking restlessly in the muddy water under the clear disclosure of the hot morning, the pervading brilliance of which was thinly blue in the high sky and yellow on the flattened land and sea. The monk stared at the craft for some time as if it were a dubious live thing with which he would have to deal. His hollowed, sickened eyes, young and deeply sensitive, were wearing the contrite expression of one who has inflicted a serious injury in the frenzy of a misled outburst; but his tall, robust body was tense and recalcitrant, as if it were being held back from battle.

"Mr. Parker," he called out in a strong tone of gentle apology.

Almost immediately Parker stuck his uncombed head out of the cuddy. His face blazed with that grin when he saw the monk. He said nothing, simply hung there grinning.

"May I come aboard?"

"Sure," said Parker, and carelessly let himself down out of sight again.

The monk climbed down the face of the dock to the deck of the schooner with the uncomfortable feeling of a man who may be performing an important, minor act in the wrong way, although there was no one in sight to watch him; and the moment he was in contact with the vessel, the moment his whole weight rested upon it, this uncomfortable feeling became heavily depressive with his impression that he had relinquished his grip on one world, the world, to drop into another in which all the rules of order as that first world knew them not merely were repudiated but unknown. He looked about uncertainly, trying to tell himself that it was incredible that the little boat he had looked down on from the dock should now have become around him this formidable jungle of tarry lines, serpents of sail-cloth and mysterious obstructions of soiled iron and wood. He did not know which way to turn in this petty labyrinth. Even his sense of direction became a trifle confused. He worked his way to a clear space in what turned out to be the bow and stood there waiting, his bundle at his feet.

He did not see Parker again until it almost was time for the schooner to cast off from the dock. This occurred shortly after the two people who formed Parker's crew, a Spaniard and a native, arrived at the head of the dock in a two-wheeled cart loaded with bales and sacks of trading material for the voyage. The monk noted as an item in Parker's favour that when the native came down and, leaning over the foot of the dock, stated dispassionately something in dialect at the cuddy, Parker arose at once into the sunshine and energetically set about helping to carry down the cargo and stow it. This habit of Parker's, however, struck few other people as being a point in his favour. It was regarded by white men as but another trick in this perverse man's irritating bag. Europeans out here did not do this sort of thing. The native carriers, lounging sleepily on the dock, felt that he deliberately was with-holding a few crumbs of money that meant much to them and nothing to him. On catching sight of the monk, the two newcom-ers paused and stared confrontingly at him from behind their arm-loads. Parker shot a casual, grinning glance over his shoulder in the direction of their attention and then commented briefly in a tangle of Spanish and Moro dialect that seemed to make of the monk a thing warranting no further attention of any kind.

The monk would have liked Parker to tell him where to estab-lish himself so that he would not be in the way, especially through the confusing moments of casting off and making sail. He even would have appreciated very much being told by Parker that he could take himself down below into the stifling little cabin, the dark, malodorous privacy of which he never would bring himself to invade without specific instructions. When he finally was driven to ask Parker where to station himself, Parker had replied, from behind the skirmishing display of his grin:

"Oh, just roost anywhere."

As a result of watching carefully for those spots most traversed and occupied by the three men, and of having been shoved aside time and again in the unconcerned manner with which one parts a door curtain, the monk came to rest on a comparatively un-molested spot in the stern, on the starboard side. He continued to live on that spot a few inches above the water, sleeping there, reading his breviary there, staring out from there for hours on end, as if from a prison cell, at the smooth glinting sweep of the damp-ly fragrant sea, at the minute swarms of virtually invisible fish and ambulant cells just beneath its surface, at the fear-driven fly-ing fish like iridescent projectiles arcing through the wild sunlight, at the passing spectacle of the incredible land: reefs like golden spectres caught within the motile, purple-green crystal of the sea . . . passionate black and brown rocks, tumbled monuments marking starkly against the sky the death place of vanquished mountains . . . islands like water-clinging drifts of heavy smoke, green and precise, that grew or diminished, distorted or changed shape entirely, as the black schooner tacked past. His oppressive situation, the unending, monotonous exaggeration of the passing world, the scorching heat which he feared was inducing a fever in him, threw him back with increasing desperation upon the boon of prayer. He found himself praying for hours at a time, relaxing motionlessly into this communion as if it were a cool, comforting reality in which was dulled or obliterated the cruelty of the sun, the relentless motion of the slightly water-logged boat, the periodic flapping of the sails, the unreality of the physical world and the heartless exclusiveness of the three other people who inhabited it. Suddenly, however, he had been deprived of this one comfort also. Not that he had stopped praying; but that this necessity had been transformed, in one horrible instant, into terms of the pressures that encompassed him. It had happened in the afternoon of the second day. On his knees, his head pillowed on the dirty gunwale, he had realized all at once in the midst of praying that he was struggling consciously, uncomfortably to go on. The well had dried up within him as before his very gaze. He had turned his head instinctively. Fixed steadily upon him from the other side of the deck, as if they had caught him in some scandalous, private act, were those two large eyes framed in the pink delight, the affront, the assault of that man's grin.

From that moment on, in the daytime, the monk prayed mostly as a matter of principle, prayed almost as an act of martyrdom under the ignoble spectatorship of Parker's hilarious eyes and grin. The man seemed to be clairvoyant. He seemed to know exactly when the monk began to pray, even when the latter tried to screen his devotion behind some casual stance of the body and neutral expression of the face. Sometimes Parker and the Spaniard would be lazing, perhaps napping, well forward in the shade of the foresail, while the Moro in a kind of implacable trance stood watch at the wheel. Observing this, the monk would seize upon it as a moment of privacy; but when he began his prayer, if he stole a glance in Parker's direction, he would find that the man had risen on one elbow and was pouring at him, a few inches above the deck, beneath the boom, around the edge of the cuddy or the mast, the corrupt, amused torrent of his attention.

Even at night, when he lay stretched out on the blanket that formed the wrapper of his bundle, the monk did not feel that he was safe from Parker's intuitiveness. He would lie there on his back, thankful for the dark, velvety shelter of the immense night, watching the mastheads and the rigging swing regularly back and forth through the patterns of the stars, and waiting for sleep to overtake that man who was carrying him to God's work. The monk was not always successful in this because Parker chose the Eight-to-Midnight Watch for a kind of musical concert the Spaniard habitually staged for him on top of the cuddy; and this often kept Parker aroused quite past the time at which the holy man found it possible to stay awake any longer, exhausted as he was by the long day of violent heat and light, the remorselessness of his captivity and the struggle within himself. When this was the case, he recklessly would launch himself into his devotions, fearful that he might fall asleep while waiting to be alone for them. Then Parker rarely failed to sense him out, bursting into a wild series of hoots and yells terminating in the shrill contemptuousness, the enraging goad of his laughter, a sustained procedure that whipped the musician up to a frenzy of execution.

This Spaniard was a middle-aged, broad-shouldered seaman from Galicia. He had a long, broad face that looked like a lump of sand-blasted mud, and dark eyes that squinted brightly with vindictive decadence just beneath the even line of the childish bang in which he wore his black, weather-beaten hair. He made his music sitting tailor-fashion opposite his patron, and gazing now up at the moon and stars, about which he often sang, and then down into his lap with his leathery eyelids lowered in a kind of corrupt demureness. His principal instrument was his voice, a throaty, rum-broken, melodious drone issuing, staccato and abandoned, from a lipless mouth that seemed grimly to begrudge opening for any purpose. His accompanying instrument was a pair of table spoons which he held back to back between the fingers of his left hand, thumping the lower spoon against the planking while he tapped the upper of the pair against the lower with the stiffened palm of his right hand. With these spoons, adroitly accompanying the provocative chant of his voice, he produced a gale of rhythmical clatter that sounded something like a combination of *castanets, clavos* and *maracas.* His triumph on these instruments was a debauched, chortling rise-and-fall of a song, half Flamenco, half West Indian, about an *aguacate,* a *panatela* and a *burro;* and it was into this composition that he stormed climac-

320

tically whenever Parker, either responding to the excitement in the music or jeering at the prayers, burst out with his yells and his laughter.

It was Parker's custom to work about the deck clad only in his shirt, loosely held upon his thin, muscular body by one or two buttons. He would go darting for the sheets, scanty shirt-tails flying, as if in the midst of sudden emergency; and when at the wheel he looked like an intoxicated man who had been summoned from his bunk, with no time for dressing, to save his vessel at the moment she was about to go on a reef. The spectacle Parker presented in this attire was so shameless, so offensive, that the monk did his best to keep the man out of his field of vision. However, perceiving this, Parker did his best to thwart it, doing all the work he could right under the holy man's eye; and finally, making an out-and-out game of it in moments of leisure when he could not doze, he took to parading up and down in front of the monk, after the manner of a Parisian dress model, his grotesque, disease-touched privates in full sun, and his face alive and insolent with that grin. This had been almost too much for the monk. The first time it happened he had blazed with rage and disgust. He had turned abruptly to the sea in a spasm of abhorrence, as if he were about to vomit or stumble over the side, while the jagged crescendo of Parker's laughter scourged at his back. On succeeding occasions, the monk simply closed his eyes with a calm movement and powerfully contracted his being into a focused, excluding memory of some rhythmical stretch of Holy Writ, which he cadenced repetitively through his mind as if he were an idiot who could not see, hear, think or feel, remaining deathly motionless there like a stone figure, one of those stone figures passive upon the sarcophagi in the mediaeval crypts of monasteries, that had been uprighted against the glittering background of the sea.

It appeared as a great mercy of God to the monk when the schooner put into a bay for a store of fruit and water. Like a person in a delirium, he found his way to the church in the village there and lunged into its cavernous, aromatic shade, a man expending the last of his strength to climb up out of the ruthless sea onto the rock of his life for safety. How Parker spent the two days in the little port it did not even occur to the monk to conjecture.

His imagination, if he had tried to face it with the burden, would probably have refused it with desperate repugnance. He, himself, spent nearly every hour of his respite from ordeal in the church, renewing his untrammelled communion with God and the Blessed Saints, refreshing his spirit, sweetening his blood; and he had regained so much of his strength by the time he took an outrigger back over the bay to the little schooner that he smiled broadly, almost burst into laughter, when he thought of that ridiculous man parading up and down like that.

At first it seemed as if the pause in the Samar village, the last safe outpost on the edge of the wild Moro waters, had wrought a change for the better in the relationship between the monk and the trader. Over the evening meal, around which they and the Spaniard sat cross-legged on the deck aft, they fell into conversation about a chanting chorus of song that came down-wind to them from a passing *vinta*. Parker explained that the natives on the *vinta* were singing their plea for a change of wind, that "they did singing for all kinds of stuff out here." The monk took this up by replying that they used to sing that way in Europe too, that remnants of the songs still existed and that farmers still sang some of them at festival times. Parker informed the monk that he had heard "a pile of songs of all kinds," but that the greatest song in the world was one he heard in Singapore that "took four people to sing it, a tune called *Rigolette*." That was the pronunciation he gave it. The monk agreed that it was a fine song and quietly, in a sonorous tenor voice that was almost a baritone, began to sing:

"Bel-la figlia del-la mo-re . . ."

When he stopped after a few phrases, Parker burst into an excited shout of a quality that astonished the monk no less than did the nostalgic fervour with which the trader then proceeded to expatiate on the song and the difficulties with which his life had enshrined it. Deeply impressed, after a fashion that he could not even have tried to put into words, the monk fell silent before the passion and mystery of the riddle that he had found amongst these weird islands of the sea. Parker, however, as soon as he had gotten back within himself, seemed to have been inspired to unlimited conversation. He used the slightest comment or question by the monk as a fresh starting point. Perhaps, intoxicated by the mem-

322

ory of the song; or relaxed unwittingly into discovering an irresistible audience whose cogent receptivity drew him out; or convinced that he was in the presence of an unequivocal respect for what he, Parker, knew, a respect untainted by any hint of listening just for the sake of placating him personally; or perhaps because he too had sweetened his strength in his own fashion ashore there and was enjoying its savour under the beguiling sedative of the vast, wine-coloured evening, he talked for hours on end about the things that seemed to beget the most response in his listener: about the tribes of the islands and what he called their "tunes," about the Moros in the region bordering the Gulf of Davao, about their government and the prejudices that inflamed them. He even adjured the monk, forgetting the status of the man before him in his absorption, "not even to blink an eye at their women. Just pretend you don't see 'em." He cocked his head on one side, as he said this, narrowed his eyes portentously and waggled the cigarette on his lower lip for a silent moment as if he were feeling that in that he had enunciated the whole secret; but he went on to say that "you daren't cheat these people like you can them northern tribes." It was, however, from his discourse on their music and their poetry, "which they just about sang as if it were songs," that the monk abstracted the best of the information of which he was so avid; for that extraordinary Parker apparently had interpreted through their music lore and habits, with an inspired, detailed accuracy that was suspect in his other observations of them, much of what was so formidably baffling in the peoples of Mindanao, Jolo and the other Moro islands. It occurred unreasonably to the monk, as he listened, that surely it was somewhere within the broad mystery of music that the man had found the device, the weapon, the chart that enabled him to sail onto and away from the deadliness of those coasts unharmed and enriched.

In the unruliness of the next day's noontime sunshine, however, all this improvement of relationship seemed to have evaporated. Parker reopened the conversation pleasantly enough, but it was only craftily to trap the monk into the most infuriating kind of religious collision. Sounding off unclearly through a mouthful of *papaya*, whose golden juice overflowed his mouth and dripped down his chest and shirt-front, Parker remarked:

"There's one thing that I wish somebody would explain to me about religion . . . and that is, why if we're created in God's image do we have to go to hell for being like him? They're always singin' and recitin' about God bein' jealous, and how his vengeance keeps up to the third and fourth generation; yet you go straight to hell if you're jealous or take out a little vengeance."

The power and the will to answer this swept urgently up through the surprised young cleric to his mind; but this rush was held up, frustrated there, for several seconds as if it could not find quite the proper intellectual outlet. The delay was seized upon by Parker to flare forth with his abominable grin and compound the difficult moment with still another question, launched precisely as the monk had found his first word of reply.

"And another thing . . . what's the idea of God smackin' a man down for gettin' hold of another man's woman, when He, His ownself, sneaked up on a poor, helpless carpenter's wife and knocked her up?"

For an appreciable instant the monk's large face, the ligaments of which seemed to have been shocked out of all co-ordination, remained an area on which could be read only that he was startled and uncomprehending; then, his features gathering themselves as if about to burst with horror and fury, his eyes staring from his face, the monk began to yell some kind of answer; but the moment he managed to get out the first word, Parker started laughing with a screeching boisterousness that filled the world and obliterated all other sound. He became an arrogant embodiment of that attitude that attacks with stinging controversy but stops up its ears to an answer. Reduced virtually to nothing but a victim of this attitude, the monk was beating his head and heart frantically against it, shouting helplessly into the omnivorous din kept up by Parker, which the man managed to increase, as if he were the devil himself, with each new attempt made by the monk to formulate speech.

All at once, stripped down to the primitive elements of simply an enraged man, the monk leapt straight at the core of that maddening furor, shooting out his hands to crush and smash at the insolent, distorted face. His foot caught in a cleat on the deck, and he fell to his hands and knees. He did not get up any further than his knees. The symptoms of a profound despair seemed to catch at every muscle in his body. Every now and then, like a sob, the black rage would resurge through him. In these diminishing spasms, he crouched tensely there, very little more than a powerful, young Irishman glaring hungrily through a red mist at his own great arms and clenched fists.

This incident restored the relationship between the monk and Parker to about what it had been at the beginning of the voyage, except that now there was in the trader's grin a quality of ominous, though contemptuous, alertness. The Spaniard, also, now had come to the point of not completely ignoring the situation, having assumed a hard, watchful attitude that relaxed only when the schooner finally reached the Gulf of Davao and the monk, going as the Spaniard was sure to certain death, stepped off the gunwale into a Moro canoe and was paddled ashore. It had not seemed possible that the precarious balance of the relationship could hold until they reached the Gulf; but it had held even through the negotiations for the monk's going ashore.

Parker had anchored, in the late afternoon, about a mile off a thick, low, neat village, stilted and the colour of pale amber, that was only partly visible from the bay. The place, strangely still and silent, appeared to rise out of the beach that fronted it and fade back into the labyrinth of the jungle behind, a massive verdure enclosing the sharp clear world of the bay in an eternity of gigantic leaves, stalks and fronds like patterns of heavy, green crystal. Shortly after the anchor was down, Parker had climbed upon the cuddy and for some minutes waved a sort of signal to the village with a piece of red cloth. Thereafter the canoe had put off from the shore and come alongside. As he had observed the five slim, graceful people in it, the absurd idea had glinted through the monk's mind that it was going to be hard to tell the men from the women if these were men all so spectacularly dressed in bright-coloured silks and precise, tight arrangements of glossy black hair. In Moro dialect, Parker had held a conversation with the people in the canoe, leaning energetically over the schooner's gunwale and grinning easily but respectfully as he talked. Now and then he casually had put out a hand to steady their craft as it rose and swayed before the groundswell, even once pushing out of the way, to do so, one of their long, broad, unsheathed swords that gleamed in the canoe like serpents that had been metallized, flattened and polished at the very moment their bodies had assumed a series of writhing curves. The parley concluded, the canoe had started to paddle away; but the monk had succeeded in halting this, explaining to Parker that he wanted to go ashore with the Moros. Although the Moros had understood nothing but his gestured command to stop and the quality of the effect produced by his words on the crew of the schooner, the monk's effort had precipitated a moment of expressionless silence, perhaps of masked but unanimous uncertainty, amongst the nine diverse people clustered there watchfully, like inexplicable symbols, on the slick, heaving breast of that faraway bay. The land breeze wafted over them a heavy breath of aromatic woods as if the jungle, fired by the red unconsuming blaze of the sunset, were giving off a mystical smoke. Then the full flood of Parker's grin had risen to his face again, with an impression of violent disinterestedness, and he had spoken a short sentence in their language to the people in the canoe. An onlooker innocent of any previous contact with those esoteric islanders could have made nothing of their silent, motionless reaction to this. Nevertheless, Parker had swung his grin at the monk and interpreted:

"Sure."

Sliding and swaying awkwardly in his dark gown, the young monk managed to get down into the canoe. He crouched there, holding onto the gunwales with both hands, just in front of the Moro in the stern and between two of the barbaric swords. He looked up at Parker, as one of the paddlers shoved the canoe clear of the schooner's side, and called back to him, smiling in a gesture of reconciliation, from out of a deep struggle for understanding:

"When must I get back?"

"Any time," the trader answered. "I sail day after tomorrow morning."

He had called out this answer in a sharp, casual tone that was genially patronizing and slightly scoffing; and he had stood grinning and blowing cigarette smoke from his nostrils, watching through narrowed eyes, until the canoe reached the land, until the sombre figure of the monk was seen to arise from it and walk up the sand into the thick cluster, brilliant with varied colours, that suddenly had appeared there, as by an eruption, in a malevolent glinting of edged steel and bizarre coiffures of jet black hair.

That night, in the midst of the Spaniard's singing, Parker, who always slept aboard in these waters, was struck literally onto his back by a swift assault of physical pain. It stunned him, devastated him, made him claw the deck and sob with fear and agony. An old, chronic case of gonorrhoea, neglected and complicated, finally had made fatal headway against his insides. In a perspiring interval between the searing, slugging rushes of the pain, Parker ordered the Spaniard to up anchor and make sail.

"Right now!" he sobbed several times, "Right now!"

Stricken quite helpless, his reason consumed by his panic, that man was obeying a frantic instinct to get home, and the only line he could travel along, the only one that would take him to a place consonant with the resistless drive of this instinct, was one that led to Manila, the place of his habits, the place where he lusted and fought and signed his name, the place where he was known and hated by men like himself.

The Spaniard, driving the native to the anchor, did not even attempt to remind his Captain of the trading to be done on the beach in the morning, or of their passenger so dangerously ashore there. It was clear that these things now did not matter. Parker wanted to feel the physical motion of his obedience to that desperate urge to get "home." He wanted to reach a doctor, he told himself, unreasonably ignoring the great time of winding sea between him and his goal.

"Christ! . . . Get under way! . . . Get under way!"

Twisting about in pain on the deck near the wheel, he kept screaming things like that every two or three minutes even after the Spaniard, steering incontinently by the stars, had gotten the schooner well under way toward the open sea.

When, days later, Parker stepped unsteadily ashore at Manila, emaciated and tottering with weakness, there was no thought in his mind but the fatuous conclusion that the respite from the pain, a respite that had lasted consistently two full days now, was to be permanent. It had done its best to kill him, he told himself, but he had beaten it and it was gone. Attached to this conclusion was the monopolizing determination to get his strength back as soon as possible. There was no thought of thanks in him for the plucky little schooner, which he always had despised, and the Spaniard who had combined to manage such a remarkable quick passage for him; nor any thought of the being he had abandoned in the remote and dangerous wilderness. For this reason, when people persistently demanded to know what had become of the monk, he was at first actually surprised; then he grew resentful of the bother this growing pressure caused him, this unsympathetic attitude in the time of his weakness and great ordeal. It was as if he had expected everybody, instead, to congratulate him on his own victory over painful death. "Christ!" he exclaimed to himself, "Why pick on *me?* Especially now that I'm down? . . . And over that priest . . . Hadn't the damn fool forced it on himself?" Powerfully colouring the conflicting attitudes, no doubt, of Parker and the town towards the fact of the monk's having been left to shift for himself out there on the coast of Mindanao was the radical difference between the two viewpoints in regarding the region: Parker did not view it with the eyes of almost absolute fear through which the other saw it.

The nastiest kind of rumours began to beat about him, the most respectable of which was that "that black-hearted bastard" had deserted the monk, in the most cowardly and swinish way, when the cleric was helping him fend off some attack in the southern islands. Men were encouraged by his weakness to demand openly that an official investigation be made, even that Parker be arrested. Two or three denounced him in an unheard of fashion to his face. The last time this happened, in a crowded bar-room, the reviler ended up by shoving him roughly aside and walking scornfully away. Parker had tried to summon from within himself the old fury of retaliation; but that long pain seemed to have emptied his body of violence. He had to content himself, swaying sickly in the wake of the man's aggression, with a loud, sneering, boastful account, while he grinned in the most revolting manner, of how he had deliberately abandoned the monk in the Gulf of Davao for a joke. As a peroration he screamed with laughter, glancing from face to face and nodding exhibitionistically as if at the fun he had deigned to evoke. A number of the people there now seemed willing to strike him; but before anyone could manage it, his sickness suddenly crumpled him onto the floor. He lay there for minutes, blighted once again by that horrible agony, unable to rise or to find his voice, his eyelids tightly clenched in a face that had turned pale azure. The afternoon sun, slanting powerfully through the interstices of the lowered bamboo door-screen, striped his body with thin vivid bands of alternate light and shade so that he looked something like an aborted zebra kicking and writhing its life away there on the dirty russet tile. A few men stood around him and stared down disgustedly until the suppressed screaming that ground from between his gritting teeth proved too much for them. Then they picked him up and carried him to one of the whores' rooms on the second floor.

The doctor's pronouncement that Parker was dying, that he would be dead any moment now, spread through the town as if it had been a just legal sentence meted out to one guilty of a revolting crime. People mentioned it in grim celebration. Parker, however, with his unfailing, obdurate perverseness, took nearly three months to die; and this delay persisted, in the most extraordinary fashion, as a public scandal before which the town remained unsettled and rebellious. He might have been a criminal staying, with all sorts of dubious writs and injunctions, the moment, awaited in righteous indignation by the world, of his execution. People asked each other relentlessly when they met at the end of the day:

"Well, is he dead yet?"

The answer to this, one evening, was the unexpected and confounding news that the monk had returned to Manila, as from the realm of the dead.

Strangely enough, this information was resented, was received with a discomfited impatience that was extended to include even the person of the monk. Not that the cleric's death was a desired end in itself; but the people had come to justify the pleasure they took in Parker's imminent death as pardonable, approval of punishment justly awarded for the most repulsive kind of murder. Confused, irritated by a rise of frustration, they were now forced to face in their feelings a still unmitigated passion for that evil man's obliteration, to face it stubbornly without having anything definite and obviously commensurate to hang it on. The first white man the monk met, four or five minutes after disembarking from the Chinese junk that had brought him north from Cebu, had told him of Parker's plight in a muddled tone that was inappropriately sullen, apologetic and aggrieved. This Spaniard, a greying Captain of artillery, had first fallen back aghast before the ragged, sunburnt apparition in the remnants of a holy gown, exclaiming in the most startled way imaginable:

"Good God, *Padre,* we thought that mad dog had murdered you!"

By a stroke of good fortune, the day on which the monk first stepped foot on that beach of the Gulf of Davao, to which the Moro canoe had brought him from Parker's schooner, was part of one of those brief, serene periods into which all communities now and then relax. Apparently, for the exotic puritans on that strand that day, their world was a pleasant and benign place which they appeared to inhabit without shame or doubt. They had been in no need of a scapegoat to drive out into the wilderness of death burdened with the projected load of the communities' pollutions. The monk had been suffered to mount among them, a guest from their friend's ship; and their sufferance had gradually become flattered amusement and welcome when they succumbed to the impression that this ridiculous, friendly youth had visited them only to improve himself, not with their favour, but with their culture. In a dim way they had suspected his religious status and that he had nothing to do with their friend's business venture; but he had obtruded upon them no offence of advice or criticism, no religious or political word. If he had tried that, it without doubt would have destroyed instantly the vulnerable stability of his acceptance.

He had been invited by a person of authority, a person who seemed to have supervision over the village's periodical dealings with Parker, to spend the night there, and, reckless of whether or not the invitation had been a mere matter of form, had grasped his opportunity, had accepted. Early the next morning when he had looked out over the polished, mist-clouded bay and found the schooner gone, he had suffered a fearful, swindled surge of feeling, a premonition of the truth. He had been helplessly marooned in that bedevilled chaos, thrown on the dangerous tolerance of those unintelligible beings who had accepted him on the say-so of

330

that man who was now gone, that man who had outdone himself in one last gesture of hatefulness toward him. So vast was his sense of being lost himself that it never even entered his head to mourn the small bundle of his personal belongings carried away in the schooner; but he was careful not to betray his consternation to the Moros, who thought it strange that so careful a man as their friend in trade should have gone off so unceremoniously in the face of the scheduled exchange of goods. With all his strangeness and rarity, their favoured infidel never had done anything like this before. They were disappointed (being always eager for the things he brought them), and they sensed something inexplicable in his sudden move. Moreover, they were keenly conscious of the responsibility he had left with them in the person of the gentle monstrosity who plodded about in the sun beneath a dark, heavy robe learning their language. However, their friend had disappeared. That was the fact. They would accept it in the sight of Allah until the days, the months of his return.

The monk had waited hopelessly for this event himself, waited until his sense of the unfitness of forcing himself on that village any longer, combined with a fear that his prestige there was waning as the Moros began to sense the truth of his situation, had become intolerable; and he had felt himself desperately unable to resist the precipitation of some issue. He had announced one morning that he was going to set out across the island on foot for the northern coast. His plan was to find some kind of craft there to take him over the smaller seas to Leyte, an island that was populated by northern tribes and Chinamen, and with which the Spaniards in Manila kept up an intermittent contact. The Moros had been astounded at his proposal of such a formidable and dangerous journey. If he had announced that he was going to kill himself on the beach they might have found it rather less startling. No expression of this, however, got as far as the tactful imperturbability of their faces or tongues. A council was held, an imposing, formalistic affair under torchlight at which decisions seemed to be arrived at mostly by silences. As it had decided his fate, the monk almost fatuously had tried to throw into it the colour, the understanding that such a journey or something similar had been Parker's and his intention all along; and he had tried to adjust his conscience to this effort by telling himself that that in the long run, in the very long run though it might be, really was his intention.

In the end they had permitted him to go; not alone, as he had proposed, to lose himself in the first jungle-filled gorge of the unknown interior, or to die under the barongs and krises of the first men he met, or to fill the mouths of wild beasts and snakes, but guided by two heavily armed youths. These led him back over mountains to a village at the head of a river that wound down a hundred and fifty miles, through a fabulous valley no European ever had seen before, to the Suriago Sea. In this village the two young Moros first explained about Parker, the friend and provider of the many powerful peoples of the Gulf, Parker, the legendary exception to the inexorable law of that inscrutable world. Next they made clear that the being with them was "of Parker" and that it evidently was the intention of Fate that he be aided and comforted on his way. Exactly what his "way" was no man knew; but it was judged to be friendly as it came from a friend, and was harmless and natural in a way that only Allah himself understood. His guides then had turned him over to the new village and had left him. These people, in turn, had placed him in a canoe and taken him to a village still farther down the river where the process was repeated, until, after many days, his progress in this manner becoming first a precedent and finally a tradition that was to persist unbroken even through his subsequent years of travel in these parts, he arrived, travel-worn but safe, on the coast of Leyte. It was not until years later, long after people had come to regard his perennial security amongst the fanatics of the Moro islands in the same baffling light now illuminating that of Parker, a security that was to be as especially incomprehensible in view of the cleric's uniformed Christianity as it had been in view of the trader's blatant depravity, that the monk suffered a clear vision of the truth: He had wandered there the rest of his life in that land, that land so bloody, gaudy and strange, safe and respected beneath the magical protection of Parker's long-forgotten cloak.

When the artillery Captain, in the first minutes after the monk's landing, had informed him of the trader's plight, the monk signified his intention of going to see the dying man. The air of grimness and of unrelenting purpose in which he framed this expressed intention, together with the aggressive tension that, on the instant, seemed to imprison his body, was impressive enough to make the army officer wonder whether he should not make an effort to calm him. Not that he, himself, felt that anybody should go easy with that scoundrel; but, after all, the man was dying and there were certain proprieties, even for a man who had been handled as nastily as the *Padre*. The monk did not linger with him long enough for the Captain to decide on a method of launching his feeling completely, but he did manage to say meaningfully in parting:

"He's dying, you know. He may be dead right now."

It did not take the monk very long to report his return to his superiors, clean himself up and procure a change of clothes; yet in that brief two hours or so the officer had succeeded in loosing a variety of cross-currents through the town that agitated it as the conflicting streams of an incoming tide rip up the waters of a shallow. There were witnesses in the street in front of the building when the monk went in at the low door, and a veritable pack of them in the bar-room to observe, as he passed through the lane they formed for him on his way to the stairs, the iron purposefulness of the dark figure from which swung a crucifix. The witnesses up in the shadowy room itself, lit with a single candle, were swept by a slow, frightful emotion that took their breaths away and weakened their insides when the monk, standing tall, silent and motionless in the doorway, confronted his murderous betrayer. It was as if the whole formidable power of the very Church were impending, materialized and vengeful, in that doorway.

The dying man knew he was there the moment the monk appeared in the doorway. He opened his great liquid eyes, which lived on stubbornly in the wild, feverish disorder of his emaciated face, and aimed them steadily at the spectre looming out of the obscurity that enclosed his ambush, an obscurity, for him, like that surrounding a man being murdered in the night, in the seconds after he had been awakened by a rustling sound in the darkness from which the knife is about to descend. Other than opening his eyes, Parker made no motion, nor did he make a sound until the monk appeared about to speak; then, his voice, gasping and twisting quietly, ill-humouredly, he said:

"You brought it on yourself . . . you . . . you forced yourself on me . . . God damn you . . . get the hell away from here . . ."

His voice failed him. The pain seemed to awake here and there down the length of his body, which writhed feebly as if he were trying to combat the agony with motion in those spots, or as if he were struggling to turn over. In the midst of this he managed another sick burst of interruption:

". . . damn . . . just get yourself to hell out of here . . .bastardly ghost in a black night shirt . . ."

He halted again, struggling with a kind of croaking disintegration that crept into his voice. A spasm of rage or pain troubled the upper part of his body and culminated in his actually raising his head, that ghastly head on which only the hair was unchanged, alive, unruly, the colour of dirty straw. Then suddenly the monk knew that there in the shadow Parker's face was contorting into the corpse equivalent of that insolent grin. The implacable figure in the doorway stiffened and vibrated as if it suddenly had been charged with an intolerable current. From the high face, indistinguishable in the flickering gloom against which it now closed its eyes, there issued silently, starkly:

"O, merciful God, remember that this is Thy child dying in the darkness, Thine own immortal soul caught beneath the evil surface wrought upon it by the world."

"Don't . . ." gasped Parker faintly but raucously, "don't come praying over *me* . . . Don't start to telling me I'm that God damn sheep that strayed . . . I won't stand for it . . ." He made a blurred, quick sound in his throat, trying to shout.

The monk's hand came up to tremble uncertainly against his breast in a gesture that would have been one of helpless distress if the hand had not been tightly clenched into a fist.

"Sure," ejected the dying man so weakly that he just could be heard, "I know . . ." the sick sound coming from him slid into what unmistakably was intended as mimicry of the monk, "you just came to help me . . . just came to do something to make my last moments easier." The thin, caricatured whine faded into the malodorous shadow of the crowded room, in which could be heard, for a long interval, only the eloquent breathing of the revolted and bewildered witnesses. In this interval Parker held his head stiffly, grotesquely up from the bed as if he were waiting, as if he were searching along the slashes and flickers of candlelight, for an access of strength. When he found it, he spat it forth in words that barely could be heard but that were intended as a yell, a yell of filth and derision and malice.

"Sure! . . . You can get me a juicy naked woman . . . and put her here alongside me . . . You can get me *ten* naked women and stand 'em around my bed . . . You can get me them four singers to sing me that tune while I . . ."

Abruptly something had happened to the atmosphere of the room. The thing Parker's spirit had been doing to it seemed to have collapsed and dropped away. The monk stepped to the side of the bed to determine if the man had died. Standing close there, he could see quite clearly now even the startled, blank expression on Parker's face and the look in his eyes, the look of a man who, on the instant, has been hurled from some casual but violent course of thought and feeling into the depths of a poignant memory. The thought of that song, the power of its remembrance, had caught him, at the unprecedented moment of his death, in his own snare. He had lost awareness of his jest, of his surroundings. He was gazing back into the memory of the song, in anguish, as one does at pleasant times that are forever past, at the face of a lost beloved or at the vista of a landscape glowing with the far days of youth. A short sound, helpless and appealing, escaped from the face still held rigidly up from the surface of the bed. The monk's hands came together in an involuntary, clutching gesture. That sound, the expression on that face, he knew, had not been meant for him, but they filled his being with a burst of driving understanding. His body seemed to lean, to sway slightly over the bed in a movement of response at once unsure and emphatic, a moment of gesture that seemed to grow and expand until it culminated in a rocket of words flashing briefly, strongly through the murk in certitude and promise.

"Hold on, my brother! . . . For just a little longer . . . Hold on!"

Then he swung about and strode from the room in the manner of one in the midst of fatal emergency.

The leader of the army band, Parker's enemy, was waiting to sit down to supper when the monk arrived at his house. Informed that "the monk that devil, Parker, murdered" was waiting in the *patio* to speak to him, he hurried out surprised and quite unready for the crisis awaiting him. The others in the house heard a minute or so of ardent, smothered controversy out there in the shadow near the street door. The musician's wife was certain that in the end she had heard the sounds of a brief scuffle.

Indignantly reluctant, a flushed figure of protest, his mustachios goring like petty tusks at imaginary obstacles in the first dark of the night, the bandmaster led his captor to the abode of a man who turned out to be the Colonel's cook and orderly. This man had a voice, an unhealthy voice, like a woman's, and he was proud of his notorious ability to sing even the difficult soprano parts of several operas; but he did not grasp readily at what tempted him as an unparalleled opportunity to indulge his talent. He was rendered timorous by the paradox in the tone of obvious disinclination with which the bandmaster truculently made their wants known and urged them upon him. Staring uncertainly from his military superior to the holy man, he evaded the dangers of his own open consent by chattering through a kind of prim desperation of a woman, "the officers' woman," who sang contralto. He was talking about a whore, a thin woman with bleached hair and a repellently painted face, who, broken and lost in this stagnant backwater of the China Seas, was expending the last spurt of her body's life in catering to an Officer Corps that affected to find in blonde Englishwomen something peculiarly choice.

This woman was getting herself together for her night's effort when they arrived at the hotel. The orderly went in to interview her while the monk and the bandmaster waited outside in the sprawling garden of the one-story place. It took him quite some time. He apparently was having difficulty. Finally the two of them appeared in a streak of lamplight on the verandah, the soldier pointing confirmingly in the direction of the monk and the bandmaster. The woman seemed very doubtful of the thing really wanted of her, repeating phrases of what the soldier was saying as if he had been talking in but semi-intelligible fragments . . . "the Quartette from *Rigoletto*" ". . . powerful men" . . . "dying." There ensued a waiting, deciding stretch of silence, a silence that actually was a fusion of established sounds: the nocturnal drone of insects in the garden, a faint current of noise from the hotel's interior, the heightened rhythm of four troubled people breathing the humid evening air. As if he could not bear this indecisive waiting any longer, the monk stepped out of the shadow and up to the railing near her.

"You will have to hurry, my child. I will see that you are paid for your trouble," he said.

"It's not that . . ." faltered the woman, ". . . I . . . I . . ." Her hand sought her mouth in a puerile gesture. A breath of freshly drunk rum drifted out from her and blended with the fragrance of blossoms on a shrub in the dusk close by.

The bandmaster seemed to relent and improve the quality of his co-operation with the affair as it came to include the presence of this woman usually so restricted to relationships with officers and men of rank. He assumed a gallant stance of body and touched one of his mustachios. A smile of amused forbearance on his face, as if he, too, were quite superior to all such child's play, he also stepped forward so that she could see him clearly. He bowed, striving for an air of condescension.

"This, madam, is the *Padre* who was abandoned to the Moros by that scoundrel. And I," he bowed again, "am Ramirez, the leader of the band."

When the procession filled into the bar-room, the bandmaster leading and the monk bringing up the rear, the faces of the men gathered along the bar betrayed graphically that they were not, as they had felt after the event of an hour ago, now prepared for anything. Their expressions were those of a mob of victims responding individually to the effect of a stupefying drug. They stood transfixed by shock and bewilderment. As the procession ascended the stairs there was no sound, save that of the eight marching feet and the single loud tap of a glass being set down sharply on the bar. The bandmaster was smiling distantly; the woman stared upward apprehensively in the direction of her climb; the soldier, a red pompon on his shako bobbing nervously, was biting his nails beneath lowered eyes; while the monk plodded determinedly like a man in a hurry but who is being delayed, his

337

breath coming a bit hard, his blue gaze driving on those ahead of him as if they were the mere slaves of his purpose and his vision. Not a man in the bar-room made as much as a suggestion to follow them up the stairs. All they could tell later was what they had heard "after that whore and the pervert went up." Through what they did hear, they remained tensely at the edge of quiet panic, darting questioning glances at each other's faces, gripped by a sense of the monstrous and the uncanny. If one of them had but given the signal they would have flung themselves in a mass out into the street.

Parker lay stiffly alone in the stench of the nearly dark room. The single candle guttered on the night-table near his head, its rays flickering noxiously amongst the smudgy patches of beard on his slick, drawn face. He did not open his eyes now as the four people lined up at the foot of his bed.

"Parker!" called out the monk compellingly, "Parker!" His voice gave the impression that he was trying to shout through a medium that absorbed sound.

The big round eyes, unchanged and alert, then opened for a long stare on which they slowly reclosed as they shifted from figure to figure in the line that bulked down there amidst the unsteady shadow.

"Listen, my brother, listen now," said the monk in a powerfully matter-of-fact tone.

The monk turned his head to look at the bandmaster, to look at him hard as a gambler flings himself through his gaze upon the blind chance of a turning card. That pudgy man put out his arm. A tremor went through the perspiring line; then it seemed to gather itself. When the arm fell, there issued from the uplifted throat of the holy man, in sublime plea, those melodious words of love.

The sharp chin of the dying man stirred faintly upward as if drawn by this first gust of the rising song, as if he were feeling it but as a keener precipitation, a mirage of his memory; or as if, perhaps, he were nostalgically striving to get without himself and into the safety, the luxury of its current, a current that all at once, with the voices of the whore, the soldier and Parker's enemy, rose into a great tide of splendorous sweetness that possessed the filthy place of death. It caught the demoniac face in its surge, relaxed it, transfigured it with rapture; and that spirit so frightfully at grips with the universe, that spirit so naked, defiant, lustful and undismayed, seemed to sink, to dissolve, to be swept out amidst the stars of the heavy night, beguiled into final, submissive ecstasy, within the great quartered cry of yearning and renunciation, of passion and despair.

20 〰️

"Bel-la figlia del-la mo-re . . ." At the last word of his story, Ensign Woodbridge's voice expanded richly into the first measures of the Duke's song. For more than half a minute it filled the small, neat wardroom, beat glamorously against the pale green walls, swirled gracefully with the tobacco smoke out the port-holes and up past the open lace-curtained leaves of the little hatch cover.

Away forward on the narrow iron deck a member of Ensign Snell's reconnaissance party, recounting his adventures to a cluster of glowing cigarettes, paused as the fragment of song rose and slowly diminished in the jasmine-scented darkness. The man grinned to himself, savouring the officer's personality rather than his song, and resumed his tale by exclaiming, the recognized voice drawing irresistibly from him an admiring aside:

"Listen to that son of a bitch singing back there!"

The brief stretch of song served to release gradually, with a desirable grace and decorousness, saving them a too vivid return, a too brutal deflation, the four friends sitting around the after-dinner litter of the wardroom table. Still, Lieutenant Fitzpatrick, as the song died, did permit his body to collapse incontinently against the back of his chair, while his breath escaped from his chest in a long exhalation that bordered on a whistle. The Captain, almost clinging to the white-clothed edge of the table, was leaning forward so that his sunburned chin hung just above the group of

339

the white coffee cup, the golden coils of fruit peel and a half-smoked cigar that he had crunched out violently in the saucer. The wrinkles of his face were held in a slight pattern of strain, and his blue eyes were open wide, fixed steadily in the direction of Ensign Woodbridge, fixed as if into the direction of a great manifestation of power that was threatening to drag the anchors of his self-possession. In his roomy, starched white uniform aglitter with gold, he hung there with an appearance of stiffness, struggling statically, helplessly in an effort to preserve, an effort that was mysterious rather than unconscious, the form of his being against a too-cogent, a too-affecting seduction of that art that was, for him, the finest, the most near to what men apprehend as the miraculous. It was, too, as if his experience were coming to an end in the area of its one beautiful release, as if this phase of his life prematurely were being destroyed by perfection, as if never again would he be able to look forward in it.

Ensign Snell, stirred by the bare, objective facts of the story, sat staring belligerently from a heavy face at the silver bowl of fruit in the centre of the table. His large hands were clenched into fists that rested about a half yard apart on the stretch of white table-cloth in front of him. He was breathing like a man on the verge of violent action.

"Anyway," said Lieutenant Fitzpatrick with a wry, exhausted gesture of speech, "when they kick you out of the Navy you can be a writer."

"Listen," said Ensign Snell, "is that story straight? Is that the truth?"

"Why, certainly," answered Ensign Woodbridge, grinning a trifle sardonically.

"You know what I mean," sullenly pressed Ensign Snell. "I mean . . . allowing for all that story-telling stuff you stuck in to get a rise, did it really happen . . . like a thing you'd read about in the newspapers?"

"Absolutely," affirmed Ensign Woodbridge.

Ensign Snell made a sudden, threatening movement with his fists that knocked over the silver sugar bowl. In slow confusion he righted the bowl, then took a cigarette from a pack on the table and lighted it behind cupped hands as if he were sheltering the match from a wind.

"It's no use," jeered Ensign Woodbridge, grinning at the big hands still cupped in front of his friend's face, "the man died before you were born."

A wave of pink rose up Ensign Snell's face and neck to disappear in his hair.

"Too bad he did," said the Captain, looking sympathetically, protectingly at Ensign Snell in a quick accession of feeling for him, "I'd like to take a swing at him myself."

"The poor old *Padre,*" mused Lieutenant Fitzpatrick. "What he's been through!"

Two evenings later Ensign Snell rose to his own defence. It was after a dinner throughout which he cumbrously had kept silent under a faintly brooding quality, as if he still were remembering his display of helpless confusion after knocking over the sugar bowl. Ensign Woodbridge was about to leave the table when Ensign Snell, turning in his chair to face his agile antagonist squarely and a little grimly, challenged him like a man who has been waiting until he was ready but who has been forced to move slightly before.

"Look here," he said indignantly, the words pouring from him in slow but cogent waves, while his heavy blue eyes glinted good-humouredly despite the fact that they were fixed on his friend accusingly, "the other night . . . that wild tale about the monk . . . whichever it was, a true report or just a story . . . it was wrong . . . gave a wrong impression . . . Made you think it happened right now, right amongst us, when as a matter of fact the whole damn thing took place before anybody but the Captain, here, was born." His tone became aggressive with self-justification. "If the thing had been told right, we'd a got that impression right from the start and all the way through."

Lieutenant Fitzpatrick began to laugh quietly, delightedly, in the second of silence that followed the vigour and sureness of this delayed explosion. The Captain raised his eyebrows in surprise and stared at his youngest officer with a look that comically expressed a combination of solicitude, deprecation and suppressed admiration for foolhardiness. This forthright statement had caught Ensign Woodbridge unprepared. He already had forgotten, until this reminded him of it, that he had told the story; but it took only the second of silence, as he stood there with one hand resting on the back of his chair as if lightly bracing himself against the attack of the big man's gaze, for him to find words of reply.

"Ah, my boy," he said in a tone deliberately coloured with condescension as a tactical measure, and despite the fact that his own maturity measured but a year and a half more than Ensign Snell's, "you will find that the highest accomplishment of art is that which enables it to demonstrate what all educated men know . . . that all epochs in history, all civilizations even, have been essentially the same. Time, in the sense you mean, is a delusion. Man, in all recorded periods of time and in whatever particular framework he may have chosen to set himself, has remained essentially the same. Time . . ."

"Come on, Woodbridge!" interrupted Lieutenant Fitzpatrick. "Quit stalling. Meet the man fairly or pipe down."

"What I just said is positively true," maintained Ensign Woodbridge.

"Sure it is," said Lieutenant Fitzpatrick, "but on a different level of analysis. Don't try your old trick of mixing up levels of analysis on us . . . we *know* you."

They all were standing now, facing each other around the table. The Executive Officer's voice, thrusting calmly forth to join the battle, its accents a trifle cooled by friendly inexorability, warned Ensign Woodbridge that he had allowed himself to be caught on false ground, that no matter how many authentic points he might now bring up to refute the original attack, this second and more alert antagonist, hungry for a rare, clear victory over him, would not let him out of the new ambush.

"Just how does my answer mix up the issue?" he demanded, smiling broadly at Ensign Snell.

"*I'll* tell you," said Lieutenant Fitzpatrick, smiling just as broadly.

"Never mind," said Ensign Woodbridge, attempting a victorious retreat. He reached into his pocket for his pipe with a gesture intended to give the impression that obviously this discussion had worked itself into boredom. "In a couple of weeks he'll turn up with the answer himself."

"And it'll be a good one too," said the Captain.

21 〰️

It is possible that the warmth of confidence the Captain was able to put into this promise for his officer was not derived solely from his loyal appreciation of that man's deliberate ability. It may have been partly a reflection of the quietly but triumphantly blazing fact that the Captain was in the very midst of fulfilling the formidable promise he had made to himself: He had got his ship back together again, and got her back in that improved condition that had so powerfully and suddenly occurred to him as being necessary in the prophetic moment down south there. His crew, too, he had got back; not "every last one of them," as he had promised; but his was a nature susceptible to the large substance in an approximation of perfection rather than to the incompleteness of its form, and he was calmly exultant.

Besides Warrington and O'Connel to be returned from the submarines, the two Carey brothers from the hospital, Ensign Snell's reconnaissance party from the jungle and Ensign Woodbridge from China, there had been some scattered twenty-three men to be "got back"; and all but five of these twenty-three, together with the Carey brothers and the new man, had been sent to rejoin Delilah on the two destroyers the Captain had observed being brought in by the tug just after the shark had attacked Wright.

The officers and Yeomen of the Personnel Office in Cavite, irritated by the stubborn tactics with which Delilah's Commanding Officer had disturbed their usual procedure, were feeling an individual, personal justification in not being able to send back those five missing men. For the permanent loss to Delilah of Wright and Mendel they could not take credit; but they could take a sort of vague satisfaction from it. As to the other three, two Firemen and a Water-tender, these were on the Galveston, then hurrying to face a possible emergency in Chinese waters, and definitely could not be considered available for transfer. The letter in which the Personnel Office informed the Captain about the men on the Galveston was impeccably impersonal and routine, but it nevertheless faintly breathed off an air of triumph. The irritation suffered by the Personnel Office, and its almost unconscious temptation to gain a point over Delilah's Captain, had not been permitted, however, to impede its persistent efforts to do for her crew what the rest of the Base was working day and night to do for her machinery and structures. The problem of the Personnel Office was the more desperate. Even if it had had one-third again as many men at its disposal to distribute, the ships and stations to which it was obligated still would have been undermanned. In the interests of this small ship and her four sister destroyers, so urgently and mysteriously bent on an increased readiness, it ruthlessly pared down the crews of all other units to the very danger point. It even speculated in future releases from the Naval Prison and hospitals, making promises on the strength of these to the helpless ships whose men it transferred to the destroyers. The acting head of the office, a tall, thin Lieutenant who resembled a traditional caricature of the early Puritan clergyman, was keenly chagrined at being able to compensate Delilah for the loss of her five men by but a single replacement. As he had signed the order transferring this man to Delilah he had felt a twinge of conscience for the element in the transfer that he could not help: the man was a Seaman, and what that ship needed were people for the Engineer's force. For another element in the transfer that he could not help either he had suffered no twinge: "Borden didn't want any new men to replace his old ones . . . Well," he had assured himself with guilty triumph, "he is going to get one and like it."

22

This new Seaman, a man named Rowe, had come out from San Francisco the week before on the collier Proteus as one of a pitifully meagre draft of reinforcements. He was tall, solidly built, about twenty-five, and his body gave a definite impression of being efficient without being athletic. The hair on his head, on the backs of his hands, on his chest was casually blond. His steady, pale blue eyes, without containing any slightest degree either of challenge or evasion, gazed easily out of his large, regular features to meet the gaze of anyone who spoke to him; and he had a quite unobtrusive habit, when he was uncertain or nervous, of gripping the thumb of his left hand in the fist of his right and gently twisting and retwisting the fist around it. He came from that part of Nebraska that had been transforming itself from cattle range to farmland just about the time of his birth, and such peculiarity as there was in his personality seemed to be a reflection of this conflict between cowboy and farmhand. The first two years of his enlistment had been spent on a cruiser, the Milwaukee, that rarely left the vicinity of San Francisco Bay; but it was clear that he was the kind of a man who was learning his work thoroughly, the kind that any ship would be pleased to receive. This pleasure could be seen as increasing to a positive eagerness in the case of any of the badly undermanned, semi-embattled craft in the Asiatic Squadron; and a hint of this had sustained him through the heavy days that had drifted past since he had been landed, beneath a blaze of exotic sunshine, on this incomprehensible shore so far in every way from what he ever had known before.

He spent a part of one of these days standing on a dock crowded with beings he did understand, a crowd of people with heads and faces like his own, who, dressed in their best clothes for the occasion that brought them there, breathed off a scent of perspiring, especial cleanliness that made him remember, with a pang, the Methodist Church far away in Alliance. He had been attracted to the dock by the sounds of a military band playing *Auld Lang Syne,* and he remained there with the crowd watching a white transport, laden with Army, Navy and Civil Service families that had served their time, turn her back on Manila and head for home. The band never ceased playing; there were flowers everywhere, small, strange, illusory flowers, most of them a passionate white, some a vivid crimson, clustering on the rail of the ship and in the arms of those on the dock; and there seemed not a face that was not smiling with an almost frantic gaiety. When the transport backed away from the dock, people shouted and waved hysterically. A woman held up her trembling child and sobbed: "See, darling! . . . It's going home . . . home!"

Many on the transport burst into tears, as though unable to withstand the wild surge of relief freed by the first throb of the ship, this ship that was to carry their yearning bodies back across the vast waters of exile to the familiar, glamorous reality their spirits never had left. Some on the dock, too, wept slowly, silently but openly; others fought back their tears with an agony of unconscious effort, not daring even thus to recognize the furor of suppressed longing that beat in their blood and glittered in the steady, smiling gazes they could not take from that departing ship. As the transport fled slowly down the slick, sepia reach of the oriental bay, its Homeward-bound Pennant streaming in a long, serpentine flick of red, white and blue from the mast-head, the band on the dock played *The Star-Spangled Banner*. Rowe, standing there stiffly at salute in the thick of that nostalgic crowd, was cut to the quick by some swift thrust of the anthem that never before had reached him save as a sustained blare of official sound; and there welled up in his calm, homesick heart a feeling of being left irretrievably behind.

Two days later, this feeling of being lost and forgotten at the end of the world was somehow alleviated when he received a copy of the orders assigning him to Delilah for duty. "She's a destroyer," volunteered the Yeoman good-naturedly, as he handed him the orders. Rowe, walking away with the paper, stared hard at the name of the ship written on it, straining, almost with eagerness, to make the name, as quickly as possible, a familiar part of his consciousness. "Delilah . . . Delilah," he repeated out loud in a commonplace voice, repeated it against a background of semi-emerged memories of destroyers he had seen skimming arrogantly across San Francisco Bay or, grey, slim and fabulous, lancing through the waves, themselves as grey and arrogant, that embattle the water off Lobos Point. "Delilah" . . . That was where he belonged, that was where he was going tomorrow, to Delilah. He sensed his destination as a veritable portion of known realness barricaded safely within steel walls against the surrounding alien void into which it had extended itself. It excited him to feel that his portion of "home," far as it had extended itself, could, if it wanted to, turn

346

like that transport and hurry back. He would be welcome there, he told himself without vanity; and he was eager to get to the ship and assume the responsibilities of that welcome.

The next day, however, when he reached Cavite and reported aboard one of Delilah's sister ships, which was to ferry him out to Olongapo, his eagerness, in the face of what it encountered, gave way to a fruitless, searching curiosity in regard to his own attitude and conduct. He passed much of the trip by himself up on the forecastle of the slowly towed vessel pondering what on earth he had said or done, or failed to say or do, in the moment of reporting, that had placed him somehow in the position of an intruder; and his general first impression, that "this Navy out here is different," received an added, dampening confirmation. He had said little more to the busy Quartermaster on watch than that he was reporting to be taken out to Delilah; but the effect of this on the Quartermaster, as well as on the nearby group of listeners-in, had been to gain for the big Seaman a perceptible stiffening of attitude and a quick glance from eyes that were impersonal but antagonistic.

"Your gang's up there by the torpedo-tube," the Quartermaster informed him, gesturing curtly with his head toward amidships. He said this in the tone of a partisan forced by duty to assume a strict neutrality.

Pausing there with the neat burden of his lashed bag and hammock balanced on his competent shoulder, a slight smile of almost shy friendliness touching the corners of his eyes and mouth, Rowe was taken by surprise. He turned promptly away in the direction indicated, with his smile still intact but with its quality transformed into that of a mask for the effect of his rebuff. As he moved toward the tight group of Delilah's returning men amidships, he tried to dismiss this effect with the silent exclamation that that Quartermaster and his ship could "go to hell." It was not with them that he belonged anyhow. Even months later, after he had listened time and again to stories and boasts of the fierce brawling around Manila and Cavite in which Delilah's men had defended themselves against all comers, stories rapidly becoming part of the influential legend of the ship, Rowe was to be provided with no key that opened up the stories as explanations for the repudiation he just then had encountered at this gangway; nor for the welcome, so different from what he had hoped for, that he was moving to receive from the small group of Delilah's men clustered there amidships.

These nine men (the rest were aboard the other destroyer secured to the tug's port side) were standing firmly together beside the torpedo-tube as with an air of being back to back in a strange and hostile place; and the sharp sense of strangeness was but emphasized by the fact that this ship on which they did not belong was identical, in even minute details, with that on which they did. They had marched aboard in a body, a few minutes ahead of Rowe's arrival alone, to recognize, in the Quartermaster on watch and a thick sprinkling of others of that ship's company, men against whom they had fought during the furious rioting ashore in the days before the temporary dispersal of Delilah's crew. The presence of these men in this crew here now—the result of the kind of permanent transferring, shifting about and healthy "breaking up" that Lieutenant-Commander Borden had opposed so tenaciously for his own ship—had instantly imbued the handful of Delilah's men with a quiet, arrogant defiance that had revived in the inhabitants of the ship a flare of the old antagonism. The progress of the nine invaders to where they now stood had been watched with sullen eyes that said plainly: "Oh, so they still think they're salty, do they?" The resentment, under the circumstances, could go no further than this; but the circumstances did not prevent a display of how far it would have liked to go; and it was this simple display, so unexpected and incomprehensible for Rowe, that had confronted him at the gangway the instant he announced his allegiance to Delilah. Just as he had had no hint that it was to the word, "Delilah," that the people at the gangway reacted, so he had no cause for suspecting that the welcome he received from the group of his future shipmates, when he arrived beside them, was not also a reaction to him personally.

As he stopped there and braced his body to lower his bag and hammock to the deck, he asked, as an initiating formality, asked in the tone of relief and assurance of one who already knows the good answer to his question, and with the diffident smile of friendliness once again touching up his face:

"You guys from Delilah?"

All the eyes of the group shifted to him for a moment of preoccupied inspection. The expression of hostile alertness in some of the eyes, an expression that he could not know had little to do with him, halted Rowe's intention to lay his bag and hammock on the deck beside those of these men. He dissimulated the initial movements of this intention, into which he was quite launched, by shifting the burden to his other shoulder.

"Yeah," answered one of them with a tone and manner that seemed to add, for Rowe, "What about it?"

"I'm reporting to her," said Rowe. His voice was steady, but embarrassed by the necessity of forcing words which, on the instant, he was convinced nobody wanted to hear.

"Where from?" asked another with a perfunctory interest that the new man, under his heavy sense of general rebuff, understood as suspicion if not hostility.

"I came in a draft from the Coast."

With this they accepted him, accepted him as being as yet but theoretically one of them, as one of whom they knew nothing and who knew nothing of them, especially nothing of the preoccupying situation in which they found themselves at that moment; and to the situation, to their open, clear defiance of it, they abruptly returned their attention.

In the face of this rebuff, too, the big Seaman's slight tentative smile of friendliness altered as he retreated, unobserved, toward the forecastle in a series of moves calculated to cover his mortification. His smile had transformed itself into not merely a momentary mask for the effect of the new check, but into a positive shield—from then on his habitual expression in the face of Delilah and her men—for his sense of having been unaccountably rejected in the most humiliating manner by those upon whom he had depended for an indispensable welcome, a burning sense which denuded him of his assurance, of his eagerness to get to that ship he had envisioned as his saving portion of "home."

The advent of destiny, the deliberate, labyrinthine approach of that pattern man egoistically emplaces on the events of his past, seemed to require that its way be strewn with the repulses and disappointments of Rowe's attempts to become one with the ship. Even his first sight of her was tainted with a diminution of what his original enthusiasm had led him to expect. He came upon her without awnings, denuded of paint and mottled with red lead, a dead, sparse-looking thing trussed nakedly up there in gloom between the two enormous, neat steel walls like a dowdy reptile caught in a trap.

Had he been able to climb up to her deck, as to a refuge, from out of his sense of being abandoned and lost in an alien wilderness, he whole-heartedly could have blinded himself to her imperfections, as many a man before him has done under similar circumstances, with the sanguine emotion that springs from the right to say, "There she is . . . for better or for worse . . . that's where I belong." However, though he had received his assignment to her with such a gush of that emotion, it was with eyes miserably clear of its saving illusion that he approached her, less than three hours after the shark had taken Wright, in the company of the returning men who did belong to her and who had put it into his feelings, by the manner in which (as he understood it) they had rejected him, that he did not. As these men tramped along in the gloom beneath Delilah's flank, seemingly following the still fresh trail of Wright's blood down the damp dry-dock floor, the coincidence placing this trail of blood side by side with their zeal to board their ship once more, gave to them, in the realm of fleeting impressions that Rowe neither stopped to think about nor take into account, a character of cruel, bestial pursuit. This impression, so unjust that Rowe would have branded as light in the head any one who might have pointed it out to him, nevertheless so inflamed his reluctance to climb the ladder to the ship, to intrude himself where he feared he was not wanted, to face another rebuff of his proffered goodwill, that he waited until all the others had mounted the ladder before starting up himself. Probably because his reluctance contained much that belonged in the Luciferic category of those impulses that men somehow force themselves to negate, that is, men who ever have been touched even indirectly by society, he permitted to it no further concession than that, a concession that could be seen as presenting the acceptable appearance of civility or modesty; yet his reluctance to climb up the ladder was a more poignant, a more exigent urge than that which made him eat when he was hungry, than that which made him drink when he was thirsty, than that which made him avoid a threatened injury to his body, or than that which finally made him climb the ladder.

His premonition of the kind of welcome awaiting him at the top of the ladder proved, from the only point of view now permitted to him, not false. Had he arrived without the premonition, and in the full flush of his original eagerness to join the ship, he would have expected nothing more than the receptive curiosity, casual but general, that usually arises about a new man reporting to a small ship; and, in consideration of the fact that he had arrived with a returning group of the crew's old shipmates, he probably would have seen but a shadow of such an attitude as natural and adequate. As it was, he perceived less than the shadow, even something quite different from it. Everybody completely ignored him, seemed pointedly to turn their backs on him, except the Lieutenant-Commander standing on the quarter-deck and the Quartermaster on watch. The latter, posted near the little desk fastened to the side of the After Conning-tower, was checking in the new arrivals. As Rowe gave his papers to the Quartermaster, whose aspect left no doubt that it was the papers rather than the man that exacted his hasty, perfunctory attention, Rowe turned his eyes for a glance at the officer. He was able to take a good look at him because the officer's smiling attention was held by the boisterous reunion of old friends going on amidships. A swift rise of liking and confidence was Rowe's reaction to what he took in from the small, durable figure and the wrinkled, wind-tempered face so unpretentiously full of matter-of-fact integrity and innocent restraint. Then, as the officer turned away toward the stern, his dry, pleasant gaze encountered Rowe. So swiftly complete was the change of expression that swept the officer's face at sight of him that Rowe, although he respectfully shifted his look to the Quartermaster reading his papers, had no chance to escape the definite repudiation and displeasure compressing the lips and narrowing the eyes that but an instant before had been alight with pleasure and approval. Once again the big Seaman's steady being was agitated by the conviction, mysterious but corrosive, that he was an intruder.

351

Although it had not been as sharply apparent as Rowe, in his prepared condition, had taken it to be, he had not imagined that glance of repudiation and displeasure from the Captain; for, at first sight of the new man, the Captain had suffered a twinge of emotion more or less like that the acting head of the Personnel Office guiltily had hoped he would feel when he assured himself that "Borden was going to get a new man and like it." Certainly, the triumphant pleasure the Captain was taking, from the return of so many of those whom he considered his rightful men, had been briefly but rudely blurred by this symbol of those he had lost; but he had no idea that the Seaman had caught any reflection of this on his face. Such an idea would have distressed him deeply; especially as the expression had nothing to do with the new man personally. His impression of the man personally, as he sized him up through the screen of a light frown for the item of defeat represented by the man's "newness," was unquestionably favoura- ble. "Sound looking fellow," the Captain told himself, "alert . . . and with plenty of stuff to him . . . nobody's fool either, unless I miss my guess."

For Rowe, the explanation of the expression on the Captain's face must have remained forever beyond him under any circum- stances: but if, to begin with, his excessive readiness to get to the ship and become part of it had not brutally been sent recoiling back upon him time after time, he would have been able to make the normal, correct judgment, and make it comfortably, that the others, still excitedly reacting to the bloody attack by the shark, had but little awareness to spare for him. Now, however, he could see his reception only in the false light shed by what a part of this crew already had prepared him to expect, hours before either he or they had known about the shark. He did not argue thus with himself; his first wounding was yet too recent, and the unexpected shock of it too monopolizing, to permit the rise of any defending doubt so subtle as one fathered by the axiom that similar effects may result from unrelated causes. He did not even think about the reception he was getting. He simply found, and was accepting, what he had climbed the ladder to face: the persistence of the inexplicable snubbing that began the moment he had stepped aboard that other destroyer back there inside the Cavite breakwater. What now helped prevent him from seeing the excitement about the shark as the cause for his being so unusually ignored, what, by its sheer existence, prevented this excitement from even occurring to him as a cause, was the fact that his eyes and ears were filled with the enthusiastic greeting the crew was bestowing upon the group that had preceded him up the ladder: yet he might have found in this greeting, if he had been able to see it in normal light, a consoling demonstration of the very "cause" that he saw the welcome as denying.

What he would have found in this greeting to the others was that, while the crew had but little awareness to waste on the arrival of a stranger, it had not very much more to waste even on the return of companions who had been given up for lost. Not that the greeting was lacking in authenticity; it literally was a burst of congratulation, rejoicing and delighted surprise; but it too quickly changed its object, too quickly became a welcome to the opportunity for recounting the details of Wright's tragedy, for which privilege men volubly competed. The returned old friends became little else than pretexts for a reversion to the sensation that had the ship in its grip, pretexts for emotioned men, victims of different points of view, once more to come to the verge of blows over the precise manner in which the shark had struck . . . for a renewal of the fierce controversy as to whether it was Corum or Forsythe who had pulled the driver of the laundry waggon from his seat . . . for Ragatzo to marvel more loudly than ever at his nearness to a danger, now remembered as having been deliberately risked, that had passed him by in favour of the unfortunate Wright . . . for Feenan to repeat his muttered judgment, punctuated by a jet of saliva over the side, that the officers were to blame for permitting the risk in the first place.

"All right," said the Quartermaster, as he finished with Rowe's papers. "Just take any empty bunk and locker you find in the forecastle."

With these words he hastily turned away from his completed chare and headed for the excitement about the shark up forward there, which he realized, had realized even before finishing with Rowe's papers, was beginning to blaze again. Left standing alone in this summary fashion, Rowe could not bring himself, immediately, to act upon this advice, which would force him to move in the direction of that crowded reunion of old friends, so loud, familiar and excluding. He simply continued to hesitate there taking it in, lonely and ignored, until he felt the pressure of the Captain's slightly puzzled observation of him; continued to hesitate there, commonplace but prepossessing, his tall, young, heavy frame slightly relaxed by an unaccustomed need of assurance, his unwavering blue eyes masked with that slight smile of altered, shy friendliness, his right fist unobtrusively gripping the thumb of his left hand and slowly, almost imperceptibly, twisting and retwisting around it.

He stood just like this, too, with no sense of participation, watching first the celebration that rose about the home-coming of Ensign Snell and his men two days later, and then the more formal but not less warm greeting bestowed upon the return of Ensign Woodbridge.

Even the great flurry of preparation to relaunch the ship left him a spectator; and his sense of being such was intensified by observing how those other recent arrivals were reabsorbed by the crew with a celerity and completeness that left no trace of their ever having been parted from it. He could not, as a matter of fact, understand the impatient, ardent quality in this preparation, the pressing, almost fanatical attention to minute details of personal and official equipment. He tended to make the mistake of attributing the long hours of persistence with which the men kept at an abnormal amount of work to a "slave-driving" temper in the officers. He was not wholly mistaken here either, for the Captain, responding both to the urgency of getting another of the destroyers into dry dock under repair and to his own burning necessity for feeling his ship in the water once more, was working the crew relentlessly; but that it clearly suited the crew's mood was what most helped to bewilder Rowe and keep him an outsider.

Furthermore, in these hurried, trying hours it was easier for the other Seamen to do all the work themselves than to break the new man in to a share of it; and Cruck, the Chief Boatswain's Mate, as a matter of course put off assigning him a definite routine area of work until after the ship was in the water again and he would have time to "size him up." This left Rowe with little else to do but move uncomfortably from place to place where work was going on in an effort to escape an impression of shirking while, at the same time, strictly avoiding an intrusion upon what almost seemed like the private endeavours of these, for him, antagonistic men. Occasionally, when there was something heavy to lift or an untechnical, bulk operation to be performed, someone would shout at him:

"Hey, you, new guy! . . . Lend a hand here."

Invariably he would give a nervous start of alacrity, then hesitate for an instant to be sure of his ground before obeying.

Not faced with the incomprehensible "antagonism," he might have gone up to Cruck and sheepishly demanded some proper share in the work. As it was, he would as soon have thought of making a public plea to the crew to relent, to take him in. By the time Cruck did get around to recommending him for specific work and duty stations, just a week after he had reported aboard, Rowe's personality, in relation to the ship, had become more or less established and set. Not that his character had changed; it simply had reacted; but it was the result of this reaction, this "personality," that conflicted with what had been Cruck's first impression of the man and what, the week later, again was his impression as he stood, fists on hips, watching Rowe paint a railing stanchion. Cruck's first impression, like the Captain's, had been decidedly favourable. Nevertheless, a sense of the faintly crippled quality now pervading Rowe's soundness and potentialities, a quality intangible but doubt-inspiring for Cruck's rough instinct, was reflected in the uncertainty with which the Chief Boatswain's Mate finally made to Lieutenant Fitzpatrick his recommendations for the new man's stationing and billeting. They placed him where any deficiencies that he might harbour, if he did harbour any, would be least dangerous to the life of the ship.

The crew also, as it came their turn to "size him up" through the succeeding days of his silent, competent adapting of himself to their routines, suffered the same kind of conflict between their instinctive approval and a perception of something faltering about him, something morbidly reserved. "He's O.K.," was the way Arnold put it. "Just a little slow on the uptake." Feenan amplified this estimate by contributing the phrase "too suspicious," which was evoked by the memory of an attempt to make friends with Rowe soon after his arrival. The red-headed Oiler not only had liked the general look of him, but he also had felt the chance to start over with this new man, the chance to resume with the stranger the kind of relationship no longer possible with the old members of the crew because of his mortifying loss of prestige. The attempt had consisted in his going up to Rowe's bunk in the deserted, sweltering forecastle one night, just after Rowe had climbed into it, and volunteering the suggestion that "out here, in this climate, nobody sleeps in the forecastle." He had said this in the slightly pompous, terse manner of an important business man who makes a cult of minding his own business but who has condescended to break his rule in order to save a lost motorist from taking the wrong road; and then he had paused to permit a genial but faintly patronizing smile to light up his large, unpleasantly freckled face. Rowe's instant, thoughtless reaction to this had been to arrest his movement of relaxing in the bunk as if he had been caught getting into the wrong one by mistake. This movement was something like the sudden starts of alacrity he made when one of these men gave him an unexpected order. Then, after the same sort of hesitating moment that followed each of those starts, a moment through which he had gazed at Feenan with alert, questioning eyes, he had realized that he was on safe ground and had replied, from behind that faint shielding smile:

"I noticed it."

"You want to get yourself a camp cot," Feenan had continued. "There's a place in Olongapo there . . ." he had paused to gesture briefly in the direction of the land with the cigar between his stubby fingers, then had prolonged the pause in order to relight the cigar. ". . . that sells 'em." He had exhaled a leisurely, authoritative puff of smoke. "I'll show you the place . . . tomorrow when we get ashore."

"Much obliged," Rowe had said in a neutral tone, as he had settled himself in the bunk with a manner of retiring from the conversation. "Thanks."

He had terminated the conversation in this fashion, not out of a desire to be rid of Feenan, but out of an anxiety to prevent the man from getting any impression of his trying to force the continuance of it; and the next day, for the same kind of reason, he had made a point, without even trying to speak further with Feenan, of going ashore by himself to find the cot. This had been enough to discourage the Oiler, for the time being, from his attempt at attaching him, discouraged Feenan to such an extent that that night, when the men were putting down their cots, he had refrained from carrying out his intention of crowding Rowe's cot in beside his own. With the new cot, still folded, under his arm Rowe had stood uncertainly in the door of the forecastle and watched every available space of the deck being taken up; but in this case his raw uncertainty and fear of intruding, his reluctance to risk further rebuff, had saved him from the error of putting his cot down in any of these spaces. Each of them long had been the accustomed and recognized property of a particular man. He finally had backed out of sight into the forecastle and gone to bed in his bunk as usual, hiding the folded cot under the head of his mattress, where it served the ostensible purpose of a pillow.

His attitude on that occasion had been one of grim resignation rather than meekness, a kind of makeshift resignation that came to colour his whole attitude toward his existence in the ship, which he usually referred to in his thoughts as "this madhouse." The other men would have been no less bewildered at knowing that he thought of Delilah as a "madhouse," a term applied to a disorganized ship in which a miserable crew is overworked, than at knowing of his purpose to get transferred back off her. This purpose, which he had arrived at in a smarting, ignominious moment of clearly apprehending himself making one of those false starts of alacrity he gave when anybody spoke to him, was now the chief solace and bolster of his self-respect. He did not care how, he repeatedly told himself with determination, but he was going to get off that ship. Nursing this comforting determination, and with his likeable, close-cropped blond head and sturdy shoulders wearing a faint shade of resentfulness, even of defiance, he went about the ship working hard and competently at precisely what it was indicated or ordered that he should do and nothing more. Never once did he offer a suggestion, nor make one of those customary intrusions of friendly curiosity up to the bridge or down into an engine- or fire-room; and such of his acts as required the slightest initiative, either in the line of duty or out of it, suffered a slight lag, a hesitation in their inception such as one might observe in the movements of a person living through force of circumstances in a house where he was of the family but unwelcome. After he had discovered that he was making them, such hesitations invariably were followed, at first consciously and later automatically, by a violent, almost angry, throwing of himself into the act he had hesitated to initiate. Once, for example, he accidentally dropped his paint brush down the Starboard Engine-room Hatchway. He naturally started down after the brush; hesitated; then, as if stung with disgust for himself over the hesitation and scorn for that which inspired it, he furiously, almost vengefully, so over-emphasized his recovery from it that he literally leapt down the hatchway, saving himself from a bad fall only by a last-second clutch at a rung of the ladder. As he climbed on down the oily steel rungs, his muscles trembling mechanically in the wake of the violent emergency they too suddenly had been called upon to meet, he assured himself with calm vehemence that "This madhouse and everybody in it can go to hell too!" Although this assurance continued, until the night he finally was free of the ship, to give light to his resignation and heat to his sense of isolation and bewilderment, the corners of his eyes and mouth were ever shadowed by the slight wounded smile, that set mask of altered shy friendliness.

23 〰〰

Rowe's painful idleness, his unattached drifting about amidst the turmoil of other men's hard work, was suddenly relieved, at dawn of his sixth day aboard, by the submerging of the dry dock in order to return the ship to the sea. As the two great walls of the dry dock gracefully, unhurriedly settled in the water, like two hands carefully placing a toy boat in a pond, everybody gazed steadily down at the sea reaching for Delilah's hull. The Captain, Lieutenant Fitzpatrick and Ensign Woodbridge were on the bridge, Ensign Snell was on the After Conning-tower, and the crew lined both rails. As one man they tensely were suffering the same naïve emotion, an experimental expectancy, an absurdly founded but breathless doubt as to what would happen when she was regiven to the water. Finally it touched her, crept up her sides. The workmen on the dock walls knocked away the supporting braces. Many of the crew made an instinctive gesture of hanging on to the rail as the ship gave a slight, abandoned roll and downward surge. Then they felt and heard her tightening about herself. She was back in the water! An audible mass sigh swept the crew, a sigh not only of relaxation from the stress of apprehending her prove that she could, but of relief for the fact that she had.

"Watch those lines!" admonished the Captain sharply.

That portion of the deck force posted in the stern gave a sudden start away from the rail, as if recovering from a trance, and alertly faced the tug which, cautiously backing in, was preparing to heave its hand-lines.

In almost no time at all the tug had her across the clear, glassy extent of the port and secured alongside two heavily loaded coal barges moored to the Fuel Dock near the mouth of Boton River. Then, while Cruck and his force rigged coaling booms on either side of the ship, the tug manoeuvred two more of the loaded barges against her free flank. Shabby and forlorn in the clear rays of the newly risen sun, she finally lay there, surrounded, half-hidden by her dully glittering hillocks of floating coal, like a derelict embedded in a black ice-floe that had drifted against a jungled shore.

The Warrant Officer in charge there, a corpulent, middle-aged Boatswain with a taciturn, red face under a white cork helmet, stood on his dock with arms akimbo and glared with a kind of pointed sympathy, which served but conventionally as a mask for his personal disapproval, while half of Delilah's crew, dressed in their oldest dungarees and whites, climbed reluctantly out upon the high-piled coal in the barges, took up shovels and grimly began the dirtiest, the most punishing routine chare that men-of-warsmen ever have been called upon to perform. Not even the old iron men in their exacting wooden ships ever regularly faced any task so oppressively dull, extended and exhausting. By force of a tradition insisting that a man-of-war be independent to the fullest extent possible of any assistance from the land, a tradition existing to no such fanatical degree in any other navy, this chare fell into the category of a drill. Therefore, like Collision Drill, Fire Drill or Abandon Ship Drill, it had to be performed by the crew itself, and performed, like any other drill, with unrelenting smartness, persistence and speed.

There were rare occasions when it was seen fit to compromise with this tradition: whenever, for example, a ship found it necessary to take on coal in ports of India, China or Japan, where the white residents would have been irritated, even outraged where the English prevailed, at the sight of men like themselves doing work that was specifically the allotment of the most abject class of natives. In such ports, multitudes of low-caste, barefooted old men, women and children were permitted to deliver the coal to the bunker holes, streaming endlessly up and down cleated inclines laid from barges to deck, carrying their loads in baskets on their heads. In some way or other this compromise also had crept into the routine management of affairs at Olongapo and firmly established itself, strangely established itself in face of the fact that almost the only, certainly the dominant, public opinion in the place was Navy. There ships were coaled by the red-faced Boatswain at the head of a numerous gang of Tagalogs and Bicols he had organized for the purpose.

When the Captain had rejected this customary Olongapo compromise and insisted that "this time I want her to coal herself," the Boatswain had fought him "tooth and nail," as the Captain had put it afterwards to Lieutenant Fitzpatrick, in defence of his function.

"What's the good of it, Commander?" the Warrant Officer had demanded with a little more aggressiveness than was permitted by the differences in their ranks and stations. Placed above the rate of the highest enlisted man but below the rank of the lowest Commissioned Officer, the Boatswain's rather anomalous status was granted, by practice and tradition, a special consideration from his superiors. He had gone on to complain: "And it'll just raise hell with us. Why, my gooks are all ready to do the job." He had turned heatedly to the Captain of the Yard, who was refereeing the contest. "You know these people. They've loaded the barges and they expect the rest of the work. Why, they got their pay for it half spent already!" He had ended on an impatiently ominous note. "This Bay is too damn restless now . . . And here we want to go an' cheat 'em out of a job of work."

What the Boatswain had been getting at underneath all this had been reasonably clear. The man had a cosy billet of it here ashore, and he was going to lose it if people started coaling themselves; but Delilah's Captain had replied with patient good humour:

"My intention is not to cheat anybody, Boatswain. I've confidence in your ability to make your . . . your Filipinos see that."

Warned by the way the word "cheat" had been reflected in this reply, and by a slight facial gesture of disapproval on the part of the Captain of the Yard, the Warrant Officer hastily had explained:

"Don't misunderstand me, Commander . . . I'm just trying to think how the Bay is going to take it." He had pushed back his cork helmet and mopped his brow with a red bandanna handkerchief. "They're a nutty crowd to handle."

"Let's hope they'll take it easier than you fear," Delilah's Captain had said encouragingly.

In the end, after fruitlessly having used every argument he had been able to think of, the Boatswain even had gone so far as to resort to a display of sympathy for Delilah's men. An "old-timer" who had risen from the vanished rate of Apprentice Boy, the Boatswain was in no sense a sympathetic man; but he had managed to say, with a kind of woeful droop to his full, hard, red features:

"It's a radical upset of the way we do things here, Captain Borden, but . . . but it's extra hard on your men . . . Those poor boys out there doing niggers' work in this weather . . . When it's not necessary." He had compressed his lips grimly over the last word.

"But that's just it," Delilah's Commanding Officer had replied, shifting his glance to the Captain of the Yard. "It's of them that I'm thinking. They've been scattered all over the place . . . And most of them have laid around the beach so long they've gotten soft, careless." He had paused to smile dryly.

The Captain of the Yard, already a trifle revolted by the Boatswain's exceptional display of sympathy, had tried to fend off the other bright, sharp point he had seen coming if Delilah's Captain continued:

"I think I understand."

Ordinarily the man to whom the victory had been thus conceded would have let it rest at that and gone about his business; for he seldom was guilty of the dangerous tactic of arguing beyond a triumph. Then, however, he had felt the necessity, the practical necessity, of putting his insistence in the clear right. He had sent the point home in a friendly tone:

"You see, I want to harden them up as quickly as possible, and get them working as a team again . . . get them back in the Navy."

Having been unable to parry it, the Captain of the Yard had taken the point in the last four words unflinchingly, with a wry smile; but his order to the Boatswain had been curt:

"If he wants to coal her himself, it's up to him. See that he gets whatever he needs."

"All right," the Boatswain almost had mumbled, slowly taking off his unregulation cork helmet and turning it about in his hands as if he had become uncomfortably conscious of it. "How many of my wheelbarrows will you need, Commander?"

"I won't trouble you for those," had been the answer in a friendly tone. "I'll coal her regulation style, with my bags."

This reply had stung the Boatswain back to a state of almost reckless resistance. As if it were not enough that the stubborn little destroyer Captain had struck a public blow at his official pride and reason for being, he now was scorning his equipment, the equipment he had had so much trouble in extracting from this "tightwad of a Station!" The Boatswain had improved on the system of having people carry the coal up in baskets on their heads; his orientals pushed it up runways in wheelbarrows. With his eyes squinting antagonistically above his beefy cheek-bones, he had exploded:

"But, Commander, you can't get steam up for your winches. She'll be as empty as a gourd!" He had turned to the Captain of the Yard and demanded scornfully, "How's he going to hoist his bags without winches?"

"That's true," Delilah's Commanding Officer had admitted

readily. Then he had exclaimed mildly in a bright, dry, friendly way innocent of any triumph, "I'll tell you . . . you *can* lend me a runway and two or three of those wheelbarrows . . . until we trundle up enough to start one of the boilers."

"I can't understand," had commented the Boatswain frustratedly, "why you want to make so much trouble for yourself."

Lieutenant-Commander Borden, much to the Captain of the Yard's relief, had seen fit to pass by this irregular remark without finding it insubordinate. He casually had said, in the tone of one who had expected, and had been receiving, co-operation:

"That point about getting up steam brings us to the question of water also. Before they float her, I thought I'd take on just enough from the dry-dock main to begin with . . . Won't do to fill her tanks while she's out of the water like that. Then if you'll send over the water-lighter at noon . . . while the men are eating . . . that'll put us on our own."

"So be it," had pronounced the Captain of the Yard, getting decisively to his feet; and he had smiled good-naturedly, a little admiringly.

On men-of-war larger than Delilah, the drill of Coaling Ship sometimes lasted for two days; sometimes even continuing, under flood-lights, into the night. Shore liberty being suspended, all hands must "Coal Ship" regardless of rate or specialty; only a certificate from the Doctor or another indispensable duty, such as being the Quartermaster or Cook on watch, could save a man from it. There were no rest periods except an hour at meal times, and this hour was cut to thirty or forty minutes if the ship was faced with emergency duty. True, about every three hours the Cook on watch would climb from barge to barge with a tall polished copper pot of coffee and a bucket of corned-beef sandwiches, which the men were expected to gulp down, much as they snatched a drink from the water pail, almost in the stride of their work. If a man had to relieve his bladder, he stood briefly at the edge of the barge, to leeward, and did so into the sea. If he had to relieve his bowels, he climbed hastily aboard ship and went to the head amidst a general, sharp observation that warned him against a repetition; and if this vigilance did not suffice, a Boatswain's Mate or a Master at Arms put the warning into plain-spoken words.

Thus did Delilah's men, snarling, cursing, barking short laughs, stand out there in the blazing sunshine and fight the mountains of coal until, just before first dark, they had moved them into the bunkers of their hollow ship. There were about eight shovellers in each of the four barges. On the starboard side, the side toward the dock, those in the sternmost barge were in charge of Cruck; those in the foremost barge in charge of the Carpenter's Mate; and the two, Cruck scowling and clenching his blunt, gnarled fists like an enemy of mankind, the Carpenter's Mate lanky, middle-aged, disdainful and grim, drove their men unrelentingly at the coal as if they alone were concerned with emptying the two barges before those in charge on the port side could empty theirs. However, Ensign Snell, who stood in a cleared corner of Cruck's barge slowly, unprofitably smoking one dusty cigarette after another, knew just how intently each of those twenty men before him was set on winning the race; so every now and then he would climb from the barge up to Delilah's quarter-deck and survey the rival shovellers on the port side, where the suave, good-humoured authority of Orlop, the Chief Gunner's Mate, dominated the forward barge, and Bidot, willowy and smiling, his long, straight, black hair confined by a blue bandanna knotted around his head, kept up the pace in the after barge with the soft, tough whip-lash of his voice and the genial goad of his bright glance. Invariably, on these occasions, Ensign Snell received from Ensign Woodbridge a smile full of sharp-edged gaiety, self-assurance and pleasant contempt for his opponent's chance of success. He sent this smile down at him from whichever of the two port barges happened, at that moment, to have the highest coal pile, upon the top of which, khaki-garbed yet well tailored, still delicately scented, and with the gold strap on his cap glinting freshly beneath its powdering of coal, he would be perched smoking his straight-stemmed pipe in a careless, competent manner.

This smile always sent Ensign Snell back to his own barges with a stubborn look on his heavy face and struggling with the temptation to take up a shovel himself; but the smile never distracted him from his purpose, for as he arrived back amongst his men he would be able to tell them what they wanted to know. Those nearest the spot to which he climbed back down would pause, sullen with fatigue and fierce with effort, clear the dripping perspiration from their grimy brows with a back-hand swipe and dart brief questioning glances at his eyes or grin at him expectantly; and he would say loudly in an even voice that could be heard in both his barges, "A couple of tons," if the other side were ahead; or, "Keep it up," if the others were behind; sometimes he could give them nothing more than, "Neck and neck."

Ensign Woodbridge did not need to make any such scouting trips; he could tell from his friend's manner, when he made his, just about how the competition was going. As soon as the other had retreated, Ensign Woodbridge would take the pipe from his mouth and shout in a cheerful, jeering tone, if he judged the starboard side to be ahead, "Better get a move on . . . Those birds are creeping up on us"; or, in the same tone but touched with enthusiasm, when apparently his side was ahead, "Keep it moving! . . . Keep it moving! . . . We've got them on the run!"

They did not need to be told to keep it moving; they would have kept it moving anyway, at the same strenuous, practised, unfrantic pace; but they appreciated the luxury of the game they were permitted to make of this black ordeal, and they expected the connivance of their officers at it, a game that shredded the palms of their hands with broken blisters, that filled the muscles of their shoulders and backs with ache, that covered their sweating bodies with ebony mud, and that plastered their hair, choked their throats, their nostrils, clogged their finger-nails, their teeth, as well as every cranny of the ship, with the heavy dust that seemed to have displaced the motionless, incandescent air.

The half of the crew that remained aboard during the drill escaped neither its smearing dust nor, with seven exceptions, a share of its drudgery. At least two of the exceptions, Stengle, the senior Chief Machinist's Mate, and Whorley, the Water-Tender, were made such on grounds of pure necessity and indispensable function untainted by prejudice, privilege, usurpation or even justice. Between them, throughout the whole day, these two kept up the head of steam in Number One Boiler that operated the winches, pumps and dynamo. Stengle, in addition, was standing all the other Engineering Force Watches, including that over the dynamo. However, if the dynamo had started acting up, he would have summoned Poe, the thin, delicate-looking Chief Electrician, who was shovelling in one of the barges on the port side. The exemption in favour of Whorley had come about simply because his regular day on watch in the fire-room had coincided with the day of coaling; that in favour of Stengle because obviously he was the man, in point of competence and official authority, to stand the combination of watches that he normally supervised.

Two others, middle-aged Ah Lee, the Captain's Steward, and Tiburcio, the Wardroom Mess Attendant, were exceptions for no such utilitarian and regulation reasons. The Chinaman and the young Tagalog, being servants, were not expected, nor would they easily have been permitted, to participate in this violent effort of the men any more than they would have been accepted as members of a gun's crew in target practice or battle. They kept out of the way, even out of sight down in the diminutive Wardroom Pantry.

Also excepted were Portness, the bandy-legged Radio Electrician, and Olgan, the Cook, who, on account of the undermanned condition of the Fleet, were the only men of their respective ratings in the crew. During the hours when the former was away from the ship on liberty, Delilah neither could send nor receive a radio message. When he was aboard, in harbour, he spent alternating three-hour periods on and off watch from eight o'clock in the morning to eleven at night. At sea, day and night, he spent every other two hours at his instruments. Radio stations whose business it was to communicate with the ship possessed his watch schedule and sent their messages accordingly. That he now was not using his three-hour off watch periods to help coal ship struck nobody as unfair. If the Executive Officer had forced him to, it even might have aroused a flurry of indignation amongst those men readily susceptible to sympathy, those whose regard long since had raised him to a kind of eminence upon the impression that "the poor bastard is always on watch." As a matter of fact, although his small, flat, froglike, uncommunicative, Welsh face never gave him away, he smiled inwardly at the sympathetic basis of his eminence; for the long, unmolested hours that he passed in the little steel shack between the foremast and the Forward Conning-tower, head-phones in place, were anything but irksome to him. They gave him larger opportunity to indulge the chief pleasure of his life and more time for the profitable little industry that helped him finance his loaning operations, which, strictly illegal and carried on in considerable fear of discovery by the officers, consisted of advances of from one to ten dollars to his shipmates to be paid back at the rate of two for one on the next bi-monthly pay day. Of the total net profit from his industry, his pay and his usury, he sent one third of the money to his mother in Detroit and spent the rest, except for the small sum that he mailed off each year for a subscription to *Adventure Magazine,* precisely as the other men spent theirs. In this magazine he found his great pleasure, especially in those of its stories that dealt with the French Foreign Legion; and he looked forward to its arrival, regularly every month if the ship were around Manila, in delayed batches of two or three if she were up along the China Coast or down amongst the southern islands, as his ancestors had looked forward to harvest time. Sitting there beside his spark-gap, his ears mechanically on the alert for the slightest disturbance within their covering receivers, he would exhaust each page of every issue. Nothing save the demands of his instrument served to distract him very long from those pages of dangerous excitement and glamorous travail. He had read them through typhoons that seemed about to pound Delilah into the depths of the China Sea. When there were no more pages to read, he worked on one of the rings, stamped with the Navy crest, that he casually peddled ashore, for five dollars each, amongst such of the Fleet's men that he encountered in what he considered a receptive mood. He beat these rings out from silver Mexican *pesos,* a stock of which he laid up whenever Delilah touched at Shanghai where they formed the principal currency, beat them out on a little anvil that belonged to his radio repair kit, while he dreamed of the fulfilment of the promise he continually made himself, a promise that, someday before he died, he was going to pull himself up out of this monotonous grind of everyday, ordinary restriction and discipline in which he was wasting his life and risk it like a man, those men in the magazine, for something worth seeing and doing.

If Lieutenant Fitzpatrick had ordered Olgan, the Cook, into the coal barges, people would have suffered no indignation. They would have been highly amused; yet Olgan's misfortune of being nearly always on duty, which he performed on a spot almost directly above the heat of the After Fire-room, was far more genuine as such than that of Portness. Each day, from five-thirty in the morning until six in the evening, this small, ignominious, milky-eyed being with a quality of stale youthfulness, dressed in an undershirt, a pair of dungaree trousers and wooden sandals that were always soppy with sweat from his flushed body and vapour from his two great steam cauldrons, scurried tenaciously in and about the galley, hung over the flaming coal stove, breathed the too close odours, touched surfaces that were forever hot, moist or greasy, preparing a torrent of coffee, stewed prunes, fresh *papayas,* ham and eggs, bread, biscuits, ice-cream, corned beef and cabbage, soups, mashed potatoes, fried potatoes or potato salad, puddings, roasts, pies, fresh fish, frankfurters and sauerkraut, fresh vegetables, navy beans, stews, steaks, canned spinach, an unending torrent that disappeared into the appetite of the crew as rapidly, as inexorably as a jet of steam into the sky. At sea, he got up at midnight besides, and again at three-thirty in the morning, to brew a further portion of coffee for the men of the oncoming watch.

Because life for him seemed to consist of one great ambush formed of a series of minor ambushes through which he lived from escape to escape, it sufficed him to know, as far as his sense of the customary working of the world was concerned, that there was to be an escape from this ambush of excessive toil also. He did not reflect upon it; for he did not reflect upon anything; he simply *felt* the *good,* in terms of imminent escape, in the unquestionably honest, repeated promises of the Captain, Lieutenant Fitzpatrick and the Division Paymaster at the Base that there was to be an escape, that they were doing everything in their power, power that he did not doubt, to get another Cook with whom he could divide the work. It actually made little difference to him that the situation had lasted almost a year now; sometimes it took ten minutes to "get out," sometimes ten years; time, duration, became a disaster for him only when its extension was greater than that within which escape, the essential, was possible: And the weight of the work, the density of his present ambush, already was so hard to bore through that a tough spot, a knot in the wood, such as, for example, his having to add to his toil, on this day of coaling ship, the periodic preparation and distribution of coffee and sandwiches, had no poignant effect on him as long as it did not tend to nullify his progress toward that point at which the lines of time and escape intersected.

There were, however, three things in his situation that he detested and one that he hated. His detestations were: first, the necessity for keeping his person and his galley clean to a degree he considered fanatical, a degree maintained by the ruthless inspections of Lieutenant Fitzpatrick; second, the fried potatoes he was forced to prepare nearly everyday because these formed the crew's favourite dish; and third, the red silk handkerchief that he wore, tied Moro style about his lobeless ears and patchy-haired head, to keep dandruff out of the food, a device hit upon and unofficially enforced, through threat of violence, by Rene, the Chief Machinist's Mate. He had not arrived at these detestations by any open, logical process, and if he had been asked to explain them he would have felt as frustrated as if he had been asked to explain why he did not like *papaya* but did like sliced bananas loaded with sugar and evaporated milk. There even was a paradox in his attitude toward the fried potatoes, for in peeling and slicing them he received, from those members of the crew detailed anew each month to serve the mess tables, the only help of any kind that was vouchsafed him. His hatred of Rene, too, was quite as unreasonable. This hatred had not arisen because of the red silk handkerchief, nor because the Chief Machinist's Mate's huge, big-faced, feline person was inevitably at the centre of those storms that broke about the galley whenever the crew judged, usually in error, that the food was off-standard. The hatred, a blind, sharp thing like instinctive fear, had arisen previous to these developments, had arisen in the instant of the pair's first proximity, before so much as an exchange of speech or a meeting of the eyes, as if Olgan had taken in through his hairs, through the alert cells of his skin the existence of an hostility between this being and himself antedating their knowledge of each other as individuals; and it had persisted with familiarity, this hatred, lying dark, heavy and dormant or rising erect and vibrant in direct proportion to

Rene's physical distance or nearness. Whenever the two were face to face Olgan invariably smiled in a way that Rene took to be placatingly; but it was the kind of mouth gesture that an animal makes when it is confronted by another that it finds formidable.

One of the things that reinforced Olgan's hatred was the fact that Rene made a point, especially before others, of using the same condescending manner and primitive English in talking to him that he used with Tiburcio, the Wardroom Mess Attendant. The big, rowdy, genial man, whose grandparents had emigrated from Figeac, France, had hit upon this unending joke as a result of listening to Olgan fretfully, plaintively contend that his rate, Ship's Cook, Second-Class, was the same as any other Second-Class Petty Officer rating, such as Second-Class Boatswain's Mate or Second-Class Machinist's Mate, and that just because he handled food, like Ah Lee, the Chinaman, or Tiburcio, the Tagalog, it was not to be confused with theirs. They "made beds, took care of the officers' clothes"; while he "fetched and carried for nobody." He did not even serve the food he cooked. He had whined out this last bit of evidence defiantly, and with sulky, evasive but pointed glances at those unfortunate Seamen and Firemen who, at the moment, had had the duty of serving the crew's mess tables. What he was trying to get at was that he was in no sense a servant; and he was not. His station in battle was at the polished, bronze nozzle of the Forward Fire Hose, Starboard Side, between the two forward six-pounders, and just below the bridge; with the men. So vivid was his sense of the distinction that if, in the drills for that emergency, Ah Lee or the Tagalog had touched the nozzle in his grip he would have dropped the heavy thing to the deck; and no threat of force or punishment, not even an order from the Captain, would have made him pick it up again. Not that the Captain ever would have given Olgan such an order; he would unhesitatingly have seized hold of the nozzle himself, if it had been necessary, and gone shoulder to shoulder with him into a blaze; but he never would have ordered him to go in with a servant.

Probably, Olgan missed the aid of a companion Cook more in this defence of his social position than in the excess of his work; and he remembered, with a sense of loss, the other, larger ships on which he had worked where there had been as many as three, even four Cooks, besides a Steward, the Chief Petty Officer rate in his branch, to take the responsibility . . . Each of those ships, too, had had a Paymaster of its own, right on board all the time . . . a regular Commissioned Officer who, in addition to paying the ship and having charge of all its stores, was the Cooks' own officer, supervising their work, approving the menus, ordering the food from the Base or buying it, the fresh part of it, on the beach himself . . . an officer who was unquestionably an officer . . . just like Mr. Fitzpatrick . . . who had a room aft all to himself . . . ate in the Wardroom . . . wore gold braid . . . and whom people saluted . . . He'd like to see anybody try to call *him* a servant just because he had to do with food!

As a result of there being no one to relieve him of his unpostponable and indispensable duties, Olgan did not get to spend much time ashore. The other men, except the venereal cases and those undergoing restrictive punishment for minor offences, usually were granted liberty every other day from five in the afternoon until midnight, half of them going one day and the other half the next; and once a week, unless there was an emergency pending, they were permitted to stay ashore all night, a third or so leaving the ship from Friday afternoon until Saturday morning, another third from Saturday afternoon until Sunday morning and the last third from Sunday afternoon until Monday morning. Even Portness was enabled to enjoy these latter extended excursions ashore each week simply by informing the nearby naval ships and stations, as he did for his shorter absences, of the exact sixteen-hour period through which his instrument would be dead.

It was the necessity for consistently depriving Olgan alone of this overnight liberty that most emphasized the Cook's irregular situation for Lieutenant Fitzpatrick, that positively embarrassed his function, as Executive Officer, of seeing to it that the men got good and sufficient liberty. He was doing everything he could think of to alter the situation favourably. He even had approached every other Executive Officer he had seen come into the Army and Navy Club in Manila with a proposition to trade a good Seaman, even a Machinist's Mate or even one of his precious Quartermasters for another Cook. He had gone so far as to try to persuade Forsythe, the Seaman from Fort Worth, to strike for Cook, Third-

Class, in the galley under Olgan, a measure suggested to him by overhearing Forsythe tell of a time, back in Texas, when he had cooked through a whole season for the hands on a round-up after the regular cook had been hurt by falling from a horse. The youthful Seaman had drawn up his long, lean, tough person in a gesture of authentic but unconscious dignity and rejected the suggestion, rejected it so firmly that the officer had given up his attempt at persuasion; but he had not given up the idea; and he was determined upon the unsound expedient, if worst came to worst, of *ordering* the man into the galley. Hardwood, after Forsythe had disclosed to him, in an outraged tone, the details of the interview between him and the Executive Officer, had sensed out Lieutenant Fitzpatrick's determination; and thereafter he had gone hooting and chortling around the ship for days, claiming that Forsythe "was jes' goin' ashore right now and get him a dose of clap so they can't make him a cook . . . in the galley . . . strikin' for Olgan!" The first time that Hardwood exploded with this jest, Forsythe had glared about him belligerently and ground out:

"If you guys think that's a joke, you're bugs . . . I'll go ashore and run down every rotten whore in town . . . I'll come back to this God damn ship so loaded with clap, syphilis, hard chancres, soft chancres, pinto, buboes, yaws, cordee and leprosy that they'll keep me shut in the paint locker under a Marine guard!"

In the meantime, the best that Lieutenant Fitzpatrick could do to ameliorate his appreciation of a slightly shameful stress in the life of the ship, a feeling that recurred each time he saw or thought of Olgan, was to give him free gangway, put him on the permanent list of those chosen few who could visit the land every day, whenever they themselves judged their work was finished, and return at their own discretion as to hours. This highly special list had contained only three names up until the time that Olgan's went on it: those of Chief Machinist's Mate Stengle, Chief Gunner's Mate Orlop and Chief Quartermaster Blood. These three were tried and trusted men of recognized responsibility whose duties, because of the nature of the ship and her circumstances, bordered on those of officers and often, besides, called them ashore, at all hours of the day, to transactions in Base storehouses, shops, armories, and magazines. Two of them, Stengle and Orlop, stood few regular watches, being always on watch in a supervisory sense, and were actually heads of departments under Lieutenant Fitzpatrick and Ensign Woodbridge.

This extraordinary distinction was a comfort to Olgan. It strengthened his confidence in the promise of escape; and it lent corroboration to his argument, of which he never quite lost waking consciousness (sometimes he dreamed he was running *amok* at a great royal banquet, stripping all the waiters and guests of their clothes, which he burned in his stove, leaving everybody completely naked), that his rate bore no resemblance to that of a servant's. The appearance of the Cook's name on the free gangway list caused little of the sensation that it might have been expected to; perhaps because the men quite realized that its position there was but an empty compensation, realized it even without knowing that Lieutenant Fitzpatrick, as he informed him he was being put on the list, had cautioned Olgan that, after all, he must not stay ashore later than midnight on account of having to get up so early in the morning. Feenan was the only person who had commented emphatically on the matter, saying with prim sententiousness:

"If they put him on, they should put Portness on too."

Olgan never once was tempted to abuse the apparent rights of being on the list. As a matter of fact, he usually was too tired to take advantage even of what there safely was in it for him. This consisted in leaving the ship every night around half-past eight, when he finished cleaning up the galley and himself after supper, and remaining away from it for about three hours; but he usually went only on Wednesdays, when the easy supper, a cold meal of potato salad, canned corned beef, cold beans, canned peaches and iced tea, left him with a modicum of energy. When he did go, dressed in his tailor-made but ill-fitting uniform and with his colourless, water-combed hair carefully parted on the side, he almost invariably took refuge in some dim, quiet, shabby place like a bar-room on the verge of bankruptcy or a brothel sheltering three or four lonely, middle-aged women, places where he could feel secure from pressure or violence of any kind; and he would sit there resting patiently, his mug of beer held with both hands, his stooped, dandruff-specked shoulders curved defensively about him, his small, milky eyes darting an occasional alert glance at the street door, until his time was up, sit there pacifically in his shadowy corner like some beady-eyed rodent fumbling unurgently with a piece of cheese.

The seventh exception to the rule that all hands must help coal ship was "Unc" Blood, the Chief Quartermaster, who always asserted the prerogative of his rate, seniority and position to assume the duty of Quartermaster on watch for the whole day of coaling. He performed this duty on such occasions, long-glass tucked under his arm in traditional fashion and strolling in view of his toiling shipmates whenever possible, with a peculiar offhand manner and dignity that in no sense apologised for the summary method by which he had escaped the drill. Rather this air was a positive emphasizing, a flaunting of his sedulous pretence, a pretence which he knew the ship regarded as ridiculous, of being a privileged if not a distinguished naval person. Aboard ship he never put this pretence into actual words save in the most roundabout way. This consisted in his perennially telling and retelling, in a quiet, harsh, contemptuous voice, of the successive periods, before he joined the Navy, when he was a surgeon, a professional baseball player, the Master of a clipper ship, an aviator, a confidant of the fabulously great, an architect, a Central American General, a prospector in the Klondike or a dancing master; which tales he always ended up with a veiled but unmistakable inference that his present situation must be of an importance surpassing those of his past or he would not deliberately have abandoned them for it. By reason of some mysterious force in his personality, even habitually scornful and tough-minded men, men who certainly did not believe him or fear the cruel glint in his steady gaze, dared listen with nothing but feigned respect to his skilful, aggressive boasting, which, according to the Pharmacist's Mate, who behind his back grimly kept a sort of clinical time chart on this irrefutable history, proved him to be nearly one hundred and seven years of age. Ashore, however, in large home ports such as Brooklyn, Boston, Seattle or San Francisco, when he found himself with people who knew little or nothing about the Navy, "Unc" Blood *had* put the pretence directly into words. His quiet, hearty, businesslike admission that he was a Naval Officer, an admission aided by his impressive, grey-streaked brown beard and mustachios and abetted by the fact that a Chief Petty Officer's uniform and cap bear a general resemblance to those of a Commissioned Officer, more than once had introduced him into middle-class fields and groves far beyond the saloons, eating places and brothels comfortably accessible to enlisted men, greener fields wherein not only his "distinction," his "high naval prestige" could graze unfettered, but also where his unsubdued though aging loins found an added stimulation amidst the relatively greater elegance, fragility and choiceness of the nymphs.

Whether the indirect, difficult, empty form of this social pretence that persisted aboard ship was but sustaining practice for the easier and fuller version that flourished ashore, or whether it was the other way round, the shipboard version of it never tainted his relationship to his work. He did not pretend in regard to that. He seemed to know precisely how much he did know about the life of the ship, which was a great deal, and what he was capable of for her; and he never once was caught presuming beyond it. He was in fact, so good at what he knew that neighbouring ships of the Fleet sometimes borrowed him when there was some exacting piece of work to be done, a sextant to be repaired, a sounding machine to be overhauled; and he would go off in the duty boat wearing his air of privilege and distinction and stroking the right wing of his mustachios in the most dignified manner imaginable; but when he got there, and had looked at what was to be done, he promptly would disclose, punctuating his curt honesty with the harsh sniffing sound he habitually made at the back of his throat, whether or no he understood the job and could do it.

The men sweating in the barges long had become accustomed to "Unc" Blood's legal evasion of Coaling Ship; but there was not one among them, not even Cavendish and Arnold whose watches he had usurped on the present occasion, who would not wryly but sincerely have admitted, if forced to judge him as he periodically passed by up there on the deck like a tough but stately old satyr strutting about amidst the slowly rising swirls of dark dust, that he was the most resourceful watch Quartermaster, the steadiest helmsman, the most experienced signalman, the sharpest look-out and, without question, the best all-round man for the watch through this long, dirty, tired day of confusion and unalertness.

Save for these seven men on duty or semi-duty, the half of the crew that remained aboard endured a share of Coaling Ship either up on deck or down in the bunkers; and they hated the black turmoil almost as much as those shovelling in the barges. Some of them, those on deck working the booms and steam winches that hauled up the huge, rectangular, sail-cloth bags the men in the barges filled with coal, were excluded from the ameliorating competition between port and starboard barges on account of having to serve both sides impartially. There were two booms forward, situated just abaft the break of the forecastle, one boom projecting at a high angle out over the forward barge on the starboard side, the other in similar fashion out over the forward barge on the port side. These two booms were served alternately by the forward winch, at the valve lever of which was Feenan, the Oiler. Handling the thick fall that coiled in and out from the winch's drum as a full bag was hoisted or an empty one lowered, was Hardwood, the Seaman. In charge there was Barnes, the Blacksmith, a large, ordinary man of thirty-seven, as genial as he was imperturbable, whose extensive baldness was of the sort most appropriately seen at the glass-topped desk of a managerial office or behind the spread of a *Saturday Evening Post* on a commuters' train.

As a matter of fact, he was a subscriber to the *Saturday Evening Post*. Most of his leisure time aboard ship, when he was not playing pinocle, he spent in either reading it or using it as a shield for his eyes while napping, both of which relaxations he enjoyed stretched out, with an appearance of lying in a porch hammock, on his bunk down in the Chief Petty Officers' Compartment, when there was a breeze coming through the port-holes, or up on the forecastle in the shadow of the Forward Conning-tower when there was no breeze. Sometimes, in such moments, he smoked an Owl Cigar; smoked it rather neatly, not chewing its end, as Feenan did, but rolling or grasping it lightly between his almost straight lips and fairly regular teeth.

He rarely smoked while at work; for then it was his custom to whistle, especially if what he was doing consisted in some sustained application of hack-saw, smaller hammers or oxyacetylene torch. He did not whistle out loud, but simply kept his lips slightly puckered in a mere rhythmical expulsion of air that was practically silent. When he paused briefly every now and then to inspect the progress of what he was doing, one could tell whether it was *Oh, You Beautiful Doll!* or *Alma, Sweet Alma, Where Do You Live?* that he was whistling (invariably it was one or the other), because in the pauses he permitted the soft exhalations to assume more force and definition. Probably, he preferred this quiet style of rendition, and would have whistled thus in whatever world he found himself working. If so, then his whistling was unrestrained; if not, then it must have been held in check by a rigidly respected taboo of incalculable antiquity decreeing that on a man-of-war, though he may hum to his heart's content or even burst into song, no officer or man may whistle. This taboo arose, according to some, out of the necessity to exclude any sound that might conflict with the call of the boatswain's pipe, an odd-shaped silver whistle which, on larger ships, still hangs on a cord from the neck of a Boatswain's Mate, and on which he pipes the eerie bars that, while in no sense competing with or duplicating the functions of the bugle, preface each routine, shouted order, that officially welcome and speed the honoured guest, that bid a formal farewell to the departing dead. However, although this explanation of the taboo's origin seems reasonable enough, there are hints, along the Frisian Sand Banks and in the Aegean, as well as amidst the isles of the Sunda, the Banda and the Sulu seas, that long before the shrill pipes of the Greek boatswains urged their oarsmen into the Battle of Salamis seamen had consecrated the whistling of their lips to the demons of the sea and the gods of the wind.

Through the morning and in the first couple of hours after the midday meal, the Blacksmith had whistled, in his silent fashion, as he went about the monotonous business of seeing that his pair of booms promptly and neutrally hoisted as much coal as the men in the two competing forward barges could shovel. As the punishing afternoon wore on, however, the genial pucker of his lips gave way to a straight, compressed line, and his broad, coal-streaked, perspiring face, in a further concession to fatigue, took on a good-naturedly grim expression; but the movements of his ample body, which displayed the beginnings of a paunch, lost little of their easy, competent tone and style. He gave the impression, the amiable impression under the turned-down brim of his regulation white hat (which bestowed upon him the droll aspect of a business man on a picnic), that he could go on like this forever, padding effortlessly back and forth across the deck between the two booms, putting his heavy but inconspicuous shoulder to first one boom and then the other in order to swing the suspended load near the bunker hole, helping the two Firemen there dump the bag, adroitly signalling Feenan and Hardwood to lower it, empty, back down into the barge, and then, before making the trip across the deck again, glancing at Hardwood to see that he was replacing the fall on the drum with that for the other side.

The two booms aft, situated just forward of the galley and served by the after winch, were similar in every detail to the two forward; and Cord, the Boilermaker, his tall, thin, calm frame overlayed with coal dust from the top of his uncovered blond head to the bottom of his long, slim, sandalled feet, ran them in a manner to which there seemed to be no suggestive style and tone. In the very midst of his management the Boilermaker presented a slightly apologetic appearance, as if in reality he were quite detached from it; and every now and then, for no apparent reason, a faint, naïve smile would flit from beneath his small, drooping mustaches across the narrow expanse of his tired but untroubled Saxon face. He did not seem to be perspiring as much as Hemple, the Machinist's Mate, who was at the valve lever of the after winch, or anywhere near as much as Ferguson, the Seaman, belligerently handling the falls on the drum; yet he was getting precisely the same efficient, impartial result with his two competing barges as Barnes, the Blacksmith, was getting up forward there.

Unlike those at winch and boom, the eight men on deck (four to a side) receiving the coal at the round bunker holes, and the twelve men below (six to a side) stowing it in the bunkers, definitely were partisans in the race between port and starboard barges. Each of them, men such as Morrow and Easterly at the two starboard holes forward or Hector and Louis Carey at the two starboard holes aft, were rated as professional coal handlers, trained at shovelling it, passing it, stowing it and burning it. Much of the decision as to whether port or starboard would win the race rested in their calloused and expert hands; because if those on a side did not make room for the new loads of coal, around the deck holes and in the bunkers, by quickly disposing of the old, then a hoist was skipped on that side and their party fell behind. Although their share of the swift work required the application of more skill and handling of more shovelfuls per man than that of the shovellers in the barges, they enjoyed a periodic change of scene and technic that dissembled the cruel interminableness of their effort. This occurred every two hours when the men up on deck at the holes changed places with an equal number from down in the bunkers, those narrow, steel tunnels where a man smothered in gloom and dust that seemed but a slightly less heavy version of the lumpy, semi-visible mass that shifted under and about him, and where almost as soon as he was confined there, he began to long incontinently for a sight of how the game was going up on the surface of that sea so smooth, so clear under the vivid airy freedom of the blue-white sky: a sea and sky that were, to those caught out there in the barges between them, little more or less than the close limits, flaming and malevolent, of the infernal field upon which they were struggling for a grimy victory which, as the meaningless hours passed, came to assume, and not unliterally, the desirability of a salvation.

People could be injured, even killed at the game, as Ensign Snell nearly proved in returning from one of his trips to scout the progress of the barges on the port side. Such casualties occurred when one of the huge, loaded bags swept a man off his feet, as it was being hoisted aboard ship by the boom, and crushed him against the bulwark of the barge, or, when the rising bag, swinging through the air above those who had filled it, fell from its hook upon them. For this reason Cruck personally attended, with a kind of pugnacious efficiency, to the hooking on and lurching departure of each bag from his barge. After he had hooked it on, he would order, "Stand from under!" and glare alertly along the path that the bag could be calculated to follow in the first moments of being dragged free. As soon as he saw that the way was clear or that the men who happened to be in it had heard him and begun to move, he would wave a signalling hand, accompanied by a yell of, "Take it away!" to Cord up at the boom; and then he would follow the bag, wrestling fiercely, semi-effectively, as with a recalcitrant monster, to keep it in the calculated path until, after lunging and slithering along dangerously for two or three yards, it fled up into the air.

All the phases of this hoisting operation developed within the same, swift, uninterrupted rhythm that dominated everything else having to do with coaling ship; consequently, when Ensign Snell dropped from the quarter-deck into the path of a load, there was opportunity for but a partial escape from it. Suffering the energy lag that victimized him every afternoon between the hours of three and four, and preoccupied with his reaction to another of Ensign Woodbridge's provoking smiles, he had been but half-way across the quarter-deck when Cruck shouted his warning, "Stand from under!" and as these shouts, continually being flung up from first one and then another of the four barges, had pointed significance only for those in their immediate vicinity, seeming no more than fragmentary parts of the general noise for those detached from them, Ensign Snell had not particularized the warning in relation to himself. He arrived at the starboard railing and began lowering himself to the barge an instant after Cruck, satisfied that the way was clear, had signalled the winch to hoist away. Once the officer had begun to lower himself, facing the side of the ship in accepted fashion and going down in a smart half-climb, half-jump, he was blind to what was going on in the barge at his back, could not see the lunging start of the bag. Cruck could not see what was happening either, because he had his sweaty left cheek and shoulder pressed hard against the bulge of the load in the struggle to keep it under control.

The men in the stern of the barge who had filled the bag, a group consisting of O'Connel, Warrington, Ragatzo, Rowe and Arnold, were in no state to observe anything, although they were only four yards or so from where Ensign Snell was descending. Shoulder to shoulder in a cloud of ebony dust, their fevered heads bent stiffly, their swollen feet stumbling in the jagged, uncertain footing, their hands, their forearms trembling with fatigue and tense with effort, their eyes stunned by glare and hypnotized by monotony of movement, they were shovelling coal, fighting the black, shifting, sliding mountain in front of them just as they had fought it all through the long tropical day. They already had forgotten the bag that, like some gorged but angry monster, was swishing and bumping along the gritty floor of the barge toward Ensign Snell. There was no reason why they should have remembered it longer than any other of the bags in the endless series they had filled since sunrise, no reason for following the course of its headlong departure, as a special case, past Cruck's shout of, "Take it away!" They were filling another one: But suddenly they were arrested, their heads turned, by a sense of something sharply amiss in the rhythm of movement and noise that immersed them. It was a chord of noise that was lacking: the dull, screaming whir of a winch had ceased out of tempo, the swish of a bag had ended too abruptly.

Cord, the Boilermaker, up at the boom, had caught sight of Ensign Snell just as the officer's feet touched the floor of the barge. The calm, quick signal of his thin hand had stopped the winch; but not in time to prevent the great bag from slugging into Ensign Snell's back at the very moment he was turning around. The officer did not know what was hitting him; but, as if the inception of the rounded impact had released in him a recourse to the wrestling and boxing tactics at which he had excelled in Annapolis, he instantly increased to a violent spin the normal turning movement his big body already had begun. This saved him from being carried along or falling in front of the bag, flung him off at a tangent to its path. He landed with a thud against the slope of the coal pile, where he kept making slight, futile, unconscious efforts to rise to his hands and knees, while the disturbed coal at the top of the slope commenced to slide noisily down about him. The bag, in the seconds before the winch managed to cease its pull, had skidded heavily on for three or four feet, then sagged to a stop against the bulwark with force enough to crush a bull.

Cruck, the instant he felt the bag relax, had jerked his shaggy head back for a glance up at the boom. Seeing nothing wrong, he stepped away from the bag and glared questioningly at Cord. The Boilermaker's fixed downward stare of consternation promptly swung Cruck around in the direction of its target, almost beside him; then he lunged for the prone form, which, on the instant, he did not realize was that of the officer, much as a heavy lineman goes for a fumbled football.

Throughout the little more than a second that it took for the Chief Boatswain's Mate to discover Ensign Snell's plight and start to his aid, the only other people in the barge who were aware of what had happened, the five men who had filled the bag, stood in a pitiful-looking line, like victims of adversity, and stared through sweat-blurred eyes, stared helplessly and without excitement, at the stunned form of the officer. They did, somehow, present a more pitiable, a more affecting sight than he as they stood there, precisely where they had straightened up from shovelling, exhausted, breathing hard, swaying on unsteady ankles. They gave the impression of beset men who suddenly and finally had been called upon to face an added ordeal that, unjust and unforeseen, betrayed their virtue and their goodwill. For them the peculiar, flabbergasting element in the accident, the element of novelty, that new twist to the familiar skein of a familiar type of event, that twist often so happily welcomed in times of normal strength and situation but now treacherously wounding the purposeful inertia that had been enabling them to carry on past the end of endurance, lay in the fact that the sprawling form embodied, not a *degree,* but a *kind* of quality that neither experience nor imagination had prepared them to encounter in these circumstances. If it had been one of themselves lying there as the result of such a blow, their capacity for reaction would have found little in the event that was not readily digestible despite their lessened strength and initiative. They would not have been haltingly scandalized, nor the prone form have been elusively but arrestingly disparaged. Thus, adjusting themselves to the shock of the novelty, the inappositeness of what their eyes were trying to take in, they stood through the long second: the formidable O'Connel, blackened, bareheaded, naked to the waist, his dungaree trousers rolled free of his ankles; Rowe, in a suit of regulation whites in lieu of the dungarees he had not yet had time to purchase, the jumper and trousers clinging to his sweat-drenched body like an uneven dip of fresh black mud, the upflaring brim of his once white hat grey with coal dust where it perched defiantly on the back of his once blond head; Arnold, the stiff rim of his old white hat turned down to protect his heat-flushed face in which the conspicuous pug nostrils were strangely rimmed with black, his worn dungaree jumper and trousers tied with cord at wrists and ankles to stem the dust; Warrington and Ragatzo, their flagrantly young, coal-tarnished bodies half naked like O'Connel's, their faces—that of the first blond, finely cut, that of the second coffee-coloured, blunt—shaded by the downturned brims of their white hats, from beneath which drooped sprigs of the fleshy green leaves that Ragatzo had gathered ashore in the meal hour as a charm against the sun. Then O'Connel tossed aside his shovel and waded vehemently through the sliding coal toward Ensign Snell. The next man to start was Rowe, but he hesitated after the first impulsive step and Ragatzo passed him, closely followed by Arnold. Warrington started last, yet he arrived beside the officer almost as soon as the rest.

As these five others crowded around, to be joined a second later by the four men from the head of the barge, Cruck, hands under Ensign Snell's shoulders, was raising him to his feet in impulsive response to the unproclaimed but almost religious tradition that an officer, like a flag, must never remain fallen. This restoration to the vertical position was so swiftly clearing the officer's head and re-establishing co-ordination that he was able to plant his feet and shake off Cruck's aiding hands. An unhappy moment more and he would have found himself being supported by other ready arms, being carried ignominiously aboard ship and down to his room. O'Connel had been reaching for his knees just as he had reasserted himself. Swaying groggily, his heavy face wearing the sullen, frustrated expression of a decent man struggling with the desire to strike out at something or somebody, Ensign Snell stood there for several seconds getting back into himself; while the ten men around him stared solemnly, silently, alertly, waiting for some sign, one way or the other, of his condition.

"Footwork," muttered Ensign Snell brusquely, "a little slow."

With this he took a stumbling, uncertain step to the spot where he had lain, the group about him parting with cautious solicitude to let him by, and stooped to pick up his cap there. As he bent over he nearly fell on his face, but saved himself by thrusting out a stiff arm into the shifting facets of coal. In this position, his free hand fumbling for the cap, the faint, deep smell of the agitated coal again flooded his nostrils. It repelled him, helped send him, with a haste that amounted to a reflexive jerk, back upright to his feet; but he had retrieved the cap, which he proceeded to adjust in its customary, solid but careless-appearing place on his head. Then with slightly trembling motions he took out a cigarette and lit it behind cupped hands that shielded the expression of his eyes and mouth. As if the cigarette were slow in lighting, he continued to shield his face in this manner during the time it took him to turn and walk, as if nothing had happened, to the corner he favoured there in the cleared corner of the barge. This evidently was the kind of sign the men about him were waiting for; because the moment he reached the corner and curtly tossed the expended match overboard, Cruck signalled Cord to hoist away, and the other nine, with quick curses of encouragement for themselves and one another, moved to resume their shovelling; moved to resume it just as the rumour that Ensign Snell had been hurt brought the men from the forward barge crowding, with scandalized faces, to find, as they had thought, that it was not true. In the barges on the other side of the ship, at the same moment, this rumour, sharpened from "hurt" to "killed," also halted the game. The men there were prevented from climbing over the deck to see for themselves only by the determined commands of Orlop and Bidot, who gathered from a gesture of Ensign Woodbridge's, as that officer impetuously made for the other side of the ship, that that was what he wanted.

Half-way across the quarter-deck, Ensign Woodbridge's face instantly, brilliantly smoothed out into its wonted, slightly sardonic expression, which had been dissolved by a rush of wild concern. He slowed his leaping progress to the rapid, confident pace that so suited him, and let the held breath out of his lungs with a short "Ha!" that could have sounded like a fragment of restrained laughter. He had caught sight of Ensign Snell's head. "Whatever it is," he reassured himself with a relief that became enthusiasm, "he's on his feet!"

When Ensign Woodbridge reached the rail, near the stern, and casually leaned over it to gaze down at his friend, his face was wearing the same smile full of sharp-edged gaiety that he had sent at him from the top of his coal piles; but his eyes quickly were noting every detail of Ensign Snell's now considerably blackened person.

"What's the matter? . . . Pace too tough for you?" demanded Ensign Woodbridge.

"Ten to five we whip you," replied Ensign Snell.

He lit a fresh cigarette from the half-burned old one, shielding his face with his cupped hands as before. This did not prevent Ensign Woodbridge from observing the stunned expression on that big, obdurate, so well-known face. He observed, too, that the hands were just visibly trembling. He turned his head and, without disturbing his slightly jeering smile, darted a sharp, questioning glance at Cruck.

"The bag . . . grazed him, Sir," said Cruck, shifting his gaze away toward Ensign Snell, a gaze of apology and appeal from one forced into not minding his own business.

In a series of rapid, casual movements Ensign Woodbridge lowered himself into the barge and faced his friend. Nobody paid any further attention to them, for the shovelling was again in full progress; besides, with the arrival there of Ensign Woodbridge the men confidently relinquished all responsibility for their officer's plight, if he was in one. "These two knew how to handle each other," was the way any of them might have expressed the consensus; and the two did know, had known ever since their beginnings at the Academy together.

A few seconds after Ensign Snell had been knocked down, "Unc" Blood hastily had climbed up the bridge ladder and called the accident to the attention of Lieutenant Fitzpatrick, who was up there with his binoculars fixed yearningly on a boating excursion that was departing from the Naval Station Dock. He, together with the Captain, Ensign Woodbridge and Ensign Snell, had been invited by the ladies of the Station to go on the excursion, but he had had to forego it in order to attend Delilah, as Officer of the Deck, through the day of coaling. At the Chief Quartermaster's urgent, informing shout, he had jerked his eyes from the levelled binoculars and stared aft at Ensign Snell's barges. The sight of the khaki-clad body in the coal had sent him dashing all of a sudden for the ladder, the forgotten binoculars swinging recklessly from the strap about his neck. He had collided with Blood in his heedless rush, sending the Chief Quartermaster staggering backwards for a step, and had gone down the ladder so unrestrainedly that he had slithered the first few steps. The effort at recovering his balance had brought the Executive Officer sharply to himself, and he had continued on down to the deck with a grim, tense deliberateness that had taxed all his self-control. He even had managed to pause at the railing, with an air of calmness that fought a stomach loaded with suspense, to watch Cruck pull "the damn little fool" to his feet. Then through the binoculars he had studied the big, groggy form until it had tossed the match over the side . . . Nothing broken, apparently. He had started walking aft with his false air of calmness at about the time that Ensign Woodbridge had arrived on the quarter-deck above where Ensign Snell was standing. He had increased his pace with a slight access of nervousness when Ensign Woodbridge had climbed down into the barge . . . "Maybe there is something wrong with him after all . . . When one of *those* bags drops on a man, something happens . . . "

The Executive Officer and the Captain encountered each other, as if by happenstance, abreast of the After Conning-tower; for the Captain, in his fashion, had rushed up there too. Through the Pantry port-hole Ah Lee, an excitable, serious man, had seen Ensign Snell's fall and had waited for no more than their having had to lift him up to fling himself into the Captain's Cabin virtually screaming something to the effect that "Mr. Snell he down . . . down . . . hurted down!" The Chinaman had run out of words here but had sustained his report with a fierce, jabbing, pointing gesture at the starboard bulkhead. The Captain, who had been writing at his desk, had at once put down his fountain-pen and reached for his spectacle case. He had taken the spectacles out and adjusted them as he had risen to his feet.

"Mr. Snell, you say?"

"Oh, yes, yes, Captain . . . Quick! . . ." was what the reply seemed to have been in a chattering moan, "You know them bag! . . . Mr. Snell . . . bad, bad!"

On the desk, near where he had tossed the empty spectacle case instead of putting it in his pocket, had lain the thin cigar he had been waiting for the proper time to smoke. (His wife had his promise that he would smoke but one every two hours.) He had taken up the cigar, lit it thoroughly, put on his cap and left his cabin with no more physical fluster than if he had been going up to have a look at the weather; but he had exclaimed to himself as he had walked through the passage-way to the conning-tower ladder. "Now if that boy has gone and got himself injured!" had been the Captain's exclamation; and it had reflected the general extent to which Ensign Snell's prestige had suffered by having been knocked down, for the Captain rarely, even in the privacy of his own mind, referred to his officer as "that boy."

The Captain had reached the quarter-deck as Ensign Woodbridge had finished climbing down into the barge. He had accepted the fact of Ensign Snell's being on his feet as evidence that the Chinaman had been guilty of excited exaggeration: and he had taken it as a good sign that Cruck was urging on the work in his usual fashion. "He wouldn't be carrying on like that," the Captain told himself, "if anything were seriously the matter." Cruck, who always referred to any group of opponents, friendly or otherwise, as a "gang of sons o' bitches," was yelling at the men in both barges:

"Come on! Come on! . . . Get going! That gang of sons o' bitches 'll get ahead of us!"

The Captain continued to stand there, just outside the conning-tower door, puffing easily now and then at the cigar, with his face turned in the general direction of the Fuel Dock, on the edge of which the red-faced Warrant Officer was standing, arms akimbo, glaring at the scene of the accident with the air of a man who has taken a strong stand and witnessed its justification. The Captain did not change his seemingly casual position or make any comment when Lieutenant Fitzpatrick joined him. There was no need to. They both knew that "if there was anything wrong, Woodbridge would haul him up out of there."

Facing each other down in the barge, their eyes no more than fourteen inches apart, the two friends were gazing a steady, clear question and answer through a silent moment, a Wardroom moment, that both recognized as one beyond the province of everyday rivalry, face-saving, sporting pretence or decent reticence. A slight, communicative smile, precisely the same smile, wrinkled the skin about their eyes and flickered at the corners of their mouths.

"All right?" was the question in Ensign Woodbridge's gaze.

"O.K." was the answer in Ensign Snell's.

Ensign Woodbridge unjustly scrupled a moment beyond the clear answer, his acceptance snagged by the thought that the man before him was one of those absurd, stubborn creatures who had seen fit to play through a whole quarter against Army without confessing to a set of broken ribs. This moment of supererogation gave Ensign Snell the ascendency. While his trace of a smile broadened to a grin that nevertheless retained a quality of discomposure, he proceeded to flex first one arm and then the other, briefly shift his weight from foot to foot. Ensign Woodbridge not only felt the touch of the barb in this gesture but realized that he was, that he could be satisfied. With this realization, as if it had been an evident signal, they were safely, comfortably free, both at the same instant but each in his distinct manner, to reclothe themselves, to not be themselves again. Ensign Woodbridge turned away, with a derisive wave of the hand of what he now pretended to consider as the other's clownishness, and headed for his own barges, where the men, reassured by a report from Cord, were again shovelling to win the game.

The patronizing smile, patronizing for Ensign Snell, that Ensign Woodbridge bestowed upon the Captain and the Executive Officer, as he passed them, tartly dispelled any remaining apprehension they may have had; and they proceeded to behave as if they never had had any.

"The Boatswain there," said the Captain to Lieutenant Fitzpatrick, "still seems put out." He accompanied his words with a smiling glance at the Warrant Officer on the Fuel Dock.

"Probably afraid you won't let him coal the other boats either."

The Captain's china-blue eyes narrowed about a twinkle that came into them in response to something he sensed beneath his officer's reply; and he commented in his innocent, dry tone, as he moved away:

"There'll be other picnics, Mr. Fitzpatrick."

Lieutenant Fitzpatrick took a hasty step after the Captain as if bent on making a protest against this insinuation; but he took no more than the first step, after which he stopped, with a grimly affectionate smile and a hopeless shake of the head for the recalcitrant quality in that otherwise so estimable man.

The Captain, puffing evenly at his cigar, strolled on forward along the deck until he was opposite the Warrant Officer standing on the Fuel Dock. He glanced across at him in a way that indicated his intention to join him there; then, after removing his spectacles and stowing them in one of the gold-buttoned breast pockets of his white blouse, went on to carry out his intention, lowering himself to the forward end of the after barge, across which he made his way to the ladder against the low face of the dock.

Abetted by Cruck and the Carpenter's Mate, the men adjacent to the Captain's path, in both barges, but simulated continuance of their work in order to keep a respectful, precautionary eye on him until he was half-way up the dock ladder; at which point Ensign Snell breathed a dizzy ejaculation of relief over the fact that, clearly, the Captain's movement was aimed at nothing concerning him.

As the Captain climbed to the dock and stood up to face the Warrant Officer, he was met by a wave of dank but fragrant coolness that poured out of the jungle close behind the dock to dissolve in the limitless blaze of heat that lay upon the water.

"You have it some cooler here," said the Captain, as he removed his cap the better to enjoy the momentarily perceived change.

"That was a nasty bang he took there, Commander," said the red-faced Boatswain, incontinently displaying his harsh air of unaccustomed sympathy that was merely a mask for his now triumphant reproach.

"I'll bet it was," agreed the Captain. He put his cap back on and took the horn-rimmed spectacles out of his pocket, but, instead of emplacing the spectacles, kept them cradled in his loosely clenched right hand. His tone was social, even placative, the tone of his purpose in making this visit.

"I saw it coming, Sir," said the Boatswain, "and tried to warn him . . . But with all that racket . . ." He paused to mop at his face with the red bandanna.

What he said was true. He had come out of his little shack of an office on the dock for a periodic glare at the progress of the coaling, and had shouted, "Watch it, Mr. Snell!"

"Does raise a din," smiled the Captain agreeably, permitting his gaze to travel from group to group of the familiar figures toiling there in the two barges between him and his ship. He was thinking that, though they looked a little soft, and a little too tired, they still handled themselves easily and well. With a hoarse, deeply vibrating roar, an excess of steam billowed from Delilah's escape valve atop the fuming stack. It was like a sustained cry of triumph, of readiness, of renewed strength. The Captain's matter-of-fact being did not apprehend her manifestation in this guise; yet a flick of something that was not inconsonant with it sprang to life at the corners of his sizeable mouth.

"It wouldn't have happened . . . couldn't have . . . with my wheelbarrows," said the Boatswain with a stubbornness of which, as he said this, he began to be faintly self-conscious.

"Without question," agreed the Captain. "And look here." He turned to face the Boatswain squarely. "I've got no objection to them. That system you've worked out is thoroughly practical." He gestured toward the barges with the hand containing the spectacles. "You can see what I was after."

While the Captain was out on the dock encouraging the Boatswain to see that what he was after had nothing to do with that veteran personally, Lieutenant Fitzpatrick went back up to the bridge for another look at the boats of what the Captain had called the "picnic." They were steering a course straight for Grande Island, out toward the mouth of the bay, two of the Station's big motor-sailers, each towing a whaleboat. The two motor-sailers, filled with white uniforms and gay dresses, were travelling side by side in order, as Lieutenant Fitzpatrick could see through his binoculars, that those in one might laugh and talk with those in the other. He did not need to train his glasses on the towed whaleboats; he knew just about what they always took in those: a couple of mess boys, a crock of salad, a load of roasted chickens, perhaps some steaks for grilling, a basketful of cake and mangoes, hunks of ice wrapped in tarpaulins and a tank of orange juice into which would be poured, with conventional secrecy, the flasks of gin carried in the pockets of the white uniforms . . . There'd be beer, too, for the "steady hands," brought down from Subic in a *banco*. He smiled a trifle condescendingly beneath the levelled binoculars at the seriousness with which some people took that absurd General Order about liquor . . . especially Commanding Officers . . . must be the age creeping up on them . . . Yet they were all in the conspiracy against that other order . . . the venereal order . . . and they could whip this one also if they wanted to . . . But the Captain of the Yard, despite his being a "hoister" from way back, never even would go on the parties to Grande, though the island really wasn't part of the Station . . . said "what he didn't know didn't hurt him" . . . And the Captain . . . His smile lost its condescending quality and he lowered the glasses for an instant of open, sympathetic laughter . . . Why the Captain would give his own grandmother a court martial if he caught her taking a drink aboard Delilah! . . . As if his bungalow in Manila wasn't filled with it! . . . But the Captain was hipped on that idea about alcohol and machinery . . .

He turned for a glance aft to where the Captain still was standing on the dock talking to the Warrant Officer. He noticed that the sun had begun to lose its scorch and that its light had grown softer. A drift of distant singing reached him from across the inert, glinting water. He turned toward the "picnic" boats again, which, some two miles off, had reached a spot directly opposite Delilah. Yes, they were singing . . . as if they already had been sampling the orange juice. As soon as he had the glasses properly focused on them he seemed to be able to hear them better . . . And he could see Laura, the Captain's wife, and that bride of the Doctor's . . . They were waving at the ship. He freed one of his hands from the binoculars and waved back. How the men ganged up on that poor kid of a bride! . . . It was disgusting . . . Just let any new white female show her face in these God-forsaken islands and they behaved like . . . He definitely could follow the words of the song they were singing . . . "We went sailing along . . . down Moonlight Bay . . ." He assured himself that the reason for his being able to make out the words so clearly was because he knew what they would be singing . . . That was the trouble with life in the Navy . . . They always did the same things in the same way . . . By the time they reached the island it would be *If I Knocked the L Out of Kelley* or, if the

Station's Executive Officer had his way, *My Little Grey Home In the West* . . . And on the way home in the moonlight . . . they would start back with *Down the Old Green River On the Good Ship Rock and Rye* . . . but they would end up, singing it over and over again, with *We Won't Go Back To Zambo' Anymore.*

24 〜〜〜

After brooms had been tossed down into the emptied barges (Ensign Snell's had won by half a ton or so), and the last remaining scatter of coal dust had been swept up into the shovels and tossed into the last bag, the men climbed wearily back aboard ship, replaced deck bunker-hole covers, broke out the hoses and began washing her down. While the tug hauled away the two port barges, one after another, Lieutenant Fitzpatrick made the engine-rooms ready for getting under way. He went about this routine procedure with a suppressed excitement, a sense of expectancy amounting well-nigh to discomfort, that brought home to him, vividly for the first time, just how long it was since Delilah had been alive as a ship. Some equivalent of this emotion must have been struggling for possession of Chief Machinist's Mate Stengle also, because his little, brown, dirty face was stressed grimly about the line of his compressed lips as if in disapproval, not of what he was calmly and ably helping Lieutenant Fitzpatrick to do, but of the excitement that it was trying to arouse in him. "All this fuss," he irritably muttered to himself despite the fact that no one was visibly making any, "just for a couple of new tubes and cylinders." Even when Stengle called a routine warning, through the voice-tube, up to the bridge that they were going to test the engines, his people, a tired pair in each engine-room, gave little sign of meriting his charge; they simply spat, or frowned, or smiled carelessly, each assuming the ordinary mask of his custom under such circumstances, and made ready to open the throttles for a brief shot of steam into the renovated cylinders.

Up on the bridge, where the Captain was ostensibly studying the weather, and Ensign Woodbridge, beside him, was refilling his pipe and faintly smiling to himself, the warning from the engine-room voice-tube produced no unusual demonstration either; nor a couple of minutes later, after the bridge had taken the proper precautions astern and so informed the engine-rooms, did the actual brief turning of the screws themselves: the blades of first the right and then the left flopped slowly, heavily over three or four times beneath Delilah's flat stern, sending a profound, healthy shiver through the ship and a spread of lively foam to the surface of the water. Ensign Woodbridge, stimulated to the point of a congratulatory exclamation by this vigorous proof of revival, quickly took his pipe from his mouth and darted an enthusiastic glance at the Captain; then he halted the exclamation on its first note, transformed it into a brief chuckle, put the pipe back between his excellent, smile-bared teeth and emulated the Captain's posture of searching for a sign of weather in the sky; but he knew that the Captain was not hunting for any sign up there. Down on the deck, however, where the men, aggressive with fatigue, were attacking every dust-covered surface with streams of sea water from the big hoses, the enthusiasm did have its moment of exclamation. As the heavy thud of the starboard propeller vibrated through the ship, Hardwood, who was directing the nozzle of one of the hoses, stopped dead in his tracks, shot a reckless blast of water at the break of the forecastle and yelled exultantly:

"God damn!"

The flare of this demonstration pierced the fatigue befogging the sensibilities of the men surrounding him, dispelled it for an interval through which they felt her living again beneath their feet, felt not only the great, preparatory stir of her limbs but the steady throbbing of her pumps, the current in her metallic veins, the hum of her breathing. Grouped there about the hoses or over buckets and scrub rags, they paused to glance around at one another with unexpected smiles of ingenuous excitement.

The Captain had told the Captain of the Yard that he wanted to take his ship, as soon as she was coaled, up Subic Bay for a little shakedown trip; he also had mentioned to Ensign Woodbridge his purpose of staying at the head of the bay long enough to put the crew through a small-arms practice on the range up there; and he had suggested to Lieutenant Fitzpatrick that it would provide a good opportunity for giving the men an overnight liberty in Subic, a larger and more lively sort of town than Olongapo, as a compensation for making them coal ship when it was not "necessary"; the fact of the matter probably was, although he believed what he said, that he just wanted to feel her move again, feel her steaming along quit and normally independent of the land once more, ready with the added strength and fitness he had envisioned, in that bygone moment down south, as being so urgent for her. Whatever his reason, he proceeded to cast her off, shortly after the tug had hauled away the two port barges, and head her up the bay. He managed the not too easy manoeuvre of getting her away from the Fuel Dock with a prompt, effortless, unostentatious skill that made Ensign Woodbridge gaze in the same sort of admiring way the Captain did at him when he told one of his stories. It occurred to Ensign Woodbridge, as he took it in, that there was something of the nature of inspiration in his handling of her, that he somehow was deriving a greater illumination from this time of rebeginning than were the rest of them. It was only six miles from where they lay up to the head of the bay, but to his officer's eye the Captain, beneath an ordinary, everyday exterior, was initiating that brief voyage as if it were one into significant, into exacting possibility.

Even after she was safely on her way, with Kalakan Point abaft the beam, the Captain continued to con her on up the bay himself. Besides Ensign Woodbridge, ready to relieve him, there were two other people on the bridge, Bidot, at the wheel, and "Unc" Blood, the Quartermaster on watch; but it almost seemed as if the ship and her Captain alone were accomplishing the leisurely sprint up the smooth reach of that narrow bay bordered by glinting masses of bamboo, palm trees and the clustered raggedness of plantains, that bay so closely framed in jungle-clad peaks and rises that it gave the impression of being a high, mountain pool played upon by airs that were warm, humid, oppressive and by a dying light that was preternaturally clear. Up from behind the dark green symmetry of Mount Maybe, on the left, delicately floated a black and yellow sunset, low in the lucent blue sky, almost precise in its arrangement of long, flat, alternate strokes of colour, like an art display of Nature. Standing there beneath the glowing shade of the bridge awning, beside the hooded breech of the three-inch gun, with his cap in one hand and his uncased spectacles in the other, the Captain spoke to nobody but the ship, spoke to her dry, brief phrases in a tone of confidence that no more were meant for the helmsman who conveyed them than were words spoken into a telephone meant for it. Through his long stretches of silence he might have been listening to the soft chatter and hiss of the darkening, blue-green water that curled up on either side of her thin bow. The faint breeze, engendered by her steadily throbbing progress, touched the cowlick at the back of his bare head; he seemed to the two men, as Bidot phrased it to himself, "on his toes"; he seemed, to Ensign Woodbridge, in a way intoxicated; to himself he seemed, without in the slightest degree consciously inspecting the state of his feelings, calmly and lucidly exalted, more joyful than he ever had felt before.

Behind him, down the whole length of the ship, the men were tiredly but uncompromisingly restoring her to the condition that is the most obvious characteristic of a man-of-war, even of a "black boat": a clean tidiness, with every object, every appurtenance in a fitting and prearranged place. They unshipped the coaling booms and stowed them below, restrung the bronze cables of the railing, restacked the spare shovels in the Engineer's Storeroom, put the heavy bags back in what still was called the Sail Locker and, as soon as they had finished washing her down, began spreading the deck awning.

It was quite dark by the time they finished lashing the last stretch of the awning in place, and more than two hours after the ship, staining the evening sky above her forward stack with light smudges of brownish smoke, had panted in over the smooth water to an anchorage a half mile or so off the mouth of the Guadagi, a slow, wild river that came down out of the monkey-inhabited jungle to scavenge and bathe the western edge of the sprawling town. Most of the men now worked with impatient, jerky energy to finish their last tasks, putting aside their fatigue much as the Romans, using a kind of contempt in lieu of the modern anodynes, disregarded their casual pains and infirmities; for, shortly after the anchor had been dropped, a list had been posted on the side of the galley naming the two-thirds of the crew who were to be given overnight liberty as soon as work was done. The faint, luring drifts of odour that a shifting breeze occasionally wafted off from the town, an exotic aroma, sour, pungent, dry, blended of heavy jungle fragrances, stale fish, damp matting, human excrement, wood fires and frying fat, seemed to spur the ordinary working movements of those on the list to a tempo that gave an impression of increasing competitively as more and more men, singly and in groups, finished what they had to do and made for their wash buckets and clean clothes, darting, as they went, grimly eager glances at the distant sparks and blots of yellow light that had begun to cluster the dark shore. As if their punishing day of fierce labour had but levelled and intensified the desire to live that had been reawakened by their return to the sea, their loins swelled at the thought of the primitive women imminent across there in the obscurity; and they became inordinately conscious of hunger for the mean kind of food available in that town, thirsted like addicts for its cheap, imported beer and whiskey, for its fiery brandy distilled from the ichor of local palm trees.

A share of the liberty party's excitement arose also from the prospect of getting, for once, all they wanted of what, in this out-of-the-way bay, was considered a rare and good thing; for men from the Station and ships at Olongapo almost never were permitted to remain away later than midnight, and the trip to Subic and back, feasible only by water, alone disposed of anywhere from two to four of their hours, depending on whether they made it fortunately in a motor-sailer or at all odds in a native *banco*. This glamorous desirability of Subic as a place in which to spend liberties was decidedly relative. It arose, not simply out of the tantalization of a persistently too brief enjoyment of it, nor out of the fact that the town was the largest collection of nipa houses on the bay; but chiefly out of the circumstance that the village of Olongapo, the only other sizeable place, was, together with the bungalows and one-story, corrugated-iron-roofed build-ings of the Navy Yard, the Hospital Ship, the floating dry dock and the Fuel Dock, at the centre of an extended area designated as a Naval Reservation, on which were tolerated no vending of liquor, no prostitution, no friendship between Navy man and native girl, no entertainment enterprise of any kind that was not strictly supervised by the naval administration. There was, in fact, but one such enterprise in Olongapo, unless a shack of a restaurant run by a Chinaman who had been a Captain's Steward could be counted also, and that was a rude, semi-open-air dance hall where, for a small price, the men soberly could dance with the village girls who gathered there nightly for the business. These very Asiatic little females, with Spanish names like Angelina, Clementina, Luz, Carmen or Dolores, and with oily, hot climate, hybrid-brown skin which they covered as thoroughly as possible with home-made, more or less American-style frocks, could not be escorted home or met afterwards; caught in the act of permitting such a thing meant, for the girl and her family, expulsion from the Reservation and exclusion from the work it provided. Going on liberty in the place was not like going on liberty at all; it was more like the off-duty hours spent aboard ship or in the Navy Yard. Even on the nights, once a week, when the dance hall was turned into a picture show, many of those who had enough time fled to the makeshift paradise up the bay. There, at the heart of a petty labyrinth of dark, mud streets, palms, plantains and stilted nipa shacks, they found a long, wide, thatch roof beneath which a man was on his own with something to drink, a plate of eggs and fried bananas, the music from eight or nine old records played on a still older Edison phonograph and a sparsely clad flock of strangely naïve little whores who, in the daytime, washed clothes in the river with their mothers, herded carabao with their brothers and gathered fruit from the topmost branches of the mango trees. True, there was the Naval Station Patrol, ten rough-and-tumble fighters armed with policeman clubs who arrived at Subic with the first liberty party in the afternoon and departed with the last at midnight; but it never interfered unless things assumed the proportions of a riot, a clash between the men and the natives or trouble with the two pompous Tagalogs who strutted about the place in uniforms of the Philippine Constabulary.

The rare event of a naval vessel steaming that far up into the bay and anchoring with an air of permanence had brought a scattered fleet of *bancos* out from the town, some paddled canoe fashion from the stern, others under the laziest of sail. A few more filled with mangoes, *papayas,* midget bananas or fish to sell, but the majority were motivated by nothing more than simple curiosity; and it was into some of these lingering empty craft, and others that hurried out as soon as the occasion was realized, that Delilah's liberty party tumbled, with an appearance of a sporadic abandonment of the ship, to fade jubilantly and abruptly away into the humid darkness.

Their work done, the third of the crew that were forced to remain aboard compensated themselves with a frank and unhampered relaxation into the fatigue they would have had to deny if their names had appeared on the liberty list; and they consoled themselves with the general feeling, only slightly infected by resignation, that when their turn came tomorrow they would be fresh and able to do it justice. ". . . And, hell," said Horner with a tired snarl, his heavily soaped body astraddle a wash bucket, "those guys ain't going to use up the place in one night." By the time Warrington, who had succeeded to the Quartermaster's Watch, had checked out no more than two or three of the first lucky groups to go down the port gangway, the stay-aboards managed an easy inattention to the rest of the departure that was positively disparaging. On the other hand, Ensign Snell, who had taken a shower and changed his clothes while the ship was making the trip, and now was Officer of the Deck, watched nearly the whole, group by group departure with an ingenuous envy that it did not occur to him either to conceal or to display. "The kind of binge those birds are piling into is just what I need," he told himself, with a cautious feel at the swollen and abrazed cheek from which he had been unable to remove all the tiny pits of coal. When the last and largest group, as spick and span as if it were leaving the ship for a liberty in Brooklyn or San Francisco, gathered beneath the electric light at the gangway to be checked out, he sighfully let his bruised body down into one of the wicker chairs on the quarter-deck. "I'm all dressed up too," were the wry, unspoken words of his sigh, "but they've got some place to go."

Ensign Snell was the only one of the officers on deck while the liberty party left. Lieutenant Fitzpatrick was down below taking a shower and putting on a clean uniform; and the Captain, who would have derived from the sight another portion of that particular satisfaction he was obtaining from this, as it were, seagoing day, had left the ship in the motor-dory, taking Ensign Woodbridge with him as a sort of aide, as soon as she had anchored. The wireless message, in code, that had provoked this unexpected withdrawal had been received just as Delilah, passing Pequeña Island, had slowed her engines to nose into the anchorage. Despite the clearly indicated urgency and importance of the message, the Captain had barely permitted its arrival on the bridge, at the hand of Portness, to ruffle the current of attention, serene, triumphant but unobtrusive, that he had been devoting to the end of that voyage. He had glanced at it, then handed it to the Signal Officer with the brief effort of a spiritually ready man for whom, at long last, the unexpected can prove neither untimely nor fatefully disturbing. Ensign Woodbridge, quieting his first rush of misgiving with the reassuring thought that so urgent and importantly coded a message could not possibly have anything to do with his missionary trouble, had taken the message aft to the Captain's Cabin for decoding; and on his way back to the bridge with the transcription, he had given Cruck orders to rig the starboard gangway and ready the dory for lowering; because the very official message had instructed the Captain to report immediately, in person, to the Captain of the Yard in Olongapo.

25 〜〜〜

For Warrington, as he went down the bridge ladder, at nine-thirty, on the routine trip along the deck to turn off the electric lights that glowed here and there beneath its awning, the ship wore a decidedly lonely if not an abandoned aspect. Perhaps it was on account of the blackness of the night, which obliterated not only land and water but surrounding space itself. Pausing at the break of the forecastle, on the top step of the next ladder, which, just below his feet, dropped through an opening in the deck awning, he took in the long, slim length of the anchored ship so warmly aglow with unbold light. She seemed to crouch there, close to the unseen water, as if intimidated by the limitless darkness at the core of which she found herself. He turned his gaze upward to the sky in a gesture that might have appeared to an onlooker as one aimed at detecting the cause of the intimidation. His gaze encountered no fabulous, predatory hovering, nothing but the infinite blackness; save where a small, sharply defined, uneven rift in it disclosed, as above the top of some chasm in the universe, and at a greater distance than he ever had imagined or dreamed, a few eerily vivid stars that gave no light, that hung there, in the sombre blue clarity above that unthinkably deep hole in black nothingness, looking awesomely, three-dimensionally like what they really were, like vast globes of molten metal, like monstrous specks of reflective dust, like spheres, glittering and iridescent, of frozen ash, like swirls of flaming gas towering higher than the world, all unconvincingly decreased by the illusion of the visible distance, frightful in itself, to a size no greater than that of animal eyes peering from thickets on summer nights.

From out of the near darkness, from a *banco* silently sailing past the ship, invisibly passing save for the unfocal, greenish silver line of deathly brightness and trailing stir of troubled luminosity engendered by its progress through the phosphorescent water, rose a softly chanted ". . . *naidasay . . . toy pusoc . . .*" The strange but earthy words of the native song uttered so close at hand, the unintelligibility of which gradually dimmed as the *banco* drifted farther and farther away, seemed to remind Warrington to lower his head; which he did with a movement as of weakness rather than of volition. He tightened his balance; for, as if dizzy, he was swaying perilously on the step of the railless ladder. His bemused eyes hesitantly brought into focus the patch of warmly lighted deck, a few feet away, at the bottom of the ladder. He descended to it in a series of brief movements that were almost uncertain, as if his sense of physical proportion had been deranged also. A faint disinclination to turn out the light there caught at the vaguer borders of his consciousness. After he turned it out, he went on to the next light with an impatient sweep at his consciousness intended to erase the impression of that formidable disclosure up there at the top of the blackness, the same sort of mental gesture a man makes to dispel an obsessional memory that keeps intruding between him and the difficult page or the problem on the paper. The gesture helped him to readjust his apprehension, to shrink it to the exactions and standards of that thin world bounded by the convex steel deck on which he walked and the taut awning just above his head, to tell himself, in comforting terms of it, that the ship's lonely, empty aspect was the result of the extraordinarily large liberty party, of there being so few people left aboard. Usually, at this hour, the deck was crowded with cots to such an extent that one hardly could make his way between them. Being out from between the sheltering walls of the dry dock, out here alone on the water again, probably had something to do with it too. As he went by the open, faintly luminous hatch of the Forward Fire-room, he glanced down into it, casually attracted by the awake humanity that the glance might reveal; but the sight of the man on watch down there in that bleak cavern, seen as in the depths of a dream lit by but a single weak bulb on the face of a boiler and the pulsating radiation from a partly opened fire-box, did not dissipate the sense of orderly desolation. The man was sitting cross-legged on the steel floor plates, his baldish head bent over a clay pipe which his fingers slowly, unrhythmically were covering with elegant cord-work, sitting there like some forlorn survivor passively concerned with nothing but a remnant of tribal culture and the heavy passage of much time.

The semi-naked men stretched out on the scattering of cots along the deck seemed, except for the two or three who were snoring, to be dead rather than asleep. Only one of them was awake. He lay on his back in an access of relaxation, his hands clasped beneath his head, a curved-stem pipe barely retained between his teeth, his trancelike gaze fixed unseeingly on the awning above as if exploring the depths of benign heavens. Warrington, remembering the rift in the black sky, wondered if the man would have kept his eyes open had the awning not been there. He remained oblivious while Warrington turned out the light near him and moved on.

When Warrington reached the area between the galley and the After Conning-tower, an area illuminated by the lights of the opposing port and starboard gangways, the only deck lights not to be turned off, he instinctively tarried in it for the comfort of the illumination. He rested his arm on the mount of the six-pounder there and gazed out past the port gangway into the impenetrable darkness that the electric light dispersed from but a few yards of slick green water. There surged through him, though the ship evinced no movement, the peculiar sense of being afloat, an uncanny sense of physical precariousness revitalized by the long abstinence from the sea. The pervading solitude was not lessened by the little sounds of life, resonant in the metal hull, that occasionally accentuated the stillness . . . a faint throbbing at the heart of the dormant machinery . . . the fall of some slight, hard object to the steel deck . . . a man briefly murmuring in his sleep somewhere up forward . . . the creak of a wicker chair aft. From off in the blackness, on the other side of the ship, a curt splash brought him upright with routine alertness for the return of the Captain's boat. "Just a leaping fish," he presently assured himself; but, taking no chances, he moved around the breech of the six-pounder and stood listening at the starboard gangway for the chug of the motor-dory, stood there—a slim, blond, very young figure nearly six feet tall dressed in a brief, round, upflaring white hat, a white sleeveless undershirt, a clean pair of worn dungaree trousers, well-polished low shoes, black socks neatly rolled to the ankles and a cartridge belt from which hung a forty-five calibre Colt automatic —stood there unconsciously displaying, despite his alertness, a contempt, not for his environment, but for his place in it; and even there in the eyeless solitude he bore himself with his definite air of being a fine and especial entity, an implicit, deeply masculine air of transcendental assurance that remained uncorrupted by the dank loneliness and heavy fatigue seeping beneath it.

His conscious listening gradually gave way to a contemplation of the three or four points and streaks of man-made light that betrayed the town off there amidst the heavier black where lay the land. On this side of the ship the land was only half a mile away. From it a barely perceptible gust of breeze brought him a blurred fragment of phonograph music accompanied by drunken singing, not the sort of singing that had just passed so unintelligibly in the nearby darkness, but a familiar song from the throat of a man he probably knew, a reminder of the revelry with those women, being used there in the distant obscurity, that his having the watch had saved him the fight of resisting . . . But he could have resisted them anyhow, he reassured himself . . . His breath quickened slightly, and a nervous emptiness spread from the pit of his stomach . . . He would prove it . . . tomorrow night . . . when he was on the liberty list . . . he would scorn that town and all it contained . . . by staying aboard . . . when he was free to go. Out through the darkness on another gust of the unfelt breeze came a muffled yell, a wild bar of inarticulate male sound full of brutal ecstasy, of abandon. No . . . that would not prove it . . . He would go ashore . . . and he would walk right amongst all that licence and unrestraint . . . closely, slowly . . . resisting every deliberately braved call of that female filth to the treason in his body . . . "O God," he cried out silently, "please, O God, help me! See to it that tomorrow night when . . ." Thus, every muscle of his body clenched, his breath held, he began the first phase of a prayer to that God who knew, even if what was simply the boy did not, that it was the wild cry of one lost in the wilderness of purity to which he had sternly fled, not merely from the general world of brutishness and anarchy, nor merely from the vulgarity drabbing the new and strange one that had enmeshed him, but from the greater ugliness, vividly realized in adolescence, of a degeneration at the very heart of the intimate world that had produced him. A movement on the quarter-deck, which now was lit only by the light that rose through the little elegantly curtained hatch, mechanically caught the attention of that superficial layer of consciousness above the deeps in which he was praying. He turned his head. Ensign Snell was still dozing in the chair as he had been for the last hour, his legs stretched out before him, his heavy bruised chin sunk on his breast. Lieutenant Fitzpatrick was the source of the movement. He had come up from below with the open, personal pages of a long letter in his hand, as if the airless heat of the wardroom had succeeded in interrupting him after he had started reading it, and driven him up to the comparative freshness of the quarter-deck. "A letter from that girl," Warrington noted with probable accuracy, as he backed a step from the gangway, turned his face away from the quarter-deck with a studiedly casual movement and, launching into the second phase of his prayer, paced in routine fashion up the deck.

The fact that he and the officer were there alone on the deck of the darkened and sleeping ship, the glimpse of each other thus, now provided them with no opportunity save one to suppress mutually suffered rises of self-consciousness, irritation and a heavy sinking feeling that neither could have identified. That the situation offered a chance for reconciliation never entered their heads, not only because they did not know what it was they had to reconcile, but because the idea of it, to get into consciousness, would have had to traverse an insuperable barrier of repugnance, not for each other, but for something unknowable deep and impending within this act of reconciliation itself. These days, when Warrington thought of the disaster that had so suddenly and inexplicably overtaken their friendship, he did so with a sickening sense of failure, of opportunity fumblingly, irretrievably missed; and it occurred to him, every time he thought of it, like a crippling blow at the heart of his integrity, that the failure had been met with at a point where he felt he was extraordinarily fit to be successful. The disaster, even though it left him fighting the misery of one left behind, of significantly not counting any more, still continued to bestow its compensatory largess of lending a meaning, none the less a meaning despite its obscure foundation, to the ordeal of his life here that had been so sterile before the first conversation with the officer on the bridge, a largess still filling that once so fatally intolerable vacuum with a continued relationship and richness of feeling undiminished by the fact that the first had become tortured and the second become pain.

There was further compensation in the phenomenon that, while he was realistically conscious of the aching distance he had been left behind and miserably aware of every parched, dragging moment of time through which their estrangement endured, calendar time seemed to be washed away so swiftly by the torrent of shame, indignation and pain that he was unable to keep up with it. Before the estrangement, perhaps it was before that first conversation on the bridge, he had counted the passing days, sometimes even the hours of the days, drearily pencilling off each day on the calendar he kept with his books, as obstacles overcome on the road to enlistment's end; but this very morning, just after he had gotten up to help with the relaunching of the ship—a "time" that now had been precipitated far back into "a long time ago," in terms of consciousness duration, not by a sense of the fullness represented by the dramatic relaunching or by the long effort of coaling, but by the latest sharp crisis, as the officer had come up with his letter, in their persistent, undemonstrative ignoring of each other—he had taken out the calendar to mark off the shortening of his time, and he had realized with a shock, almost with bewilderment, that more than thirty days had passed since last he had obliterated a single unit in that inflexible series. The discovery of that sizeable stretch thus miraculously slashed from the time left him to serve had brought an actual, audible shout of joy to his lips, a shout that had made the three or four others in the forecastle dart sharp glances at him and shake their heads hopelessly.

"What's the matter?" Hardwood had demanded sleepily. "Goin' more nuts than yo' are already?"

In defence of the shout, Arnold, observing the neglected calendar in Warrington's hand, had replied for him:

"You'd pour it on too . . . if you suddenly woke up and found only a year and a butt to do."

The joyous shout had been no more than the upward darting ray sparked off by the discovery: there had been a downward piercing ray also, a ray that lividly had confirmed, with its display of a swiftly passing time he had not wanted to keep up with, the permanence of the breach between him and the only fellow being, the only mitigation of his isolation, the only access to valid, living spiritual communion, he had found in this smother of negation to which he was condemned until either death or the current of time, the orderly progress into the past of all those little subdivided squares on the sheaf of flimsy paper he had held in his hand, released him. Although the passionate reluctance to have time pass at all that was harboured by the part of him devoted to his tortured relationship —a part now monopolizing the foreground of his consciousness and in which time rushed perversely on by virtue of the very reluctance—was chiefly responsible for inducing time to pass swiftly in that part of him now relegated to the background of consciousness, there had been another element that, lately, had furthered the speeding. He had managed to foreshorten the result of time perception by somehow setting up and concentrating on the re-launching of the ship as the end and aim toward which the days and hours were passing; as if that event were a hill in time behind which would be revealed a valley flowering with the solutions to problems, a translucent hill that seemed to block or blur all his eager vistas down duration, save the one that, partaking of distance as much as of time, was unsusceptible to measure by countable units, that far significant future, that nameless glory beyond the farthest horizon. Perhaps without thinking he had selected the re-launching of the ship as a marker because some breath of the Captain's tacit attitude toward that coming event had infected his intuition without informing it; or perhaps O'Connel's persistent, prophetic phrase, "all this means something," had affected his curiosity, as it had that of others, to such an extent that the future was dominated by the disclosure that might be brought about by the completion, with the relaunching of the ship, of all those frantically hurried repairs. It may have been, too, that the style of the prose to which of late he had been devoting himself had contracted his sense of time to the appositeness of nearer markers, the opportunistic, ephemeral style whose essence is "a few hours ago," "right now," "in a few hours," the style of the newspapers from Manila and home in which he read of the war, a war so far away and in so different a world that, when he looked up from the immediacy of the page, it partook of unreality, that war in which men were flinging themselves to death rather than survive the triumph of injustice, and in which he, himself, longed with an intensity that increased day by day to fling himself also, that inaccessible war of which he read in a style devoid of the significant implications of those larger extensions of duration, of permanence, of reality, devoid of the sense of the past, the continuity of the present, the eligibility of the future to become the past, and therefore devoid of the very identifying essence of poetry—the element so enabling, so enriching the style of his former reading, the novels, verses and histories he had carried aboard in his sea-bag. However, he may have selected the relaunching of the ship as a target for the days and hours simply because he had been looking forward, with exclusive, unreasoning hope, to the end of that stranding on the land that had brought a withering of friendship, to the return to the sea upon which his conversations with the officer had begun and upon which they might revive. Whether it was one of these influences, or a combination of them all, that had tended to restrict the trajectory of his time sense to the near event, he had so swiftly, vividly and completely lived through the shorter arc, while neglecting to remain, as formerly, alert to the greater, of which the smaller was but an integral segment, that he had extracted the extent of the smaller, virtually without realizing it, from that of the greater.

Now that the looked-forward-to event, the relaunching of the ship that morning, had been reached, passed and even, in consciousness time, relegated to the distant past, Warrington could face the fact, without actually facing the worded thought, that nothing of the vague expected had happened; nothing save that he and his former friend had just met back there, almost face to face in the obscure loneliness, and had turned away from each other. As he climbed to the forecastle deck, praying steadily, precisely amidst the third phase of his entreaty that he be enabled to resist those women in the darkness tomorrow night, he confronted with a shudder that became physical the vast, empty stretch of time between "now" and the end of his enlistment, an intimidating desert of time across which he was to move with infinite slowness, with no conscious division point yet in view to which he could again plot an engrossing trajectory and thus shorten time by expanding the importance of a segment of it. True, "tomorrow night" was a division point in view; but it was so near in calendar time that it made a regrettable waste of the headlong speed with which he was rushing at it on the wings of a fear that he might not be able to pass the test of temptation by the flesh that formed the point; that point in calendar time that was as near at hand in consciousness time as it would have been far away if, for example, he was to have consummated, at the point, an arranged and impatiently awaited reconciliation with his friend.

"The reading of that letter he had in his hand," he told himself on a level of consciousness above those on which he was praying and facing the emptiness of time, "from the girl he's in love with, was a rereading . . . must be a rereading . . . The new mail hadn't come yet . . ." The thought of that girl he did not know suddenly filled him with the memory of the one he did. The memory took him unawares, shook his heart, tore prayer and time from his consciousness, exposed the raw wound made by the failure where he had felt he was extraordinarily fit to succeed, dissolved him to the verge of those dreaded tears to which once, back in eternity, her gaze had brought him as he stood on the platform before the jeering crowd. Standing there in the blackness, one supporting hand against the rounded steel side of the conning-tower, the other clutching his trembling throat as if to strangle a savagely resisted rise of self-pity, he suffered the dawning of a monstrous premonition, suffered the premonition, lost there on that infinitesimal mote of metal floating in a dark beam of endless and beginningless time, that there was to be no distant perfecting of his love like iridescent white fire . . . no namelss glory of a future for which he sacrificed his all in the meaningless present . . . no . . . The wave of terror subsided as swiftly as it had come; but it left behind a scar of tragic lucidity, the kind of lucidity that engulfs a confirmed alcoholic through a moment of sobriety, a pitiless lucidity that he watched take possession of his whole being as crystals of ice creep through a freezing pool. With eyes thus cleared he thought he saw, too, the explanation for his seeming abandonment by that being back there in the receding distance: There never had been any friendship in the first place! . . . No finding of a kindred spirit! . . . He had thrown himself forward at a mirage, at a fervid, unclear "friendship" the illusion of which had been able to arise and bewilder his restraint only because of his isolation, far from everything that had given his life meaning and form, at the heart of this emptiness barriered by equivocal hills, by a chaos of incredible vegetation, by beaches like pale expanses of something living and secret reluctantly exposed in the unravelling foam of a sea that could blaze cruelly by day and glitter inimically by night; a mirage that still had been able to lead him on and on, even after friendship's end, toward that "reconciliation," as resisted as it was desired, harbouring a danger inexplicable and nameless. Shame, acrid, corrosive, smothering, rose in an irrepressible defiling flood from the depths of his being to fill his throat, his eyes, his nostrils, to overflow as cold perspiration at the pores of his burning skin. It had been all his fault! He had forced himself upon the officer, a person who was significantly a part of all that was understanding and worthy to be understood. He, Warrington, ignominiously had tried to force himself upon a being like himself, had revolted him with his advances, had forced the man publicly to reject him! He stiffened, bolt upright but swaying, as if a high-tension current had leapt through the steel of the conning-tower and electrocuted him. He suffered the outright necessity of jerking the automatic from his belt and firing it into his seething brain, into his freezing heart, of blasting out of existence the abomination, the ignominy that pervaded him like a stench; but he seized the grip of the pistol with a disabling reluctance that drew its strength from the very source of the shame itself. He could not kill himself in the face of that man's contempt! The humiliation that he wanted to destroy expanded intolerably as he felt the impact of the interpretation that would be put upon his death where he had offered himself and been rejected, rejected where he could not admit, even by killing himself, that he was not extraordinarily fit to be accepted. Reasoning with himself that after he had fired the shot he would not then be aware of the unbearable interpretation, of the increased humiliation, did not negate the power of his burning prescience of it; he even obtained a measure of relief, deliverance from the foretasted increase of the humiliation, by rejecting this counsel of reason. He regretted with ferocity, with the despair of his new-found lucidity, that he had not flung himself down into the churning propellers as he had started to in that long ago . . . before he had been tricked into delivering this hostage to relentless shame . . . "But I shall find a way!" he said distinctly in a wild, cold voice that flickered abhorrently in address, in reference between first person, second person, third person and between the qualities of self-reassurance, plea and defiance, "You must help me . . . I have done my best . . . deep in my heart . . . that I have done my best . . . This shall not stop me

... especially not now ... Nothing shall stop me ... never fear ... You must help me, O God ... I must ... I shall find a way to die so that nothing ... A death that can't be compromised ... a clean, swift, splendid ..."

26 〰〰

Sometimes leaning against the side of the conning-tower, occasionally standing rigid and tense to face the darkness, but more often pacing shortly up and down the narrow strip of forecastle deck leading from the ladder to the bow, Warrington so passionately had thought and felt and dazed through the consciousness time of his Eight-to-Midnight Watch that chronometer time had lost synchronization with it. There is no telling how long he might have remained on watch in this fashion if Ensign Snell had not stumbled drowsily up the ladder in search of him.

"Quartermaster?" The officer's voice seemed to grope through the darkness that his eyes could not penetrate.

"Here, Sir."

Ensign Snell did not try to make him out; he simply gave his order to the dim motion in the blackness that had responded.

"Be sure and tell your relief to notify Mr. Fitzpatrick ... instead of me ... as soon as the Captain's approaching ..." He could be heard stifling a yawn. "... lying down in his cabin."

"Aye, aye, Sir."

"Goodnight," said Ensign Snell with sleepy amiability, and felt his way heavily back down the ladder.

Warrington returned the "goodnight" with the sinking feeling that there was something amiss in the officer's having had to come up in search of him to give this order. He found out what it was when, after giving Ensign Snell time to get aft and go below, he followed him to the now deserted quarter-deck and looked at the chronometer fastened to the side of the After Conning-tower: He had not been back there, had made no round of the ship, for over two hours! It was a quarter-past midnight!

He was twenty-five minutes late in waking up Arnold, his relief;

a thing he was supposed to have done at eleven-fifty, so as to give the relief time to dress and slosh his face with cold water before taking over the watch at twelve. When he laid his hand on Arnold's shoulder and said sharply in his ear, "It's after twelve o'clock," Arnold, who was as easy to wake up as Cavendish was difficult, sat up immediately, aroused more quickly even than usual by something irregular in the awakening words.

"What time?" he demanded thickly, shoving a hand through his dust-covered hair.

"Twelve-fifteen."

"Thanks for the extra," commented Arnold with a grim, sleepy smile, as he swung his legs over the side of the cot in the recognized gesture signifying both that he was officially awake and that he was to be molested with no further attentions to achieve that end.

It was going on toward one o'clock by the time Warrington had filled in the Rough Log Book, turned over the watch and was unfolding his cot in his habitual sleeping space on the port side of the deck close to the Amidships Torpedo-tube. The contact with Ensign Snell and Arnold had restored his surface mind and emotions to their customary guise of assured, almost arrogant control, restored them except for a new, strange, permanent feeling that reached up into them, a kind of irremediable sadness, more like a changed condition than a disturbance, which, he promised himself, he would identify as soon as he was safely on his cot. The postponement of this identification helped keep his consciousness focused on the superficial level, on the details of going to bed without waking up the Blacksmith, whose cot lay at the foot of his, on his lateness in turning over the watch, on reassuring himself with the recollection that he had encountered Ensign Snell in darkness and that Arnold had been too preoccupied with clearing his own sleep-distorted consciousness to notice anything disturbed about him; but, he told himself, that kind of display just would not do; he could not give himself away like that, even to Arnold, even when there was no one to see; and he must not permit himself to get so absent-minded either. He could not understand it; he had heard the noisy Olongapo liberty party going home in their boats . . . he remembered distinctly that he had heard them . . . which should have warned him it was after eleven. Fortunately, the time lapse had done no harm, except cheat him out of an hour's sleep . . . Bad enough . . . but what a lucky thing there had been no officer to call or anything like that, as on the morning watch, or no bells to be struck every half-hour as on larger ships. One of these days, if he was not careful, he was going to let a duty boat drift away . . . or be caught with an anchor light out . . . or . . . The next thought was so suddenly disquieting that he dropped the corner of the cot against the Blacksmith's, causing its slumberer to shift his big, bald head about restlessly . . . If he had let the Captain's boat get into the gangway without a hail! That would have been the end, just the end! Perhaps the slight sounds of a boat approaching the other side of the ship had made him think of this. It was not the Captain's boat, he noted, not a motor-boat. Probably some of the liberty party returning to sleep aboard after all.

"Boat, Ahoy!" sang out Arnold's still sleepy voice from over by the starboard gangway.

As Warrington stooped to undo his shoes, he automatically listened for the boat's answer. No naval people in it, he concluded, when the hail remained unanswered; or if there were, they were all dead drunk and the native boatman too ignorant or too frightened to answer himself. It could be an ugly business, checking in drunks. He had not been late enough to let himself in for that anyhow, he congratulated himself.

"Boat, Ahoy!" This time an aggressive alertness had displaced the sleepy quality in Arnold's voice.

From the now quite close boat came a sharp, uncertain murmur in broken English.

"What do you want?" demanded Arnold's voice with tense brevity.

"Captain." This answer was gasped close at hand, and as if its speaker had just ceased paddling with all his strength.

"Captain's not aboard," was Arnold's slightly uncertain reply.

This provoked a torrent, spotted with interjections by another but precisely similar native voice, of low strident words that gave an impression of bitter indignation, of terror, of need. Warrington made out the words, "drunk . . . break everything . . . kill . . . steal girl . . ."

Startled and curious, Warrington slipped on his shoes again and, without bothering to lace them, walked quickly aft to where he could get a view of the starboard gangway. Arnold, standing at the edge of the deck, just above the first step of the gangway ladder, was staring down through narrowed boxer's eyes at an apparition that seemed to have risen to the level of his waist from the water close beside the ship: two Malay faces lividly illuminated by the gangway lights against the background of heavy night. A trembling hand, slick with blood, clutched at the ladder stanchion to hold in their *banco.* The mouth of the one doing most of the talking had been mangled by a heavy blow and was bleeding profusely; the face and uniformed breast of the other were so smeared and drenched with blood that it was difficult to discover either the location or the importance of the wounds from which it was flowing.

"Hang on," said Arnold grimly, "I'll call the Officer of the Deck."

As Arnold moved toward the quarter-deck, Warrington called out:

"What's up?"

Without stopping or turning his head, Arnold said:

"Watch it a minute, will you? . . . 'Till I get Mr. Snell."

The two Tagalogs in the *banco* paid no attention to the advancing newcomer save that the spokesman darted him a brief, fevered glance before looking at the fingers he had placed to his bloody mouth; the other swayed, covered his face with his hands and sat down in the *banco* so suddenly that he seemed to have dematerialized.

It was Lieutenant Fitzpatrick, with Arnold at his heels, who came up almost immediately. Dozing on his bunk fully dressed, waiting for the Captain to return, he had heard the Quartermaster call Ensign Snell, already thoroughly in bed and asleep, and tell him that "those two Constabularys from Subic are at the gangway asking for help, Sir . . . Trouble ashore . . . Sounds like bad trouble too . . . They've been pretty roughly handled themselves." Lieutenant Fitzpatrick's questioning of the Tagalog still on his feet, whose face, at the appearance of indubitable authority, instantly had become an oriental mask with a crimson, liquid mouth, brought him no further than the general conclusion he expressed to Ensign Snell when that officer, at the end of five or six minutes, arrived on deck buttoning up his blouse.

"Hell seems to have broken loose ashore . . . Our men."

"Shall I send over a party to bring them back?" asked Ensign Snell, his sleep-hazed glance coming to rest on the Tagalog's mouth. He invariably betrayed all his actual youngness in the first few moments after having been waked up.

The answer he received to this question caused him to shift his eyes to Lieutenant Fitzpatrick's with a surprised expression that lasted through the long instant it took him, also, to realize that, with two-thirds of the crew ashore in a drunken general rampage as serious as this seemed to be, there were not enough of the right kind of men left aboard to send; and there was no room for what clearly would be a mere bluff adorned with police clubs, a bluff that, failing, would but add what remained of the crew to the chaos, and leave the ship an unmanned derelict. If they did send what they had, they would have to empower them with firearms and the intention to use them; a measure that these two officers could not, at this point, bring themselves even to contemplate in relation to those particular men who were said to be running wild over there in the town, a measure, impossible to be seen except in the tragic light of last resort, that was likely to result far more disastrously than anything it would be aimed at ameliorating.

"I don't think that will be necessary," had been the answer in a level voice, "I'll go over and attend to it myself."

Above and beyond the personal, physical risk of going alone to face a violence that called for the use of a powerful patrol, this proposal involved a daring gamble that was full of a greater danger not only for the Executive Officer and the men ashore, but for the very prestige and discipline of the Navy itself. Ordinarily, Lieutenant Fitzpatrick would have abided by the rigid custom of avoiding personal contact with angry or drunken enlisted men; for he was thoroughly indoctrinated with the supreme necessity of never subjecting either the Navy or its men to the risk of having an officer defied or attacked. Such offences, seeds of fatal confusion, the mere awareness of which established mutiny as a possible event, were so rare in the Navy as to be practically non-existent; more rare than homicide; so rare that they had no place in rumour, precedent, tradition or lore; and the faintest, shameful shadow of them, whenever it fell, was met with such opprobrium, such swift and merciless punishment that even the idea of these most serious of all naval crimes, which technically can have no extenuating circumstances, never entered a man's head save as a spurt of ridiculous fantasy or to indicate an extreme in the way that a civilian says, "I'd as soon think of jumping off Brooklyn Bridge!" As a matter of fact, no crew ever has gotten as far as a mutiny in the American Navy. Once, eighteen years before the War Between the States, a forgotten Midshipman and two Seamen attempted to incite one aboard the Somers. The Captain and the rest of the crew promptly hanged them at the yard-arm, despite the fact that the Midshipman was a son of the Secretary of War.

Lieutenant Fitzpatrick probably was more sensitive than most officers to the practical value that lay in this naval morality and the traditional sanctity of the commissioned rank; besides he had been a witness, a beneficiary of what this morality and sanctity could do, had watched himself and his two friends, alone and far from the bases of their authority on an antiquated, failing ship, yet with the sure efficiency of unimpaired confidence, drive their short-handed, overworked crew of formidable human beings through outlandish isolations, into crisis after crisis that punished the body, tried the spirit and fevered the brain, on unreasonable appearing missions that seemed to have no other object in view than the courting of disaster and death. He knew what he was risking, for himself, for his men and for the Navy, when he expressed his decision to go ashore alone, knew it fully and with a sense of responsibility; but he knew also that what might be happening on that dark beach of an alien and unwilling colony held a possible threat to the transcendental thing of which the Navy was but a preserving part: he could not, for the sake of no matter what other considerations, stand by and watch his men set ablaze another of those ugly local revolts that endangered the nation's international security. The stakes of the gamble were high and the odds long; but what was on his side was not contemptible. He counted on the sobering effect, in his experience infallible, of his appearance amongst those men, of the appearance amongst them, for the purpose of giving them orders, of a commissioned officer, counted on the appearance amongst them (although he did not analyze it to this extent) of one of those all-powerful, privileged beings so apart, so vested with superiority and prestige, so little known in the familiar, personal sense, so little known at all save as repositories of authority and fate.

It entered Ensign Snell's head to propose that his friend at least might take a couple of the men with him; but he did not make the suggestion. He could not have explained clearly on the instant why he had not made it; he would have had to say, with thorough but wordless conviction, "Well, it's got to be one thing or the other." However, it was quite clear to Lieutenant Fitzpatrick why he, himself, had rejected the same idea when it had entered his head: If what he was counting on was to be displayed in the most apprehendable, the most emphatic and unmistakable manner, it would have to remain undiluted by any weak intrusion of the other kind of force, an intrusion which not only would be too weak to justify itself, too weak even to defend itself on its own grounds, but one that easily might, in the excitement over there, becloud and give impulsive opportunity for the evasion of the only issue he intended should arise.

"We could," said Ensign Snell, as he came to a realization of the situation, "wireless Olongapo for another patrol . . . It's their job anyway."

"The radio operator is ashore," said Lieutenant Fitzpatrick, stepping into the gangway. "Besides, there's no patrol over there now."

"What in the world happened to it?" demanded Ensign Snell in a troubled and, what was for him, startled tone.

The Tagalog constabularyman, pausing in his effort to make room in the *banco* for Lieutenant Fitzpatrick, felt called upon to answer this question himself. His bloody lips sputtered quite vindictively with the affirmation that he, personally, had requested the patrol to stay. He had not liked the look of the way things were tending, especially with all those unmanageable men planning to remain in the town all night; but the patrol had not consented to stay. They had gone off at eleven-thirty in the boats with the Olongapo men, saying that if the ship wanted a patrol she could send one.

"Go down and get Mr. Fitzpatrick's pistol," said Ensign Snell to Arnold.

As the Quartermaster hastened away to get the automatic always kept oiled and ready on his desk, Lieutenant Fitzpatrick smiled tartly at his friend; but the disapproving, witty pucker of the small, brunette, superior features did not, for once, abash Ensign Snell. His own lips compressed so stubbornly that it set up dimplelike gatherings across the front of his broad chin, and he said, on the verge of a mumble:

"Might as well be regulation about it." Then in a quiet, hopeful burst of inspired pretext, "You never can tell . . . Maybe these birds," he gestured with his head at the Tagalog standing in the *banco*, "have got the cart before the horse . . . Maybe it's our people that need the protection."

The Tagalog, in the face of this, taking it to be consummate effrontery or stupidity, merely lowered his eyelids with slow, scornful grace.

When the holstered pistol and cartridge belt arrived, Lieutenant Fitzpatrick shrugged his shoulders lightly and fastened the belt around his waist. As he went down into the *banco*, Warrington suffered a deep pang of concern for him, a concern so purely personal and intimate that he permitted not the slightest open manifestation of it; yet perhaps the conflicting rush of feeling with which he instantly met and obscured the concern did faintly break the surface for the officer's sensitivity, resulting, as if in answer to Warrington's impetuous assuring of himself that "all this means nothing to me! . . . It would serve him right if he did get hurt over there," in a slight blemishing of the officer's attitude, in the barest touch of swaggering impudicity, in his enjoying an instant, for Warrington's benefit, of showing off. When he was seated firmly upright in the *banco*, however, and while it was being quickly shoved away from the ship's side to disappear across the glassy patch of illuminated water into the blackness, his attitude lost the blemish: He became simply the Second-in-Command of the ship going to recall his men, whom he trusted to be in no such fantastic mess as was reported, to their senses.

From the palm grove where Lieutenant Fitzpatrick landed to the structure that sheltered the trouble, it was about one hundred and fifty yards along a straight, fairly wide, malodorous street cluttered with mud holes, weed-tufted hillocks and the projecting leaves, cumbrous and ragged, of bordering plantain trees. He walked directly up the centre of it, with the two constabularymen at a gradually increasing distance behind him, as if the business that called his small, elegant person to that place up ahead there, the only house in town that showed a light, was some casual, routine bother. He seemed preoccupied only with the effort of making his deliberate way through the heavy darkness without stumbling. The stilted nipa houses on either hand were as silent and barren of movement as if deserted; but the two long, uneven masses of them gave the officer the impression that they were quivering in their darkness with tension and expectancy. He did not alter the air of his progress by so much as a turn of the head or a shortening of the casual, sophisticated rhythm with which his hands swung to his stride when he sensed that behind him and the constabularymen there was forming, recruited silently from the blackness, a tensely following crowd; neither did he seem to take notice of an abrupt sequence of sounds from up ahead, a quick rending of wood, a gush of abject female screaming.

As he neared the building, a big thatched roof above an enclosure walled but here and there with cane lattice or braced matting, the braid on his cap, the stripes on his epaulets, the buttons of his blouse caught a far-flung radiation from the four or five kerosene lamps in the place, to give him the appearance of an undismayed white shadow, faintly aglitter with gold, approaching through the obscurity. Someone within or just outside an opening in the wall must have observed and appreciated the dull glitter of this appearance, for there arose the familiar warning shout:

"Gold braid!"

The warning, furtive and exigent, was uttered only once; but it provoked the brief tumult, reassuring for the officer's ear, of leather-shod feet stampeding away into the darkness. As he found himself, he could ask for no more satisfactory recognition of what he had counted on than this. He felt warmly thankful to those fleeing men who had not failed him; they elicited his admiration.

On reaching the doorway, he paused in it to estimate what there was left of the crisis for him to face. An unconscious native, covered with blood, his chest heaving exaggeratedly, was sprawled on the floor almost at Lieutenant Fitzpatrick's feet. Another, his head framed by a pool of blood, was lying with his face to the farther wall. A third, stretched out face down, was crying stertorously. On the floor near him was the long, leaf-shaped blade of a work *bolo*. The bar was turned over amidst a heaped chaos of glasses and bottles, many of which were broken. From this debris spread streams of pungent liquid. Every place his eye rested around the floor there seemed to be a welter of spilled food, a splatter of broken crockery or a fragmented bottle in a puddle. One of the lamps had been shattered by a missile, but through some miracle its dripping oil had not caught fire. All the chairs, to his hasty glance, were in pieces. Blood-smeared tables seemed to have been piled up in the centre of the floor and then the pile knocked over. A piece of garment was snagged on one of the up-ended table legs. High up under the roof, above the pile of overturned tables, a girl perched on a cross-beam, her hands clutching frantically at the hard, rough thatch close to her head, from which the long, straight, blue-black hair was falling in disorder. Her trembling brown legs, which were very slim and much longer than was usual amongst these tribes, were doubled so tensely that the skin over the knee-caps glistened in the lamplight like the officer's buttons. She was holding her breath as if about to fall, and her wide-open, slanting eyes, in a flat, pert, pock-marked face that had turned a sickly yellow, were glaring steadily down with the wildest desperation. This glare was directed at O'Connel, who, evidently having failed to reach her by climbing up the wall, the elements of which had proven too weak to sustain his weight, and then up the pile of tables, which had toppled with him, was smashing and tearing down, piece by piece, the whole wall-frame supporting an end of the beam on which she crouched. Spotted and smeared with other men's blood, and emitting through clenched teeth streaks of sound that were half-moan, half-whine, he was flinging his great body into this destruction with a kind of insane ferocity. Never pausing or relaxing for a fraction of a second, he would hurl his shoulder against a timber in an apelike lunge and then, while the wood was still cracking under the impact, lash his body backward with the timber gripped in his hands as if it were the throat of an enemy.

As Lieutenant Fitzpatrick walked toward him, the startled realization that the constabularyman had been right, that a woman was being attacked here, and by O'Connel of all people, was succeeded by the apprehension that at any moment the roof would come tumbling down upon them; and then this in turn was succeeded by the definite impression, which subsequently turned out to be virtually correct, that O'Connel alone was responsible for all this damage. Coming to a stop so close to the oblivious man that he was in danger of being struck by one of the backward lunges, and fastening a steady gaze on the spot where O'Connel's eyes would be when he turned around, the officer spoke in the same level tone with which he had announced his intention of coming ashore alone.

"All right, O'Connel . . . that'll do."

At the sound of this particular voice saying this kind of thing in this way, O'Connel, like some blazing arc light whose carbons suddenly have been jerked apart, instantly ceased all display of activity and purpose. His stilled body did not lose its impression of being charged with frightful danger; but its white rage seemed, not to disappear, but to subside darkly and poise within itself. Only his big, swelling hands continued to show movement, a very slight movement: they were gradually relaxing their grip on the timber as if adjusting themselves to the demands of a new and unexpected necessity by which they have been diverted. Then he turned around, swiftly but without an appearance of suddenness, to tower above the officer. His hands, which sank to the level of his hips, rigidly spread apart their fingers and remained thus as if paralyzed on the verge of clenching into fists. His heavy eyelids were lowered enigmatically. His breath, reeking with liquor, came in even jerks through the quiver of thick, flat nostrils that had become an ugly white. The lines that curved down from the nostrils had deepened violently to seethe with perspiration and grey, intimidating shadow; and he kept baring the repellent golden row of his upper teeth in a spasmodic gesture, a tight, rectangular retreat of the lip, that was neither smile nor snarl!

As the officer stood there persistently seeking for the lowered gaze of all that destructive power flaring with irresponsibility, he was conscious of little more than that everything he had risked was hanging in the balance. The other things that tried to dart into his mind, things that if permitted to enter would corrupt the steadiness of his calm gaze, the assurance of his prestige before this man, were in the nature of reflections that should have been made before, and not after, he had arrived face to face with him . . . "He couldn't drink . . . everybody knew that . . . He went mad when he drank . . . He was crazy anyhow and now he was crazy drunk . . . It was worse than insanity to try to do anything with him when he was drunk . . . He didn't know what he was doing, the men said, on account of the silver plate in his head . . ."

All at once—at the very instant that the officer, after nine or ten interminable seconds of this confrontation, was beginning to succumb to the notion that he was enmeshed in the great error of his career, of his life—O'Connel's arms, the arch of his back, the angle of his neck, the muscles of the long prognathous face, framed by brutal upflaring ears and unplentiful brown hair that had a tendency to crinkle, seemed to sag almost imperceptibly, fatalistically, as if he were an Aegean warrior suffering, in the midst of combat, a fatal intervention of the gods.

"Come along," said Lieutenant Fitzpatrick then, in the same tone as before.

As he said this the officer turned and walked to the door, which he went through without a backward glance, a person, for the eyes crowding the shadows around the building, into whose head had not even entered the possibility that he might not be obeyed.

He did not glance back either on the way down the street to the beach through clots of natives who withdrew into the blackness before his advance. Anyway, he did not need to, for most of the time he could hear O'Connel treading heavily along behind him. The gait and manner of the officer's departure was the same that had made his arrival appear so casual, even though now the going was harder because there was no beacon ahead filled with lamplight and danger to guide him. It was harder, too, because he had much more to conceal beneath the air of being concerned only with the uncertain footing and the inability to see. Not now, any more than before, would it do to show his trepidation; nor would it do to disclose his immense, relaxing sense of relief over the fact that the trouble had not proved so disastrous after all, over the fact that he was settling so easily what did exist and that he was winning the gamble involving the great danger, not merely to himself, but to what he represented.

At the phosphorescent edge of the sea, which manifested itself more as a tranquil lapping sound in the darkness than as something for the eye to take hold of, Lieutenant Fitzpatrick had a little trouble in manning the *banco* that had brought him. The two constabularymen flatly, though with official respect, refused to paddle it back to the ship. They preferred to accept the ignominy implied in the officer's unavoidably scornful assurance that, as they could see for themselves, he was in need of no further help from them save in this mere matter of transportation. At a carefully preserved distance of two or three yards from the dangerous man the officer was taking back, they smoulderingly reiterated what amounted to a statement that there was much left for them to do there, wounded to take care of, investigations to be made, the populace to be calmed . . . They were sorry, extremely sorry . . . but they could not continue to enjoy the honour . . . He must permit them to stay and put the town in order.

This reminded Lieutenant Fitzpatrick to say to them, to say it in an offhand tone despite a sharp goading anxiety to hurry back to the ship before anything could disturb the balance of that tense motionless towering beside him:

"If those men in there are really hurt," he gestured with his head toward the lamplight up the street, "take them down to Olongapo. Tell the hospital ship I sent them."

"They're hurt," assured the spokesman of the two constabularymen with an obdurate reproachfulness that irritated Lieutenant Fitzpatrick, and which he was afraid would irritate O'Connel also.

"I'll be over in the morning to make a full investigation."

The officer said this in a tone that O'Connel, if he had not been monopolized by his struggle for breath and integrity amidst a vortex of humiliation, would have recognized as his most arrogant. The two constabularymen attempted to take it as their dismissal; but Lieutenant Fitzpatrick stopped them with the command, sharp contemptuous and containing a threat:

"Get me someone for this *banco* immediately."

The leader of the two Tagalogs turned in a manner that should have been accompanied by a shrug of the shoulders and faced the part of the darkness that was the land. He called out a name. They waited in silence for the reply. When it did not come, the constabularyman called out another name. Lieutenant Fitzpatrick seemed to feel the crowded blackness, as if it were the thing summoned, brace itself against a reply. He felt a tremor, that was somehow intimidating, go through the cause of this silence. He restrained the impulse to place a calming hand on O'Connel's arm.

"Then go get one of them," ordered the officer in the same sharp tone as before.

The constabularyman who had called the names stepped noncommittally away up the softly crunching sand into the darkness. A moment later he could be heard murmuring curtly. He seemed to be talking insistently to himself in there. A few seconds later he was near them again, accompanied by a deliberately moving being of whom the officer could gain no other impression in the sightlessness than that of great age, of withered oriental toughness. The newcomer went straight to the *banco* despite the darkness. Lieutenant Fitzpatrick felt the canoelike craft slip away from the side of his shin. He realized that he had been bracing his leg tensely against it. Making a definite effort at dispelling what this implied, he waited until he heard the *banco* stop grating across the sand, then he said, taking O'Connel's arm in a gesture that could not be understood as other than one of guiding:

"Get in." But as he felt the big elbow stiffen, almost quiver, he added in explanation of his touch, "It's right here . . . the other side of me."

When the *banco,* under the strokes of the invisible ancient in the stern, had travelled no more than fifty or sixty feet over the water away from that shore so heavily buried in night, there could be heard a murmuring rush back there as if the unseeable land suddenly had charged forward, in relief and triumph, to engulf the sea. There was even a long, intermittent ripple of cautious, excited laughter. The paddle strokes leapt into a more hurried tempo.

Lieutenant Fitzpatrick, himself, no longer could resist the relief, dangerously premature up until this moment, that had been surging against the bulwarks of his attitude of unquestionable self-assurance. It swept in and took possession of him in the darkness behind O'Connel's back, permitted him to relinquish the set of his shoulders, to pass a hand across his perspiring brow, to face in the sober emphasis of retrospect the details of the disaster his ending venture might have become. His lips very nearly puckered to exhale a relaxing, appreciative whistle. It did not matter, he assured himself; in a moment more they would be back aboard ship and everything automatically would be taken care of . . . even his attitude would be taken care of, disclosed though it then would be in the glare of electric light.

Once, when they were about half-way back to the ship, O'Connel braced his hands against the gunwales of the gliding *banco* and turned his head with the intention to speak; but through the two feet of blackness that separated him from the officer he seemed to get an impression of unresponsiveness, of impassive relentlessness, that made him turn his head back again with the intention abandoned. This impression from the officer behind him vividly intensified O'Connel's swirling sense of being helplessly, shamefully, frustratedly in the wrong. Because he considered Lieutenant Fitzpatrick to be, despite his habitual air of natty arrogance, the most warmly human, understanding officer in the ship, "good Irish" was the way he put it, it occurred to him, unprecisely but passionately, that if *he* was going to feel this way about it there was no use in trying to explain anything to anybody; and he suffered a moment of fierce, drunken self-pity.

What really preoccupied Lieutenant Fitzpatrick as O'Connel turned his head was a deep musing into which he had retreated from the consciousness of relief, a musing over the situation in which he had found his man. He was still too shocked to laugh secretly at it, as he later would laugh openly and sincerely when relating the thing to the Captain and the others. What shocked him was that this was the first time he ever had known or heard of even an attempted rape by one of the ship's company. That it should have been O'Connel was doubly shocking. The big man was more than typical in this respect, typical of the vast majority of the Navy's enlisted men who, "scum of the earth" though many branded them, very rarely ever went so far even as to molest a woman on the street unless she took notice of them, or was there to be molested.

O'Connel would have been as astonished as Lieutenant Fitzpatrick was if it had entered his head that he had been caught in the act of an attempted rape. It is true that if he had gotten at her he would have given her a thrashing, which he was convinced she deserved, and then carried her off into the darkness and possessed her; but there would have been as much difference, from his point of view, between that culmination of the woman's having "led him on" and the detached crime of "rape" as there actually was between "the truth" and the way he felt things looked to Lieutenant Fitzpatrick when he arrived. An important part of the wild and heavy misery that now beset him, his acute embarrassment, his silent frustration, lay in his inability to organize into words, even for himself, the difference between that disgraceful appearance of things and this "truth."

He had, he felt, been sitting quietly in that place minding his own affairs and drinking beer when the girl, who had a lot of Spanish in her, had begun on him. Her long, slim, shapely legs and pert manner had taken his eye, there was no doubt about that; but he had not tried anything with her because he had observed that she had not gone out with any of the others; and he had concluded that she was not "on her back like the rest of those wenches," that she was there simply to help with the bar, that she was different. Even when she had begun to dart him an occasional interested but derisive glance he had not brought himself to an overcoming of his hesitancy. He had continued to sit there with a strained smile on his bony face, irked by the silly, helpless feeling that invariably flooded him when he was faced with doing something about a woman who was not a whore. Once or twice she had swung close by him, lithe, insolent, enticingly aromatic, and he had felt that she had done it on purpose; but he had not been sure; so he had not succumbed to the temptation to reach out and lay hold of her. Then the silly, helpless hesitancy had been consumed by a flame of mortification; she had been making a fool of him all the time! She had begun the same set of tricks on another one, a leisurely but cocky Swede from one of the other destroyers in Olongapo. Fortunately, his rival had been a big man, like himself, so he had been able to take him outside with an easy conscience and beat him senseless before the patrol could stop the fight. This had solved a great deal; for, having become empowered by the idea that now he had won her in fair fight, he had walked back into the place, taken her by the arm and sat her down at his table. The way she had accepted this and stayed there had made it clear, to him at least, that there was now something between them, that it had become definitely a private thing between her and him. At the moment when he had been getting up his courage, and for some reason it still had required courage, to take her arm and lead her out to one of the shacks in the same way he had led her to his table, she had begun to taunt him about drinking beer. He had not been able to understand the provocative gabble of her words, but her pantomime, charming, natural, eloquent, clearly had insisted that he drink palm liquor like a man. Carelessly he had downed a glass of the formidable native liquor in response to what he had considered her whim; then, giggling delightedly, she had made him drink another. Evidently she had counted on the vodka-like stuff to save her from the looming, intimate encounter to which subsequent events proved she had determined not to submit; but alcohol only released O'Connel into Homeric fury; it never weakened him. When she had tried to make him drink a third, he had made it a condition that she also drink glass for glass with him. Then he had caught her dribbling her glass down the table leg. At the end of a long, scornful, half-angry glare through narrowed lids he had gotten to his feet and said, with a curt gesture of his head towards the door:

"Come on, babe, let's take a walk."

It had been clear that she had understood his tone and the gesture of his head if not his words. As she had risen, she had darted a glance over her shoulder preparatory to flight; but O'Connel had got his arm crooked firmly around her before she had been able to get as far as a step. For a moment they had stood thus exchanging a look of stubborn defiance; then the girl had suddenly writhed downward out of his arm. She had not been able to scramble away, however, because O'Connel had dealt her what he had intended to be merely a halting slap across the back of the neck. It had knocked her flat on her stomach, from which position he had picked her up in his arms and, flashing a glare about that had challenged interference, had started for the door. The challenging glare had met with little but tense neutrality in the native eyes it had encountered; in others, the eyes of those who knew him, there had been a smiling glitter of expectancy. Portness, the Radio Electrician, had rasped out:

"Go ahead, Harp, don't let her play you for a sucker."

The struggle, which the girl had seen fit to postpone for the moment, had been renewed with instant violence, with a guilty sort of franticness, on the arrival in the doorway of a long-haired native with a work *bolo* sheathed at his side. She had fastened wildly appealing eyes on this new arrival, eyes dramatic with a helplessness they had not displayed before. The native had drawn the *bolo* and, a doubtful aggressiveness stiffening his small, reptile-like body, had barred the way. O'Connel had permitted the girl to escape, had snatched up a chair and with it met a swing of the *bolo* so forcefully that the huge knife had been knocked from the man's hand. Another blow from the chair had sent the man back against the railing; another had floored him. Then O'Connel, dropping the chair and pausing only to pick up the fallen *bolo* and fling it out into the night, had swung about to retrieve the girl, who had fled behind the bar. The chase around the bar had done most of the damage there; and when it had been turned over, the girl had fled from corner to corner of the room, amidst the upsetting tables, with O'Connel so close behind her that she had not had time to climb the fairly high railing that bridged the gaps between the stretches of wall. O'Connel had managed to keep between her and the door, and every time he had passed the heap of overturned bottles he had grabbed up one and hurled it at her in an attempt to bowl her over. Another native, evidently a friend of him who had gone down, had rushed in *bolo* in hand and made for O'Connel's back. That had been the only occasion on which any of the rest of the crew had participated in the violence. Before the *bolo* had been able to reach O'Connel, Louis Carey had hit the native over the head with a chair and Saunders had followed this up with a blow from a bottle that had finished him.

At the moment that O'Connel had finally got the girl trapped again in one of the walled corners, the two Tagalog constabularymen and a hardy villager had intervened, each of the constabularymen laying a restraining hand on the Irishman's arms. As he had swung around to face them, the girl had seized the opportunity to climb swiftly up the framework of the wall to the crosspiece under the roof. The battle with the constabularymen, ending in their flight for assistance, had been short, for they, the only ones in that strictly disarmed region permitted to carry pistols, had not dared to use them on a Navy man. The villager, O'Connel had knocked down and tried to kick out of the way; but the man's body had jammed against a table leg, so O'Connel had snatched him up and hurled him across the room.

O'Connel neither had desired nor had intended to do damage to anything or anybody except that girl between whom and himself there had arisen a personal, private relationship. If other people and things incidentally had gotten in his way, that was their fault, or hers; and the more openly violent he had become, the more damage he had done in his pursuit of her, the further had he seemed committed to his purpose. Even now that he had abandoned it and was going back to face an uncomprehending justice, the incommensurate fury, the almost independent fury, that had been loosed by that girl, by those men, by the roof that had tried to frustrate him, kept rising up into his struggle for self-control like the acrid contents of a retching stomach. For the officer behind him, who could not see the slightly pathetic droop to the huge shoulders, he monstrously clotted the darkness with power, with irresponsibility, with rage, with unrestraint that swayed in precarious balance above the bow of the *banco* like a ledge of mountain top on the verge of avalanche.

O'Connel was so oblivious that he seemed not to hear the ship's hail, which Lieutenant Fitzpatrick himself answered; but as their craft slid into the circle of light framing the foot of the starboard gangway O'Connel spasmodically stiffened his shoulders, and as he mounted the gangway ladder to the deck his massive blood-spattered body assumed a perceptible swagger of defiance; yet his eyes failed to meet those of Ensign Snell who, backed by the solemnly curious Arnold and Warrington, confronted him there.

"Go forward and turn in," said Lieutenant Fitzpatrick to O'Connel, who stood expectantly, as if at last he were going to get a chance to explain.

428

"Listen, Mr. Fitzpatrick," apologetically ground out the big Irishman, accompanying his verbal effort with a slight lifting of the long, thick arms that hung at his sides in a helpless, almost a despairing fashion, "I wasn't . . ."

He was interrupted peremptorily with:

"Never mind that now . . . You can tell your tale to the Captain, at Mast in the morning."

Lieutenant Fitzpatrick felt that a drunken wrangle with the man could serve no purpose whatsoever, that the thing should come to a proper end there and then, must come to an end as far as he was concerned. As he spoke he turned back to the gangway to toss a coin to the boatman, but the ancient creature already had sped the *banco* off into the darkness, concerned with no other reward than to be distantly free of that stern, iron place, that brightly lighted source of incomprehensibility and danger. Balked in this punctuational gesture, the officer darted a sharp, meaningless look at Ensign Snell and withdrew toward the quarter-deck. Ensign Snell followed him, lighting a cigarette behind cupped hands, and, as he caught up just before they reached the conning-tower door, demanded in a low voice that was not sufficiently low to escape the ears of the group left by the gangway:

"That all there is to it?"

"It was enough," breathed Lieutenant Fitzpatrick quite as audibly and with the humorous emphasis of extreme relief.

From beneath the heavy, jutting arches of bone that shadowed his eyes full of trouble and frustration, O'Connel, with an air of hopeless, fevered calm, watched each of Lieutenant Fitzpatrick's abrupt gestures of withdrawal. His swelling heart was shouting, and his whirling, battered brain putting into inept words that never reached his throat, the phrases of his justification . . . "I didn't do anything! . . . *They* . . . those dirty hypocritical sons of bitches over there . . . they did it to *me*! . . . I didn't try to start anything . . . or hurt anybody . . . I just aimed to teach that woman!" The wildest sense of being belittled flamed in him when he caught the humorous flavour in Lieutenant Fitzpatrick's reply to Ensign Snell as the two approached the conning-tower door. He clenched his fists. They were going down below to laugh at him! With that, he remembered, realized for the first time the significance of the sound that had followed in the wake of the *banco's* departure from the beach. That town had laughed at him too! . . . Made a fool of him! . . . And then laughed at him! "By God, I'll show those bastards what happens when I *am* trying to hurt somebody!" Now the current of phrases finally managed to reach his bursting throat, to explode through his tightly compressed lips and grinding teeth in spurts of fury and anguish that woke the ship, that destroyed Arnold's and Warrington's ability to think or act, that stunned the two officers to a halt at the conning-tower door.

"All right!" he yelled insanely, striding to the gangway and shaking both fists at that laughter hidden in darkness. "I'll show you! I'll rip your lousy town apart! I'll tear your dirty guts out and stuff 'em down your throats!"

Before he reached the last word, he dove with swift fury and sureness out over the gangway deep into the illuminated patch of water at its foot. So cleanly did his body pierce the water that it made little sound, and there was left behind, at the centre of the glittering green surface, no more than a foaming pucker from which unctuous rings spread away into the blackness.

For a moment no one moved. There was no sound save a creaking from the cots of awakened men. Then Warrington sprang to the gangway and stared helplessly into the implacable darkness. Arnold turned his head to glare in a suppressed panic of uncertainty at the startled faces of the two officers in the shadow on the quarter-deck; finally he shouted, in a voice dubious with bewilderment:

"Man Overboard!"

Up the length of the deck men tumbled to their feet. Lieutenant Fitzpatrick, with a tired, defeated gesture, put his hand to his forehead as if a sharp pain had struck him just above the eyes. Ensign Snell stepped to the rail, snapped his cigarette over the side and fixed his wide eyes on the spot where O'Connel had disappeared. There was no sign, for eye or ear, of the enraged man who had flung himself into that sea so heavily smothered in darkness. His dive must have carried him deep, and he must have remained down there, swimming under water, until he was a considerable distance

430

from the ship. Lieutenant Fitzpatrick, moved by a tangle of impelments, the fear that a shark might get O'Connel, a determination that discipline and authority should dominate, the dread certainty of what would happen if the man now returned to the town, dropped his hand from his forehead and said loudly, colourlessly:

"Quartermaster."

"Sir?" tensely answered Arnold, stepping toward him.

"Call Cruck. Tell him to lower a couple of boats."

As Arnold swung about to execute this order, Ensign Snell suggested:

"Better call all hands, hadn't he?"

"Yes," agreed Lieutenant Fitzpatrick, "and call all hands."

Without turning around or pausing, Arnold acknowledged this with an "Aye, aye, Sir," and strode off up the deck, turning on the lights and shouting exigently:

"All hands! . . . All hands on deck! Show a leg, there! All hands! Hit the deck, you guys! . . . All hands!"

When he reached Cruck's cot, up near the washing space, the Chief Boatswain's Mate was on his feet, sleepily jerking into his trousers. His bulky, hairy body, not yet having retrieved its co-ordination, was swaying and stumbling about like that of a wounded animal; and his voice, when he spoke, was more dully harsh than usual because of the phlegm that invariably filled his throat as he slept.

"What in Christ's name's this all about?"

"Man overboard," answered Arnold. "O'Connel . . . He dove off . . . Jumped ship."

"That batty Harp," grumbled the man in the next cot, as he stomped into his shoes. Another, still asleep though on his feet, uttered something in a small, clear-sounding voice about "pressing into him . . . that silver plate . . ."

"Mr. Fitzpatrick says," continued Arnold, "to lower a couple of boats."

Cruck, with fists doubled belligerently, faced aft and, despite the fact that the whole long narrow space beneath the awning was by now aferment with groggy, partly dressed men, bellowed angrily:

431

"Hit the deck, you dopes!" Then, in a change of tone suggesting that the activity already prevailing had arisen but in mollifying, prompt obedience to his order, he roared a degree more formally, "All hands stand by the starboard whaleboats!"

27 〰〰

The two boats, which got away from the ship's side at about the same time, pulled at full stroke along the shortest course to the town, leaving behind them, cometlike, two long wakes of spectral radiance in the phosphorescent water. Notwithstanding the fact that they were moving nearly side by side, only about fifteen yards apart, the two crews would have been unable to see each other in the obliterating darkness, which even gave an illusion of muffling the noise of the oars, if Lieutenant Fitzpatrick and Ensign Snell, one in either boat, had not been carrying paraffin bunker lamps, the small, stubborn, free flames of which pulsed gutteringly backward in the still air before each forward thrust of the boats. In Lieutenant Fitzpatrick's boat Hardwood was at the tiller, Horner at stroke and Warrington, Petrie, Whorley, Feenan and the Blacksmith at the other oars; in Ensign Snell's boat Cruck was at the tiller, Ferguson at stroke, while behind him pulled Forsythe, Rowe, Hemple, Rene and the Carpenter's Mate. Although those in the boats displayed no excitement, nor much other emotion save a sleepy, sullen sense of hurry, every one of them realized the extraordinary, emergency quality in this chase; for the ship had been left with no more than eight men aboard her, and in command of Arnold, a Second-Class Petty Officer. It was startlingly unprecedented for the ship to be thus left without a commissioned officer aboard, but Lieutenant Fitzpatrick had not hesitated; it had occurred to him, unanswerably, that if one of the boats encountered O'Connel, it must have an officer with which to face him.

The officer's plan was to get the boats close in shore, between the beach and the swimming man, as fast as possible. In that position they stood the best chance not only of intercepting him but also of arriving in town right on his heels if he got past them.

He was confident, despite the swimmer's headstart, that the boats could get in there first; and he hoped that the sight and sound of these in front of him would send O'Connel, an O'Connel cooled off by his swim, back to the ship. If he did swim back, Arnold had instructions to signal this event to the boats by turning off and on the gangway light.

Without discovering a sign of the swimmer, the two boats pulled swiftly into the spot from which Lieutenant Fitzpatrick and O'Connel had put off in the *banco*. Standing up in the drifting boat and holding the bunker light above his head, Lieutenant Fitzpatrick called out into that limitless smother of darkness floored by a burnished surface that disclosed itself, beyond the beams of the paraffin torches, only in streaks and shimmers of ghostly green fire kindled by the dart of a fish, the eddy of a current, the thrust of an oar, called out impatiently, authoritatively:

"O'Connel!. . . Where are you, O'Connel?"

When there was no response of any kind to this, everybody in both boats listened intently for a sound of swimming. Perhaps the sound they were listening for could not filter through the foreground noise of the men's heavy, audible breathing after their spurt at the oars, or was lost in the subtle background din of the still sea surging and lapping against the shore; they heard nothing else; nothing, save occasionally the rise of a tentatively renewed revelry at the heart of the town. Then Lieutenant Fitzpatrick ordered the other boat to patrol back and forth between there and the mouth of the river; his own boat would take care of the waterfront for a half-mile in the opposite direction. "Watch for the phosphorescence," he admonished, "that will give him away."

As Ensign Snell's boat made off, with Cruck periodically shouting, "O'Connel . . . Hey, O'Connel," Lieutenant Fitzpatrick hastily landed Wembly on the beach armed with a Very signal pistol. Brought along especially for this, the Gunner's Mate was to fire up a couple of the pistol's roman-candlelike balls to summon the boats if O'Connel reached the town.

Although the boats, on their way in, had found no trace of O'Connel, they had, as a matter of fact, passed right over him. Swimming fiercely, his great body seething with his unmitigated intention to "show that town," he had turned his head, in order to check his course through the blackness by the ship's lights, just in time to see the bow of one of the boats, luminous with the magic water through which it was cutting, about to run him down. Instantly he had plunged beneath the surface, and had remained there as long as his brief, emergency intake of breath had permitted. When he had allowed no more than his head to rise to the surface again, amidst the softly flaming turbulence and foam of the boat's wake, he had taken in the fact that there were two of them, the ship's boats, he had realized; and he had not doubted for a second that they were going in there to help that place against him!

His long, heavy, efficiently shaped legs treading water to the increasing rhythm of his rage, it never had entered his head, as Lieutenant Fitzpatrick hoped it would, to return to the ship. Instead, there had shot through him a pang of abandonment, an unreasoning, goading conviction that everything, even his own world, was turning against him. His anger, his vengeful purpose had neither cooled nor relaxed; it had grown more Achillean, more deliberate, more inclusive, more absolute. He had begun swimming along in the brilliant but non-illuminative wake of the boat that nearly had run him down, half-instinctively concealing in it the luminosity of his own progress. He would swim under those boats to get at the town, he had told himself; but if they discovered him, he would smash his way through.

Treading water again, five or six yards away from where the boats stopped, he heard Lieutenant Fitzpatrick call out his name. He smiled scornfully; felt strangely freed by the smile. Noticing that the cloud of glow left behind by the boats had begun to subside around him, he ceased all motion in the coruscant, tell-tale liquid, cannily relaxed, permitting the water to take him as it would. Most of what Lieutenant Fitzpatrick said escaped him because the water rose to fill his ears, to engulf all of him save the front of his upraised face; but then, irked by the feeling of submission and helplessness that his drifting posture gave rise to, and by a sense of being alone and lost rather than embattled that was evoked by his view of the devastating, star-topped crevice at the apex of the blackness beneath which he lay buried, he finally braved the risk of slowly resuming control of and erecting his body. He accomplished this in time to hear the words about the phosphorescence giving him away. Again the scornful smile distorted his face; and the double-edged possibilities of the inflammable sea became a fixed tactic of his mind instead of a mere recourse of his instinct.

The movements of the boats now, however, confused him. His eyes were so close to the water he could not make out precisely what they were up to. One of them definitely was moving away somewhere, he was sure about that; but as to the other one, he could not guess whether it intended to guard this approach to the beach or make a landing. His first, impulsive solution for this confusion was to dash in and fight his way past the boat's crew. The idea of it landing like this to side with "those rats" against him, O'Connel, tormented him so heavily that for a moment he seemed incapable of any other course of action; but the obsessional fury of his purpose to avenge himself on that sly, laughing town drove him to evade this diversion of his efforts. That was what they wanted, "the double-crossing sons of bitches!" He porpoised beneath the water and swam deep.

O'Connel's curt surface dive did not go unnoticed by the people in Lieutenant Fitzpatrick's boat. Hardwood and Whorley, simultaneously, called attention to the swirling cloud of phosphorescence; but after a moment of watchfulness, the officer decided that the swirl of submerged glow, from above which expanded circular ripples of nebulous brilliance, was too carelessly near the boat to be O'Connel. It must have been, he decided, a shark or one of the large fish that, disturbed by the violent traffic unwontedly agitating their still, tropical bay, had begun to leap and dart on all sides. He ordered the boat, as a concession to the two men's co-operation, to pull over the spot and then down the shore in pursuance of his plan of patrol.

It was Ensign Snell's boat that, a few minutes later, discovered O'Connel. His long underwater swim, intended to carry him up the beach to an unobserved landing, had gone astray to such an extent that when he came to the surface he found himself a considerable distance out toward the lights of the ship. As if his bulkily clinging clothes were to blame for this error, he began vindictively ripping them off. A glance had shown him that the torch of

435

one boat appeared to be quite a distance away on the left, while that of the other was far down the shore on the right. Rash with growing impatience, goaded by the frustration in his erroneous swim and wildly rebellious against the first creeping approach of fatigue, he probably would have thus ridden himself of the clothes even if the boats had been nearer; but in that case he would have maintained a defiant alertness while he tore away jumper, trousers and underwear (his oxfords had gone long before). As it was, with the boats' distance giving him the idea that they would not see him, he neglected to observe that the torch on his left had begun to draw rapidly closer. He obliviously jerked and kicked at his entangling trousers as if they, too, were in league with that hatefulness he was raging to bring to account.

The men in Ensign Snell's boat, their eyes so bewildered by tense staring at evanescent clouds of bright, lifeless fire that they had lost all real optical sense of whether those ghosts of light were in the black of the sea or in the darkness above it, had no hope that the distant glimmer they now were pursuing was anything more than what the boat already had sped at fifty times; but Ensign Snell was performing his duty in characteristic fashion. He had orders to investigate every likely patch of that phosphorescence, and he was doing so with stubborn thoroughness.

Then all of a sudden Cruck, inspired by a flash of certainty that the persistent milky conflagration in the water ahead was, really at last, what they were looking for, yelled:

"Lay on them oars!" and, to increase the stroke, continued rhythmically with, "Heave! . . . Heave! . . . Yo! . . . Heave! . . . Heave! . . ."

This urgent, torchlit shouting, unexpectedly close at hand and sweeping down upon him, stung O'Connel with the realization that he had blundered again. He whirled around in the water, with clenched fists and grinding teeth, to face that sneaking boat; then he heard Ensign Snell shout:

"If it's he, keep in between him and the shore."

O'Connel, beside himself, reacted instantly to the challenge in this shout and sent his naked body streaking recklessly in toward the beach at a wide angle to the course along which the boat was approaching.

"Hold water, port! . . . Give way, starboard!" yelled Cruck, as he took in the direction of the turbulent line of vague, greenish brilliance extending swiftly through the blackness.

Ensign Snell stood up in the stern of the turning boat and, waving the paraffin torch back and forth, hailed:

"Ahoy, Mr. Fitzpatrick! . . . Mr. Fitzpatrick, there!" Then, as some kind of answering shout, accompanied by a waving of the distant torch, came readily back through the darkness, "We've found him!"

When the bow of the boat overtook O'Connel, Ensign Snell started to speak to him, but before he could pronounce his name the man had plunged beneath the surface.

"Oars!" yelled Cruck.

While the boat continued to cut ahead through the velvety water under its own momentum, every gaze in it tensely struggled with the broadening, patchy area of incandescence astern that had been boiled up by the swimmer, the oars, the hull of the boat and by startled fish. Finally, someone, to relieve his eyes, glanced out into an undisturbed vista of darkness and caught sight of O'Connel, an eruption of foamy glitter, breaking the surface some sixty yards off to starboard, just abaft the beam.

A bolt of exultation, a sense of domination, illumined O'Connel's rage as he saw the boat promptly turn and make for him anew, the kind of feeling that encouraged him in the ring when an opponent led unhesitatingly into a feint. He waited until the boat was within a couple of yards of him, then he dove under its bow to swim beneath its speeding keel and on up into its effulgent, concealing wake. Aimed directly for the shore again, triumphant over the headstart he had tricked the boat into giving him and renewed by the rise of his second-wind and reserve strength, he swam with all his great might in along the cloaking path of restlessly glowing water. He got far in toward the shore before the outmanoeuvred boat rediscovered him. This did not happen until after he had progressed more than a hundred yards past the end of the glow, out of which he heedlessly had rocketed on into the unstirred blackness, blazing as with the intensity of his need to run *amok* in that town, to smash and rend, to obliterate contemptuous mouths, to feel laughter and complacency, turned to blood,

437

spurting between his fingers. He roared victoriously into the scattering surface of warmly tingling water through which his head, rhythmically oscillating for breath, cut like a prow. By the time they got that boat around and overcame his lead, he would be in there!

A flare of inspiration like the demoniac fire with which his lunging body was bestrewing the sea promised him that, once in the town, he could use its dark streets and houses just as he had been using the trails and patches of phosphorescence . . . He would shift around through them, away from the treachery of that pursuit as fast as it turned up . . . while he gave "those snickering yellow bastards . . . every dirty bitch and mother's son" he could lay hands on . . . what they were looking for! . . . He would . . .

With a blow that almost stove in its side, he crashed head-on into Lieutenant Fitzpatrick's boat, which, hugging the shore as a precautionary measure, had been pulling up as fast as it could in response to Ensign Snell's hail. During the last fifty yards or so of his dash for the shore the people in this boat had been watching the swimmer come in, and had kept the boat directly in his path. Lieutenant Fitzpatrick, obscuring the light of the torch as much as possible, had hoped that O'Connel would not see them until the last moment; but he had not counted on his not seeing them at all. An instant before the collision, he had shouted a warning to O'Connel, which he had not heard, and a sharp admonition to the port oarsmen, Warrington, Whorley and the Blacksmith, to "watch out with your oars!" Their efforts to obey this order were not wholly successful, and the moment following the crash became a tumult of entangling oars, O'Connel's threshing body and the wildly rocking boat, from which O'Connel finally emerged, after furiously having tried to jerk away two of the weighty oars, in a spurt that took him up along the shore toward the river. The shore here was lined sporadically with native fishtraps the tops of which, at and three or four feet above the surface of the shallow water, manifested themselves in extended rectangular labyrinths of bamboo stakes; nevertheless, O'Connel managed to swim and writhe through these obstacles with so little difficulty that Lieutenant Fitzpatrick and Hardwood, the coxswain, after the boat had gotten reorganized and ready to resume the pursuit, failed to realize that the course into which they sped it was not a clear one. In the hurry and darkness, hardly ameliorated by the little bunker lamp, the whaleboat promptly leapt head-on into one of these fish-traps to enmesh itself amidst another chaos of oaths, tumbling bodies and oars that clubbed and swept about as if infected with the revolt of the swimming quarry.

Ensign Snell's boat, however, was now cutting in directly across O'Connel's path; and it had the luck to do this at a deep spot clear of the fish-traps. Ensign Snell, during the pull in from where he had been tricked, had figured out a way of handling the situation, and the boat was proceeding to carry out his orders to:

"Keep close to him . . . in between him and the beach . . . but not so close he can double back under us again . . . When he's swum himself out, we'll pick him up."

Thwarted and irritated by this clinging tactic after three attempts to repeat the manoeuvre by which he had escaped the boat before, attempts in which his pursuer would come so close and no closer, stopping when he stopped, even backing swiftly away when he swam toward it, O'Connel's fury suddenly, but without his realizing it as a mutation of his original purpose, came to conceive of the pursuing boats no longer as mere interfering nuisances, but as actual mocking parts of the "laughter" he had plunged in to destroy. Like an unrecreant bull glaring about an arena full of bright enemy he has been unable to reach with his horns, O'Connel paused, treading water, to determine where and when to make his next effort. A few seconds of this enabled him to take in, with the calmness of profound, sustained rage, the facts that his manoeuvring had again carried him a considerable distance out from the occasional steady points of light that marked the shore, and that there was some kind of consternation beneath the torch off there a few yards away. They had lost track of him! For some reason or other his phosphorescent wake had not followed him to the spot in which he was treading water. He, himself, could see where his trail of glow ended, half-way to the boat. The fragmentary clusters of annoyed, anxious words that dropped through the gloom as if sputtered off by the torch informed him that his enemies, thinking that he had dived under at the place where the phosphorescence ended, were waiting, with growing restlessness and uncertainty, for the blaze of his coming up again. He clenched his fists in an exaltation of triumph, seared by the conviction that at last the fight was going his way, that a miraculous sympathy had parted the sea of its fire in his behalf. The fact of the matter was that his last attempt to lure the boat on top of him, so that he could double back under it, had carried him opposite the mouth of the river, from which poured a slow, spreading channel of fresh water free of and dispersing the teeming source of the phosphorescence, the infinite horde of salt-water animalcules, the glow-worms of the sea, that become points of cold fire when disturbed. O'Connel swam a few quiet strokes toward the land, then paused to inspect the blackness through which he had come: there was no slightest spark of wake! Boldly, with a hardly suppressed shout of triumph, he struck out for that objective from which the boats had been trying to keep him.

Like a knowing goal-keeper, Lieutenant Fitzpatrick's boat, having freed itself from the fish-trap, was again moving up along the shore to the new scene of action as it had been doing at the time O'Connel collided with it. When it was just opposite the now not distant torch that represented the other boat, the officer and Hardwood, at the same instant, observed a speeding streak of fire suddenly begin in the darkness between them and the other craft and then bend precipitately out of sight again.

"Oars!" shouted Hardwood, then, "Stern, all! . . . Stroke . . . two . . . three . . . Oars!"

Lieutenant Fitzpatrick stood up in the stern of the now virtually motionless boat and, using his white and gold breast as a reflector, tried to project the light of the bunker lamp out toward where the broad line of green fire so cleanly had ended. "The man must still be there," he thought. "The line hadn't ended in a dive . . . not enough disturbance for that." As he readjusted his grip on the little tin reservoir of the bunker lamp, unpleasantly hot and greasy to his hand, he listened intently at the sultry darkness into which he was trying to project his gaze and the beams of the torch. His hearing could not get beyond the commotion of heavy exhausted breathing that rose from the oarsmen at his feet. He darted his gaze impatiently down at them, a glance that informed him that "this thing can't go on much longer." The men were reaching the end of their endurance, their flushed, sweat-drenched faces uniformly bent into the moment of rest, their doubled elbows resting tiredly on the looms of the balanced oars, their bare, drooped shoulders and the Blacksmith's bald head glinting wetly in the torchlight, which touched also the moist hair on the backs of dangling, used-up wrists and hands that seemed to stretch in an endless line off into the blackness. A puff of breeze cleared away the musk of violent human effort, leaving fleetingly dominant only the subtle aroma of the boat itself, the fragrance of wood persistently steeped in sea.

"Better pull over there," said Lieutenant Fitzpatrick to Hardwood.

O'Connel, seduced by the darkness-freed tendency of all thought and motion to curve back on itself, had begun, as once before, to swim in a circle whose circumference had carried him again into water that blazed; but he too, on taking a rearward glance for a bearing on Ensign Snell's torch, had become aware of his reigniting wake almost as soon as his enemies had; and he had hurled himself back into the general direction of the safe dead blackness from which he had been swerving. Swimming furiously as for cover, his head held high for repeated backward glances at his betraying trail of fire, he had concentrated his whole frenzied anxiety on the moment when it should cease. What he consciously had wanted out of that cessation was another chance, like the one with which he had been provided after the first discovery of himself in uninflammable water, to get his bearings for the advantageous renewal, once again, of the conflict; but when suddenly his trail of fire had ceased, his body had incontinently relaxed into a semi-floating condition, as if this diminution of effort had been his real need in taking cover. He maintained but the least exacting motions of a vague breast stroke, while his powerful lungs gasped with a breathlessness that was the looming of an exhaustion which he would not face. After a moment of such equivocal resting, safely hidden there just within the dark, unkindling current, he erected his body to tread water and, like some beset demon of the sea, swing his head bellicosely back and forth in search of his foe. The torch of one, which one his now disorientated memory and senses could not tell him, and which his water-tortured eyes glimpsed

441

uncertainly as ringed by an iridescent corona, was close at hand and coming down fast; the other seemed almost as close. He ground breath between his teeth in an access of his fury, pounded the water with his feet, flailed at it with his long arms and huge fists, protesting the wane of strength in those traitorous appendages of a being now come to understand its wrath as directed solely at the persistent effrontery of that boat about to close with him. The pressure of his unfaced, intolerable inadequacy to long continue the fight erupted in a necessity, a frenzy, in a mighty forward lunge from his hiding place at annihilation.

Lieutenant Fitzpatrick, observing the sudden reappearance of the path of green fire that charged recklessly through the blackness toward the very bow of the boat, thought that the man had come to life with the intention of diving out of the way beneath them; but before he could convey this idea, Hardwood, deriving a more correct guess from the directness and fury in the charging line of brilliance, apprehended through his intimate respect for its cause, shoved the tiller over and yelled frantically:

"Oars, starboard! . . . Give way, port!"

The evading turn of the boat did not save it from the thing that, as he had been struck with the prescience of it, had sent a stab of fear through Hardwood. O'Connel missed the bow, up around whose narrowness he had intended to reach his arms for a grip on either gunwale, but he got in under the straining port oars amidships and seized the gunwale there with both hands. As O'Connel furiously jerked himself waist-high up the side of the careening boat, Whorley and Petrie, the men nearest him, shrank instinctively away from the mass of snarling, maddened nakedness, Petrie to a fall between the thwarts; the rest abandoned their tangled oars and clung frantically. Hardwood snatched out the tiller and brandished it defensively with one hand while with the other he clutched the stern thwart, on which the officer beside him also had a grip with tense hands that trembled. The dropped bunker lamp was threatening to sputter out in the damp bottom of the boat.

"Clear his hands from there," ordered Lieutenant Fitzpatrick, retrieving the little torch.

Before anybody could attempt to obey, O'Connel plunged his body, like a gigantic plummet, violently beneath the surface, while still clinging with exultant ferocity to the gunwale; for it was not his design to climb aboard. He wanted to spill "those bastards" out where he could get right at them. The whaleboat almost capsized, went so far over that she shipped a great scoop of water; but of her frenziedly clinging crew only Petrie was splashed into the sea. As O'Connel, still gripping the gunwale of the writhing boat, hoisted himself for another drop, Whorley managed to claw one of his hands loose, and O'Connel toppled back sideways out of control; promptly Whorley tore and pounded loose the other hand. The disorganized boat, whose way had carried it into the non-phosphorescent water, rocked stormily toward an even keel at the centre of the shadow-tossed nimbus maintained by the torch in the calm, encompassing blackness.

"Man those starboard oars," said Lieutenant Fitzpatrick, holding out the bunker lamp so they could see better. "The rest of you keep him clear of the gunwale."

"Petrie's missing, Sir," complained Feenan in a voice that was half-whine, half-gasp.

"Never mind that. Give way the two of you . . . and keep pulling."

As Feenan and Horner, the other remaining starboard oarsman, feverishly struggled to reship their oars, O'Connel contrived to right his floundering body and secure another grip on the gunwale. Feeling his hands being torn loose again, he did not wait to raise himself for the greater effect as before but simply gave a savage downward tug, trying to carry the gunwale under with him as he shot, feet foremost, beneath and across the bottom of the boat. It was almost enough. Although his hands gave way, the fierce tug, aided by the momentum of the rolling and by the unbalancing rush of the water it had shipped, threw the boat's starboard side high in the air as if it were clutching, like a drowning man at the sky, for that hole at the top of the blackness glittering with a far, fragmentary reminder of where the heavens were. Perhaps only the fact that its occupants, instead of being tumbled to the low side, managed, not merely to cling to their positions, but to extend their weights to starboard, saved the boat from going over this time. It hung heavily on its beam for an instant, flooded by another swirling gulp of sea, then swept back in a breath-taking reverse roll so severe that the men now flung their balancing heads and torsos into the direction against which, but a flash of time before, they had frantically rebelled.

"Give way, starboard! . . . God damn it, give way!" Lieutenant Fitzpatrick found the breath to grind out. Holding on with but one hand, so that the other could retain the torch, it was he who had nearly been tossed out under the last assault.

O'Connel, whom nobody had kept track of, gave the whaleboat and its drenched crew no time to steady themselves. Bursting to the surface to starboard, he again hurled himself in to the attack; thus unexpectedly taking the boat, unfortunately for the officer's plan to keep it circling away from him, on the side where the two oars were reaching desperately for the water. As his charge carried him slithering onto the blade of one of these oars, Horner, its wielder, threw his body down with all his might across its loom in order to retain it; the oar snapped at the neck, tumbling Horner headfirst into Hardwood and Lieutenant Fitzpatrick.

"Give way, port," said Lieutenant Fitzpatrick, striving to balance himself against the impact of Horner's body and the lurch of the boat, "Oars, starboard."

The snapping blade had dumped O'Connel eye-deep into the water at the very moment he had been gasping in a breath. With a coughing roar he tried to clear his choked windpipe, clawing and beating the water confusedly to recover and sustain himself. Even before he had quite accomplished this, he charged blindly back in across the foaming, torchlit obscurity at where he judged the boat to be; but it had begun to swing under a stroke of the port oars, and its bow took him heavily on the shoulder, sprawled him backward. As it started to plough him under, he grabbed vindictively at the cut water, got a grip on it with one hand, then with the other, then between his doubled knees.

Lieutenant Fitzpatrick, feeling the boat stumble and balk over the weight that continued to cling to its bow through a lengthening moment, hoped it meant that at last O'Connel was exhausted and was hanging on there as to a life-preserver.

"Get up there and man that idle starboard oar," he said to Horner, seizing the opportunity to get the pull of the boat at least partially rebalanced.

Horner, who had been shoved summarily back in place by Hardwood, squirmed and edged adeptly past the heaving handle of Warrington's oar to the empty thwart where Petrie had been pulling.

The fact of seeing the man vouchsafed the time to plant himself securely there and hastily begin hauling in on the lash of the trailing oar, bestowed upon Lieutenant Fitzpatrick a slight but grateful diminution of the harrowing feeling that he could not seem to get hold of this situation. He even felt free to risk diverting his attention from it long enough for a glance around in search of the other boat, noticing for the first time as he did so, noticing in passing and without room for surprise or conjecture, that he had gotten out of phosphorescent water. Ensign Snell's boat, however, some forty or fifty feet away, was still in it, swerving and bobbing about beneath the tiny golden flame of its torch like a phantom craft immured in a spreading patch of ghostly lava. It was picking up Petrie, who, having been flung out over O'Connel's submerging head and so having escaped his notice, had been able to flee panic-stricken off in the direction in which he had found himself sightlessly swimming. Fortunately, the closed circle of his course, one semi-circumference of it a trail of green glow, the other blackness, had kept him more or less in line with the alert approach of Ensign Snell's boat.

"Please come up, Mr. Snell," shouted Lieutenant Fitzpatrick.

O'Connel, having succeeded in getting his head above the smothering rush of water parted by the stubbornly circling bow, was reorganizing his breath into a workable rhythm. He shook himself truculently, as if to free himself of the crowding sea, while the realization burnt redly, hazily through him that he had the boat in the grip for which he had aimed in the first place. He slid his left hand up and grasped the starboard gunwale, then his right up to grip the port. Clenching his teeth exultantly, he began see-sawing his weight from arm to arm with such precipitate violence that the boat, keeling further and further with each shift, was all of a sudden like a rearing, plunging animal at whose throat an enemy has leapt from leeward darkness. A tight, startled cry burst from somebody in the boat; the port oars fouled wildly; the Blacksmith, in the bow, simultaneously lost hold of his oar, flinched forward onto his knees and faced around.

"You in the bow there," shouted Lieutenant Fitzpatrick, "get hold of this tiller!"

He had grabbed the heavy stick of wood from the Seaman beside him and was displaying it unsteadily near the torch. With his last word, he tossed the tiller over the heads of the intervening men at the Blacksmith, whom it hit on the chest as he turned in answer to the officer's shout. The robust, bald-headed man groped jerkily after the rebounding tiller amidst the swirl of water at the bottom of the capsizing boat. The officer shouted again to demand:

"Got it?"

"Yes, Sir," curtly called back the Blacksmith a split-second later, his voice flattened by the pressure of desperately divided attention.

"Knock him out," ordered the officer.

The men, having abandoned all pretext at rowing, screwed their heads around and glared tensely forward as the Blacksmith got a leg crooked under the foremost thwart, braced himself and raised the tiller clubwise above his head. His physical movements had betrayed no sign of hesitancy in preparing to carry out the order. In fact, his body had responded with an imperturbable alacrity that nearly had caused it to be tumbled from the rolling and pitching boat; but so distinctly had he given off an impression of something like irresoluteness that Lieutenant Fitzpatrick had shouted again:

"Hit him, I tell you! Hit him!"

As the club lashed downward at the end of the Blacksmith's powerful arms, a gust of terror sucked at Warrington's bowels, a terror compounded both of acute sympathy for his friend in the water and dread of the retaliatory cataclysm the blow might provoke if it did not finish him; and when the blow landed, Warrington's startled reaction, as if he had not been really prepared for it, was a sharp inward gasp accompanied by a spasmodic click of the teeth. The club landed partly on O'Connel's shoulder, partly in the water at his back. A shrill roar, filled with all the horrible murderousness that Warrington had feared, was the response from the darkness beneath the bow of the boat; but the explosion of emotion of which this yell had been but the froth had blasted away all O'Connel's control and cunning. He began heaving and jerking maniacally at the bow as if trying to rend it apart.

"Hit him!" again came the order in a rapierlike thrust at the Blacksmith's tensed back; then the officer leant across Horner's vacated thwart to shove the torch at Warrington, saying urgently, "Here, you, Warrington, pass it forward."

As the Blacksmith set himself for another blow, the tossing light of the nearing bunker lamp gave him a clear aim at the patch of O'Connel's wet, crisp hair. He brought the club down straight at it; but in this same instant O'Connel's now chaotic fury drove him, in an excess of last-ditch opportunism, into a try at flinging himself up over the bow into the boat. The blow caught him solidly on the brow of his upturned face.

The hollow, fatal detonation of it might have been a peremptory warning signal from the powers hiding that scene of fury and strife in darkness, so instantly did a choked stillness close in about the boat, which ceased to plunge and vibrate, the men held their breaths. Even the obscure surface of the bay seemed furtively anxious to resume its dead-level, non-committal slickness. The Blacksmith, as if rendered immobile in the midst of readiness for another quick blow, knelt in the bow with the club poised above the glossy, troubled spot where O'Connel's head had sunk. Toward this spot, over the Blacksmith's shoulder, Feenan rigidly extended the flickering glare of the little torch in the manner of a man trying to shield himself from danger.

When O'Connel's head did broach the surface, however, the Blacksmith forbore to strike at it. Thrown far back, so that its face seemed to float like a heavy brutal mask beneath the distorting light of the torch, it sought the surface so slowly, so unaggressively that neither danger nor even very much life could be attributed to the submerged body barely sustaining it. The large animal-like, habitually narrowed eyes were open wide with astonishment and some kind of fundamental reproach. As they fixed those of the Blacksmith, which were staring steadily down from less than three feet directly above, the tortured blue mouth that floated with them gasped a wordless cry like that of a drowning man, save that it was the colour and tone of a curse; then, while the blood again began to flood the gaping wound left by the club,

447

a great, vertical almond-shaped wound in the exact centre of his forehead, he sank out of sight, like a dead weight, and in the very midst of another cry, an uprise of words this time, which, even though water-clogged and quite deliriously helpless, was understood, with a shiver of apprehension, by most of those in the boat.

"All right, Blacky! . . . I'll get you for this . . . You'll see . . ." was what he had tried to shout.

"Haul him into the boat," came the order from the stern.

"He's . . . he's gone down, Sir," said Feenan in a loud, shocked, plaintive voice.

The attitude of everybody, including that of those in Ensign Snell's boat, which just had come alongside, instantly took its tone from Feenan's voice. Men stared hard, in every direction, at where they knew the water to be. The Blacksmith swung slowly around, wiped his brow with his forearm, resumed his seat on the thwart and handed the tiller, with a leisurely gesture of finality, to Whorley, who hastily passed it on to Horner as if he did not want to be identified, even for an instant, with the thing. When Horner handed the tiller to him, Warrington leaned aft and laid it on Lieutenant Fitzpatrick's knees. The officer picked it up absently and refitted it in the rudder post.

"Forsythe," Ensign Snell was saying, "kick off your duds and go in after him. You too, Cruck."

"That's it," agreed Lieutenant Fitzpatrick, "but circle around us . . . Maybe he's drifted off a bit." As he said this, he hastily took a rough bearing on the lights of the ship and a light in the town in order to maintain position over the spot where O'Connel had gone down.

With Forsythe and Cruck grimly readying themselves for the water, their boat very slowly oared away again to carry out the circling manoeuvre.

"There he goes, by God!" suddenly sang out the Carpenter's Mate, who was pulling the bow oar in Ensign Snell's boat.

It was true. A considerable distance away off there, on the far side of the dark current pouring from the mouth of the river, a thick line of luminosity was crawling heavily through the blackness in the direction of what the officers judged to be the desolate, jungled head of the bay. With a suppressed cheer, a ragged, impulsive outburst containing strangely within it the expression of conflicting emotions, the crews of both whaleboats responded, amidst the night's first enthusiasm, to the order to pursue.

There is no doubt that O'Connel, all at once bereft of his immense physical strength, had begun quietly to drown when he had gone under in the midst of his threat against the Blacksmith. However, as his body, which he had seemed to be discarding because of its inability to keep up with him, had tumbled passively and with infinite slowness over and over down into the sable, solitary, womblike depths, some indissoluble clot in the dazed current of his ebbing power and consciousness, perhaps a clot of the profoundly horrible stuff that inspired its discoverer to conclude that not even a rat dies in a trap without a consenting act of will, had induced his arms and legs to assume more or less the stance of a primitive swimming stroke. Apprehending, as if dreaming within a nightmare, that his body had been able and trying to do at least this much, he had accepted the effort, accepted and empowered it with the something like disdain that had been expanding in a tingling, continuous explosion from the incandescent centre of what was not his body but himself. He had accepted, not because he had been beaten . . . he never could be beaten! . . . but out of condescension to a moment, a passing moment, controlled by the weakness of the vehicle that confined him, condescended precisely as a Captain accepts the necessity of heading his ship away from his course into a storm. Thus, sluggishly flexing his arms and legs frogwise, he had drifted on and on, like some monstrous specimen of man's amphibious embryonic stage condemned to everlasting life in a laboratory fluid, drifted thus until he had floundered to the surface, to an awakening of heavy, choking, physical agony, to the realization that now the water, too, was his enemy. It was seeping and soaking into him, feeling for him, cloying his movements and his breath. It seemed to have grown thicker, heavier in order the better to weight him down, catch at his armpits, his elbows, gag his throat.

He had not known when he had swum out of the dark river current into water that brightened, nor had he even thought or felt about the direction in which he had moved subsequently; but he knew, although consciousness of individual body parts long had been consumed in the vast blaze of his pain, when his feet touched bottom amidst one of the periodic flounderings into which the water kept dragging him. He managed to stagger upright, to keep moving upright in the same direction he had been swimming, until, like some great dripping creature retreating from sea to jungle in search of a renewal of strength, he had tottered out of the water.

Of O'Connel's landing, all that the eyes of the two officers and their coxswains in the sterns of the nearing boats could take in, through the blackness, was the scatter of phosphorescent water flung off by his emerging body. There seemed to rise up out of the night, a few boat-lengths ahead of them, an invisible tower of failing strength that disintegrated in showered beads of light. Then, either because O'Connel had plunged on into the jungle, which here almost mingled with the bay, or because the rain that suddenly began driving earthward through the darkness had washed him clean of radiant sea, their eyes lost him.

"Way enough!" came Lieutenant Fitzpatrick's rain-muffled order.

The boats slowed until they barely were moving, creeping heavily, uncertainly forward to feel for the darkness-hidden shore as if being vanquished, at long last, by the unexpected torrent of water pounding down in an infinity of precise thrusts to reinforce the sea. Although this rain was but one of the customary regional downpours, in other parts of the world it would have been regarded, awesomely, as a cloudburst; and it abruptly augmented the wash of water in the boats, obliterated the mile-distant lights of the ship, beat into the men's faces, drummed engulfingly upon their backs, upon their bare close-cropped heads, seemed to smother, as easily as it had the little flames of the torches, their will to continue. Nevertheless, all but two boat-keepers landed on the narrow beach in a drenched, close mob to confront unseeingly the monumental flank of a jungle that made itself felt as an inimically alive, insensate presence, that corrupted even the flood of rain with its aggressive odour of a fecundity that was ceaseless, intricate and monstrous. They made no effort to penetrate that black chaos of vegetation. The utter meaninglessness of trying to look for the man in there probably prevented the idea from so much as taking cogitable form in anybody's mind. The best they could do was to explore the quarter-mile of beach, which was impassably blocked at either end by spurs of jungle. Shoulder to shoulder, chest to back, they trudged blindly up and down the desolate, rain-boiled margin of sand, now and then dejectedly shouting appeals to O'Connel that the downpour seemed to drown within a yard of their mouths. As far as most of those who had been at the oars were concerned, these shouts were a mere pretence insisted upon by the officers. They did not say so, but the suspicion grew strong amongst them that Hardwood, Cruck and the two officers had been victimized by wishful thinking or some other illusion when they had thought they had seen the wounded man wade into the beach; and by the time the search was relinquished and the order curtly given to take again to the boats, this suspicion had solidified into the conviction that the truth of the matter was that O'Connel had gone down to his end out there in the water under the Blacksmith's club.

Whatever O'Connel's fate was, the boats now abandoned him to it and pulled off down the black reach of bay, fumbling wearily through the obscuring rain for the lights of the ship. Ensign Snell, still vividly remembering his recent march through that jungle filled with dangerous snakes and animals, was not happy about this abandonment; but there was no course of action he could think of to suggest in place of it; and he knew, by his own feelings, how uneasy his friend must be at having so insecurely left the ship, for so long a time, with no officer and virtually no crew aboard her. Anyhow, the most important thing they had been after had been achieved: they had prevented O'Connel from "raising further Cain in the town." Ensign Snell would have agreed, also, with Lieutenant Fitzpatrick's opinion, if they had exchanged any words on the subject, that O'Connel was now in no condition to swim out of that pocket of sand and jungle for the town; or if by a flattering stretch of the imagination he could be granted the strength and stamina still to manage it, it was impossible to think of him as fit to do any damage after he got there, not much damage, at worst, before a warning from Wembly would again bring help from the ship. Lieutenant Fitzpatrick assured himself, with growing ill-humour, that he had done all he could or should do about it. In the morning, provided this rain stopped, he would send over a party to look for him, and when he was "damn good and ready, too . . . If the stubborn ass is lost in there, it's his own fault . . . nobody to blame but himself . . . If he isn't, well and good . . . maybe it'll grind a little sense into his thick head to take it all alone in that wild hell-hole for the rest of the night . . ."

As a matter of fact, the night was near its end when the two boatloads of used-up men, soaked to the skin and surly with doubt over the result of their long, miserable venture, secured the boats alongside the ship and climbed from them up through the bronze cables of the railing to the deck. They did not bother to dry themselves off; they simply peeled away their liquid-heavy garments, bunching closely, unnecessarily beneath the electric bulbs to do so, and then stretched out incontinently on their cots, surrendering with closed eyes to the appreciation of effort's end and of shelter finally reached, to the sense of having regained with their return to the ship, lost at the heart of far distance and nothingness though she was, their share of security and normality, to the sense of having been opportunely reprieved from the darkness and violence, the disorientation and madness choking that glow-haunted bay on the outside there. The promise of this had inundated them, terminated their resistance to the dissolution of strength, the moment the boats had sighted the vague looming of Delilah's lights. Mere yellow, rain-curtained blots of ordinary electric light, these nevertheless had illuminated the men's ability to see the ship behind the screen of rain and darkness, to see with the eyes of long familiarity, as clearly as if she had been exposed to them in full sunlight, the whole of her slim, tense gracefulness, the admired arrogance of her high, thin, dangerous bow, the touch of warm breath above the first of her rakish funnels, the waiting embrace, stern, pure but consoling, of her rounded steel deck and trim insides.

28 ∼∼∼

Because the boats' crews were so brutally spent, their mood so intimidatingly one not to be questioned, and their turning-in so abrupt, those who had remained aboard forbore to question them until the opportunity for trying to satisfy intense curiosity almost had escaped. Five or six of the exhausted men, however, whose sleeping gear had been moved because it had been within reach of the rain, were forced to suffer a few attempts at questioning in the brief delay provided by their necessity of finding their cots before they could retreat to unavailability upon them.

"Did you bring him back?" asked Corum, the Electrician, voice and logic addled, on the instant, in the face of Horner's silent, rancorous rejection of help with his cot.

"Don't see him, do you?" snarled the Seaman.

"Leave him in the town?" Naylor placatingly asked of Forsythe.

"No," was all there was to the reply.

Even Petrie, the red-faced Seaman who had been hurled from the boat, was unable to maintain his characteristic amicability when Arnold and Easterly, standing on either side of the puddle spreading away from his bare feet, demanded to know in apologetically good-humoured tones:

"Did you ever come up with him?"

"Any kind of a mix-up?"

The thoroughly done-in Petrie made no response whatsoever. He stretched himself out on the cot as if he were alone and unbadgered, flung an arm over his bright black eyes, which had narrowed stubbornly, and went to sleep.

The curiosity, before those whom it possessed were forced to leash it for the night and go to bed also, did get some satisfaction, an unsettling sort of satisfaction, from the tardily passed on information that first Stengle and then Bidot had succeeded in gleaning from the officers themselves. What Stengle had learned had resulted from his having approached the officers, as soon as they had come aboard, with a silent but assured questioning attitude, the clear, rightful attitude of the senior Chief Machinist's Mate in charge of the Engineering Force seeking information about one of his men. He had continued to stand near the officers in this patient yet pressing fashion until Ensign Snell had felt constrained to vouchsafe heavily:

"We had to sock him . . . in the water . . . Guess it almost did for him."

This blunt statement had inspired Lieutenant Fitzpatrick to tell Bidot, who had returned to the ship at four o'clock to relieve

Arnold of the Quartermaster Watch, not to bother with entering "anything about this business in the Rough Log," that he would do it himself in the morning.

"Will O'Connel come back to the ship tonight, Sir . . . or what?" Bidot had seen fit to ask in reply to this instruction.

"I don't think so," the Executive Officer had replied tiredly, irritably. Then he had added, with an indicating jerk of his dripping head toward the head of the bay, "He's marooned off there in the jungle."

Although Warrington, lying miserably on his wet cot as if asleep, had not heard this conversation, it would not have affected his own conviction that O'Connel could and would come back to the ship to carry out his threat against the Blacksmith. He did not believe, as did most of the other oarsmen, that his friend had drowned out there under the blow. His confidence in O'Connel's unvanquishableness, together with a vivid return of the demoniac impression that had accrued from their first encounter, writhed threateningly in and out through every obstacle that his sleepless brain tried to set up. It would have been a heavy punishment to have had to sleep in the forecastle on such a hot, humid night; but he had suffered a twist of apprehensive disappointment, that had become transformed into a mounting fear, when the rain, a few seconds after they climbed aboard, had stopped its drumming roar on the awning as suddenly as it had begun, thus permitting everybody to spread their cots as usual on the open deck. The deck was so narrow that a torrent like the one that just had ceased invariably splashed and dribbled in along most of its length. When O'Connel did get back, it would have been harder for him to have found the Blacksmith if he had not been sleeping, exposed and almost alone, in his known place; and that would have given the ship an opportunity to arouse itself and stop what was going to happen. Warrington could not face what was going to happen! It was not simply because of the big, fleshy, genial man lying on the cot at his feet, nor because of the fact that the horror looming over the ship was in the person of the irresponsible invincibility that had made itself his friend; but because the coming event itself, as no more than an isolated reality, was going to be so ghastly with ugliness and unappeasable ferocity. He knew, and it was profoundly dismaying

454

that no one else seemed to, what that last terrible cry in the water meant! His consciousness tossed and turned beneath the unrelenting goad of the certitude; and it but increased his oppression that his body was too inert, too submerged in fatigue to correspond to this apprehensive restlessness.

Inert as his body was, a tremor of fear, of impendence, vibrated through it when Bidot turned off the electric light above the torpedo-tube beside his cot. His tension, his unbearable feeling of waiting for the dreadful thing to happen increased degree by degree with each light that Bidot turned off up the length of the ship. He wanted to cry out against this stupid setting of the stage for the insane murder swimming through the blackness at the ship. He sought for calm by silently jeering at himself that such an attempt at a warning would be just the kind of rare thing that they expected of him, wanted of him so that they could feel superior to him in a moment of importance. The jeer restrained him but brought him no calm; neither did the caustic reminder that this whole tranquilly sleeping world around him could not be wrong and he right. The heavy, waiting darkness that now enveloped the deck seemed to clear and make ominous the silence, so that he was constrained to listen tensely, to listen with fearful expectancy, for the slightest flaw in it. He lost, as if it were a retreating hope, the sound of Bidot's discreet footfalls on the hollow metal deck.

His head began to spin as if he were losing consciousness; it was simply, he finally understood, that he had been holding his breath too long in order to listen the better. He let the breath out in cautious, panic-checked spurts. The realization that the film of perspiration between his eyes and their shielding arm was icy cold sent a shiver through him. Anything was preferable to this! The burst of desperation empowered his exhausted body to sit up with a climactic movement; then he got to his feet as if in doing so he were flinging himself into the very vortex of terror. He glared over the torpedo-tube into the darkness there, then recklessly swung around to probe the deeper blackness past the railing where a leaping fish had splashed. His breath was coming in soft gasps; yet he felt better, even began to suffer a general, aiding sense of indignation. Under the impulse of the different orientation of his consciousness provided by his erect position and the feel of the warm metal under his bare feet, he moved close to the Blacksmith's cot and peered down purposefully at the big, naked, darkness-blurred form lying on its side with its back to him. He no longer could resist giving the warning; but before he could find any words with which to begin it, the Blacksmith said, without turning around:

"What do you want, kid?"

It was clear from his tone that he had not been asleep at all, and that he had heard Warrington get up and move to his side. On the instant, Warrington, in his abject need of fending off the looming event, found himself making a concession he never had made before, found himself trying to speak in the aggressively apologetic, "common-sense" style that seemed to move these men.

"Look, Blacky," he whispered, "it may be just a cockeyed idea . . . but I'm sure O'Connel's coming back!"

"All right," said the Blacksmith, still without moving.

"The thing is, he's got the idea now . . . that all this is just between you and him."

"I can't help that."

Warrington tried to speak carelessly and not lean tensely over the Blacksmith:

"You heard what he yelled at you in the water . . . And it doesn't make sense . . . Why should you take it, all alone, for the ship? . . . And that's the way it'll be . . . He'll find you here . . . all alone . . . on your back . . . and he'll be on you before you even have a chance to get on your feet!"

Strangely enough, it was not the boy's imitated "common sense," but the ordinarily distrusted intensity of personal power trying to hide behind it, that now caused the Blacksmith to turn on his back as if he were giving consideration to the whispered exhortation. Warrington leapt at this receptivity with:

"Let the officers and the rest handle him! . . . Nobody can say he's got you bluffed . . . you've already proved he hasn't . . . Besides, it's the ship's fight . . . everybody knows that."

Although he had gone so far as to turn on his back, the Blacksmith could not permit his gaze to rise up into the darkness from which he knew the boy's grey, impassioned eyes were boring down at him. He was humiliated not only at having to receive this counsel from one so ineffectively young and unimportant, but also at having to give heed to a streak of his notorious "craziness"; nevertheless he sat up on the edge of the cot as if he were being persuaded.

"You can go back and sleep on a bunk in the Chief's compartment," urged Warrington, his effort at restraint merely blurring his eagerness. "He'll look for you here first . . . and that will give Bidot and the others time . . ."

This was precisely the temptation the Blacksmith had been resisting ever since he had lain down on his cot. He ran his hands tightly back across the smooth, hairless convexity of his big head; they came away coldly wet.

". . . when he looks down there, you'll hear him coming . . . and be ready."

The Blacksmith, his nakedness relieved by nothing save a pair of drawers, got to his feet in a leisurely manner, secured the sizeable hammer hidden under the cot and rolled it up in his thin mattress. In the same leisurely manner, the mattress tucked carelessly beneath his arm, he walked aft as if it were but some casual inconvenience that had driven him away, or as if he were motivated simply by consideration for Warrington's anxiety; yet his lips were struggling, tremulously, with the shadow of a smile that was at once abashed and wounded.

So great was Warrington's relief at the Blacksmith's retreat that he was deluded into apprehending it as covering more ground, much more ground, than it actually did. He found this out a few minutes after he had let himself back down on his cot, where, by favour of the sudden release into comparative peace, he had quickly fallen asleep, found it out when, his head raised tensely and his whole trembling body covered with cold perspiration this time, he realized himself as awake again and listening, in the wake of an appalling nightmare, for the something that was gathering, crouching within the hushed obscurity. He had to summon, positively summon, the moral courage to relax from this listening attitude and recompose himself on his back; but his arms kept alert at his sides ready to propel him into some movement of flight or defence. Notwithstanding the fact that he definitely gave up the idea of going to sleep again and resigned himself to thus waiting out the rest of the darkness, he eventually relapsed, at the end of some evanescent and unmeasurable interval, to the brink of that slumber he now resisted as a disarming, as a danger. He was so nearly over the brink that the returning nightmare arose avidly to mingle with the failing remains of waking consciousness . . . *swimming with but the faintest of occasional sounds through the glow-haunted darkness* . . . So that was what he had been dreaming back there! The brief illusion of hearing O'Connel swimming toward the ship had him wide awake once more. He turned, cautiously, with the manner of one hiding from a near and listening enemy, over onto his stomach; but this augmented his feeling of insecurity, and he turned again onto his back . . . and he would have to let his eyes close . . . there was no holding up the lids . . . it did not matter . . . it did not muffle his hearing as he had feared . . . he still could hear clearly . . . *O'Connel's great, wild hands reaching up out of the green inflamed spume for a grip on the anchor chain* . . . He shook himself free of the treacherous drowse and breathed consciously, guardedly. He made an attempt at laughing silently at himself. Now he had another piece of the hidden nightmare! . . . This was ridiculous . . . He must not let this go on . . . He was just lying here wallowing in fear . . . He would get up . . . that was the thing to do . . . it was nearly morning anyway . . . yes, he would get up . . . as soon as he had gotten himself together . . . Only for an instant . . . but only for an instant he would let his eyes stay closed . . . until he had gotten himself together . . . that was the thing to do . . . get up and find Bidot and talk to him until daylight . . . But now he couldn't! . . . The tingling cells of his skin erected eerily . . . It was too late! . . . *There it was!* . . . *all wet and insane and bloody!* . . . *climbing up the anchor chain with ravenous hands!* . . . *He could hear the clink of the chain* . . . now he could hear the wet pad of its bare feet coming down the deck . . . It was pawing about over the surface of the Blacksmith's empty cot! . . . Red light came aglow upon his translucent eyelids . . . It was morning! . . . It was, O God, O God, the light of the sun! . . . He opened his eyes. The great, long, dripping horror was leaning exigently over him from out of the darkness. There was a slight grin of apology, repellent, demoniac, on O'Connel's face. The edges of the vertical, coagulating wound in the centre of his forehead, the deep lines on either side of his mouth, his close, crisp, wet hair were horrent with a madness of death-hungry strength. His teeth were chattering with a hysteria of purpose. In one of his half-extended hands he held a flaming bunker lamp, in the other an open razor.

"Where is he, kiddy, where is he?"

There was no stoutness of heart, no intention in Warrington's failure to answer this vibrant whisper. His being was suffocating in more violence and horror than its heart, nerves and brain had been evolved to withstand. Perhaps the sight of his face, stiff, immobile, from which the eyes glared fixedly as from the face of one dead by terror, convinced O'Connel that, whether he knew or not, there could be no answer from him. O'Connel straightened up and, with the air of a huge, frantically scenting animal, glared indecisively up and down the deck. Then another frustrated glance at the Blacksmith's cot loosed an inspiration which he acted upon as if it were winged with certitude.

Upon the sudden withdrawal of the musky reek of that fevered body, Warrington seemed enabled to refocus his sense of meaning, to refocus it to such an extent that the assured swiftness, with which the footfalls sped away aft could trouble his deathly, spinning torpor with the idea that perhaps he had disclosed to O'Connel where the Blacksmith had taken refuge . . . Then it was he, himself, at no matter what risk, who must retrieve the saving moment he had abbreviated! . . . The ship must not lose its opportunity to intervene in time! . . . Then it was he, himself, at no matter what risk . . . He fought clear of his spinning mind and sprang from the cot to his feet; but his body did not follow him; it remained there, trembling and choking over breath, betraying no more than a tethered straining at obedience. Again he made the agonizing effort. This time all of him landed with a resounding impact, the result of a paralysed roll, face down on the deck.

In response to this heavy sound from out of the darkness, Hardwood and Cruck, at widely separated spots on the other side of the ship, sprang to their feet as if they had been lying awake waiting for just some such warning. Hardwood snatched a short length of brass pipe out from under his mattress and, with his breath coming fast, faced in the direction from whence had come the sound of the fall. Cruck's weapon, one of the boat tillers, was in his hand when he got to his feet. He had been lying there with it beside him all along. Now he held it half-raised, so ready to beat back what might be advancing upon him through that darkness at which he was listening that his thick feral body, poised heavily on slightly bent knees, seemed about to sway into a lunge. The Fireman on watch, hidden by the dark, warned Cruck in a stricken, awed whisper:

"He's got his razor! . . . He just came out of the forecastle with it and grabbed my bunker lamp!"

From some deep place aft came a yell, a curt, screaming, triumphant yell full of discovery and deadly threat, that burst like a shell amidst the sleeping ship.

Cruck got to a light and turned it on; then, silent for once, he began hurrying from cot to cot, tugging at the shoulders and staring ominously down into the wide, startled eyes of those whom the murderous cry had not yet brought to their feet.

The depth from which O'Connel's yell had risen was the little square hatchway, on the port side of the illuminated area between galley and After Conning-tower, that led down into the Chief Petty Officers' Sleeping Compartment. When Lieutenant Fitzpatrick and Ensign Snell, who had been promptly aroused by Bidot in the wake of the yell, reached this hatch, it already was ringed by a rapidly swelling crowd of perspiring, semi-naked bodies and set faces. The faces were uniformly aglitter with a tense non-committalness; yet taken as a single massed impression, with the detail of the faces submerged in it, the crowd glowed and trembled with an effort at suppressing the blackest sort of panic. They might have been a mob conscripted to station itself around the crater of a volcano seething to erupt, and deprived, in some mystical fashion, of the right to communicate, even of the right to recognize clearly, the dreadful rise of what would engulf and destroy them. Only three or four were gazing steadily down into the hatch, from which was ascending an intermittent shuffling and slapping noise, punctuated by the vicious strike and scrape of metal and accompanied by a high-pitched, bestial snarling that rose and fell but never ceased.

The crowd opened, as with heavy reluctance, to let the officers and Bidot through; perhaps the feverish shadow of opposition in this movement was cast, in some degree, by their knowledge that the officers' arrival meant they would now have to become part of what was happening down there. Characteristic of all the prevailing movement, orderly and unvociferous, like the sullen, abdicating manner in which Stengle moved from the hatch to lean, his eyes unraised, against the side of the galley, this opening of the crowd, seen through the distorting haze of intimidating stress, nevertheless appeared as a frenzied swirl amidst an expanding cloud of confusion.

When Bidot glimpsed what was at the bottom of the hatchway, which was only about nine feet deep, he retreated a step and stared aghast, and with expectant challenge, at the backs of the officers' heads, at first one and then the other, as though he were staring into their faces. Lieutenant Fitzpatrick's small, dark head, still sprucely combed despite the fact that he had been asleep, may have recoiled a fleck of an inch as he looked down there, and he almost audibly caught his breath, but the generous cut of his pongee pyjamas fairly concealed the shiver of sudden reaction that rippled the length of his neat body. Big Ensign Snell, clothed only in a pair of khaki slacks and his uniform cap, went nervously white and his eyes narrowed belligerently. He was the first to speak into the hatch.

"Get the hell up out of there!"

The unnerving quality in what was to be seen below there probably was not so much in what was happening, as in the impact provided by the monstrous, unabating ferocity of intention that had combined with weakness, disproportionate, self-conscious and horrible, to transform O'Connel's formidable person. He now no longer was a noble savage, a comprehensible Samson pulling his world down about him in a burst of natural rage and confident strength; he had become a great, sick, grisly creature slashing hysterically at flesh with a razor.

O'Connel seemed to pay no attention to Ensign Snell's order; or if he did, his acknowledgment of it was simply to make another cobralike lash with the razor at the Blacksmith's blood-covered body, which was wedged defensively within the air-compressor compartment at the forward foot of the hatchway ladder. The Blacksmith had made a dash from his bunk for this steel-doored niche, a recess but six feet high, three feet deep and as wide as a man, when he had heard O'Connel start down the ladder; but he had been able to do no more than crowd in with the air-compressor and get but the bottom half of the divided door closed before O'Connel was upon him. Beneath the dripping welter of blood that curtained his nakedness, at least one of his wounds was to be clearly discerned, an enormous gash beginning over his heart and extending to the right bulge of his stomach. No panic displayed itself on his large, white, blood-littered face, and there was a calm stubbornness in the way he was parrying the razor with his hammer. It was evident from the new blunt wounds on O'Connel's chest and arms that the Blacksmith had struck some blows in his own defence; but now the best he seemed able to do, by the uncertain light of the bunker lamp on the deck at his enemy's feet, was to fend the attack, meet it with short, clumsy, pushing thrusts of the hammer which, catching O'Connel on the hand or arm, as often as not kept the razor from his body.

"O'Connel!" shouted Lieutenant Fitzpatrick at the hatch, "Get up here!" His voice flared through his customary manner of giving an order as if it barely had been restrained from escaping in a scream.

Heedless, O'Connel slashed again with the razor.

"Engage him with that tiller," Lieutenant Fitzpatrick ordered in the same inflamed, nearly trembling voice, "While the rest of you jump down there and get hold of him."

As Cruck, tiller in hand, dropped sullenly to his knees beside the hatch, the front rank of the others facing Lieutenant Fitzpatrick across it, those who could not escape considering themselves as having been included by the order, suffered a spasmodic tightening of the muscles and briefly raised hard, expressionless eyes to meet the officer's glare. Then, one after another, Horner, Rene, Corum, Easterly, Feenan and Arnold also dropped to their knees around the rim of the hatch. Cruck, tight-lipped and unconfident, began an effort at striking down through the hatchway with the tiller, but the opening, was too small to permit of much more than a badly aimed jabbing.

"For Christ's sake, Harp, cut it out and come on up," pleaded Horner in an aggressive whine.

"Sure, Harp!" begged Corum appeasingly, his voice thin with intimidation, "He's had enough!"

Although O'Connel seemed unaware of the tiller slugging for his head and worrying at his shoulders, he definitely made a response to this pleading. It took the form of a quick upward glance full of disdain and recklessness, followed by a wild series of lashes with the razor that seemed to recognize the possibility of an interruption feared only as a distraction.

"Enough of that stuff . . . Jump down there on him!" raged Lieutenant Fitzpatrick.

The Blacksmith's fending hammer caught and snagged the blade of the razor as it was whipping downward in full swing. The blade was knocked from O'Connel's hand and sent flying back off into the darkness of the empty web of bunks behind him. Instantly O'Connel grabbed at the bloody hammer, got hold of it with both hands, fought wildly for possession of it in a manner that left no doubt that the issue of the struggle was but a matter of seconds.

Even this did not break the grip of wavering hesitancy, an oppressive hesitancy though it was lasting through but a flash of time, that held those men around the hatch from obeying the officer's order. Unfortunately, there were not present people like Cavendish, the blond Quartermaster, or the two Carey brothers or Heller, the Pharmacist's Mate, people who would plunge with unfeeling precipitancy into personal combat against anybody regardless of consequences. Virtually each of the men who was present would be unhesitant in any formal battle, even the most hopeless battle, into which the ship might carry them; and where the Pharmacist's Mate, strangely enough, would be frankly irresolute. Furthermore, most of them, sufficiently incited, would have been prompt to close with O'Connel in precisely this situation if they had not known him personally; but there now, pitted against that intimate, frightful, fighting thing, that intimate thing under which it was their custom to live submissive, they were almost powerless. Easterly, for example, who had dived so incredibly into the terrible

463

midst of the sharks after Wright, was not merely slow to fling himself upon O'Connel; he just could not bring himself to do it at all. Rene, the huge Chief Machinist's Mate, however, who turned sick to his stomach every time he remembered Easterly's heroic act, was on the very point of hurling himself down the hatch. The expiration of five or six seconds more would have found him down there grappling with the possessed man; and he would quickly have been followed by Rowe, the new Seaman, who, not yet having had time to become subjected by O'Connel or his reputation and being one of those who swiftly can bring themselves to disregard even an unexpected assault of physical fear, would have obeyed the officer's order in the very instant it had been given if he had not hesitated, after the fashion that was crystallizing into a habit with him, to intrude himself past where there was a faltering of the others, those others who knew and were so personally a part of that hateful ship's life from which he had been excluded.

That Rene and Rowe were not granted the moment more to escape from what withheld them, was owing to the fact that Ensign Snell, after a wide-eyed, astonished taking in of the crowd's reluctance, shoved his way roughly to the hatchway ladder and started down its narrow steel rungs moved by his added indignation over the thing he had understood. At this, Lieutenant Fitzpatrick got hold of the automatic in Bidot's holster and, slipping off the safety, held it ready but unobtrusively at his side.

Instantly aware of Ensign Snell's descent, O'Connel swung around to glare up at him with a fury shot through by some quality ranging between surprise and outrage; but this did not cause him to let go of the hammer, which he continued to grip with his left hand alone. The Blacksmith also continued to cling to the hammer, with both hands, in a manifestation of undaunted stubbornness rather than strength.

"Don't!" screamed O'Connel warningly. "Don't come down, Mr. Snell!"

Ignoring this, the officer, barefooted and naked to the waist, his uniform cap jammed firmly upon his head, kept on descending with his air of indignant deliberateness into that steel well of violence and blood that seemed to quiver as much with the maniacal screaming as with the chiaroscuro flung by the flickering torch. He betrayed a sense of danger only by the fact that he climbed down with his back to the ladder, poised to make an attacking leap.

"This is different!" O'Connel had continued to yell threateningly and with a sincerity that was beyond question. "Don't come down, Mr. Snell! . . . I'm warning you . . . remember that!"

As he landed on the deck at the foot of the ladder, the officer struck with his left fist at O'Connel's face. The blow missed because of a sudden movement O'Connel made in giving a fierce, unexpected jerk at the hammer, which tore it from the Blacksmith's hands; but he did not hit Ensign Snell with the hammer; if he had made so much as the first gesture leading to that, Lieutenant Fitzpatrick, who on the instant had aimed the automatic down the hatch, would have fired at his blood-spattered chest. The aimed pistol was not the reason O'Connel did not strike; he did not even see it, for he was glaring with all his stricken ferocity at Ensign Snell's narrowed and for once unresponsive eyes. What seemed to restrain him was some recalling force generated within himself by his having begun to repeat in a tense, harsh voice, first threateningly, then with expostulation, again pleadingly, as he backed away step by step into the dark sleeping compartment:

"Mr. Snell! . . . Mr. Snell! . . . Mr. Snell!"

The officer kept following him up with his deliberate relentlessness, seeking for a chance to send in another blow at O'Connel's face. As the two disappeared from the sight of those hanging over the hatch, Ensign Snell was seen to strike out again, first with his left then quickly with his right; although afterwards, in their official testimony, these witnesses evaded to a man any mention of this fundamental breach of Naval Regulations. Again, however, the blows had missed. O'Connel had raised neither the hammer nor his free hand to block them; he simply had bobbed his head to one side barely to avoid the first one and had backed briefly, skilfully away from the second.

The Blacksmith, with the violence thus receding from him, slumped back against the air-compressor, which had become so flooded with his blood that it appeared a crimson, tangled shapelessness, and closed his eyes as if to shut out a glare. Rene dropped into the hatch, hung for an instant by both hands from the coaming, then landed below with a turning movement that sent him spinning in after Ensign Snell and O'Connel even as he landed. Cruck, the tiller still clutched in his hand, almost dropped on Rene's back. Horner went down as soon as there was room, and Rowe, then Arnold, followed him.

"Get the handcuffs," said Lieutenant Fitzpatrick unevenly to Bidot, "in the bottom drawer . . . under my bunk."

As Bidot shoved his way out of the taut, silent ring of quickly breathing men, Lieutenant Fitzpatrick gazed unseeingly at the hatch from which there now were coming no sounds of violence. A light was turned on somewhere down there, obliterating the dull waver of the little torch. He shifted his gaze to the casual discomfort at his right thigh; it was the pistol, hanging heavily from his sweating hand against his leg. He put on the safety and handed the pistol to Petrie, who continued to guard it in both slightly outstretched hands in the way that one holds a small animal.

The Carpenter's Mate unurgently lowered his bleak, middle-aged body down the hatchway ladder and stood, with grimly compressed lips and folded arms, staring into the compartment where O'Connel, backed against a tier of bunks, had just received a hard blow on the jaw from Ensign Snell. O'Connel made no attempt to retaliate or to defend himself against any further blows that might be aimed at him. A faint, unnamable smile flickered about his big mouth, a disturbing smile that could have been compounded of such dissimilar things as superiority, shame and weakness, an expression that unaccountably seemed to extend itself to his massive, drooping shoulders. It was much the same sort of smile that had trembled about the Blacksmith's mouth when he had retreated from his cot after Warrington's warning. Although O'Connel's face was not lowered, his gaze was dropped straight down in a way that made his eyes appear to be almost closed. In an uncertain gesture imbued with the quality of his smile, he held the hammer out to Ensign Snell. The officer glanced but briefly at the blood-smeared thing and then, with a disdainful movement of his hand, knocked the hammer to the deck. The five men lined up at his back, of whose presence he was not yet aware, said afterwards that they received the very definite impression that Ensign Snell *"wanted* O'Connel to start something."

"Get up the ladder," said the officer.

O'Connel swayed unsteadily from the ankles for an instant, an instant through which Ensign Snell seemed about to hit him again, then moved slowly, with a kind of resigned shuffle and without raising his eyes, past the officer and the backing men. When he neared the ladder, he stopped and looked up to watch Bidot reach the handcuffs down to the Carpenter's Mate.

"Put them on him," ordered Lieutenant Fitzpatrick's voice.

O'Connel and the Carpenter's Mate confronted each other across but two feet of space; in a harsh, unintimidated manner the Carpenter's Mate held out the open manacles. As he stared at these, an enigmatic expression displaced the strange tremulousness beneath the splashes of drying and wet blood on O'Connel's face. When he did not immediately make a move to place his wrists in them, Ensign Snell, with a personal, heated impatience the men never had observed in him before, stepped to O'Connel's side, took the handcuffs from the Carpenter's Mate and vehemently snapped them on, being forced to raise in turn each of the big, life-lessly hanging arms to do so.

For a second it appeared as though O'Connel were going to speak to the Blacksmith, still sprawled obliviously about the air-compressor; but instead he looked fleetingly at his wrists, almost as briefly proved the length of the short chain linking them, then turned to the ladder and began mounting it. The periodic clanking of the chain against the rungs, as he went up, sounded out ominously against the vigilant silence. Ensign Snell, without taking his gaze from this ascent, gestured his head curtly at the Blacksmith and said:

"Take him up on deck."

On emerging from the hatch, O'Connel seemed to have some difficulty in maintaining his balance. Warrington took hold of his arm with both hands to steady him. Feeling the hands, he initiated, in the midst of his imbalance, a spurning movement to free himself of them; but when a quick glare identified the source of the assistance, he simply ignored it, relaxing his fierce movement, and stepped clear, through the backing crowd, to a position near the six-pounder.

"Get a line," said Lieutenant Fitzpatrick to Hardwood, "and lash him by that chain to the gun-mount."

With eyes commencing to smoulder above an expression as unreadable as the one that had masked his face when the Carpenter's Mate held out the handcuffs, O'Connel watched the Seaman move quickly but unostentatiously away in obedience to this order. Then he lowered his gaze to his long, shackled, encrimsoned arms, which, in seeming response, tensed and stretched miserably toward the deck as if God were down there in the black depths beneath the sea instead of above the awning in the high heaven that now had begun to conceal itself, as yet unnoticed by anybody, behind a diffusion of grey, pre-morning light. Even while the crowd stared uneasily at this singular manifestation of his fettered arms, these became fused, transformed without any apparent motion into a mighty club, a transformation that perhaps only Warrington sensed as an acute shrinking from the red-dripping, mutilated mass Cruck and Rene were tugging and shoving up through the hatch. The crowd began easing backward, their eyes fixed hypnotically on this murderous, steel-tipped weapon the arms had become. Lieutenant Fitzpatrick resisted the impulse to take a backward step also; but the fact that O'Connel had not yet made the slightest purposeful movement confused his search for an admonishment. Then, before he could find and finish uttering an edged, "Stop it!" O'Connel had raised his eyes to dart about him, in all directions save at the hatch, a glare that was a torrent of frenzied repudiation. An instant later he had shut his eyes, clenched his bared teeth and was whirling round and round toward the gangway, the club of his stiffened arms held straight out in front of him. When he hurtled over the gangway into the water, the emotion of the crowd burst in a sharp, meaningless yell.

"Pull him in, God damn it!" shouted Lieutenant Fitzpatrick, "Pull him in!"

As the officer went by the hatch, he noted that Cruck had arrived on deck and, with his gaze fixed warily on where O'Connel had gone over, was pulling the Blacksmith through the hatch by the arm-pits. He said to him:

"Quick! . . . In there after him, Cruck!"

The Chief Boatswain's Mate finished hauling Barnes through the hatch with an abrupt heave, relinquished his hold on him and padded to the gangway. There he lowered himself into the water and began swimming the four or five yards to where O'Connel was threshing wildly about, doubling and jerking his body like a gigantic waterworm, in the passion of his effort to flee the ship. Forsythe, who had been the first to dash to the gangway, felt Lieutenant Fitzpatrick's hand laid so impellingly on his shoulder it seemed to be giving him a shove toward the water.

"You help him."

Virtually from where he stood Forsythe managed a fairly accurate dive for a spot behind O'Connel; but when he came up, treading water, he was right beside him, O'Connel having swerved in an attempt to hit Cruck with the handcuffs. The Seaman flung himself on O'Connel's back and grabbed him around the waist. This foundering attack enabled Cruck to get a grip on the handcuff chain with his left hand and begin slugging frantically with his right. Then O'Connel spun over in Forsythe's arms so violently that he broke Cruck's grasp on the chain. He got in only one chopping blow at the new enemy, however, because Cruck, now at his back, clenched a strangle-hold on him from which he could not writhe free and which he knew, by the savage finality with which it crushed off his breath, was meant to kill him.

The haggard men lining the rail of the ship gazed in surly detachment upon the struggle shattering the glassy surface of purple water, from which the beamless, steel-blue light was clearing the darkness. There was no phosphorescence now, the mere first rise of day having exorcised that ghost of fire. Observing the inescapable hold Cruck had achieved, the men expected to see the Chief Boatswain's Mate kick back toward the ship with his captive in the way that one brings in a drowning man; but when he made no other effort than to maintain and tighten his hold, they too concluded, without revolt and without excitement, that he was going to kill him. They even remained untouched by suspense when Hardwood, carrying the end of a line, jumped from the gangway and swam into the spread of white foam boiling away from O'Connel's desperately kicking legs.

Forsythe, lunging up out of the depth into which he had slipped to escape the swing of the handcuffs, took in with relief the unbreakable clamp that kept O'Connel helplessly on his back. He trod water for a moment, clear of them, in order not to interfere with Cruck's getting started back toward the ship; then, when he realized that no such thing was happening, he ducked in, clutched O'Connel by the armpit and began to push the two of them in himself.

O'Connel's arms, although again tensed together at full length to form a club, had begun flinging about to such little purpose that Hardwood had no great difficulty in getting at the handcuff chain and bending on the line; but progress toward the gangway, which was gradually increasing its distance with the swing of the ship, still was slow. Every time those aboard hauled in on the line faster than Forsythe and Hardwood could kick along supporting them, the two in the death grip sank beneath the surface. This was largely caused by the fact that Cruck, eyelids and teeth clenched as brutally as his thick, shapeless arm about O'Connel's throat, had taken Hardwood's appearance for an attempt at interfering with his purpose and had abandoned treading water to reinforce his position. He had lashed his legs in a scissors'-hold around O'Connel's waist. Once, hoping that the immersion would force Cruck free, Lieutenant Fitzpatrick shouted at the Seamen to let them sink. After a few seconds of this they did rise to the surface unaided, propelled by Cruck's treading feet; but his arm remained crushed just as tenaciously as ever across the throat of that great body whose violent threshing of the water came now in spurts spasmodically.

It needed a struggle, as ugly as it was brief, to drag the Chief Boatswain's Mate clear of the unconscious man's throat even after the two were got within reach of the many hands ready about the gangway. This victory, complicated by the breaking of the handcuff chain under a too suddenly vigorous heave on the line, had finally been speeded only through the aid of some *bancos* filled with an early returning portion of the liberty party.

For a moment after he was hauled up to the deck, a moment during which Lieutenant Fitzpatrick exhaustedly gathered himself for a resolution of the baleful discord, O'Connel was suffered to lie unmolested on his back in the thick puddle of blood spreading from the body of the dozing Blacksmith; for whom nobody knew what to do. This moment came to an end when O'Connel, the sea dripping from him to dilute the puddle of blood, made a gasping, reflex effort to rise to his hands and knees. Instantly Cruck had hurled himself into an attempt at again reaching the man's throat, an attempt that it took Rene, Chief Gunner's Mate Orlop, who had returned in one of the *bancos,* and a half-dozen others to block. Confronted by Ensign Snell with an angry, "Stay away from him! . . . Understand?" Cruck subsided into a hunched, sullen posture, his breathing ruffled, his puckered, unsentient eyes glinting feverishly, an unaccustomed tremble worrying at his knees and grimy, blunt hands; but he acknowledged the order in a tone that, under more organized circumstances, would have been taken up as insubordinate:

"I'll stay away from him!"

As O'Connel's body made another faltering try at raising itself, Lieutenant Fitzpatrick ordered:

"Lash him down . . . there on the deck." Then, sensing a surrender to the almost triumphant disorder in having this done amidst all that blood, he amended, "Over on the starboard side."

Rene, Horner, Ferguson, Arnold and Hemple picked up O'Connel; but the heavy burden, blood-slippery and convulsive, proved so hard to carry and the footing so precarious that they had to be joined by two others, the Carpenter's Mate and Warrington, before they could slither and ease with it out of the red welter to the other side of the six-pounder. There, while Rene kept a knee on his chest, Horner and Ferguson lashed him down on his back spread-eagle fashion, an arm to either side of the gun-mount base. The big, vertical wound on his forehead had begun to bleed again, but much more slowly than the fresher injuries left upon his chest, his arms and amongst the fractures of his hands by the Blacksmith's hammer; and where the edges of the manacles, now reduced by separation to the guise of mere barbaric adornments, had jagged in the efforts to haul him out of the sea, circles of welling blood also matted the dark hair into the line being bound about his wrists. The lashing of these concluded, Rene removed his knee and stood up. The deep breaths that this permitted

O'Connel to heave in seemed to be restoring him. He opened his sunken eyes to gaze expressionlessly at the Seamen while they curtly went on to secure, at railing stanchions, first one ankle and then the other with long, ruthless, self-tightening bights of the line; but he made not the slightest effort to impede them. When the last knot was tied, he gazed slowly around the crowd encircling him, as if without seeing, until his eyes met and held Lieutenant Fitzpatrick's.

For as long as he could, the Executive Officer bore the quiet, unblinking gaze from those eyes into which it had been a custom of his life to look with confidence, to look as into any other depth of the ship that had come to submit itself, in such full assurance, to his care; then he turned irritably away and moved across the deck to the side of the Blacksmith, relying, perhaps, on a sight of what O'Connel's violence had brought upon the ship to adjust, to smother the unreasonable tumble of uneasiness, like a strange, restless receptivity to reproach, that O'Connel's eyes had released somewhere beneath his heart. "Christ!" he exclaimed silently to himself; and if he had not instantly followed it with the thought, as his gaze flickered over the Blacksmith's destroyed body, "There's nothing to be done for him . . . a dozen tourniquets would be lost in that mess," he might have recognized the exclamation as a defensive one flung into the face of the uneasiness that had gripped him before he had arrived within this view of the dying man.

"Boat ahoy!" hailed Bidot's voice in a long, formal quaver from the other side of the ship.

Out of the not-far distance was coming the urgent chug-chug of a two-cycle engine. Lieutenant Fitzpatrick took for granted that it was the ship's motor-dory returning with the Captain, a presumption confirmed by its answering hail:

"Delilah!"

On his way over to the starboard gangway to meet the Captain, the officer did not so much as glance down at the supine figure lashed out alongside it; and the position he took up, opposite Ensign Snell, left little before his eyes save the far, mist-hung mountains, blue, cool and exotic, towering out of the feathery line of fragrant shore, across that still surface of a bay ready for the spangling of the not yet risen sun. Standing there, in his official capacity of waiting to receive the Captain aboard, he seemed actually to have turned his back, for the interval that it took the motor-dory to make the gangway, on that turbulent world of a ship that persisted in reaching him with its early morning scent, mingled with that of the brewing coffee and frying bacon and eggs Olgan finally had nerved himself to prepare for the men's breakfast, of tobacco smoke and raw metal deck oxydizing under the dampness of recent rain.

The Captain, who had made the forty-minute trip up the bay with his cap on his knees while the slight, deceptively cool breeze of the motor-dory's progress fluttered the sandy cow-lick at the back of his head, promptly donned it and stepped onto a rung of the gangway ladder virtually in the moment that his craft slid alongside; but full as he was of the urgent instructions and portentous advices he had received at the night-long council in the Captain of the Yard's office, he mounted the smartly railed and varnished little ladder with quite his usual unstudied manner, neither hasty nor deliberate, of a man for whom a display of the dramatic in personal conduct, either in his own or in that of others, was more or less disquieting. However, he could not wholly keep out of his appearance the fact, obscured for Lieutenant Fitzpatrick by the intensity of his own cruel preoccupation, that he was being carried along in a current of eagerness. The faint, dry light of it seemed to leak from the corners of his innocent, practical eyes to illuminate, just barely illuminate, the deep wrinkles and tanned contours, the decent pleasant ordinariness, that harboured the impressiveness of his face; and it was fairly evident that all the way from Olongapo he had guilelessly held in his hand, held it out before him, as it were, in the way that a youth holds a thing of triumph, of personal justification on the way home to show it to his family, the symbol that had to do with this eagerness, a long official envelope. The starched whiteness of his ample uniform was blemished a bit, at the collar, by an absorption of perspiration and at one arm and leg by splashes from the sea. His air of disregarded weariness was made more obvious, no doubt, by the seeming complete lack of it in Ensign Woodbridge, who followed him up the gangway with a supporting elation, worn easily like some subtle patrician adornment, as unwilted as the carelessly elegant expanses of his own uniform, which had remained unrelieved by any save their proper blemishes of gold.

Reaching the deck, the Captain stopped suddenly, but without an appearance of suddenness, before the sight of O'Connel lashed out like that; and the hand holding the envelope sank slowly to his side. O'Connel's eyes did not meet his gaze. Their lids, darkened to a deep purple by the long blazing of violence, had lowered at the first glimpse of the Captain on the gangway. The Captain shifted his gaze only after he had got out his horn-rimmed spectacles and put them on; then he looked briefly about at the scene into which he had returned, looked about it in the heavy silence that would be maintained until he should see fit to speak in a way that could be replied to. Everybody else's eyes met his when he looked at them, but did so, he noted, with a kind of miserable reluctance. Lieutenant Fitzpatrick could not be included in this observation, he being engaged in facing away to say to the coxswain of the motor-dory:

"Hold on. I want you to make a trip back to Olongapo . . . to the hospital ship."

The Captain noted also the spots of blood on the legs of Lieutenant Fitzpatrick's pyjamas, the blood on one of Ensign Snell's hands and unclothed shoulders, the fact that some of the rest of them had actually been wading in blood. His eyes dwelt longest on the two whaleboats secured alongside and still untidily awash with the sea and rain shipped in the chase.

Within Cruck's spent and benumbed spirit this dwelling glance at his boats ignited, even as it restored his functional personality, a flare of acrid emotion, a resentment, a frustration, that could not have been produced, in this exhausted moment, by any cruel recollection of the punishing night. A shadowy, irrelevant fragment of an act occurring in the midst of what was so much more significant, the glance yet had the power to prejudge, to belittle his unsparing participation in what there had been to do and crown it with unjust accusation. He could not know that the gaze, as it lingered on the boats, had become thoughtful rather than seeing, and that it contained no censure of the fact that they were not hoisted high and dry at the davits as they should have been.

It was with seeing eyes, however, that the Captain patiently watched while Lieutenant Fitzpatrick supervised the carrying of the Blacksmith to the gangway and his lowering into the motor-dory. Throughout this grim operation he asked no more than a dry, "Any others beside O'Connel and Barnes?" directed at Ensign Snell. He seemed to learn all he wanted to know, for the moment, from his officer's subdued, almost mumbled answer of, "Well . . . no, Sir." The stumble in Ensign Snell's answer had been caused by the thought of the injured natives ashore and the uncertainty as to whether the scope of the Captain's question had included them. As the motor-dory continued to cling at the gangway, with its coxswain, Ragatzo, urgently coiling a pull-line around the engine's flywheel to get it started, the Captain stepped to the rail and looked down in quiet, sincere pity at the part he was losing from his ship, losing it forever it was clear, in the very moment for which, all these weeks, he had fought so hard, and so in the dark he admitted, to reintegrate and preserve her.

Behind his back Ensign Woodbridge, having instantly precipitated his reaction to the Blacksmith's condition from off the casual splendour of his surface into those private depths of which many denied the existence, was smiling ironically at Lieutenant Fitzpatrick and Ensign Snell. They knew that if the Captain had not been within hearing he would have accompanied the smile with some such equally perverse words as, "Nice little party you're having here." Lieutenant Fitzpatrick's quick irritation and the other's slow resentment, begot by this attitude that pretended to see with gay approval their dejection, their physical distress as felicities in the stride of a debauch, was nevertheless accompanied by an astringent effect that did for the two officers much of what the Captain's glance at the boats had done for the Chief Boatswain's Mate. Lieutenant Fitzpatrick abruptly turned his back and moved to the Captain's side to face out, recklessly if that were necessary, the whole tragic business; while Ensign Snell became conscious of, and pulled in from before the eyes of that "incorrigible bastard" to whom it seemed to be affording such amusement, the ragged display of personal indignation that had continued to linger about him since his descent into the hatch upon O'Connel.

At Lieutenant Fitzpatrick's emphatic arrival beside him, the Captain turned from looking after the motor-dory, which had gotten its engine started and was heading around, to listen attentively, but with his eyes regarding the man lashed out at his feet, while the Executive Officer said:

"If you care to come below, Captain, I'll clear this thing up for you."

The Captain did not reply at once. He was telling himself that the essentials of the "thing" already were "clear" for him . . . He had lost another man, lost another valuable man at the very last minute (the word "valuable" functioning for him with the force that, had it been Lieutenant Fitzpatrick thinking, would have required some phrase like "as much a part of the ship as one of the propeller shafts") . . . and if it was O'Connel there who had killed him, then he had lost still another.

Without O'Connel's realizing it, his lips had relaxed, under the scrutiny his closed eyes would not meet, to remain set in a wide, sick, helpless gesture that was in no sense a smile even though it disclosed both rows of his unclenched teeth. The Captain's eyes turning away from this lighted on the envelope in his hand. The reminding sight of it caused him to suppress the nearly launched words of an affirmative answer to his officer, and to say instead:

"Mr. Fitzpatrick, please have the crew called to Quarters."

Cruck, standing close by with Bidot and Stengle, the three of them waiting with a kind of sullen patience for some word as to how the ship was to end what had been the night and begin the day, heard this and needed only Lieutenant Fitzpatrick's glance, passing the order on to him, to set up a hoarse, weary shout of:

"All hands to Quarters!"

There were only thirty or so of them aboard, surly, exhausted and incapable of wonder, to shuffle into double rank along the starboard side of the deck with Ensign Woodbridge and Ensign Snell at their front; and though most of them were semi-naked, without shoes or with them unlaced on bare feet, though they were soiled with blood, and wrung to the point of collapse by long striving, by lack of sleep and by assaults of tearing emotion, and though a murderer who had been one of them was even now lashed out there on their flank like a massive, naked, gold-toothed,

Irish Christ crucified on steel, a monstrous stigma gaping in the centre of his brow and the blood of a friend splattered over his body, they yet managed to impress themselves and their Captain —who faced them with the Executive Officer at his left elbow— as a ship's company, as a collective being that had sustained itself, its peculiar, sedulously patterned self, in the face of what had proved too much for nearly each of the individuals composing it.

"Atten . . . tion!" ordered Ensign Woodbridge.

A brusque little wave of response rippled over bare, sweaty muscles, swept along those ranks of beset men to leave them silent, cleansed of relaxation and of restlessness, beneath the taut grey awning that still was damp from its drench of rain. To these lines of wan faces, the expressionless faces of a crew at attention, the Captain disclosed, of all the urgencies with which he had returned so full, only what was in the envelope he carried in his hand. Out of this he took a flimsy, folded paper of the size upon which copies of Navy radiograms were made. As he did so, a gust of sunrise breeze fluttered it, nearly snatched it out of his hand, causing Ensign Woodbridge, standing rigidly at attention, to remember, for some unaccountable reason, the Captain's story about the eager man from whom the wind had snatched a Gorgonian note just in the moment when finally it was to have been read.

"April, the Sixth, Nineteen-hundred and Seventeen," read the Captain in a voice that, for all its simplicity, seemed to be a vehicle for an expression of calm, personal justification. "From: Secretary of the Navy . . . To: All Ships and Stations . . ." He paused to remove his spectacles and for a brief raising of his eyes to those men who now could begin to understand why he had pressed them so uncommonly of late.

With the last word of what he had continued to read, he turned unhurriedly to Lieutenant Fitzpatrick and handed him the copy of the radiogram before adding, "Have it tacked up on the bulletin board." Then he walked aft, with the Executive Officer's "Aye aye, Sir," conventionally clipping the routine silence in his wake, walked away in precisely the same definite but unpointed manner, the trustful manner, in which he always walked away from these formal confrontations with a ship that never failed to understand him. The words he had continued to read were:

"The President signed an act which declares that a state of war exists between the United States and Germany."

"Dismissed," said Lieutenant Fitzpatrick.

The ranks slumped, began to dissolve in a renewal of jaded murmur that had as much to do with the imminence of breakfast as with the declaration to which they had just listened. Standing close upon the wreckage of a violence that had touched them, their emotions were unavailable for the terse little tale about one that had not touched them. It could take them for no rise into the fervid conjecture that had gripped them ever since the ship had become the subject of such frantic and mysterious preparation; nor had it the power, in that moment, to revive and illuminate with a beam of vindication the assurance that "all this meant something." They understood the declaration, most of them, simply in the sense that now, one way or another, there had become part of their daily work a fabulous chaos blazing somewhere half-a-world away, amidst still other scenes and peoples their eyes had not looked upon before.

"All right, you guys," snarled Cruck, "get them boats up!"

a note about
the production
of this book

The text of this special edition of *Delilah* is set in Times Roman. The text was photocomposed at Time Inc. under the direction of Albert J. Dunn and Arthur J. Dunn. The book was printed and bound by J. W. Clement Co., Buffalo, New York. The cover was printed by Livermore and Knight Co., a division of Printing Corporation of America, in Providence, Rhode Island.

✕

The paper, TIME Reading Text, is from The Mead Corporation, Dayton, Ohio. The cover stock is from The Plastic Coating Corporation, Holyoke, Massachusetts.